NUN

Headlines

By the same author

Rich
Railroad
Solitaire
Maiden Voyage
Lady of Fortune

HEADLINES

Graham Masterton

C

CENTURY
LONDON MELBOURNE AUCKLAND JOHANNESBURG

ACKNOWLEDGEMENTS

For their interest and assistance, the Chicago *Tribune*, the Chicago Fire Department Academy, the University of Chicago Press, Rockwell International Graphics Division, Jean Quinn at Marshall Field, the Chicago Police Department, the Drake Hotel, the Ambassador East Hotel, the Chicago Historical Society, Michael Halperin, and Lloyd Wendt.

© Graham Masterton 1986

First published in Great Britain by Century Hutchinson Ltd
Brookmount House, 62–65 Chandos Place, London WC2N 4NW

Reprinted 1986

Century Hutchinson Publishing Group (Australia) Pty Ltd
16–22 Church Street, Hawthorn, Melbourne, Victoria 3122

Century Hutchinson Group (NZ) Ltd
32–34 View Road, PO Box 40–086, Glenfield, Auckland 10

Century Hutchinson Group (SA) Pty Ltd
PO Box 337, Bergvlei 2012, South Africa

Photoset by Rowland Phototypesetting Ltd
Bury St Edmunds, Suffolk
Printed and bound in Great Britain by
Anchor Brendon Ltd, Tiptree, Essex

ISBN 0 7126 9485 4

For Wiescka, and for the three sons you gave me, with love.

1

Morgana had lost so much weight on Dr Holman's Dried-Apricot Diet that the black and white Dior original which had cost her father $780 now looked positively *flaccid*. That was her own word for it, *flaccid*. It was finishing-school lingo for anything saggy or *démodé* or drab. Only two hours to go before the first guests were expected to arrive for her twenty-first birthday party, and the outfit with which she had been confident of wowing the whole of Chicago high society was draped around her like a New Look bivouac.

'I look like *Hell*,' she told her eleven mothers, each of them sharply reflected in the mirrored doors of her dressing room.

Her eleven mothers arched their eyebrows *en masse*. 'What else can you expect, after living for six weeks on nothing but dried apricots? Dried apricots! I never heard of anything so sickening. Your bowels must look like sunset over Oahu.'

'Dried apricots are good for the figure, Momsy. And for the psyche, too.' Morgana spun around on her bare heel and critically appraised the way her full pleated skirt flared out.

'The psyche,' said her mother, scornfully. 'The nearest thing that any of our family ever had to a psyche was your Uncle Gerard's predilection for topiarizing his yew hedges into the shape of misbehaving couples.'

'That's not what psyche means, Momsy. Psyche means the way your mind adapts to your surroundings, and vice versa.'

'Exactly,' her mother retorted. 'Your Uncle Gerard had a lewd mind, and he adapted his surroundings to match it. Mind you, I scarcely blame him, the way that Ethel was. Even a hedge is better than nothing.'

Almost as an afterthought, she added, 'She always made him change them into chickens.'

'She always made him change what into chickens?'

'My dear! The misbehaving couples. And for God's sake don't keep calling me Momsy. You're twenty-one today. You can call me Eleanor, if you like. Anything but Momsy.'

'I like Momsy,' said Morgana, trying to tug in the waist of her dress at the back. 'It reminds me of when we were little. You know, the nursery, and going for rides in the dogcart, and brushing our hair before he came to say good night.'

'Heaven preserve us,' said her mother, snapping open her little white kid bag, and taking out her white enameled cigarette case. 'I thought our relationship had developed since then. Apart from that, if you tried to ride in the dogcart now, you'd kill the poor dog. Listen – Loukia can take in that waist easily. Let me call her.'

'But Momsy *means* something,' Morgana insisted, turning around; and in spite of the crowd of reflections, there really was only one mother, after all. 'We're friends now, aren't we? Grown-up friends. But that doesn't take away the fact that you're still my Momsy.'

Morgana's mother pretended to look – what? severe? sophisticated? thoroughly exasperated? But her pursed red lips couldn't conceal her affection and her amusement. She held out her lemon-gloved hands, and held her daughter around the waist, and looked into those autumnal-colored eyes that were exactly level with hers, and said, 'You are absolutely and eternally forbidden from making me feel my age.'

'Momsy, you're –'

Her mother lifted one hand, and melodramatically closed her eyes, as if she could neither hear nor see the evidence of the passing years. 'I wish I could say to you – Morgana, don't be twenty-one. Be seven again; or eight at the most. Your dolls are all waiting for you, out in the playhouse. Remember that china doll Catherine? The prettiest, but always the naughtiest. My dear, if only we *could* go back! If you were seven again, I would be twenty-nine. I was in full bloom, at the age of twenty-nine.'

Morgana kissed her mother on her right cheek; then on her left.

'What's that? An official award for longevity?' her mother demanded, and mock-irritably brushed her away. 'Now, look – you have less than two hours left to get ready. Let me call Loukia for you.'

'It's no use,' Morgana protested. 'Even if she takes the waist in, I'm still going to look like Hell.'

'No daughter of mine ever looked like Hell,' her mother retorted. She went through to the large cream-painted bedroom, and picked up the cream boudoir telephone that connected her through to the staff quarters.

'Edmundo? This is Mrs Croft Tate. Would you send Loukia up to Miss Morgana's dressing room, please? Very well, good. And did the salmon arrive? Well, praise be. But still no sign of the flowers? You can call Karpathian and tell him that if those flowers aren't here within twenty minutes flat, he's never going to be given another order from Weatherwood, ever, and I mean for the rest of human history.'

She put down the telephone and lit her cigarette, drawing in her cheeks as tautly as a stockyard auctioneer in between sales. 'Kenneth is always trying to tell me that Chicago is civilized now; but I have to admit that I'm seriously beginning to doubt it. Do you know that when we went to the Bransons' last week, for dinner, they were hacking at their bread rolls with their knives? I was quite expecting to see them lick their plates.'

'Momsy, you're such a stickler.'

'Of course I'm a stickler! I believe in standards. Before the war there used to be standards. I believe in consideration for other people, and cutting your bread roll with your knife is just about the most inconsiderate breach of etiquette I can think of.'

'I don't see why.'

'Don't argue. It offends me, that's all, and I get worried that the bread rolls might tumble off the table. How can anybody expect me to enjoy my dinner if I'm offended and worried?'

'Oh, Momsy,' said Morgana. She took another twirl in front of the mirrors, and then she said, 'It's no use. I'm going to have to wear the Worth instead.'

'You can't. Your father will detonate.'

'Let him detonate. I'm twenty-one now.'

'Yes, and quite old enough to know better than to upset your father. Just remember that he made a grotesquely uncharacteristic effort to get you this dress. You know what he thinks about fashion. The quickest way to a man's wallet, that's what he always says. If your father had his way, the whole family would be walking around in loincloths. I wouldn't mind so much, but your father would look quite awful in a loincloth. He's not exactly Johnny Weissmuller, let's face it.'

'Momsy –'

Eleanor Croft Tate extravagantly blew smoke, and waved her hand around as if she didn't want to hear anything that Morgana had to say. 'The dress will be perfect, anyway. Just you wait and see.'

Morgana and her mother were unnervingly alike. They were both tall, so that when they were wearing their spike-heeled New Look shoes, they were almost always eye to eye with the men that they met; and the men that they met almost always found this disconcerting. They both had alarmingly dark, large, intelligent eyes; and fashionably short, straight noses. They both had cheekbones that could cut their way through a crowded cocktail party like the prows of twin icebreakers.

Eleanor Croft Tate, however, had the kind of heart-shaped mouth that had been all the swoon in the 1930s, very Carole Lombardish; whereas Morgana had inherited the wide, full-lipped mouth of her maternal grandmother – a mouth that Larry Keane IV, her last boyfriend but one, had described as looking 'just as if it never stops kissing.'

Morgana had dark, upswept hair, fastened at the crown with combs and then falling on to her shoulders. Her mother's hair, fair, was brushed back in a simple but elegant coif.

There was no doubt, however, where Morgana's figure came from. Even at forty-three, Eleanor was still full-bosomed, narrow-waisted, and long-legged. Her husband had grumbled for days when she first started wearing the new long skirts, only twelve inches above the ground. 'I married you for your legs, Eleanor. If it hadn't have been for that flapper frock of yours, I probably wouldn't even have looked at you. Great grief, if I wanted to ogle fabric, I would have gone into the garment business. And how much does all of that extra material cost, I'd like to know?'

It was a long-running pretense played out by Morgana's father that he was the world's greatest tightwad. In fact, provided they kept strictly to the rules of his pretense, he would indulge his wife and his daughters beyond all reason, and always had done. Anyone approaching Weatherwood on foot stood a fair to middling chance of being knocked down on any day of the week by any one of a constant procession of delivery vans bringing gowns, flowers, hats, chocolates, pocketbooks, and furs.

It was only when she was feeling isolated and blue – during her period, or after breaking up with a boyfriend – that Morgana thought about her father's overwhelming generosity, and recognized it for what it probably was. A way of compensating her with money for that last precious ounce of love which he had never quite been able to give her. That last ounce of love which would remain forever bottled up inside of him, because he had reserved it, as most men do, for a first-born boy.

Eleanor patted her hair in front of one of the mirrors. 'I'm not sure I care for this style any more. It makes me look like a schoolteacher.'

Morgana looked at her mother's exquisitely cut day dress, in pale lemon wool, and her strappy lemon-colored high heels. She looked at her five-strand pearl necklace, and her pearl-cluster brooch, and she laughed. 'A schoolteacher? What subjects do you take? Second-grade *haute couture* and beginners in calculated extravagance?'

Just then, the family's Greek seamstress Loukia knocked politely at the door. She was diminutive and dark, with popping eyes like Bette Davis. Close behind her – still swathed in her floor-length salmon-pink silk bathrobe, her blonde hair still tangled up in curling rags – came Morgana's younger sister Phoebe. She was smoking a pink cigarette in a long white holder, which was a new affectation of hers, and she walked into the bedroom with an exaggerated prance, and spread out her arms as if she were acknowledging the screams and the applause of her adoring public.

'The ever-devastating John has arrived,' she announced.

'Already?' asked Morgana.

'He said he was so desperate to see you again, he couldn't hold himself back any longer. He said he was foaming at the mouth.'

'What a disgusting thing to say,' said Eleanor. 'I thought he was a man of manners, when I first met him.'

'Actually, he didn't say that at all,' said Phoebe. 'He wasn't foaming at the mouth – nor anywhere else, so far as I could see. But I think he's got a surprise for you, my dear Morgana.

He's downstairs rehearsing with the band and I *hate* to say it but I think he's going to sing. I do like his smile, you know. That's one thing I'll say about John. He categorically has more teeth than any man I ever met. It must be like kissing the front of a Buick.'

'Don't be odious,' Eleanor snapped. 'Now, Loukia dear, I want you to take in the waist of Miss Morgana's dress like so. That's it; and fold over that pleat at the back. I'll hold it if you pin it.'

Morgana looked at herself critically in the mirror, tilting her head a little to one side. Phoebe stood right next to her and examined her own reflection, pouting out her lips now and again, and perching her hand on her hip.

Phoebe was three inches shorter than Morgana, although she wore the most dangerously high heels that she could find. She was prettier, in a pert, heart-shaped kind of way, with curly blonde permanent-waved hair and startling bright blue eyes. Anyone could tell that she and Morgana were sisters. There was a distinctly similar shape about their noses and their mouths. But Phoebe was always the sparkly sister, the sister who was giggling and dancing and teasing the boys. Although she was only just eighteen, Phoebe had smoked before Morgana, a Chesterfield, in the back of their father's new Packard. She had drunk champagne before Morgana, learned to drive a car before Morgana, and found out all about sex before Morgana. She had first kissed a boy (real, tongue-in-the-mouth kissing) when she was ten; and when she was fourteen and three days old, she had enthusiastically given what remained of her virginity to the sullen handsome boy who used to weed their rosebeds. His name was Eric. Phoebe still liked to unsettle Morgana by talking about him, and saying that 'Eric was the only boy who ever meant anything.'

It was all a tease, of course. Phoebe couldn't even remember what Eric looked like, apart from his magnificently curling lip. But it was a splintery little reminder to Morgana that *she* could always attract the boys; whereas Morgana had always seemed unapproachable to would-be suitors. Distant, selective, and even frightening.

'I think you and John are so well suited,' said Phoebe, making big sky-blue eyes at herself in the mirror. Loukia was down on her knees now, with her mouth crammed with dressmaking pins, trying to adjust Morgana's waistline.

'What makes you say that?' Morgana asked. 'I think he's rather shallow, to tell you the truth.'

'Well, I don't know,' Phoebe replied. 'He may be shallow, but he's so serene, so self-confident, and so are you. You and he are like two magnificent swans, gliding together across the glassy surface of society.'

'What claptrap,' put in Eleanor.

'Oh, mother, you don't have any sense of romance,' Phoebe protested.

'I have a fine sense of claptrap,' said her mother. 'Now, go get yourself dressed, madam. Just for once, on your sister's twenty-first birthday, I want you to be ready.'

Phoebe sucked with hyperbolic elegance at her cigarette holder, but made no move to go. 'Did you hear the news?' she asked, trying to blow smoke rings.

'What news?' asked Morgana. 'About Margaret Mitchell, you mean? Edmundo told me this morning.'

'Please, Miss Morgana, holding still,' begged Loukia, who had been shuffling around behind Loukia on her knees, like a penitent.

'Oh, no, not that. No – they found Robert Wentworth.'

Eleanor, who had been systematically tugging at her gloves to make sure that there were no folds between her fingers, suddenly stiffened, and stared at Phoebe as if Phoebe had just announced that she was having a baby, or that President Truman had dropped dead, or that Hitler had been found alive and well and living in Scranton, Pa. Morgana – alerted by her mother's abrupt and unexpected change of mood – said, 'Where did you hear that?' and then looked quickly back at her mother to see what effect Phoebe's answer would have on her.

'It was a special flash on the radio,' said Phoebe, apparently unaware of the way in which her mother had reacted. 'Robert Wentworth, playboy and socialite, found by horrified whitefish anglers floating off Indiana Harbor.' In the Croft Tate household, they were all used to talking in headlines.

'He was dead?' asked Morgana, unnecessarily; but only because she sensed that her mother wanted to hear everything about it.

'Of course dead,' said Phoebe. 'Half-eaten by fish, poor man. The police only managed to identify him by his clothes and shoes. The first body they'd ever dragged out of the lake wearing a Savile Row suit and handmade Alan McAfee brogues.'

'*Phoebe,*' said Eleanor, in a voice as white as paper.

Phoebe turned. 'It's true. That's what they said on the news bulletin. Ask father.'

Both sisters half expected their mother to say something else; but Eleanor turned away, first to the left, then hesitated, then to the right. She couldn't seem to make up her mind which way to leave the dressing room.

'*Momsy* –' said Morgana, following her, and dragging in her wake the flustered Loukia.

Eleanor paused at the door, one hand gently touching the doorframe, but with her back to Morgana as if she were not prepared to wait for very long; and as if she didn't want Morgana to see her face.

'Momsy,' Morgana repeated, more quietly, and laid a hand on her mother's shoulder.

'Well, I'm just being silly,' said Eleanor, briskly but somehow off-balance. 'It came as a shock, that was all. I knew Robert Wentworth quite well. He used to come and stay at our house in San Francisco when I was young. He was only a toddler then, of course. I used to push him in his cart around our orchard. A lovely little boy, so pretty! With curly hair.'

Phoebe came over and took her mother's arm, trying to turn her around. 'I'm sorry, mother. I didn't realize. Please – I'm sorry.'

'That's all right, my darling,' said Eleanor, but still she didn't turn around. Morgana, with her hand on her shoulder, could feel her quaking.

Without another word, Eleanor left Morgana's dressing room and walked quickly away along the green and white corridor, her fair hair shining for a moment in the light from the clerestory windows above the stairs. Phoebe made a baffled face at Morgana and said, 'I wonder what brought that on? I didn't know mother knew any of the Wentworths. I always thought she considered the Wentworths *un peu grossier*. Do you remember her saying that Mrs Wentworth looked exactly like Fred Allen in a frock?'

Morgana stood thoughtfully by the door while Loukia finished pinning her dress.

'Perhaps Momsy's just over-excited. You know what she

was like when we held that garden party for the Warren Austins. And just now she was telling me how old she felt. She *is* forty-three, after all. Maybe the news about Robert Wentworth brought it all back, what it was like when she was younger, and everything.'

'She's too young to be going through the change,' remarked Phoebe, picking up a bamboo-framed photograph of John Birmingham Jr and peering at it minutely. It had been taken on their yacht last summer at Bailey's Harbor. 'You know something, I never noticed that birthmark on his neck.'

'That isn't a birthmark, that's a mole.'

'Ugh! I can't stand men with moles. Do you remember Chet Marshall? He had so many moles that people used to mistake him for a chocolate-chip cookie.'

Loukia asked, patiently, 'Would you mind taking off the dress now, Miss Morgana?'

Morgana carefully unfastened the Dior dress and stepped out of it. Underneath, she was wearing a white lace brassiere and white silk step-ins, trimmed with the same lace. She went across to the French rococo dressing table, cream-painted and decorated with gilded curlicues, and perched herself on the frilly-covered stool to finish off her make-up. Phoebe stood behind her and watched her.

'They think it was deliberate,' said Phoebe. 'Robert Wentworth, I mean. They think he drowned himself.'

Morgana dabbed powder on her nose with a powder-puff as large as a chrysanthemum. 'They didn't say why?'

'Unh-hunh. But from what Marissa was telling me, he was burning the candle at all three ends. Gambling, drinking, sex orgies, and dope. Not to mention voting Republican.'

Morgana intently plucked out a single undisciplined eyebrow-hair. 'You know something, Pheeb, you're too darned cynical for words. He probably drowned himself for love.'

Phoebe sat on the end of Morgana's bed and posed herself like Marlene Dietrich, puffing at her cigarette holder without inhaling.

'Love? Love isn't worth drowning yourself for. Especially these days. My God, sometimes love isn't even worth getting your lips wet for, let alone your whole body.'

She paused, and puffed at her cigarette-holder some more. 'Still,' she added, 'it's a *ta-air-able* tragedy.'

Morgana glanced up at her in the dressing table mirror.

'Don't you think you ought to start getting yourself dressed?'

'I suppose,' Phoebe agreed. 'You won't mind if I wear that pink off-the-shoulder thing with the roses on it? If I'm going to be playing the part of your cute little kid sister, I might as well dress for it, wouldn't you say?'

'Is Bradley coming?' asked Morgana, ignoring Phoebe's gibe. She wasn't sure if she cared for the turquoise-green shade of her eyeshadow.

'I hope not. I've told him I'm bilious. I've asked Donald Crittenden, if that's all right.'

'What if Bradley shows up regardless?' Morgana wanted to know. Bradley T. Clarke had been Phoebe's steady date for almost seven months, although she had never stopped walking out with other men, sometimes secretly, sometimes not. Bradley was the youngest of the Skokie Clarkes, good political friends of the Croft Tate family. They had made their fortune out of a popular brand of bright-pink processed pork called Ham-I-Yam. Bradley was lopsidedly good-looking, and occasionally funny in a collegiate kind of way, although his ears were far too large, and he glowed the same color as Ham-I-Yam whenever he was embarrassed. Phoebe was stringing him along for three or four different reasons. He was very rich, he was always on call, he didn't ask questions, he was engagingly innocent in bed, whenever she allowed him to take her to bed. Also, she never knew when she might need a passable husband in a hurry. She had seen too many society girls suddenly and unpredictably burn themselves out – booze, abortions, accidents, a bad affair – and she wanted to make sure that what usually happened to them didn't happen to her. What usually happened to them was that they were left on the shelf, embittered and haggard before their time; or else they wound up making a disastrous marriage with some middle-class brute who insulted their friends, couldn't hold down a decent job, couldn't play bridge without losing his temper, drank, hit them, and put proprietary sauce bottles straight on the table.

Donald Crittenden, on the other hand, was a dangerous male. Married, alluring, with a Hell's Kitchen background and appalling manners, too old for Phoebe by fifteen years, and one of the most controversial actor-managers since Monty Woolley, leaving out *Miss Tatlock's Millions*. Phoebe had been making time with Donald for two weeks now, while

Mrs Crittenden (Joanie to her friends, *La Noosance* to her husband) was visiting her epileptic sister in Savannah, Ga. For eleven-fourteenths of those two weeks, Phoebe hadn't been home nights, and had regularly appeared at breakfast in yesterday evening's frock, with bruised lips and mesmerized eyes.

'If Bradley shows, they can fight it out between them,' said Phoebe. 'I love being fought over. Do you remember the Kellerman twins? They practically killed each other trying to decide who was going to take me to see *Carousel*.'

'Supposing they fight and Donald wins,' said Morgana, sensibly. She turned around on her boudoir stool and confronted Phoebe with a tart, inquiring smile.

'Oh, they won't fight,' said Phoebe. 'And even if they did, and Bradley did win, he'd only apologize, and offer Donald a dozen cases of Ham-I-Yam.'

'Are you going to get dressed?' Morgana asked her, in amused exasperation.

'Well, I guess I ought to. You won't mind the pink dress, will you?'

'If you really want to upstage me on my twenty-first birthday, go ahead.'

Phoebe came over and laid her arms around Morgana's neck. 'You know I'd never upstage you. You're too-too beautiful, and too-too clever, and too-too cool with a capital C.'

They heard swing music from the gardens outside. 'Boogie Bop Blue', by Duke Ellington, and 'You're Just An Old Antidisestablishmentarianismist'. 'That must be John rehearsing,' said Phoebe. 'If you ask me, he secretly believes that he's Alfred Drake.'

She pecked Morgana on the forehead, and affectionately squeezed her, and said, 'Happy, happy coming of age, sister dear,' and then she went trucking off, waving her long cigarette holder and jiggling her bottom and singing 'Boogie Bop Blue' off-key.

2

Loukia came bustling back with the black and white Dior arranged carefully over her arm. 'This should fit you fine now, Miss Morgana. I took in the waistband just one quarter of an inch.'

Morgana stood up and slipped the dress carefully over her head, as if she were diving upwards into a raincloud. She made sure that she didn't smudge the wide white collar with foundation, and then she tugged the dress straight. Loukia started to button her up, awkwardly fox-trotting behind as she paced undecided from one mirror to the next, trying to make up her mind whether she still looked flaccid or not.

'I don't know,' she said, worriedly. 'Maybe I'm too thin for it. Do you think I'm too thin for it?'

'Miss Morgana, you cannot have the bosom any tighter. Nor the hips. It is all perfect. It fits perfect. It fits you like a dream.'

'A dream? Well – just so long as I don't wake up.'

'All this apricot you eat,' Loukia chided her.

'Loukia, dried apricots are very good for you. You should try them yourself. They're a wonderful source of natural sugar.'

'But so thin! You think Mr Birmingham like you this way? Skeletonkey?' The Croft Tates had called skeletons 'skeletonkeys' ever since Eleanor (on the yacht, before the war) had thrown down the Chicago *Star*'s crossword in exasperation, and protested to Howard that the answers were quite absurd. 'I've heard of a monkey and a donkey, but what on earth is a skeletonkey?' she had demanded.

There was a brisk rapping at the door. Postman's knock with a complicated flourish at the end. Morgana's father always knocked like that. He seemed to feel that it was obligatory for a man who lived in a household of women to use a secret code if he wished to enter their private boudoirs; as if he were a constant martyr to the sex of his own children. 'I want to talk All-Stars, but they want to talk underwired brassieres, and so I'm outvoted, three to one. These days, I think I know more about Didos than I do about football.'

His thick, harsh voice said, 'Is everybody decent?'

'I'm dressed, if that's what you mean,' Morgana replied. Her father leaned in through the door with a puggish frown and a spectacular bouquet of fresh pink roses.

'These aren't from me,' he assured her, at once. 'These are from Ernie. He can't make it to the party but he sends his devotions. And so he should, the amount of money I spend in the Pump Room.'

Morgana held the roses in her arms and inhaled their fragrance until she was almost delirious with it.

'They're glorioso,' she said. Then she opened her eyes, and smiled at her father, and said, 'You didn't just come to bring me these.'

'Well . . .' her father admitted.

'Loukia,' said Morgana, 'could you ask Minnie to put these roses in water? And tell her not to forget to crush the stems. And tell her not to forget to add a teaspoonful of caster sugar to the water. And tell her not to forget to soak them all day before she arranges them.'

Howard Croft Tate stepped into the bedroom, tiptoeing like a giant Fred Astaire over the white carpeting in his black patent-leather shoes. He looked at his elder daughter with cautious appreciation.

'Well, then, it's been twenty-one years,' he told her. 'How do you like the dress?' This was more of a statement than a question, because as far as Howard was concerned, a gown that had cost him that much trouble and that much money, she just had to like.

'I just hope I'm not too thin for it, that's all.'

Her father made a peculiar noise in his throat that could have been interpreted as 'yes, you are' or 'no, you're not' or 'what the hell are you girls coming to, that's what I'd like to know.' He said, abrasively, 'Don't worry about it. If you're too thin now, you won't be by two o'clock this afternoon. You should see the food down there. Fresh salmon, suckling pig, prime rib, lobster, you name it. You could put on weight just looking at it.'

'Pops, you spoil me,' said Morgana.

'So I spoil you. Who needs an emasculated daughter?'

'Emaciated.' She was pinning up her hair now. She hadn't meant to correct him, but he had made sure from the day she had first talked that her English was perfect, unlike his; and the correction had slipped past her tongue before she could stop it.

'Sure, emaciated, that's what I said,' he replied, irritated by his own shortcoming but not offended. 'Anyway, life is too short not to spoil you. What do you want me to do, hunh? Limit your allowance to five dollars a week and make you ride around by public conveyance? And what's the matter with your mother?'

'Momsy? Why?'

Her father shrugged, and leaned sideways so that he could see his reflection in the mirror, and adjusted his necktie. 'She's incarcerated herself in her dressing room, that's all. I came up to ask her to join us downstairs for a small glass of champagne; and what did I get? Silence, that's what I got. I knocked, I called, yoo-hoo, but she didn't answer.' He sniffed, and then he said, 'You know what that means, don't you – no answer? A Grade A certified tight-lipped silent disagreement. That's right. But don't ask me why, not on your birthday, because I don't know the answer to that question.'

He dragged across a silk-upholstered armchair, and sat down heavily. He was a tall, massively built man, and the chair creaked sharply as he made himself comfortable. He wore a dove-gray cutaway morning coat with striped pants and a matching dove-gray vest, with silver buttons. He was always well dressed, but this morning he looked exceptional. He was brushed, brilliantined, and his barber had shaved him twice.

Eleanor had often remarked that Morgana and her father were strikingly alike, but Morgana could never see the resemblance. Her father was a big-shouldered giant from the city of the big shoulders; thick-fingered; thick-ankled; with a head that wouldn't have looked out of place on the side of Mount Rushmore, between Roosevelt and Lincoln. His forehead was broad and looked as if it had been etched into furrows with platemaker's acid. His eyebrows were wildly tangled, and his eyes were black and deeply embedded and gave nothing at all away.

Perhaps there was some similarity between Morgana and her father around the mouth: weakness, maybe, or sensuality, or self-indulgence; but Howard Croft Tate's day-to-day pugnacity had permanently puckered up his mouth like Rocky Graziano's. He had an explosive sense of humor, and he was rarely mean, but he had been fighting for fifty-two years, ever since he was born, and he wasn't going to give up now.

He watched Morgana pinning up her hair, and then he looked around at the bright, cream-painted bedroom; glancing quickly without interest at the frilly bedcovers and the pink-bordered prints of French shepherdesses tending their flocks. He rarely came up here, this was female territory, and he rarely spoke to Morgana about anything else but himself and the newspaper business.

Whenever he wanted to discuss anything personal, his conversations always seemed to Morgana to be stiff and linear and very much to the point, almost rehearsed – as if he had asked one of the *Star*'s leader writers to sketch them out for him at the office, and memorized them in the back of his limousine on the way home. Morgana knew that he found it difficult to talk to her about family matters, and she tried hard to make allowances. After all she had committed the double felonies of being born a girl, and of shining academically at school. Howard's own father, although rich, hadn't seen the need for Howard to go to college, and had sent him down to the composing room of the Chicago *Star* the day after his fifteenth birthday, in a brand-new printer's apron. Consequently, almost all of Howard's knowledge was twentieth century, mid-Western, and sensational. He had acquired it not only piecemeal, as each successive daily edition was published, but upside down and backwards, because his first job in the composing room had been to count the lines of freshly cast type before the formes were tightened up.

He knew everything there was to know about President Harding and the Teapot Dome scandal; he knew all about 'Bathhouse John' Coughlin and 'Hinky Dink' Kenna and the other boodlers of Chicago's First Ward; and he could talk for hours about the Chicago meat-packing factories in the bad old days, when government health inspectors had been bribed to certify tubercular cattle and hogs dying of cholera as fit for human consumption, and poisoned rats had been regularly tossed into the mincing machines along with the pork.

His only attempt at self-education had been to read and reread the complete works of Longfellow, and he could quote Hiawatha by the long ton. But his grasp of art and science and political philosophy was desperately limited, and it frustrated him more than he could ever explain to anyone, even Eleanor. Perhaps he could have explained it to a son. He certainly couldn't explain it to Morgana.

Alexander Woollcott was supposed to have said of Howard Croft Tate: 'He knows only three questions. One – are they famous? Two – were they naked? And, three – how many copies will it sell?'

Morgana gave herself a final critical examination in the mirror and decided that she was ready. 'I don't think that Momsy's angry about anything, Pops.'

'Oh, no?' he asked. He reached into his inside pocket and took out a Partagas No. 7 cigar, and sucked at the end of it.

'Well, she just heard about Robert Wentworth being drowned, and it upset her, that's all. She used to play with him years ago when they were children.'

'Yes, I knew that. Cy Wentworth was a friend of your mother's father. And what a pair of drawing room hoodlums they were. Cy Wentworth made all his money out of crooked paving contracts. Next time you trip over a badly laid slab on the sidewalk, you know who to blame. And your mother's father wasn't any saint, either.'

Morgana said, 'Give Momsy a little time. She's bound to get over it. You know how romantic she is.'

'Oh, sure, she's romantic all right. Romantic's the word for it. Sometimes I think I'm living in a Hollywood movie. *Blanche Fury*, or whatever.'

'I liked *Blanche Fury*. It made me cry.'

'Well, there you are, then. That's what I have to put up with.'

Morgana leaned over her father and kissed his shiny, twice-shaved cheek. He never knew what to do when she was affectionate; and he irritably sawed at his collar with his finger, and cleared his throat in a series of rapid bursts, like a motorboat trying to start up.

'Don't tease Momsy about it, will you?' Morgana begged him.

Howard made three different kinds of face, surprised, offended, puzzled, as if he were a television commercial. 'All right. Well, I wouldn't have done, anyway. What do you think I'm made of? Marble? But Robert Wentworth wasn't worth a toot. If Cy hadn't kept on wining and dining the police commissioner, Robert would have been charged with more dope offenses than days in the year. Robert cost his father a fortune. Do you remember that time when he was driving drunk, and killed that little girl? That cost Cy more than twenty thousand dollars.'

'I didn't know that,' said Morgana, with genuine surprise. 'So much for your headline in the *Star*. What was it? "Grieving Mother Forgives Drunk-Driving Heir For Death Of Only Daughter."'

Howard sniffed philosophically. 'The story was *mostly* true. It was just that Cy asked us not to mention the payoff, as a personal favor. But the mother did forgive him. And who wouldn't, with twenty gs in the bank? She told Larry Harman that she was much happier with her new mink coat than she had ever been with her daughter. You don't have to feed a mink coat, right? and you don't have to put it through school.'

'Are you kidding me?' asked Morgana.

'Why should I kid you?' said her father, innocently spreading his hands. 'That's what the world is all about. Life, death, and money in the bank.'

'You didn't come up here just to talk about life, death, and money in the bank.'

'No, I didn't. I came up here to ask you what was wrong with your mother, and whether you'd like to come downstairs for a glass of champagne.'

'Nothing else?' Morgana inquired. Her father hadn't delivered his editorial yet; and she couldn't believe that he had come all the way up to her bedroom just to ask her two silly questions and to take a look at her new dress.

'Well,' her father confessed, 'it is your twenty-first birthday, your coming of age. You're a woman now. You can vote. You can marry any lowbrow idiot you like, without asking my permission.'

'John isn't a lowbrow idiot.'

'I didn't mean that. In fact, I think he's the most likely candidate you've ever brought home. At least his folks are wealthy, and he doesn't chew tobacco.' Howard smiled at his own joke.

Morgana sat down close beside him on the side of the bed. 'Well?' she asked him. 'What did you come up here to tell me?'

Howard took a deep breath. He looked down at his hands, and meticulously dry-washed them as he spoke. 'Let's put it this way, Morgana – nobody can say that you and I have been tremendously close, can they, during the years of your growing up. Maybe that's the way it is with most parents. Maybe that's just the way it is with me. I know that I can be sore-headed sometimes, and irrational, but that's what makes me the man I am. I know – and you know, too – that maybe I expected something out of my family life that I never quite managed to get. To be frank about it, a son. A boy to carry on the Croft Tate empire, after I've gone. I'd be fooling myself and worst of all I'd be fooling you if I ever tried to pretend that I wasn't disappointed.'

'Don't worry, Pops,' said Morgana. 'You've been making your disappointment quite obvious ever since I was three years old and wouldn't play baseball with you.'

Howard looked up at his daughter with those dark, glittering eyes of his, and she was surprised how hurt he looked. 'If that's true, then I'm sorry.'

'You know it's true,' she said, gently. 'But the point is that I don't mind and it doesn't matter. I'd probably feel the same way, if I were you.'

'You fox me sometimes,' Howard told her, with a smile.

'Then you have an advantage,' Morgana replied. 'You fox me all of the time.'

Morgana laid her hand on his. On the fourth finger of her right hand sparkled a six-diamond ring, with a centerstone of twenty-two karats; an oval brilliant, top Wesselton, flawless, worth a quarter of a million dollars. It had been Howard and Eleanor's principal gift to Morgana on her coming of age – that, and a brand-new Dodge Wayfarer Sportabout, in bright firetruck red, which was parked outside.

'Go on,' Morgana coaxed her father. He appeared to have lost the thread of his argument. Either that, or she had genuinely upset him.

He patted her hand. He looked at her, and tried out a smile.

It didn't work very well, but it was more appealing than the combative Rocky Graziano pucker.

'The thing of it is,' he said, 'that, male or female, daughter or son, you're still my child; and I've been watching you lately, over the past six months or so, and what I've been gradually coming to realize is that the qualities that make me what I am, if you can call them qualities – the love of newspapers, the love of everything that newspapers stand for, the urgency, the stress, the political power, the ability to be able to say something and have three million people pay attention to what you say; and not just that, but the telephones ringing and the typewriters clattering away, and then the presses starting to turn over, so that the whole building trembles like it's being shook by an earthquake – the love of that, and not only the love of it but the desire and the ability to make all that happen, every day of the week, three hundred sixty days a year – those qualities – well, you've got them, too.'

Morgana had never heard her father talk like this before, and so she stayed silent. She was aware that this speech wasn't at all easy for him, either as a businessman or as a father, and so she sat up straight and tried to look as open and as encouraging as she could: the mature and intelligent daughter, the respectful child.

Her father played absent-mindedly with her diamond ring, twisting it from side to side and watching the blue-white fire leap out of its facets. 'I was talking to your mother about something appropriate to give you for your twenty-first birthday. Not just jewelry, or cars, or dresses. Something for the future; something you could build on. And, well – of course we thought about the *Star*. I know how much time you spend down at the offices, talking to Grant and Reuben and all the rest of them. I know you like to stay up late to watch the paper put to bed. You have printing ink running in your veins, don't you? Just like me. Your grandfather dragged his printing press all the way across the plains in a Conestoga wagon – well, more of a broken-down buggy if the truth were known. When he died, I took over the *Star* and the *Nightly News* and built it up from there. When I die, it'll be your turn.'

'Pops, this is my birthday. Don't talk of dying.'

'This is the right moment, sugar. A birthday means one

year older. And anyway, you're old enough to think of it now. The *Star*, Morgana.'

Morgana looked at her father for a long time, then gently took her hand away from him and stood up. He sat watching her as she crossed to the mirror, tall and svelte in black and white. She was beautiful with the kind of incomplete beauty that is made up of eighty-five percent natural good looks and fifteen percent wealth. Her cheekbones were a fraction too hard; her eyes were a little too deep set. But the best hairdressing and the best cosmetics had softened her features and widened her eyes. Only her family knew what she looked like when she was un-made-up, and angry.

She stood facing her father's image in the mirror because she felt that his reflection would reveal if he was telling her the truth or not. Real faces can dissemble, but mirror faces never can. He understood her gesture, because to him the truth had always been a mirror image, dıurı ədı.

Howard stood up, too, and laid his hand on Morgana's shoulder. 'When I finally get fitted for my mahogany suit, Morgana, the Chicago *Star* will be yours. Not just a part of it, but all of it. That's my twenty-first birthday present; my real twenty-first birthday present. The legal documents are being drawn up on Monday, and by the middle of the week they should be ready for signature.'

He paused, and then he said, 'You'll have your share in everything else, of course. The small-town newspapers, the magazines, the radio stations. But the *Star* will be for you, and you alone, and if what Grant Clifford says about you is anything to go by, you won't ever let me down, nor the newspaper neither.'

Morgana turned around. Her father suddenly had tears in his eyes. They looked like two glass beads. She understood then that he had made his ultimate gesture of contrition. He had been unable to give her his heart. Instead, he had given her the most precious possession he had ever owned, his newspaper. She was twenty-one now, she was a woman, and that was the most that he could offer her. A thirty-six-story building, a staff of one hundred and ten, and a daily circulation of 935,000. If she wanted fatherly love, she knew that she would have to seek it elsewhere.

She hardly knew what to say to him. She was stunned not so much by the magnitude of what he had bequeathed her, but by the fact that – in bequeathing it – he had confessed at last the inadequacy of his feelings for her.

'Celebrated News Magnate Sobs On Daughter's Birthday,' she said, gently.

'What else can I say?' her father asked her, in a hoarse voice. 'Do you want me to say something else?'

'No,' whispered Morgana. She opened her arms to him, and he held her tight; and they stayed like that, holding each other, for a long moment of uneasy intimacy. Her father smelled of tobacco and English cologne. Close up, she could see the perfect stitching on his gray coat. She could feel his breath on her shoulder.

'Pops,' she said, 'thank you.'

Howard held her away from him, and stared at her, his face crowded with emotion, but he made no attempt to tell her how much he loved her, or to beg her pardon for twenty-one years of imperfect fatherhood.

At last he looked away, and released her. 'Maybe you'd like some champagne,' he said unevenly. 'Somebody has to drink it.'

'The loved as well as the unloved?'

He couldn't help smiling. 'Yes,' he said. 'The loved as well as the unloved.'

She replaced her hands together as if she were offering him a prayer. In a quiet voice, she told him, 'I shall never be able to thank you properly for the *Star*. Never. But *please* realize that you have made me happier and more excited than I have ever been in my entire life; and that what you have given me will always make me happy and excited.'

Howard was embarrassed. 'Come downstairs and have some champagne,' he insisted. 'Come on, it's your birthday.'

Down on the lawns, John Birmingham was singing, by way of diversion,

> 'Pepsi Cola hits the spot,
> Twelve full ounces, that's a lot.
> Twice as much for a nickel too,
> Pepsi Cola is the drink for you!
> Nickel, nickel, nickel, nickel
> Trickle, trickle, trickle, trickle.'

3

Half a dozen bottles of Dom Perignon '34 were opened in the morning room; a discreet fusillade of expensive little explosions, each tastefully suppressed by the wine butler in a clean primrose napkin. Howard stood under the moon-like countenance of his father, Gordon Croft Tate, the founder of the Croft Tate newspaper empire, whose portrait hung above the fireplace, and proposed in a sporadic but happy speech the health and prosperity of his first-born daughter, and the family applauded, and cheered. 'To Morgana! Happy birthday!'

Phoebe was industriously organizing everybody. 'Go find *John*, somebody, for goodness' sake! And where's mother? Hasn't she come down yet? Father, *do* get mother!'

Up came Cousin Arthur, in a lovat-green suit, with his strangely upside down looking face bristling with hostile bonhomie. He seized Howard's shoulder, and shook him as if he were making sure that nothing were loose. 'What do you say, Howard?'

Howard grasped his hand. 'Hallo, Arthur. What do I say about what?'

'Come now, Howard, you can't fool me,' winked Arthur. 'You get all the inside dope. You get all the gossip from behind closed doors. Is Barkley going to marry this widow-woman, or not? What do you say?'

'I say good for him if he does,' put in Morgana's Aunt Mimi. She was seventy-nine, and an enthusiastic advocate of autumnal love. She herself had remarried at the age of sixty-eight; and so far as she was concerned, the heatedly publicized courtship between Alben Barkley, the Vice-President of the United States, and a widow from St Louis called Mrs Carleton S. Hadley, was not only acceptable but highly commendable. Full marks for being a frisky old goat.

Howard said to Arthur, 'I'm sorry, Arthur. I don't know any more than you do.' He gave one of his famous biscuity coughs, and then he added, 'I made the mistake of beating Alben at golf, the last time we played, and he hasn't dropped me a crumb of scandalous information since.'

Thirty or forty of the Croft Tates' immediate family were jostling each other in the morning room, all invited early for vintage champagne. Outside, the day was humid and overcast, and the light that gleamed in through the diamond-leaded windows had the quality of clouded pewter. The family smoked and drank and bayed at each other. None of them was as rich or as powerful as Howard and his brood and they knew it, and hated it, but at the same time they were glad that they were there. In the middle of the room there was a seventeenth century hexagonal table, on which stood a huge white porcelain bowl, filled to overflowing with pink and white sweet peas. The servants' brilliantined hair shone through the cigarette smoke as they noiselessly and relentlessly refilled the family's flutes. Get them merry, but quick, Howard had instructed. Crystal and silverware sparkled; teeth glittered; diamond rings were waved around like fireworks.

Morgana, smiling in that aloof way of hers to uncles and aunts and cousins and old family friends, walked over to the French windows, and stood there for a moment alone, looking out over the East Lawn.

Six billowing marquees had been pitched on the grass – magnificent canvas palaces with gold-painted crenelations and wind-whipped banners, like the tents of some medieval king and queen. The band played 'Wunderbar' beneath the forbidding sky, and Morgana's Uncle Leonard was patting his swollen houndstooth stomach in time to the drum. The air was electric with excitement and the threat of a thunderstorm; laughter burst out obediently, as if the family were the audience at a radio show.

Cousin Stephanie approached Morgana and stood close up to her, smiling. Stephanie was overpoweringly dressed in a calf-length day-frock of clamorous turquoise, with a wrap-around front that had been embroidered in gold sequins with an eagle's wing design. She was Uncle Leonard's youngest and arguably his most obnoxious, although she had inherited her wiry Titian hair from her mother, and her prominent nose from somebody Semitic whom every preferred to forget.

'Well, then, how does it feel to be twenty-one?' asked Stephanie. 'Real old, I guess!'

'Oh, yes, old,' Morgana agreed. 'But wise, too. Definitely wise.'

Stephanie theatrically peered this way and that way across the lawn. 'This is some party,' she said. 'Doesn't it make you feel *embarrassed*?'

'Pops always likes to go over the top,' said Morgana. 'It's *his* party, as much as mine.'

'All the same, my dear,' and Stephanie's voice was lower now, 'the purr-*ice* must have been astronomical.'

Morgana shrugged. She was too happy today to allow Stephanie's jealous needling to upset her. Stephanie always needled. Stephanie lived in Forest Park and she detested it.

Morgana said, 'I don't really think that any of us should worry about the cost, do you? As long as Pops is having a good time, and as long as you and yours have enough champagne.'

'Well, pardon me, I'm sure,' Stephanie retaliated. 'I just thought it was incongruous, what with the *Star* running a fund for the destitute peoples of Europe. I mean, just look at all this, and then think about the destitute peoples of Europe.'

'You think Pops should have invited them along, as well?'

Stephanie let out a supercilious horse-like noise through one nostril. 'It's true what they say about newspaper people, then, being cynical?'

'Is that a question or an observation?'

'Neither, my dear,' said Stephanie. 'Simply a prejudice confirmed.'

Morgana stared at Stephanie and she could feel herself growing hot with annoyance. She could very easily have asked for a champagne cooler, and tipped it straight over Stephanie's Shredded-Wheat hairstyle. But instead, she managed to lip-wrestle her mouth back to a sort of a smile, and, with a sudden inspiration, clap her hands, and call out, 'Everybody!' and clap her hands again.

Forty faces looked around; bright with pleasure and amusement, and pink as jelly babies with vintage champagne.

Morgana waited until they were all quiet, and then she linked arms with Cousin Stephanie, and smiled at her, and announced, 'Cousin Stephanie has had such a marvelous idea. She's so concerned – and *rightly so* – that we're having such a lavish birthday party today while millions of people are starving in Europe that she's volunteered after the party to donate her new gown to the *Star*'s European Aid Fund; and I'm going to donate mine too. Isn't she marvelous? I think we all ought to give her a round of applause for her charitable idea!'

Stephanie's arm twisted furiously against Morgana's; but Morgana held her tight while everybody in the room put down their glasses and propped their cigarettes between their lips, and clapped.

Only Stephanie's mother, the sensitive and ever-woeful Aunt Beatrice, realized what Morgana must have done. On the opposite side of the room, her pale face rose wobbling and inquisitive like somebody balancing a dinner plate on the top of a stick. Morgana had no doubt at all that she would have words with her father before the day was done. Pale, whining words.

It was then however that Morgana's boyfriend, John Birmingham Jr, pushed his way into the room, dressed in a loud gray checkered suit and a checkered bow tie to match, patting his face all over with a bright green handkerchief, the kind favored by jazz musicians to dab their foreheads and to soak up the saliva which runs from the bells of their trumpets.

'What's this, what's this?' he wanted to know, with a wide toothy smile. 'Did I miss something? I *missed* something!' He collected a glass of champagne from the silver tray that was immediately diverted towards him; and then he shouldered his way through the uncles and the aunts (colliding, and then dancing for a moment with the furious Stephanie). He came up to Morgana, and took her hand, and kissed her once on the left cheek, once on the right cheek, and once on the tip of the nose.

'Happy birthday, sweetheart,' he told her. He reached into his pocket, and brought out a small flat package wrapped in pink tissue paper and tied with a pink silk bow. 'This is for you, from me.'

'May I open it now?' Morgana sparkled.

John frowned, and blinked and then smiled. 'Haven't you forgotten something? Where's your etiquette? Aren't you supposed to throw your arms around me and say, "Oh

Darling, you shouldn't have"? That's what ladies do in the advertisements.'

Morgana kissed him. 'You're the first person today who's called me a lady, instead of a girl.'

'Open it, then,' John urged her.

While she picked at the bow with her long red-painted fingernails, John said, 'I'm note-perfect now. Did you hear me? And that band out there is a smash! Wilbur T. Henry and the Marquettes. Do you know something – if I hadn't spent so long in law school, I'd take up singing professionally. The trumpeter said I had a natural jazz voice. "Mr Birmingham," he said, "you have pitch, you have timbre, you have tone."'

'Maybe you could sing in court, on behalf of your clients,' put in Cousin Stephanie, who had returned from a three-minute sulk to see if she could needle Morgana a little more. 'You'd have a captive audience then.'

Stephanie's bile was lost on John, who was too pleased with himself to notice anybody being ill-tempered; and who was incorrigibly good-humored in any event.

To the tune of The Children's Chorus from Act IV of *Carmen*, he sang, 'Oh, please your honor, let this fellow off. He stole a million – he's not a scoff – Law in fact he's good and decent and he takes a bath. Three times a day!'

Everybody laughed and clapped and raised their champagne glasses, and Stephanie withdrew in a round-shouldered temper, pushing Morgana's twelve-year-old cousin Eddie out of the way with her pointed turquoise elbow. Eddie said, 'Watch who you're jabbing, beanface.'

Morgana opened her present. Inside a plain black box, a star the size of a sheriff's badge sparkled, a white gold star pavé-set with diamonds. Morgana looked up at John in astonishment, and the reflections from the diamonds danced in lighted prickles on her cheeks.

'Your parents gave me some intimation of what your main present was going to be,' said John. 'I wanted to give you something to mark the occasion. Happy birthday, Miss Newspaper-Proprietor-To-Be.'

Phoebe appeared, chewing sugared almonds. 'Handsome Atty Busses Heiress At Intimate Society Smoker,' she remarked. Then she jerked her head toward Stephanie, and said, 'What's eating *her*?'

'The green-eyed googlybird, as usual,' said Morgana. She held up the diamond star that John had given her, and added, 'Mind you – just take a look at this. Enough to make anybody jealous.'

'Do you know something, dear, you spoil her,' Phoebe told John. She was all dressed up in her tight-fitting off-the-shoulder Charles James dress. It was silk, flamingo-pink, with a notched neckline, large buttons all the way down the front, and a tight narrow belt. She wore matching pink cotton gloves and pink high-heeled shoes with five ankle straps.

'Well, *you're* in the pink,' John joked, and kissed her on the hairline, which was about as far down as he could reach.

'How you doin', McEwan?' Phoebe asked him.

'Absolutely fine, McShine,' John replied.

Morgana said protectively, 'Any sign of Donald yet?' She knew that John was one hundred percent keen on her, but she didn't trust Phoebe an inch, not where men were concerned. Phoebe believed that all men were created equal. In other words, she was entitled to flirt with all of them equally, whether they were single or married, rich or poor, whether they were walking out with her older sister or not.

John was prime meat for Phoebe. He was six feet four in his Marshall Field's menswear department socks; muscular, thick-necked, with a curly Steve Canyon hairstyle and a broad, well-boned, well-fed mid-Western face. His father was John P. Birmingham, of Birmingham Wallis Ingate, one of the most prosperous company law partnerships in Chicago. His grandfather had acted for Marshall Field in the days when Field was first setting up his department store – hence the socks, which the Birmingham family had received every Christmas for forty years, gratis, by the four dozen. In 1909 that little gift had cost $10.88; today, in 1949, in spite of deflation, it was worth $60.72.

Morgana had been dating John for four months now. They had met at a charity evening at the College Inn in aid of the new veterans' hospital wing at Broadview. It had been the first really warm night of May. The stars had been sprinkled across the sky like sugar spilled on a black velvet cushion. Vic Shoen and his Orchestra had been playing 'Rum And Coca-Cola' and 'Oh! Look At Me Now!' and John had danced with Morgana almost all evening – even during the excuse-me, when he had fended off potential challengers like an All-Stars linebacker. 'Their' song, when they had danced their way out through the French windows on to the cool verandah outside, was Mairzy Doats; and they still sang it together whenever they went out for a drive.

> Mairzy doats and dozey doats
> And little lamsy divey ...

John and Morgana had made love twice. Both days shone in Morgana's memory as brightly as stained glass windows. Once, in a field, in the country, on a picnic for two, with the crickets chirruping and the orange poppies fluttering like scores of little fires breaking out in the grass. Then, at John's house, when his mother and father were away in Fort Lauderdale a whole dark and dreamlike afternoon, drinking very cold Chablis and eating raspberries and playing 'Doin' What Comes Naturally' on the Columbia.

For some reason, however, their lovemaking had not continued. Morgana one morning, tired after a late-night party, had said no; and John had not pressed her; and after that they seemed to have decided without discussing the matter that they should wait until they were married. They kissed a lot, they were as intimate as lovers, and Morgana often felt that if John were to try again to take her to bed, she wouldn't say anything but yes please, delighted. But in a strange way she liked the way they were. She liked the respect that John was showing for her: she liked the tension of waiting for the wedding night. And they were such a perfect, perfect couple that who could believe they wouldn't be married?

'You haven't told me what you think of *my* dress,' said Morgana, pointedly.

'I was going to save that for when we were alone,' John told her.

'You mean you hate it that much?'

'I love it, you dope. I just wanted to tell you in private.'

Morgana took hold of his arm, and kissed his smoothly shaven cheek. Taut skin, with a hint of a Florida tan. A taste of spiced cologne. 'You're an ace, McFace,' she told him.

Howard Croft Tate came over and shook John by the hand. 'How are you doing, John? Are they keeping you topped up with champagne?'

'Don't worry, sir. They're looking after me real well.'

Howard said to Morgana, 'I went back up and spoke to your mother. Well, it's nothing. She'll be down in a while. She let herself get too darned excited, that's all. She's been overdoing it, as usual, organizing this party. The flowers, the tents, the caterers. I guess the news about Robert Wentworth was the last parrot that brought down the tree.'

'I heard about Robert Wentworth,' said John. 'That was too bad.'

'Well, maybe,' Howard replied, trying to suck his extinguished cigar back to life. 'But if you want my opinion, he was doomed from the very beginning. That happens sometimes, you know, to the children of wealthy parents. I've seen it before. They use up all of their energy trying to burn themselves down to the ground.'

He turned to John, and gave him a friendly little prod with his finger. 'By the way, young Birmingham, I hear you're thinking of running for city councilor.'

John blushed a little. He hadn't shared his budding political ambitions with anyone outside of his family yet, not even Morgana.

Howard laughed harshly. 'Don't worry, I had lunch with your father last Thursday, at the Chicago Club. He was interested in knowing if the *Star* would back you, if you decided to run.'

'Well, of course we'd back him,' said Morgana. 'John – you didn't tell me about this! I think it's marvelous!'

'Well, I still haven't made up my mind for sure,' said John. 'I may wait until I've finished all of my legal studies.'

'You may be right,' Howard agreed. 'Even a politician should know how to make an honest living, if the need ever arises. How are your studies coming along?'

'I'm taking a week away from them, as a matter of fact. I've had about enough of *Jarowski vs Durham's Pure Leaf Lard* as I can stand.'

Morgana laughed. 'What was *Jarowski vs Durham's Pure Leaf Lard?*'

John raised his hand as if he was swearing an oath in court. 'Believe me, you don't want to know.'

'Tell me,' Morgana insisted.

'Okay, if you insist, but you won't thank me. *Jarowski vs Durham's Pure Leaf Lard* was a famous case in which Mr Jarowski – who tended a scalding vat in a tank room at

Durham's Pure Leaf Lard factory – fell into the vat without anybody noticing. He was overlooked for four days until they drained the vat and found his bones. The rest of him of course had gone out to the world as Durham's Pure Leaf Lard. His widow sued the factory for $5,000 plus 163 pounds of lard which was the equivalent weight of her dissolved husband. She said she had to have something to bury.'

Howard bellowed in amusement. 'Now, that's what I call a court case. Cases like that sell papers. Tremendous!'

Morgana said, 'Totally disgusting. I shall never be able to look at another pound of lard ever again, without feeling sick.'

Howard laid his hand on John's shoulder. 'More seriously, though, young man – if you do decide to run for city councillor – you must come downtown and have a talk with Grant Clifford – and we'll see what we can do to back you up.'

'I'll be running on a pro-labor platform,' John warned him.

'So long as you're not sponsored by the Chicago Typographical Union,' Howard replied. 'I may be a Democrat, but believe me, there is no race of people on this planet so awkward, so arrogant, and so downright rapacious, as typographers. They're a breed apart from the rest of us, believe me. Smutty-fingered, ink-stained, and utterly lacking in any form of human loyalty whatever.'

'As you can gather,' Morgana told John, 'Pops is not a great lover of printers. In fact I do believe he hates printers even more than Robert McCormick does.'

It was then that Morgana looked toward the doorway and saw that her mother had made an appearance. It was a shock. Her mother looked as if she had been stricken down with a sudden illness; or as if she had lost everything that mattered to her, for ever.

4

At eleven thirty, the first guests started to arrive, and by a quarter of twelve they were turning up in hundreds. The mile-long driveway that led up to Weatherwood glittered with Cadillacs and Chrysler Imperials and Pontiac Silver Streaks, the first of the truly post-war models, shining and streamlined and grinning with chrome. Over two thousand guests had been invited: minor royalty and major motion-picture stars, writers and producers and literary geniuses, artists and fashion designers, restaurateurs, radio comedians, industrialists, labor leaders, and city politicians.

The lion would rub shoulders with the lamb; the elite would eat canapés with the effete. The attraction of power and wealth and free publicity was irresistible to all.

Morgana and John went out on to the lawns to greet the arriving guests. The temperature was in the low seventies, but there was an unpleasantly humid wind blowing, and so Morgana wore a white angora bolero with black sequins across the shoulders.

As each limousine drew up beside the front portico, its doors were opened by blue and white liveried footmen, and its occupants were escorted up the wide front steps to shake hands with Howard: and then to be led into the huge domed hallway, where they were relieved of their hats and coats, and directed onward to the garden. There were flowers everywhere, sweet peas and roses and gladioli like bloodstained swords.

Morgana stood waiting to receive her guests under a white-painted archway decorated with red roses. Two more footmen stood just beside her, to take the birthday gifts which everybody had brought, and carry them by relay to the Long

Conservatory, where they would later be displayed, with hand-lettered name cards identifying their donors. Howard Croft Tate was an old hand at caressing egos.

The very first arrival, Henry Morgan the radio comic, led in a white baby goat on a pink-ribbon leash. 'This little lady's for you, because even if you've reached the age of adulthood, you've got to remember that you're still a kid at heart.'

After that, the gifts seemed to multiply not only in quantity but in size. Gil Lamb brought a box of Belgian fondants that could have ruined the appetites of a capacity crowd at Soldier's Field. David Bennett, the president of the Albert Verley perfume company (currently under Senate suspicion for five-percenting) brought five hundred cakes of scented soap and enough toilet water to canoe in.

None, however, could beat the giant blue package brought in by Jack L. Warner. It was almost fifteen feet high and twelve feet across, and when torn open, proved to contain a young strawberry tree, *arbutus unedo rubra*.

'For spooning under,' Jack Warner grinned, as he embraced Morgana. 'Each time you kiss you reach up and pick yourself a strawberry.'

Even under a dull and churlish sky, Weatherwood and its gardens had taken on the air of a country fairground. The house itself was a Gothic-American fantasy, the pride of the Gold Coast, a forty-bedroom mansion with turrets and spires and wrought-iron balconies and weather vanes. It had been designed in 1881 for the stockyard millionaire Nathaniel Beedy, but after the tragic death in 1900 of his young wife Doris (choked on a fish bone), he had rarely used it, and it had declined gradually into disrepair. Howard Croft Tate's father had bought it in 1917, and had organized the complete restoration of the floors, the staircases, the gilded drainpipes, and the peacock-blue roof tiles.

Weatherwood had variously been described as an architectural monstrosity; the Château Migraine; and as a railroad terminus masquerading as a private house. But Morgana adored its lavish eccentricity, and her mother always made it seem like a home, in spite of its colossal size. In summer, the reception rooms were always crammed with flowers; and in fall there were always fires crackling.

Today, Weatherwood was at its happiest, decked with banners, noisy with music, and thronged with hilarious people. Morgana welcomed Adlai Stevenson II, the governor of Illinois, who had always been a friend of the Croft Tates; she welcomed Kenneth Doyle, the mayor of Chicago, energetic and Irish and wildly talkative; she welcomed Agnes Moorehead; Ben Hecht; Senator Arthur Vandenberg; Constance Moore; Dave Garroway; Hughston McBain from Marshall Field; and one of the wealthiest of the new television personalities, Milton Berle. Prince Serge Obolensky brought a silver caviar service; Veronica Lake brought a pair of modern glass lamps; Hubert Humphrey, the mayor of Minneapolis, brought an oil painting of pink lady's slipper, the Minnesota state flower; and Senator Wayne Morse, whom Morgana's father had been trying to woo away from the Republican Party, brought a bronze sculpture of a horse from his native Oregon.

The David O. Selznicks brought a 35 mm print of *Gone With The Wind*, for Morgana to screen at home.

'Have you heard any more news about Margaret?' Morgana asked them. Margaret Mitchell, the author of *Gone With The Wind*, had been knocked down by a taxi-cab in Atlanta last night, and seriously hurt.

David shook his head. 'John said that she was still critical, but she's having an operation today. We've been praying for her. John's going to let us know if there's any improvement.'

Johnny Weissmuller arrived next, looking like a small building in a sport coat; then came Garry Moore and Dorothy Fields, the lyricist of *Annie Get Your Gun*. Salvador Dali swept in wearing a trailing white cape and a white hat folded out of paper. He kissed Morgana's hand, and bowed low, and said that he was painting a picture of her, as a birthday present, entitled 'The Fragmentation of the Innocents', but that it was not quite finished. 'Plenty of fragments, but no innocence,' he declared.

Blue-jacketed waiters weaved in and out of the crowds carrying aloft trays of (non-vintage) champagne. The band played a medley from this year's hit musical *South Pacific*. The craggy-faced Oscar Hammerstein was sitting with his drink on a low stone wall among the trailing white *saxifraga*. He remarked, as the band struck up with 'Bali Hái', 'I hope they're paying us a royalty for this.'

Groucho Marx, not far away, was describing his earlier life on the South Side of Chicago. 'Even in those days, it was a pretty good-sized slum. Most of the wealthier natives had scrammed further south; or up here, on one of the North Side roads. I was always afraid to come up here in case I accidentally wound up in Milwaukee.'

At noon, with immaculately stage-managed timing, a huge black and beige Rolls-Royce tourer drew up outside Weatherwood; and out stepped the reigning king and queen of the motion-picture business, Larry Olivier and Vivien Leigh. They were applauded on all sides as they emerged on to the East Lawn. Olivier had just won an Oscar for *Hamlet*: Vivien Leigh had starred last year in *Anna Karenina*. Their chauffeur came up behind them carrying a large box wrapped in dazzling gold paper, and tied up with an extravagant gold bow.

Olivier kissed Morgana, and then held her away from him, so that he could look at her. He looked fit, tanned, but a little tired. There was something in his eyes that silently spoke of stress, and disappointment, in spite of all the glories of the past year. 'Well, my dear,' he announced, 'you've grown up at last. I can no longer expect to see you in liberty bodices.'

'I'm sorry that you never did,' smiled Morgana.

Vivien was wearing a perfectly cut gray suit, and a stunning hat. It was wide-brimmed, gray, with a giant white rose on the front and a diaphanous white veil. She looked around, and took hold of Morgana's hand, and said, 'I can't believe it. This is more like the French Revolution than a birthday party! Look at all these people! There's Cole and Linda over there, I thought they were going to Europe. And Jean Dalrymple!'

The chauffeur noisily cleared his throat, and Olivier turned around to take the golden box out of his hands. He passed it to Morgana with a small courteous inclination of his head, and then he said, in his clear Shakespearean accents, 'For the most beautiful daughter of any newspaper proprietor anywhere – a token of our friendship and esteem.'

'And you must open it now,' Vivien insisted. 'If you really and truly hate it, we can always take it back.'

Morgana gave the box to John to hold, and tugged loose the golden bow. Then she stripped off the golden paper, and there it was, a gilded birdcage, in which a gilt and enamel bird was perched, with bright diamond eyes.

'You wind it up, you see,' Olivier explained, and twisted a small key at the side of the base. 'It's French, eighteenth century, but you can change the tune to anything you like. Even "The Darktown Strutter's Ball" or "Juke Box Saturday Night", if you know the notes.'

He turned the key, and then released it. The little gilt and enamel bird began to flap its wings and open and close its beak, and then it started to whistle a pretty and plaintive love song.

To Morgana's delight, Olivier began to sing the lyrics, taking her into his arms, and waltzing around the lawn with her, while the other guests gathered around to watch, and to cheer them on.

> 'Don't tell me it's sunset
> It can't be so soon.
> Don't tell me that lamp which lights the garden is the
>   moon . . .'

At last the mechanism wound down, and Olivier bowed to Morgana and kissed her hand. 'I'm sorry I sang so flat,' he apologized. Vivien clapped, and came forward to link arms with him. 'Happy birthday, my precious,' she began to Morgana. 'I'm glad you're only going to have one twenty-first. I couldn't bear to hear him singing again.'

John remarked, as Morgana returned to the rose-bedecked archway, 'I could be jealous of him, you know.'

'Of Larry?' asked Morgana, half-joking and half-irritated. 'You're kidding.'

'I'm not kidding at all,' John retorted.

'Well, how jealous?' Morgana demanded. 'I mean, be specific.'

'Well,' said John, thoughtfully, 'jealous enough to do some serious damage to his maxillae bones and his malar bones; as well as his lacrimal, turbinal, and vomer bones.'

'What does that mean?'

'You want it in Italian?'

'Any language you like.'

'In Italian, it means I break-a his face.'

Morgana slapped at his shoulder. 'You're a lawyer. And a politician. You're supposed to be serious.'

'I am serious. I love you.'

Morgana slapped at him again, but this time he caught her wrist, and held her tight – so tight that if she had tried to pull herself away, it would have hurt. He looked at her quite intently. She thought (not for the first time) how good-looking he was. Halfway between Errol Flynn and Dana Andrews. But she also thought (not for the first time) that something was missing between them, although she couldn't work out what it was. He said, quietly, almost as if he were threatening her, 'You've heard what people say about us, haven't you? The perfect match.'

She looked away. 'The perfect match doesn't always light fires.'

'Well, that's a smart remark. Does that mean you don't love me?'

'John – it means that today I don't want to think about anything else but enjoying myself. It's my birthday.'

'All right, then,' said John, pretending to be hurt, 'in that case, I won't ask you to marry me.'

'Good,' Morgana retorted, with a wicked little smile. 'If you proposed to me now, do you know what I'd do? I'd scream, for the rest of the day, without pausing for breath.'

John laughed, and kissed her. 'When I graduate from law school, you she-vixen, I'm going to ask you to marry me, and by God I'm not going to take any kind of a no for an answer. You hear me? I love you. And seriously, too. Not flippantly.'

'Flippantly? You make us sound like a pair of performing seals.'

'God Almighty, maybe we are.'

At that moment, bustling and flouncing, Marlene Dietrich arrived, wearing a huge hat smothered in bouncing white ostrich plumes, like a one-woman interpretation of Busby Berkeley's famous fan dance; and a white dress with a deep plunge neckline. Since Marlene immediately demanded everybody's undivided attention, Morgana had to kiss John quickly, and turn around to welcome her. Marlene planted two kisses in mid-air on either side of Morgana's face, darling, mmm, *plick*, *plick*, and then presented her with a white-wrapped gift, decorated with a flower fashioned from white Brussels lace.

'Oh, you don't have to open it yet; it's perfume,' she said, in her growling quaver. 'Very exclusive, distilled especially for me by Farina Gegenüber. It is supposed to arouse in men insatiable *lussst*.'

She looked John up and down with her heavy-lidded eyes, and John grinned at her and gave her a finger-wave, and said,

'How're you doing? I loved *A Foreign Affair*.' She leaned close to Morgana, and added *sotto voce*, 'Use *lots*,' and made an extravagant sprinkling gesture.

One o'clock chimed with a sound like one of Edgar Allen Poe's brazen bells from Weatherwood's highest tower, and Winton Snell, the Croft Tate family's portly and imperious major domo, ascended to the band rostrum at the side of the lawns and raised both his arms for silence. A stray flicker of sunlight passed across him, as if he had been acknowledged by Heaven, and for a moment he was quite saintly and dazzling, his shirtfront, his gilt buttons, his gold teeth, his black varnished hair, and his magnificent gentian nose.

'Your royal highnesses! Archbishop! My lords! Ladies! Gentlemen, luncheon is served.'

He stepped down from the rostrum with a corseted sway while the band finished playing 'Green Eyes'; and then he advanced on Morgana with all the dignified bulk of a killer whale making its way through a school of pilot fish. He excused himself to Jane Wyman and Santos Ortega, with whom Morgana had been chatting, and said, 'A very joyful coming of age, Miss Morgana. Would you and his honor the mayor care to lead the way into luncheon?'

The swing band were leaving the rostrum now, to be replaced almost immediately by Shep Fields and his Orchestra, the radio band with the 'rippling rhythm', who had been booked by Howard and Eleanor to play through luncheon. There was an enthusiastic spattering of applause as they broke into 'Slow Boat To China'.

Mayor Doyle bustled over to Morgana and bowed so enthusiastically that he looked for a moment as if he were going to dive head first into the rose bed. He was silver haired, thin as a birch-branch, wiry, Celtic, and beady eyed; crammed with that energetic agitation that makes poets, wits, priests, and politicians. He wore a crumply gray suit and the same Dick Tracy Official watch that he had borrowed from his son fifteen years ago. He was no fool, though, politically. Morgana had heard her father describe him as the wiliest mayor since Tony Cermak.

'Morgana, happy birthday to you!' he smiled, and took her arm.

'Thank you, your honor,' Morgana replied, and kissed his cheek. 'Isn't Mrs Doyle here?'

'Later, I hope; but her Pekinese was sick on the mat this morning, and she's a fearful one for her dogs. If you ask me, it's the food she gives them, far too rich for a dog, she'd have them eating with knives and forks if she possibly could, and finger-bowls, or *paw*-bowls wouldn't it be? with slices of lemon. Calves' liver, with gravy, and *petty-pwuh*! Well, she's a good woman. No man could wish for a better. But I sometimes feel like I'm living in the city pound.'

He took hold of Morgana's hand, and patted it as if it were two pounds of best butter. 'She'll be here, though, my Kate. She wouldn't miss this little bash for the world. And she's passionately in love with Laurence Olivier.'

'I think all women are,' Morgana told him, warmly. 'I know I am.'

Just then Phoebe went storming past, looking all hot and flustered. Morgana said to Mayor Doyle, 'Please excuse me – just for a second,' and intercepted Phoebe before she could disappear into the crowd.

'*Phoebe!*'

'Oh,' said Phoebe, 'I was looking for you.'

'What's the matter? Aren't you coming into lunch? You look like Grim Death.'

'Well, so would you. Everything's absolutely chaos. Mother was here for five minutes and now she's disappeared, and father's blaming me. "Go find your mother!" Well, *I* don't know where she is! And damned Donald hasn't shown up; and bloody Bradley has; and he keeps trailing around after me like a three-year-old kid with wet knickerbockers.'

Morgana frowned. 'Surely Momsy wouldn't have –?'

'Wouldn't have what? *I* don't know! I've tried her room and she isn't here. I've tried the kitchen and she isn't there either! And oh, God damn it, there's bloody Bradley again. Look at him. That innocent eager little face. The Mickey Rooney of processed meat.'

Morgana said, 'I'd better get back to the mayor.' But Mayor Doyle had already caught up with Morgana, and taken hold of her arm again.

'Hallo there, Phoebe,' he greeted her. 'Morgana, we'd better go in to lunch. If I know anything about crowds, they grow dangerous when they start getting hungry. I always used to tell your father that, you know, back before the war when he was campaigning for Congress. One hot dog with everything on it is worth ten speeches.'

Morgana quickly smiled, and then said to Phoebe, 'Let me know when you find her. Even if you give me a wave, nothing more. I must go now.'

Kenneth Doyle proudly led Morgana into the nearest of the six marquees. The orchestra played 'Geraniums In The Winder', and then 'Chicago'. Kenneth Doyle waved and Morgana smiled. They were applauded on all sides as they walked through the elaborately draped entrance to the marquee, between bursting banks of crimson American Beauties. The flowers alone for this party had cost $11,000, which was more than The Drake spent on their florist in a year.

Inside the marquee there were four trestle tables, each one hundred twenty feet long, spread with crisp white linen and arranged collectively with five hundred full place settings of English silver, one thousand crystal wine glasses, and eighty vases of yellow gladioli. At each place there was a handwritten card, with the guest's name on it, and a single yellow rose placed across a decoratively folded white napkin.

Kenneth Doyle was telling Morgana about his latest fishing expedition. 'Do you know something, I played that marlin for four hours – four hours! – and in the end I had to cut it loose. For the first time in my life I understood what Hemingway was writing about.'

'Well, you'll have to tell him all about it,' said Morgana. 'He's promised to come. In fact, he should be here already.'

Groucho Marx, who was closely following Morgana, said, 'You'll have to excuse me. I like to get in first, just in case I've been seated next to a cluck. Then I can switch the place cards.'

'No clucks were invited,' smiled Morgana.

'I still want to make sure that I'm sitting next to somebody rich and pretty. And I don't mean you, Mr Mayor, so it's no use winking at me like that.'

They walked up to the far end of the marquee, where the sunlight filtered through the canvas roof to lend a magical golden quality to everything inside, like a Hollywood interpretation of a pasha's tent. Here, twelve chefs in traditional white aprons stood sentry-duty over a hot and cold buffet of heroic proportions: a mountain range of extravagantly embellished food, glistening and rich and strongly aromatic.

Guests were invited to collect from a warming wagon a

large gilt-ringed plate, and then to proceed from one end of the mountain range to the other, selecting whatever they wanted from what the *bon-vivant* and gastronome Lucius Beebe was later to call 'the last plausible buffet in the history of American eating.' There were heaps of freshly shucked Atlantic oysters; as well as oysters *poulette* and oysters Rockefeller. There were whiskery cascades of Guaymas shrimps; and lobsters by the score – either cold, with *sauce verte* or mayonnaise – or hot, with drawn butter. There were quires of smoked salmon; sheaves of fresh Colorado trout; and thick slices of sturgeon. There were cold shoulders of spiced pork; chickens boned and stuffed with French chestnuts. Périgord truffles, and curaçao; accompanied by chilled asparagus, vinegared artichokes, pickled walnuts, and green salads as deep and verdant as South American jungles.

On command, the chefs would slice for the guests thick and appetizing pieces of hot roast beef, or hot Virginia ham, or hot corned beef, and pass these over on warm rye bread, fresh from the ovens.

At the center of the table, under the chilly supervision of six immense butter sculptures of eagles and swans and unicorns, there stood a massive cut-crystal bowl, embedded in ice and decorated with lemon wedges, which contained forty-eight pounds of fresh Beluga caviar, and from which the guests (with outsized tablespoons) were invited to help themselves.

As the guests sought out their places, with their plates stacked threateningly high, the first of the wines was being poured: a premier-cru Chablis, $4.19 a bottle, three hundred cases of which were reclining in the small pink-tiled swimming pool at the side of Weatherwood's tennis courts. The pool had been drained of water and refilled with seven truckloads of crushed ice, especially for the occasion. Meanwhile, in the North Conservatory, three hundred cases of Gevrey Chambertin were comfortably raising themselves like dusty maroon-bodied babies to room temperature.

Morgana took her place at the center of the top table, while her guests cheered and applauded. She sat between Kenneth Doyle and her father. A little further down sat the Oliviers, and the Adlai Stevensons, with the Jack L. Warners and the Selznicks judiciously separated on either side, and Prince Serge Obolensky sitting opposite. Next to Larry Olivier, however, Morgana's mother's chair remained conspicuously empty;

and although he was abrasively playing the part of the good-humored host, Morgana could tell by the way in which her father was drumming his fingers on the tablecloth that he was incandescently angry; and growing angrier.

David Selznick had been married to his new wife Jennifer Jones for little more than a month. They hadn't had time to take a honeymoon yet, although they had promised themselves a trip to Europe when Jennifer finished shooting *Gone To Earth*. David told Morgana, as he tidily rearranged his salad, carrots here, coleslaw there, 'This party is almost as good as a honeymoon. What more do we need? Good food, good wine, music, conversation. Maybe you could keep it going for a day or two, and we'll stay on. How about it, Howard? We could shoot around Jennifer until Wednesday afternoon.'

Jennifer tossed an olive at him, and it bounced off the shoulder of his white wool sport coat. 'Stop being such a cheapskate,' she protested. 'I want a proper honeymoon in Europe. I want London and Paris and Rome, and I want to be kissed under the moonlight in a gondola in Venice.'

Garry Moore, who was passing close by with a plateful of food, said, 'I wouldn't mind being kissed in a closet in Sheboygan, just so long as I was kissed.'

It was twenty minutes before Eleanor appeared at last at the entrance to the marquee, looking white. There was applause from the guests as she came in, and several of them lifted their glasses to her. She acknowledged their greeting with a quick, tight smile, and then came around to her place and sat down. One of the waiters leaned over her shoulder and asked her what she would like to eat.

'A little cold salmon will do, thank you,' she said.

Howard was picking furiously at his potato salad. His whole plate was a mess of dismembered, uneaten food. Morgana heard him say hoarsely, 'I'm glad you could make it.'

'I apologize,' Eleanor said, without looking at him. There was a steel-spring sound in her voice which was an obvious warning to him not to make a scene.

'I was concerned that you might have forgotten what day it was,' said Howard, under his breath, but still emphatically enough for everybody sitting within fifteen feet to catch the general implication of what he was saying.

'Oh, my dear Howard, there was absolutely no risk of that,'

Eleanor replied. 'It is exactly twenty-one years to the day since I was lying in the Fox River Clinic giving birth to your very first daughter – while you, my dear, were in New York having dinner at the Colony with Governor Al Smith and John J. Raskob, discussing ways in which the Chicago *Star* was going to soft-pedal the Democratic low-tariff doctrine.'

'*Touché,*' said Mrs Howard Linn, rather too loudly.

'Is that your reason for being late?' Howard demanded, out loud. The company at the top table bristled with anticipation. Was this the overture to yet another of the Croft Tates' famous public arguments? It was a social credential of no mean value to have witnessed a Croft Tate spate, and if their bouts of ill temper had been at all predictable Henry and Eleanor could have sold tickets, with souvenir photographs by Marty Black, of the *American*.

Howard insisted, 'Are you trying to get your own back, simply because business kept me away from your bedside while Morgana was being born? Was I supposed to be pacing the waiting room, with a breast pocket crammed with cheap cigars? You seem to forget that while you were trying to produce one small infant girl, I was trying to save the nation from financial collapse.'

Eleanor turned to her husband tartly. 'At least, out of the two of us, I succeeded in what I set out to do.'

Howard stared back at her, his chin quivering; but then he couldn't help smiling; and, at last, laughing. 'Damn it, Eleanor, you always have the last word, don't you? Damn it to hell.'

Eleanor said, 'I won't ever let you down, Howard, you know that. I never have done and I never will. Please forgive me for being late.'

'Eleanor,' put in Larry Olivier, leaning toward her, 'you look more beautiful by the minute, and younger by the year. Come on, tell us your secret.'

'It can't be marriage to this old grouch Howard that keeps you so young,' Jack Warner teased. 'My God, I think it would be more peaceful being married to Louis B. Mayer.'

Eleanor laid her hand on top of Howard's, and said clearly, as an open gesture of reconciliation, 'Howard is a very special husband. Here I am – late for my daughter's twenty-first birthday lunch, and as awkward in my demeanor as ever a wife could be – and he has forgiven me. Or at least I think he has. And I hope you all forgive me, too.'

There was a strange, tense moment; as if time were being pulled out like salt-water taffy, longer and tauter and still refusing to snap. But Howard then reached over, and kissed Eleanor's cheek, and somebody at the back of the marquee let out a wild Ohio hog-call, and there was tumultuous applause and table-thumping and relieved laughter.

Prince Serge Obolensky raised his arm in a flourishing salute. 'Anyone who can lay on a meal of this magnitude has no need of forgiveness,' he cried. 'If anything, they should be canonized. Saint Eleanor of the Ecstatic Luncheon.'

'The prince is a worshiper at the shrine of his own digestive system,' put in Russell Lynes, the editor of *Harper's*. But of course Russell Lynes would have been irritated by anything that Obolensky happened to say; because Obolensky had taken the last available suite at the Ambassador East Hotel, and Lynes had been forced to stay at the Michigan Palace, which he hated.

'Better to thrust one's snout into the dishes of the gods, than into the trough of human folly,' Obolensky replied. He had breakfasted on lightly scrambled eggs and a bottle of Perrier-Jouët champagne, and he was already lyrical. 'When there are more television sets being sold per week in the state of Illinois, than there are twenty-four pound cans of Beluga caviar throughout the entire United States – why, surely we must be on the brink of complete barbarism. A new Dark Age, in which palates like mine will become extinct, and the flickering eye of the television will hypnotize all!'

'Oh, you're wrong there, prince,' said Howard, shaking his head. 'Television, believe me, is the single most important step forward in human civilization since movable type.'

'What kind of a testimonial is that?' Obolensky retorted. 'What earthly benefits did movable type ever bring us?'

'The Gutenberg bible?' Johnny Weissmuller suggested, amazing everyone, probably including himself.

'The Gutenberg bible!' cried Obolensky. 'Did you ever read the Gutenberg bible? No, *mon ami*, what movable type brought us was *Forever Amber*, God help us, and *Tales of the South Pacific*! The *Katzenjammer Kids*, and the Chicago *Star*! And what is television bringing us? *Hopalong Cassidy! The Goldbergs!* The Texaco Star Theater!'

'Now, you just hold on a minute,' interrupted Milton Berle, turning around from the next table. He was the host of the Texaco theater, and the highest paid performer in American television history. 'You can't tell me that your palate is superior to my program. Maybe your palate is more refined. Maybe your palate can tell the difference between pâté de foie and chlorophyll toothpaste; and maybe your palate never does anything for a cheap laugh. But how many people would sit down for sixty minutes each week and watch your palate? *And* pay you $6,500 a week for the privilege?'

There was a burst of laughter. Prince Obolensky said, '*Zut! Quel paien!*'

Next to Morgana, Howard joined in the noisy bantering conversation with gusto – his harsh voice rising above the clamor with all the insistence of a buzzsaw on a busy construction site.

'You can't lead the American public around by the nose,' he put in. 'They know what they want, and they know what they don't want. Right now, they want romance, and they want excitement. They want to escape. And if they're prepared to pay good money for books like *This Side of Innocence* and *The King's General* – well, now, who are we to criticize them? If they want to watch Howdy Doody, or Milton here –'

'Not necessarily in that order,' cracked Milton Berle.

'– well, maybe not,' smiled Howard, 'but a little bit of fun never hurt anybody. A little bit of self-indulgence. God knows, we deserve it. You hear so much criticism of material wealth, but where's the harm in wanting security, and fine new possessions? An automatic dishwasher, why not? A new Kaiser to park in the driveway, to impress your neighbors, why not? There's nothing delirious about material possessions.'

'Deleterious,' Morgana corrected him, quietly.

'Tell me,' Prince Obolensky interrupted, 'what kind of world do *you* want, Mr Croft Tate? What *you* believe in, what *you* want you can express in your newspapers and broadcast through your radio stations, to millions of Americans, from one coast to the other. Your opinion matters. It is influential. So what goes on inside your head is of crucial importance.'

Morgana answered before her father could even think what to say. She held her father's hand, and squeezed it reassuringly, and said, 'My father is a Democrat, and a man of great humanity. What he wants is printed on the masthead of the *Star*, six nights a week. "To Inform And To Entertain". He wants his readers to know the truth, so that they can make up their own minds. He also wants to amuse them. Nobody could have two better ambitions than those.'

Dick Maney, the public relations wizard, leaned forward and said to the prince, 'If you want to know where America is headed, sir, I don't think you need look any further than the new ice cream sundae I saw advertised the other day. Eight different flavors of ice cream, all in one glass, topped up with bananas, nuts, cherries, raspberries, tutti frutti, and whipped cream. The epitome of mindless, tasteless appetite. And appropriately named, too – the Moron's Ecstasy, price one dollar.'

'Let's discuss this after we've eaten ourselves sick,' joked Russell Lynes.

'I think I am already sick,' said Prince Obolensky.

Morgana said, 'There's a place for everything, so long as it's the best.'

'Is that your motto?' asked Woolworth Donahue, dryly. 'I mean – is that the principle that you'd apply, if you ran the *Star*?'

'That's right,' Morgana told him. 'The best – or *whewpff*,' and she cut her throat with her finger.

'You'd be more frightening to work for than Attila the Hun,' Milton Berle gibed.

'My dear old pal,' said Jack Warner, 'you have to be ruthless to run a newspaper. It is the very best ingredient of good management. Same as a motion-picture studio. Attila the Hun couldn't have run a newspaper. He wouldn't have been ferocious enough. Besides, they didn't have newspapers in those days.'

'They did too,' Milton Berle replied. 'Haven't you heard of *The Evening Pillage* and *The Daily Rape*?'

The waiters gathered around them again, to clear away all the buffet plates. Then the drapes over the marquee entrance were drawn back, and six buglers marched in single file down the length of the tent, and took up position on either side of Morgana's chair. They wore the full dress uniform of musicians of the United States Heavy Artillery of 1882, with brass-spiked *pickelhauber* helmets and red-striped jackets and blue-striped trousers. They lifted their bugles to their lips and played 'Happy Birthday To You', followed by a high-speed version of 'Twenty-One Today'.

Morgana laughed and clapped in delight. Then, as the buglers stepped back, six white-uniformed pastrycooks entered the marquee, carrying between them a ten-tier birthday cake, frosted in pink and white, with swags and tails of white sugar, and twenty-one silver candlesticks. Everybody stood, spontaneously, and sang 'Happy Birthday'.

The cake was paraded around the marquee, followed by twelve members of the swing band in strawberry-colored tailcoats and straw skimmers, playing 'Garryowen'. At last the cake was set on the table in front of Morgana, to deafening applause; and Winton Snell came forward with a silver cake knife as long as a Civil War saber.

Morgana, her eyes sparkling with reflected light, blew out all twenty-one candles with one breath; and while everybody roared '*Wish! Wish! Wish!*' she closed her eyes tight and wished for this: for something to happen today that would change her life for ever.

Kenneth Doyle said, 'You wished?'

She nodded. She couldn't help laughing.

'I wish I had a wish,' said Kenneth, ambiguously.

Morgana kissed him on the cheek. 'You shall,' she told him. 'People like you always get their wish, in the end.'

Eleanor came around and hugged Morgana tight. 'Happy birthday, my darling,' she told her.

Morgana said, in a soft, inquiring undertone, 'Are you all right?'

Eleanor glanced at her keenly, and then looked away, and nodded. 'Yes, dear. I'm all right.'

She hesitated, and then she added, 'I'm sorry I was late. I had to talk to somebody.'

'About Robert Wentworth?'

Eleanor said, without looking at her, 'Don't start being too perceptive, my dear.'

'Momsy,' said Morgana, 'thank you for everything.'

'Thank your father.'

Then a young photographer from the *Star* came shouldering his way through the guests and the buglers, and lifted his hat to Morgana, and said, 'I have to get some pictures for tomorrow's special. Could you spare a minute, please?'

Almost at the same time, Phoebe came up behind Morgana, and hissed, 'He's here!'

'Who's here?'

'*He!*'

'Not Donald?'

'You're damned right Donald.'

'What are you going to do?'

'Get rid of Bradley, of course!'

'How are you going to do that?'

'God knows. Can't you think of anything?'

Morgana said, 'Tell Donald the truth, that's all you have to do.'

'That's easy for you to say, but you don't know Donald's temper. He's very passionate about everything. Right at this particular moment he's passionate about me. He'll probably *kill* Bradley, if he sees him following me around. Cut him to ounces.'

'Miss Morgana?' the *Star* photographer repeated.

'Pheeb, I have to have my picture taken,' said Morgana. 'Let's discuss it when I'm through. How long are we going to be?'

'Ten minutes, tops,' replied the photographer.

'Oh contentious fates,' Phoebe complained.

Morgana followed the photographer out of the marquee into the open air. The sky was dark and threatening, and there was a wind that smelled of storms.

'Some birthday weather, hunh?' the photographer asked her. 'Double, double, toil and whatever.' He jerked his head back toward the marquee, and said, 'What was eating that sister of yours?'

'Are you here to take my picture?' Morgana asked him.

'Sure,' he nodded.

'Then, please, just take my picture.'

'Gulp, ahem,' the photographer replied, lifting his hat to acknowledge his indiscretion. He was almost a parody of a young newspaperman. He was pale faced, with boysenberry-colored circles under his eyes, and a pencil mustache. His hair was naturally blond and curly, but he had greased it back into brilliantined waves. He wore a wide-brimmed hat with his union card stuck into the hatband, and a huge big-shouldered sport coat in vivid green and orange check. To complete the picture of downtrodden pizazz, his necktie was one of those wide hand-painted jobs with a palm tree and a sunset on it.

'We can take something pretty dramatic here,' he remarked, fitting a flashbulb into his Kodak. 'You, the house, the thunder and lightning.'

'Who do you think you are?' Morgana demanded. 'Philippe Halsman?'

'Oh, you know your photographers?' the boy retorted, haughtily. 'Well, if you know your photographers, you could say that I'm more like a mixture of Dan McNutt and W. Eugene Smith. Newsy, gossipy, but artistic with it. Actually, my name is Joseph K. Proski; but you can call me Woozy. Everybody else does.'

Morgana smiled. 'All right then, Woozy. How would you like me?'

5

Woozy took picture after picture as the warm, overpowering storm came rolling over Chicago and its north-western suburbs from the south. His flashbulbs popped and crackled in fits and starts, illuminating Morgana in her black and white Dior dress like a front-page photograph that was already flickering off the presses.

'Don't smile,' he kept telling her. 'These days, you have to look like you're in the dumps to be classy. In the prints, anyway. That's good. I caught the lightning then. That's by way of being something.'

'This is supposed to be my birthday,' said Morgana. 'Can't I smile even a little?'

'Well, I guess,' Woozy agreed. 'Dugald did say he wanted some *joie-de-vivre*.'

'*Joie-de-vivre?* You speak French?'

'No, do you? I used to date a French-Canadian girl once, her name was Justine. The only trouble was, her folks disliked me intensely. They wanted her to marry a hotelier.'

'That was peculiar.'

Woozy took another picture, and wound on the film. 'Not when you think about it. They wanted someplace to live when they retired. They didn't take to the idea of living in a darkroom, which was all that I could've offered them; so they picked on a hotel.'

He sniffed, and then he said, 'Not everybody gets what they want. Look at me. I wanted to go into the Navy.'

'What happened?'

'The Second World War ended, that's what happened. Nobody left to fight. Apart from the fact that I was rated 26–Z for physical fitness. Hold that pose, that's it, that's sublime.'

'How come you started working for the *Star*?'

Woozy bent over and collected up his spent flashbulbs. This, after all, was the Boss's private lawn, not the Loop, or the steps of the Cook County courthouse. 'One of the city reporters recommended me. He was a pal of mine, when I was younger, we were both brought up in Roseland. You probably heard of him, Harry Sharpe.'

'I can't say that I have,' Morgana admitted. At that moment, simultaneously, the first few drops of rain began to fall, warm and widely spaced and as metallic smelling as a pocketful of wet money; and John Birmingham came out of the marquee to see what had happened to Morgana.

'This your intended?' asked Woozy. 'Want to get a picture with him?'

Morgana smiled, and John wrapped his arms around her. Morgana advised him, 'You're supposed to look down in the dumps.'

'Down in the dumps? What for?'

'No, no, cheerful,' Woozy urged him. 'Down in the dumps is for fashion plates and solo ladies. Together, you're supposed to look cheerful.'

Morgana and John grinned widely as Woozy took their picture together. Morgana said, 'What about this for a caption? "Print-cess Beams In Arms of Beau."'

Woozy busily wound back his film, opened up his camera, and inserted a new reel. Ash dropped into the back of the camera from his dangling cigarette, and he had to blow it persistently away. 'You'll have to talk to Harry if you want to suggest a caption. Harry believes that reporters should do the reporting and bosses should do the bossing and that never the twain should whatever.'

'Harry sounds like a union man,' John commented.

'Harry's the best reporter the *Star* ever had, excepting for Duncan McReady, back in the old days.' Woozy sniffed. 'You should've met him, you come down to the office just about once a week, don't you? I've seen you there, talking to Solomon.'

'Solomon?' asked Morgana. 'I don't know any Solomon.'

'Solomon is what everybody calls Grant Clifford. Didn't you know that? They call him that on account of the fact that he'd cut a baby in half, just to be fair.'

'I heard that he was very impartial,' Morgana commented.

'Impartial? Harry says that Grant Clifford can see two sides to a golfball.'

Woozy took three more pictures, and then began to pack his camera away.

'Is that it?' asked Morgana.

'That's it. You want contacts? I'll send some up.'

John took Morgana's arm. 'Let's get back to the party, shall we? I'd like you to hear me sing my songs before it starts to bucket.'

Morgana held John close to her. She adored the smell of his cologne and the soft feeling of his clothes. She always found it easy to convince herself that she wanted to stay with him forever, not only because he was tall and good-looking and relaxed – not only because he could sing and dance and sail and ride and smile to all the right people – but because he had a way of making her feel prettier whenever she was with him. Woozy took two or three more photographs, in spite of the rain, and Morgana knew exactly what it was that he was trying to capture on his film – the golden couple of the gilded mid-West.

'You know something,' said John, kissing her hair. 'I do believe I love you.'

'I always knew you were nuts,' Morgana retorted.

'Hey – you have to be nuts to be a lawyer. It's a condition of employment.'

Woozy said, 'Let me tell you, Miss Morgana, you ought to be a model. With a dial like yours, you'd easy make the cover of *Glamor*. Maybe *Vogue* even.'

'I'm not sure my father would approve of that,' said Morgana. The rising wind was beginning to flap at her long Dior skirt.

'Hey, you're twenty-one now. You can do what you like.'

'Are you through now?' John demanded, with mock impatience.

Morgana said, 'I may be twenty-one, Woozy – but when you're an heiress, you can never do what you like. Not totally. You see all of this? This house? These gardens? The newspapers, too, and the radio stations. One day they're all going to belong to me, and so is the responsibility of taking care of them, and of all the people who work for them.'

Woozy had packed away his camera and his flashlight, and

now he shouldered his leather camera bag and gave one last editorial sniff. 'That sounds very depressing to me.'

'Why should it?' asked John, defensively.

'Why do you think?' Woozy retorted. 'All *I'll* ever get to inherit is a stamp collection, and a pile of jazz records, and a '37 Terraplane with a body condition that looks like leprosy.'

Morgana laughed. 'Don't worry, Woozy, when I get to take over the *Star*, I'll make you chief photographer.'

'That's a promise?'

'Come on, beat it,' John urged him. 'We have to get back to the party.'

As Morgana returned to the marquee, the guests were eating birthday cake and drinking champagne. She stopped to talk to Babe Palmer, of the Potter Palmers, who had founded the store that eventually became Marshall Field; and to Jack Velie, one of the wealthier inheritors of the Deere plow works in Kansas City. Within olive-throwing distance, there were forty or fifty socialites and celebs, from Alan Jay Lerner to Paul Draper, from Hope Williams to Peggy Fears, money and talent rubbing shoulder to shoulder, knee to knee, diamond to diamond, because Morgana Croft Tate's twenty-first birthday party just happened to be the place one ought to be seen at, this Friday August 12. It was more than a birthday party, it was a chance for everybody who was anybody to get together; to show off their burgeoning wealth; to talk; to exchange slanderous gossip; to make deals; to assert their success. They knew most of all that their presence would be flatteringly reported in every one of Howard Croft Tate's 138 newspapers, from the flagship Chicago *Star* to the Cockeysville (Maryland) *Courier*. The Croft Tate empire also embraced ten popular household magazines, including *Mitchell's* and *Excellent Housekeeping*, and fifty-five radio stations.

For everybody here, the publicity value alone had been worth an extra day's stopover between The Super Chief and The Twentieth Century Limited, or vice versa.

Morgana resumed her place at the head of the table, and Howard stood up and lifted both of his hands for silence. There was laughter, clinking of glasses and cake forks, and, at last, quiet.

'Your royal highnesses. Archbishop. My lords, ladies, and gentlemen. Let me tell you something. My father once said to me, Howard, with you, I intend to start a dynasty. I intend the name of Croft Tate to be emblazoned all over America every day, on a newspaper or a magazine; or heard every day on a radio station. I want Croft Tate to be equally familiar to the American public as Coca-Cola or Charles Lindbergh or Hershey.'

He turned, and looked down at Morgana. He winked at her once; a provocative fatherly wink that didn't go unnoticed throughout the assembled company.

'Well,' he said, 'the good Lord saw fit to give me daughters, instead of sons, and so the Croft Tate name won't be guaranteed the future that my father envisaged. But let me tell you this. Today, on my first daughter's twenty-first birthday, her coming of age, I know for sure that the *spirit* of the Croft Tates will live on, nourished and cared for in the same way that I nourished and cared for it. I know for sure that by the time I reach the end of my life, and St Peter asks me what my name is, and I say "Howard Croft Tate, your honor," he's going to say to me, "Ah – you must be Morgana's old man."'

Howard raised his glass, and proposed a twenty-first birthday toast, and everybody stood and raised their glasses together, and shouted out, 'Morgana! Happy birthday!'

Morgana stood, with the glint of tears in the corners of her eyes, and said, 'Thank you all for being so generous; and for being so warm. Somebody told me this morning that to run a newspaper, you had to have a heart of stone. Well, perhaps that's right; perhaps you do. But I know something about my heart of stone, and that is that your love and your kindness have cracked it.'

Afterwards, the guests poured out on to the lawns, flushed with wine and amusement. The worst of the thunderstorm had passed by now; and could just be seen flickering its tongue like a snake toward Lake Michigan. The swing band were making their way back to the rostrum, and John came over and kissed Morgana on the forehead, agitated and pleased with himself. 'I'm going to sing for you now,' he told her. 'Two songs I wrote for your birthday. What you're going to see now is the debut of a great musical career. Or maybe not. But either way, it's all for you, sweetheart.'

John went over to the rostrum, and climbed up the steps to a roll of snare drums from the swing band. There was echoing applause, all over the garden. Not far from Morgana,

Clare McCardell the fashion designer said, 'Surely that's not Frank Sinatra? He's far too bulky.'

Just as the band was tootling and strumming and tuning-up, Morgana looked around and saw Donald Crittenden approaching her at high speed. He was wearing a killer of a white sharkskin suit, and his wide trousers bellied and flapped as he strode with all the menace of a fully rigged man-of-war.

'Morgana, my darling,' said Donald. He took her hand, and kissed it. He was very handsome, if you cared for Errol Flynn lookalikes, cleft jaws, pencil mustaches, black curly hair and staring eyes that were one billionth of an inch too close together. 'Have you seen that sister of yours anywhere? I've been right around the garden with a nit-picker.'

'She was here just a moment ago,' said Morgana, unhelpfully.

Donald propped his hands on his hips and looked around the lawns in annoyance. 'She's making a fool out of me, your sister. Well, to hell with it. If she doesn't want to see me, she doesn't want to see me. I'm not killing myself over some eighteen-year-old tease in Stadium Girl lipstick.'

'This is my birthday party,' Morgana reminded him. 'Nobody is allowed to be irascible at my birthday party. Besides – were you invited?'

'I should hope I was,' said Donald, cryptically, and went storming off across the lawns again, in search of Phoebe.

Wilbur T. Henry and the Marquettes swung into action, and John came forward to the microphone, and began to sing. Morgana had to admit that his voice wasn't all bad, although the words he was singing were more than mildly embarrassing. Oscar Hammerstein came over and put his arm around Morgana's shoulders and gave her one of his craggy but diffident smiles. 'What does that fellow of yours do for a living?' he wanted to know.

'He's studying law.'

Oscar Hammerstein nodded. 'I'm pleased about that. I'd hate to think of him trying to make a crust out of being a song-writer.'

> 'Morgana, now you've come of age
> You'll be witty, you'll be sage
> You'll be wise as well as divine
> You're one and twenty, and you're mine!'

Oscar Hammerstein said, 'Is that true? Are you his?'

'We're supposed to be unofficially engaged,' said Morgana, cautiously.

'You don't sound too sure about that.'

'Don't you think he's suitable?' asked Morgana.

Oscar Hammerstein shrugged. 'That's not for me to say. He's good-looking enough.'

'But?'

'Did I say but?'

'Not exactly, but the implication was there.'

Oscar Hammerstein lifted his arm away from Morgana's shoulders, and sipped at his glass of champagne. 'I don't know. It seems to me that you're tough. I don't mean tough insensitive; I mean tough resolute. Most of the rich girls I've talked to, they've had the same kind of toughness; inherited, I guess. It just seems to me that you're going to need a husband who's at least as tough as you are. That young fellow's okay. Well-mannered; personable. But where's the muscle?'

Morgana looked at Oscar Hammerstein for a very long time, saying nothing. Then she told him, 'That was very forward of you, you know. That was almost rude.'

'Well, if it was, forgive me.'

'There's nothing to forgive. I like people when they're forward, and I like them even better when they're rude.'

'You must take after your mother,' Oscar Hammerstein remarked.

John sang,

> 'Morgana, you go to my head
> I can't wait until we're wed.
> Morgana, if you get my drift
> I'll give you my morning gift.'

Oscar Hammerstein laughed. 'You hear that? You may be unofficially engaged, but that young man is definitely proposing to you for real. And publicly, too. And cleverly. He's even managed to tell you that he's not marrying you for your money.'

Morgana frowned. 'How do you work all that out?'

Oscar Hammerstein smiled at her. 'You've heard about morganatic marriage? That's when a prince from one kingdom and a princess from another kingdom get married – but they agree that neither of them will make a claim on the other's kingdom if the other one dies, or if they get divorced. The reason they call it morganatic marriage is because the princess is only entitled to the traditional morning gift, the present that every husband gives his wife after their wedding night. Morning in German is *Morgen*. Hence, morganatic. And hence, of course, Morgana. Pretty name. Sensible arrangement.'

Morgana took hold of Oscar Hammerstein's hand and squeezed it. A big, square hand, with a single gold ring on it. 'One day, I'm going to have *you* write a song about me.'

Phoebe came around the corner of the marquee, looking desperately flustered, all roses and shoulders. 'Have you finished your photo-call yet?' she wanted to know. She was about to add something about Bradley, but then Bradley appeared in person. He was wandering after her as if he considered it lacking in masculinity to follow too close behind, but anxious all the same not to let her disappear. His champagne glass looked as if it had been empty for some time. His ears were pink in the sudden sunshine.

'*Bradley,* how are you?' asked Morgana, more gushingly than she had meant to.

'Morgana,' said Bradley, in that squeaky half-broken voice of his. He leaned forward to kiss her, and almost missed, his lips skidding across the side of her cheek. He was dressed in a powder-blue summer suit that was far too smart for him, and clashed with his ears. 'I haven't had the chance to wish you a happy birthday yet. I left my gift along with the others. You'll know it's from me, it's twenty years' supply of Ham-I-Yam. No, really, I'm only kidding. It's a ruby brooch in the shape of a pig. No, I'm kidding! It's a surprise. But it has my name on it. I hope you like it when you get around to opening it.'

Phoebe said, tersely, 'Morgana . . .' She didn't have to say 'help.' Morgana knew that she needed it; and badly; and quick.

'Bradley,' said Morgana, 'have you seen the vine, in the hothouse? We've had so many grapes this year that Popsy's thinking of making our own wine. Château Croft Tate. Why don't you come take a look at it? It's really something.'

'Well . . .' Bradley demurred.

'Oh do go, Bradley,' said Phoebe. 'It's quite a sight. And I can change my shoes. These high heels are like some kind of medieval torture.'

Morgana took hold of Bradley's arm and began to lead him away. Oscar Hammerstein said, 'See you later, Morgana,' and Morgana gave Phoebe a quick look which meant go sort out Donald and sort him out pronto – I can only spend so long giving a canned-ham heir a tour of a hothouse grapevine.

The timing was nearly perfect, but not quite. Just as Morgana began to usher Bradley away, Donald reappeared around the corner of the marquee, hotter and flappier than ever. 'Phoebe, there you are, for Christ's sakes!'

He seized hold of Phoebe as if he were playing the Sheik of Araby, and kissed her quite violently on the lips. Bradley stared at this performance in amazement, and when Morgana tried to tug him away, he hooked up his arm to stop her.

'*Bradley* –' Morgana protested. But Bradley's ears had reddened and his nostrils had flared, and with a double twist of his wrist he broke free from Morgana and advanced on Donald and Phoebe, perplexed, hurt, and obviously ready to defend his claim to Phoebe with a fight.

Donald said to Phoebe, 'I've been looking for you all over. What have you been trying to do, give me the run-around? I brought you a present. I even brought your sister a present.'

Phoebe looked mildly sick. She tried to say something, but couldn't, and it was then that Donald noticed Bradley, who was standing only a foot away from him, staring at him with morbid intensity.

'Who's this?' Donald asked Phoebe. 'Why is he looking at me like that?'

Phoebe flustered, 'Donald – oh, Donald, this is a friend of mine – you must have heard of Ham-I-Yam – well, this is Bradley T. Clarke – you know the Skokie Clarkes –?'

Donald genially held out his hand. 'Hey, pleased to meet you, Bradley. I was raised on Ham-I-Yam. Who wasn't? Tell me, is it true what they put into it?'

Bradley ignored Donald's hand, and snuffled with nervous aggression. 'You just kissed this young lady, is that right?'

Donald was baffled. 'Yes, that's right. That's what I call it, anyway, kissing. What do you say, Phoebe-baby?'

'Erm, excuse me, this young lady isn't your baby,' said Bradley. His voice had a peculiarly tired, carping tone; as if he were being monumentally patient with Donald, even though Donald didn't deserve it. Donald, of course, bristled, and stared back at Bradley in disbelief.

'What did you say?' he demanded. 'Do I have wax in my ears, or did you say something completely out of line?'

Bradley cleared his throat. 'I said, this young lady isn't your baby. She's my date, and it seems to me that you're horning in here, or trying to, and believe me you're not welcome. I'd consider it a favor if you'd leave us alone.'

Donald stared at Bradley, and then at Morgana, and then at Phoebe. 'Does this make any sense to any of you?' he wanted to know.

Phoebe said, 'Donald, please – don't make a scene.'

'So this does mean something to you? You know what he's talking about, young Mr Ham-I-Yam here? *He's* your date, your one and only, and I'm just the bug that fell in the lemonade?'

'Donald,' said Phoebe, growing desperate, 'it doesn't mean that at all. Bradley and I have known each other for a coon's age.'

'And that's supposed to make it okay? Listen, dear Phoebe, I flatter myself that I'm something of a man of the world. I don't expect any of the women who come into my life to be nuns. If I wanted nuns, I'd go to a nunnery. But similarly I don't expect to have to fight for the attention of the women I fancy by trading insults with some beardless kid with big ears and nothing to recommend him but a family connection to some bright pink brand of canned meat.' He reached out and touched Bradley's arm solicitously, and said, 'No personal offense, Bradley, old boy. The meat's terrific. This sure as hell wasn't your fault, either.'

Bradley said, 'Excuse me, sir, how would you care for a punch on the nose?'

'Well, no thanks, all the same,' said Donald. 'Maybe if there was something worth fighting for.'

'Donald!' Morgana interjected, 'that's my sister you're talking about. I think you'd better apologize.'

Donald looked at Morgana sharply, and then let his gaze drop sideways. 'Very well, I'm sorry. It isn't like me to behave like a punk. I may not be a gentleman, but I guess there's no harm done in being polite.' He turned to Phoebe, and bowed his head, and said, 'So long, Phoebe-baby; sorry I couldn't stay. I'm due for tea at the Wackers in a half-hour, and then I have to walk the borzois. Toodle-oo, it's been fun.'

Without any further formalities, he turned and walked away, leaving Phoebe standing with her cheeks completely drained of color, her pink-painted mouth open; two frustrated tears already sparkling in her eyes.

'Donald!' she called, trying to sound imperative. But her voice was too high and Donald had already committed himself to a *Third Man*-style exit, walking off into the distance without turning his head; and he disappeared around the side of the house leaving Phoebe furious and bereft. They had both been acting for each other's benefit, and now Donald had acted himself offstage.

Bradley tried to take hold of Phoebe's arm, but Phoebe snatched it away. 'God damn it!' she cursed. 'That's just my Goddamned luck!'

Bradley said, 'Phoebe, for Pete's sake! Would you mind please telling me what goes on here? What did I do? What's happened? Phoebe!'

'Oh, *ce n'est rien*, Bradley,' Phoebe told him, and blew three wildly erratic kisses at him, as if she were deliberately trying to make sure that they didn't make contact with him, even visibly. 'You were just as manly and protective as ever. God, you should go talk to Johnny Weissmuller, you and he would get on. Tarzan, and Acquaintance of Tarzan. I'm surprised you didn't come to the party dressed in a loin-cloth.'

She went stalking off toward the house, lifting her champagne glass as if she meant to smash it against the stone balustrade that bordered the East Lawn, but at the last moment she set it down carefully on top of the parapet, and then smiling and nodding with mechanical politeness as she negotiated the milling guests, she went inside. Howard came strolling up, and called after her, 'Phoebe?' but she didn't hear him; or pretended that she didn't.

'What goes on?' asked Howard, swizzling his champagne around in his glass. 'Phoebe looks upset.' He shook Oscar Hammerstein by the hand, and then shook Bradley's hand, although Bradley was still completely thrown by Phoebe's burst of temper, and kept opening and closing his mouth, silently appealing to the world to explain to him what had happened, and what he had done wrong.

'A misunderstanding, I think,' said Morgana. 'Excuse me, won't you?'

'Your fiancé is singing again,' Oscar Hammerstein pointed out. 'Don't you want to hear him?'

Morgana smiled tightly, and said, 'Another time, perhaps,' and went after Phoebe toward the house.

The swing band were playing a slow, romantic melody, all warbling clarinets and oozing saxophones. John approached the microphone with his hands tucked into his coat pockets, and crooned softly,

> 'Who needs the moonlight, who needs the stars?
> Who needs the fireflies, or headlights from cars?
> Your smile . . .
> Is all the lighting I need
> Your smile . . .
> Is so bright I can use it to read . . .'

Inside the house, up on the third floor, in the chaotic inner sanctum of Phoebe's bedroom – a pretty, blue-wallpapered room, smelling of Chanel No. 5 with a white French rug and white-painted furniture but always a maelstrom of discarded stockings and kicked-aside shoes and stepped-out-of step-ins – Phoebe was sitting at her dressing table powdering her nose as if noses weren't fashionable any longer. Morgana sat down beside her, uninvited, and picked up the white telephone that connected her to the servants' quarters.

'Millicent? Would you bring coffee for two up to Miss Phoebe's room, please?'

'And two brandies,' Phoebe added, fiercely. 'Two damn great brandies.'

'And two brandies,' said Morgana. She put down the phone, and then helped herself to a cigarette from Phoebe's white onyx cigarette box.

'I thought you liked men fighting over you,' she remarked, trying to sound offhand.

'I do.'

'Then what's all this temper about?'

Phoebe put down her huge swansdown powder puff. 'If two men fight over me, I *do* expect the right one to win.'

'I thought Bradley was rather good.'

'Well, so did I, as a matter of fact,' said Phoebe. 'That's the whole damned trouble. He's so nice. He's so *earnest*. And the trouble is you can't help liking him even when you dislike him.'

She picked out a cigarette for herself, and twisted it into her long cigarette holder. 'Damn Donald,' she said. 'He made me feel like a tramp.'

'I thought that was part of his attraction,' said Morgana, watching her sister narrowly through the clouds of cigarette smoke.

Phoebe stood up. 'I suppose it is. But he's so exciting. No matter what you're doing, he always makes you feel as if you're doing something dangerous.'

'You are doing something dangerous, especially if his wife finds out.'

'His *wife*,' said Phoebe, in a mocking tone. She walked over to her closet, and opened one of the doors. Inside, the rails were packed with summer dresses by Mainbocher and Pauline Trigère, and cocktail gowns by Charles James. Both Charles James and Main Rousseau Bocher were friends of the Croft Tate ladies. Mainbocher had designed the long crêpe wedding suit for the Duchess of Windsor (in the special shade he had named 'Wallis Blue'); and he had promised to design Morgana's wedding dress, although she personally preferred Norman Norell. Phoebe noisily ran her hand along the tissue covers in which Loukia had protected every dress, and smoked, and sighed, and said, 'Damn.'

Morgana said, 'I wouldn't normally offer, but do you want me to go talk to him?'

'To Donald?'

'I could explain that Bradley was just a good friend.'

Phoebe said, 'He must have gone by now.'

'Maybe. But the cars are parked six deep down there. It's going to take him a while to get out.'

'It won't do any good,' said Phoebe.

'Let me try,' said Morgana.

She left Phoebe's bedroom just as Millicent was coming up with the coffee. 'Won't be a moment, Millicent, don't pour it out yet!' she called, and ran down the wide Italian marble staircase.

Well, she thought, maybe Phoebe shouldn't be messing with Donald; but she didn't like to see Phoebe unhappy, especially today, and more than anything else she didn't want Phoebe to have to get on the telephone and beg Donald to take her out again, which she knew Phoebe would. Phoebe was alarmingly lacking in pride when it came to men, and if Morgana could protect her even a little, she thought that talking to Donald was worth the mild embarrassment.

Outside the front porch, she danced her way in between the shining bumpers of Packards and Cadillacs and Chryslers, looking for Donald's distinctive blue Lincoln. The rain had cleared almost completely now, and the collected hoods of seven hundred automobiles shone like the stepping stones to Heaven. There was a sharp aroma of wet tarmac and dripping fir trees; and all the puddles were streaked with rainbows of oil.

One of the footmen was sitting inside a Daimler, reading the sports pages. His powdered wig was hanging on the gearshift. Morgana went up to him and said, 'Did you see a light blue Lincoln leaving here, just a moment ago?'

'Yes, ma'am. Any problem?'

'No, no problem,' said Morgana. Not for me, anyway, she thought. She hesitated for a moment, wondering what she ought to do next, but there really was nothing she could do. If Phoebe wanted to go on seeing Donald, she was going to have to make the obligatory humiliating phone call, or write him an apologetic letter, and that was all there was to it.

Morgana was just crossing the driveway when she heard the sound of an engine, and a motor horn honked at her. She stepped back, and a small green Nash tourer drew up beside her, its engine beating irrhythmically and its patched-up canvas roof shaking like a Boy Scout tent. Woozy leaned out, and tipped his hat, and said, 'So long, Miss Morgana, I have to scoot.'

'Where are you going?'

'The office just called me. There's a humdinger of a fire down on 31st Street.'

'A fire?'

'That's right; and it's not going to wait while you and me talk about it.'

Morgana turned her head quickly back toward the house: toward the music and the laughter and the flapping flags. Then she twisted open the doorhandle of Woozy's Nash, and said, 'Take me with you.'

He stared at her. 'Are you nuts? I can't do that. What about your party?'

'I'm the boss's daughter, aren't I?'

'Well, sure, but this is a five-alarm fire we're talking about here. This is not your average safe and nondescript foot-of-the-pager, three pairs of long johns immolated in Chinese laundry conflagration.'

'I know. That's exactly why I want to come with you.'

Woozy puffed out his cheeks, and shrugged, and then engaged first gear, and jerked the car forward. 'It's your funeral,' he said, as Morgana slammed the door, and settled herself down in the passenger seat, and tugged her skirt straight. 'Don't expect a free ride back home, that's all.'

There was a plaster madonna mounted on the dashboard. Morgana said, 'Why do they call you Woozy?'

6

They could see the smoke from the burning tenement building from as far away as Division Street. It looked like dark brown cauliflower curds, heaped up into the sharp blue afternoon sky. The traffic everywhere was confused and tangled; Woozy had to take a right on Chicago and then a left on Rush; and then he had to show his press card to a whistle-blowing Italian traffic cop on Michigan Avenue in order to cut through to the Loop, and make his way south on Wabash. He hardly spoke at all; keeping his cigarette dangling from the side of his mouth, and his hat tilted on the back of his head, wrenching the Nash from one gear to the next as if he were trying to disembowel it.

South Canal was barricaded off. The burning building was almost directly in the center of 31st Street between South Canal and South Normal, next to Share's Grocery & Market. There were FWD firetrucks parked everywhere, and the wet pavement was tangled with hoses. Woozy parked his car right up behind a delivery truck, and climbed out, reaching into the back seat to fish out his camera and his flash-gun. Morgana climbed out, too, and immediately she could hear the terrible deep thundering of fire. It was accompanied by an extraordinary moaning sound which rose and fell, and which at first she thought was the wind, drawn off the lake by the rising heat of the fire; but which she quickly realized was the sound of human voices.

It was the most frightening sound she had ever heard. It was like a thousand people about to die; a thousand people on a ghost train. She stared at Woozy in horror, but all Woozy did was to pinch out his cigarette and ostentatiously flick it across the street. 'Fire department regulations,' he remarked.

'The whole darn neighborhood may be going up in flames, but nobody's allowed to smoke.'

Morgana followed Woozy toward the police barrier on the corner of 31st Street. The barrier was almost irrelevant, because the street itself was already crowded with hundreds of sightseers – mostly Negroes, because this was a Negro neighborhood – and the police were making little effort to do anything but keep them out of the way of the firemen. Woozy produced his press card, but the cop on duty waved them through without taking his eyes off the burning tenement. Woozy and Morgana pushed their way forward through the crowd, and Morgana was dazed and deafened by the noise and the heat and the sirens and all the running backward and forward, and by the asphyxiating stench of burning. It was the horrifying and unmistakable smell of human lives being incinerated: not just their flesh and their bones and their hair, but their sofas and their rugs and their beds and their armchairs, and all their folded-away clothes and their letters and their shoes and their wallpaper.

Morgana snatched at Woozy's shoulder, and shouted, 'My God! What's that?'

The sidewalks next to the tenement were thick with scarlet glistening mush. For a moment, Morgana thought that people must have been jumping out of the burning building, and smashed themselves to a pulp on the concrete.

Woozy said, 'Canned tomatoes. That's a food market next door. The cans must've exploded in the heat.'

At last Woozy and Morgana reached the front of the crowd, where a line of fifty or sixty cops stood red faced, arms linked, their tunic buttons untouchably hot, holding the gawpers back against the storefronts opposite the fire. The temperature was almost unbearable, it must have been well over a hundred degrees, and every now and then a cat-o'-nine-tails of water was blown back by the wind from one of the fire hoses. The crowd flinched, as if they had been whipped, but stood their ground, their eyes wide, their fists clenching and unclenching, moaning in chorus with every fresh outburst of flame, and with every thunderous collapse of timber or masonry.

The tenement was seven stories high, one of the old flat-fronted neighborhood buildings that had been put up at the time of the World Columbian Exposition in 1893; a building in whose partitioned rooms thousands of nameless Negro families had lived and died; and out of whose grimy windows countless eyes had peered hopefully over the city streets, dreaming of making good. A building at last that was scabrous, rat-ridden, half-derelict; and which was now coming to its deafening and spectacular Valhalla.

Two aerial ladders had been drawn up on either side of the building's façade, and firemen were directing torrents of spray into the third-floor windows, but every now and then the fire would lick back at them, and the crowd would moan, and the flames would give lewd and incendiary cunnilingus to the voluptuous clouds of brown smoke that billowed above them.

Woozy edged his way along to the front of the crowd until he found a gathering of newspaper reporters and photographers. Morgana kept close behind him. She recognized Edward Mason, the award-winning reporter from the *Tribune*; and Vincent Geruso from the *Daily News*; and Murray Mellish from NBC; but the rest of the gathering were unknown to her. They were instantly identifiable as press, however. They were all wearing fedora hats that looked as if they had all been purchased at the same lease-expiry sale, and then all rendered shapeless in the same rainstorm. They wore loud sport coats with sagging pockets, and neckties that were more pyrotechnical than the fire they were supposed to be covering. They watched the blaze with a kind of irritable concentration, as if they wished it would hurry up and burn itself out so they could get back to the office and write it up in time for a quick drink at O'Leary's, followed by the eighteen-thirty kick-off tonight at Soldier's Field.

Woozy waved his hand in diffident greeting to one or two photographers, who on the whole were older and shabbier than most of the reporters. Then he delved his way like a ferret in between the reporters to tug at the sleeve of a broad-faced young man in a brown and white houndstooth coat and a brown butterfly tie. The young man was keeping his attention fixed on the burning building, but at the same time he was arguing out of one side of his mouth with Vincent Geruso about the Montgomery rape case, and systematically feeding the other side of his mouth with broken-off pieces from a Baby Ruth bar.

'It's as plain as the nose on your face,' he was saying. 'Hi, Woozy, it's as plain as the nose on your face. The chief of police was a leading member of the Klan; and so was the county state's attorney. So what kind of a chance did Montgomery ever have against people like that? I ask you?'

Geruso, dark-chinned, round-spectacled, nasal, said, 'You're playing violins, Harry. The truth of the matter is that Montgomery was guilty and just because he was black that don't make him innocent. Come on, he took her into the shed and he did the business. The only reason they decided to release him was because it was politically expedient.'

'Expedient my fanny. The man was innocent. Twenty-six years in jail, and he was innocent.'

Woozy said anxiously, 'Harry – sorry to interrupt ya, but.'

'But? But what?' said Harry. 'What are you hanging around for? Go take some pictures. Make a name for yourself.'

Morgana said, 'There isn't anybody left inside the building, is there?'

Harry stared at her in barefaced surprise. Woozy grunted at him in warning, *hnh! hnh!* and tried to indicate with a complicated eyebrow-mime that she was important; that whatever she did, whatever she said, Harry should restrain himself. Everybody at the *Star* knew that Howard Croft Tate had a good-looking elder daughter; and everybody at the *Star* had seen her picture. Not everybody, however, had seen her in person; and not everybody was certain to recognize her without hesitation in a smoke-choked downtown side street on a crowded August afternoon, especially when today of all days was her (much-publicized) twenty-first birthday, and she was supposed to be up at Weatherwood, celebrating her majority with two thousand celebrities and enough bottles of wine to intoxicate the entire editorial staff of the Chicago *Star* for a year and a half.

'So far as they know, the building's empty,' said Harry. 'But five people were burned.'

'Badly?' asked Morgana, before Harry had time to ask who she was and why she wanted to know.

'Dead,' he said. 'Is that bad enough? There was one old man, who was probably the super. Then there was a woman of maybe twenty. Then there was three kids.'

Morgana said, 'That's terrible.'

'It was terrible. Yes. You're right.'

Morgana looked at him closely, her head to one side. 'You don't seem to be very upset about it. You don't even seem to be very *excited* about it.'

Harry said, 'I'm not. This is the tenth major fire on this block since July first. The five people who died today make it sixteen, altogether. Sixteen people dead, in a month and a bit.'

'Ten fires?' Morgana asked him, in disbelief. 'You mean this is arson? Somebody's doing it on purpose?'

Harry slowly unwrapped the last piece of Baby Ruth. The heat of the fire had melted the chocolate, and he sucked it off the tips of his fingers. 'Are you somebody I ought to know?' he asked Morgana. 'Woozy here keeps grunting and puffing and pulling stupid faces. What are you, City Hall or something? One of his honor's keen young social services staff?'

Morgana said, with gentle amusement, 'You don't know me?'

Harry chewed his candy and looked Morgana up and down. Smart, he thought. Expensive. And out of his class.

For her part, Morgana had to admit to herself that – apart from his terrible clothes – Harry was quite attractive. He wasn't particularly tall; by Morgana's usual standards, he wasn't tall enough. But he was well built, solid-shouldered, as if he boxed, or played weekend football; there was an attractive *density* about him; and his face was strong, sharply angled, with blond eyebrows and eyes that were deeply buried but bright blue like Indian turquoise.

Harry said, emphatically, 'You're not press.'

'Oh, yes,' Morgana told him. 'I'm press, all right. Press with a capital P.'

Harry looked perplexed. 'You're television? *Women's Wear Daily? Life* magazine?'

Woozy mouthed, 'Croft Tate, for Christ's sake,' and clenched his teeth.

Harry's face flickered through half a dozen different expressions: suspicion, curiosity, alarm, concern, anxiety, and finally something that was supposed to be slitty-eyed indifference. He pointed a finger at Morgana, and said, accusingly, 'Morgana Croft Tate. The Press Princess. It's supposed to be your birthday.'

'It is.'

'Well, then, happy birthday,' he said, with considerable bravado. 'But what are you doing here? You were supposed to be having some kind of a lallapalooza, weren't you, up at the Château Migraine?'

'I was. I mean, I am.'

Vincent Geruso had caught only a fraction of this conversation, and he leaned across to Harry, and said, 'What? What's going on here? Did somebody mention the very-much-less-than-sacred name of Croft Tate?'

'Can it, Vinny,' Harry snapped at him.

'Can it?' Vincent frowned at Morgana, and said, even more emphatically, 'Did you hear that, young lady? This hound from the *Star* has no more delicacy than Tennessee Williams.'

'*Vinny*,' Harry repeated, and this time there was no mistaking the warning in his voice. Vincent Geruso shrugged, and took off his spectacles, and held them up to the sky as if he had never seen them before.

'Ash,' he said. 'Would you look at that?'

'Pardon this quasi-hoodlum,' said Harry.

There were more sirens. The fire had now taken hold of the tenement's third story, and the Engine Co. 29 had called in two more twenty-six-foot extension ladders. The endless thundering of the flames was punctuated by the crackling and pealing of broken windows, and by the clanging of falling girders. Grunting and shouting, the police started to back the crowd further away, in case the building's façade collapsed into the street.

'This your idea of a party?' Harry asked Morgana.

'I wanted to come. I wanted to see it.'

'You just walked out on everybody? Isn't Laurence Olivier one of your guests? And Crown Prince what's-his-name?'

Morgana smiled airily. 'They're all right. There's plenty of liquor.'

'But what are you doing?' Harry insisted. 'Just rubbernecking, or what?'

'I wanted to see it, that's all. I wanted to see it the same way that you do.'

Harry took off his shapeless hat, and wiped the sweat from his forehead with the back of his hand. The heat in the street was unrelenting, and the fire was consuming oxygen so fiercely that everybody was panting like dogs; reporters and cops and firemen and spectators alike. The only refreshments were the spasmodic sprays of icy water from the firemen's hoses; and bottles of warm Royal Crown Cola from two enterprising Negro boys who were dragging a crate around and charging twenty cents each, no refunds.

Harry asked, 'Does your old man know you're here?'

Morgana shook her head. 'He wouldn't approve. Even if it weren't my birthday.'

Harry pulled one of those faces that only Polish people would understand. Life is a pickled herring. 'Well, you're twenty-one today. I guess you can do whatever you want.'

Morgana said, 'You didn't answer my question about the fires.'

Harry looked indifferent. 'What do you want to know? It's a business. They insure the building for twice its market value, then they burn it.'

'Haven't we written about it in the *Star*?' asked Morgana.

'You mean an exposé? Not a hope.'

'Why not?' Morgana demanded.

'Because the lawyers say not, that's why. Because all of this area, from 29th Street to 39th Street, from South Wells to South Union, is owned by gentlemen whose touchiness is legendary. If you printed a story saying they used to criticize their mother's *sfincuini* when they were eleven years old, they'd sue you without a second's hesitation. They could even do worse.'

'But people have died here,' Morgana protested.

'Not the first, not the last,' said Harry. 'Listen – believe me – I'm not being hard-boiled about it. But what can you do? The police can't prove anything; nor can we. Even if we could, the district courts are presided over by judges who prefer things they can hold in their hands, like girls and twelve-year-old whiskey and large denomination bills, to the abstract concept of justice. You can't fight these people. You can only write what you see, not what you know.'

Morgana shielded her eyes with her hand as the flames began to pour out of the top of the tenement. 'I never had any idea,' she said. 'How can they kill people, just for the sake of money?'

Harry glanced at her, and smiled wryly at her naiveté. 'I guess that isn't too easy to understand, when you've always had more than enough. But believe me, the going rate for a human being on the Near South Side is not much over seventy-nine cents. Less than its value as fertilizer. Cheaper than salt pork.'

The fire chief came over, his cheeks ruddy with heat, his nose smudged with ashes. He lifted his arm in magisterial greeting to the press, and two or three photographers took pictures of him. He was a stubby, fire-haired Irishman, with pale froglike eyes, and an accent that declared him to be the son of a Waterford man. He twisted open the buttons of his rubber coat, and held out his hand. Without a word, Edward Mason passed him a brown-paper bag with a bottle of bourbon in it, and he knocked back a mouthful, and then wordlessly handed it back.

'How's it going, chief?' asked Harry, taking out his notebook.

'Sure, it's burning up well enough,' said the fire chief.

'Any more bodies?'

'None so far. I've got two of my own men, injured by the blazing varnish. Jones and Kutiowski. They've both been taken to Michael Reese.'

'Was it set deliberately?' asked Morgana.

The fire chief's eyes flicked across at Morgana as quickly as a chameleon's tongue catching a fly, and then back to Harry. 'Who's this young lady?' he demanded, hoarsely; with a larynx cured by four thousand Chicago fires, burning fish and burning furniture and burning sulphur and burning beef.

Harry said, 'I don't think she meant it quite the way it sounded. Don't worry about it.'

But the fire chief said, 'Introduce me, why don't you? It's not often a working chump like me gets to meet a smart elegant young lady like this; and full of provoking opinions, too.'

Harry looked uncomfortable. 'Miss Croft Tate, this is Chief Bryan, of the Chicago Fire Department. Chief Bryan, this is Miss Morgana Croft Tate.'

'Well, well, I should have recognized you, shouldn't I?' said Chief Bryan, dragging a handkerchief out of his pants pocket so that he could smear off the soot and the sweat before he shook hands. 'But what's all this about this fire being set deliberate? That's no way to talk.'

Morgana could see by the apprehensive expression on Harry's face that the topic of arson was not one to which Chief Bryan was particularly partial. She guessed that if she started to discuss deliberately burned buildings, and attributed her newly acquired knowledge to Harry, the Chicago *Star* might have difficulty in the future getting help and information out of the Fire Department. So she smiled in the way that she thought the daughter of a powerful and wealthy newspaper proprietor ought to smile, with patronizing empty-headedness, and said, 'It was only an inquiry, Chief Bryan. I was just wondering how on earth a huge building like that could catch fire, unless someone did it on purpose.'

Chief Bryan grinned, and sniffed, and rested his hands on his hips, and looked around at the assembled reporters with a great display of fatherly indulgence, as if he were challenging them to tell him why God had permitted this dolled-up young girl to bother him with senseless questions, when he was doing his duty to Chicago and the human race just as well as always.

'You see, my dear, there are dozens of different ways that a fire can start,' he replied, and one of the reporters laughed. 'An oil stove, a cigarette, faulty electrical wiring. Kids playing with matches. The old Florence Hotel burned down because of a blazing pan of whitefish.'

'So this was probably an accident?' asked Morgana. She could feel her cheeks flushed with embarrassment and heat.

Chief Bryan stared at her for one long moment, and then nodded. 'Oh yes. Without a doubt.'

He looked at Harry pointedly, a warning now, young fellow-me-lad, keep this young lady away, and then he walked over to talk to some of the other reporters.

'What upset him so much?' asked Morgana.

Harry leafed through his notebook, pretending not to be talking to Morgana at all. 'Would your old man sack me if I told you to use your brains?'

'You mean –'

Harry nodded. 'That's exactly what I mean. We've had ten fires here in less than a month, sixteen people killed, but not one of those fires has been shown by fire department investigators to be arson. Not even a sniff of it. Genuine accidents, every one.'

'And Chief Bryan?'

'I didn't accuse anybody of anything,' said Harry. 'All I said was, use your brains. Apply your gray matter to the fact that while ten fires and sixteen deaths have been officially reported as accidental, Chief Bryan is running a new shamrock-green Studebaker Champion Regal De Luxe, not to mention a fifty-foot fishing boat, and that he and the unlovely Mrs Bryan spent two weeks vacationing in Fort

Lauderdale this spring. All that, on a city salary of $9,275 a year.'

'I'm shocked,' said Morgana. 'I have to admit it, I'm shocked.'

'Why? Didn't your daddy ever tell you what this city was like? I would have thought that it was part of your basic education. After all, your daddy knows Chief Bryan, and most of the people who grease Chief Bryan's palm.'

Morgana turned around to look at the fire chief. He was laughing loudly, and punching Vincent Geruso in a friendly fashion on the upper arm.

'Life and soul of the crematorium,' Harry remarked.

Morgana said, 'My father did tell me this city was hard. He told me all about the gangsters he used to know, men like Hymie Weiss. He even met Al Capone once or twice. But he didn't tell me that people burned other people for money, and then laughed about it.'

'That's the way it goes,' said Harry. 'Life is hard, then you die. If you're lucky you get paid a little along the way.'

'But if we know all about these fires, why won't we publish anything in the *Star*?'

Harry pushed his notebook into his sagging pocket. 'Are you kidding me, Miss Croft Tate? You can *know* something until your bean swells up to twice its normal size; but there's a mile of difference between *knowing* or *proving*. There isn't a judge or a jury anywhere in Cook County or the State of Illinois for that matter who wouldn't shake Chief Bryan by the hand for his honesty and diligence and sense of public duty.'

'But why?' Morgana insisted.

'Two reasons,' said Harry. He raised his eyes toward the top of the tenement building, where smoke was now billowing out so dense and dark that it looked as if a volcano had erupted. 'The first reason is, *they're* all on the take, too, and if any one of them gets exposed, then there's a danger that the rest will. The second reason is, none of them wants to end up as an accident statistic. Your old man told you about Hymie Weiss. Let me tell you that the men who control this city today are ten times more civilized than Hymie Weiss, ten times more intelligent, and ten times more dangerous.'

Morgana thought of some of the men who had visited her father's late-night dinner parties and roulette sessions. Not the celebrities, the movie stars or the politicians; but the smooth-faced men with pristine shirt fronts and perfectly tailored tuxedos; the men who said hardly anything at all; and yet whose presence in the house always seemed to create a sense of intense disquiet.

There was a hideous bellowing crash, like two locomotives being shunted together. More girders and masonry collapsed within the shell of the blazing tenement. On one wall, there was a painted advertisement for Sweet Georgia Brown hairdressing, with a black girl smiling and holding up a large jar. Half of her face suddenly dropped away, and collapsed on top of Share's Market.

Morgana said, 'We must meet, after this. We must talk.'

'We can talk all you want,' said Harry. 'You're the boss. Or the boss's daughter, same thing. But believe you me, it won't do you any good. There are some things you can fight, and there are other things you have to step around.'

'I'm going to own the *Star* one day, when my father dies.'

'And then what? You're going to tear this town to pieces, brick by brick?'

'If there's any of it left,' snapped Morgana.

'Whewsh,' said Harry. 'You sure have a lot to learn.'

As he spoke, however, a strange high-pitched cry went up from the crowd; an extraordinary ullulating shriek, followed by a low-keyed indrawing of breath. A fireman came splashing across the roadway, calling out to Chief Bryan. 'Chief! Chief! There are people on the roof! There are people on the roof!'

7

Morgana looked upward in horror. At first, the swirling cloak of smoke made it impossible for anybody to see anything at all; but then the wind changed around, and the smoke eddied away from the front of the building, and there, on the topmost parapet, stood three people, all Negroes, a man and a woman and a small girl. They were waving their arms and calling out for help, although their voices could hardly be heard over the furious rumbling of the fire. Every now and then, flames jumped up behind them, and it was obvious that it was only a matter of minutes before they would be burned alive.

Chief Bryan began to stalk quickly back toward the building, his rubber coat protesting loudly. The newsmen followed him en masse, taking advantage of the broad swathe that his determined bulk cut through the lines of police and firemen. Morgana followed, too, mainly because she didn't want to lose contact with Harry Sharpe in the noisy half-hysterical crowd. Woozy spring-heeled along beside her, and remarked laconically, 'What a rush! Do you see how quick these bums move when they think there's a story? You could almost believe they were keen.'

'Photographers,' retorted Vincent Geruso. 'The jackals of the news business.'

'One picture is worth a thousand words, Mr Geruso,' Woozy hit back.

Chief Bryan walked over to his parked car, and reached inside the open window for his microphone. At the same time he beckoned to a tall fireman not far away, who looked as if his white firecoat was several sizes too large for him and his helmet was several sizes too small for him. 'Melvin, I want the life-net deployed, and as quick as you damn well like.'

'Already on the way, chief.'

Chief Bryan said to himself, 'Not that it's going to save any lives; not from seven floors up. Might just as well dive straight into the concrete.'

The crowd was screaming in horror as the three figures on the rooftop balanced their way like tightrope walkers along the parapet, right to the very corner of the building, with the flames licking and lunging after them. The man stripped off his shirt and waved it from side to side, calling and calling for help, but the woman and the young girl reached the brink of the rooftop, eighty-five feet above the street, and crouched there without moving, without crying out, as if they were sure that they were going to die.

Chief Bryan switched on the loudspeaker on top of his car, and called out raucously, 'Duveen! Get that aerial ladder slap-bang up to that corner, close as you can!'

He must have known even while he was giving the order that it was hopeless. The tallest aerial ladder only just reached eighty-five feet, and the sidewalk was a landslide of bricks and rubble and charred beams, making it impossible for the turntable which carried the ladder to back up near enough to reach the parapet. The engine driver did his best; with his truck's wheels spinning and roaring up the heaps of broken brick, but the closest he could get was twenty feet away, and that was too far, especially with the truck resting at an angle. And as if the fire had a malevolent mind of its own, a staircase suddenly collapsed inside the building, directly beneath the corner where the three people were huddled, crashing forward against the front windows on the fourth and fifth floors, blazing fiercely, a stairway to hell, and its flames engulfed the ladder for almost twenty feet of its height. Nobody could have climbed or descended that ladder and lived.

'Douse those damned flames, will you?' Chief Bryan roared, and his voice bellowed through the loudspeaker on his car like the voice of God Almighty. Two hoses were immediately directed on to the staircase, but it was constructed almost entirely of wood and laid with linoleum, and already it was so hot that wherever it was extinguished, it burst into flame again. The hoses chased the fire from one window to another in a terrifying game of hide-and-seek.

'Let's have that life-net!' Chief Bryan called out. A crew of eight firemen came hurrying up with the canvas and cotton-padded net, and the fire officer in the small helmet hastily maneuvered them around so that they were as close to the building as possible, and directly below the three trapped people. Beside them, a large placard announcing Dr Sach's Eye Service, Free Examination, Easy Credit, suddenly curled up and turned as crisp and brown as a shower of dead leaves.

'My God,' said Morgana, clutching Harry's arm. 'How can they possibly jump through all those flames?'

Harry said, 'It won't make any difference. They're going to die anyway. The life-net won't do anything but kill them more comfortably.'

'Oh my God I can't bear it,' Morgana told him.

'You'll have to bear it, it's going to happen. Anyway – isn't this what you came for? True life action drama.'

'I never saw anybody die before.'

'If you want to know the truth, neither did I. I'm as scared as you are.'

The Negro crowd were abruptly hushed. The fire had taken hold of the pitch waterproofing on the roof, and it had flared up to demonic heights. The thundering sound of the flames was awesome, and even Chief Bryan slowly lowered his arms by his sides and stood staring up at the building in complete hopelessness. Morgana turned to look at the crowd, and the orange inferno was reflected in everybody's eyes, hundred upon hundred of tiny dancing fires.

It was then that somebody started to sing. It wasn't a hymn. It was that old Negro song of death and resignation, 'Take This Hammer'. It spread through the crowd, one voice after another, until they were all singing it, and the sound of their lament was louder than the rumbling of the fire, and even the three terrified and desperate people up on the roof must have been able to hear. There were tears on almost every face, tears that were dried almost at once by the heat. The man on the roof stopped waving his shirt, and stood still, a black silhouette against the fire.

> 'Take this hammer ...
> And carry it to the captain.
> Take this hammer ...
> And carry it to the captain ...
> You tell him I'm gone, man. You tell him I'm gone.

If he ask you, was I running
If he ask you, was I running
You tell him I was flying. You tell him I was flying.'

Then the man on the roof spread his arms wide as if he believed that he could rise up into the air and fly steadily away; away from the heat, away from the smoke, out over the lake where the mute swan fly with their whistling wings. The crowd still sang, but quieter now, watching him with solemn fear, as he stood for a long, long moment on the edge of the parapet, his head thrown back. Morgana couldn't take her eyes off him. He was alive. He was a man and he was alive. And yet already the heat of the flames must have been shriveling the skin off his back, and a small blue puff of smoke from the back of his head showed that his hair was alight.

He stepped off the parapet and the crowd screamed and the eight firemen holding the life-net shouted, '*Jesus God!*' almost as one man.

The man fell through the flames, his arms outstretched. The firemen juggled their life-net first to the left, then to the right. The man missed the life-net by less than a foot, and dived feet first into the rubble, penetrating the first three feet as easily as if it were water instead of broken brick. The noise of his fall was explosive. He flung his arms up into the air and clapped both hands above his head, like a high diver triumphantly saying *voilà*! But then his hipbones burst out of his sides, and he fell forward, face down, his legs still standing upright in the rubble, and the glistening tops of his femurs protruding like two chair handles.

The firemen had clustered around him in an instant, lifting him out of the debris and smothering him up in blankets.

'Is he dead?' Chief Bryan shouted. He kept his hand over the microphone, so that the crowd wouldn't be able to hear what he was saying.

'Still breathing, chief,' one of the firemen called back. 'His back's broke, though, and his legs have gone, and he's been burned pretty bad. I wouldn't lay much on his chances.'

Morgana covered her eyes with her hands, even though she was far too late to shut out the abrupt horror of the man's fall. Harry laid his hand on her shoulder, and squeezed it gently, and said, 'Are you okay? Miss Croft Tate? Listen, you'd better leave. This can only get worse.'

Morgana was shaking wildly. She could feel the blood draining out of her face. For a few moments, she was unable to hear; but then the noise of the crowd and the sirens and the rumbling fire suddenly came back to her, as if it had all been muffled behind a closed door, which had now been opened up again.

'Miss Croft Tate?' Harry repeated, seriously and urgently. 'I really think you ought to leave. I'll have Woozy drive you back home.'

Morgana obstinately shook her head. She had come down here to see for herself what was going on, and she was determined to see it through. She felt hot, frightened, very shocked, but she was steadied and sustained by what she could think of only as a kind of internal incandescence. She had felt it before, in moments of stress and anger and uncertainty, and even in moments of passion, but never so fiercely as she felt it now. It was almost as if she were alight, like the building – her bones and her nerves and her brain – alight, and burning bright.

'I'm staying,' she said.

Harry shrugged, as if to say what the hell, like a poker player folding his hand in a game which didn't particularly interest him anyway.

The crowd continued to sing. The fire roared around the rooftop like a goaded lion. Morgana looked up to the top of the building again, and she could just make out the woman and the little girl, their dresses tugged up over their heads to protect their hair from the scorching heat. They had edged right up to the very brink of the seven-story parapet, and their only choice now was to jump or burn. The crowd's voices seemed to rise and fall, almost to sway, as if they were trying to provide a spiritual cradle into which the woman and the girl could safely fall.

'Lady!' Chief Bryan shouted, over his loudspeaker. 'Do you hear me up there? You have to jump!'

'Jump!' screeched a Negro woman, who was hysterically dancing and pirouetting on the sidewalk in big white Minnie Mouse shoes. 'Jump!' bellowed the firemen, an extraordinary chorus of Irish and Italian and Polish accents. And more and more people in the crowd took up the chant of 'jump! jump! jump!' until it sounded like a huge locomotive pulling out of a station.

The cacophony of the fire and the screaming of the crowd was hellish. Morgana raised her hands to cover her ears. But as she did so, there was a sudden hush, because the woman had risen, and was standing erect on the parapet with her arms by her sides. The crowd cried, '*ohhh*. . . .' The woman was alight. Her dress was smoking and her hair flickered and burned with a crown of orange thorns. She didn't cry out; she stood silent and motionless, staring out across the slums of the city and burning. Then she pitched forward and tumbled down the side of the building, flaring with fire as she came.

They caught her in the life-net. Her body bounced, two black arms flailing for a moment. Then they smothered her with blankets, extinguishing the flames, and lifted her out with tragic care to lay her on a stretcher. For one split second, the pose of the firemen and the burned woman almost exactly echoed Michelangelo's *Pietà*, the taking down of Christ from the cross, and Woozy photographed it with unerring nonchalance, and sniffed, and wound on his film ready for the next shot.

'Well, dead then, dammit,' Chief Bryan remarked, without having to be told. He smeared sweat away from his upper lip. 'But maybe she's better off, with burns like that. There's nothing on earth that hurts like a burn.'

There was a complicated series of lurching and cracking noises from the inside of the burning building. The blazing staircase had collapsed inside the stairwell, and had brought down with it one interior wall after another. The tenement was now very close to collapse – but it was the moment that Chief Bryan had been hoping for. The leaping flames had suddenly shrunk away from the windows, and the firemen were able to maneuver one of their aerial ladders right up close to the corner of the parapet, only five or six feet away from the little girl.

Chief Bryan didn't have to ask for volunteers. A young fireman with a blond mustache was already running up the ladder, and the crowd stopped singing their lament, and began to cheer him on. 'You go boy! You go! Hallelujah! Hallelujah!'

'Oh God, please,' said Morgana, her hand over her mouth.

'Melvin – I want an ambulance ready to go just as soon as we get that little girl down,' Chief Bryan ordered. 'And let's get all of these people clear of the street. This building'll be coming down before you can say there's good news tonight.'

The young fireman ran up to the top of the aerial ladder as easily as if he were running upstairs. He hooked his feet into the uppermost rungs, and Morgana could see him holding out his arms toward the little girl. But the ladder was still too far away. Only feet, only inches, but still too far away.

'Can't you get that Goddamned ladder any higher?' Chief Bryan yelled.

'I'm sorry, sir, that's it, that's full reach,' the fireman in the small helmet told him.

The crowd's shouting and whooping suddenly died away. A strong wind blew through 31st Street like a ghost with an appetite for young souls, breathing ash and sparks and suffocating dust. Smoke began to billow out of the building even more thickly, occasionally swallowing up the fireman at the top of the ladder altogether. He was shouting to the little girl, *'C'mon, sugar! C'mon, sugar! You can do it! Just one little jump, and I'll catch you!'*

'Jesus and Mary,' growled Chief Bryan, gnawing at the knuckle of his left thumb, the hand that held the microphone. He had forgotten to switch his Tannoy system off, and his hoarse blasphemy was carried across the street. But nobody protested. Their eyes were fixed on the crouched-up girl, more than eighty-five feet over their heads, and on the flames which were spitting and wriggling so close up behind her – curtseying sometimes, when the wind blew stronger, but then leaping up again, to tease her, and scorch her, and lick at her arms and her hair.

The young fireman's hands were lifted in desperation, only four feet away from her, but still the girl crouched where she was, refusing to jump.

'C'mon, sugar, c'mon, darling, you can do it,' the fireman kept begging her, but she stayed where she was, a little brown fledgling who wouldn't try to fly; wide-eyed and terrified and almost about to burn.

'Mommy . . .' she called. 'Mommy . . .'

Her thin cries were audible from the ground; even over the spiteful crackling of the fire. The crowd sighed in pity and horror. They had all seen the child's mother die. And yet still she called, 'Mommy, mommy!' as if mommy alone could save her.

'Trust that man, child!' a black man wept, his brown suit covered in ashes. 'Jump, child! Trust him!'

Inside the building, there was a devastating crash. A supporting wall had come down, along with floor supports and stonework and most of the second staircase. The young fireman at the top of the ladder twisted himself around and cupped his hands around his mouth and shouted down in panic, 'She won't jump! She won't do it! She says she wants her mommy!'

'God Almighty, her mommy's halfway to the morgue,' Chief Bryan growled. 'Lefkowitz – I want this whole street clear. No arguments, this structure's coming down. O'Hare – what's that officer's name – the one at the top of the escape?'

'Ford, sir.'

Chief Bryan picked up his microphone, and bellowed out, 'Ford! You have fifteen seconds dead! If you can't bring her down in fifteen seconds, then come down alone! The building's going! Fifteen seconds, and that's an order!'

'She won't jump without her mommy!' the young fireman shouted back, almost hysterical.

Morgana stepped forward, and grasped the sleeve of Chief Bryan's warm rubber coat. 'Chief Bryan,' she urged him, and that incandescent feeling inside her was so bright that she was almost dazzled by it.

'What the hell do you want?'

'I want to go up the ladder.'

'Are you crazy? What's the matter with you? You can't do that. Now, please, I'm busy, if you hadn't noticed.'

But Morgana wouldn't let go of his sleeve. 'Chief – listen – the girl wants her mommy. I'm a woman. Maybe I can help.'

Chief Bryan stared at her with smoke-reddened eyes. 'Out of the question.'

'She's going to burn to death unless somebody does something.'

Chief Bryan wrenched his arm away. 'Listen, you're a civilian. Just climbing up an eighty-five foot ladder needs training. And what happens if you go up there and miss your footing? What happens if the building collapses and you get yourself crushed?'

'What happens if that little girl dies and you haven't done everything possible to save her?' Morgana retorted. 'How do you think that's going to look on the front page of the *Star*? Fire Chief Sacrifices Baby?'

High up above them, the little girl cried out, 'Mommy! Mommy! I'm hurting! Save me, mommy! Save me!'

'Please,' Morgana implored him.

Chief Bryan kept his eyes riveted on Morgana and his face was explosive with questions and doubts and furies which there was no time for him to let out.

'Melvin!' he roared.

'Yes, sir?' Melvin replied.

'Melvin, we're going to try something.' Ferociously, he began to unbutton his rubber coat. 'This lady here is going up the ladder to try to talk that young girl into jumping.'

'Sir?'

'You heard me,' Chief Bryan snapped. Underneath his coat, he was wearing a blue double-breasted uniform jacket, which he quickly yanked off, one sleeve after the other, revealing a big belly in a striped shirt and red fireman's suspenders. He roughly helped Morgana to slip her arms into the jacket and to button it up, and he raised the collar to shield her hair at the back.

'O'Hare!' Chief Bryan ordered. 'Give me your helmet!'

A freckle-faced fireman came up and handed over his helmet. It may have fitted him, but for Morgana it was enormous, a huge heavy bell on top of her head. Chief Bryan tightened up the chinstrap for her, and snarled, 'You heard what I said. You don't have any time at all. Apart from that, you volunteered for this job, and if anything goes wrong, I'm not responsible, and nor is the Fire Department. Now, get up that ladder and get up there quick. Officer Melvin will go up right behind you. And – believe me – this is a solemn promise, I swear on the Bible. If you get yourself killed up there, I'm going to murder you. In fact, I'm going to murder you whatever.'

'Yes, sir,' said Morgana.

Harry was right up beside her as she kicked off her New Look high heels and stepped into a big wallowing pair of thick-soled firemen's rubbers.

'This is insane,' he said, tersely. 'What the hell is your old man going to say? You're going to lose me my job!'

Morgana handed him her shoes. 'Would you take care of these, please?' she asked him. 'And as for my father, and what he's going to say, I don't know and I don't care and I don't have time to discuss it.'

Harry turned around to Chief Bryan. 'Chief!' he shouted. 'Chief Bryan! You're going to catch hell for this!'

But Chief Bryan waved Harry aside with a dismissive sweep of his arm. 'I want this whole street evacuated. That means you too, fellow. Let's beat the retreat before we all get flattened.'

Morgana was climbing up the ladder now, closely followed by Officer Melvin.

'Chief Bryan!' Harry persisted, pointing up at her. 'That is Morgana Croft Tate you're sending up there! Howard Croft Tate's daughter!'

Chief Bryan snapped his head around and stared at Harry angrily. 'And that little girl on the roof, whose daughter is she?'

Harry couldn't think of an instant retort, but as Chief Bryan walked away, he said loudly, 'Maybe you should have thought of details like that before. I mean, before this fire even got itself started.'

Chief Bryan visibly flinched, but he didn't look back.

Morgana was only a third of the way up the aerial ladder when she began to have doubts about what she was doing. The metal rungs were slippery and coated in soot, and about as hot as saucepan handles that have been left over the hob. The smoke from the building blew directly into her face, and most of the time it was impossible for her to see anything at all, except her own hands, with elegantly painted nails and a nineteen karat diamond ring, as she scaled the ladder. When the smoke cleared away, however, she almost wished that it hadn't, because then she could look down and see the street, and even when she was less than halfway up, the street seemed as if it were nearly a mile beneath her, choked up with tiny people and toy-like firetrucks and hoses that were tangled everywhere. In the distance, toward the east, she could see the Michael Reese Hospital, and the haze over the lake. Her knees and elbows began to tremble with the strain of climbing, and her throat was choked up tight with smoke and fright. Officer Melvin didn't help matters, either. He kept on coming up after her relentlessly, making it impossible for her to stop and rest, and what was worse his steady climbing shook the ladder alarmingly. All that brightness that had filled Morgana when she had volunteered to climb up the ladder began to flicker and dim, as if each successive rung were a switch, and the higher she climbed, the more lights were extinguished inside her. Two thirds of the way up, regardless of Officer Melvin, she had to pause, and press herself close to the ladder, in a concentrated effort to restore her courage, and to get her breath back.

'Oh, please, God,' she prayed, squeezing her eyes tight shut.

Officer Melvin said, 'You want to go on? We don't have too much time.'

The last few rungs were so difficult for her to climb that by the time she found herself facing the black rubber boot heels of the young fireman who was standing at the very top of the ladder, she was practically unable to speak. She didn't dare to look down. She had never before realized how overwhelming the human fear of falling could be. She held on to the ladder so tightly that her fingers were cramped, and what had started off as the trembling of tiredness had become an uncontrollable juddering in every single muscle.

The fire on the roof blasted her face with wind-blown waves of intense heat; and the crackling and thundering were even more frightening up here than they had been on the ground.

The young fireman looked down at her with a frown, and shouted, 'What the hell goes on?'

Morgana leaned a little to the left, so that she could see past the fireman up to the curved stone parapet of the building, where the little Negro girl was clinging. From here what had appeared from the ground to be a narrow gap between the top of the ladder and the smoke-stained brickwork seemed like an unbridgeable gulf. Up above their heads, the little girl sat with a pink gingham dress tugged over her head, the way that her mommy had told her, with her braids sticking out on either side. She couldn't have been older than six or seven, and she was clutching a rubber doll with a bright pink face.

Morgana turned away, to give her face some relief from the devastating heat. It roasted her throat and tightened her skin and dried her eyeballs. Every now and then, for what seemed like minutes on end, a thick cloud of smoke would swallow them all, and the little girl would vanish.

'I came up to help!' Morgana told the young fireman. Her voice didn't sound like her own voice at all: it was a high-pitched strangled shriek. 'The girl wants her mommy! I thought I could help!'

'Did the chief send you or what?' the young fireman demanded. 'You can't do anything!'

Morgana said, 'This is the chief's jacket!' But she didn't relinquish her grip on the ladder to show him the gold lapel badge.

'I can't reach her!' the fireman explained. 'That last section of pitch roof is going to ignite any second now, and then we've had it!'

Morgana cried out, 'Little girl! Little girl! Can you hear me? Little girl!'

The girl shook her head wildly from side to side, and called, 'Mommy! Mommy! Mommy!

'I've come to take you to mommy!' Morgana shouted. 'But you have to be quick! You don't want the fire to get you! Mommy said she wants you to jump – just the way that she did! But you don't have to jump down to the ground! The fireman will catch you! But you have to jump! Mommy wants you to!'

'I want mommy!' the little girl screamed. 'I want mommy!'

'Jump!' Morgana pleaded. 'Mommy says jump!'

There was another rumble from inside the building, and they were engulfed for a moment in a blinding eruption of smoke and red-hot sparks. Morgana heard Chief Bryan's amplified voice, urging the cops to speed up the evacuation of 31st Street, and then commanding in the same abrasive tone, 'That's it, Ford! That's it, Miss Croft Tate! Time's up! We're bringing you down whatever!'

'*No!*' shouted Morgana, although her larynx was so constricted with smoke that Chief Bryan couldn't possibly have heard her. She felt the ladder sway as the turntable crew prepared to swing it away from the building and wind it down. '*No!*' she shouted, again and again. '*No!*'

'Miss, you've got to come down,' Officer Melvin instructed her urgently. 'Come on now, chief's orders!'

Morgana hesitated for a second, but then she knew what she had to do. She clambered up three or four more rungs, right next to the young fireman at the top, and shrieked at him, 'Hold me! Hold my legs! If I stretch out, I can reach her!'

The fireman stared down at her with alarm and indecision. His face was grimy and sweaty, but in spite of the dirt and in spite of his mustache, he still looked very young.

'*Hold me!*' Morgana ordered him, and climbed up next to him, clinging on to the ladder with one hand and on to his white canvas fire-coat with the other.

The fireman swallowed, and blinked, and then nodded.

Morgana scaled her way up to the highest rung she could manage unaided, and the young fireman grasped her with both arms around the shins, to support her, and to prevent her from tipping forward. Officer Melvin climbed up higher, too, so that he, in turn, could hold on to the young fireman's belt.

At the very top of the ladder, with her feet hooked on the fourth-to-last rung, Morgana gradually and fearfully released her handhold – one hand first, then the other – and balanced herself until she was standing up straight. She reached out once, twice, and at last her hand touched the building's hot brickwork. Just above her, only nine or ten inches out of reach, the little girl looked down at her with fascinated terror, still not moving, still tightly clutching her doll.

Pressing one hand against the building to steady herself, Morgana lifted her other hand up toward the little girl. 'Come on, now,' she cajoled her. 'Take hold of my hand. Your mommy's waiting for you. Come on, now, she's waiting!'

There was a moment of utter desperation in which Morgana thought that the little girl was never going to move; that she was going to be burned alive in front of her eyes. But then yards of roof structure sagged and collapsed close behind the little girl, and the pitch waterproofing suddenly roared into flame, and fiery fragments of black canvas whirled all around them. The little girl screamed and screamed. Her dress was alight; and she scrambled up on to her feet and fell toward Morgana without any warning at all.

Morgana screamed, too. The little girl tumbled straight into her, knocking her forehead against Morgana's teeth. Morgana snatched at her dress, but it tore, and the little girl almost fell right over her shoulder. It was then, however, that the young fireman caught hold of the little girl, and smacked her back where her dress was burning, and Officer Melvin yelled down to the turntable crew, 'Get us out of here, will ya?' and the ladder began to revolve and sink while Morgana clung wordlessly to the very top rung, gasping, bruised, and the young fireman gently lifted the little girl from her shoulder and passed her down to Officer Melvin with care and triumph, while she sobbed with that miserable hooting noise that always gladdens adults because it means that no matter how miserable she happens to be, the child is alive, and well enough to complain.

The young fireman helped Morgana to climb down the last few rungs of the ladder, and back to the ground. Her legs felt as if they were dissolving underneath her. Chief Bryan came marching over, closely accompanied by Harry and Woozy and the rest of the press. Flashbulbs popped and clattered like castanets. Chief Bryan without any ceremony unbuckled Morgana's chinstrap, and lifted the fire-helmet off her head.

'Your mouth is bruised,' he remarked, flatly. His Irish accent was very emotional, very strong. 'What's your father going to say about that?'

Morgana said, shakily, 'The little girl's head – she sort of hit me when she jumped.'

'You're a heroine, I suppose you know,' said Chief Bryan.

Morgana said, 'I think I'm going to have to sit down.'

'Here,' said Harry, 'my car's parked right around the corner.'

'Miss Croft Tate! Miss Croft Tate!' the reporters begged her. 'Come on, now, just because your daddy owns the *Star*! Give us a comment! Were you frightened up there? What did the little girl say to you? What did you do to make her jump?'

'Miss Croft Tate's saying nothing,' Harry insisted.

Morgana slowly unbuttoned Chief Bryan's jacket. Chief Bryan laid a hand on her shoulder and said, 'Keep it, Miss Croft Tate. I think you've earned it. Do you want one of my men to drive you home?'

'Miss Croft Tate, please!' the reporters cried out. 'Come on, now! Don't give us the freeze!'

Morgana saw Officer Melvin standing close by. 'Is the little girl all right?' she asked him, anxiously.

Officer Melvin took off his helmet. 'She's fine, thank you, Miss Croft Tate. Second-degree burns on her back, some on her hands, but she's going to survive, thanks to you. You did something real special up there. You impressed me. You didn't do what we told you to do, but you brought her down.'

'Okay, that's it,' interrupted Harry, possessively, and took hold of Morgana's elbow, and steered her away between the firetrucks and the snaking hoses. The street was almost clear now, but a few straggling Negroes followed Morgana all the way back to Harry's car, cheering and clapping their hands. 'We thank you! We thank you! Hallelujah! Hallelujah! We thank you! You is the business, ma'am, you surely is!'

They reached the corner of 31st Street and South Normal. Behind them, there was a deep and sinister rumbling; and they turned to see half of the tenement's façade collapsing into the street, half-burying one of the firetrucks. A rolling cloud of thick brown smoke filled the air. Harry said, 'You see that? You were lucky you weren't killed.'

His yellow Ford Woodie was parked up on the sidewalk. He reached into his coat pockets for his keys, and opened the passenger door. 'You always have to lock your car around here,' he said, reaching inside and clearing a stack of old newspapers and popcorn cartons off the seat. 'That's if you want to come back and find you've still got some seats to sit on.'

'You're not taking me home,' said Morgana, as she climbed in.

Harry leaned on the open door and stared at her. 'What's that supposed to mean? Where do you think I'm going to take you? The Triangle Hot Doggerie?'

'Now you come to mention it, I wouldn't mind a hot dog one bit,' Morgana retorted. She felt shaky but she still felt determined. 'But I thought we had a story to file. Infant Rescued From Blazing Tenement.'

'Ho-ho, now, hold up there,' said Harry. 'Don't let's forget who you are, Miss Morgana Croft Tate. You're my boss's daughter, that's who you are; and what do you think my boss is going to say when he hears that I let you climb up a fire-ladder and practically kill yourself, and then didn't take you home?'

Morgana said, 'Listen, Mr Sharpe, you're supposed to be a newspaper reporter. That means your first priority is to go back to the office and file your story. And, yes, I am your boss's daughter; and believe me your boss is going to have something to say to you if the *Star* fails to carry this story when every other paper has it splashed all over the front page. Now let's go, we're wasting time.'

Harry drew in his breath, and then slammed the station wagon door shut. 'May God preserve your father,' he breathed.

'What did you say?' Morgana demanded, as he climbed behind the wheel.

'I said may God preserve your father. Because when he dies, you take over – and without any personal offense meant – I don't relish that at all.'

Morgana pulled down her sun vizor, and examined her white smoke-smudged face in the vanity mirror. 'Is that because I'm a girl?' she asked Harry. 'I should say woman now, shouldn't I? God, I look positively bleached.'

Harry started up the engine, and jolted the Woodie into gear. 'It's because you're so damned unreasonable, that's why,' he told her, and drove off the curb with a loud clonk of worn-out suspension.

'Did you get that little girl's name?' Morgana asked him.

'Did I what?'

'Did you get that little girl's name? For the story.'

Driving one-handed, Harry lifted his notebook out of his pocket, and held it up so that he could read it. 'Doris Wells, aged six and a half. The woman who died was Mary-Beth Wells, aged twenty-four. They haven't identified the man yet. He wasn't her husband.'

Morgana drew the fire chief's jacket closer around her. Although the day was humid and warm, she was beginning to feel chilled; so chilled that her teeth chattered together.

'Are you okay?' Harry asked her.

'I'm a little shocked, that's all. I'll get over it, once we get back to the office and you buy me that hot dog.'

'You should let me take you home, you know that? You're in no condition to come back to the office.'

'I didn't know you cared,' said Morgana.

'Well, I'm not such a bad guy, when you get to know me,' Harry told her. 'Besides, I want to keep my job, such as it is. I don't fancy going back to the *Polish Daily Zgoda*.'

'Is that where you worked before?'

'Sporadycznie,' said Harry. 'That's Polish for "on and off."'

They reached the corner of South Normal and West 30th Street, another broken-down corner in a broken-down neighborhood, with scabby three-story buildings, shacks, lean-tos, garages, and dilapidated stores. As they drew up at the intersection, a huge black Cadillac nine-passenger limousine came dipping into South Normal, crossing right in front of them.

Harry stepped on the brakes of his station wagon, twisted the gearshift violently into neutral, and yanked open his door.

'Where are you going?' Morgana asked him, in perplexity. 'What are you doing?'

'Give me one minute,' said Harry. 'You know what *that* is, don't you?'

8

Harry would have missed the Cadillac altogether if half of South Normal Avenue hadn't been blocked up with smashed packing cases and garbage. The limousine was forced to slow down and stop only a few yards behind them because a huge and filthy meat truck was grinding up the avenue in the opposite direction, and hogging all the available space. Harry caught up with the limousine and hammered with his fist on the roof. Morgana had twisted around in her seat and was watching Harry through the Woodie's rear doors, and she could see the passenger window of the Cadillac being wound down, and Harry starting to talk with furious intensity to whoever was sitting inside. He kept waving his notebook like a baseball referee, and turning around to point toward the scene of the fire.

Morgana waited patiently for two or three minutes; shivering a little; but then, curious, she opened the passenger door and stepped out. She walked cautiously toward the Cadillac, watched with unabashed interest by three small Negro boys in patched-up dungarees who were playing in the trash, and a Negro man who was leaning on a rickety upstairs balcony smoking a handmade. A radio was playing 'Good Night, Irene', by Leadbelly.

Harry was shouting, 'That's five human beings dead – you understand that, sir? *Five!* And what am I supposed to write about that? "Another extremely unfortunate accident in another South Side firetrap?" You listen to me, Mr Vespucci, they had to jump off the roof and they were *alight*.'

Morgana reached the car and stood beside Harry with her fireman's jacket clutched around her. 'Mr Sharpe?' she said, pointedly.

Harry turned around. He was so furious that his face was red like a beef tomato. 'You should have stayed in the wagon,' he told her, although he seemed quite glad to see her. 'I was just asking Mr Vespucci here a few pertinent questions about what happened on West 31st Street today. "The owner of the tenement, Mr Enzo Vespucci, 62, well-known millionaire, man about town, and friend of everybody in Chicago who has money and influence, expressed his sincere regret at the death of his tenants, and gave a notarized assurance that next time he would try to fully evacuate any of his buildings before burning them down."'

'Now, come on now, my friend,' said a smooth, cultured, Italian-accented voice from within the depths of the limousine. 'You know better than to talk like that.'

Morgana came closer to Harry and peered inside the open window of the limousine. Perched on the cream-colored velour seats was a small, delicately featured man in a light gray summer suit. He wore a well-brushed gray fedora and a Chicago Club necktie. There was no question about his ancestry. His skin was the translucent yellowish shade of handmade lasagne, and his eyes were dark and sad. He had the prominent nose of a Sienese cardinal, or a painted disciple by Giotto. On his lap sat a Colorpoint cat, which stared at Morgana with mesmeric hostility. As the man caught sight of Morgana, he stopped stroking his cat for a moment, and he courteously took off his hat.

'Mr Sharpe here should introduce us,' the man said, with mannered politeness.

'Mr Sharpe here is going to do nothing of the kind,' Harry retorted. 'This young lady was almost killed today because of you. If she has any sense at all, she'll sue you for every bent nickel you've got. Let me tell you something, Mr Vespucci, today you stepped way out of line. From now on, lawyers or no lawyers, the *Star* is going to be after you.'

Enzo Vespucci seemed to be quite unperturbed by Harry's ranting. He said, vaguely, 'So much for the objectivity of the American Press,' and called to his driver, 'Ambrogio? Is the street clear?'

Morgana leaned forward a little toward the limousine's window, and asked him intently, 'Was that your building? The tenement that burned down just now?'

Harry turned to Morgana in disgust. 'Believe me, Miss

Croft Tate, you'd be better off talking to one of the rats in one of Mr Vespucci's slums. At least the rats don't pretend to be human.'

At this, the driver's window of the limousine was unevenly wound down, and a bulky man with a face like an auto-parts yard leaned out and said to Harry in a thick, unearthly whisper, 'You there. *Cimabue*. Remember who you're talking to.'

Enzo Vespucci frowned at Morgana and said, in a clear voice, 'Miss Croft Tate? Surely you are not one of Mr Howard Croft Tate's daughters?'

Harry tried to tug Morgana away, But Morgana resisted him. 'You're right, Mr Vespucci. I'm Morgana. I've seen you up at Weatherwood, haven't I, having dinner with my father?'

'But my dear,' said Enzo Vespucci. He indicated with some bewilderment the outsized blue jacket that Morgana was wearing; although he was too much of a gentleman to remark on her smudged face and her flyaway hair. 'What are you doing here? This is no place for you. And, surely, today is your birthday. I was going to call up at Weatherwood later to give Howard my congratulations. This is no place to celebrate!'

Morgana unbuttoned the fire jacket and showed Enzo Vespucci her Dior dress. 'I came down to see the fire. Even we society girls like a touch of excitement now and again.'

'You must forgive me, Morgana,' Enzo Vespucci said, 'for leaving you standing in the street.' He said something in Italian to his driver, and the driver climbed out and opened the passenger door. 'Come inside and sit down, please. You must forgive me for not standing up myself. I have been suffering lately from bursitis.'

'Deepest apologies,' Harry interrupted. 'The lady can't stay. We have a deadline to meet. A building just burned down, remember? Five people were killed.'

Morgana said to Enzo Vespucci, 'Mr Sharpe seems to think that the fire was started on purpose.'

Enzo Vespucci stroked and stroked the head of his Colorpoint cat as if there were some kind of unnatural symbiosis between them; as if the stroking were necessary to keep Enzo Vespucci's heart beating, and to discourage the cat from leaping viciously and self-destructively at anyone who approached her master. 'It is with great sadness that I learn of this fire,' he said. 'Of course, people will always make accusations. That is what you get, when you try to help the poor. I have come down here simply to see if there is anything that I can do to compensate those wretched people who have lost their homes and their loved ones.'

His tone was so quiet and so modest that Morgana found herself almost believing him. But Harry said, 'Mr Vespucci, you're breaking my heart,' and pursed his lips, and spat into the roadway.

The bulky driver got out of the car and approached Harry. He stood right next to him, as tall and as ponderous as a bear standing on his hind legs. He wore a baggy blue serge suit with shiny knees and elbows, and a cascade of dandruff down each shoulder. Harry glanced up at him with exaggerated indifference, and said, 'What's this, Monte Forfora? Come on, pal, get back in the car. You're blocking the light.

Enzo Vespucci said quietly, 'Ambrogio, get back in the car.' He continued to stroke the cat, and the cat closed its eyes in pleasure. With an expression that rivaled anything in Moon Mullins, the driver returned to the car and heaved himself back into his seat, but he continued to stare at Harry and his stare didn't waver once.

'We have to go,' said Harry. He took out his notebook, and held his pencil poised. 'Is there anything else you want to say, Mr Vespucci?'

'You just write your story,' Enzo Vespucci replied. 'But before you start waging a war against me, Mr Sharpe, you make sure that you know what it is that you are doing. I am a private citizen. I work hard, I vote Democrat. I am an American, don't forget that. I gave thousands of dollars to the Government during the war. There are laws in this country which protect people from persecution, you understand me? And there are also times when aggrieved citizens have the right to protect themselves.'

'You mean if I go to press with the word Arsonist, you'll have Ambrogio rub his scalp over me, and bury me alive in dandruff?'

Enzo Vespucci's smile faded away, like the sunshine fading from a bedroom wall. 'You're a funny man, Mr Sharpe.'

Morgana said, 'Maybe you should explain your side of the story, Mr Vespucci.'

Enzo Vespucci turned his dark dead eyes towards her. 'What does this mean?'

'It means why don't you let the *Star* interview you properly on the subject of being a slum landlord?'

'This "slum landlord", please. I don't like this.'

'Maybe you don't,' Morgana insisted. 'But that's the way that ordinary people think about you, isn't it? Maybe you could set the record straight. Let me come talk to you over the weekend,' Morgana suggested.

Harry tugged wildly at the sleeve of her fireman's jacket. 'Are you *crazy*?' he demanded, in a high-pitched whisper. 'I mean – are you totally *crazy*?'

Enzo Vespucci was growing impatient and anxious. He said to Ambrogio in Italian, 'Come on. Come on, let's get a move on. I can't spend all day talking with an over-excited girl.'

But Morgana said, 'I'm not over-excited. I'm simply interested in finding out the truth from a man who seems to have forgotten the truth – as well as his manners.'

Deeply embarrassed, Enzo Vespucci flushed, and said, 'Forgive me, please. No offense was intended. I didn't realize that you spoke Italian.'

'When can I meet you?' asked Morgana.

Enzo Vespucci sucked in his cheeks thoughtfully, as if he were extracting the last juices of lunch from his dentures. Then he said, 'On Sunday afternoon I shall be out at Winnetka, viewing my racehorses. The Crown Park Stables, your driver will know where they are.'

'Very well,' said Morgana. 'On Sunday, at three. I hope you won't be late.'

'Your father is to be complimented on his beautiful and spirited daughter,' Enzo Vespucci replied, although his voice was quite expressionless. 'This lackey from the *Star* should take better care of you.' Then he leaned forward and said to Ambrogio, this time in English, 'Now, go. I do not care to stay in this neighborhood for too long. It smells bad, and I am never safe here. Thirty-first Street.'

The Cadillac swung around the landslides of garbage, and burbled away.

'Quite a cookie, isn't he?' said Harry, with ill-suppressed anger.

They walked side by side back to his Woodie. Harry opened the passenger door for Morgana and she climbed in. 'Thank you,' she said coolly.

'The pleasure is totally mine,' Harry replied, equally coolly. He slammed the door and the glass dropped out of his side mirror, and broke on the pavement.

'That's seven years of bad luck,' said Morgana, as he started up the engine.

'So I understand,' he replied. 'And if I'm any judge of anything, it starts on Sunday afternoon, at three.'

They drove northwards on State Street toward the Loop, passing block by block through the squalor of the Near South Side. They passed leprous rows of condemned houses with grimy façades and sagging rear porches. They passed sidestreets strewn with garbage and lined with rusting automobiles. They passed parking lots and elevated railroad tracks and billboards with out-of-date posters that flapped in the wind like peeling skin. They passed intersections where Negroes sat hopeless and shabby, their eyes hidden in shadow by the brims of their hats, watching the traffic go by. They passed automobile dumps and boarded-up stores and dilapidated nineteenth-century hotels with flaking stone façades and windows like empty eyes.

Morgana had driven through the South Side before, of course. The slums of State Street were only a few steps away from the bristling glamor of Wacker Drive and North Michigan Avenue. But up until now, she had only seen the South Side as an ugly abstract landscape; somewhere unpleasant that you had to pass through to get from the south shore of Lake Michigan to the Gold Coast; a blighted area of low buildings and smoking chimneys, where Negroes lived. She had never before seen the appalling unhappiness of it. She had never really stopped to think that these people who walked the streets or looked out of windows or leaned against the rotting back porches weren't movie extras, but real people, living out real lives. They played here, went to school here, worked, shopped, prayed, and brought up their families. Here – where the streets were littered and the houses half-derelict and everything seemed drab and brown for mile after mile after mile. Brown faces, brown clothes, brown buildings, brown sky.

'You know why Enzo Vespucci makes me so angry?' Harry told her, as they drove past East 21st Street. 'You look at that block there. Three months ago, I wrote a story on that block. There are thirty-seven buildings between 20th and 21st; and in those thirty-seven buildings, there are two hundred fifty-three families. Each of those families pay forty dollars for the privilege of living there. Can you imagine that? Forty dollars, for two overcrowded rooms in that cockroach circus, and no toilet.'

Morgana looked at him, but said nothing.

His phrases were short and clipped, as if he were reciting from memory. 'This area here – the South Side from 20th Street to 47th Street – this is the largest contiguous slum in any city in the United States. You've been lucky. You've only seen the outside of these buildings. Inside, they've got water running down the walls. Not to mention rats, and dry rot, and bugs by the billion. Can you think what it's like to have to live here? No, you can't; because I can't, either.'

'Did the *Star* publish your story?' asked Morgana. 'I don't remember reading it.'

Harry shook his head, and sniffed. 'Spiked by lawyers. Too provocative. Too dangerous. Vespucci would sue, and the *Star* would lose.'

'But you called him an arsonist and a liar right to his face,' said Morgana.

'Sure I did. I've done it before. He doesn't care. He enjoys it, if you ask me. He knows we all know what a racketeer he is; and he also knows that we can't do one single darned thing about it.'

Harry took out a cigarette, and offered one to Morgana, but she declined. He tucked it into the side of his mouth, and lit it by snapping a match with his thumbnail.

'Enzo Vespucci wants the South Side to stay like it is. In fact, he's been fighting very hard to make sure that it does. For him, the slum is a business, an industry, and he's got it just the way he wants it. I mean – you think about it – what better tenants could he possibly have than frightened, uneducated Negroes? They never complain to City Hall about overcrowding or insanitary conditions, because they're scared of authority, and City Hall wouldn't listen to them anyway. They never complain to the police because half of the time they've been stealing automobiles to pay the rent or selling their kid sister's body or shooting up drugs because they don't have anything else to do. And they sure as hell *never* complain to Enzo Vespucci himself because people who complain to Enzo Vespucci himself get their ribs broken and their wife raped and their furniture burned, and that's if they're lucky.'

Harry was silent for a while, and smoked, and drove. Then, as they pulled up at the traffic signal at the intersection of East 9th Street, he said, in a gentler tone, 'You can see why I called you crazy. A man like Enzo Vespucci doesn't need publicity. He doesn't need anybody to interview him, or try to understand his point of view. He doesn't *have* a point of view. He isn't even human. If you go out to Winnetka Sunday afternoon, you'll be talking to a two-legged creature who thinks that burning down people's homes is good business, and who cares if half a dozen people get themselves barbecued, too. You'll be taking tea and looking at racehorses with a creature who to my certain knowledge has ordered the killings of over thirty rival gangsters; and who has been arrested eleven times for extortion; seven times for conspiracy; twice for selling narcotics; and once for perjury. But none of the charges ever came to trial, Vespucci is a murderer, a drug runner, a pimp, a pervert and a running sore on the body of Chicago.'

'Aren't you afraid of him?' asked Morgana.

'Are you kidding? I never walk down dark alleys at night without my Tom Mix tri-color flashlight. I sleep with a rolled-up copy of the Sunday paper under my bed. I look left and then right and then left again whenever I cross the road, and I never accept rides in black Cadillacs.'

'You're not afraid of him, are you?' Morgana persisted.

Harry made a face. 'There's afraid, and then there's *afraid*. Sure I'm afraid. But not afraid enough to back off.'

Although they were still driving along State Street's skid row, the tall glittering skyscrapers around the Loop rose clearly up in front of them; concrete and glass shining like cathedrals against a dark afternoon sky. The Drake Hotel, the Palmolive Building, the Allerton Hotel, the Medinah Athletic Club, and the Wrigley Building. Then, as they came closer, they saw the *Tribune* Building, with its Gothic crown, and the *Star* Building, on Wabash Avenue, thirty-six stories of Art Deco blocks and balconies, with its distinctive five-pointed star revolving slowly on its roof, and the clouds reflected in its windows.

Harry said, 'You're quite sure you don't want to go home?'

'I'll file my story, then I'll go home.'

'You mean you'll wait around while I file *my* story, then you'll go home.'

'No, I mean I'll file *my* story. *You* file *your* story.'

Harry jammed on the Woodie's brakes. A taxi that was driving close up behind him gave him a blast on its horn, and the driver yelled out, 'What's your problem, you jerk?'

Harry leaned out of the window and yelled back, 'Who are you calling a jerk, you jerk?'

'Can't you ever keep your temper?' Morgana demanded.

'What temper?'

The cab driver climbed out of his taxi and walked toward them, rolling up the sleeves of his shirt. 'You see?' said Harry. 'All they know is violence.'

Just as the cab driver came up to his open window, Harry drove off, leaving the man yelling and shaking his fist at him in the road, and a line of backed-up traffic on State Street that was honking and hooting at the abandoned hack.

'You're trying to tell me that *you're* going to write a story about this fire?' Harry asked Morgana. Now they were driving along the swankier blocks of State Street, past the Palmer House Hotel, and Marshall Field's department store. This was Morgana's usual territory – the wide bustling sidewalks under the Marshall Field awnings – the 28 Shop and the cocktail lounges and the expensive hotels. She began to feel more relaxed and more confident, and she could feel the color coming back to her cheeks. She felt almost as if she had returned to civilization from a dangerous expedition to darkest Africa.

Harry steered the Woodie around a northbound bus, and then took a right on Lake Street toward Wabash Avenue. He puffed at his cigarette without taking it out of his mouth.

'What are you trying to do?' he asked, after a while. 'You use your position as the daughter of the newspaper proprietor for whom I work – only as a lowly minion of course – to write up a story which by rights should carry my byline. It's a question of – what can I call it? – taking the crust right out of my stretched-open mouth.'

They crossed the Wabash Avenue bridge, and turned almost immediately in to the *Star* Building, which rose up from the banks of the Chicago River like a shining glass cliff. Three large barges were tethered up beside the building, and huge rolls of newsprint were being swung out of the barge's holds with cranes and chains. At the gate of the *Star*'s underground parking lot, Harry waved to Tomahawk Billy, a full-blooded Arikara Indian who always looked murky-faced and uncomfortable in his peaked cap and silver-buttoned parking attendant's uniform. Tomahawk Billy peered back at him sourly, and then wound up the red and white barrier. Harry drove down into the parking lot with squealing tires, and made a performance of backing the Woodie into the space marked Jerry Hamner, Advertising Manager. He scraped the fender noisily against the wall, leaving yellow paint on the concrete.

'All I can say is that you have a galloping persecution complex,' Morgana told Harry, as they walked with brisk echoing footsteps toward the elevator.

'Well – who do you think you are, that's what I want to know,' Harry told her. He jabbed the button for up, missed, and jabbed it again. 'Your father owns a whole editorial department, populated at any one time with thirty of the mid-West's best and most ambitious journalists, all of whom are over-talented and under-employed. Jack Wollensky! David Tribe! Nathan Caldicott!'

'Harry Sharpe!' Morgana interjected, as the elevator arrived, and the gates crashed back.

'All right, if you like, Harry Sharpe,' said Harry. He pressed the button for the twenty-third floor.

Morgana could see her reflection in the mirror at the back of the elevator car, and she looked appalling. She was whiter than ever; there were plum-colored smudges under her eyes; and her hair was all windblown and wildly lopsided.

The elevator doors hummed open at the twenty-third floor. City Desk; Foreign News; Cartoon Editor. Harry beckoned Morgana out of the elevator and along the corridor, with its green waxed floors and its dark mahogany doors, until they reached a door that had been scratched and marked by a million hands going in and out. Harry swung open the door, and allowed Morgana to go through first. She said, lightly, 'I do know the way,' but Harry retaliated, 'Not to my desk, you don't. Nobody can ever find my desk, and that includes me.'

The first person they bumped into was Dundas, the copy boy, a smart-talking young Irish lad with silver sleeve suspenders and circular spectacles and hair that was cut like a hedgehog. 'Harry?' said Dundas, lashing out an armful of galleys. 'Gordon wants you to check through that Walgreen's hold-up story. He says something about you haven't made it clear whether the hostages were hurt or not.' He glanced at Morgana's smudged face and fireman's coat, and said solicitously, 'How're you doing, Miss Croft Tate? Are you okay? I thought this was your birthday?'

'It started out that way,' said Morgana. She tried to smile. She was beginning to feel very weak and tired and shocked, and cold, she couldn't believe how *cold* she was; and somehow the idea of writing up her own account of the 31st Street fire didn't seem so alluring any more. The floor moved sideways, and then the walls moved with it, but she managed to keep her balance by pressing her hand against the nearest partition. It was only then that she realized how painfully the fire had blistered her fingers.

'Well,' said Dundas uncertainly, 'happy birthday to you.' Harry gave him a quick jerk of the head which meant vamoose, and Dundas walked off toward the foreign department on excruciatingly squeaking rubber-soled shoes.

'You want to use my desk?' Harry asked Morgana.

Morgana nodded.

'Okay, then, come with me,' Harry told her, and he led the way round the editorial floor.

It was comparatively quiet on the twenty-third floor at this time of day; only a half-dozen reporters and feature writers sat in their waist-high pigpens, clattering away at their typewriters. The rest of the partitions into which the main editorial department was divided were empty, a maze of cluttered desks and tilted chairs, file-cabinets and heaps of paper, an indoor landscape of triumphant untidiness. Two or three telephones were ringing but the reporters steadfastly ignored them. A large clock on the wall announced that it was nine minutes of three – far earlier than Morgana had imagined.

'Here,' said Harry. He led her around to a pigpen right next to the window. There was a swivel chair with a worn-out velvet cushion on it, a battered mahogany file-cabinet that Harry must have been using as a dart target ever since he had been at the *Star*; and a desk that was buried under an avalanche of copy paper and week-old newspapers and Baby Ruth wrappers and cigarette packets and cups of cold coffee. Harry pushed aside the central section of rubbish to reveal an upright Underwood typewriter, in which there was a piece of copy paper with the smudgily typed words,

gas shortage 1   hs
T threat o an immediate severe gasoline shortage i t Chicago area lessened last night as local 705, AFL teamsters union, announced tt

Harry ripped out the copy paper, shuffled in one of his drawers for a handful of fresh paper, reeled one sheet into the typewriter platen with a sharp zizz, and then said to Morgana, 'Here, go ahead. Five folios should do it.'

Morgana sat unsteadily down on Harry's chair. Behind her, the window overlooked Wabash Avenue, facing north-west, with an unprepossessing view of the State Street Bridge multi-story garage, with its huge poster for Fox Head '400' Beer; and a clutter of flat rooftops and water towers; beyond which rose the Berkshire and the Devonshire Hotels. In the hazy distance, however, the sun still shone on the suburbs, and the clouds were folded over the prairies beyond Albany Park and Forest Glen like thick gray comforters. On the side of the file-cabinet, Harry had pinned a lithograph of Thaddeus Kosciuszko, the Polish patriot who fought on the side of the colonists in the American War of Independence; and next to it, a pin-up of Alexis Smith.

'I suppose you can type?' Harry asked Morgana.

Morgana said tartly, 'They taught me at finishing school. I can type seventy-five words a minute without even chipping the lacquer on my nails.'

'I should have known,' said Harry. He checked his wristwatch. 'Let me just make one phone call, then I'll come back and give you a hand.'

'You're being very solicitous, all of a sudden, for a man who's having the bread snatched out of his mouth.'

'Well, so what, it's only bread,' Harry told her. He draped the yard-long galleys of the Walgreen's hostage story over the side of his pigpen, and went off toward Gordon McLintock's office, whistling the 'Tennessee Waltz'. He called out, 'How're you doing?' to a bald-headed feature writer who was typing so fast that everything on his desk was gradually juddering off the edges, and the bald-headed feature writer raised a hand in reply, but didn't look up.

Morgana sat with her hands in her lap for a moment. Then she slowly stood up, and eased Chief Bryan's jacket off her shoulders. She hung the jacket over the back of the chair, and then sat down again, and tugged the chair right up to the desk, to sit staring with watery eyes at the blank sheet of copy paper that Harry had rolled into the typewriter for her.

She knew that she was being ridiculously brave. She had actually climbed on to the top of an eighty-five foot ladder and rescued a child from a burning building. And now she was going to sit down here and write about it as if it had happened to somebody else. Still – the way she felt at the moment – it seemed much more likely that it *had* happened to somebody else. She felt so tired and so swimmy and so distant. The telephones seemed to echo like bells in a bucket, and the noise of the typewriters was curiously muffled.

She found the crumpled-up sheet of paper on which Harry had been writing his gasoline strike story, and slowly typed,

blaze rescue 1   mct
Today I rescued a six-year-old girl from a burning tenement building on the Near South Side. While a thousand-strong crowd stood in the street and watched me, I climbed up a fire department ladder, right to the very top, and

She stopped. It didn't sound real, any of it. It didn't sound true. She couldn't believe it had happened, and if she couldn't believe it, how could she expect the readers of the *Star* to. And even if it *were* true – which her shocked mind was seriously beginning to doubt – didn't it sound too much as if she were blowing her own trumpet?

She snatched the copy paper out of the typewriter, and wound in a fresh piece. She typed:

blaze rescue 1   mct
If anybody had told me on the morning of my 21st birthday that I was going to

She ripped that piece of paper out, too, and rolled it up between the palms of her hands.

It was then that Gordon McLintock the City Editor appeared. He was a short, stocky man, more like a neighborhood grocer than a journalist, with black brilliantined hair and bright black eyes and a good beer belly which sat round and comfortable between his jazzy red and yellow suspenders. Gordon McLintock was one of the finest city editors in the country: Morgana's father had engineered his poaching from the Philadelphia *Inquirer* after he had presented and edited an extraordinary four-page supplement in 1944 entitled 'Philadelphia At War'. He was pragmatic and quiet, and he had a reputation for summing up the public's taste to a T.

He nodded affably to Morgana, and said, 'Good afternoon, Miss Croft Tate. And happy birthday, too.'

'Well, thank you,' said Morgana. She pushed a third piece of copy paper into the typewriter, and typed:

blaze rescue 1   mct

Gordon McLintock watched her and smiled, his hands in his pockets. 'Harry tells me you deserve a medal for what you did today. Tomorrow morning's front page, a feature on Sunday; no question about it.'

'That's what I'm doing,' said Morgana. She typed 'Five people died in a blaz' and then stopped, and covered her mouth and her nose with her tented hands, and stared at the paper as if she half-expected the words she had written to crawl off across the page like little black curled-up caterpillars. She added 'ing tenement today' and then immediately pulled the paper out of the machine, and crushed it up.

'You look like you could use some rest,' said Gordon McLintock, gently. 'Maybe you'd like to lie down on my office couch for ten minutes. I could ask Dundas to bring you some coffee.'

'Please – I'm all right,' Morgana insisted. 'I just want to get this story finished.'

Harry came back across the editorial floor, and Gordon turned around and raised a querying eyebrow at him. Harry winked, without humor, and took off his sport coat, hanging it up on the bentwood stand that he shared with David Tribe and Nathan Caldicott. "Is Woozy back yet?' Gordon asked him, and Harry nodded, 'He's down in the darkroom. He should have the prints up here in ten minutes.'

Morgana began to type her story again, while Harry and Gordon watched her.

Harry lit up again, and noisily blew out smoke, and perched one buttock on the edge of the next desk while he watched

Morgana type. The smoke curled blue around the partitions, and the sunlight silently fluted it, and when Morgana glanced up at Harry he looked almost as if he were standing in church. Gordon cleared his throat, and then wiped his nose with a wagging gesture of his index finger.

'There really isn't any *need* for you to do this, you know, Miss Croft Tate,' he said, as she hesitated at the end of a sentence. 'Harry could talk to you, and write down what you say, and that would make a fine story in itself.'

'But Harry would write it the way that *he* sees it, wouldn't he?' Morgana retorted. 'I want to write it the way that *I* see it.'

'Well . . . it still has to be sub-edited, and passed by Mr Clifford,' said Gordon, trying to sound reasonable.

'Mr Clifford will pass it,' Morgana said, with regal certainty.

'Well, I'm afraid, Miss Croft Tate, that not even the Lord Almighty –' Gordon began; but Harry gave him a quick shake of the head, and Gordon shrugged, and thrust his hands into his pockets, and contented himself with standing where he was, watching Morgana as she typed out her story.

blaze rescue 1   mct
After it had happened, they called me a heroine. But when I climbed up an eighty-five foot aerial ladder to rescue a little Negro girl from a blazing tenement on 31st Street yesterday afternoon, being a heroine was the furthest thing from my mind.

Twenty minutes went by, and the sun moved around the newsroom. Walter Dempsey the sport reporter came shuffling between the pigpens, a fifty-five-year-old who looked sixty, splendidly raddled, with a disastrous tweed hat studded with fishing flies and a nose that could have been mistaken for a bright crimson mangosteen. He was wearing a huge grass-green necktie, fastidiously knotted, although most of his shirt buttons were either missing or unfastened, revealing cotton underwear of a suspiciously gray hue, and the crotch of his pants hung down voluminously between his thighs. He smelled strongly of whiskey and cigarettes and Listerine mouthwash.

'You're looking rather more elegant than usual, W.D.,' Harry remarked, as Walter managed to bicycle his disobedient feet to something like a standstill. 'Where'd you get that necktie?'

'It was hand woven by the mountain peoples of Mexico,' Gordon grinned.

'No, no, he cut it out of the top of a pool table,' said Harry. 'Either that, or he's been going to those Sinn Fein meetings again.'

Walter Dempsey snorted contemptuously. 'Ignoramuses! What do you know about the Dempsey heritage? My father was the finest Irishman who ever stepped on to American soil. He could sing like a linnet! God in Heaven, did I ever tell you that my elder brother was walking along the street one evening in the summer of 1915 whistling and singing, and a fellow came up to him all excited, and wrote down the tune on the back of an old envelope? It turned out to be "When Irish Eyes Are Smiling". Did I ever tell you that?'

'Yes, you did; and it's a lie,' Harry replied, quite kindly. '"When Irish Eyes Are Smiling" was written in 1912. Music by Ball, words by Olcott and Graft. I looked it up in the morgue.'

'Blasphemer,' Walter Dempsey told Harry, slapping him affectionately on the back. 'How about a cigarette, then? By God, I could do with a snorter. Is anybody coming down to O'Leary's with me? I have to go to Soldier's Field in half an hour, we'll just have time to sterilize the tonsils.' He paused, and swayed, and reached out for the cigarette that Harry offered him. '*Heritage*,' he said, trying to aim the tip of the cigarette toward Harry's lighted match, and at last having to cling on to Harry's wrist so that he could aim straight. 'What do you know of heritage? You were conceived in the back seats of the Marbro movie house, that's what. My heritage is Ireland, the Emerald Jewel! Yours is a popcorn palace on Madison and Crawford!'

It was then that Walter Dempsey focused at last on Morgana, as she sat typing. He frowned at Gordon, and spread his fingers interrogatively over his chest, as if to say, what's this, what's this? Then he approached Morgana with his head slightly tilted to one side, and scrutinized her minutely. Morgana knew that he was there, but she ignored him, because she had almost finished her story, and she was just about ready to faint.

'This is ...' Walter Dempsey began, and then turned

around to Harry, and said, 'A new recruit, hey? Well, what's she writing? May I see what it is? I sense an air of expectancy not to mention terror! Miss Morgana Croft Tate, no less. My respects, young madam. We've had occasion before, haven't we? At your command!'

Morgana turned, and smiled wanly, acknowledging Walter Dempsey with a nod.

'Come on now, W.D., leave the lady alone,' said Harry. 'Get off to your football interviews before you say something you don't really mean.'

'But – now, now – she's *writing*,' Walter Dempsey persisted. 'What's she writing, that's what I'd like to know? The elder daughter of the Great White How's-your-father, gracing our miserable newsroom with her beauty and fashionabil-ability. And *writing*! Come on, now, men! We must inspect!'

Gordon tried to head him off, but Walter Dempsey snatched up two or three folios of Morgana's copy, and held it up, squinting at it with exaggerated curiosity.

'Well, well!' he said. 'This is powerful stuff! Have you read this, Gordon? Listen to this now, pin back your aural receivers!'

Unsteadily, he read Morgana's story out loud. 'Today's tragic fire was not an accident or an Act of God. What happened today was quite deliberate, the work of evil men who prey on human weakness and human suffering. If there is anything heroic in what I did, it is that I refused to allow the greed of corrupt men to claim the life of an innocent child. But there is nothing heroic in all of us standing up against such men, and refusing to allow them to claim any more lives in their reckless pursuit of easy wealth. It is simple human decency. It is –'

He came to the end of the folio and he couldn't find the continuation. In the end, he returned the copy to Morgana's desk, and said with slightly detached reverence, 'That is stirring stuff, Miss Croft Tate! That is blistering stuff! The reckless pursuit of wheezy wealth. By Jiminy! That will either sell us a million and a half copies tomorrow, or else it'll close us down for good!'

At that moment, Gordon reached out and touched Walter's arm. There was something about that touch that alerted Walter at once; and it abruptly sobered him up. He played the idiot drunk to great effect; but he was also the very best sport writer in the state of Illinois, if not America, and his years of top-level reporting had given him a finely tuned sense of mood. Joe di Maggio had candidly said that Walter Dempsey could read a player's mind, almost as if he had a cartoon bubble floating out of the top of his head – the way that Walter had described the pain he had been suffering from that bone spur this season, that was uncanny; and Casey Stengel had said the man was simply tree-mendous and who ever needed to read anything else but Walter Dempsey's column except maybe the menu when you sat down for lunch?

Morgan sensed that something was going on, too, and she turned around in Harry's revolving chair, and looked toward the opposite side of the newsroom. There, half-hidden by cigarette smoke, stood her father, with Phoebe and John.

Morgana looked quickly at Harry. Harry eased his backside off the desk, and crushed out his cigarette, and said, 'I admit it. It was me, I called them.'

Morgana tugged the last sheet of copy paper out of the typewriter. 'I'm not cross with you,' she told him. 'In fact, I'm rather glad that you did.'

She carefully collated the six folios of her fire story, and handed them to Gordon. 'If there's anything else you need to know, you can call me at home,' she told him. Gordon accepted the copy as if he had won the booby prize in a weekend raffle.

'You take care of yourself,' he told her. 'Mr Clifford will take a look at this just as soon as he gets into the office.'

Phoebe came hurrying up to Morgana, and hugged her. 'Oh, look at you!' she cried out. 'They called from the office and said you went to a fire!'

John came over and laid his arm around Morgana's shoulders. 'Mr Sharpe here told us all about it,' he said, looking toward Gordon.

'I'm Mr Sharpe,' Harry corrected him.

'Well, we're very appreciative,' said John. 'Now, come on, Morgana, we'd better get you back home. Everybody kept wondering where you were!'

'You're having the best birthday party of the decade and you're not even *there*!' Phoebe told her; her voice so high it was almost hysterical.

Morgana said, 'I'm sorry. Woozy told me there was a fire and I wanted to go see it, that's all.'

'Woozy?' demanded Howard Croft Tate, gruffly. 'Who's Woozy?'

'One of our photographers, sir,' said Harry. 'His real name's Joseph Proski, but everybody calls him Woozy, after Plastic Man's sidekick.'

'*Plastic Man?*' Howard frowned, in complete bewilderment.

Morgana said, 'It's all right now, Pops. I just want to go home.'

'Come on,' John told her. 'This is no place to be on your twenty-first birthday.'

'My coat!' said Morgana. 'I mustn't forget my coat!'

She turned, and Harry came toward her carrying the dark-blue uniform jacket that Chief Bryan had given her. It was big and shapeless and it reeked of smoke.

'Here,' he said. 'You earned it, remember?'

9

She woke up and her bedroom was suffused with sunlight. She lay on her rose-patterned pillow for a long while, dozing, and then she held out her hand in front of her face. Three fingers were bandaged; and her wrist was bound with surgical tape. She lifted her head and stared at it, and then she sat up. Everything that had happened on 31st Street and back at the Chicago *Star* office came tumbling back to her as if somebody had suddenly emptied a box of souvenirs all over her head. The fire, the ladder, the little girl jumping at her like a jack-in-the-box and banging her forehead. And then the strange dreamlike interlude at Harry Sharpe's typewriter, trying to describe in tiny and disobedient black letters the anger she felt.

The bedroom door opened and her mother came in, wearing a simple pink and white day dress with a ruffled neckline by Pauline Trigère. She looked paler than usual, but very composed, and she was perfumed with Chanel No. 5, which usually indicated that she was feeling well balanced and quite in control of herself. She drew up a white basketwork chair (she never sat on beds) and smiled and took hold of Morgana's hand.

'You've been on the television,' she said. 'You're quite a celebrity.'

Morgana said nothing, but held up her bandaged hand.

'Dr Lemmon came, and made sure that there was nothing seriously amiss,' her mother explained. 'You frightened us all, you know! Poor John was hunting for you everywhere. He was going to propose. You knew that, didn't you? Is that why you ran away? But you frightened us all so much! John was quite distraught! And I can't begin to tell you what your father had to say. He was raging about it all night.'

Morgana found it difficult to focus on her mother clearly.

'All night?' Morgana asked her. 'What do you mean, all night? What day is it?'

'My dear, it's Saturday, and it's past lunchtime. You've been asleep.'

'You mean my birthday's over?'

'The guests have gone, the tents are down, the tables have been taken away. In an hour or two, you won't even know that it happened.'

'Oh my God, Popsy must be absolutely *furious*! Oh, Momsy, I'm so sorry! I went down to see that fire – I don't know – on *impulse*. I didn't think that it would take more than an hour.'

Her mother swept her hand through her hair, and airily looked away. 'We're pleased you weren't hurt, that's all. A few blisters on your right hand; shock; and some singed hair. But apart from that, you're very well, especially for somebody who has been subsisting on nothing but dried apricots.'

'Oh, Momsy,' said Morgana, in genuine sorrow.

'Oh, Momsy,' mimicked her mother. 'Well – at least your father doesn't seem to mind. In fact, he's indecently proud. You were on every television news bulletin this morning; and the front page of every paper whether it was Croft Tate or not. Movietone News are supposed to be coming around at four o'clock to interview you.'

Eleanor hesitated, then laid her hand on the cream silk cover of Morgana's bed. On the wall behind her, a Maxfield Parrish shepherdess lifted her billowing dress to the wind. She said, seriously, 'I couldn't believe it when your father told me what you had done. I'm not sure that I can believe it even now. I have none of that kind of courage, myself. You certainly didn't inherit it from me. Perhaps it comes from your father. I don't know. I always thought that his bravery was more calculating than that. But what you did was quite remarkable, my darling, and if I seem offhand about it, well, it's only because it still scares me to think about it. You were marvelous, and please believe me when I say that I'm very proud of you.'

Just then, the door opened and John came in, smiling, in a white sport coat and white trousers, carrying a huge bunch of yellow roses. 'Who's that little chatterbox?' he asked.

'I hope you realize you're talking about your future

mother-in-law,' retorted Eleanor. 'Have you brought the ring?'

John spread his arms wide, like Frank Sinatra. 'It's so easy to keep a secret around here. It's like *The Romance of Helen Trent.*'

He laid the flowers on the foot of the bed, and came up and kissed Morgana tenderly on the forehead. Morgana held him around the neck with her left arm, and kissed him back; and the smell of him and the warmth of him was even more comforting than ever; and she couldn't think what it was that made her think that he was stiff and unfeeling. Maybe she was frustrated. Maybe they needed to forget their pact of celibacy and make love. He suddenly seemed very reassuring and very desirable. She patted the quilt, and John sat down close to her, his weight pinning her tightly beneath it.

'Your mother's given everything away,' he told her.

'Don't worry about it. Momsy always gives everything away.'

He laughed. 'Yes,' he said. She couldn't help looking at his teeth.

'Well,' she said, feigning coyness. 'I'm sorry I wasn't around yesterday.'

John touched her cheek, and his smile sank away. 'I don't want you doing anything like that when we're married. I'm serious, Morgana. You could have been killed. I know what you did. I know you saved that little girl. But, phew.'

Morgana said, a little unbalanced, and quite close to tears, 'You know what we Croft Tate ladies are like. Rather impetuous, what?'

'You saved the little girl's life,' said John; and by the expression on his face she could tell that he was more impressed by what she had done than he cared to admit.

'Is she all right?' Morgana asked.

'She's fine, according to the papers. She's at the 15th Street Clinic, with minor burns.'

John shifted off the bed, and knelt down close beside her, and she buried her face in his white coat and felt secure. When he spoke, she could hear his voice rumbling in his larynx.

He said, 'I always wanted to do this properly . . . you know, down on one knee. I believe in the old traditions. I guess I'm just an incorrigible Phi Beta Kappa man at heart. But here . . . look . . .' and he straightened up, and produced from his pocket a dark blue ring box, and held it up so that Morgana could see it.

'Morgana,' he said, with well-rehearsed sincerity, 'I love you more than the whole world. I want to spend the rest of my life with you. I want to make you happy – so happy that you forget for ever what it's like to be blue.'

Morgana looked over John's shoulder toward her mother and there was an expression on her mother's face which she couldn't understand at all. Was it regret? Was it sorrow? But then a smile passed over her mother's face as quickly as a bird flying past a window; and Morgana could only suppose that she was probably all right – that she was nothing more than tired after yesterday's party.

John said, 'Will you marry me, Morgana?'

He paused, and then he said, 'I've written a special song to sing if you say yes.'

'That's what I call a disincentive,' put in Morgana's mother. She may have been looking wistful for a moment, but she hadn't lost her waspishness.

Morgana couldn't help laughing. She buried her hands in John's hair, and pulled him close, and kissed him, and said, 'You're not *that* bad a catch, I suppose.'

'Hey, mmmff,' he protested, as she kissed him again and again. 'Is that a yes or what?'

'It's a yes. Besides, I want to see the ring.'

'Ah, the *ring*. You see what girls are like these days, Mrs Croft Tate? Gold diggers. They're not interested in love and romance. All they want is jewelry.'

'I want to see the ring,' Morgana demanded.

'All right, all right,' John agreed, and opened up the box. Inside, on a white satin cushion, was a delicate antique ring fashioned into the shape of a lover's knot of sapphires and diamonds. John carefully lifted it out, and took hold of Morgana's hand, and slipped it on to her finger.

'It's not worth a million dollars,' he confessed. 'I don't come into my inheritance until I'm twenty-five. But it belonged to my great-grandmother. She was engaged at the family home at York, Pennsylvania, on the night before the battle of Gettysburg, 1863; and this was the ring that my great-grandfather gave her.'

Morgana held up the ring so that the sapphires sparkled. 'Oh, John,' she said, and the tears started to slide down her cheeks because yesterday she had thought so meanly about him, when all the time he had wanted to love her and cherish her.

There was a knock at the bedroom door. John climbed up off his knees as Morgana's father came in, closely followed by a tall, shy-looking man with close-cropped white hair, wearing a double-breasted gray suit that was smart, but oddly loose and out of style. He was Grant Clifford, the editor of the *Star*; and he and Morgana had become particularly good friends during her frequent visits to the editorial offices and the press room. In fact, whenever she visited the *Star*, she spent most of the time sitting in his office, watching him at work. She adored his maddeningly quiet manner, and the way in which he would set up the most sensational of stories as if he were presenting an account of a women's club meeting. Diffident, restrained, a gentleman of the press. He came in this morning with a fresh white carnation in his buttonhole and a copy of the *Star* folded under his arm.

Howard glanced at Eleanor but Eleanor turned away. For one disconnected moment Morgana had the impression that they had been arguing. But then her father briskly rubbed his hands together and said, 'Well, now, how's the party pooper?'

'Oh, Popsy, I'm so sorry,' said Morgana. She dabbed away her tears with the edge of her sheet. 'That marvelous party, all those people. You must feel like disinheriting me.'

Howard thrust his hands into his pockets and grunted with amusement. 'All I want to know is, did you have a good time? You're twenty-one now, if you prefer climbing up firemen's ladders to dancing the light fantastic, who am I to criticize? Come on, don't worry about it. Everybody else had a good time, back here, and most of the guests were too pie-eyed to realize you'd gone. I did the same thing myself once. My father gave a party when we opened the print works at Gary. You know what I did? I went automobiling out to Diamond Lake with three friends and a bottle of Old Devastation. Didn't go home for four days. Worst hangover in living memory.'

Grant Clifford came forward, smiling gently. 'I'm glad you're well,' he told her, in his hushed, Down East accent. 'When Harry Sharpe told me what you did – well, I don't know of any other young lady who would have had the *chutzpah*.' He opened up the newspaper, and held it in front of her, so that she could see the huge eight-column photograph of herself, right up at the top of the aerial ladder, with the little Negro girl about to fall into her arms, and the banner headline, THE HEROINE.

Underneath, a thirty-six point strap said *News heiress in daring rooftop blaze rescue.*

Morgana tried to sit up in bed. John plumped up her pillows for her, and helped her to sit straight. Then, as everybody watched her, she took the paper and quickly leafed through it. It took her only a few moments to realize that her own story hadn't been run.

She looked up at Grant. 'Where's the piece I wrote?' she asked him.

Grant suppressed a small, dry, artificial cough in his fist. Howard turned toward Eleanor again, but Eleanor had withdrawn from the circle around the bed, and was sitting with her arms drawn protectively up in front of her, as if she were tired, or cold, or afraid of being hurt.

'You didn't *run* it,' Morgana persisted. 'I was the person who actually went up that ladder to rescue that little girl, and you didn't run my own first-hand story!'

Grant said, 'We, er, we used parts of it. Well, Harry used parts of it in his story – look, you see here, like quotations.' He obviously didn't know what else to say.

'But why?' Morgana demanded. 'Wasn't it good enough?'

Grant pulled a wry face, but Howard laid a hand on his shoulder as if they were comrades in arms, and said, 'What you wrote, honey, was good – but it was also libelous. You libeled Mr Vespucci. He could have taken legal action against us and cost us a small fortune.'

'But it was the truth! How could it be libelous?'

'You *think* it was the truth,' Howard replied. 'Maybe it *was* the truth. But you had no proof, no evidence, nothing in black and white which you could have taken into a court of law, and said to the judge, I called Mr Vespucci this, that and the other because here's my evidence. Mr Vespucci would've crucified us, nailed us to the wall. I mean, he's a business friend, you know that, but he still would've done it, and rightly so.'

'He's a slum landlord,' Morgana said, hotly.

'He owns some low-quality housing, that's for sure. He

wouldn't deny it – even though he holds most of it through holding companies and proxies. But, you know, there has to be some rock-bottom housing in every city. Where are your poor people going to live? And Mr Vespucci has never been accused of any housing code violations.'

'Popsy –' Morgana protested. But Howard sat down next to Morgana and took hold of her hands and squeezed them together with affection.

'I'm sorry. It was a fine story. Stirring stuff, that's what Grant said. I can understand that you're sore about it. But, you know, maybe we'll fix Mr Vespucci some other day, hunh?'

'Did the lawyers *really* say that we couldn't run the story?' asked Morgana, her voice wavering. 'Or did you kill it yourself, because Mr Vespucci happens to be one of your late-night men's club gambling buddies?'

Howard made a wry face. It was the same face he always made when he was about to say anything intolerant and patronizing. *Come on, now, young lady, we've talked about this like grown-ups, I've told you what I think and that's the way it's going to be. That kind of face.*

'It's a responsibility, running a newspaper,' he said. 'You can't just . . . run around accusing everybody you suspect of doing wrong, just because you suspect them, or just because you don't happen to like the look of their face. I expect my newspapers to crusade, certainly I do. I expect them to campaign continuously for justice and freedom. We run the American flag on our masthead and that's the greatest symbol of justice and freedom that ever was. But we belong to a community, too. Do you understand that? We serve the community and we have to serve it with responsibility.'

'The same way Mr Vespucci serves it with responsibility?' asked Morgana, with deep sarcasm.

Grant rubbed his forehead in embarrassment and looked around at Eleanor but Eleanor wasn't smiling at all.

Howard said, 'Mr Vespucci owns property, and a trucking corporation, and a juke box factory, he's as much a part of daily life in Chicago as me, or Colonel McCormick, or Kenneth Doyle, or any of those men who keep this city moving. Now – if he ever commits a misdemeanor and we can *prove* that he's committed that misdemeanor – then we can do something about it. But we can't start running blistering personal attacks on him just because my daughter doesn't care for the way he parts his hair.'

'Popsy, I'm not interested in the way he parts his hair. I'm interested in the way he sets fire to buildings and burns people alive.'

Grant put in, 'I'm sorry, Morgana, your father's right. There's nothing we can say about Mr Vespucci right now. If only there were.'

John said to Howard, 'Morgana's a little overwrought, sir. You know, the shock and everything.'

'Don't *you* start patronizing me!' Morgana protested; but John ignored her, and leaned over to take hold of her left hand. He lifted it up, and waved it from side to side so that Howard and Grant could see her antique engagement ring, and he beamed with pride.

'You see this? I did it at last. I popped the question and Morgana said yes. Please say congratulations to the future Mrs John Birmingham III.'

Morgana was about to tug her hand out of John's grasp, but again her mother caught her eye. This wasn't the time and this wasn't the place. Something had happened between Howard and Eleanor, Morgana couldn't work out what it was, but it was clear that Howard was quite quickly running out of fatherly indulgence, and that Eleanor had completely run out of any family feeling whatsoever.

Howard leaned forward and kissed Morgana on the cheek but she couldn't smile. She felt as if everything she had done yesterday, saving the girl, writing the news story, had been deceitfully compromised, by her father, by Harry Sharpe, and even by Grant Clifford, the man she had always respected as the fairest of the fair.

Perhaps it was Grant's very fairness that was wrong. There were times when you *had* to take sides, at least as far as Morgana was concerned – when you *had* to be hot-headed. A newspaper wasn't worth buying if it didn't speak out for what it believed in. A tangle of lies was a tangle of lies and Enzo Vespucci was a rat and there was no possible way in which anybody could be fair about that.

'We're so pleased for the both of you,' smiled Howard, taking hold of Morgana's hand and admiring her ring. 'John did actually broach the subject with me, of course, a couple of weeks ago. Not that you need my permission any more.

You're a woman now, you can do what you like! But I'm real pleased you said yes. I just hope this doesn't mean we have to throw another party!'

Grant Clifford came forward now and leaned over the bed to kiss Morgana his congratulations on the cheek. He looked her straight in the eyes, and Morgana could see that he was trying to tell her something without using words. A message sent directly from his gray-green eyes with their pale experienced stare to her dark-brown eyes where vivacity and youthful curiosity still burned hot. A message that said, I'm sorry, it couldn't be helped, there was no other possible way. A message that said, I tried.

'You ought to let me buy you lunch, to celebrate,' Grant told her. 'When are you planning on coming down to the office next?'

'Monday,' said Morgana, decisively. She glanced at her father, and the challenge was unmistakable. 'I have an appointment to interview Mr Vespucci Sunday afternoon. I'm going to grill him. Then I'm going to go back to the Near South Side and find out everything I can about him. After that, there's going to be something to print. Something not only dirty but legal.'

Howard let out an odd burst of mirth, like somebody laughing into a drinking glass. 'You don't think our reporters haven't been trying to do just that for years, my darling? Listen, Mr Vespucci isn't anything like you think he is; and even if he were, you'd never be able to get anything out of him. So, please. Leave him alone.'

'I'm going to talk to him Sunday, Popsy, and that's final.'

Howard shook his head. 'I'm sorry. Mr Vespucci's secretary called me this morning to say that he can't keep his appointment with you. He had to alter his weekend plans and drive up to Milwaukee. But – he sent his compliments. He said you were the sweetest young lady. He said you were truly *dolce*. *Dolce* means sweet.'

'Popsy, I took Italian at school and he promised to meet me.'

Her father shrugged. 'Honeybun, I'm only passing on a message. His secretary said urgent business. I don't know.' For some reason, he seemed fretful and distracted.

Grant squeezed Morgana's hand again, and then stood up, tugging at his gray silk bow tie. 'Come talk to me anyway,' he said. 'I'll buy you lunch at the Well of the Sea. And, you know, remember that life is full of possibilities.'

Nobody else in the bedroom appeared to understand what Grant had meant by that last remark, or even to hear it – or even if they had heard it and had understood it, to care. But Morgana was sure that he had been trying to reassure her that the matter of Mr Enzo Vespucci was by no means concluded. Perhaps she had misjudged Grant. Perhaps his apparent unwillingness to attack Enzo Vespucci had been forced on by him Morgana's father. She would have to wait until Monday to find out.

Meanwhile Grant bowed his head respectfully to Eleanor, and took her hand, and said, 'You're going to enjoy a wedding, Mrs Croft Tate. All those arrangements. All those bridesmaid's dresses to be made. Some bliss.'

'There isn't any question at all that children and particularly daughters are a direct punishment from God Himself,' said Eleanor.

'That's nonsense,' Grant smiled. 'You know you love it.'

Howard and Grant left together – Grant to return to the office for an editorial meeting with Jack Fawcett, the executive editor of the Sunday *Star* – Howard to eat a cold smoked chicken salad before going off to play golf with Kenneth Doyle. Eleanor and John and Morgana sat talking for a while about the possible date of the wedding. June next year seemed like the most appropriate date.

'A ten-month engagement,' Eleanor nodded, peering at her tiny kid-bound diary with the gold pencil. 'Long enough to prove you're not pregnant and short enough not to be too frustrating.'

'Are you going to put on some weight?' John asked Morgana. 'You've been looking like you're all skin and bone lately.'

'I promise I'll give up apricots,' said Morgana. 'I'll start on dried kumquat instead.'

After a while, Morgana began to feel tired, and Eleanor got up to leave. She said to John, 'Don't stay too long, Sir Galahad. I don't want my daughter worn to a frazzle.'

John smiled when she had gone, and said to Morgana, 'Your mother seems pleased.'

'Oh, she thinks pretty well of you. You have all the right connections and you say all the right things.'

'Is that all?'

'Isn't it enough?'

'Well, I don't know,' said John. 'I would have thought that the first priority was that her daughter was madly in love with me.'

'Love? What on earth are you talking about? Momsy doesn't care about love – not when it comes to the care and welfare of her two divine daughters, anyway. Love comes, and love goes, that's what she always says, but a good name is worth money in the bank and money in the bank is even better.'

John looked around the bedroom, almost as if he expected Eleanor to be standing there with cue cards. 'She's some woman, your mother.'

'Her daughter's some woman, too, I hope you realize.'

John was silent for a moment. Then he said, 'You do really want to marry me?'

'Do you think I would have said yes if I hadn't?'

'I don't know. I'm not sure. We don't seem to have been too close lately.'

Morgana stroked the back of his hand, the fine line of hairs along the edge of it, turned blond by the summer sun. 'We said that if it was worth having it was worth waiting for. It has more value that way.'

'We *are* talking about value? We're not talking about avoiding it, in case it doesn't turn out too good?'

Morgana lifted her eyes and looked him directly in the eyes. 'It was good that time in the field, wasn't it? It was good for you?'

'Well, sure, it was good for me.'

Morgana said, 'It was good for me, too. I just think sometimes that you hide yourself. You're not hiding yourself now, but you do sometimes. You don't share what's going on inside of you. Those are the only times when I don't like you. I don't know. I don't think I mean that I don't like you. It's just that I feel that I'm looking at your face but there's nobody home.'

John raised an eyebrow. 'I don't hide myself on purpose. I don't even know that I'm doing it.'

Morgana kissed him. 'Next time, I'll tell you when you're doing it, so you can stop doing it. Do you know what Oscar Hammerstein said about you?'

'No, I don't know what Oscar Hammerstein said about me.'

'He said you were good looking but you didn't look as if you had any muscle.'

'Muscle?' John demanded, indignantly. 'What does he mean, muscle? I'm training to be a lawyer, not an all-in wrestler.'

'Gorgeous John!' Morgana teased him.

'I'll sue that Hammerstein for everything he's got,' John retorted, pretending to be annoyed. He looked at his watch. 'Listen,' he said, 'I have to go now – and your mother did tell me not to tire you out. But I just want to tell you that I love you.'

'I love you, too, John,' Morgana heard herself telling him.

John stood up, and looked down at her.

'You're doing it again,' she said.

'Doing what again?'

'Going all distant, as if your brain just went out for a stroll in the park.'

'It did, as a matter of fact. I was wondering how many children we were going to have, and what we were going to call them.'

'*Children?*' squeaked Morgana.

'I'm going, I'm going. I'll call by tomorrow afternoon if that's okay.'

'Come for lunch,' Morgana invited him. She suddenly thought of her canceled interview with Enzo Vespucci, and added, less happily, 'I'm not doing anything else.'

When John had left, Morgana rang down for Millicent to bring her a cup of lemon tea and smoked salmon sandwich. Then she called Loukia to lay out a fresh nightdress for her – a pure cotton creation in pale lemon with white broderie anglaise collar and cuffs, by the Belgian designer Aimée. She showered, and then wrapped in her lemon cotton peignoir, she opened the French windows of her bedroom and stepped out on to the curved balcony, sipping her tea.

Millicent asked, as she straightened the bed, 'Is there anything else, Miss Morgana?'

Morgana shook her head. 'No, thank you, Millicent. I'm going to read the paper and then I'm going to sleep for a while. The newsreel people are supposed to be coming at four.'

She stood on the balcony, holding on to the ornate cast-iron railing and looking out over the gardens. Her bedroom faced south, over the rose beds, with the golf course and the woods beyond. It was a hot hazy day, and insects floated through the air like flecks of gold tumbling slowly through the muddy water of a prospector's pan. There was music playing from somewhere, an open window down by the servants' wing, and somebody was singing 'Almost Like Being In Love'.

Mrs Morgana Birmingham, she thought to herself. Mrs John Birmingham III. It did have quite a ring to it. Less fluffy and snappy than 'Croft Tate.'

A phoebe suddenly fluttered up, and perched on the guttering next to the balcony. It cocked its head from side to side, and then started chirping feebee, feebee, feeblee, over and over. Morgana looked up at it, and said, 'What do you think? Do you think that I love him?'

Feeblee, chirruped the phoebe. Feebee, feebee, feeblee.

'Well, you're no judge,' said Morgana. 'You're only a bird.'

She was about to leave the balcony and go back inside when her eye was caught by the sharp reflected sparkle of a French window being opened downstairs. Out on to the pathway that led to the rose garden stepped John, closely followed by Phoebe. Morgana was about to call and wave when the bird on the guttering suddenly flirruped away, and something made her stay where she was, inside the doorway, concealed from the garden by the darkness of the bedroom and the wind-stirred drapes.

She could hear Phoebe laugh. Then she heard John laughing, too. She didn't know what it was that compelled her to stay where she was, watching. She never usually spied on people, it wasn't her nature. But there were Phoebe and John, laughing together, and somehow she found the sight of them fascinating. Phoebe was wearing a simple blue and white Thai-silk afternoon dress by Mainbocher, and a curving straw hat. John was holding her hand.

Morgana was unable to catch what it was they were saying. One of the gardeners had started up his mower on the East Lawn, where they had held the party yesterday. But quite unexpectedly, Phoebe stood on tiptoe and kissed John directly on his mouth. It wasn't a long, passionate kiss, but it wasn't a peck, either. Morgana felt flushed, and then cold. It was a kiss of affectionate familiarity.

John held Phoebe's shoulders and kissed her back. Then, he lifted up one hand in a short, choppy salute, and walked briskly off toward the garages, his white pants flapping in the sunshine like the sails of a small boat.

Phoebe stood at the doorway, waving. Then she went back inside, leaving the French windows open.

Morgana remained where she was, both fists clenched tightly. She felt madly confused, and angry with both of them, although she felt guilty, too, for having spied. She turned back, setting down her teacup on the white-painted bureau, and then she looked at herself in the mirror on the opposite wall, the French mirror with the frame of gilded ribbons.

Perhaps she was imagining things. Perhaps those kisses had meant nothing at all. Why should John propose to *her*, if he was really in love with Phoebe? Phoebe was just as eligible, as long as a fellow was prepared to chase away her various casual suitors, like Donald Crittenden and what was his name? – that awful race driver with the magnificent profile and the tattooed buttock.

No, it was hogwash. They hadn't been doing anything more serious than saying goodbye to each other. She should be glad they were friends, not jealous. She had seen so many society families in which the brothers-in-law could quite happily have cat-o'-nine-tailed their sisters-in-law around the morning room. Sisters-in-law, after all, did come under the *Encyclopedia Britannica* classification of major pests.

Morgana climbed back into bed. She lay back against the puffed-up pillows for a moment, thinking. Then she picked up the newspaper and stared at the blurred photograph of herself, right at the top of that aerial ladder, and the little black girl falling toward her, head forward, almost as if she were praying rather than falling.

She wondered if her mother would allow her to have a small glass of brandy.

10

The late afternoon sunlight fell across the Lakeshore golf course like a golden shawl that had frayed into rags.

Rashly, Howard had used a number three wood on the long hole by the lake, and it had skyed his ball way past the green into the woods. Now he was rooting through the ivy with his putter, while Kenneth Doyle helped him in a spasmodic, Irish kind of a way, and chattered a lot, and kept trying again and again to light up his S-shaped Sherlock Holmes briar with a cheap lighter that sparked like a firecracker but scarcely ever lit, and when it did light, promptly blew out again.

'You're not concentrating your essences,' Kenneth remarked.

'My *essences*? What do my essences have to do with it?' Howard replied, in well-suppressed rage. He had more on his mind than a lost golf ball.

'Your essences determine your demeanor,' Kenneth explained. 'Your blood controls your loyalties, your bile controls your temper, your phlegm controls your sensibilities, do you see? and your urine controls your impetuosity.'

'Well, Kenneth,' said Howard, 'it's pretty hard for anyone to concentrate anything with you constantly scratching away at that damned lighter. Why don't you let me buy you a decent one, that works?'

'That could easily be construed by certain unprincipled hacks from the yellow press as bribery of an elected official,' said Kenneth. 'Don't you think I'm having enough trouble as it is with the Negroes accusing me of taking money from the Sicilians, and the Sicilians accusing me of taking money from the Irish, and the Irish accusing me of taking money from the

Lithuanians. The only people who don't think I'm taking money from anyone are the Poles, and they suspect me of getting my *kabanos* cheap from the Czechs.'

'Well, nobody ever said it was easy, being mayor,' said Howard.

He suddenly said, 'aha!' and leaned forward into the undergrowth to pick up a ball. He scrutinized it closely, and then said, 'Damn it,' and dropped it back again. A little further off to his left, his caddy was thrashing at the brambles with his stick, so wildly and so furiously that there couldn't have been any chance of him finding anything. Perhaps he was imagining that the brambles were Howard.

Kenneth managed to get his pipe going, and for a moment or two he stood sucking at it blissfully with his hands in the pockets of his baggy plus fours and his wedgie tucked under his arm. 'You know something, Howie,' he said, and then sucked some more, and then said, 'that was a rare act of coolness, don't you think, the way Morgana rescued that little girl? There are not many people you'll find in this life with coolness like that, and the more I think about it, the cooler it seems to be.'

'Morgana has always been the cool one,' said Howard, still tussling with the ivy. 'She's a sweet girl, you know. Soft, too. But when she's determined to do something, by jiminy she does it. And works it out, too, up in her mind.' He tapped his temples, with great significance.

'Good at concentrating the essences, then,' said Kenneth.

'You know something,' Howard told him, 'I remember when she was – what, now? – eight or nine years old. She wanted a pony so bad, but Eleanor kept saying no because she thought we ought to draw the line somewhere, when it came to giving the girls everything they wanted. Now *Phoebe* – if it had been Phoebe who wanted a pony, she would have cuddled me and kissed me and oh-Popsy'd me until I couldn't stand it any longer, and I would've bought her the darned animal just to get some peace.'

He stood up straight, easing his stiff back with his hand. 'Not Morgana, though, no! Do you know what Morgana did? She called up Deke Oliver – you remember old Deke, he used to be City Editor before Gordon McLintock – and she asked Deke to run a story on the front page of the Metro section no less, right where she knew that I'd see it, and I opened the paper over my breakfast and there it was. Morgana Croft Tate Dearly Desires Pony. Begs Dad To Relent. Can you believe that? It was just like a news item, you know? "Morgana Croft Tate, nine, pleaded with her father this morning to buy her a pony. She told *Star* reporters, 'I promise to take care of it and love it for ever.'" Well, I had dozens of telephone calls from readers, telling me what a mean old moth-wallet I was, and why didn't I let Morgana have her pony right away.'

'Did you buy her the pony?' asked Kenneth, slyly.

'You're asking me that? A sentimental old Celt like you?' Howard retorted.

He ripped some more ivy away from the floor of the woods. Behind him, the sun-gilded trees dipped and waved. He said, 'She has ink instead of blood, that girl. That's what Grant thinks about her.'

'Yes, he's a good fellow, Grant,' said Kenneth, ingenuously. 'I can't say that I have quite the same regard for Larry Trench, at the *Tribune*.' He paused, and puffed smoke, and then he said, 'Morgana must have been pretty annoyed with Grant, though, don't you think, when he wouldn't run her story about the fire.'

Howard slowly turned around and gave Kenneth what was generally understood to be an 'old-fashioned' look.

'Who the hell told you that?'

'Howie, Howie, Howie. Watch that bile of yours. I'm the *mayor*, Howie. Who tells me anything? I have to deal with those reporters of yours day by day. We trade news, you know, your reporters and I. I'll bet I know most of them better than you do.'

'It wasn't Grant who told you,' Howard asserted, aggressively. 'Nor Gordon, neither.'

'And would you sack them if it were? Of course not. But it's true, isn't it? Morgana wrote her own story about the fire, six impassioned pages from what I hear, and you refused to publish it.'

'Kenneth,' said Howard, 'it was libelous. The lawyers nixed it from the second line.'

'Was it libelous, Howie, or was it simply truthful?'

Howard sniffed dryly. 'Whether an article is libelous or whether it's simply truthful depends on the sensitivity of the person you're writing about. In this case the person we were writing about was Enzo Vespucci, and that meant we couldn't run any of it without laying ourselves wide open to a seven-million-dollar action in the district courts.'

'And *worse*, of course,' said Kenneth, with exaggerated sagacity.

'Well, you know Enzo as well as I do. A generous friend and an enemy to curdle the blood.'

Kenneth looked down with some sadness at the bowl of his pipe. 'Yes, no doubt about that. You remember what happened when the *Tribune* tried to run those articles on dope-peddling, don't you? Three newsbutchers beaten half to death; two newspaper trucks set on fire; two hundred thousand dollars' worth of damage at the printing plant. Not to mention those hayseeds in Springfield accusing me of fiddling while Chicago burned. That rankled.'

He looked up, and added, 'I'm not saying it was Enzo, of course. I wouldn't be such a fool. But I'm not saying it wasn't either.'

'Kenneth,' said Howard, emphatically, 'I feel the same way about Enzo as you do. But, he's a fact of life, the same way that sharks in the sea are a fact of life. You can ply your boats from shore to shore and he won't ever bother you; you can even take a swim now and again. But don't start churning up the water, by God, or he'll be after you, and he'll bite your damned legs off, *gnanng*!'

'Does he scare you that much?' asked Kenneth.

'Don't tell me that he doesn't scare you.'

'Well, to be truthful, he doesn't scare me personally, not for myself,' Kenneth replied. 'But whenever I see him angry at all, I get scared for other people. And, you know, in a way, that's worse, being scared for other people. It's the helplessness. My old mother always used to say that a sense of responsibility was a heavier burden than a sackful of broccoli bottoms.'

'I'm beginning to thank God that I never met your old mother.'

'She wouldn't have liked you, either. She thought that newspapers were the work of the Devil. Satan's Advertisements, that's what she used to call them. The flysheets of Hades.'

'You ought to be impeached just for having had parents beyond the call of reason,' Howard told him.

'Howie,' Kenneth appealed, 'I didn't ask you to play golf with me this afternoon purely for the sake of your health.'

'Well, I know that, Kenneth,' Howard replied, trying not to be testy. 'I don't think that you've asked me once to play golf with you purely for the sake of my health ever since you were elected mayor. And quite honestly I don't think that my health ever recovered from the shock of you being elected. To think that Kenneth Doyle who never led anything but the Milwaukee Avenue St Patrick's Day Parade should be wearing the mantle of Big Bill Thompson.'

Kenneth laughed, and shook his head. 'You're the best cure I know for an over-inflated ego, Howie, the very best. But you know what I want to talk about, don't you? And it's not a million miles distant from the very fellow that we've been discussing up until now.'

Howard didn't look up. 'You want to talk about Enzo and you want to talk about slum clearance. I know, Kenneth. I know what pressures you're under.'

'I need your help, Howie,' Kenneth said, acutely.

'All right then, if that's what you're after, let's talk *tachlis*.'

Kenneth kept his eyes down. The afternoon breeze made his white hair flap like someone waving a handkerchief from a faraway balcony. 'Howie,' he said, 'it's been four years now since the war was over, and let's face it the talk everywhere is of prosperity and new houses and a better standard of living. Happy days are here again, Howie, that's the very nub of it. But they haven't reached the center of Chicago, these happy days. There's no sun shining in the Near South Side. In fact, things are worse than you know.'

Howard said nothing, but listened, and prodded impatiently around for his ball.

Kenneth said, 'It's desperate now, Howie, do you know that? Almost beyond saving. And *I'm* desperate, too. Do you think that I want to go down in the history books as the mayor who presided over the final collapse of America's Second City? Do you think that? But by God it's going to take some rare guts to change the way things are. It's going to take some rare guts.'

'Not to mention some very rare money,' Howard commented.

'Well, it's billions, isn't it, if we're going to be truthful,' said Kenneth. 'But what have I got? Most of my best taxpayers have gone to live in the suburbs. And what am I left with? The poorest of the poor, those who can't leave, and certainly can't afford to renovate the houses they live in. Oh, Howie, the worse it gets the worse it gets. Those people living in the slums, God help them, they're caught up in a whirlwind, a self-perpetuating disaster, like Dorothy, except that they're not going to Oz, they're going to hell. They don't have the money to help themselves, and they don't have the skill; and to make matters worse they don't even have the will. And on top of that, there are men like Enzo who are feeding off their misery, feeding off their degradation, and who are making quite sure for their own profitable purposes that they *never* escape.'

He paused for a moment, breathless. He was very upset. Then he said, more quietly, 'The slums have to be cleared, Howie, the city has to rise up again. But that means that legitimate businesses and legitimate organizations have to be encouraged to invest their money in the city center. Well, not just encouraged, *urged*! And that's where the *Star* comes into it. The *Star* has to help me to break the grip of men like Enzo Vespucci, and bring back honest money.

'Have you looked at those slums, Howie? It could make you cry.'

Kenneth shivered, and turned to Howard with an expression that Howard had never seen before. White, haunted, cornered.

'You know, Howie,' he said, 'a Negro came and stood outside my office last month, every day for a whole month. He stood there from six o'clock in the morning until it was dark. In the end I walked outside and asked him why he was standing there, who did he think he was, Mrs Mudd or something? I was tired, I suppose, and not so patient. But do you know what he said? "Your honor, I've been standing here because you killed my little girl, not your personal fault, your honor, but my girl was eleven and went out and worked as a whore, and in the end she was taken by five men, the day before her twelfth birthday, and they did everything to that little girl that you could do, five of them, and then when she asked them afterwards for money they beat up on her and they killed her." That's what this Negro said, and I couldn't think what to tell him, but he didn't want an answer. All he said was, "This is your city, your honor, you clean it up. Otherwise go home, and never set foot back in City Hall for as long as you live."'

Howard said, with dense hoarseness, 'You can't blame yourself personally, Kenneth. There isn't too much you can do. Cities are like people. They grow old, they get wrinkled, they get sick. You can't change history.'

Kenneth whacked his golf club on to the ground. 'I *have* to change history! I have to fight back! I have the death of that girl on my conscience, Howie, and the continuing daily misery of thousands of others! Do you think I can sleep? I feel like a rat in a trap!'

Howard was watching Kenneth with care. Howard was influential, Howard was a power. When Howard had an opinion, his voice spoke from coast to coast through millions of newspapers and scores of radio stations and dozens of magazines, an Hallelujah chorus of assenting voices. But Howard did not lend his influence easily, and he was not a political evangelist, not about anything. He believed in law and order and the American Way. He believed in individual freedom. But he also believed in letting things find their own level. He was not a William Randolph Hearst or Robert McCormick. He didn't hold with creating the news. His father had always told him, 'What happens is what happens, and that's sufficient.' And Howard had other considerations, too, private considerations: considerations that he wasn't at all sure that he was prepared to risk because of Kenneth Doyle's latest moral upsurge. He had heard Kenneth talk this way before. Kenneth always talked this way when he was panicking about his politcal security; and, of course, who else could Kenneth turn to, when all the other major newspaper publishers were so fiercely Republican?

Kenneth for his part harbored no illusions about Howard. He knew that Howard was not an indiscriminate crusader, and that he always chose his causes with care. Howard was not at all like Stephen Leacock's hero, who 'flung himself from the room, flung himself upon his horse, and rode madly off in all directions.' By being parsimonious with his political commitments, Howard had remained powerful, sought-after, and overwhelmingly rich. All the same Kenneth was going to persist. His career was crumbling and so was the city of Chicago. He felt, too, that his friendship with Howard was showing its age. It had lost so much of its humor; and almost all of its boyish closeness. They didn't talk about horses any more; or women; or liquor. Perhaps, in truth, they were no longer friends at all, but golfing partners, political acquaintances, two weary opportunists shaking out the memories of what they once used to be for whatever they could get, like a railroad bum shaking out his pants for a lost nickel.

The trees around the golf course worriedly rustled; but the clouds sailed past, serene.

Kenneth said, 'It's true, you know, Howie, that I've got my troubles. The state legislature is still holding up funds for rebuilding until I can show them what they call realistic plans. Realistic, I ask you! They're farmers, the lot of them, what do they know about cities? My own people at City Hall are accusing me of being too soft on the slum barons; while the other lot are accusing me of interfering with the constitutional rights of private landowners. Unless I can show some results, Howie, they're going to be sharing out my tripes in a pudding bowl.'

He paused, and then he said, 'We have a chance, Howie, do you see that? A real chance for a new beginning, and we have to take it. Both the Michael Reese Hospital and the Illinois Institute of Technology – well, you know for yourself what's been happening to them in the past ten years. They've been surrounded by slums on all sides. But I've been talking to their planning committees lately, and they have both decided not to move, not to relocate, but to stay where they are. They want to bring together as many local businesses as they can, and they want to plan and finance private rebuilding all around them, right where they stand. A new beginning, Howie, knock down the slums, rebuild, think where it could lead to.'

Howard said, 'What about Enzo? Most of that district belongs to him, doesn't it?'

'Come on, Howie,' said Kenneth, although he was not quite as convincing as he would have liked to be. 'There's a fighting spirit in Chicago now! The spirit of '71, all over again! And not just on the South Side, either. You ought to hear them in the Hyde Park–Kenwood district. People want to clear away the slums for good! The University of Chicago has all kinds of magnificent plans for rebuilding the area, magnificent! and there are scores of neighborhood groups who want to help them. It's a holy war, Howie! Just the thing for the *Star* to support!'

'A holy war,' Howard repeated, unconvinced. 'Do you think that Enzo's going to see it that way?'

'Enzo's a dinosaur,' Kenneth retaliated, impatiently. 'Enzo and his kind are the last of a tiresome, vicious, small-brained breed, long overdue for extinction.'

'Oh yes? And who are you going to tell that to?' Howard asked. 'The courts? The cops? The Fire Department? Me?'

He held up his fist, and brandished it in front of Kenneth's face, as if he had caught hold of a handful of moths, and crushed them. 'Enzo has this city there, doesn't he?' he demanded. 'Enzo and all the other Enzos.'

Kenneth turned away. 'You know, Howie, you've made me feel genuinely disappointed.'

'Oh yes?' Howard retorted. 'Enzo may be a dinosaur, but he's still powerful and very dangerous. And what about Francesco Lorenzo and Orville O'Keefe and Danny Sabatini, and that's just three of them, without talking about neighborhood housing rackets and the tenements run by Germans and Hungarians and Czezskis.'

'And Irish,' put in Kenneth.

Howard couldn't help grunting with laughter. 'You'd take the credit for anything, wouldn't you, you stupid bastard?'

'I'm not afraid of Enzo,' Kenneth repeated.

Howard paused and lifted his head, and said, 'It's going to rain. I can feel it. I have this pain in my left knee, always the left knee. You mark what I say, it's going to rain.'

'For God's sake, Howie,' said Kenneth.

Howard turned on him. 'You were talking about your sense of responsibility, your sackful of broccoli bottoms. Well, just remember that I have to think about *my* responsibilities, too. I have to think about my business, and all the people who work for me. Four thousand, six hundred eighteen, as of yesterday morning. All of them depending on me personally to put a chicken in their pot, not just for today, but tomorrow, and every day. Chickens, Kenneth. Four thousand, six hundred eighteen chickens a day, seven days a week. That makes thirty-two thousand, three hundred twenty-six chickens.'

Kenneth stared at him in astonishment.

'*Chickens?*' he said, and then suddenly they both burst out laughing.

Howard hadn't laughed so much in months. He barked like a big hoarse dog, while Kenneth went 'sss-sss-sss' between his teeth. Howard felt so weak that he had to lean against a tree to catch his breath, while Kenneth promptly sat down amongst the ivy.

It was then that Kenneth frowned, and reached down beneath him, and produced Howard's golf ball, just as if he had laid an egg. This finished Howard completely. He barked and barked, and wept as he barked, and punched the tree again and again.

The caddies came up, and stood watching Howard and Kenneth in silence. At last Howard said, 'I think I'd better play that ball now, or this game's going to take us the rest of the day.'

'Are you going to play it as it lies?' Kenneth wanted to know.

'Well, morally, yes, I ought to,' Howard replied.

'In that case, concentrate your essences,' Kenneth advised him. 'Concentrate your essences, and you should be able to get it back on to the green.'

'Oh go piss on your essences,' said Howard; and that led them to burst out laughing all over again. Howard's caddy covered his face with his hands, as if he were asking the Lord God to intervene, and to cut this game short.

Not long afterwards, as they began walking uphill toward the fourth hole, the caddy's prayer was answered by a bellowing of summer thunder, and the sudden rushing of rain. They stood under the trees for a while, watching the spray that danced across the greens, and then Howard looked at his watch, and said, 'Let's call this a day, shall we? Can I give you a ride downtown?'

'Are you going to consider what I said at all?' asked Kenneth. His white face was tinged with luminous green, from the leaves of the chestnut tree which sheltered them. There was a fresh smell of ozone in the air.

'Give me the weekend, then we'll talk some more,' Howard replied.

Kenneth took out his pipe, and tapped it against the tree trunk. 'Right then,' he said, as if he wasn't discouraged in the slightest.

11

They drove downtown along Lake Shore Drive, and the lake on their left-hand side was the color of gray serge suits, while the elegant 1920s apartment buildings rose up on their right like thermometers filled with shining mercury. The tires of Howard's dark blue Chrysler Imperial limousine sizzled on the wet pavement, and drops of water shuddered on the long highly waxed hood. It was eighty-three degrees and steamy – so steamy that Howard felt as if he could scarcely breathe.

Kenneth said, 'You'll call me Monday morning, won't you, then? Ernie's back; perhaps I can buy you some lunch.'

Howard said nothing, but laced his fingers tightly together and continued to stare out of the window.

They passed the 1500 block where William Wrigley the chewing gum millionaire had once lived in a twenty-room duplex; and George Wood had occupied a thirty-room rooftop apartment with a spacious garden and an unchallenged view of the lake. Nearer the city center, however, the grand old, red granite mansions built by Chicago's wealthy merchants were beginning to look shabby and shrunken. And then they turned west, away from the Gold Coast, and into the tenement area of Clark and Wells streets, the area that Harvey Zorbaugh more than twenty years before had called 'the jungle of human wreckage,' and which today was far worse.

The rain that had paved Lake Shore Drive with silver had turned this district into a mean canyon of dripping awnings, glistening sidewalks, wet-streaked windows, puddles, and alleyways choked with sodden trash. On a steamed-up storefront, the words 'Good Eats Pervided' had been boldly whitewashed, and seven or eight men with copies of the *Star* draped wetly over their heads were standing in line outside.

'Seems like your newspaper's doing *some* good in the slums,' Kenneth told Howard, with well-enjoyed sarcasm.

Howard briskly cleared his throat, but didn't reply. He didn't like Kenneth when he nagged. He had listened studiously to what Kenneth had said about slum clearance, and about the plans that the Michael Reese Hospital and the I.I.T. had worked up for private rebuilding. Now he wanted to think it over, worry it around the house, and decide what the *Star* was going to do about it, if anything.

Howard let Kenneth off at South Michigan Avenue. Howard's chauffeur held a large black umbrella over Kenneth's head, on to which the rain drummed tautly and then dripped on to the shoulder of Kenneth's coat. A taxi beeped loudly.

'It's too wet to get down on my knees,' said Kenneth. 'Besides, I never would. But if there's any way of begging you, Howie, without losing your esteem, then that's what I'm doing.'

'You haven't lost my esteem, Kenneth,' said Howard.

'I've annoyed you, though.'

'Just give me some time to think.'

'All right, Howie. Will I see you for lunch?'

'Call me. And give my love to Kate. And that sickly Pomeranian of hers.'

'Pekinese, Howie.'

'That's right, Pekinese.'

For one dissolving instant, there was a look on Kenneth's face which betrayed a longing for real friendship, the kind of friendship they could have had if they had been boys. Then Kenneth stood up straight, catching his forehead on one of the ribs of Charles's umbrella, and gave a stiff funny salute, and said, 'I'll be seeing you, then. And, um, you know ... good luck with the chickens!'

Charles drove Howard smoothly back toward the *Star* building. The limousine's door was opened for him by Freddie, the *Star*'s uniformed doorman, a flat-faced ex-pug whose white cotton gloves concealed fists like lumps of roughcast concrete.

'You play golf today, Mr Croft Tate?' he asked, through whistling nostrils, opening the wide door that led into the lobby.

Howard stopped and looked at him with curiosity. 'How

come you can always tell when I've been playing golf?' he wanted to know. 'Does it show on my face?'

'No, sir, Mr Croft Tate. But it always rains.'

The lobby of the *Star* building was floored in shining green marble, and its walls were clad in burnished steel. From the ceiling, three stories high, a gargantuan chandelier was suspended, in the shape of an exploding Art Deco star, and there were lighted balconies curving all around the lobby, behind whose stainless-steel railings secretaries and reporters and advertising staff moved to and fro as if they were extras in some futuristic movie like *Just Imagine*.

The science-fiction feel to the *Star*'s lobby was heightened by the echoing of voices and footsteps, and by the deep thrumming noise from the press room in the basement. It was the beating of the newspaper's twenty-five ton hearts: the rotary Goss Headliner presses which were finishing off the late editions of Sunday's newspaper at a speed of five hundred copies a minute.

Howard was acknowledged on all sides as he walked across the lobby to the curving stainless-steel reception desk. Behind this desk sat two girls, each as pretty as a beauty-pageant queen, one blonde and one redhead, both in black wool jersey dresses with padded shoulders, with diamanté star brooches. Howard had always insisted that the Star's reception staff should be perky and bright and 'so darn helpful they set your teeth on edge.' In his father's day the desk had been manned by a cantankerous chain-smoking woman called Mrs Schocolad who had once shouted at Mayor 'Big Bill' Thompson for walking mud into the lobby on a wet day.

'Good afternoon, Mr Croft Tate,' the girls chorused.

'Anymore calls from Ogden Avenue, Mandy?' Howard asked them. Then, 'You two girls are a sight to set an old man's heart racing.'

The girls giggled. Howard rested his arms on the top of the desk, and leaned over. 'Have we had any interesting visitors this afternoon? Anybody that I should know about?'

The redhead leafed through her notepad. 'Mr Yablonsky from the Albert Verley company came to see Mr Perez in features.'

Howard raised an eyebrow. 'Did he now?' He made a mental note to dictate a memo to Alfons Perez. The Albert Verley company was being investigated by a senate subcommittee on political bribery, and Mr Yablonsky was their chief attorney. Howard didn't like other people's attorneys paying calls on his editorial staff. Ninety percent of the time, they came only for one purpose: to suppress the news.

'Is that it?' he asked the redhead, and the redhead smiled him a sassy smile. 'All except for that gentleman over in the corner. He said he wanted to see you personally, but he doesn't have an appointment, and we told him you wouldn't be back.'

Howard turned around. Over in the far corner of the lobby, half-concealed by the leaves of an overhanging fern, sat a well-built man of about sixty-five years old, his hands clasped patiently in his lap.

'Did he give his name?' frowned Howard.

The redhead shook her head. 'He said you'd know him.'

Howard left the reception desk and walked cautiously across the marble floor toward the group of chairs where the man was waiting for him. As he approached, he saw the man's face: sallow, with pale blue eyes, the face of a long-term invalid. The man had white hair that had been grown quite long and then greased straight back from his forehead. He wore a brown sport coat with leather-patched elbows that looked as if it had been bought from a thrift store, and mismatched brown pants that bagged at the knees. On his head he wore a brown hat, with a press card stuck ostentatiously in to the band.

Howard decided that whoever the man was, he didn't want to know him, and he turned away. Just as he did so, however, the man called, 'Mr Croft Tate! Please! One moment!'

Howard waited where he was as the man hurried over on creaking shoes. 'Mr Croft Tate! I've been waiting for you for two hours now!'

'Well, I'm afraid I'm a little busy right now,' said Howard, with a humorless smile. 'Why don't you call my secretary and make an appointment?'

The man circled around Howard until he was facing him. He was grinning. 'You don't recognize me, do you?'

Howard gave him a cursory look. 'I'm sorry, I don't. Is there any reason why I should?'

'What did you say to that receptionist girl when you walked in here?'

'I said "Good afternoon." Now, if you don't mind –'

'No, no,' the man enthused. 'Before that. What did you say before that?'

'I said, "Any more calls from Ogden Avenue, Mandy." It's a *Star* tradition. We always say it.'

The man rubbed his hands together. From close to, he smelled disconcertingly like vinegar. 'The girl's name isn't Mandy,' he said.

'No, it isn't,' said Howard. He was growing quite testy now. 'The reason we say it is because of the one and only time that a *Star* reporter earned himself a Pulitzer prize. He called in his story from Ogden Avenue, and it was taken down by a receptionist called Mandy because there was nobody else who had fast enough shorthand.'

'The Ackland Gang Massacre, at the Standard Oil filling station on Ogden Avenue and LaGrange Road, 1935,' the man said, triumphantly.

'That's right,' said Howard. 'Now, you're really going to have to forgive me.'

'Lenny Mutken,' the man interrupted.

'What?' asked Howard.

'That was who it was. That famous *Star* reporter. Your one and only Pulitzer prize winner. His name was Lenny Mutken.'

'Yes,' Howard agreed. He raised his head to look over the man's shoulder and catch the eye of the *Star*'s doorman. At first the doorman was engaged in conversation with a little old Negro lady, but then he turned and saw that Howard was silently appealing for help. He came through the doors and marched across the lobby with the arm-swinging stride of an ex-Marine.

'But don't you understand?' the vinegary-smelling man was saying. 'That was *me*! Look – look at my press card. There it is, in black and white, photograph too. Lenny Mutken. That's me.'

'Well, how about that?' said Howard, uncomfortably. 'To tell you the truth, we thought that you'd gone to meet that Great Deadline in the Sky. Glad to see you again. You've changed. I wouldn't have recognized you.'

'I was sick for a long while,' Lenny Mutken explained. 'Very badly sick. But you don't want to hear about that. What I really came here for was to see if you needed some extra help.'

The doorman came up and stood close to Lenny Mutken with his hands clasped emphatically behind his back.

Howard said, 'I appreciate the offer, Lenny, believe me. But as it is, I'm overstaffed. Tell you what, though – leave your number at the reception desk. If anything comes up, I'll call you.'

'I'm still the best, believe me. I can get stories out of a stone.'

'I'm sure you can, Lenny.' Howard reluctantly laid his hand on Lenny Mutken's shoulder. 'But the genuine truth is that we don't have any vacancies right now. You can always try submitting freelance articles. They pay good money.'

Lenny Mutken grinned and bobbed his head and shuffled his feet. 'I don't think you understand, Mr Croft Tate. It's the paper I miss. The noise, the bustle, the teamwork.'

'I'm sorry,' said Howard, unnecessarily checking his wristwatch. 'Now, I really have to go.'

'Mr Croft Tate –'

'Talk to Grant Clifford, he may be able to give you something. Meanwhile, it's been good to see you.'

Lenny Mutken threw up one hand; but as he did so the doorman took hold of his elbow. Affronted, the white-haired reporter tried to tug himself away, but the doorman turned him around and steered him toward the exit.

'Believe me you don't know what you're turning away!' Lenny Mutken called back to Howard, not violently, but in the sonorous tones of a Biblical prophecy. 'You don't know what a scoop you're going to miss!'

Howard watched unhappily as the doorman maneuvered Lenny Mutken out into the street. The blonde girl behind the reception-desk said, 'That's Lenny Mutken? I always thought he was a hot-shot.'

'He was,' said Howard, 'and don't let anyone tell you different.'

Lenny Mutken was outside now, arguing with the doorman. Howard walked across to the elevators, to be closely and busily joined by young Dale Perk, the deputy features editor. Dale Perk always reminded Howard of a free-range egg in spectacles and a tight striped vest. He said, 'Mind if I ride with you, sir?' and Howard shrugged. Dale said, as the doors closed, 'Lenny Mutken used to be my hero. Can you imagine that?'

'We all grow old,' Howard remarked. 'Some of us even have the effrontery to die, when the time comes.'

'Well, of course we do, sir. But I can't imagine the *Star* without *you*.'

Howard looked at him, and gave him a smile that wasn't really a smile at all; more like the shorthand outline of a smile. 'You *do* know that I'm going to die one day, don't you?' he asked Dale Perk. 'I don't expect the *Star* to cease publication, just because of a minor incident like that.'

Dale Perk was embarrassed. He was carrying galleys over his left arm as if he were a waiter carrying a towel, and he patted them a little too loudly, and said, 'We have a really excellent piece on the Navy Club scandal, sir. Really excellent. All the dope on those phony orphans' outings.'

'I'll make a point of reading it,' said Howard. He was edgy and depressed – partly because he was tired, and the weather was so sticky – but mostly because of the way that Kenneth had been chiseling on at him about the slums, and the grotesque personal choice that he was now forcing him to make. He knew, of course, that Kenneth was right. He knew that it was his moral duty as a Democrat and as a captain of public opinion to give Kenneth's slum-clearance campaign all the fire and all the thunder that the *Star* at its most indignant could muster. Bulldoze The Near South Side! he could imagine the banner headline right now. But Eleanor, damn it, Eleanor. Even the continuing crucifixion of Chicago's slum-dwellers didn't make it any easier for him to crucify his wife.

Dale Perk said, 'We also have the most comprehensive automobilist's guide to out-of-town restaurants and road-houses ever. And, do you know, it's amazing. There's a little place in Hinsdale, the Green Plover Restaurant, and Connor rates it even higher than the Whitehall Club. They do curried Maryland crab, blue trout, prime rib smothered with mustard, quails with chestnuts; isn't that amazing; and doesn't it sound mouth-watering? And all that, right out in Hinsdale, of all places.'

'Well,' said Howard tightly, 'Hinsdale's quite a tasteful little suburb these days, that's what I hear.' He couldn't imagine why Dale was trying to tempt him with the menu of a restaurant in which he would never eat, in a town which he would never visit. It seemed that everybody he had met today was trying to make him feel as if it was his personal responsibility to make the world a more cheerful place; as if he alone could do it; and *should* do it; and why was he being so darned slow and reluctant about it?

'This is my floor,' said Dale Perk, as the elevator doors opened on twenty-two. 'Have a fruitful weekend, sir.'

'Well, yes, you too,' Howard replied, and leaned thankfully back against the rear of the elevator car as Dale Perk went bustling out, his galleys rustling noisily. *Fruitful*, what an extraordinary thing to say. It made him sound more like an Old Testament patriarch than a newspaper proprietor. Be fruitful, and multiply. His head was going around.

Grant wasn't in his office, although Jack Fawcett the Sunday *Star* editor was there, arguing with Adeline Duveen about her proposed three-page fall fashion special for next week's paper. Jack was tough and short and sandy, with sandy hair and sandy eyebrows and sandy-colored tweed suits that looked as if he had been rolling in burrs. Adeline Duveen was tall and leggy and desperately thin, with hooded eyes and a hooked nose and a nasal Bryn Mawr accent. She was wearing a corrugated John-Frederic hat in pale coffee, and the pale coffee corrugated pocketbook which she had bought to match it was perched on the edge of Jack Fawcett's desk. Her thin frame was draped in a brown Hattie Carnegie dress with pale coffee corrugated cuffs.

Jack was smoking furiously, and saying, 'This is supposed to be duds for the ordinary suburban hausfrau, okay? And look at what you've brung me! Look at this outfit! A checkered umbrella, a checkered hat, a checkered blouse, a checkered skirt, and checkered gloves. Women want to look like women, Adeline, they don't want to look like some kind of a walking crossword puzzle.'

'Jack Fawcett, it's the *fashion*,' Adeline drawled back at him. 'Matching is *very* strong this fall. And all our Chicago couturiers are producing lines of matching frocks and matching accessories. Charles James has even designed a matching coat for one's *dog*.'

'Well, thank the good Lord above that you didn't bring me no picture of *that*,' Jack growled.

'I did, dear. It's here,' said Adeline, and held it up.

Jack crushed out his cigarette in a battered Century of Progress ashtray. 'I got a headache,' he said, in resignation. He looked up, and saw Howard standing just outside the doorway, and beckoned him in. 'Don't stand on ceremony, Howard, come on in. Miss Duveen and I were just trying to decide whether the squares on the hips were equal to the sum of the squares in front of your eyes.'

He picked up one of the photographs, and said, 'Will you look at these things? If my wife tried to walk out the front door dressed in anything like this, she'd break every window in the neighborhood.'

Howard shook hands with Jack and lifted Adeline's languid hand to his lips. 'It's good to see you, Adeline. I'm sorry we didn't have a chance to talk at the party yesterday. Didn't I see you talking to Salvador Dali?'

'Oh . . . yes,' Adeline replied. 'I can't possibly tell you what he was proposing. A fashion spread with – I don't know – dead donkeys in it, or something disgusting.'

'That daughter of yours deserves some congratulations,' said Jack. 'Not many people would have done that, now would they?'

Adeline gathered up her photographs and her copy, and tapped them neatly together on the very edge of Jack's desk. Jack said, friendly but dismissive, 'Let's talk about this Tuesday, Adeline. Maybe I'll be driving home on Grand Avenue and suddenly I'll see the light. You know, like Saul. Meanwhile, do me a favor, would you? Look out some fashion that isn't quite so bizarre.'

'*Bizarre,* he calls it,' Adeline retorted. 'A man who still wears sleeve-bands.'

When she was gone, Jack looked from one sleeve to the other, stretching out his sleeve-bands with his finger. 'What's wrong with sleeve-bands?' he wanted to know. 'These are classic.' He pushed the telephone button on his desk. 'It's incredible, you know, that woman does something to my blood vessels. Every week, she brings me right to the brink of death. Did you look at her? All dressed up like a chocolate cupcake? Jesus.'

From the telephone speaker, an aggressive, nasal voice said, 'Press room.'

'Hank? Is that Hank?' Jack demanded.

'Hank ain't here. This is Morrie.'

'All right, Morrie, is Mr Clifford down there?'

'He's on his way back up. You want me to go after him?'

'No, no, so long as he's on his way back up.'

Morrie put down the phone without so much as a grunt. Jack threw himself backwards into his swivel chair, with its burst-open cushion that he had brought from home, and propped his feet up on the desk. 'Did you see the paper?' he asked Howard, 'There's a good feature on that little Negro girl Morgana rescued.'

Howard glanced toward a scrambled-up half-dismembered copy of the Sunday *Star*, lying on a side table. 'I prefer to wait until Sunday. I guess it's a fetish. I feel guilty if I get to see what's happening to Terry and the Pirates before I'm supposed to.'

'Walter wrote a humdinger of a piece on the football game,' said Jack. 'You heard what happened, though, did you?'

Howard shook his head. 'Don't tell me he fell down drunk again.'

'Dear God, Howard, if only he *had*. No – what happened was, he went for a leak and went straight into the ladies' powder room, and there was Mrs Beaumont the chairlady of the Women's Club sitting on the john with her unmentionables around her ankles.'

'Oh my God, Mrs Beaumont,' said Howard. He knew Mrs Beaumont socially; or at least Eleanor did. Mrs Beaumont was a hundred-percent Helen Hokinson-type Women's Club member, and whenever she met Howard she was always slapping at his elbow with her gloves and telling him to tone down the drawings on the funny pages, especially Howard's favorite, the Dragon Lady.

'That wasn't all of it,' said Jack. 'Instead of leaving, Walter tried to engage her in conversation. Something political, the way I understand it. Why the only solution to the nation's problems was to bring back the ten-cent cigar and the three-dollar whorehouse.'

'Oh my God,' said Howard.

At that moment, Grant Clifford appeared, looking tired. 'Hello, Howard. I see that Jack's told you about the Mrs Beaumont fiasco.'

Howard growled, 'If that man wasn't the best Goddamned sport reporter that ever drew breath, I'd have his back end out of this building before you could say lawbreakers always lose.' He drew back the tails of his coat, and stood with his fists on his hips, but he couldn't help grinning. 'I'll tell you something, though. I would have given a month's profits to have been there. Mrs Beaumont, with her drawers down, trying to fend off Walter Dempsey in full flood. That must have been the bout of the century.'

'I thought you were playing golf with his Irish honor,' remarked Grant. He turned momentarily to Jack, and said, 'They've sorted out the paper-feed problem. They should have finished the run by five.'

Howard said, 'We were rained off. Besides, Kenneth's got some bee in his bonnet about slum clearance, and you know what Kenneth's like when he's got a bee in his bonnet. He thinks it's time the *Star* started running another campaign against the slum landlords.'

Grant glanced at Jack again, and then asked, 'Is that so bad? Maybe he's right. Maybe it is time. There's quite a groundswell of feeling about it – particularly from the business community.'

'Grant,' said Howard, 'our job is to report the news, not to make it.'

'That's not totally true, Howard,' put in Jack, trying to be light-hearted and diplomatic. 'I understand your daughter's going to be making news again on Monday. A five-column picture, with three inches of maple syrup by Margaret Drzal. News Princess To Wed Blue-Book Yodeler.'

Howard gave Jack one of his unamused puckered-up expressions. 'Well, you know, it's high time she settled down. She can't go on flibbertigibbeting around for ever. I mean, *she'd* disagree with me, first off. But that John Birmingham is going to do her good, stabilize her, you know? But you can't say that she didn't go out without making a darned good display of it.'

Grant said, 'How did you leave things with Doyle?'

Howard frowned. 'I told him I'd think on it, that's all.'

'Howard – I have to say that in my opinion slum clearance is a fundamental issue,' said Grant. His voice wavered a little, because it was clear that Howard didn't want to talk about Kenneth Doyle and his slum crusade anymore. 'I think his honor's right, Howard. It's time the press spoke out. The slums are the single most pressing crisis in Chicago right now. They affect the city's finances, they affect the city's morale. They affect the city's future as a city. Worst of all, they're not showing any signs of receding.'

Howard repeated, 'I'm *thinking* on it, Grant.'

'Well, for my money, and with all due respect, there's nothing to think about,' said Grant, quiet but impassioned. 'The suburbs continue to grow, the city continues to shrink. There are three and a half million people living in this city, and that's less than seven percent more than there were ten years ago, in 1939. This city's dying. And it's not as if you have to drive miles away from the center to find the slum districts; it's not as if they're hidden out of sight, and out of mind.' He pointed southwards out of Jack's rain-patterned window, toward the wet huddled rooftops of South Wabash and State Street and Dearborn. 'We can see them from here, Howard. And, what's more, we know exactly who owns them, and who wants them to stay the way they are.'

'I *said* –!' Howard interrupted, with a bark, and then more gently, 'I said that I'll think on it, okay? I'll think on it, all weekend, and then on Monday we'll have a policy meeting about it, and decide what we're going to do. But, until then, the subject of slums is taboo. For legal reasons; for publishing reasons; and for the reason that I don't want to see anything in the *Star* about slums until I personally decide.'

'You're the boss,' said Grant.

'You're damned right,' said Howard.

Just then, Harry Sharpe appeared, in shirtsleeves, a pencil stuck behind his left ear, eating a Baby Ruth. 'Grant?' I've been looking for you. I've had a call from Dan Rogers at the 36th Precinct. It seems like there's been a homicide out at Jefferson Park. Messy, in the extreme, according to first reports. Maybe you want me and Woozy to go out and take a look.'

Grant said, 'You were supposed to have a half day today. How come you're still here?'

Harry glanced at Howard, and gave him a quick army-style salute. 'How're you doing, Mr Croft Tate? How's Morgana?'

'Morgana's feeling very much better, thank you,' said Howard. He didn't add 'no thanks to you,' but the intonation in his voice was enough to suggest it.

'Morgana's gotten herself engaged,' said Jack, taking his feet off his desk and shuffling through the heaps of proofs and photographs that covered it. He lifted up a ten by eight of Morgana standing on the lawns of Weatherwood, the dark clouds stacked up behind her.

'That was taken yesterday,' Harry commented, his mouth

full of chocolate. 'Nice picture, hunh? That frock was something. But I'd still say she looks better in the real. Who's the lucky beau?'

'John Birmingham, Jr,' said Jack. 'Son of John Birmingham, Sr.'

'You don't say. You want me to take a look at that homicide, Grant? I wasn't planning on knocking off yet anyway.'

'Well . . .' said Grant, looking at his watch. 'Busby's not here. I guess he wouldn't mind.' Busby Brill was the *Star*'s ace crime reporter, and he was always somewhat touchy about police stories being allocated to what he called the 'cat-up-a-tree patrol'.

Harry rolled up the Baby Ruth wrapper between the palms of his hands, and tossed it toward Jack's waste basket. Unfortunately his aim was off and the wrapper bounced off the top of Jack's head. Jack slapped his hand on top of his bald spot, and roared, 'What the hell do you think you're doing, you *yekl?*'

'I'm going, I'm going,' said Harry, and backed out of the office.

When he was gone, Howard turned to Grant, and said, 'You were having some trouble with the presses?'

'Paper feed,' replied Grant, flatly. He was sulking a little, because Howard had reminded him in words of one syllable that the ultimate decision on what went into the *Star* and what didn't was still in the hands of the publisher, rather than the editor. In his own quiet way, Grant was quite an authoritarian himself; and like most authoritarians he very much resented being told what to do.

'Was it the paper or was it the press?' asked Howard.

'The paper. It's the first consignment we've taken from Calgary Mills, and it stretched widthwise more than we'd like. Hank's taking it up with the buyers, don't worry.'

Howard said to Grant, 'Come up to my office. Maybe we can have a word.'

The two of them walked along the elevator bank; where Grant performed the duty of pressing the button for the thirty-sixth floor. The elevator doors opened and Walter Dempsey promptly appeared, lindy-hopping sideways to catch his balance. He was wearing a tan raincoat that was so stiff and new it seemed to have a life of its own, and – in contrast – a terrible old hat crammed with fishing lures.

'*Mr Croft Tate!*' he cried, so loudly that Howard momentarily turned around to see if Walter was calling to somebody further back down the corridor. 'Mr Croft Tate! What an unheralded pleasure! Well, well! Yesterday we were illuminated by the presence of your beautiful daughter, and lo! here it is, only tomorrow, and here you are in the worsted! I trust, sir, that you read my latest piece on last night's football game? By the stars, that was a game. All other football events were as zircons compared with last night's affray.'

Howard clasped his hands together and stood stern and unmoving like a displeased teacher. 'Good afternoon, Walter. I heard about Mrs Beaumont.'

Walter frowned, and patted himself all over, as if he were searching for a written excuse. 'Mrs Beaumont,' he repeated. 'Mrs Beaumont?'

'Mrs Beaumont the president of the Chicago Federation of Women's Clubs,' Howard reminded him.

'Ah,' said Walter. He suddenly snatched the elevator doors to prevent them from closing again. 'Ah,' he said again.

'I suppose you know that Mrs Beaumont is not only a very influential member of the community; and that her husband is president of the Chicago general services administration; but that she is a personal friend of my wife?'

Walter rubbed his chin and looked intensely thoughtful. 'It was one of those social torts,' he said, 'one of those social torts into which only destiny at large can possibly lead a man's footsteps.'

'You're saying that destiny at large took you into the ladies' powder room at Soldiers' Field?'

'Well, sir,' said Walter, 'if it were not destiny at large, then it was certainly a grave misassemblage of navigational errors. I have composed a letter of regret to the good lady which is almost Byzantine in the glamor of its apologies.'

'I gather you subjected Mrs Beaumont to some kind of political harangue,' said Howard. He could see that Grant was having difficulty in keeping his face straight.

'I did have something to say on the subject of Taftite Republicanism, I seem to recall,' said Walter. 'It seemed to me that Mrs Beaumont was confusing New Dealism with communism, and I was simply trying to set her straight.'

Howard laid his hand on the padded shoulder of Walter's

raincoat. 'All right, Walter. I suppose that by your own lights you were trying to do something commendable. But, next time you come across Mrs Beaumont, can you please make sure that your lights are not quite so brightly lit up?'

'Yes, sir,' said Walter humbly; and then stepped back with an extraordinary Fred Astaire shuffle to allow Howard and Grant to enter the elevator.

Howard and Grant rose in silence to the thirty-sixth floor. It was up here, in the penthouse office that had been especially designed for Howard by Ieh Ming Pei, the *Star* building's architect, that Howard retreated whenever he was seriously troubled. The main office was vast, covering almost half of the floor space of the entire thirty-sixth story, with floor-to-ceiling windows on three sides. Its main view was not toward the city but toward Lake Michigan, and when Howard stood close to the window and stared out toward the flat blue-gray waters he sometimes felt that he was suspended 450 feet in midair, like a kite.

The floors were laid with blue-gray rugs that mirrored the misty hues of the lake so that it was sometimes difficult to decide where the office ended and the shoreline began. There was a single huge desk standing in the center of the office, more of an altar than a desk, but highly contemporary, because it was molded out of a single sheet of plywood. Behind the desk there was a plywood chair, similarly molded. Both pieces had been specially commissioned by Howard from an enterprising young furniture designer from Los Angeles called Charles Eames.

The desk was bare except for a pure white blotter, a black and white photograph of the Croft Tate family in a stainless steel frame, and two conical stainless steel lamps designed by Lazlo Moholy-Nagy at Chicago's New Bauhaus.

Nobody who had visited Weatherwood, with all its Gothic pomposity, could ever have guessed that Howard had an office like this. It was almost oriental in its calm and in its simplicity. He rarely came here; but it was good to know that he could come here whenever he needed to.

'Sit down, Grant,' said Howard, indicating one of the curved modern chairs. 'Would you care for a drink? Martini?'

'No, thank you, Howard. I think that would just about put me to sleep.'

Grant perched uncomfortably right on the edge of the chair

and crossed his legs, while Howard walked right over to the window, with his hands in his pockets, and stared out at the gathering twilight. The clouds flew past like wind-tangled skeins of wool.

'There's nothing wrong, is there?' Grant asked him, quietly.

Howard continued to stare out at the lake. 'That lake,' he said, 'contains 1,180 cubic miles of water. Did you know that? One thousand one hundred eighty cubic miles.'

'Who told you that?' asked Grant, with a gentle smile.

'Oh, it's in that . . . what-do-you-call-it feature. "Fascinating Facts", that thing we run at the foot of the funnies.'

'Something's bothering you,' said Grant, trying not to be too persistent; but anxious to get home now, after a long day at the office.

'I don't know, life seems to change sometimes,' said Howard. 'I mean turn itself upside down, without warning, as if an hourglass had suddenly emptied, and God came along and turned it back up the other way.'

Grant sat with his left foot jiggling and said nothing.

'Grant,' said Howard. It was growing quite dark now, and gradually Howard's face was appearing in the window as a white reflection, an insubstantial life mask of worry and age. 'Grant . . . is there any way, do you think, of finding out whether a woman really loves you or not?'

Grant stiffened. This sounded dangerous. He knew of course that Howard had an eye for pretty young girls; and that from time to time he had been seen having dinner at the Drake with dancers and actresses, and girls from the *Star*'s reception desk; but as far as he was concerned, his publisher's floozies were his own affair, and he preferred to keep his opinions to himself. He was not jealous. His own wife Enid was all he had ever asked for.

Howard came away from the window and stood facing Grant with his hand over his mouth. 'I mean – do you think there's any kind of a *test*, something you can ask a woman to do, to prove whether she loves you?'

Grant shook his head. 'I don't think so, Howard. After all, love isn't like hamburger. You can't send it to the public analyst to find out whether they've ground up cows' lips in it, instead of steak.' Grant's stockyard heritage sometimes showed itself in startling and unexpected ways.

'Cows' lips?' said Howard.

'What I'm saying is, you can only judge love by the effect that it has on you. There isn't any empirical test. And sometimes, somebody can love you and you don't even realize how much, because you're looking for the wrong clues. You're looking for sympathy, for instance, at a time when somebody who really loves you should be kicking your butt. You're looking for agreement, when what you're doing is wrong – and anybody who really loves you should be telling you so.'

Howard thought about this, and then sniffed, and cleared his throat. 'I don't know . . .' he said. 'It seems like there's a wall.'

'A wall?'

'Come on, Grant. You and I go way back together. You remember when Enid was sick, and she didn't tell you how worried she was? You and I talked, didn't we, man to man?'

Grant nodded. He understood that Howard was asking him for complete confidentiality – in the same way that Howard had kept Grant's confidence when Enid had been suffering that cervical erosion, and had been terrified all the time that it was cancer.

'It's me and Eleanor,' said Howard. 'I don't know, I never suspected how she felt. I never knew what kind of a woman she was. I knew she was *strong*. Oh, yes. I knew she had her passions. And, of course, she's bright, and intelligent. Not just a wife to hang on your arm, Grant. I mean, not just your average Lake Shore Drive hostess, with a social calendar as full up as a beehive and a head as empty as a pisspot. I don't know. I was vain enough to think that I was enough for her; that she could never be interested in anything else, apart from the Croft Tate business, and me.'

Grant licked his lips. He didn't speak. He sensed that it wasn't the right time yet.

Howard dragged over another plywood chair, and sat so close to Grant that occasionally as he spoke, a fleck of saliva landed on Grant's suit. 'She always said that she loved me. But I guess those words are pretty easy to say. It's what they mean when you say them that counts. And, I don't know, Grant, I'm not so sure that Eleanor means them anymore.'

Grant asked, with great care, 'Is there anything in particular which has made you feel this way?'

Howard took a thick deep quivering breath. 'I don't know, Grant. You don't want to be burdened with this.'

Grant's greatest desire at that moment was that he were already on his way back to his apartment on Oak Street. Enid's brother was coming over, and they were having Enid's special, country captain. But he tried to smile and to look sympathetic, in spite of his hunger and in spite of his tiredness, and in spite of his deep unwillingness to be privy to Howard's marital difficulties. Howard was awkward with women, as many rich and powerful men are, but he could be startlingly intimate with his men friends.

Howard wrung his hands together so fiercely that they squeaked. 'This is a hard thing for any man to have to say about his wife, Grant. But you and I, we go way back, don't we? You'll understand, won't you, that I'm not telling you this to – what's the word – *demean* her. Not to demean her, Grant, not in any way at all. I respect Eleanor one hundred percent. But yesterday, you know, before all of this fire business with Morgana ... Eleanor was acting so ... unfriendly. She came down late for the lunch, and then she disappeared for a while, and even when she did appear she seemed like she had something on her mind ... you know, forgetting what she was saying in the middle of a sentence.'

Grant waited, his foot jiggling.

Howard said, 'Of course, when all this fire business happened ... it kind of got forgotten. But late last night I went up into Eleanor's dressing room and I found her crying. I guess I'd had a few drinks. I asked her what in hell was wrong. She said she wasn't going to tell me, I wouldn't understand if she did. I said damn it, look here, I've been your husband for thirty years, I can understand you better than anybody. And she said –'

Howard sat back, his hands in his lap. In spite of the soft controlled lighting in the office, Grant suddenly saw how haggard he was; how old. A man whose certainty in the world around him had died in the night.

A tear sparkled in the corner of Howard's left eye. 'She said that I hadn't understood anything about her for years, that I hadn't been interested in her for years. She said that I'd been living my own life and all the time just assuming that she was going to be there. She said she still loved me, but, well, what I'd been giving her, *of myself*, if you understand what I mean, well, that hadn't been enough. She'd been living her own life for quite some time.'

Grant folded his arms. The lemon had to be bit into sooner or later. 'You mean that she's been seeing somebody else, another man.'

Howard gave a sharp, unbalanced nod, and made a gruff noise down in his throat.

Quietly, Grant asked, 'Is it somebody you know?'

Howard nodded. The tears were sliding into the wrinkles around his eyes, the way that dewdrops slide into the wrinkles of autumn leaves.

'Is she still seeing him?'

'No. No she's not. I'm certain of that.'

'Quite certain?'

'Don't ask me how, Grant. That would give it all away. But, yes, I'm certain.'

'She says she still loves you,' Grant reminded him.

Howard dragged out his handkerchief and noisily blew his nose. There was a very long silence between them, during which the Lindbergh beacon on top of the Palmolive Building winked six times. It was growing even darker now, and the city on either side of them was beginning to sparkle, a thousand square miles of brilliant rectangles formed by straight streets and buildings.

Howard said, 'You go along for year after year, believing you're happy ... and what? You suddenly find out that you shouldn't have been happy at all.'

Grant shook his head. 'Howard, you can't start recriminating. You can't look back: not if you want Eleanor to stay with you, and I assume you do. If you were happy, you were happy. You led your life the way you wanted to. You had your own attachments, outside of your marriage. How can you blame Eleanor if she did the same?'

Howard frowned at Grant, and then swatted away the implication of what he was saying in the same way that he would have swatted a midge.

'Come on, Howard,' Grant reminded him. He was taking risks now, but he sensed that Howard wouldn't object to being pushed a little. 'Who was that dancer? That French lady with the dark hair? Lois Xenon, wasn't that it? And people were saying all kinds of things about you and Jane Wyman.'

'There was nothing at all between me and Jane Wyman. She's a beautiful lady and I took her to dinner, that's all.'

'Now you're being aggressive,' Grant told him.

Howard leaned forward again, and covered his face with his hands. 'I don't know, Grant, to hell with it. It seems to me that everything I believed was firm and certain is all made out of jello.'

Grant with carefully modulated camaraderie rested his hand on Howard's shoulder. 'I'm sorry, Howard, what else can I say? Listen – I have to go now, anyway. Enid's been waiting on me since five. The only advice I can give you is, don't blame Eleanor. Don't be jealous of what she did; and above all don't be vengeful. What's done is done. And if you're vengeful, all you're going to do is burn yourself up inside, and push Eleanor even further away from you.'

'You're a wise owl, Grant,' said Howard, laying his hand on top of Grant's, and patting it a couple of times. 'Thanks for your time.' Then, 'You're sure you won't have that martini?'

'I have to get home. Enid's going to kill me.'

'Sure,' said Howard.

Grant stood up and walked stiffly toward the office door, like Lee J. Cobb in the last act of *Death of a Salesman*. Howard remained where he was, hunched on his plywood chair. Grant hesitated by the door, and said, 'Goodnight, Howard.'

Howard lifted his head and peered at Grant as if he had already forgotten that he had been there. Grant closed the office door behind him and went as quickly as he could to the elevator, in case he was called back.

12

Irving Park Road east of Milwaukee Avenue was crowded with so many police cars at so many different angles that it looked as if they had just been filming a chase scene for the *Keystone Kops*. Harry drove his Woodie all the way along the sidewalk, and parked it right outside the murder house, an odd two-story frame house with a sagging fence all the way around it and a single plane tree whose life had been mercilessly extinguished by neighborhood dogs. The house was painted green, and the paint was flaking, and it was a curious throwback to the 1920s; a suburban dwelling that had somehow survived the development of stores and apartment blocks all around it.

The night was warm and sweaty. A collection of neighbors and passers-by stood by the police trestles in silence. Harry sometimes thought that the same crowd of the same people collected to watch whenever anything ghoulish happened, no matter where it was in America. He would have written a short story about that for *Amazing Stories*, if he had ever been able to find the time, or the talent. 'The Crowd'. It could have been really creepy.

Dan Rogers was standing outside the house smoking a bright green stogie. He was a big, ugly man, with a slabby face pocked with acne scars, and eyes that looked as if they were black buttons, sewn on. Dan Rogers was a friend of the press. He had done duty as a detective sergeant in the 32nd Precinct for fifteen years, and his permanent beef was that the suburban policeman never got publicly recognized. That was why he called the *Star* and the *Tribune* and the *Daily News* whenever Jefferson Park was the scene of a crime of any magnitude.

Dan was in his element tonight. He stood with his hands jammed into the pockets of his shapeless gray suit, his body bulging, while photographers and coroners' assistants and uniformed officers came and went, and flashbulbs lit him up like summer lightning.

'Well now, the Pole,' said Dan, without taking his stogie out of his teeth. 'What happened to Busby tonight?'

'Even ace crime reporters have to go home to wash their smalls sometimes,' Harry remarked. Woozy, coming up close behind him, took a quick shot of Dan Rogers looking contemptuous.

Harry said, 'What happened here? Have you taken the body away yet?'

'The coroner's still busy,' Dan told him. 'We're still looking for the liver.'

Harry glanced toward the house, and wiped his nose with his finger. 'That messy, hunh?'

'Didn't I tell you on the phone? You boys are going to be having a field day with this one.'

'Do you know the victim's name?' asked Harry, taking out his notebook.

'Anne with an "e" Leonidas with an "a", twenty-four years old, Greek-American extraction. Married, two children of her own, she was baby-sitting for a friend of hers who lives here, Georgina Attalides, separated from her husband.'

A siren wailed in the distance; a police radio blurted and crackled, and a voice said, 'Car 23, Car 23, where are you?'

'Is that you, Car 23?' Harry asked Dan, with a cheeky smile. 'If so, where are you?'

Dan ignored him, and doughtily plowed on. 'An unknown assailant rang the doorbell here at four fifteen approximately. That's about as near as we can get. Twenty minutes later a man was seen leaving, a man in a brown fedora and a brown suit. He had a ticket stuck in his hatband, maybe a baseball raincheck. At five ten or thereabouts, a neighbor called to borrow some chick peas. She found the front door ajar, and so she went inside. How she found the victim Mrs Anne Leonidas – well, you can go right inside and see for yourself.'

Harry finished writing, and then he said, 'This man in the brown fedora and the brown suit. What did he look like?'

'He wore a brown fedora and a brown suit.'

'Well, that's very helpful, sergeant; but out of two million men in metropolitan Chicago, at least one million must have a brown fedora and a brown suit. Either you're going to book them *all* on suspicion, or else you're going to find a few more details that kind of help to narrow things down.'

Dan Rogers looked away. Harry stood and waited for an answer, but no answer appeared to be forthcoming. Woozy took another picture of Dan Rogers, looking petulant, and then he moved around and took another picture of Dan Rogers, looking irritated.

'So far, all we have is the hat and the suit,' he said, keeping his temper.

Harry wrote that down, repeating it out loud as he did so, in a deliberately cretinous accent. 'All-we-have-is-da-hat-un-da-soot.'

'I don't *have* to call you people, you know,' said Dan.

'Ah, but you do, Dan, that's just the point,' Harry told him, squeezing his arm. 'If you didn't call us, what would be the reward for being a cop? A pension? A group photograph? Nothing to show for twenty-five years' service but a letter from the commissioner and a two-roomed apartment overlooking the Proviso Yards?'

'The man was Caucasian,' said Dan, unwillingly. 'The witnesses weren't all that clear, but they think he was old, maybe sixty or sixty-five.'

'Well, that's good, that narrows it down to six hundred thousand,' said Harry. He jerked his head toward the house. 'Mind if we go in?'

'So long as you didn't eat,' Dan told him. 'I don't want anybody throwing up all over the evidence.'

'There speaks a man who has never eaten one of O'Leary's hamburger sandwiches,' said Harry. 'Come on, Dan, we're press. We've seen everything. Stomachs of steel.'

'Yeah, and brains of pure mahogany,' said Dan.

Harry slapped him on the back. 'Don't you worry, Dan. You solve this, and you'll be Captain of Detectives by Christmas.'

'All right, then,' said Dan, and led Harry and Woozy up the weather-blistered front steps to the front door. There was multi-colored glass in the door itself, one pane of it cracked. The hallway was dazzlingly lit by a 150-watt police inspection light, which revealed without pity the sadness of the brown flowered wallpaper, the chipped ocher paint on the skirting boards, and the damp-foxed calendar picture of the late King George II of Greece. There was a strong smell of dry rot and stale olive oil. A police photographer was squatting awkwardly on the floor taking pictures of a bloody footprint. He glanced up at Harry and Woozy as Dan Rogers led them in, and his eyes were as neutral as two green grapes. Harry began all of a sudden to dread what they were going to see.

'No doubt about it, whoever did this, man or woman, for whatever reason, they're a maniac,' said Dan.

'Oh, yeah?' said Harry, trying to sound nonchalant.

A baby carriage half obstructed the passageway. Policemen pushed their way past it, carrying pieces of evidence in cellophane bags, a pink plastic comb with black hairs in it, a slipper squiggled with blood. Dan Rogers led Harry and Woozy through to the living room, and it was here that the homicide had taken place. There were lights set up everywhere, the room was unnaturally bright like a stage set, and moths were fluttering and pinging off the bulbs.

This was obviously Mrs Attalides' best room. In the opposite corner, there was a veneered Grand Rapids china cabinet, with a set of ruby-colored ouzo glasses in it. Close beside it there was a small table covered with a crocheted cloth, on which stood a ten-year-old Zenith radio, with zigzag fabric over the speaker; the radio itself topped by framed photographs of Mrs Attalides' children and two clumpy china dogs.

Harry turned toward the long brown sofa. A tall thin man with a crewcut was leaning over it as if he were a visitor at an exhibition of modern art. On the center cushion of the sofa was the exhibit itself, and for the first few seconds Harry couldn't believe that what he was looking at was real, it was all so pink and scarlet. Then suddenly he made sense of it, and the shock was so devastating that he felt as if he had dropped down an open elevator shaft. 'Holy Christ,' he said, out loud, although he couldn't hear himself speak.

The tall thin man stepped away from the sofa and started to rummage with some vexation through a black leather bag. Harry stood where he was, thrilled and horrified, staring at the mortal remains of Mrs Anne Leonidas with his hands by his sides and his mouth dropped open.

'Who are you, press?' asked the tall thin man, without looking at him.

'Yes, sir,' Harry replied.

'Make sure you spell the name right, in that case. Dr Charles Mischeff, with two ffs.'

'Mischeff, two ffs,' Harry repeated, woodenly.

He kept on staring at Mrs Anne Leonidas and Mrs Anne Leonidas kept on staring at him. Her naked trunk, pale and bloody, had been propped upside down on the center cushion of the sofa. Her head and her arms and her legs had been sawn off. Her head had been balanced on top of her inverted body, her chin resting in the cleft of her buttocks, and her arms and her legs had been stacked up beside her. She had thick curly black hair, still clipped up on each side with pale green plastic barettes. She was sallow-faced, brown-eyed, as sad-looking as any madonna, her lower lip slightly caught by one protruding upper tooth as if she were trying to puzzle out how such a grisly catastrophe could ever have been visited on an innocent woman like her. There were dark red stains all over the sofa, all over the rugs, all over the chairs. In some places the blood still crackled quietly as it soaked into the furnishings.

Close behind Harry, Woozy made a noise that was halfway between a cough and a retch. 'I'm not taking no pictures of that. Jesus.'

Harry at last tugged his eyes away from Mrs Leonidas' sad dead staring face, and touched Woozy's arm. 'Take a couple of quick ones, will you please? I'm sorry, but we're going to need them for the record.'

While Woozy took his photographs, Harry went back outside to talk to Sergeant Rogers. Vincent Geruso from the *Daily News* had arrived, looking crumpled and unshaven and smelling of beer; and so had Bill Keen from the *Tribune*, in a smart brown houndstooth sport coat and a necktie with a seagull painted on it.

'How's Howard Croft Tate's favorite boy?' asked Vincent, sarcastically.

Harry said, 'Don't start needling, Vinnie. This isn't the time and this isn't the place.'

'Take a look, did you?' Dan Rogers asked him, nodding toward the house. 'How's your hamburger now?'

'Actually, it was corned beef and cabbage,' said Harry. Then, without saying anything else, he smartly walked away from the house, crossed the road, and found an alleyway at the side of a filling station where there were oil drums and discarded bumpers and worn-out tires. His stomach arched and heaved, and he was painfully sick. For a long time he leaned against the wall, sweating and watery-eyed, trying not to think of Mrs Leonidas and her severed head. Then he wiped his mouth, and walked back across the road.

'Stomachs of steel, hunh?' gibed Dan Rogers, chewing his bright-green stogie.

'Corned beef must've been bad,' Harry replied. He sniffed, and flipped open his notebook. 'You want to make some kind of guess who might have killed her?'

Dan Rogers opened up his shirt pocket and produced a roll of peppermint-flavored Life Savers. He carefully peeled off the wrapper and held one out to Harry, who accepted it with silent gratitude. Dan Rogers said, 'We've talked to the husband. Alex Leonidas, also known as Willy the Greek, also known as Alex Metaxas. Twenty-six years old, one seven-month stretch in Joliet in '41, for larceny. He sells second-hand iceboxes on Grand Avenue, along with a guy called Czestowski. He was working all day today, all through the time of the homicide, clearing a house on Green Street.'

'So he's not a suspect?'

'Not unless he commissioned a hit. And this wasn't a hit.'

'How about boyfriends?' asked Harry. 'She was separated, right? Did she have any boyfriends?'

Dan Rogers shook his head. 'The last man she dated was John Kavanagh, twenty-eight years old, works for Youngstown Sheet & Tube. During the time of the homicide he was working a double shift down at Indiana Harbor.'

'So who are you left with?' asked Harry. The peppermint Life Saver rattled against his teeth.

Woozy rejoined him now, looking almost as bloodless as Mrs Leonidas. Close behind him, with grins like Hallowe'en pumpkins, came Vincent Geruso and Bill Keen, and the *Tribune*'s photographer Hamlin O'Neal. All of them were swallowing repeatedly, as if they were trying to keep their lunch down, and when Vincent Geruso reached into his pocket to take out his notebook, he scattered loose pages all over the pathway, and said desperately, 'Shit!' Dan Rogers watched him stooping to pick them up with policemanly satisfaction.

'A loony did that, right?' asked Bill Keen, unsteadily. 'I mean, that had to be a loony.'

Dan Rogers rocked backward and forward on his heels. He was playing this one for all it was worth. 'I wouldn't care to say loony, Mr Keen. Loony, that's not scientific.'

'Deranged, then? You'd say deranged?'

Dan Rogers shook his head. 'Let me tell you something, gentlemen, all we know so far is that the murderer was more than likely a stranger, somebody that Mrs Leonidas didn't know. We say this because there were signs of a struggle in the hallway, the rug all rucked up, a small side table knocked over. Also – we've talked to Mrs Attalides, and she says that Mrs Leonidas was perfectly happy this evening, and obviously wasn't expecting to be called on by anybody who meant to do her harm. In fact, she told Mrs Attalides only a week since that she was really content with her life. Life was all honey, those were her actual words.'

Bill Keen licked the tip of his pencil, and said, 'You're looking for some kind of random butcher, then? Somebody who killed her and cut her up just for the hell of it?'

Dan Rogers made a disapproving face, then abruptly grinned for the benefit of the *Herald-Examiner*'s photographer, who had just arrived. 'Butcher? Well, butcher may be right. One of our patrolmen came across Mrs Leonidas' underslip about seven hundred fifty feet west of here, in an ash can just behind the Jefferson Park Drugstore. It was soaked in blood, and it had apparently been used to wrap up two metal instruments, although both of those metal instruments had dropped out of the underslip because of their weight and fallen to the bottom of the ash can. They were, namely, one Diamond-A skinning knife with a ten-inch blade and a beechwood handle; and one Fulton beef-splitting saw, with a thirty-two-inch blade and a hardwood handle. Both instruments were heavily stained with blood and the teeth of the splitting saw were clogged with bone and human tissue.'

'So you could be looking for somebody from Packingtown?' asked Harry. 'Somebody from Armour or Cudahy? A professional butcher, who knows how to cut up a carcass?'

'That's a possibility and we're looking into it,' said Dan Rogers.

'Are you going to give some advice to single and separated women living on Milwaukee Avenue?' asked Vincent Geruso, and he was jotting down the answer even before Dan Rogers could open his mouth. There were certain basic requirements to every news story; and it was a basic requirement to every unsolved homicide that 'police warned single and separated women to be on their guard, and not to open their doors to strangers.' For the next few days, the Fuller brush salesmen were going to have a difficult time in Jefferson Park, doors slammed in their faces, 'What do you think, lady, I'm going to hack you to death with a toilet brush?'

After ten minutes talking to Dan Rogers, Harry walked over to the Jefferson Park Drugstore and used the telephone to call rewrite. The drugstore smelled of gumballs and coffee and cinnamon, and there was a rack next to the phone booth crammed with dog-eared copies of *Police Comics* and *Blackhawk* and *Sheena Queen of the Jungle*. A fat old man who looked like a Greek version of W. C. Fields was serving behind a dangling frieze of dried sausages. In front of the counter, five dozen copies of the Sunday *Star* were already stacked up, bound tight with string.

Harry tucked the telephone under his chin and picked up a copy of *Sheena*, leafing through it while he waited for the *Star* switchboard to connect him. 'The B'wali tribe! Ho, witch doctor, what means the attack?' For some reason, he found himself thinking about Morgana Croft Tate. Maybe Sheena looked like a blonde Morgana. Tall, lithe, athletic, totally confident. He tucked the comic book back in the rack, and beckoned to Woozy to pass him a cigarette. Woozy, still nauseated from taking pictures of Mrs Leonidas, gave him the whole pack.

Later, as they drove back to the *Star* building in Harry's Woodie, Woozy said, 'Let me out, will ya.' Harry drew over to the curb, and waited patiently, his face illuminated by the orange glow of his cigarette, while Woozy bent over the gutter and puked.

'How can anybody *do* that?' he asked Harry, as they turned southward on Michigan. The city lights rose up ahead of them like Christmas.

'I don't know,' said Harry. 'Hate? Maybe he hated women.'

'But jeez, to cut her up like that. And *arrange* her like that.'

Harry said nothing. There was nothing to say. Both of them knew that they would probably have nightmares about it tonight, and for nights to come, Mrs Leonidas' face, so bruised and so bloody and yet so curiously beatific, nestling in her own pubic hair like some extraordinary and terrifying creature from ancient mythology. The image refused to go away, and Harry was beginning to understand already that it would *never* go away.

Harry overtook a glossy Buick Roadmaster convertible that was curb-crawling between Huron and Erie, its wide-hatted driver whistling at the girls in their tight calf-length skirts and uptilted bonnets who were already strutting along the sidewalks looking for six o'clock clients. 'How about a drink?' he asked Woozy. 'You can print those pictures up later. We can't use them, whatever.'

'A drink? Sure. How about two?'

They parked in the basement of the *Star* building. Tomahawk Billy was sitting in his little wooden booth listening to *Mr and Mrs North* on his Arvin radio. He scowled at them as if he was quite prepared to scalp them both. They walked across Wabash Avenue to O'Leary's Pub, which was right on the corner of Wabash where it curved north again after having angled itself to cross the Chicago River. The air was sullen and heavy and somewhere off to the west, there were thunderstorms banging over the prairies.

O'Leary's was the blood rival to the Billy Goat, under the Wrigley Building, where the more inebriate of the *Tribune* reporters always gathered. It was furnished in the style which could best be described as Victorian Irish, all dark mahogany and frosted glass partitions and black cast-iron tables with marble tops. It was named, of course, for Mrs O'Leary, whose cow had kicked over the lamp that had started the great Chicago fire of 1871. The proprietor's name was really Roy Chamberlain and he was English, all belly and mustaches. He and his wife Betty were standing behind the bar polishing glasses when Harry and Woozy came in. Without the need for a spoken order, he set up two beer mugs and two shot-glasses and poured out two Hamm's and two Four Roses.

'Hard day at the office, dear?' he asked. It was the way he greeted everybody. Harry tugged his necktie loose and picked up the shot-glass of whiskey, tipping it back in one mouthful.

'That bad, huh?' asked Roy.

'A murder,' said Woozy. 'A real hack-'em-up job. Worst I ever seen.'

Harry looked around the smoky bar to see who was in. It was early yet. The die-hard drinkers usually came in after the football games were finished. All the same, he could see Walter

Dempsey in the kingly gloom of his favorite booth, holding forth to two young *Tribune* staffers about the glories of baseball before the war. Harry waved to Walter and Walter waved regally back.

Betty Chamberlain came over with a dish of salted peanuts for them. She was a motherly peroxide blonde, with teeth that were always tinted with lipstick and a bosom on which many a *Star* reporter, drunk and maudlin, had metaphorically and sometimes literally rested his head. 'Harry?' she said. 'You're not looking too clever.'

'A murder,' Woozy repeated. 'Some Greek woman, totally cut to pieces. I never saw anything like it.'

'Urgh, it sounds *terrible*. Do they know who did it?'

'Not a clue,' said Harry, shaking out a cigarette. 'Maybe some professional hog-hooker. Anyway, do you mind if we don't discuss it?'

Betty said, 'Do you know who came in lunchtime?'

'Walter Dempsey, and he hasn't left yet.'

'No, no, you'd never believe it. Lenny Mutken.'

Harry turned around and leaned his elbow on the counter. 'Lenny Mutken? You mean *the* Lenny Mutken? I thought he was dead.'

'He bloody near looked it,' said Roy, as he unscrewed a fresh bottle of gin.

'Well, well,' Harry remarked. 'The man who made Ogden Avenue famous.'

'Before your time, wasn't he, Lenny Mutken?' asked Roy.

'Oh, sure,' said Harry. 'I don't know when he quit, maybe two or three years before I joined the *Star*. But they were still talking about him, even then. They still talk about him now.'

'I think he just wanted to chat to some of the old faces,' said Betty. 'Relive old times. Walter was here. He talked to Walter for a while. He didn't look well, though. And you wouldn't credit how *old* he looks.'

'Lonely, if you ask me,' put in Roy.

'I wish I'd seen him,' said Harry. He lit his cigarette, and blew out smoke between his teeth.

'Well, he might be in again,' said Betty. 'He said he missed the old days, especially the pressure. That's what he said, the pressure. The trouble with being retired, he said, there were no deadlines. You just woke up in the morning one day and realized there was no reason to get out of bed.'

Harry scooped up a handful of nuts. 'Did he say what he was doing these days?'

'Writing little articles I think, and fillers. Anything he can turn his hand to. He said something about polishing furniture as well. I wasn't quite sure what he meant.'

'Maybe he's polishing furniture as well,' said Woozy, helpfully.

Walter Dempsey came over, balancing like an overloaded hod-carrier on the ridge of a third-story roof. He flung his arms around Harry and Woozy, and cried, 'The hounds of truth! The indefatigabubble seekers after fact!'

'How're you doing, Walter?' asked Harry.

Walter peered at him blearily. 'I am not doing well, sir. I am doing poorly. I finished my last drink nearly an eon ago, and those parsimonious college boys from the *Tribune* have done nothing but sit and stare at me in impertinent amusement, as if their mothers sewed their pockets up before they let them out, that's if they have mothers.'

'Give the man a drink,' Harry told Betty. 'Walter without a drink is like Chicago without a lake.'

Walter passed over his glass, and beadily watched Betty half filling it with whiskey. 'You're a hero, Mr Sharpe,' he told Harry, without taking his eyes away from his drink. 'A hero in homespun.'

'Betty tells me that Lenny Mutken was here,' said Harry.

'Ah, yes! Leonard Alward Mutken, the only hack of any distinction apart from myself that the miserable Croft Tate empire has ever spawned. It was almost like the old days for a moment, except that Lenny doesn't drink now, not the way he used to. It was Lenny Mutken who taught me to hold my liquor, you know. That was in Prohibition days, of course. Great days, you know, incandescent days! Lenny was as close as – as close as – well, as close as *something* with Al Capone. We used to go round to Capone's place at the Hawthorne Hotel, Lenny and me, and they would treat us like princes! All the liquor we could gargle down, and the premium stuff, too. Do you know what Capone used to say, he used to say that when he sold liquor, everybody called it bootlegging, but when that same liquor was served on a silver tray on Lake Shore Drive – that was hospitality. A friendly fellow, Al Capone. All for Al and Al for All. Lenny used to think that Al Capone was the finest son this city ever produced.'

'Is he coming in again?' asked Harry.

Walter frowned at him as if he were mad. 'Capone?' he asked.

'Not Capone, Walter, for Christ's sake. Lenny Mutken.'

'Ah!' said Walter. 'Well ... yes. The answer to that is probably. Yes, he said he might. He's still ... illuminatory, you know. You can keep your Ben Hechts. Lenny Mutken was the man who made newsprint sing.' He blinked, and shuffled a little, and then said, 'He sang quite a lot himself, too. In his cups, you understand.'

Then he said, 'Robert and Slobert Hink.'

'Robert and Slobert Hink? Who the hell are Robert and Slobert Hink?'

'They were the identical twins in *Vic and Sade*, correct? And that's how close Lenny was with Al Capone. Robert and Slobert Hink. I was trying to think of their names.'

A little after eight, hungry but still sick to his stomach, Harry drove Woozy back to his apartment block on 73rd Street, and then headed south through the jostling Saturday evening traffic on 111th Street and Michigan, the district known as Roseland, where his mother lived. He visited his mother only once or twice a month, but today he felt the need for some normality, some quietness, and some unshakable evidence that there was still human affection left in the world.

Roseland was a community of brick bungalows, two-story frame houses and small 1930s apartment buildings. Its heart was the corner of Michigan Avenue and 111th Street, where the Parkway popcorn palace still stood, and Tysons Liquor Store sold muscatel wine by the tap. The Sczanieckas had been one of the first Polish families to move into the area twenty-five years ago when it was mainly Swedish and Dutch. These days its streets were crowded with Lithuanians, Italians, and Negroes. It was growing tatty, a little run-down, but as Harry came around that odd familiar kink in Michigan Avenue and drove past the lighted windows of the stores that he had known as a boy, he still felt a sense of homecoming.

He turned right into 111th, and drew up outside Palmer Apartments, right next to Zyzniewski's Food Mart. He leaned forward and looked upward so that he could see his mother's third-floor window. The living room light was on, the brown cotton drapes with the red roses on them were drawn tightly across. Harry sat back in his seat and took out another cigarette. He would smoke it, and then go up.

.

13

After church on Sunday morning the Croft Tates were driven back to Weatherwood, where they climbed out of the limousine and dispersed, saying nothing to each other. There was an atmosphere: the kind of atmosphere that in the words of Morgana's maternal grandmother would have gassed rats. Howard went to his dressing room to change out of his churchgoing clothes. His accountant Wendell Wiley was coming up to Weatherwood later in the morning to talk about floating a new television station in the Cleveland area. Phoebe went to her room to write one of her passionate letters to Donald (to his office address, of course, where his secretary would sniff the envelope and smile, but never give him away). Donald had refused to come to the phone yesterday, and Phoebe was already vexed and frustrated. 'He's such a sleech.'

Morgana went into the garden room to take coffee and read the Sunday *Star* while she waited for John to arrive. The garden room was furnished with white wicker armchairs and flouncy floral fabrics, with potted ferns everywhere, and white Portuguese planters. The sun had decided to act as sulkily as the Croft Tates this morning, shining on and off, waxing and waning, and so the room was alternately dull and bright. Morgana was consistently bright however in a daffodil-yellow linen suit with a calf-length box-pleated skirt, her hair combed back and tied with yellow ribbons.

She read the *Star*'s feature on Doris Wells, the little girl whom she had rescued from the burning tenement. There was a photograph of Doris sitting up in bed at the burns unit, with a bandage over one side of her head. She was smiling and clutching a toy bear.

'Did you see this?' Morgana asked, as Eleanor came into

the garden room, balancing a cup of coffee. Eleanor was dressed in gray, and she looked elegant but somber. A large flower made of white silk ribbon was pinned to her breast, but that was the only decoration she wore. She sat down next to Morgana and leaned over to look at the paper.

'So, that's the little girl. She's sweet, isn't she? You ought to go down to the clinic and see her.'

'I was planning to. John's going to drive me down after lunch.'

'You ought to drive *him*. You haven't tried out your new car yet.'

'Well, I don't know, Momsy. I'm still a little shaky.'

There was silence between them. The light faded, giving the room the appearance of a colorless photograph. Eleanor set down her coffee cup and sat with her hands clasped in her lap, looking distant and unhappy. Folding up the paper, Morgana said, 'Momsy? Are you all right? You haven't had a spat with Popsy, have you?'

'I'm perfectly all right, thank you, my dear. Never better, as Martin Luther said to his shirtmaker.'

'Momsy, something's wrong,' Morgana persisted. 'There has to be. You've been walking around ever since the morning of my birthday party with a face as long as a fiddle. And you've been acting so completely – I don't know, *streptococchal*.' That was another finishing school favorite.

'For goodness's sake, Morgana, will you mind your own business!' her mother suddenly barked at her.

Morgana went pink. 'Momsy – it *is* my business! You almost ruined my party! And now the whole house is full of gloom and doom! Popsy wouldn't even sing in church this morning. And when was the last time that Popsy wouldn't sing in church?'

'*Morgana!*' her mother screamed.

There was a moment of utter quivering silence. Eleanor was twisting a lace handkerchief between her hands, as if she was trying to wring tears out of it that she was unable to cry herself.

'You *have* had an argument with Popsy, haven't you?' Morgana asked her.

Eleanor lifted her head, and took a breath. 'You could call it that, in a way.'

'What happened? It wasn't about me, was it?'

'Of course not. It was about . . . us, that's all.'

Morgana was suddenly alerted to her mother's deep unhappiness. She dropped the newspaper on the floor, and leaned forward and touched her mother's hands.

'Momsy? What's *wrong*? Tell me!'

Eleanor tried to make her words sound light and careless. But the gravity of what she was saying gave her words the gradually-descending rhythms of a requiem. 'I had to tell your father something that was very unpalatable. It caused both of us a considerable amount of anguish; but I suppose it had to be said. There is no future in keeping secrets from a man like your father. If you do, you succeed only in punishing yourself. He's that kind of man. He's more than a man, you see. Over the years, he's become an institution. Keeping secrets from your father – well, it's rather like keeping secrets from the IRS. Its profitability is tainted by the overwhelming sense of guilt that it brings with it.'

Morgana watched her mother in bewilderment. Usually, her mother was a mirror. She could look at her mother and know exactly how she looked herself. And usually, her mother was sharp-eyed and clear-jawed and beautifully self-possessed. A woman of wealth and intelligence and caustic opinions. This morning, however, she looked haggard, and the skin around her neck was crumpled like peach-colored tissue paper.

'Momsy, I don't understand what you're talking about. What secrets?'

Her mother's long varnished fingernails traced a pattern on the knee of her gray dress. She attempted a maternal smile. For the first time Morgana was aware of the skull-like furrows around her mother's mouth. That sudden awareness was almost more of a shock than what her mother actually said.

'It was Robert Wentworth, you see. Young Robert. Well – what I told you was true. I *did* used to play with him when I was young, in San Francisco. But that wasn't all of it. I happened to meet him again, by chance, four years ago, when your father was in Washington, sorting out all that business with the War Assets Administration. I suppose you could say that I was lonely. There was plenty to keep me occupied, of course. All those fund-raising committees; and all that work I did at the Chicago Beach Hotel, when they turned it into a hospital. But, you know, for a woman like me –'

She hesitated. She raised her hands, and pressed them together, as if she were trying to think of a suitable prayer.

Then, in a quieter, contralto voice, she said, 'I knew of course that your father had his girlfriends. Well, I don't know whether they were girlfriends or not. He used to take some of his secretaries out to dinner. Whether anything ever happened between them or not, who can tell? And who cares, really? He always returned. You know, just like a dime returns, when you can't get connected. But that wasn't it. I didn't do it out of anger, or revenge. I did it because I needed something which your father seemed unable to give me – which I didn't even expect him to give me.'

She stared at Morgana appealingly, desperate to be understood. 'Risk, Morgana! Chance! That's what I did it for! The sheer excitement of it! Quite apart from the fact that Robert was so much younger than me, and he still found me attractive.'

Morgana said, softly, 'You were lovers.'

Eleanor grimaced. 'How ironic it all was! How bitter, how tragic, how sweet, how painful! And worst of all, we are *well* past the age of shedding tears, aren't we? We are all far too experienced and far too worldly-wise for that! God, but when we cry, doesn't it hurt? Doesn't it hurt, hurt, hurt!'

'You told Popsy?' said Morgana.

'Yes,' whispered Eleanor. Then, louder, quicker, 'He took it quite well, all things considered. He's not a spontaneous man, is he? He didn't shout, he didn't break anything priceless. He sulked a bit. He's still sulking. He's locked himself in his dressing room and he's opening and closing drawers and whistling fraternity songs. "Here's One In The Eye For Phi Sigma Pi" or something equally inane. And he never even went to college. God, Morgana, if my mother were still alive, I'd go back to mother.'

'Did you *have* to tell him?' Morgana asked her.

Eleanor thought about that for a moment, and then said, 'Yes, I think so. For Robert's sake, really more than my own. I always kept my love for him secret, when he was alive. The very least I could do was to confess it when he was dead. I suppose you think it very ill-considered but it was sort of a memorial. I expect he would have haunted me, too, if I hadn't told your father about him.'

Morgana sat back on her creaking basketwork chair. 'Well,'

she said, off-balance. 'It's quite a shock when you suddenly find out that your a mother's scarlet temptress.'

Eleanor said, 'Don't try to mock me, my dear. The situation may seem ridiculous but I can assure you that the distress is quite genuine. He was my lover, I loved him, and now he's drowned.'

'I don't know what else to say,' Morgana told her. 'What happens next? Are you and Popsy going to stay together?'

'Probably, I don't know. We haven't really had the chance to talk about it.'

'Do you love him?'

'What kind of a question is that?' Eleanor demanded.

'It's very simple, do you love him?'

'Well – I don't know what to say! That's like asking me if I like eating. I eat to stay alive, I eat because I enjoy it. Sometimes I eat something and five minutes later I've forgotten what I've eaten. Sometimes I eat something and enjoy it and then I wish I hadn't.'

Morgana said, 'Did you see Robert very often?'

Eleanor picked up her coffee cup, peered into it, realized the coffee was stone cold, and set it back down again. 'I don't know. Twice a month; sometimes three times, if we were lucky.'

'Did you ever think of leaving Popsy, and going to stay with him?'

Eleanor shook her head. 'I thought about it, yes, but not very seriously. For all of his faults, for all of his tempers, Howard isn't the kind of man you find every day. Not that Robert was, either. But if I had gone with Robert, I would have had to throw everything away. You, Phoebe, this house, my whole way of life. If I had gone with Robert, I would have lost almost everything. And that, I'm afraid, if you want the sordid unromantic truth – *that* is why I didn't think of leaving. You can call me a coward, if you like, as well as a scarlet woman. The Benedict Arnold of true romance. But Robert had youth and I didn't. I liked my risk, I liked my adventure, but I certainly wasn't going to live in a two-story frame house on Avenue G, with nothing but a cloth coat and two pairs of shoes, frying corned-beef hash and wondering when the gas company was coming to disconnect my stove.'

'Robert wasn't as poor as that, surely?'

'He would have been, if ever Cy Wentworth had found out

what was going on. And don't think for one moment that your father wouldn't have crucified me financially if I had walked out of the door. Your father can take a great deal. He's a tough man. But I very much doubt if he could have taken the humiliation of his prized socialite wife deserting him for some gambling wastrel straight out of F. Scott Fitzgerald.'

Morgana held her hand against the blue and gold Herend coffeepot. It was cold now; so she reached behind her and rang the bell for Millicent to bring them some fresh coffee. She rather thought that her mother needed it.

'Momsy,' she said, 'I'm really sorry.'

'Well, dear, you don't have anything to be sorry for. I don't deserve any sympathy, do I?'

'What are you going to do?'

'Do? There's absolutely nothing I can do. I told your father that I wasn't expecting forgiveness; but that I do still love him; and that I do want to stay; and that I hope in time that this can all be forgotten.'

Eleanor paused, and then she added, 'It's already been two days now, since Robert died. Tomorrow it will be three. Eventually, so many days will have passed that I will be able to go from morning to evening, and not think about him.'

Morgana said, 'Do you want me to talk to Popsy about it?'

'No, dear. I don't think that would be a good idea.'

'I'm over twenty-one.'

'Only just, and you're lucky you're alive to see it. Climbing up firemen's ladders like that.'

Morgana knelt down beside her and put her arms around her. She could smell Chanel. She could smell brandy, too. It was only eleven o'clock in the morning and already her mother had been drinking.

Morgana said, 'Perhaps we're the same, you and I. Perhaps I was looking for the same kind of things as you.'

'Well,' said her mother, 'let me give you a word of advice. If that's the kind of girl you are, think twice before marrying John.'

Morgana was startled by her mother's directness. 'But I love John!'

'You could say that as if you meant it.'

'I do, I love him.'

'And I love your father. But look at me now. On second thoughts, perhaps you'd better not.'

Eleanor stood up, and went to the window of the garden room. Outside, there was a view of the golf course, bordered by Moline elms which looked almost blue. The sun shone brighter for a moment, and made a halo out of Eleanor's hair. She held herself close, arms tightly crossed, as if she had lost any confidence that anybody else would. 'John is an excellent young man,' she said. 'He's hard working, and well connected, and he seems to have some kind of sense of humor. It would not be a social disaster if you were to marry him. It would, however, be a romantic disaster.'

She turned around now, and her eyes were as fierce as a bitch's. 'Ask any woman what death is, what real death is. The subjugation of the spirit, my dear. The daily acceptance of decisions made by inferior minds. Death is always being beautiful; death is cocktail parties; death is smiling on your husband's arm. Death is sitting caged up in his mausoleum of a house waiting for a man who may or may not decide to come home, while your real lover wastes his life away, out of your reach.'

'Momsy,' said Morgana, reaching out for her, and there were tears in her eyes.

'Well, hah, you don't have to take any notice of me,' Eleanor told her. 'I'm mourning, that's all. I thought I might be able to conceal it, but I can't. My heart has been cut out of me. I'm sorry. You mustn't listen. Your life is nothing like mine, and you are nothing like me. Marry your John, and be happy. Let him sing you his silly songs until the sun goes down.'

Morgana stood up and walked over to her mother and embraced her. But Eleanor was stiff, unholdable, and after a while Morgana stepped back.

Eleanor lowered her head. 'He took me out to dinner, the very first night,' she confirmed. 'It was a little Italian restaurant on the North Side. I hadn't eaten in a place like that in years. We had *arrosticini all' abruzzese*, and *pizza rustica*. I can close my eyes now and remember what it tasted like. And the wine, Corvo. Then he took me back to his father's apartment 999 Lake Shore Drive. My God, Morgana, I felt like a girl again.'

Morgana held her mother's hand but there was very little else she could do; and very little else she could say. Eleanor smiled for a moment, as if she were remembering something that Robert had said, and then her smile died away.

At that moment, Phoebe came in, noisily, flapping in one hand the letter she had written to Donald Crittenden. 'I'm *darned* if I can say what I mean,' she said. 'This is the fifth letter! I can't get it right! Either I sound too difficult, or else I sound too easy. And I don't want to sound *too* rude about poor Bradley – who incidentally is coming to lunch today, if that's okay.'

Morgana gave her mother's hand one last squeeze, and then turned to Phoebe with a smile. 'Come on,' she said, 'let me have a look.'

The letter was on pink paper with scalloped edges, and Phoebe had already sprayed it heavily with Norell perfume. Phoebe's writing was round and enthusiastic, with six or seven scratchings-out. 'My dearest darling Dondon, How you could have walked out on me I don't know what were you thinking about!!! Bradley is a dear and nothing but a friend you should know that!!! If you think I'm going to spend the rest of my life being Mrs Ham-I-Yam well you've got yourself another think coming!!! You didn't even give me the opportunity to explain!!! Still I like you when you're angry!!! Please call me whenever so that me and you can get together again!!!'

Morgana couldn't help laughing. 'Phoebe, this is terrible! Apart from the grammar, what do you think Donald's going to think?'

'I don't care what he thinks, just so long as he calls,' Phoebe protested. 'Besides, what's wrong with the grammar?'

'It's full of mistakes.'

'So what? Even great literary geniuses make mistakes. Didn't you hear Max Sackheim talking about that on Friday? He was a scream. Do you know what he said? "Between you and I, I can't hardly help making mistakes myself." Don't you think that's a killer? Anyway, it was something like that.'

She opened the porcelain cigarette box on the table and took out a cigarette. Morgana said, 'Donald's going to think you're so *cheap*.'

Phoebe pouted. 'Well, if my big sister had interceded on my behalf, instead of chasing firetrucks, I wouldn't have had to write to him at all. But who cares. He's pretty cheap, too. He and me can just be cheap together. A couple of cheapies.'

She took back her letter, and folded it up, and kissed it, and then she said, 'We can't *all* be betrothed to classy young lawyers, you know.'

'Don't tell me you're jealous of John,' said Morgana. She had meant to sound amusing, but somehow her throat caught at the word 'jealous' and instead she sounded tetchy.

'Jealous, my dear, why should I be jealous?' Phoebe asked her. 'Anyway, I'm never jealous. What shall I wear for lunch? What do you think about that gray and white dress I wore at the Bessenhausers'? Or maybe that green one, with all the pleats? No, you're in pleats. We don't want to look de-pleat-ed, do we? Goodness me! I'm funny this morning!'

Phoebe lit her cigarette and then suddenly caught sight of her mother, sitting as hunched and angular as Picasso's portrait of a 'Woman Ironing'. The distress of Eleanor's posture was extraordinary; all of her pain and all of her uncertainty were concentrated in the single coathanger line of her shoulders. She was masking her face with her hand: a hand on which three huge diamonds shone.

'*Mother?*' said Phoebe, frowning.

14

Enzo Vespucci arose from his scented bath and stood naked as a child waiting for his manservant Carmino to drape him with a huge warm snow-white Turkish towel. The steamy mirrors in his bathroom showed that he must have been a dark and sinister child; the kind of child who might have been suspected in the Middle Ages of being a changeling, left in a Sienese crib one morning in a whirl of sulphur smoke.

Once he had been dried by the silent, pomaded Carmino; and puffed with powder; Enzo slipped into his blue silk dragon bathrobe and blue silk mules, and slip-slopped his way through to the dining room, where he would take his breakfast.

The dining room was decorated in soft yellows in the classical style; the circular table was laid with a soft yellow cloth. A huge oval mirror allowed Enzo to watch himself as he ate. His apartment had mirrors everywhere. There were so many mirrors that sometimes his servants had the unnerving feeling that thirty people lived there, instead of six.

His maidservant Eufemia was waiting with his napkin. She was handsome, in her mid-twenties, but not too distractingly pretty. He sat down and Eufemia laid his napkin over his lap for him, and poured his coffee, and then went to fetch his food. He rubbed his hands together, squeezing his fingers so that his knuckles cracked. All the Sunday newspapers were lying tucked in a brass magazine rack right next to him, but he didn't lift any of them out. He was thinking about sex, and the opera.

Eufemia came back with a tray. She placed a plate in front of Enzo, and raised the polished metal cover. The plate bore his monogram EV, and a steaming arrangement of *spaghetti alla carbonara*, spaghetti with raw eggs, Italian *pancetta* bacon, white wine and *pecorini romano* cheese. Enzo leaned forward infinitesimally, breathed in the aroma of the spaghetti, and then nodded so slightly that anyone who had not been paying microscopic attention to him would have missed it altogether.

He began to eat. The room was silent, except for the clicking of his fork and the muted sound of the traffic outside on North Lake Shore Drive. Occasionally, a distant bright glitter from the lake would pierce the soft lace curtains which screened Enzo from the world outside. He lived on the top floor of 1540 Lake Shore Drive, at the south end of Lincoln Park, a sixteen-story apartment block built in the style of a French château.

He was unusually uninterested in family for a man of his nationality in his walk of life; although his trucking concern in Cicero was taken care of by his sister's three sons the Piccagge brothers. He had never married, he had no sons of his own. He lived a quiet, formal, concentrated existence, indulging himself expensively but sparingly in everything he loved best. He adored food, but he never ate too much. He adored wine, but he never drank too much. He visited the opera only once a month. He consorted with the five women in his life only at weekends; and not always then. He believed that every single experience should be one worth holding one's breath for.

In the late 1930s Enzo had quickly acquired control of vast tracts of the Near South Side, through a complicated series of negotiations with other major racketeers. Very few of these negotiations had been legal and very few of them had been bloodless. The police and the FBI had been trying for years to unravel exactly what had happened, and how much property had fallen into Enzo's hands, but they hadn't been trying too hard, in case they revealed just how closely Enzo's interests were intertwined with those of union presidents and politicians and business notables, not to mention police officials and judges. Enzo paid dues wherever dues were payable. Enzo kept everybody happy. But Enzo was also a man capable of killing other human beings who disturbed the quiet and equilibrium which he prized so much. He had killed a man with his own hands when he was fourteen; a man who had cuckolded his father. He had cursed his father for a coward and he had cursed his mother for a slut. But he had gone to church afterwards and thanked God that he had discovered the secret strength that would make him powerful and rich. Normal people find it almost impossible to stand up against somebody who is quite prepared to kill them without compunction.

Enzo was winding the last of his spaghetti around his fork when Ambrogio came in. Ambrogio stood with his cap in his hand waiting in silence while Enzo finished eating, and fastidiously cleaned his mouth with his napkin.

'Well?' Enzo asked him.

'I was wondering what time you wanted to go out to the track, sir,' said Ambrogio.

Enzo thought for a while, and then said, 'What time did Marcella say that she would be there?'

'Two o'clock, sir, or thereabouts.'

'In that case, let us make it two o'clock. It is too long since I saw Marcella last.'

'Yes, sir. And . . . you'll forgive me, sir.'

Enzo looked at his coffee cup; and almost as if summoned by thought transference, Eufemia came back into the dining room, walked quickly across the yellow carpet, and poured him a fresh cup. Enzo picked it up, sipped it, and waited with a mask-like expression for Ambrogio to finish what he was saying.

'Carlo Aceto is outside, sir. He says he begs to talk to you.'

Enzo set down his cup. The mask broke. '*Carlo Aceto*? That pig's offal has the nerve to come here? I thought he was in Nevada.'

'He says he begs forgiveness, sir.'

Enzo suddenly stood up, and slapped his napkin against the table. '*Forgiveness*? A man who has betrayed his brothers? A man who would sell his sister's vagina for the price of a worn-out car tire? Didn't I say to Carlo Aceto that if ever he set foot in Chicago one more time I would nail his head to a tree?'

Ambrogio listened to this invective with noticeable tolerance. Enzo enjoyed insults and threats. It was only when he stopped insulting and threatening that the people around him had cause to be really frightened. Enzo paced up and down the dining room, appealing every now and then to the huge Guido Reni painting of St Michael which overlooked the gilded sideboard, as if only a saint could understand what a racketeer had to put up with. 'Didn't I say to Carlo Aceto that I would feed him on *pane integrale* mixed with concrete, and drop him into the North Pond?'

'Do you want to see him?' asked Ambrogio, patiently.

'Carlo Aceto? That dog-vomit?'

'He came at seven, sir. He's been waiting in the gallery since then.'

'Well . . . all right, then. You can show him through to the library. Make sure he sits on newspaper.'

'As you say, sir.'

'And make sure you tell him how much he tests my hospitality. Make sure you tell him that I am angry like the fires of all hell, excuse me, San Michel. Make sure he understands that he is right on the razor's edge; that he will have only to sneeze and I will cut him from nose tip to belly button and stuff him with marjoram. *Carlo Aceto al maggiorana.*'

Ambrogio couldn't help laughing; a deep, slow reverberating guffaw.

Enzo returned to the bathroom and meticulously brushed his teeth with chlorophyll toothpaste. As he was swilling out his mouth, the bathroom door opened behind him and a short, voluptuous, black-haired girl stepped in, and came right up to him, and draped her arms around his shoulders. 'Enzo,' she coaxed him. 'I woke up, and you just weren't there any more. Aren't you coming back to bed?'

Enzo regarded their reflections in the mirror, the two of them jostled up close. He with his curiously immobile aristocratic features, and his hooded eyes. She with her tangled hair and her high cheekbones and her pouting crimson-painted lips, just like a girl from a movie poster, sultry, torrid, passionate, reeking richly of Chamade and sexual juices. She was all wound up in a silk wrap of palest eau de nil, with beige lace edging, beneath which her heavy breasts wallowed, and her pillowy hips rose and fell like the sea.

'Enzo, Enzo, Enzo,' she pouted, and her lips drew back over her teeth in a smile of such overpowering lust that Enzo turned around and looked at her face to face, and visibly quaked. She laughed then, as if she had won something from him, and kissed him, face and neck and cheeks and forehead and nose, and said, 'Enzo, come on, Enzo, come back to bed; come and let me fit my house over your chimney.'

Enzo caught her left wrist, then her right wrist, and gradually prized her away from him. 'I have business. Go back to bed.'

'Business? Business? It's Sunday! What business can any man do on Sunday? Are you a priest, Enzo, do you have to take confession?'

Enzo smiled faintly. 'You could call it that, Nana. A confession, yes.'

Enzo

'Enzo, let me fry your eggs, Enzo?'

Enzo pushed her away flat-handed. 'First I have business. Go back to bed. Brush your hair. Find something to do.'

'Oh, Enzo, you are so wicked,' Nana blurted, and kissed him again and again.

Enzo reached inside her wrap, and twisted her pubic hair around his fingers.

'Enzo!' she gasped, and clutched at his shoulder.

He twisted tighter; as tight as a lover might, in a moment of high sexual excitement; except that he was not aroused, he was dispassionate as marble. Then he twisted tighter still and Nana's smile poured sideways with fear.

'Enzo don't hurt me,' she whispered.

'I don't want to hurt you. I want you to listen to me, that's all. Is it too much to ask, that you should listen to me? I have business. Go back to bed. Later, you can play houses, chimneys, eggs, whatever you like.'

Nana closed her eyes. There were tears clinging in her eyelashes. She knew what she had to say. 'I'm sorry,' she whispered. 'Forgive me.'

He released her. He removed his hand from her wrap, and raised it very slowly to his nostrils, and dispassionately breathed in the smell of her. He didn't take his eyes off her once. 'I forgive you,' he said. 'I am a kind man. You can ask anybody.'

'Yes,' she said. She looked drained.

Enzo waited until she had gone back to the bedroom and closed the door behind her. Then he carefully washed his hand in the basin, and dried it. His face in the mirror was completely expressionless. He admired the human face that gave nothing away. He loved sculpture, especially Bernini. He thought of last night, of Nana screaming, with her big thighs stretched wide apart, his fingers buried like claws in her breasts. He thought of *Tosca*, his favorite opera, the scene where Tosca realizes that Cavaradossi has really been killed by the firing squad. Intense moments, moments worth holding one's breath for. 'His gaze is like the gaze of statues, and his voice, faraway, calm and grave, speaks with accents of those who were dear and are now silent.'

Enzo wept for himself, making no noise. Nothing showed on his face but a slight tightening of the muscles around the mouth, and two tears.

Carlo Aceto was waiting for him, sitting quite unnecessarily on the small advertisement section of the Sunday *Tribune*. The library was not a library because Enzo kept all his books in his bedroom, but Plotke & Grosby in their original prospectus for 1540 Lake Shore Drive had described this room as a library and that as far as Enzo was concerned was what it was. The room was pale green, almost the same color as Nana's wrap. The sun was shining in through the window, and gleaming on Carlo Aceto's scalp, even though he had combed his hair across it in an attempt to hide his baldness.

Carlo started to rise to his feet with a crackle of newspaper. But Enzo waved at him dismissively and he sat down again. Carlo was a square, big-shouldered man, with one of those large heads that looked as if they were the product of extraneous bony growth. He kept his short-fingered hands jammed together, and his ankles tightly crossed. His gray suit couldn't have been tighter or worse-fitting if he had gone to his tailor's and asked them specially to run him up something with a matching vest to make him look like a *schlemiel*.

Enzo stood over Carlo with his hands thrust into the pockets of his dragon wrap and stared at him with contempt.

'Carlo Aceto,' he said, after a while. Aceto wasn't Carlo's real name: it was Italian for 'vinegar', and Enzo made sure that he pronounced it with vinegar. Carlo had been given the name Aceto because he always left a sour taste in people's mouths; even those of his friends.

'Mr Vespucci, I know that I promised,' Carlo fumbled. 'I know what I said, about getting out of Chicago, about never coming back. But, I couldn't find work. Nobody would give me a job. Not even the Salvatores, in Reno. I begged, but they wouldn't have me. I had to come back. There wasn't anyplace else.'

Enzo sat down opposite Carlo in a rope-back armchair,

and folded his arms and stared at Carlo without blinking for an unnaturally long time.

'They wouldn't have you,' he repeated. 'Are you surprised by that?'

'No, sir.'

'So, what makes you think that *I* will have you?'

'Well, sir, Mr Vespucci –'

'I am not a generous man,' Enzo interrupted him. 'I am not a forgiving man, either. You can ask whoever you like. I don't have to be. Is there any law in the United States which says that I have to be generous or forgiving? I am *kind*, yes. Ask anybody about that. But kindness is something special.'

Carlo Aceto stared at him. His face was yellow, like uncooked parsnips. 'I have heard people say that, Mr Vespucci. That . . . you are kind.'

'Should I be kind to you, do you think, Carlo Aceto?'

'Mr Vespucci – I don't ask much. I know I made some bad mistakes. I had no money then. My brother was in trouble, I had to raise bail. I didn't want my brother to go the same way that I did. What had he done, you know? Nothing but grand theft auto. He would've given the car back, if he hadn't wrecked it. An accident, nothing else. But how could I leave him to take the rap? You can understand that.'

Enzo said, with some relish, 'I don't have a brother, Carlo. One sister, that's all.'

Carlo dragged an off-color handkerchief out of his pants and wiped his face with it, all over. 'I wouldn't of come back, you know, if I hadn't of had some kind of a bird in the hand, you know, something to offer.'

'I see,' said Enzo. 'You have something to offer?'

'I don't take all the credit for it, Mr Vespucci, believe me. I'm not trying to say that I'm somebody special. But I heard what I heard, and I guess that's worth something, because nobody else heard it.'

'You heard something?' asked Enzo, rather prissily. 'What did you hear? And where?'

'A friend of my sister's works for City Hall; she's a stenog. She's been typing some letters for the mayor.'

'Well, really?' said Enzo. 'You *are* well connected. Do you have copies of these letters? Do you know what they say?'

'Oh, yes sir, I know what they say all right. The slums,

that's what they're all about. They're all about clearing the slums.'

Enzo rose from his armchair and walked stiffly around the library until he was standing right behind Carlo Aceto's chair – so close behind that Carlo Aceto couldn't see him, even when he tried to shift from one side to the other.

Enzo said, 'You know what these letters say. Well then, tell me what they say. That is what you came here for, isn't it?'

'Mr Vespucci – forgive me –'

'I've already forgiven you. You want me to forgive you twice?'

Carlo sniffed unhappily. 'What I mean is, these letters. I know what they say and I know what Mayor Doyle is planning to do. But, I have to have some kind of guarantee, you know? Like, before I tell you what's going on, I have to have some guarantee that nobody's going to come after me for what I did before. I mean, that wasn't my fault; that wasn't all my fault, anyway, no matter what you say, what happened to Benny and Genaro.'

There was a small reproduction desk in the corner of the library. Enzo walked over, and opened it up. 'Go on,' he said, to Carlo. 'You were talking about a guarantee.'

Carlo twisted around in his chair. 'Well, sir –'

'The paper,' said Enzo, indicating the newspaper that Carlo was sitting on. 'I haven't read that yet. Don't crumple it.'

'I'm sorry, Mr Vespucci, but what I was going to say was –'

But Enzo didn't give Carlo the opportunity to say anything. Enzo knew what it was that Carlo wanted, and it was nothing more and nothing less than the chance to stay alive, unhounded, without a price on his head. The holy protection of the *consigliere*. That was a guarantee which Enzo certainly had the power to give him: but Enzo never gave guarantees to anyone, because he didn't believe in guarantees. To give a guarantee was un-American. Those who gave guarantees forfeited their future freedom of action; they surrendered their God-given right to exact revenge.

Enzo said, softly and harshly, sandpaper being rubbed against a cat's fur, 'I still remember what you did, you cow's caul. I saw Benito and Genaro for myself, dead. Shot through the head, with their brains on the wall. And you who betrayed them – you have the effrontery to ask me for a life-guarantee!'

'Mr Vespucci, mercy –'

Enzo twisted his left arm around Carlo's neck, almost strangling him. For a small delicate-looking man, Enzo was alarmingly powerful, and even though Carlo's hands immediately flew up to clutch at Enzo's sleeve, he was unable to prize him loose.

'*Consigliere,* my family –'

It was then that Enzo raised a silver-handled letter opener which he had taken out of his desk, and jabbed the point of it right into the very top of Carlo's bald head. It was not very sharp, but Enzo drove it down with sufficient force to pierce the skin, and a thin runnel of blood slid down the side of Carlo's head and into his grubby collar. Carlo roared out *eeeugghhh*! and tried to heave himself off the chair, but Enzo twisted him even more tightly, and dug the letter opener even more viciously into his scalp.

'Listen to me, you dog's abortion, you're lucky that I haven't killed you already. You expect to come back to Chicago, do you, on your knees, weeping and tipping ashes on your head, begging for forgiveness, and now you're asking me for guarantees, too? Well, here is a guarantee for you. I guarantee not to drive this thing right up to the handle in the top of your head if you tell me what Mayor Doyle is saying in his letters.'

Carlo gasped, 'My mother, Mr Vespucci, she's so sick.'

'Benito and Genaro are even sicker. And so will you be, unless you speak.'

Carlo's voice was almost a babble now. 'Mr Vespucci, if only I could turn back the clock.'

Enzo tightened his grip on Carlo's throat, and gradually twisted the letter opener from side to side. Carlo shrieked, and shouted, 'No! No, Mr Vespucci, no! Please! I'll talk, Mr Vespucci – please!'

Enzo lifted the letter opener a half inch away from the top of Carlo's head, and waited, his whole body tensed up underneath his wrap. Carlo winced, and swallowed, and then blurted out everything he knew in garbled rushes.

'The letters didn't go out yet. They was just typed. They're all supposed to be secret or something, that's what June said anyway, June she's the stenog my sister knows. Anyway it seems like Mayor Doyle says he's going to tear down all of the South Side slums, that's what he says, and he says by hook or by crook he's going to do it, those are his words. He says he can't tear nothing down, though, until he elbows out the people who own the slums, you know, namely you and Franny Lorenzo and Orville O'Keefe. He's got his list, maybe twenty or thirty names, and yours is right at the very top Mr Vespucci, top banana.'

'Go on,' Enzo urged him.

Carlo swallowed and shifted on his newspaper. 'Mayor Doyle says he's got to have help if they're going to tear down the slums, you know like help from the people and help from the newspapers and help from the teevee people. He says he wants a public whatsisname, public outcry, everybody saying they got to tear down the South Side slums and what a lot of bums they are that own them.'

Enzo could see himself in the mirror on the other side of the room. He wondered without emotion what it would be like to watch himself poke Carlo Aceto's eyes out.

Carlo was sweating. 'He says he doesn't want nobody to be scared of you no more, not even the people you got on your payroll. He says the district attorney is going to turn this blind eye to anybody who comes up and confesses you've been paying them off, provided they promise they're going to give testimony against you and Franny and all the rest. He says it's like some kind of holy war. I don't know what he means by that, but June said that Doyle kept talking about it over and over like it was pretty important. Holy war, holy war. Anyway another thing is that June thinks that Doyle is after you more than anybody else on that list.'

'What led her to think that?' asked Enzo. One eyeball, then the other eyeball, nothing simpler. Pop, pop.

'Well she saw these guys in Doyle's office when she was picking up his mail and one of them she knew for sure was Orville O'Keefe, she recognized his mug from the newspaper. She says Doyle and O'Keefe was talking pretty damned friendly, and they was talking about rent collecting and stuff like that. I don't know for sure but my guess is that Doyle wants to hang you out to dry and he doesn't care who helps him.'

'So that's it,' Enzo mused. 'He's given O'Keefe a guarantee. You see how freely these guarantees are given, Carlo? You see just how little they mean? The only guarantee that means a squat in this world Carlo is the guarantee that one day you'll be dead, with lilies in a jelly jar, and your photograph on your headstone smiling at everybody and saying "looka me, folks, looka me, I'm dead."'

Carlo grunted and gritted his teeth. The pain in the top of his head felt as if it were spreading, and it gripped his temples like a paralyzing migraine.

'*Unh* – that's it, Mr Vespucci – that's it – I swear to you!'

'That's it? That's it? Don't you think that's enough, all of my friends turned against me?'

'It's Mayor Doyle, Mr Vespucci, he's your man – *unh* – he says he's going to break you. That's what he says in his letters, he's going to break you. He's going to get the newspapers to tear you down, the newspapers and the radio stations, and he's going to get the district attorney's office to tear you down, as soon as people turn against you and start coughing up information. He's going to indict you for arson, insurance fraud, peddling narcotics, pandering income tax, whatever you want to name. That's what the letters say.'

Enzo paused for a moment, and then slowly released his stranglehold on Carlo's neck, and turned away. Carlo immediately took out his handkerchief again and dabbed the top of his head with it.

Enzo walked across to the other side of the room. His feet moved like ballet dancer, full of energy and quick menace. He was strange to watch. He cupped his right elbow in the palm of his left hand, and then he said, with great preciseness, 'You know something, Carlo Aceto, this is true. I have indeed been feeling some sort of unease lately whenever I have been visiting my friends. I feel that they are looking at me as if I have some fatal disease, and the only person who does not know that I have it is me.'

He paused a moment longer, and then he said, '*Bastards*. And so many of them taking so much of my money, too. And I am the very last one to hear about it; and I hear about it from you, Carlo Aceto, the rat's cack who sold the lives of Benito and Genaro! I am left grinning in my innocence while everybody else is gradually edging their way out of the door!'

He confronted Carlo with a face the color of pizza dough, rolled in flour. 'Bastards! There will be blood! Bastards! On the life of my mother I swear that I will grind them into pies and feed them to their own children.'

Carlo unhappily inspected his handkerchief. 'My collar is all soaked with blood.'

'Your collar is already so greasy that a louse would slide off it,' Enzo retorted. He picked up the telephone on the desk and said, 'Ambrogio? Mr Aceto is going home now. Perhaps you would like to take him.'

Carlo stood up, lifting a hand like a son-in-law begging not to be served another helping of mother's pie.

'All I need is your say-so, Mr Vespucci.'

Enzo put down the receiver. He said nothing. His tongue was arched up so that it touched the back of his upper teeth. The underside of it was pale blue and bumpy, like the underside of some sea scavenger.

Carlo without warning dropped on to his knees. 'All I need is your say-so, Mr Vespucci. A say-so will do.'

15

Just as Carlo Aceto was being assisted into the back seat of a beige Nash Ambassador which the concierge had brought round to the *porte-cochère*, Enzo was closing his bedroom door behind him and melodramatically loosening the belt around his wrap.

Carlo refused to duck his head at first, so that Ambrogio could force him into the car. He gripped the roof, and wedged his scuffed two-tone shoe against the side of the seat, and Ambrogio was obliged to press down on his shoulder and tug at his waist in an attempt to bend him sideways. The concierge who had been well tipped and was always well tipped stood and watched this silent wrestling match with a face as expressionless as an empty pie dish. He had already noticed that a shabby middle-aged man had alighted unsteadily from a passing bus, and was making his way toward them, but it was not his duty to give Ambrogio any warnings.

'I will break your back,' growled Ambrogio. Carlo's rigid face gave every indication that he believed him.

Nana giggled, and writhed beneath the single yellow sheet, her eyes twinkling at Enzo in lust and amusement and also in anticipation of the diamond bracelet which he had promised her for afterwards. Enzo allowed the wrap to slither down to his ankles, and then he climbed on to the bed, sallow and naked. His chest was hairless, his nipples were the color of rose petals, pressed between the pages of a book. There were small moles all over his back and his shoulders. The first time Nana had seen him naked, she had asked him what would happen if she joined up all the dots with a pen, like one of those children's puzzles, what picture would appear. Enzo had smiled at her and touched her lips with his fingertip and said, '*Il Diablo.*'

Enzo tugged back the sheet with three systematic wrenches. Nana pretended to resist him, and giggled even more, and rolled away across the bed, wrapping herself up in the sheet as tightly as she could, to hide her nakedness. Enzo let out a hiss of pleasure, and came after her.

Tussling with Ambrogio, Carlo twisted his head around and suddenly caught sight of the middle-aged man who was making his way toward the entrance of 1540. He shouted out, '*Sir! Sir!*'

The middle-aged man stopped, but didn't look around. Instead, he remained where he was, his hands buried in the pockets of his coat, frowning to himself as if he had heard a voice from Heaven; or from within the depths of his own guilty soul. It was, after all, Sunday.

'*Sir!*' cried out Carlo, more desperately this time. Ambrogio heaved at his waist, and one of Carlo's fingernails caught on the drip rail over the automobile's door, and was bent right back.

Carlo's last cry, however, coupled with a sudden scuffle of activity next to the car, attracted the middle-aged man's attention. He peered over at the Nash uncertainly, and then he started to walk toward it, his legs moving with the cumbersome grace of a diver walking over the bottom of the sea.

Enzo did not attempt to unwind Nana from her sheet. Instead he ran the fingers of his left hand deep into her thick black hair, and grasped it tight, so that she let out a '*yah!*' of genuine pain, and lay back panting, and staring at him, her eyes darting from side to side, trying to understand what he wanted, trying to judge just how far he would go.

'*I want you naked,*' he said.

She hesitated for a single second, and he wrenched at her scalp a second time.

'*I want you naked,*' he repeated.

Slowly, without taking her eyes off him, Nana hooked her thumbs into the top of the sheet and edged it downwards. One breast was bared, then the other. Nana was sixteen years and seventeen days old. Her breasts were big and round and white, and as Aretino had once described the flesh of an urgent young nun, 'softer than a mill mouse born and raised in flour.' Her tiny pink nipples crinkled tight. Her mouth opened slightly; her breath smelled of stale wine and fresh peaches.

She drew the sheet down even further, baring a soft white stomach, slightly curved, and wide restless hips. Enzo took his fingers out of her hair, and held her face instead, in that kind of possessive grasp that immediately establishes superiority, one human being over another. Normally, you only hold children and animals like that; because when you hold a woman like that you are either going to kiss her whether she wants to be kissed or not; or you are going to hurt her badly.

Ambrogio grunted, 'Shit! Get into the car!' And almost as an afterthought, he punched Carlo very hard in the kidneys. Carlo squealed, and fell to the pavement, but Ambrogio picked him up by the collar, and swung him around.

At that moment, however, the middle-aged man intervened. 'What's this?' he wanted to know. He peered down at Carlo's gasping beetroot-colored face. 'What's this? What in the blue blazes are you doing to this man?'

Ambrogio said, 'Come on, eh, mind your own business, shove off.'

The middle-aged man refocused his eyes, and swayed. 'I'll have you know I'm a representative of the press, my good fellow, and unless you release this man instantly, I shall call for the plodders.'

Ambrogio pushed the man square in the chest. Not hard, but enough to make him stagger backwards three or four paces. Both Ambrogio and the dish-faced concierge paused to watch him as he staggered, quite certain that he was going to fall over, but the usual laws of gravity and balance seemed to have been temporarily suspended, and he came lurching back again, one finger censoriously raised, his chin quivering with wounded rectitude.

'Assault is a serious matter, you ruffian. And to a district judge a push is as good as a punch. Concierge, I want you to call up to apartment 20–1, Mr Vespucci's apartment, and tell him that Mr Walter Dempsey of the Chicago *Star* newspaper has arrived, but that I shall be momentarily delayed while dealing with a hooligan.'

Ambrogio paused in his attempts to swing Carlo into the back seat of the Nash. 'You are visiting Mr Vespucci?'

Walter gripped his lapels firmly, although he was leaning

at such an impossible angle that it seemed as this was the only way in which he could hold himself up. 'I'll have you know that Mr Vespucci invited me personally out to the track today, to write an article on his racehorses.'

'In this case, I beg to say sorry,' said Ambrogio. With a last effort, he managed to push Carlo into the automobile, and press the door closed against Carlo's shoulder. 'I am Mr Vespucci's chauffeur. I am simply carrying out Mr Vespucci's instructions to remove this man who was attempting to annoy Mr Vespucci, and take him away from the premises. There is no harm here. You will know what a kind man Mr Vespucci always is. Please, accept my apologies for the pushing.'

Walter sniffed, and blinked, and looked as if he hadn't understood a single word. But nonetheless, he turned to the concierge, and said, 'You may cancel that instruction. You may call up to 20–1 and announce me.'

In the golden landscape of the bed, Nana lifted one plump knee so that the sheet slid slowly down the inside of her thigh until it revealed the first curls of pubic hair, black and glossy. Enzo raised his left hand as slowly as a spider stalking its prey, and extended his long middle finger with the sapphire signet ring on it, and hooked the top joint of it over the hem of the sheet. His hooded eyes were fixed unblinking between Nana's thighs. He didn't even seem to be breathing. Nana herself was watching him now in fascination, her breath catching harshly in the back of her throat. Her black hair lay spread across the pillow in waves. She had been brought up by a welder, reared in the drab industrial turmoil of Calumet, cheap brown wallpaper, dingy brown curtains, a mother who nagged like a toothache and a father who drank beer until it sluiced out of the sides of his mouth. A childhood of radio laughter and skimpy cotton dresses and boiling carrots and endless uncertainty. 'What are you drawing?' 'A princess, with a white fur coat and a crown all made out of gold.'

Her family were all Catholics, though, and blitheringly pious, 'from the deceits and crafts of the Devil, O Holy Mother deliver us,' and that in a way was why Nana had been so mesmerized by Enzo, because he put her in mind so much of a priest or a cardinal. He was holy, that was it. Enzo was holy. And no less holy because of his cruelty and his sexual obsessions.

His single finger drew down the sheet. He had seen her

naked before, of course, but somehow he managed to electrify her with this single act of revelation. She felt herself flush; and there was nothing at all that she could do to stop it.

Enzo stared at her vulva with academic prurience. The shadowy line of it beneath the hair, the enclosed mystery. He followed the line with his fingertip, and Nana, still watching him, shuddered. He smiled. He did not raise his eyes. 'Your lock, your door, your garden,' he said, in a voice that was oddly pitched. 'Your nest, your scabbard, your Colosseum.'

He laughed. His laugh startled her. He placed both his thumbs against the swelling of her vulva, side by side, and gently parted it. He revealed glistening leaves of sugar-pink flesh that peeled away from other leaves of sugar-pink flesh with almost audible succulence. He stared for a long time, and then he bent his head forward, and ran the extreme tip of his tongue between the leaves. Nana closed her eyes. His very gentleness was threatening. With the heels of his hands he pushed her thighs wider apart, so that she revealed herself even more deeply.

His head bent forward again, and then again. She opened her eyes again and stared at the French-style plaster moldings on the bedroom ceiling. A reflection from the surface of the lake fluttered brightly in one corner of the room like the ghost of a once-trapped butterfly.

'Enzo . . .' she murmured, blurrily.

Walter Dempsey was leaning with the flat of his hand against Enzo's doorbell. He suppressed a burp with an exaggeratedly smart movement of his fist, almost like a salute, and wished very much that he had chosen either the salami for breakfast or the muscatel but not both. 'Murder,' he said to himself, thinking of what was going on inside his stomach. 'Sheer Shakespearean murder.'

Carmino opened the door and stared at him with hostility. 'Yes? What do you want?'

Walter swayed, and sniffed, and then burped. 'God damn salami,' he said, trying to sound cheerful.

'They do not permit mendicants in the building,' said Carmino. 'You shall have to leave.'

'Mendicants?' Walter demanded. 'Mendicants? My name is Walter Dempsey and I am senior sport reporter for the Chicago *Star*. I have an appointment with Mr Vespucci, to look at his horses, Mendicants, for God's sake. Here's my – card – a little dog-eared, I'm sorry – I'd like it back.'

Carmino put on a pair of half-glasses and read the card carefully. Then he said, 'Mr Vespucci is expecting you, yes, Mr Dempsey. I regret however that he is tied up at the moment in a meeting. But, if you would care to wait in the gallery for a little while, I will bring you coffee and a magazine to read.'

Walter followed him into the gallery. It was long and narrow, without windows, its walls painted in Sienese marble effect. There was a single gilt chair with a green seat and a single gilded table. Opposite the chair and the table there was a painting of the Christ child by Duccio di Buoninsegna that must have been worth several hundreds of thousands of dollars. Walter turned around and around, his hands still jammed in his pockets.

'You don't mind if I take a raincheck on that coffee, do you? And, listen, don't worry about the magazine. I hate to read. Reading is always full of other people's opinions and I'm afraid they only confuse me, other people's opinions. But I wouldn't say no to a nip of brandy, if you had such a thing.'

'Brandy, sir?' asked Carmino, coldly.

'Well, maybe a little seltzer in it, since it's so early.' Walter laughed, and wiped his nose with his finger, and nodded towards di Buoninsegna's holy baby. 'Cute little fellow, don't you think?'

Carlo sat locked in the back of the Nash as Ambrogio drove him southwards through the slums. He had tried once or twice to bang on the windows of the car, but hardly anybody had taken any notice; and those who had looked closer had been immediately reassured by Ambrogio's smile, and by the little twiddle he had given with his finger to indicate that Carlo was on his way to the mental hospital. At length Carlo had given up, and sat on the edge of his seat, his hands crossed over his chest, his left pants leg soaked dark with urine, waiting for the acting out of Enzo's revenge. He made no appeal to Ambrogio. He knew that Ambrogio would only laugh at him; and in his final moments on earth the very last thing he wanted was to be laughed at. He started to pray, but he found that none of the words would come out properly. They tangled themselves like fish hooks and wool. He repeated his wife's name several times, but the sheer uselessness of it started him weeping, and so he stopped. The run-down streets passed him by like a war documentary of a blitzed European city. Vacant lots, garbage tips, dilapidated wooden houses, garages, second-hand stores, hotels you wouldn't have booked into even to commit suicide.

This was Vespucci territory. This was the heartland of Enzo's business enterprises. This was the area about which Louis Kurtz had recently written, 'I have seen pitiful, pathetic, deplorable, rotten and damnable shacks, hovels, lean-tos and hell-holes in my travels, but the Black Belt of Chicago beats them all when it comes to Misery at its worst.'

Ambrogio sang a little. 'Night and Day', his favorite song. He had met Sinatra once, one summer weekend in Miami when Enzo had visited Lucky Luciano. Ambrogio was happy. He was always happy when Enzo gave him something responsible to do. It made him feel bigger inside. It gave him stature. The fact that he was already six foot three inches tall and weighed 241 pounds didn't seem to count.

He drew up at last on Honore Street, between 35th and 36th Streets. This was one of the filthiest and most collapsed of Enzo's properties, a row of wooden houses with wooden steps leading up to the upper floors from the back yards, and broken palings and ash-houses and line after line of washing flapping in the dusty summer wind. Negroes clustered on the back verandas to stare at their washing or at nothing at all, or to share a bottle of liquor. Crackling radio music played; dogs yapped; children screamed as if they were frightened that the sky was falling down.

The residents of Honore Street called it Outhouse Alley because none of the houses had sanitary facilities, and it was characterized by its rows of wooden privies.

The Negroes watched without interest as Ambrogio climbed out of the Nash, and then unlocked the back door for Carlo. Carlo climbed out and stood in the dust blinking against the sunlight. He took off his hat and the light gleamed on his head. The wound that Enzo had made in his scalp was already forming a crusty scab. Ambrogio took his arm and at the same time checked his watch. 'This way,' he said. He dragged Carlo along the alley at the backs of the houses and Carlo followed him, still clutching his hat.

They reached a privy with its door hanging open. There was a star-shaped hole cut in the door, the kind of hole that Lem Putt would have frowned on as too fancy, because it throws a ragged shadder. Ambrogio pushed Carlo into the privy. There was a momentary scuffle in which leaves of the Sears, Roebuck catalog flew about. Then Ambrogio hit Carlo hard in the stomach and winded him and Carlo sat down on the wooden seat whining for breath.

Ambrogio kicked the door shut and said, 'Stay there, you got me? One move out of you and that's the finish. You know what Mr Vespucci said.'

He checked his watch again. It was three minutes of eleven o'clock. He reached into his gray sport coat and lifted out a Colt .45 automatic, dull black, smelling thinly of oil. He pulled back the slide to cock it, and then he checked his watch yet again. It didn't occur to him that he could have fired right away and Enzo would never have known.

Walter Dempsey leafed through a copy of *Fortune* magazine, in the front of which was pasted a grandiose gold-printed bookplate announcing that it was *Ex Libris* Enzo Vespucci. At length, halfway through an article on deflation, and how it had brought the price of pie *à la mode* down to one cent, and at the same time hiked unemployment up to four million, Walter dropped the magazine on to the floor from nerveless fingers, and growled, and stood up, and hammered on the wall with his fist.

Carmino appeared from the servants' quarters, and said, calmly, 'Yes?'

'My good man,' said Walter. 'I came here by appointment, and at considerable personal inconvenience, and for Christ's sake don't ask me to say *that* again. But let me make this quite clear, if it was reading I wanted, I would have gone to the library, and taken out *The Complete Works of John Keats*. "He entered, but he entered full of wrath; his flaming robes streamed out behind his heels." Do you know what that is? "Hyperion, A Fragment". And weren't you bringing me some brandy?'

Unruffled, Carmino said, 'Mr Vespucci apologizes if he has kept you waiting, Mr Dempsey, and promises to join you shortly.'

'We-e-ell,' sniffed Walter. He was unused to people apologizing to him. Most of the time it was the other way around.

'And I will bring your brandy, sir,' Carmino added; and that mollified Walter completely.

In the bedroom, only thirty feet away from the chair where

Walter was sitting; Nana was panting thickly, her eyes tightly closed, her cheeks flushed. Gradually the flush spread across her chest, and she released her grip on the sheets and held her hands over her breasts, so that the flattened palms just touched her nipples. She rotated her hands around and around, deliberately skimming her nipples as lightly as she could, an act of self-stimulation which was all the more arousing because her immediate urge was to grasp both of her breasts tightly and squeeze them until they hurt.

The room was utterly silent, except for an occasional liquid lapping sound, as Enzo attended with his tongue to what classical authors of erotica would have called 'the pages of her missal.' Enzo was a great collector of erotica, books and drawings and sculptures and novelties. To him, having sex with Nana was as much an intellectual experience as a physical one. And, of course, it had its own twisted and mysterious aspects which gave him a unique pleasure beyond all normal description. Sometimes it was like being slithered over, naked, by snakes. At other times it was like being electrocuted. It was invariably so intense that he felt as it came toward its crescendo that he could no longer remain conscious. He always did, however, blindingly conscious, and he always craved to do it again.

'Enzo,' whispered Nana, as if she were in pain. Then she cried '*Enzo*' and her voice was as deep as a man's.

Enzo heard the carriage clock beside the bed click slightly and its chiming mechanism begin to whirr. It was almost eleven o'clock now, split seconds away from the hour. Enzo flickered the tip of his tongue as quickly as a hummingbird's wings, and just as delicately. Nana rotated her hands around her nipples faster and faster, but at last she could bear the swelling sensation no longer, and she jammed her fingernails deeply into her flesh and screamed out loud a scream that was scarlet as flags, scarlet as flames, scarlet as firetrucks, scarlet as blood.

Eleven o'clock began to strike. Nana cried, 'Ah – ah – ah – ah – ah!' and thrashed uncontrollably on the sheets. Enzo, untouched by any stimulus except what was happening both here and on Honore Street, fell flat on to his back with his eyes wide open, like a fifteenth-century pilgrim struck by a holy vision, and released fountain after fountain of leaping liquid pearl.

At the identical instant, Ambrogio lifted his .45 automatic in both hands, and fired into the side of the wooden privy, at about the height of a man's head, if that man were seated. There was a deafening bang and a cloud of blue smoke, and the bullet tore a hole right through the privy from one side to the other and left something red that looked like gristle or sinew hanging from the far hole. Ambrogio fired again and again and again, until the Negroes on the back porches held their hands over their ears, and Ambrogio's own ears were singing with the noise. The privy was punched and splintered and broken, and fragments whirling in all directions.

Ambrogio fired five times in all, and then approached the privy with the automatic hanging down by his side. Smoke and dust drifted away. A distant radio sang about 'the pee-kle in the mee-dle and the mustard on the top.' Ambrogio wrenched open the privy door, and peered inside. The sunlight shone through the bullet holes, and illuminated the slumped and bloodied figure of Carlo Aceto, exactly as he would appear on the front page of tomorrow's *Star*.

Three small Negro children and their brown mongrel dog came up to Ambrogio and stood staring at him in awe. Ambrogio tucked away his .45, buttoned up his coat, and then reached into his pants pocket for a handful of loose change. He picked out three dimes, and handed one to each of the children in turn. Then he reached into another pocket, and took out a small paper poke of aniseed balls, tossing a handful into the air for the dog to catch.

He walked back to the Nash, found his keys, started up the engine, and backed out of Outhouse Alley, waving in a friendly way to an old Negro woman who stepped back with her basket of washing to let him past. Lieutenant Dan Sorensen of the 9th Precinct remarked later that morning how wonderful it was that nearly ninety people were standing on their back porches or hanging out their washing or playing with their kids, all within thirty yards of Carlo Aceto's shooting, and yet not one of them saw or heard anything at all noteworthy, except for one toothless old man who admitted 'I might of hayed a car back-farrin.'

Walter stood in the gallery of Enzo's apartment, his eyes wide, his brandy glass clutched tight in his hand. He had heard Nana scream, and shout out, and was wondering if he ought to put his shoulder to the door and rescue her from

Enzo's bedroom, or call the police, or knock back his drink and make a run for it before Enzo did the same to him.

Carmino opened the door again. 'Is everything all right, Mr Dempsey?'

'Did – did you hear that? That wasn't my imagination, was it?' Walter asked him.

'I beg your pardon?'

Walter stared at him, with his mouth hanging open. Then he slowly sat down. He was beginning to understand that he might have made a fool of himself. He sipped his brandy twice, then swallowed the whole of the rest of the glassful in one. For some reason he couldn't completely understand, he had a sense of dread.

Enzo stood by the window wrapping himself up in blue silk dragons. Nana lay back on the pillows watching him through slitted eyes.

'Why don't you come back to bed?' she murmured. 'Come back to bed, and put your obelisk in my Colosseum.' She giggled at her own cleverness in using one of Enzo's classical euphemisms.

'I am satisfied,' said Enzo. There was a stony quality in his voice which discouraged any further discussion on the subject.

'You know something,' said Nana, slowly rubbing her bare thighs together in a circular movement, 'you are closer to a god than any man I have ever met.'

'God the father,' he said, and smiled to himself, because she would never understand what he meant, and she would never understand why he was so satisfied. Her ignorance in fact was part of his satisfaction. She would never know that she had been made to climax this morning at the very instant when a man had been killed; and that for Enzo the stimulation had been that he personally had orchestrated both acts. The 'little death' and the real death, both at once.

Nana would never know that sixteen years and seventeen days ago, on the day that she was born, Enzo had sent her mother an envelope containing $2,000 in cash, with the promise of $5,000 more when she reached her sixteenth birthday. All that her mother had been asked to do was call Enzo on the very morning when Nana was sixteen, and let him know where she could be found. As it happened, she had been working as a waitress in Siebens Brewery on Larrabee

Street on the North Side, and living with a girlfriend's family two blocks a way.

In a way, Enzo had a right to know where Nana was, because in common with every one of the five girls with whom he was presently practicing his regular sexual rituals (not *too* frequently, of course, the anticipation was always the thing) Nana was his daughter.

16

Lunch at Weatherwood that afternoon was congested with misery. The family sat around the large oval dining table, spread with a snow-white cloth that looked to Morgana as wide and as icy as Chignik Bay in winter. Howard sat at one end of the table, speaking only when he was spoken to, and leaving it to Winton Snell to carve the roast ribs of beef. Eleanor sparkled with self-destructive humor, her voice rising high and tight, chatting and flirting with John and Bradley, while Morgana and Phoebe sat opposite each other, exchanging looks that varied from ironic to highly alarmed to downright despairing. Morgana was reminded of the opening of *Anna Karenina*, 'All happy families resemble one another, each unhappy family is unhappy in its own way.'

Outside the French windows, the garden was bright, but the dining room had always been gloomy. Above the sideboard there were oil paintings of Walter Beedy, who had built Weatherwood, and his choked bride Doris; both unsmiling; both dressed in black, as if they were in mourning for their own impending deaths.

Morgana was dressed in black too: a wide-shouldered Norell suit with a spray of diamonds on the lapel. Phoebe wore a silk summer dress by Anne Miller in green. Eleanor wore white.

Eleanor said, 'You and John are going down to the clinic this afternoon, then, to see that little Negro girl?'

Morgana reached for the pepper. 'Momsy, I've told you that twenty-eight times if I've told you once.'

'Twenty-eight times? Is that all? Usually you tell me a hundred at least. No thank you, Millicent, no squash for me. Somebody once told me that there is a vitamin in squash which can make a person unnaturally elated. Howard? What do you think? It wouldn't do for any of us to become unnaturally elated, would it?'

Howard looked up from his plate, and focused on Eleanor as if she were a distant ship. 'Elated?'

Bradley, blinking, transferring his fork from one hand to the other and then back again, said, 'You are what you eat, you know, that's true. There are pretty strict health department controls on what we put into Ham-I-Yam. For instance we're only permitted a certain proportion of cereal or bone or coloring.'

'Bradley, I'm eating my lunch,' John complained. 'The very *name* Ham-I-Yam as far as I'm concerned is an emetic. Particularly since I happened to read the full grisly transcript of *State of Illinois vs Clarke Meat Processors, Inc., 1937*.'

'That was all a misunderstanding,' said Bradley, his ears glowing aggressively.

'It was a misunderstanding that fifty-six pig carcasses riddled with cancer were ground up and canned and sold to the public as premium-quality luncheon meat?'

'I didn't know you used coloring,' put in Eleanor, trying to steer the subject away.

John humphed in amusement. 'Coloring? Of course they use coloring! You don't think that if you mush up pigs' lungs and pigs' livers and rendered-down trotter jelly and boiled-off tail meat – you don't think that stuff is going to turn out pink, do you? That's gray, that stuff, when it comes oozing out of the mincers. It looks the same color and consistency as pulped newspaper. They *have* to color it. Would you eat anything *gray?*'

'Oh, for God's sake,' said Phoebe. 'This is all too revolting for words.'

Eleanor said, 'Well ... I suppose one ought not to close one's eyes to such things. You're going to make a fine lawyer, John! If I were in the jury, I think I would have convicted Ham-I-Yam without any hesitation whatsoever! Five years in Joliet, no parole, and a steady diet of Ham-I-Yam morning, noon, and night.'

'Now, you're being very unfair here, Mrs Croft Tate, if you'll forgive my saying so,' Bradley began. But Howard raised his hand and although he said nothing it was quite clear that he didn't want to hear any more about meat packing.

'Let me just say this,' Bradley added. 'Why don't you all come up to the factory one day and I'll show you around it personally. How would you like that? And maybe some lunch afterwards, in the executive dining room.'

'So long as it isn't Ham-I-Yam,' John replied.

Eleanor cut the tiniest piece of beef, and chewed it over and over and over, as if she found it impossible to swallow. Howard prodded a roasted potato around the rim of his plate. Phoebe glanced up at Morgana and fixed her mouth in a ghastly smile, like Lon Chaney playing the Phantom of the Opera.

Morgana said to her father, 'How was his honor?'

'Kenneth?' Howard queried. 'Oh, Kenneth was just the same. Gallarous.'

'Garrulous,' Morgana corrected him. 'What was he being garrulous about?'

Howard shrugged, and put down his knife and fork. 'Slum clearance, that's his latest hobbyhorse. He wants to start tearing down the Near South Side.'

'Well, good for him,' said Morgana.

'It's not as easy as that,' Howard replied. He sipped his red wine, and wiped his mouth with his napkin.

'It's not as easy as what?'

'As knocking down buildings, that's all. There are all kinds of considerations.'

'Well, such as what?' Morgana wanted to know.

Howard had obviously not intended to get himself drawn into a conversation of any kind. He gave Eleanor an odd, noncommittal look, and then he said, with undisguised impatience, 'All of those buildings have owners. Not all of those owners are enthusiastic about seeing their property taken over and demolished. There's a lot of money involved here, both public and private. There's a lot of political influence, too. Before Kenneth can tear down the Near South Side, he's going to have to tear down fifty years of tradition at City Hall. Not so easy – especially for a mayor who doesn't have too many friends.'

'I thought *you* were his friend,' said Morgana.

Howard took his eyes away from Eleanor for the first time and looked carefully at his elder daughter. 'I am,' he said.

'Then why don't you support him? Why doesn't the *Star* support him?'

'Because the time isn't right. Because the public are going to be asked to throw good money after bad. Because Kenneth hasn't yet worked out what he's going to do, and how he's going to do it. You know Kenneth. An Irish firecracker. Full of noise, but not so hot when it comes to getting the sparks to fly.'

'Nice metaphor, Mr Croft Tate,' John remarked, cutting into his inch-thick rib.

But Morgana said, 'Don't you think the *Star* ought to be doing everything it possibly can to get those slums cleared away? I mean – when *is* the time going to be right? And surely it's costing much more now in terms of human degradation than any amount of public taxes could ever add up to? Popsy – we've *got* to say something!'

Howard was silent for a moment. Then he said, 'I think I've already made it quite clear that the *Star* is not going to be carrying any editorial material on the question of clearing slums. It's a legal and a political morass, the whole thing, and I don't happen to want the *Star* to get caught up in it. What's more, it doesn't sell papers. It's not a subject that Chicagoans want to read about, especially our advertisers. If you want it in terms of bald figures, we're now 11,000 short of beating the *Tribune* out of the top circulation spot. I don't want to jeopardize Grant's chances of beating them out simply for the sake of one unpopular topic.'

'One unpopular topic?' Morgana demanded, and slapped the flat of her hand on to the tablecloth. 'Popsy, you're talking about people's whole lives!'

'Young lady, I'm not talking about anything,' Howard retorted. 'This whole question is closed, as far as I'm concerned. We report the news, we don't invent it. And we don't abuse our public trust by using our newspapers and our radio stations to push our own social prejudicials down people's throats.'

'Prejudices,' Morgana corrected him. 'And since when? The *Star* was screaming for Doyle in 1947, and so were all our radio stations. And what about all this business of putting up rail freight charges? The *Star*'s been ranting on about it for weeks, just because Buddy Mullet of the Chicago & North Western Railroad happens to have nominated you on to the board.'

Howard looked as if he were about to detonate. He was gripping the edge of the table with his left hand and Morgana could feel the whole table top shuddering. There were teardrop pendants on the Tiffany silver and crystal cruet in the center of the tablecloth, and they began to tinkle, as if an earth tremor were imminent.

Eleanor said, in an English-toffee voice, 'Morgana, I think you ought to apologize to your father.'

Morgana turned back toward her father, but Howard slowly shook his head from side to side. 'I don't want an apology, thank you. I've learned enough about the women in my family this weekend to understand that they wound without any kind of conscience, whether they say they're sorry or not. If you say you're sorry, my dear, I'm not going to believe you, I'm just going to eat my lunch and pretend to myself that what I heard from you was nothing but somebody's knife squeaking on their plate.'

With that, he picked up his fork and began steadily to eat, his eyes lowered, leaving everybody else to stare at each other in embarrassment.

Bradley was the first to break the silence. He said, 'Phoebe and me were thinking of driving out to see the Palmers this afternoon. They're having some kind of tennis tournament. Well, amateur of course; but Margaret Osborne duPont is going to be there, you know, just for fun, to give us a few pointers.'

'How sensitive you men are,' said Eleanor, and for a moment nobody understood that she was replying to Howard's outburst against women; and that she had not been listening to Bradley at all. She raised her eyes, and looked directly at Howard, and said, 'You torture your wives day after day, night after night, without even a thought for their continuing agony. And yet one scratch on your precious skin, and the howls!'

'Eleanor, I'm telling you here and now to stop,' Howard commanded her.

'Momsy, please,' said Morgana. 'I know you're both feeling upset, but please.'

Eleanor pressed her napkin against her mouth, and said, 'Excuse me,' and abruptly left the table. Howard didn't make any move to stop her, even when she passed him close by. Phoebe said, 'I think I'll go see what's wrong with mother,' but Howard said hoarsely, 'You'll stay where you are. We're having lunch.'

Phoebe looked toward Morgana appealingly, but Morgana quickly mouthed 'no.' The family was right on the brink of falling apart; and even though Morgana knew that she was just as much to blame as either her father or her mother, she didn't want today's lunch to split them up any further.

John said, 'My mother once played with Pauline Betz. My mother's a real ace at tennis. And bridge, too. An absolute killer at bridge.'

Phoebe said, 'I've always wanted to arm-wrestle. You know, in the Yukon, with bearded men in red flannel long johns whose names are Pierre the Merde.'

Morgana closed her knife and fork together. She had scarcely eaten anything. Howard continued to chew his beef with offended stolidity, his eyes fixed on the Croft Tate crest on the rim of his plate, and the atmosphere in the dining room was so chilly and hostile that none of them could do anything but sit and look at each other and pray that lunch would soon be over.

Bradley said to Phoebe, with the brightness born of sheer desperation, 'Your father owns the *Star*, and you can make a grammatical blooper like that?'

Phoebe said, tautly, 'Like *what*, Bradley?'

Bradley sniggered. 'Like, "men in red flannel long johns whose names are Pierre the Merde." I mean, what you're saying is that their long johns are called Pierre the Merde. Not *them*, their long johns.'

'Oh God, Bradley,' said Phoebe.

'I'm sorry,' Bradley sniggered.

Howard took a very long time finishing his beef. No clock ticked; there were no clocks in the dining room. All four of them watched every mouthful that Howard cut for himself in painful fascination. When he had nothing left on his plate but the gravy *au jus*, he broke pieces of bread roll and mopped it up until his plate was completely clean. When he was a boy, his father used to cuff him viciously if he didn't finish everything on his plate.

Millicent came in and asked asked if they wanted the prune pie or the cranberry sherbet. They wanted neither; but Howard asked for the prune pie, and so they nodded and smiled with faces like Hallowe'en masks and all asked for a small slice of the same, with cream.

John said, 'I plan to go to Colorado this winter. You know, for the skiing. I didn't ski at all last year because of my exams.'

Phoebe said, 'Really? I love to ski. Morgana hates it. Maybe you should take me with you, instead of her.'

John laughed. Morgana didn't like the sound of that laugh at all; nor did she like the idea of what he was laughing at. Millicent served out the prune pie and they all sat in silence and looked at it. Howard started to eat his slice with belligerent steadiness. At that moment, however, Winton Snell came gliding into the dining room on patent-leather feet, and bent himself down to Howard's right ear, his hand cupped, and whispered, 'The telephone, sir. Mr Mmhm-Hmhm.'

'Who?' queried Howard, out loud, coughing a fragment of pastry out of his throat.

'Mr Mmhm-Hmhm, sir,' said Winton, and then straightened himself up a little, and allowed his eyebrows to rise slowly up his forehead, to make sure that Howard had understood him.

Howard twisted his napkin out of his shirt collar, and tossed it on to the dining table. He scraped his chair back, and said to nobody in particular, 'You'll pardon me,' and walked out of the dining room. Morgana and Phoebe and John and Bradley were left alone with the funereal portraits of Walter and Doris Beedy and their platefuls of prune pie.

'Well,' breathed John.

'I'm sorry,' said Morgana. 'It was all my fault.'

John smiled at her winningly. 'If you say you're sorry my dear,' he mimicked, 'I'm not going to believe you. I'm just going to pretend that it was somebody squeaking their knife on their plate.'

Phoebe said, 'This is dire. And my God, I can't tell you how much I detest prune pie.'

'If you don't like it, don't eat it,' said Bradley.

'Oh, yes?' Phoebe challenged him. 'And top off the day's disasters by making the cook quit? Alice is absolutely the most domineering cook since, I don't know, Fannie Farmer.'

'For goodness' sake don't *panic*,' said John. 'This is all very easily fixed. Does anybody else dislike prune pie? Hands up who dislikes prune pie?'

All of them put up their hands.

'Okay,' said John. He took out a quarter, and flipped it up. 'We're going to toss a coin, and whoever loses has to smuggle the prune pie out. If Bradley or I lose, we have to put it in our pockets. If you or Phoebe lose, you have to carry it in your purses. Is that agreed?'

Morgana called against Bradley. 'Heads!' she cried, and John snapped his hand away from the coin and it was heads. Phoebe called against Bradley. 'Tails!' she cried, and it was tails. 'Now it's the two of us,' John grinned. 'Do you want to call?' Bradley called, 'Heads! I mean tails!' and it was heads.

'Darn it to hell,' said Bradley.

'Stand up, my man,' John ordered him, soberly.

Bradley stood up and one by one they scraped their dessert plates into his held-open pockets. As a final touch, John took out Bradley's breast-pocket handkerchief, and replaced it with a neat triangle of pie. Bradley peered down at it in disgust.

'Are we all finished?' said Morgana. 'Right now, let's wait for Popsy. Phoebe — would you ring for Millicent? We might as well have some coffee while we're waiting.'

John leaned forward on the table, displaying his starched white cuffs and his Chicago Club cufflinks, and asked Morgana in a very lawyerish way, 'There's nothing wrong between your mother and your father, is there? It does seem to me that things are — well, hot-tin-roofy.'

'I'll tell you later,' said Morgana, and extinguished John's next question with a warning look.

Bradley complained nasally, 'This pie feels disgusting. It's soaking through to my lining.'

'I'm sorry, old man, you lost the toss. You have to take the consequences.'

Howard had taken the telephone call in the study. He hadn't known exactly who it was. He had several friends and business acquaintances whom Winton always introduced as 'Mr Mmhm-Hmhm.' Howard was no special friend of the Mob, but it was almost impossible to be wealthy and influential and a Democrat and a regular negotiator with typographical unions and not have some day-to-day dealings with those whom Kenneth Doyle usually described as the 'Knights of Canneloni.'

The voice on the telephone was silky and distinctive.

'Good afternoon, Howard. Did I disturb your lunch?'

Howard wiped his mouth with his handkerchief. 'That's all right, Enzo. I was almost finished up anyway.'

'I wanted to congratulate you, Howard. That's a spiritied daughter you have there.'

'Well, I just hope she wasn't rude.'

'Not at all. I enjoy a girl with a mind of her own.'

Howard said, 'What can I do for you, Enzo?'

'How is your charming wife?'

'She's well, thank you, Enzo.'

'Good, good. You have a wife in a million, Howard. There are many men who would commit serious crimes, just to have a wife like yours.'

'I hope that's a joke,' said Howard.

Enzo chuckled. 'I called about Kenneth, as a matter of fact.'

'Kenneth? What about him?'

'Have you seen him recently?'

'I played golf with him yesterday afternoon. What of it?'

Enzo sniffed sharply. 'Did he happen by any chance to broach the subject of housing with you?'

'As a matter of fact yes. It was just about all he talked about.'

'He is starting some kind of a drive to clear up the South Side, yes? And he is asking the newspapers and the radio stations and the television people to help him? Is this so?'

'In essence, yes,' said Howard.

'Well, I have been given information about this,' said Enzo. 'But, you know, it would be very unfortunate if Kenneth were allowed to have his head. Kenneth is Irish, you know. He doesn't understand economics. He doesn't understand good business. Good business is low overheads, low maintenance costs, and a product which you can sell over and over again and it still belongs to you. That's why prostitution is good business. In fact, prostitution is even better business than being a landlord. If I wasn't such a moral man, Howard, I might almost be tempted.'

Howard didn't like conversations like this. He knew that Enzo was needling him, playing with him, and he didn't enjoy having his one serious vulnerability swung backwards and forwards in front of his face as if it were a dead kitten.

'You want to get to the point?' he asked Enzo.

'There is no point,' said Enzo. Howard could tell that he was smiling. 'All I wanted to do was to reassure myself that the *Star* would not be supporting Kenneth Doyle; nor would any of your radio stations.'

Howard ran his hand wearily through his hair. 'Did you have to ask?'

'I always like to make sure, Howard. I always like to double check.'

'Well, there's no need.'

'This makes me feel comfortable, Howard. This will also make Marcella feel comfortable. The best love that a man can give is the love that costs him dear. You know who said that?'

'Is that everything, Enzo?'

Enzo let out a thin, mannered sigh. 'You are not a man for idle conversation, are you, Howard? Perhaps that's why I like you so much. I love to see the pressure inside you, always trying to burst out. You are a good man.'

'Marcella's okay?' asked Howard, glancing up toward the half-open library door to make sure that nobody was listening outside.

'Marcella is an angel like her mother. She is coming out to the track today. So is that drunken sport reporter of yours, the one who keeps falling over and vomiting and offending every lady he meets.'

'You mean Walter.'

'Yes, Walter. If I didn't love you so much, my friend Howard, I would never allow him anywhere near me. Marcella calls him the Tower of Pisa, because he's always leaning over sideways. Quite a clever girl, don't you think?'

Howard said nothing. He saw Millicent carrying a tray of coffee past the library door, and then Winton peeped in and gave him a courteous wave that was simply an inquiry that 'all's well?'

Enzo said, 'Strictly between you and me, Howard, I have to tell you that Kenneth isn't going to be staying in office too much longer. I don't mean that anybody's going to do a Tony Cermak on him, but the man doesn't have what it takes. This city is a big city and it needs a boss, not a parish priest.'

Howard took the reference to Tony Cermak seriously. Cermak had been elected mayor of Chicago after the decline and fall of 'Big Bill' Thompson; but he had been shot and fatally wounded while visiting Florida with President-elect Roosevelt in 1933. The official explanation for the shooting of Mayor Cermak had been that the assassin Giuseppe Zangara had been aiming for the president-elect, and missed. But it was common knowledge in Chicago that Zangara was one of Enzo Vespucci's plug-uglies; and afterwards Enzo had quietly let it be known that any future attempts by City Hall to regulate his private affairs would be similarly dealt with.

Enzo had always been courteous, however: he had sent to Mayor Cermak's funeral the largest wreath of all. A pushcart made of chrysanthemums.

Howard said, 'You're going to have to be careful, Enzo. And, believe me, that's not a friendly warning. Kenneth is a friend of mine, and I believe in what he's doing. If I've agreed to keep quiet on this slum-clearance business, that's one thing. But that doesn't mean I'm going to tolerate anything like that Cermak nonsense.'

'Howard, Howard, not so angry,' Enzo chided him. 'Everything's going to be fine. So long as I know that Kenneth is going to be out on his own.'

'Well you know that Colonel McCormick won't support him. Colonel McCormick wouldn't support him if he were Christ Almighty.'

'Colonel McCormick is a weasel's bladder,' said Enzo. 'There is only one great newspaper publisher in the mid-West, Howard, and you know what his name is. Howard Croft Tate!'

Howard returned to the dining room to find Morgana and Phoebe and John and Bradley drinking coffee and talking about Communism. John was accusing Bradley of being a 'parlor pinko' because he believed in Government intervention to keep meat prices up; Bradley was accusing John of being a 'ring-knocker', somebody who flashed his fraternity status at every possible opportunity.

'Everything all right, sir?' John asked Howard, boldly, as Howard sat down.

Howard allowed the side of his mouth to tip up slightly in acknowledgement. 'Everything's fine, thank you.'

Morgana reached across the table and touched her father's hand. She said nothing; she couldn't think of anything that would mitigate his distress. But she tried to show him by the look in her eyes that she still loved him.

'Was that anybody special?' asked Phoebe, scraping her pie plate with her spoon to make it appear as if she had finished her dessert completely.

'Special?' asked Howard. He shook his head. 'No, that was just ...' He paused, and cut off a piece of pie, and then said, 'A man about an airplane. You know, ever since Bert McCormick bought that B-17 and turned it into a private office ... well, I've been thinking we ought to do the same. You know, a question of status. If the *Tribune* can have its own airliner, then so can the *Star*. There's a DC-3 out at Orchard Place. I thought maybe that Grant and me could go take a look at it next week.'

'That would be marvelous!' Phoebe enthused. 'We could have dance-parties in the air!'

'Bring a bottle and a parachute,' grinned John.

'Society Sisters Fly High,' said Phoebe, headlining again.

Howard tried to smile, but Morgana, when she looked back at him, suddenly realized that he was in pain. His eyes had started to water, and he was wiping them with his fingers. His mouth was puckered up in an unsuccessful attempt to hide his grief.

'Popsy ...' she said.

'Nothing, nothing,' he told her, shaking his head. 'Just a piece of pie went down the wrong pipe. If you could just pass me the water jug, and maybe ...' he patted his pockets '... could I borrow your handkerchief, Bradley?'

Bradley said, '*Ah*,' and sat up straight in his seat, but he was too late to stop Howard from reaching out toward his breast pocket and pinching the slice of prune pie between finger and thumb.

Howard took his hand away from Bradley's pocket, and peered shortsightedly at his prune-stained fingertips. Then he leaned forward, and patted the front of Bradley's coat.

'Bradley,' he said, 'you have dessert in your pocket.'

'Yes, sir.'

Morgana handed her father one of her own lace-trimmed handkerchiefs, and he wiped his eyes with that, but he kept on staring at Bradley with relentless curiosity. Bradley was bright pink in the face, and sweating.

At length, however, Howard finished his own dessert, and drank his coffee, and excused them all from the table. Morgana waited behind after the others had gone through to the long conservatory, and laid her hand on her father's shoulder.

'Momsy told me all about it,' she said.

Howard nodded. 'I was hoping that she would. She needs to talk about it.'

'Do you think you two are going to be able to get over it?' asked Morgana. 'You know – forgive and forget?'

'I don't know. It goes a little deeper than that.'

They linked arms and walked out of the dining room toward the conservatory. Morgana said, 'You can forgive her, can't you? I wouldn't like to see you two fall apart.'

Howard said, 'I do love your mother. I want you to know that. I just don't know how I could cope with things if I found out that she didn't love me.'

'Oh, Pops, I'm sure she still loves you. The way she talks about you, I don't think there's any question of that at all.'

They had reached a leaded window which gave them a view out of the parquet-floored corridor into the gardens around the conservatory. Howard stopped for a moment, and shaded his eyes, so that he could see out over the lawns. Bradley was standing by the ornamental pond, surrounded by ducks. He was scooping prune pie out of his pockets and feeding it to them in handfuls.

'I wonder what the hell that boy's up to?' Howard mused. 'Are they eccentric, his family, do you know? I'm not sure that I want Phoebe getting herself all tied up with a boy who puts dessert in his pockets.'

Morgana kissed her father's cheek. She hoped and prayed that he and her mother could be reconciled. But she wondered why he had lied about the airplane. She had overheard him talking about it much earlier this morning to Wendell Wiley, and he had been emphatic that he didn't want it. Who could have called him during lunch and upset him so much? Who in the world apart from her mother could make him cry?

17

Harry came into the newsroom shortly after one o'clock, carrying a crumpled brown bag of bologna and pickle sandwiches that his mother had made for him, and which he hadn't yet had time to eat. He carried his coat over his shoulder, his finger hooked into the tag. His fedora was perched on the back of his head and his palm-tree tie was tugged loose.

Monday's first edition was almost completed. Reporters, rewrite men and copy editors were bent over their desks, some of them almost invisible in the smoke from eighty cigarettes burning at once. Gordon McLintock was over on the far side of the office, talking to Busby Brill about the front-page story HACKER WILL STRIKE AGAIN! Busby had taken over the homicide of Mrs Anne Leonidas as soon as he had arrived at the office this morning, and he had immediately sent his four crime staff scurrying to all points of the compass. He was still bitter about the way in which the *Tribune*'s veteran police reporter James Gavin had so thoroughly scooped him on the George Heirens homicide case three years ago. Heirens had been another hacker: murdering one woman on Kenmore Avenue, shooting and beating several others, stabbing and shooting another woman on Pine Grove Avenue, before kidnaping and completely dismembering a six-year-old girl called Suzanne Degnan.

Busby had sent his greenest young girl reporter Jenny Crowe to talk to one of the detectives who had worked on the Heirens case. This detective had told her solemnly, 'This was ritual murder and if I know anything about ritual murder you're going to get more. So single women had better bolt their doors including you, tootsie.'

Harry hung up his coat, saying hi to David Tribe, who was hunched over his typewriter in the next pigpen, his glasses on the tip of his nose, writing up a fatal road crash at Elk Grove, two truck drivers burned to death. Harry sat down, and opened up his sandwich bag, taking out a doorstep of rye bread, and biting into it hungrily. He was tired, too. He had been up since six o'clock. First of all he had interviewed Alex Leonidas, the dead woman's husband, who had been friendly and talkative and completely unhelpful, drinking beer out of the bottle ('this is breakfast, see? better than four platefuls of Post Toasties any time') and patting the huge fat-pillowed thighs of his Greek girlfriend while he chatted ('Anne, you know, well what can I say, she musta had it comin'). Then he had run down Mrs Leonidas' last-known lover John Kavanagh, who had sat in his single room in Calumet with his thin arms crossed on the green oilcloth tabletop in front of him, saying almost nothing and refusing to turn off the radio while Harry asked him questions.

Harry zipped a piece of copy paper into his typewriter, and began to hammer away at it, still chewing away at his sandwich. There really wasn't much to write, but he knew that Gordon expected a full description of Alex Leonidas and John Kavanagh, right down to their socks, even if he never ran it in the paper.

Downstairs, nineteen floors below the newsroom, nearly fifty young women were clattering away at varitypers, which were like typewriters except that they justified the columns of news both left and right. These columns were taken away to be cut out and pasted on to page forms of the *Star*, and then photographed and engraved on to stereotype plates. Normally, all of the typesetting in the *Star* would have been set on Linotype machines in hot metal, but local No. 16 of the Chicago Typographical Union had been on strike since November, 1947; obliging all the major newspapers to set their type photographically.

Colonel Robert McCormick of the *Tribune* had said that he didn't care how long the strike went on; Marshall Field III who owned the *Sun-Times* was equally determined not to be blackmailed; and Howard's views on typographical unions were legendary. So far, the strike showed no signs of breaking, or being broken.

Harry typed,

> hacker 1 hs
> Twenty-seven-year-old Alex Leonidas, the victim's estranged husband, sd ystdy at his walk-up apt o Green-st, 'Anne ws a gd wife and a gd mother b

Opposite Harry, in a pigpen decorated with astral calendars, Peter Donleavy was typing out the last of Monday's horoscopes. Peter was a young wavy-haired history graduate from the University of Michigan, who had always yearned to be a journalist. Out of sympathy, Grant had given him a part-time job writing 'Your Stars In The Star', under the byline of Madame Tzizane. He was allowed five lines for each horoscope, no more, and since there were thirty characters in each line, he simply typed a row of thirty dots at the top of his sheet of paper, and wrote his copy underneath the dots to fit.

> ....
> ARIES * Somebody close to you
> will cause you to question their
> loyalty. Beware of money-saving
> offers. You will receive news
> midweek that will make you happy.

Peter counted the characters on the last line under his breath, decided that two 'ms' and two 'ws' made it a little too tight, in spite of two 'ls' and two 'is', and crossed out 'happy' and substituted 'sad.' On such considerations was the daily destiny of a million Chicagoans decided.

Next to Peter sat John Sebastian, who wrote the *Star*'s weather. John had been taught at a Jesuit school, and he headed every page of copy AMDG, which were the Latin initials of the Jesuit motto, 'to the greater glory of God'. At the foot of each page he typed LDS – 'praise to God always'. Gordon McLintock had not forbidden him to do so, but any copy editor who let those initials slip into the paper's weather report knew that he would face the full fury of a Gordon McLintock temper.

Harry was still typing when Busby Brill came over and leaned against the side of his pigpen. 'Sharpe by name and sharp by nature, is that it?' he asked, lighting a cigarette.

Harry took another bite of his sandwich and propped it on

the edge of his desk. 'Two minutes, Busby, and you can have everything I know.'

Busby watched him through narrowed eyes. Busby was small and brisk and vain, with oiled-back hair and bulbous eyes and a toad-like mouth, Edward G. Robinson's smooth-talking brother. He wore a green hound's-tooth suit and tan-colored shoes and a green necktie which proclaimed him to be a member of the Lake Forest Yacht Club, although he had never sailed in anything more sporting than a ferry from Milwaukee, Wis., to Ludington, Mich. He was good, though. He knew all the gangsters and all the cops and all the fingerprint men and all the coroner's assistants, and somehow because of his sheer repulsiveness he was acceptable to all of them.

Busby had scooped the *Tribune*'s police reporters again and again. Only the Heirens case still stuck between his teeth. It was obvious to Harry that if he managed to solve the murder of Mrs Leonidas, his pride might at last be restored. Pride meant a lot to Busby Brill.

'You could have called me,' said Busby, watching Harry finish his copy.

'Sure, yes, I could.'

'Then why didn't you?'

'Because you were off duty. Because you were at home, doing whatever it is you do when you're at home. Yachting, or whatever.'

Busby sucked at his cigarette, and let the smoke escape from between clenched teeth. 'This was a ritual murder, right? You should have called me.'

'I didn't know it was a ritual murder until I saw it, and when I'd seen it I wished I hadn't. So don't get any ideas about my leaning over to mop the gravy up off of your plate. This kind of gravy you can keep.'

Harry tugged his copy out of his typewriter and handed it to Busby with an exaggerated flourish. 'They're not guilty, either of them. Well, maybe Kavanagh could have done it, but the police don't seem to think so and neither do I. He was too introspective. He was more interested in himself than he was in her. Besides, he didn't look as if he had the strength. He had arms like a stick insect.'

'Better than having brains like a stick insect,' remarked Busby, leafing disdainfully through Harry's three folios of copy.

Harry took another big bite of sandwich, and chewed it stolidly. 'Do you know something?' he asked Busby, as he swallowed, once, and then again, 'there's an old Polish saying. Do you want to hear it?'

Busby flicked Harry's copy with his middle finger, so that the paper cracked loudly, and said, 'If your old Polish sayings are anything like your old Polish copy, then forget it.'

'No, no, you should hear this. My father was always saying it. "He who goes digging for gold up his own ass should beware of taking a sharp shovel."'

Busby stared at him. 'You're crazy, you know that? But let me tell you this. That story you wrote about the Leonidas killing was first rate. One hundred percent. I couldn't have written it better myself. But don't expect me to repeat myself, and don't expect me to say that to anybody else. You're damned good, and you're a crazy Polack.'

Without saying anything else, Busby walked back to his pigpen, leaving Harry at his desk swallowing the last few fragments of rye bread and wondering if the end of the world were imminent. That was something that Jack Wollensky had said, a couple of months ago: if you ever got praise from Busby Brill, that meant the end of the world was imminent. David Tribe stopped typing and took off his glasses and looked at Harry with a mixture of pity and deep respect.

At five after two, Harry drove his Woodie out of the *Star* parking lot. Tomahawk Billy came over to open the barrier for him, and Harry saluted and tossed him a pack of Red Man tobacco. Tomahawk Billy caught the tobacco and examined it, stone faced.

'Is this some kind of joke?' he demanded, in accents as solid as granite.

'Joke? What joke? White people like to chew this, just as much as Indians.'

'You are man of shit,' said Tomahawk Billy, but pocketed the tobacco all the same.

Harry drove out on Lake Shore Drive and Sheridan Road to Winnetka, the lake twinkling on his right, the sky as white and neutral as a fluorescent lamp. It was two thirty by the time he turned off by Elder Lane Park toward Indian Hill Golf Club and the Crown Park Training Track, and drove up a dusty sloping road until he reached the white-painted bleachers and the green-painted stable block. Enzo Vespucci's

Cadillac was parked nearby, as well as a Chrysler Royal station wagon with 'Crown Park Stables' emblazoned on the doors. There was also a pre-war Buick convertible in bright gold, with the top down. Harry parked next to it, and then sat in his Woodie for a while, and lit a cigarette.

Eventually a short square man with a flour-white face and shoulders like a linebacker came walking over and rapped on the window of his Woodie with blue-scarred knuckles. Harry wound down the window, allowing the cigarette smoke to escape.

'Yes?' he asked.

'Dis is private proppidy,' the man told him, in the catarrhal voice of a boxer.

'I know that,' said Harry. 'I was supposed to be meeting somebody here.'

'Oh yeah? Who are you?'

Harry took out his press card. The man examined it with a frown, his lips moving as he read the name. At last he handed the card back and said, 'Repawduh, hunh?'

'Dat's right,' Harry mimicked him. 'Noospapuh repawduh.'

The man had no ear for accents, not even his own. 'Who ya supposdah be meetin?' he said, his eyes flicking from side to side, casting around the racetrack for some sudden intruder.

'Miss Morgana Croft Tate. Is she here? She had a date to meet up with Mr Vespucci.'

The man shook his head so that his cauliflower ears waggled. 'No ladies here today, buddy. Only Miss Marcella.'

'Oh,' said Harry. 'Maybe she didn't get here yet. But Mr Vespucci's here, isn't he? That's his car.'

At that moment, Enzo came strolling over, dressed in a hunting jacket and jodhpurs and tall shiny boots, smacking a crop into the palm of his hand as if he were lightly punishing himself for being so intolerably stylish. He was closely followed by Ambrogio, who seemed at peace today, mountainous and scurfy and smiling.

'It's all right, Guido,' said Enzo, waving the boxer away. 'This particular ferret is known to me. How are you doing, Mr Sharpe? Did you come out here for the country air?'

Harry climbed out of the Woodie, and breathed smoke out of his nostrils. 'I thought I'd give myself the Sunday off,' he said. 'You know – just to see how the other half disports itself. Is Miss Croft Tate here yet?'

Enzo smacked his palm with his riding crop, keeping his eyes fixed on Harry's face as if he were concerned that it might suddenly change itself into somebody or something else. 'Miss Croft Tate won't be coming. You want to see my horses? There are six of them here today. The very finest. They were driven up last week from Kentucky. Your friend and associate Mr Walter Dempsey is here. He's going to be writing an article about my horses.' Enzo paused for a moment, and then added, 'When he wakes up.' He began to walk back toward the stable block, and Harry followed him. 'You're sure my station wagon's going to be okay there?' asked Harry. 'That mutt of yours isn't going to try stealing the hubcaps or anything?'

'He's not a Pole,' said Enzo.

Harry sucked hard at the butt of his cigarette. 'We have a saying in Poland. "Don't trust men who look as if they might steal your hubcaps. They probably will."'

'I don't speak the language,' said Enzo, with a tight smile.

'Oh, I'm sorry. It means, don't trust men who look as if they might steal hubcaps. They probably will.'

They reached the stable block. There was a strong smell of freshly cropped hay and horse manure. 'Good for roses,' said Harry, as a stableboy led past an elegant and nervous chestnut mare, which was pouring out droppings with every step. 'I've heard that you can dry it, and smoke it, too. Mind you, I'm not so sure. I might walk a mile for a Camel, but I don't think I'd go more than two or three blocks for a horse.'

Enzo said, 'That mare is called Daughter of Hyperion. She is worth almost half a million dollars.'

Harry whistled. 'Can she run?'

'If she were human, she could dance *Coppelia*.'

As the mare was backed into her stable, she let out a reverberating blast of stomach gas. Harry said, 'I bet she can go like the wind,' and prided himself that he kept a straight face.

Enzo led Harry the length of the stable block, showing off his horses. They were all magnificent; and the finest was a black stallion called Prince of Darkness, bred in Lexington by D. D. Thomas. He stood fifteen hands tall, a furious muscular animal with a coat like poured oil.

'Well, that's some horse,' Harry had to admit. 'It's a pity that animals don't recognize each other; you know, like Prince of Darkness looking at you and recognizing that you're a rat.'

A clear voice said, echoing, 'You mustn't talk to my father like that.'

Harry turned around. A tall girl with a huge mane of curly black hair was walking into the stable block, the heels of her riding boots clicking sharply on the crisscross-patterned tiles. She was silhouetted against the daylight at first, and Harry could scarcely see what she looked like, but then she walked around him and stood facing him, her hands on her hips, as if she were quite ready to fight him to a standstill; or at least to a guarded apology.

She was strikingly handsome, this girl, and in a strange way she reminded Harry of Morgana, except that her skin was more sallow, her hair was thicker and more wiry, and her eyes were intensely dark. Like Enzo, she wore a jacket in hunting pink, and which was tailored to make the most of her heavy Jane Russell breasts; and jodhpurs so tight that Harry could see the subtlest of clefts between her thighs. She looked Italian; her lips were pouting and sensual; and there was an intonation in her voice which reminded Harry of the girl from Naples who used to work Saturday mornings at Zyzniewski's (full-bosomed, puppy-fatted, with dreaming green eyes and an irresistible lisp.) This girl smelled of some heavy and hypnotic perfume like musk and cloves and oil of oranges; and she looked at Harry directly and never took her eyes away from him.

Enzo smiled. 'You haven't met my daughter Marcella.'

Harry said, 'You're right, I haven't, how's tricks?' to Marcella, and then, to Enzo, 'You never told me you were a family man.'

'He's not,' Marcella interrupted. 'My father doesn't believe in families. He is far too selfish for that, aren't you, father? But in the year of 1919 he happened to go to a party given by Governor Lowden, and at that party he happened to meet a beautiful lady from South Bend, Indiana, and two weeks later they went to Reno and got married. My mother always used to blame the champagne. I don't blame anybody.'

'The marriage lasted for seven weeks and two days,' Enzo added. 'Marcella's mother was quite impossible. She used to ride a bicycle around the bedroom, ringing the bell, when I was trying to sleep.'

'Well, well, this is something new,' said Harry. 'How about a feature story on your secret marriage and your undisclosed daughter, Mr Vespucci? Maybe the public will warm to you for once. Or will you break my legs?'

'I'll break your legs,' said Enzo, cheerfully.

Guido came over and said, 'A telephone call for ya, Mr Vespucci. Mr Di Angelo.'

'Ah, yes, Mr Di Angelo,' Enzo said, with exaggerated emphasis. Harry shrugged and made a point of looking the other way, out across the track, as if he were completely uninterested. 'Mr Di Angelo' was unlikely to be anybody but Mike Di Angelo, alias Mike Constant, alias The Neapolitan, one of the Mob's most powerful captains, and the virtual dictator of all vice on the West Side. Enzo took Marcella's hand, and kissed her cheek, and said, 'You'll forgive me, hah?' and went off to take the call. Ambrogio pulled a self-satisfied face and tugged sharply at the lapels of his coat before following his master.

Harry and Marcella were left alone. Harry nodded toward Marcella's hunting jacket, and said, 'You ride?'

'Do you really think I would dress up like this if I didn't?'

Harry offered Marcella a cigarette but she shook her head. 'There used to be a city alderman who dressed up in a tutu, but I never heard that he danced any ballet.'

Marcella smiled. 'I'm going out on the track to try out my horse. Do you want to come?'

'Should I be laying any money on it?'

'One day soon, when it is properly trained. You are a newspaper reporter?'

'Does it show?'

'Perhaps it's the necktie. Only hoodlums and newspaper reporters wear neckties like that. I should be careful what I say, shouldn't I? We have another newspaper reporter here, but he is asleep in one of the stables. I think he is probably drunk.'

Harry couldn't help noticing that Marcella walked with a highly provocative swaying movement, and that the rounded cheeks of her bottom jiggled up and down inside her jodhpurs. He glanced down at her riding boots. He had heard of a trick used by beauty-pageant queens of cutting a quarter inch off one heel, to give themselves an extra-jiggly walk, but Marcella's movement seemed to be natural. He stared at her and she caught him staring at her and they both stopped and looked at each other.

Marcella pointed across the scrubby grass on the track to a wonderfully elegant roan, which was being led toward them on a short rein. 'There, that's my horse. What do you think? Isn't she beautiful? Her name is Secret Kiss.'

'What a romantic family you are,' said Harry. He lit his cigarette, although he would much rather have unwrapped a Baby Ruth. He was hungry and tired and he felt a little nauseated, as if there were grease on the roof of his mouth. He also had a nagging feeling that he would soon have to go for a leak. And apart from which, he was more disappointed than he would have thought possible that Morgana hadn't shown. He watched edgily as Marcella patted her horse's nose, and affectionately slapped its flanks. The stable lad grinned at her like Frankenstein's Igor, a fifteen-year-old boy with a humped shoulder and a seventy-year-old face.

Harry thought to himself: whoever said that you can't judge a book by its cover was talking out of his ass. In his experience, gangsters looked like gangsters and corrupt politicians looked like corrupt politicians and whores looked like whores. He glanced down at his necktie, and added newspaper reporters to the list.

'Hold her still, Kermit,' Marcella said to the stable lad. She took hold of the horse's reins, and turned to Harry. 'How about a leg up, Mr Newspaper Reporter?'

Harry propped his cigarette between his lips and came up close to the horse and cupped his hands together. 'Harry Sharpe,' he said. 'It's short for Sczaniecka.'

Marcella stepped into his hands, and he hoisted her up until she could swing her leg over the saddle and slip her riding boots into the stirrups. 'Thank you, Mr Sharpe,' she told him.

'Well, I know my place,' Harry replied. 'I've only known you five minutes and already I'm offering to let you tread on me.' He slapped the horse's shoulder as if he were used to slapping horses' shoulders. 'This is a nice piece of living vehicle. Did your old man cough up for it?'

'You are far too inquisitive,' she told him, and clicked her tongue, and went cantering off on Secret Kiss toward the other side of the track. Harry shaded his eyes against the overcast glare of the sky and watched her go.

Harry blew out smoke and watched Marcella trotting first one way around the track, then the other. He didn't know anything at all about horses, although he occasionally placed a bet on a runner at Arlington Park; but he thought that Marcella looked remarkable. Straight-backed, chin lifted, her black curls waving in the wind. She may have been Enzo Vespucci's daughter but she had all the class that anybody could have asked for.

Walter Dempsey appeared from the direction of the stable block, blinking and coughing and running his hand through his hair. He caught sight of Harry and obviously couldn't believe his eyes to begin with. But then he came shuffling over, and rested his hand on Harry's shoulder. 'What am I doing here?' he asked.

'You came here to write a piece on Enzo Vespucci's racehorses.'

'Ah, that's it! I'm glad you reminded me. Where are they? Is that girl riding one of them?'

'No, that's Marcella, she's Enzo's daughter. She has her own horse.'

Walter nodded, absentmindedly, and then masked his eyes with his hand and stood stockstill saying nothing for almost a minute. There was no sound but the soft thundering of the wind against their eardrums and the hard tattoo of Secret Kiss' hoofs.

'Something happened and I'm trying to think what it was,' said Walter.

Harry smoked and didn't answer. Walter at last took his hand away from his eyes, and said, 'Something happened, Harry. Something I was going to tell you about. I wish I could just . . . I don't know, my memory's going. Maybe I'm getting too old for this kind of thing.'

At that moment, however, there was a high-pitched whinny from Secret Kiss; and Harry looked across the track and saw the horse rearing right up on its hind legs, its front hoofs thrashing the air. Suddenly it bucked and kicked up again, whinnying and snorting, and Marcella had to clutch it around the neck to save herself from being pitched off.

'Princess! Princess!' Igor cried, and began to scuttle bandy-legged across the turf.

Harry hesitated for a second, and then ran after him, throwing his cigarette aside. He was far faster than the hunchback, and he overtook him when he was less than a third of the way across the field. Up ahead of him, Harry saw Secret Kiss kicking and bounding and twisting. Marcella lost one stirrup, and Harry thought she was going to be thrown off, but somehow she managed to grip the horse's mane and keep herself from sliding off.

He reached the horse and it pirouetted on its hind legs. From close up it looked about twenty feet tall. 'What shall I do?' he yelled to Marcella; but Marcella's answer was nothing but an indistinct blurt of sound.

Harry decided there was only one possible thing he could do, and that was to make a grab for the horse's reins. He danced awkwardly from side to side, trying to anticipate which way the animal was going to rear up. Walter, trotting up behind, shouted out, 'The throat-latch, Harry! Catch the throat-latch!'

Harry half-turned and then Secret Kiss whinnied wildly lashing out as she did so. Her left hoof caught Harry a glancing blow on the side of the chin, and he felt the hard-packed earth come swinging up behind him to bang him on the back. He saw sky, and beady little stars, and Walter's face peering down at him like a man peering down a well. Then, for a moment, he lost consciousness.

He heard drumming, and shouting, and he thought it was 1945 again, and he was listening to a victory parade on the radio. He heard his mother arguing with his father, '*Siedzisz caty czas na kanapie, nie robiac nic!* All the time sitting on the sofa, never working!' He heard somebody laughing; and then daylight returned, and he was helped up into a sitting position, and everything was bright and headachy and his jaw felt as if it were ten times its usual size.

Marcella was kneeling down beside him. Walter and Igor were holding Secret Kiss, whose hoofs were still twitching and whose eyes were still rolling, but whose sudden temper now seemed to have subsided. Marcella reached out toward Harry's jaw, and asked him worriedly, 'Is it broken? Can you move it? You have such a bruise!'

Harry tried to say, 'It's all right, thank you, I can move it,' but the words came out more like 'Hawhi, hanhu, hihan hoohih.'

He climbed to his feet. The world seemed peculiarly flat and ordinary. He patted his chin but it didn't feel as if it belonged to him. 'I'm okay,' he managed to say. 'I guesh I wash lucky.'

'Kermit, take Kiss back to her stall and rub her down for me, would you?' Marcella asked him. 'Mr Sharpe, let me take you for a drink. You look as if you could use it.'

'I'm all right,' said Harry, wiggling his jaw from side to side. 'It wasn't as bad as it looked. I just won't be able to eat any of my mother's sandwiches for a month, thank God.'

'Is there something wrong with your mother's sandwiches?' frowned Marcella.

'That's a little like asking if there's something wrong with dry rot,' said Harry.

Walter said, 'Shall I join you? I think I could use a small palliative myself.'

'You stay here and get your story,' Harry told him. Then he turned to Marcella, and said, 'Shall we take my car?'

'Which one is yours? That station wagon? I'm sorry – we'll have to take mine. The nearest cocktail lounge is at the Indian Hill Hotel, and station wagons are not permitted there. The management feel that it lowers the tone.'

Unexpectedly, Marcella took Harry's hand, and led him across the track toward her highly polished Buick convertible. 'One drink, and that's all, for medicinal purposes,' she said. 'And you must promise not to talk about your work. All I want to talk about is horses; and how beautiful you think I am; and what flowers we should choose for our funerals.'

'Are you kidding? Lilies,' said Harry.

Marcella waited while Harry opened the door of the car for her, and then she climbed behind the wheel, keeping her ankles together and her back straight. Harry eased himself into the passenger seat and Marcella smiled at him and said, 'Fat face.'

'Thanks a million,' said Harry. 'I was almost beginning to feel human, until you said that.'

'Oh, you will have to get used to me,' said Marcella. 'I always say what I mean.' She started up the engine, and swung the convertible away from the stables and back along the white dirt track toward the Indian Hill golf club. 'You wouldn't like it, anyway, if I said you looked wonderful. You know that your face is fat. It's not your fault. When I first saw you, I thought you looked quite handsome.'

'Do you know what my father used to say to me, when I was a kid?' said Harry, leaning his elbow on the car door. 'There isn't a single Polish man on this whole planet who doesn't look like the bottom end of a kitbag. That's you and me included, he said. But do you know what else he said? You'll get all the women you want, Harry, my son, because you look so stupid. I mean, that really build up my confidence, you know?'

'But did you get the women?' asked Marcella.

Harry shrugged, and smiled. 'Sporadycznie. That's Polish for now and then.'

'What is the Polish for, "what are you doing here?"'

'You really want to know?'

'Yes,' said Marcella. There was such a wealth of inflection in that one word – passionate, Italian, self-controlled, European, provocative, almost angry.

The cocktail bar of the Indian Hill Hotel looked out over the golf course. They perched on stools while an over-familiar bartender called Irving noisily shook up drinks with unprepossessing names like The Divot and The Bunker Blaster and The Nineteenth Hole, and grumpy fiftyish couples came in and complained loudly about the weather and the condition of the greens and what the hell was happening to the world today.

Harry drank Four Roses with a Hamm's chaser. 'I have to tell you the truth,' he told Marcella. 'I've been after your father for a long time. It's no secret.'

'Because he's a mobster? Is that it?'

Harry looked at her without saying anything for a moment. Then he took out a cigarette and said, 'You ever call him that? To his face?'

Marcella shrugged.

'Are you close?' asked Harry.

'He's my father, and I acknowledge that fact. That's all. Somehow, we've worked out a way to live with each other.'

'What about your mother?'

'My mother wouldn't mind if they used my father to test out the effects of circular saws on the human neck. Your father's a crook, that's what she tells me. Just make sure that you don't go the same way.'

'Some mother,' said Harry, raising an eyebrow.

'Yes,' said Marcella. 'Some mother.'

'Some daughter, too.'

Marcella smiled at him. 'I like you. I like your style. You don't beat around any bushes, do you? Tell me, why are you after my father? What has he done to you?'

Harry lit his cigarette and blew out the match with a puff of smoke. 'I didn't really want to spoil a very pleasant cocktail hour.'

'Tell me,' said Marcella, softly.

'Well . . .' said Harry. 'The fact is that your father owns a very extensive amount of real estate on the South Side.'

'That's true.'

'Do I have to say any more?' asked Harry. 'Don't tell me you've never driven along State Street, or Cottage Grove Avenue? Your father owns the whole of the 3400 block on Cottage Grove Avenue, and in one four-room apartment in one building, there are six families. That's a total of twenty-seven people, including twelve under the age of five. You can imagine what kind of life they lead.'

'Here – let me buy you another drink,' Marcella urged him.

'I don't think I ought to. Already I'm shooting my mouth off. Maybe I'd be better going home.'

Marcella waved to Irving the bartender to bring some more drinks, and he saluted and snapped out, 'R-r-r-right away, Miss Vespucci,' and went along the bar to fix them up. Harry waved smoke away from Marcella's face and said, 'I'm sorry. But it all kind of came to a head on Friday. You heard about that fire on 31st Street? You know the fire where Morgana Croft Tate saved that little Negro girl? Well, you know, seven people died in that fire, and that makes it eighteen people burned to death on the South Side since July first. Your father did that. I can't prove it but as God is my judge he did it.'

Marcella sipped her drink contemplatively while Harry himself sat agitated and upset right next to her, smoking and drinking and shifting around on his barstool. In the end, he said, 'I have to go to the men's room.'

He stood in front of the urinal looking at the golfing cartoons. There was a drawing of a man playing golf on his living room carpet, and his sour-faced maid with a vacuum cleaner saying, 'D'you mind if I play through?'

He was buttoning up and just about to leave when the door

swung open and Guido came in. Harry tried to maneuver past him, but Guido pushed him square in the chest.

Harry said, 'All right, King Kong, what's going on?'

'It's a message,' said Guido. 'Mr Vespucci says go back, get your car, and gedarah Winnetka pronto.'

'Mr Vespucci can shove his head where the sun never shines.'

Guido smiled. He bunched up his fist, and for a second Harry thought that he was going to punch him in the face. Instead of that, however, Guido opened up his fist again, and patted Harry one brisk pat, right where Secret Kiss had kicked him.

'Dah!' Harry shouted out, and lifted his arm to protect his face.

Guido simply smiled, and opened the men's room door again, and gave Harry a wave. 'You go back, you get your car, and dat's final.'

Marcella was still waiting for Harry in the cocktail bar. She had seen Guido go into the men's room, and she watched Harry tensely as he came back to finish his drink.

'He didn't hurt you?' she asked.

Harry shook his head.

'But he told you to get out of here, as fast as humanly possible? That figures. My father doesn't like me talking to men whose apparent incomes are less than $25,000 a year.'

'Is that what I look like?'

'I told you. It's the necktie.'

Harry lifted up the palm-tree tie and peered at it closely. 'I like it. If I was making $25,000 a year, I wouldn't change it, I'd just buy a couple dozen more.'

'Look,' said Marcella, 'you have to go. I mean it, for your own safety. But meet me here at eleven o'clock. Just make sure that nobody follows you up to my apartment.' She reached into her pocketbook and handed Harry a card with her address on it, 333 West Burton Place.

Harry turned the card over between his fingers. 'Okay,' he said, nodding slowly. Marcella smiled and Harry smiled back; and both of them realized with a satisfying sense of pleasure that they liked each other.

18

The little Negro girl Doris Wells was asleep when Morgana and John went to the 15th Street Clinic to see her that afternoon. Her head was bandaged and her lips were puffy and blistered. Her aunt sat by her bedside, a large silent Negress who obviously had little time for white folks, because all the time that Morgana was there she sat and stared at her with suspicion; and as Morgana was leaving took the Steiff teddy bear that Morgana had brought her off the bed and shut it away in the bedside cabinet. Morgana distinctly heard her say, 'Boojums,' which was a derogatory ghetto word for whites.

The ward sister said, 'Don't mind her. She doesn't really mean you any harm. She's still grieving for the child's mother.'

Morgana went to the bursar's office and made out a check for $1,000 to ensure that Doris Wells was well looked after, and then she and John left the clinic and returned to Morgana's bright-red open-topped Wayfarer Sportabout.

'I feel like just driving,' said Morgana. 'Do you mind?'

John opened the door for her. He was wearing a cream-colored wool blazer and a red and green tie, and he looked dazzlingly handsome and smart. Morgana had chosen a pale gray Dior suit of slubbed silk, with padded shoulders and a pencil skirt, and a hand-knitted silk jumper by Williams of San Francisco. On the lapel of her Dior suit she wore the diamond star which John had given her at her birthday party; and on her finger she wore his antique engagement ring.

In her pocketbook, she had hidden a surprise for him – an heirloom ring which had belonged to her grandfather, slim and gold, with a square-cut emerald set into it. She was going to give it to him when they said goodnight tonight, a kiss and a ring.

They drove north-westwards, along Lake Shore Drive. Without realizing it, near Foster Avenue Beach, they passed Harry Sharpe coming the other way in his yellow Woodie. John sat back in the passenger seat with his legs crossed and his fingers laced together, admiring the passing scenery. He was straining so hard to appear relaxed that Morgana deliberately drove a little faster and a little more daringly, in order to see how long he could keep it up. Her gray-gloved hand shifted proficiently up and down through the gears.

'All right?' she asked him. 'Enjoying yourself?'

'You were going to tell me what your parents were being so bear-jawed about,' said John.

'Oh – Momsy and Popsy always have at least one monumental row per annum,' Morgana lied. 'This just happens to be one of them.' She had calmed down since lunch; she didn't really want to tell John the truth, particularly since they had only just gotten engaged. On the day after your fiancé proposes, you tell him that your parents are almost on the point of splitting up?

John said, 'They're lucky they have one only once a year. My folks are *always* arguing.'

'I think your folks are sweet!'

'So do they. That's the trouble. Mommy thinks she's sweeter than daddy, and daddy thinks he's sweeter than mommy, and they keep trying to outsweet each other, which usually ends up in a blazing argument.'

'Well, I hope *we* don't argue like that, when *we're* married,' said Morgana.

'Why should we? We love each other, don't we?'

'Of course we do,' Morgana agreed. 'And there can't possibly be any argument about who's the sweeter.'

They drove all the way up to Lake Forest, and there they stopped at the Onwentsia Club, where Howard Croft Tate was an honorary member, in spite of being a Democrat. They had a couple of gin rickeys in the bar and then they went out to watch the tennis for a while. Although the sky was still quilted with cloud, the afternoon was sticky, and Morgana took off her coat and left it in the car. They sat by the tennis courts and a waiter brought them out two more drinks. Morgana began to feel a little dizzy.

They met several people they knew. The Morton Tylers were there, playing mixed doubles with the Gerry Underbergs, the two wealthiest real-estate dealers in the mid-West and their wives, doing their darnedest to wipe each other out with furious smashes and erratic backhands. 'Yours, partner, for God's sake!' 'Get off my damned foot, Henrietta!' They met the Willard T. Forbeses and the Nathan Petries and the Daniel K. Ryersons, and there was a great deal of shaking hands and kissing cheeks and congratulations on Morgana's exploits up the fire ladder and her as-yet-unannounced engagement. John was always perfect. He always knew the right thing to say and the right woman to compliment and the right man to address as 'sir' more often than most.

They had two more cocktails in the bar with the Biff McHenrys. Biff himself was a steelman, one of the old Chicago McHenrys. He was big-bellied and wonderfully prejudiced. As far as he was concerned, it was an inexplicable disappointment that the United States, having developed and successfully used the atom bomb, had not already dropped it on the Russians and the Chinese and at least threatened to drop it on the British. Biff's wife Marjorie wore a turquoise dress and clashing bangles and gasped 'is that *so-o-o*??' in response to everything that anyone told her.

It was growing dark when they drove back along the lake. John said, 'You're sure you don't want me to drive? Those are pretty hefty cocktails they serve at the club.' But Morgana adored her new car and wanted to drive all the way. They sang 'Mairzy Doats' three times over in various hilarious harmonies, ending up with Morgana trying to sing bass and John singing falsetto.

'Mairzy doats and dozey doats and little lamsy divey...'

After they passed through Highland Park they drove for a while in silence. Morgana had the feeling that they were at the very center of the known universe, that Chicago stood like a glittering castle at the hub of the twilit world. It was a warm, strong, romantic feeling, driving fast between the lake and the prairie, being wealthy and being beautiful and being in love.

'What are you thinking about?' John asked her, after they had driven for nearly a quarter of an hour in silence.

'Us,' said Morgana, cheerfully.

'Oh, yes? And what conclusion did you come to?'

'I came to the conclusion that, socially, we must be the ideal couple. Tailor-made for each other.'

'You make us sound like a couple of pairs of pants.'

Morgana laughed. 'We are, though, aren't we? Ideal, I mean?'

'I guess we are.' He leaned over and kissed her shoulder, then her cheek. She turned her head to kiss him back, but John said, 'Unh-hunh. Keep your peepers on the road.'

'I like to live dangerously.'

'So I've noticed. I just hope you're going to give up moonlighting for the Fire Department after we're married.'

'Well, who knows?' said Morgana, steering the Sportabout from one side of the road to the other. 'If a fire just *happens* to be blazing, and if somebody just *happens* to need rescuing, and if I just *happen* to be passing by . . .'

John kissed her again. 'You're crazy. Mind you, I think I like you when you're crazy.'

'You think I'm crazy? I think *you're* crazy. Who else but a crazy would want to marry a crazy?'

'Hey, let me tell you a crazy story,' said John.

'A crazy story?' Morgana giggled.

'I promise you it's totally crazy. There was this stupid little guy, and his wife used to like to sit out on the porch fanning herself, but one day, you know – her fan broke, and so the stupid little guy went to the fancy-goods store to buy her a new one. And he looks through hundreds of fans, you see, *hundreds*, and he can't make up his mind which one to buy, and the owner of the store is getting more and more irritated. Finally it comes down to two fans, one is fifty cents and the other one is a dollar, and the stupid little guy asks the owner of the store, what's the difference between them? And the owner says sarcastically, "With the one-dollar fan, you keep yourself cool by waving the fan from side to side, like this; and with the fifty-cent fan you have to hold the fan still and wave your head from side to side." And the stupid little guy looks at these fans for ages and ages, and finally he says, "You know – I wonder if my wife is going to think it's worth the extra fifty cents."'

'That's *crazy*,' said Morgana, playfully punching John's shoulder. 'That's the craziest story I ever heard.'

John nuzzled her neck, and the car slewed halfway across the road. 'Hey come on now,' Morgana told him. 'We're trying to do some serious driving here. Some very serious driving.'

'Of course,' said John. 'In fact, I'm thinking of entering you for next year's Indy 500. You could lick Bill Holland any old day of the week.'

For some reason, Morgana began to giggle, and couldn't stop. 'I thought you didn't want me to live dangerously any more,' she said.

'I don't,' said John, stroking her shoulder. 'After the 500, I want you to settle down.'

'Settle down? What will I do?'

'What do you mean, *do*? You're going to be my wife, that's what you're going to do. And with any luck, you're going to be the mother of my children, too.'

'There you go again. You've got me pregnant and we're not even married.'

'But that's part of it. I mean, we have to carry on the Birmingham name, don't we? We have to produce John Birmingham IV. My father will never forgive you if you don't give me an heir.'

'I'm not going to marry your father, I'm going to marry you.'

'Morgana, you're going to be busy, busy, busy! You don't have to worry about what you're going to do! You don't think that the wife of one of the most brilliant young commercial lawyers in the whole of Illinois is going to be able to sit on her bohunkus all day eating candy?'

'John,' Morgana protested, although she was still half-giggling, 'I don't want to be a *housewife* ...! I do have ambitions of my own, you know ... quite apart from the fact that I'm going to inherit the *Star*. And opinions! I have opinions on everything! And *feelings* too. You just think about that poor little girl we went to see today! And think of all the other people living in the slums.'

John shook his head in amusement. 'When you get on to a hobbyhorse, you sure ride it until it drops, don't you? People will always be living in slums. It's the natural way. There are poor people and rich people; there are stupid people and clever people. If you gave two people a hundred dollars each and told them to do what they like with it, within five years one of those guys is going to be in debt and the other guy is going to be rich. You can't change human nature!'

'*John* –'

'Hey, come on, just hush up and drive. Drive me through the park, Happy as a lark, Even when it's dark, We'll go driving through the park. You and me, we're going to be the happiest damned couple that ever were.'

John reached over and kissed her hair. Then he laid his hand on her right thigh, and started slowly to massage it through her silk skirt. There was the finest slippery friction between silk lining and nylon stocking, a friction that charged her clothes with warm perfumed electricity, a crackle of Chanel, and it made Morgana shudder, partly out of irritation, partly out of arousal.

John said, 'You're the most beautiful girl I ever met. About you I am completely nuts. I worship you. You're my queen! Believe me, when we get married, it's going to be the Fourth of July every day.'

'Independence every day?' Morgana teased him.

'Dammit, no, fireworks!'

As Morgana light-headedly steered the Sportabout along Sheridan Road, John slid his hand down and caressed her calf. Since her foot was pressed down on the gas pedal, there was nothing she could do to move her leg away. He kissed her cheek again, his lips were warm and dry, and then he slid his hand up her calf toward her knee, lifting her skirt higher so that he could stroke around and around her kneecap.

'John,' she giggled, 'I'm trying to drive!'

'You're driving like a wheeled angel! Don't stop!'

'You're drunk!'

'Well, dammit, so are you!'

Morgan giggled some more, but tried to sober herself up. 'John this is *dangerous*.'

'You said you liked a little danger, now and again. Climbing that fire ladder was more dangerous than this. This is nothing! What are you doing? Forty-five? Nothing! Climbing that fire ladder must've been much more of a thrill!'

'I was *terrified*, if you want to know the true story.'

'Oh, sure, sure you were terrified! Were you really terrified? But what else? It must have been a kick, too!' His hand had slid up inside her skirt now, and he was caressing her stocking top, working his fingertips underneath the tight nylon to touch her bare flesh. She shivered, and said, 'John,' but there was no indication in her voice whether she wanted him to stop or whether she was urging him to continue.

She was driving at nearly fifty miles an hour now, and the dusk that had gathered over the lake was now clinging to the trees on the shoreline, and clogging between the lighted apartment buildings, and it was difficult for her to see the oncoming traffic whenever she passed another auto. The wind snapped at her headscarf, and her face was cold, cold as ice, in strangely erotic contrast to the warmth between her thighs, where John was fondling her.

'Tell me what you felt,' John asked her, and this time he spoke huskily and quietly, so that she could hardly hear him. A limousine flashed past in the opposite direction, its horn blowing a warning at her in a hair-raising Doppler howl.

'I felt . . .' Morgana whispered, but then she forgot what she was supposed to be saying. She wanted him to stop caressing her; and yet she knew perfectly well that all she had to do was pull the car over to the side of the road and make him take his hand away. There was nothing to compel her to go on driving through the dusk at fifty miles an hour, while his fingers traced the softest of traceries on the inside of her thigh. Maybe she wanted him to go on. Maybe his caress was the reassurance she needed that he loved her deeply and completely and forsaking all others, and that he didn't hanker secretly or not-so-secretly for Phoebe, and that their long abstinence from lovemaking had really been for the sake of mutual regard, rather than the disconcerting reason that they didn't actually love each other quite as much as they tried to convince themselves. They always seemed so right together. They always *looked* so right together. Besides, Eleanor was already drawing up the guest list for their engagement party, on the fifteenth of September.

John's index finger slipped under the loose elastic of her French silk step-ins, then his middle finger. He stroked the crisp tight-crushed fur that he found there, and at the same time kissed and nuzzled at Morgana's neck. He murmured hotly in her ear, she could smell the alcohol on his breath. 'Do you know much I desiiirrre you,' he growled, and then he went 'grrrffff!' and bit at her ear lobe.

'Stop,' she mouthed, but almost silently. She pressed her foot a little harder on the gas pedal and the red speedo needle began to rise gradually upwards and quiver like a live thing.

It was dark. The avenue flashed past them as if it were being hurled at them piece by piece out of the night: mailboxes, trees, bollards, parked cars, buildings. Only John's fingers were slow and warm as they stroked her. The rest of the world was a riot.

'Stop,' she repeated, a whisper that was snatched away by the blustery wind. 'Oh stop, John, please stop.'

She began to feel that she was burning again, the way that she had burned just before she had rescued the little Negro girl from the top of the tenement. Whether he knew it or not, John had been remarkably intuitive to ask her what she had felt when she had climbed that fireman's ladder. She felt the same incandescence now. She shone, she was almost incandescent, she sped through the twilight like a beautiful comet, leaving behind her a tail of fire, and whipped-up sheets of newspaper, and the lingering smell of hot-burned gasoline and Chanel No. 5.

There she goes! Morgana Croft Tate!

John's fingers parted her as silently as petals part. She didn't know whether she was driving fast or slow. The lighted windows of the lakeshore apartment buildings streamed past her in an endless procession, ocean liners, freight trains, fortresses. His finger slipped in quick and deep, and she pressed herself down on the Sportabout's leather seat, undulating slowly, feeling her chest tighten, her breath quicken.

A feeling like spilled ink began to spread inside her, wider and wider. She could hear John's breath harsh in her ear. Her stomach muscles tensed up and began to quake.

'*Stop,*' she might have begged him, but already it was too late to stop. The ink flooded her completely, and she let out a strange high-pitched scream, as if she were trying to hit the B at the very top of the piano.

She closed her eyes for one split second. She ran straight through a red light. She missed the rear end of a huge truck carrying steel girders by inches, a huge dark bellowing incarnation of hell on wheels, and it roared its klaxon at her, and she screamed out loud.

'*John!*'

Jerkily, she pulled over to the side of the road, parking at an awkward angle. She was shivering with terror and exhilaration. John reached out to touch her again but she pushed him away. He sat and watched her without saying anything as she took one deep breath after another.

'My God, I could have killed us both,' she said.

John took out his gold cigarette case, lit two cigarettes at once, and passed one to Morgana. She inhaled so deeply that the cigarette squeaked. Then she loudly blew out smoke, and nervously tapped away ash that hadn't even formed yet.

'My God,' she repeated.

'I think I've suddenly sobered up,' said John. His face looked very yellow in the street light.

'Do you want to take me to bed?' she asked him. She was still so shocked that her voice was all wobbly and uncontrolled. 'Is *that* it?'

'Of course I want to take you to bed! Morgana, I love you!'

'Then, please, take me to bed,' she told him.

He kissed her. She turned her face away; not because she didn't want him, but because she needed to know what he was thinking. John sat back in his seat and looked at her for a while, the tip of his cigarette glowed scarlet in the darkness, and then he said, 'It isn't long to wait, is it? It's only ten months.'

'John, I don't understand this at all. You don't want to take me to bed until we're married – but we've been to bed together before – and that was good, wasn't it? Wasn't that good? And yet you can do what you did to me tonight.'

'I'm sorry,' he said. His voice sounded very withdrawn. 'I guess I had one too many rickeys.'

Morgana clasped her hand together into a fist and gently pounded at his shoulder in frustration. 'John, I *love* you! I love you, I love you, I love you. I want to go to bed with you, but I want to do it properly, not like two high school kids, in a car. The way we did before. It was *good*, the way we did it before, why can't we do it like that now, instead of this?'

'Morgana, my darling, we're not – we're not *married* yet,' John protested. His voice rose half an octave in mystified amusement, as if he had unexpectedly found it necessary to explain to her that people in polite society don't normally drink water out of their finger bowls.

'But we went to bed before,' Morgana retorted. She could scarcely believe what she was hearing.

John nodded. 'We did, and it was good. It was wonderful,

I admit it! In fact, that was one of the things that convinced me that you and I were going to be perfect together.'

'Yes?' Morgana demanded.

'Well, that's it. I wanted to marry you. It's official now, we're bespoken. And it doesn't really do for a fellow to be sleeping with his bride-to-be, does it?'

Morgana took one long drag at her cigarette, looked at it, and then tossed it out of the car. 'Oh, John,' she said. 'What a proper gentleman you are.'

'I hope so,' John told her.

'I suppose I ought to be thankful about one thing,' said Morgana. 'At least I know now that the reason you've been treating me like a porcelain ornament is to be socially correct. I was really beginning to wonder whether your feelings for me had gone on the blink.'

She felt tensed up and unsettled. She knew that her words sounded sour. Perhaps it was natural, this irritability, after such a near-miss with sudden death. It wasn't every evening that she was brought face to face with extinction and ecstasy, both at the very same instant. She gave John a quick, wan, noncomittal smile, and started up the Sportabout's engine again.

John said, 'I'm sorry, Morgana. Really. Listen – I'll tell you what I'll do. I'll buy you dinner at the Pump Room, how about that? We haven't been there since that very first time. Let me show you how romantic I can be, when I try.'

Morgana looked at him, and then relaxed, and laughed, and kissed him on the nose. 'I'm sorry,' she said, and she was.

'No, no, I'm sorrier than you.'

'That's ridiculous! I'm much sorrier than you!'

John leaned back in his seat. 'I hope you realize that this is how my parents' arguments always begin.'

Morgana winked at him. 'The question is, dearest John, how do they end?'

A police car drew up alongside them, and the officer next to them probed into their car with his flashlight.

'You people all right?'

'Yes, officer, thank you,' Morgana called back.

'Suggest you move along then; you're causing an obstruction right here.'

'Right away, officer,' said John, cheerily waving. Then,

'Come on, Morgana, we'd better absquatulate. We don't want to get picked up for driving under the influence.'

Morgana drove John back to his parents' apartment block on Walton Street, where the doorman opened the car door for him and saluted Morgana with an ingratiating grin. John said, 'I'll pick you up at nine; in my car. And be careful going home.'

'Your wish is my command, O Master,' said Morgana, and U-turned in the street with an echoing squeal of tires.

19

Morgana drove the three miles back to Weatherwood to change her dress for dinner. The huge house stood brightly lit under an overpoweringly dark sky. Thunder was beginning to boom, and there was a restless wind around. She left her car for the chauffeur to drive into the garages for her; and Liley their black maid took her upstairs to her bedroom suite, turned on her lights for her, arranged the cushions on the chaise longue and went into the bathroom to draw water.

'Is my father around?' Morgana asked her, unpinning her hair in front of her dressing table mirror.

'Your father gone downtown,' said Liley, as she took out an armful of towels. 'That Mr Donato come by, from the Newsboy Union. They hardly ask howdy before they was arguing something terrible.'

'*That* doesn't surprise me,' said Morgana. Ever since before the war, Howard Croft Tate and the newspaper deliverymen had been tussling with each other like two small boys trying to share out seven marbles. Howard had seriously upset the Newsboys in 1931 by denouncing their president Daniel A. Serritella as a lackey of Al Capone, and whenever Howard made extra demands on them, or rejected their claims for better pay, they made a malicious ritual out of calling meetings at an impossible hour, or (in this case) of interrupting his family Sunday.

Not that there was very much more that anybody *could* spoil, not this Sunday. Morgana's mother had locked herself in her rooms again ('to catch up with my letter-writing,' she had told Millicent, although Phoebe had pressed her ear to the door and heard her mother crying, Phoebe herself was in a crisscross mood, flouncing, smoking too much, and flinging 'damns' and 'hells' around. Ill-bred but irresistible Donald had called her, but he had abruptly slammed down the receiver halfway through their murmuring conversation because his wife had walked into the room, *La Noosance* herself, back four days early from Savannah, Ga. The servants were agitatedly hurrying all around Weatherwood, changing flower-water, dusting, polishing, pressing suits, anything to break the threatening atmosphere, like children when their parents are arguing.

Morgana told Liley to leave, and closed the door behind her. She kicked off her shoes one after the other and they tumbled right across the dressing room. A moment later Millicent rapped at her door and asked her if she wanted a cocktail. Sometimes Morgana had a martini or a rickey round about now. But she called back no. She stood in front of the dressing room mirrors and took off her coat; then she loosened her skirt and stepped out of it. Loukia knocked at the door and asked her if she wanted any help in dressing, but again she called back no. For an hour at least, she wanted to be completely alone. Her mind felt like the inside of a child's kaleidoscope, crowded with all those bits and pieces of brightly coloured glass, and she wanted to see if she could make some kind of a pattern out of them before she talked to anybody else. There were so many questions, some of them dull and some of them hair-raising; some of them irrelevant and some of them crucial. Some of the dull ones were crucial and some of the irrelevant ones were hair-raising; but all of them needed answering. Did John really love her? He had obviously enjoyed exciting her, but how excited had *he* been? Did he really have an eye for Phoebe? Why had Oscar Hammerstein been so down on him? Why had her mother warned her that marrying John was going to be a romantic disaster? Did she love him? Did she really, truly love him?

Morgana switched on her television. The 'Croft Tate Inspirational Hour' was featuring a hymn service, and so she switched it off again. That's just like life, she thought. If you hit a truck, you die instantly, just like the tube of a switched-off television. One minute 'Rock of Ages' from the Croft Tate studios, the next minute oblivion. But if you marry the wrong man, you can never switch the television off. It stays on from *Howdie Doody* until close-down, by way of *Art Godfrey*, the *Goldbergs*, *Dave Garroway*, *Hopalong Cassidy* and the NBC nightly news, week after week, month after month, year after year.

She considered that analogy to be very profound; so profound that she opened the drawer of her dressing table and took out her diary. Under Sunday she wrote 'Marrying the wrong man is like owning a TV you can never switch off.' Then, after a moment's hesitation, she drew a vertical line down the middle of the page with her gold propelling-pencil, separating it into two columns. One column she headed 'John Plus'. The other column she headed 'John Minus'.

Under 'Plus' she wrote, 'Gd looking! Very!' Then 'Sexy'. Then 'Absolutely 100 p.c. manners.' Finally, she added, 'Socially impeccable.'

Under 'Minus' she wrote, 'Can be lawyerish.' Also, 'Flirting with P.??' Also 'Expects wife to be wife with capital W.' Then, 'Others have warned, why??'

She read and reread what she had written. Then, boldly, she wrote right across the page, 'Trouble is, do love him!!!'

She undressed. Her French silk briefs were damp. She stood holding them in her hand for a moment, watching her own eyes in the dressing room mirror. Who are you, Morgana Croft Tate? Everybody thinks that you're so composed; everybody thinks that you're so wealthy and witty. Everybody envies you. Your looks, your money, your dresses, your social connections. Laurence Olivier danced with you on your twenty-first birthday. You climbed up a fire ladder and took everybody's breath away. And yet, look at you. Unsure, uncertain, questioning yourself; and questioning the life around you, too, for the very first time. You nearly killed yourself tonight. Wasn't it exciting! But what if you *had* killed yourself? What a way to die. What a useless, meaningless, unprofitable way to die.

She finished undressing. She looked extremely thin. Her breasts were still quite full, but her hipbones were prominent under her skin. She slid into the warm perfumed water of her pale-pink bathtub, under the merry eyes of golden dolphin faucets, and slowly soaped her arms. She felt disconcertingly like a child; for the first time in her life she began to realize that the more you knew, the more you realized you didn't know.

After a minute or two, Phoebe came in, without knocking, and leaned against the doorframe in her pink ruffled robe, watching Morgana through blonde-lashed eyes that were creamed clean of make-up, so that she was still pretty, but strangely blank-faced. She was smoking a cigarette in her extra-long holder, and she leaned forward to tap the ash into one of Morgana's soap dishes.

'Bradley went home,' she explained, more to herself than to Morgana.

'I thought he was taking you out to dinner tonight.'

'He *was*, the little pink-eared darling, but he had to go home. Something about his mother feeling sick.'

'So what are you going to do?'

'I don't know, what are you going to do?'

'John's supposed to be taking me for dinner at Ernie's.'

Phoebe primped her hair with her fingers. 'That's a bit heavyweight, isn't it?'

'I'm only going to eat something light.'

'At *Ernie's*, my dear, something light is a five-pound lobster.'

Morgana climbed out of the bath, and wrapped herself in a large pink Fieldcraft towel. Phoebe followed her into the dressing room, still smoking, and talked to some of her reflections. 'I could *kill* Donald, you know. I could quite happily poison his salt-beef sandwiches.'

'I didn't know that he ate salt-beef sandwiches,' said Morgana, peering at herself in the dressing table mirror with one eye closed and trying to decide what to do about her lashes.

'I don't know whether he does either. He just *looks* as if he does. Do you think mommy and daddy are going to p-a-r-t?'

'*Part?* I don't think so.'

'Well, it's incredibly racy to have one of those mothers who goes around fornicating with younger men, don't you think so? I know *other* girls' mothers do it. Philipa Kogan's mother used to do it with everybody. Gardeners, chauffeurs, laundrymen, kings, princes, garage mechanics, you only had to say the word, and she did it with them. But *our* mother; the brilliant and glacial Eleanor Croft Tate, society's answer to the death of a thousand cuts, can you imagine her doing it? With somebody like Robert Wentworth? I think not, exclamation point!'

Morgana began to apply foundation to her bare face. 'I look terrible,' she said. 'Look at these bags under my eyes. I had about six gin rickeys up at Lake Forest. God. I feel like a boiled owl.'

Phoebe said, 'You were lucky you weren't here, *ma chérie*. Father was storming around and slamming doors, and mother was gliding from room to room as if she was on ice skates. Actually, I think father was quite relieved when that awful Doughnutto showed up. It gave him an excuse to get out of the house. And if you ask me, Bradley's mother wasn't feeling half as sick as Bradley.'

Morgana turned around on her seat. 'Phoebe ... you mustn't upset them, Momsy and Popsy. I know they're our parents, and I know this Robert Wentworth business seems as if it's – well, as if it's *funny* in one way, but really upsetting in another – and I know you're probably just as off-balance about it as I am –'

'Off-balance? Who's off-balance? They're grown-ups, aren't they? They don't have to ask our permission to do anything. Who are we to say that they can't fornicate if they want to?'

'Phoebe!' snapped Morgana, shocked.

'Well,' said Phoebe, making an exaggerated gesture with her cigarette holder. 'We *are* their daughters, after all, aren't we? And it wasn't all that long ago, was it, when father was bouncing us up and down on his knee, and mother was showing us how to braid our hair, and we were a family. Now look at us!'

Suddenly, alarmingly, there were hot tears in Phoebe's eyes. Morgana stood up and came over and held her in her arms. She suddenly realized how much Phoebe needed her parents to be together, in spite of the fact that she herself was so dizzily promiscuous; or perhaps because of it. '*Shush*,' said Morgana. 'You don't want me calling you a bawl-baby.'

Phoebe pushed her away, and wiped at her eyes with her knuckle. 'It's all right,' she said. 'I'm quite all right. I'm just angry, that's all.'

'Do you want me to stay home with you tonight?' asked Morgana.

'No, no, you go out. You haven't had a chance to celebrate your engagement yet, have you? I expect I can find something amusing to do, like look through some old copies of *Vogue*. You're going downtown tomorrow, aren't you? Maybe I can meet you in the afternoon and we'll go to Field's and buy some clothes. I mean *lots* of clothes.'

Morgana held Phoebe's hand and squeezed it. 'Don't be upset,' she said. 'I'm sure that Momsy and Popsy can find some way of making it up.'

Phoebe shrugged, and then started looking around for an ashtray. 'I could kill them, you know. I could poison their breakfast.'

John picked Morgana up sharp at nine, driving his father's conservative gray Kaiser. Morgana had chosen a simple white taffeta evening gown by Nettie Rosenstein, with low shoulders and a huge taffeta bow at the back. She wore three strings of pearls, and carried a smooth white mink wrap. Her matching hat was small and curved, with a bow and a veil and three rows of seed pearls sewn on to it.

'You look like a bride already,' John complimented her. He wore a white tuxedo, with a white carnation in his lapel. Only his eyes were slightly pink.

He drove to the Ambassador East Hotel, and escorted Morgana through to the Pump Room restaurant. There were smiles and bows from staff on all sides, and the glossy-haired night manager himself came forward and greeted them. 'Miss Croft Tate! I read about you in the paper yesterday. I hope you will accept the compliments of the Ambassador East Hotel.'

Morgana and John walked into the restaurant itself; a high white-pillared room with walls of cobalt blue, buzzing like a stately beehive with conversation, flickering with spirit-burners and staffed by waiters in red tailcoats and knee-britches. There was a general murmuring and a turning of heads among the clientele, and then when Jimmy Hart the hotelier came over and welcomed Morgana with a kiss and John with a firm shaking of the hand, there was applause from one side of the restaurant to the other.

'It isn't every day that we entertain a heroine,' Jimmy Hart smiled. 'Here, please, come over and use my personal booth.'

They were seated at a table decorated with fresh-cut white roses. 'You'll have the champagne, of course,' said Jimmy. 'Krug private cuvée.'

'Actually,' Morgana confided in John, 'I think I could use a very strong cup of coffee. Either that, or one of their king-size martinis.'

John said, 'That's a brilliant idea. Waiter – before you bring the champagne – could we have two of the large martinis.'

The Pump Room's gargantuan six-ounce martini had been devised by Ernie Byfield in the restaurant's early days in the hope that customers would all the more rapidly lose their inhibitions about ordering some of the more expensive items on the menu, and make a long and profitable night of it. The effect of two or three of these pre-dinner drinks, however, had been to render most customers semi-conscious before they had managed to order anything at all. The bon-vivant Lucius Beebe had described them as 'the only really plausible cocktail between New York and San Francisco', but these days they were strictly limited to one per person.

While they sipped their ice-cold, wryly flavored gin, John and Morgana considered the menu.

'I have to admit that I thought of coming here for one special reason,' said John. 'You know how much they love to set everything alight here. Well, I thought we might have everything in flames. Just to celebrate the way you saved that little girl from the fire.'

Morgana laughed, bright-eyed. 'I was thinking of picking at a spinach salad. But – all right. You're paying, husband-to-be. *You* order.'

The meal was hilarious and spectacular. The Pump Room's food was customarily rolled to the table on mobile open-hearth furnaces, since it had always been part of Ernie Byfield's philosophy that food should not only entertain the palate but also entertain the eye, and this usually meant setting it on fire. John ordered crabmeat *crêpes louise*, crackling with flames; followed by a roast pheasant blazing with cognac; and rounded off the dinner with peaches *flambées* and two beakers of *café diable*; which meant that they had four roaring conflagrations at their table between the first martini and the last sip of Krug champagne.

Morgana was so delighted by the meal that she couldn't help herself from laughing at anything and everything. That dark near-accident on the lakeshore highway was forgotten already, in fact it had drained away in the last chilly drops of the six-ounce martini. She had forgotten her doubts about John, too, and it made her feel sparklingly happy just to watch him smiling and talking even though most of the time she wasn't even listening to a single word that he was saying.

At last, when it was nearly midnight, John called for the check. But Jimmy Hart came over personally, and took Morgana's hand and said, 'Please, accept this meal with our compliments. A true Chicago heroine.'

'There's one thing more,' said Morgana. She opened her pocketbook, and took out the small blue ring box which she had been carrying all day in anticipation of this very last moment. She passed it across to John and said, 'Open it. It's for you.'

John held Morgana's gaze for a moment that poured slowly into her consciousness like honey off a warm spoon. It was a moment of utter unashamed romance; of warmth and caring and mutual understanding. 'Before I open this,' said John, 'before I even look at it and see what it is, I want you to know that I love you.'

Then he opened up the box and took out the emerald ring, and its facets prickled at his face with reflected green fire. He held it up, and turned it from side to side, and he was plainly delighted with it. When he tried it on his finger, however, he found that it was far too small. He couldn't even wedge it on to his pinkie. All the same, he leaned across the table and kissed Morgana's lips and told her, 'It's wonderful. It truly is wonderful. I'm going to treasure it for ever.'

Morgana said, 'Do you know your ring size? I'm going to Field's tomorrow; they'll enlarge it for me. Oh, I'm so disappointed. I wanted you to wear it right away.'

'I'll tell you what I'll do,' said John. 'If you can come back to my apartment for a nightcap, I'll give you my old frat ring, and you can take that along to Field's so that they can compare it.'

They left the Pump Room, bowed out on all sides by waiters in knee-britches, and John drove them back to his parents' house on Walton Street. His parents were out of town this weekend. John explained that they were burying his Aunt Hilda in Peru, Indiana, and that they had not only attended the funeral but taken the opportunity to visit a few of his mother's Hoosier relatives. 'Aunt Hilda was a character. She disapproved of just about everything, but she always used to say, "there's three things in life I cannot tol'rate, boys, cats, and chewing wax."'

Only a few minutes away from Walton Street, the Lincoln began to run a little rough and uneven, and when the doorman came out to park it, John asked him to take a quick look under the hood to check if there was anything wrong. 'My father'll kill me if I mess up his car.'

They went up in the elevator to the 11th floor. John held Morgana in his arms and kissed her deeply as they rose up through the silence of the expensive apartment building.

'Where do you think we're going to live?' he asked her. 'Lake Forest, maybe?'

'Too far out. The Loop will do for me.'

'You know what your trouble is?' John teased her. 'You're one hundred percentile natural-born Chicagoan. You never take no for an answer.'

'Well, you know what *your* trouble is,' Morgana retorted. 'You're a one hundred percentile natural-born lawyer, and that means you'll never take *yes* for an answer.'

They were admitted to the Birmingham apartment by their black maid Annie. John ushered Morgana inside, and Annie took her wrap for her.

'One last celebratory toast?' asked John, and led Morgana through to the living room.

The Birminghams' apartment had an oppressive opulence which had already probably remained completely unchanged since the early 1930s, when John's father had first become wealthy. The carpets were beige, with green and black scalloped borders woven into them; the ceilings were cream combed plaster. There were massive odeon sofas in white leather; and tables and sideboards in garish walnut veneers. The paintings on the walls were worth hundreds of thousands of dollars – dark green and maroon leaf paintings by Arthur Dove, cubist cities by Lyonel Feininger. On almost every table top there was an Art Deco nude in bronze or alabaster. There was a smell everywhere of overheated furnishings and money.

Morgana flopped on to one of the leather sofas, and said, 'A very very *very* small martini. I think I'm about to enter my third hangover of the day.'

'But what a day, hunh?' smiled John, opening up the cocktail cabinet.

After John had given Morgana her martini, in a black-stemmed martini glass, Annie came into the living room and stood patiently by the door.

'Annie?' asked John. 'Did you want something?'

'If I can speak with you a moment, Mr Birmingham.'

'Of course you can. What is it?'

'Something private, Mr Birmingham.'

'Well, won't it keep till later?' John asked her, irritably, sitting down next to Morgana.

'I'm sorry, sir, it won't keep.'

'All right, then, Annie, if you really must. Would you excuse me for just one minute, my darling?'

John was gone only for half a minute, but when he came back he seemed flustered.

'Is something wrong?' Morgana asked him.

'No, no, nothing serious. Well, nothing *too* serious. It just seems that one of my father's clients called up and needs some urgent advice. He's going to be coming round here first thing in the morning. Meanwhile, I've got to bone up on *Untermeyer vs First Trust Bank of Illinois*.'

Morgana took hold of his hand. 'Oh, come on, John, you don't have to worry about me. I'm tired anyway. If you have work to do, I don't mind if you run me home.'

John kissed her on the forehead. 'You're an angel. Did you know that?' He went across and picked up the white apartment telephone. 'Hallo? Freddie? Yes, it's Mr Birmingham here. I have to take Miss Croft Tate home. Would you bring the Lincoln round to the front for me?'

He paused, and then he said, 'Oh,' and then 'Oh, is it that bad?' He listened for a little while longer and then put the phone down again. 'I'm sorry,' he told Morgana. 'Freddie says that the oil pump's gone, or something like that. Anyway, I can't use the car until he's arranged for the mechanic to come fix it. Would you mind terribly if I put you into a Checker?'

Morgana smiled. 'I have *occasionally* been known to stoop to riding in cabs.'

They said goodnight outside the apartment building with a cool night breeze ruffling the fur of Morgana's white wrap. The cab driver waited with amusement while they kissed and kissed again; and Freddie the doorman watched them with his white gloves held behind his back and a silly smile on his face. He had always had a soft spot for Morgana, ever since John had first brought her home to meet his parents.

Then Morgana climbed into the cab and said, 'Weatherwood, please,' and gave John a last wave as the cab pulled away from the curb.

'I saw your picture in the noospaper,' the cab driver told her, his disembodied eyes staring at her in the rear-view mirror. 'That was quite something, the way you saved that Negro kid. They going to give you some kind of medal for that or something? They should.'

'The fire chief gave me his coat.'

'You mean Bryan? Well, believe me, you're the first person in living memory who ever got squat out of that guy, pardon my French. I took him and his old lady down to the Fireman's Ball once, maybe four, five years ago; and he was all dressed up in his white tie and tails, and his old lady looked like Astor's pet horse; and all the time they were trying to tell me how grand they was, and do you know what they tipped me? Two lottery tickets for the firemen's draw. And when I says, what's this? Bryan says to me, you could win a vacation for two in Miami, Florida, and I says to him, sure, and on the other hand maybe I couldn't. And do you know what? I didn't.'

They had almost reached the long stone wall, topped with black iron railings, that guarded Weatherwood from Lake Shore Drive. Morgana opened her pocketbook to find some money for the cab driver, and then she saw something flash, down in the dark silk lining. It was John's emerald engagement ring. He had hurried her out of his parents' apartment so quickly; and she had still been so tiddly; that she had forgotten to ask him for his fraternity ring.

'Please,' she said to the cab driver, 'do you mind if we quickly go back to Walton Street? I've forgotten something important.'

'You only gave him one hundred ninety-nine goodnight kisses, instead of two hundred?' the cab driver grinned. All the same, he quite happily turned the Checker cab around, and drove her back toward Walton Street.

'Could I ask you a question?' he said, as they drove southward again.

'Go ahead.'

'Well, you know that question page, "Dear Gloria" . . . you know the one with all people's problems on it. Well, those letters they print, don't tell me those letters are true?'

'Oh, they're true all right,' said Morgana. 'At least, they're all real letters, from real people, and we do try to make sure that they're authentic.'

'Is that right?' the cab driver asked her. He shook his head slowly from side to side. 'You know something. I can't believe that. What a world we live in. There must be half the population of Chi-town out of their box. Did you see that one the other day? Did you see it? The one where the guy thinks his wife's been whoring all day, while he's at work, and his evidence is that she sends so many towels to the laundry.'

'I'm afraid I didn't see it,' said Morgana. She was beginning to feel very dopey and sleepy, and her head was going around like a very slow carousel, horses up, tigers down, tigers up, horses down. She hoped very much that she wasn't going to be sick.

They turned into Walton Street and the cab driver drew up outside the apartment block. Freddie opened the door for her, and said, 'Back already, Miss Croft Tate? That was a short night.'

'Mr Birmingham was going to give me something important,' said Morgana. 'But don't worry – I'll just go straight on up and ring at the door.'

'Whatever you like, Miss Croft Tate. I should keep on ringing, though. Their maid went home about ten minutes ago, and sometimes they don't hear you if they're in the bathroom or the bedroom.'

Morgana took the elevator up to the eleventh floor. The tigers and horses were beginning to speed up; to rise and to fall; to dip and to rear; and her stomach let out a loud anguished gurgle that made her glad she was in the elevator car alone. The elevator doors opened and she walked along the thickly carpeted corridor in silence.

At the door nameplated Birmingham she rang and rang, but there was no reply. John must already be taking a bath, or studying his lawbooks in bed. Morgana was about to leave when the elevator doors slid open again and Freddie appeared.

'No reply?' he asked her. He came up and tried the bell himself. He waited, and then he shook his head. 'He's home okay: I didn't see him leave. But he's probably taking a shower. Here, why don't I let you in? Then you can give him a nice surprise.'

'Are you allowed to?' asked Morgana, as Freddie tugged out his bunch of keys, and selected the master key to the apartments on eleven. Freddie gave her a conspiratorial nod. 'It's okay, I know you enough to trust you. I mean, what are the odds against Miss Morgana Croft Tate lifting any of Mrs Birmingham's jewelry, or walking off with any of her furs?'

He opened the apartment door, and let Morgana in. The hallway was in darkness; even the living room lights had been switched off now. But there was a sharp chink of light showing from under one of the bedroom doors at the far end of the main corridor. Morgana turned to Freddie and whispered, 'You'd better disappear. You don't want to get into any trouble. I can always say that I tried the door and found that it was unlocked.'

'Goodnight, Miss Croft Tate,' Freddie smiled, and touched his hat.

'Oh, wait,' said Morgana, and opened her pocketbook and gave him a dollar.

When Freddie had gone and the elevator had sunk to the ground floor, Morgana tippy-toed along the darkened corridor until she reached the door with a light under it. She pressed her ear against it. She could hear a murmuring sound, as if a radio had been left on low: a kind of continuous conversational burble, like a news commentary. Morgana waited for a moment, and then reached out and grasped the door handle.

'Surprise!' she cried out, flinging open the door.

The bedroom was brightly lit by two white bedside lamps. There, right in front of Morgana's eyes, crouched John and Phoebe — Phoebe with her face half-buried in the pillow and her bottom lifted, naked except for pink garters and pink silk stockings — John behind her, naked too except for his open dress shirt, thrusting himself into her with fierce, quick strokes, as if he were right on the brink of his climax.

The radio beside the bed was obliviously reporting on the day's news.

John stopped thrusting and stared at Morgana as if she had thrown a bucket of cold water over him. Phoebe opened her eyes and caught sight of Morgana through a tangle of blonde curls. Morgana stepped back, very stiffly, like an actress in a very bad amateur play. It was impossible to tell which of them was the most horrified.

Morgana saw everything in relentless detail, the kind of detail which she would go over and over in her mind's eye for months to come. The red scratch marks on John's thigh. The crushed look of Phoebe's pink lips. The skewed sheets, the rumpled quilt. John's necktie on the floor. And the very worst thing of all was the smell of Phoebe's perfume and fresh sex.

Suddenly, without understanding how it had started happening, Morgana found the corridor was jumbling its way past her, and she was out of the door, and clapping the flat of her hand against the elevator button again and again in a desperate and hysterical attempt to escape. She heard John calling her, but his voice sounded very slow and blurry, like a film run at the wrong speed. '*Maaawwhhhghaaaanaaaaahh . . .*'

The elevator doors opened in front of her. She collided with its far wall. It carried her downwards on a journey that seemed to last for months. It was cramped and stifling, the elevator car, and the face that watched her in the small vanity mirror was almost gray. She walked out through the lobby of the apartment building and there was Freddie smiling like a mortician and of course he must have known all along that Phoebe was up there, that was what the Birmingham's maid had wanted to tell John in private, that Phoebe had already arrived.

The lukewarm night air tightened her stomach and churned up the crabmeat crêpes and the pheasant and the peaches *flambées*, not to mention the six-ounce Pump Room martini and all that champagne. The Checker cab driver opened the door for her, and held out his hand to assist her, but she waved him away, burking, and leaned over the gutter.

Freddie and the cab driver watched in silence as the heiress to the greatest daily newspaper in the United States was wretchedly sick down the front of her $700 evening gown.

20

Grant Clifford was at home only a block away from Walton Street, playing a last hand of poker with his friend from the apartment opposite, Dennis Pekko, before turning in. He sat at the card table in his shirtsleeves, wearing an eyeshade that Howard Croft Tate had given him as a joking present when he was first appointed editor of the *Star*. Dennis was retired now, but Grant liked him because he remained witty and knowledgeable and pragmatic, and most of all because he knew nothing at all about newspapers. Dennis had made a respectable amount of money out of confectionery, and now he spent his time reading, walking in the park, cooking, playing cards, and talking to his wife. 'When I was working for Brach's, I didn't talk to Hettie for thirty years. We've got a whole lot of catching up to do. Do you know something, in thirty years, I never found out she hated chocolate?'

Dennis was expounding on the evils of the forty-hour week when the telephone rang in the hallway, and Enid went to answer it. Grant lifted his hand for a moment to indicate to Dennis that he should be quiet for just a moment. There was something very Norman Rockwell about the scene at that moment: two men playing poker under a circle of lamplight in a modestly furnished living room, with dark traditional furniture, and antimacassars on every chair, and walls papered with twining roses, while outside in the well-lit hallway a silver-haired woman in a yellow dressing gown answered the phone, her own watercolors of poppies hanging reassuringly all around her.

'Yes,' said Enid. 'Yes.' Then she laid down the receiver, and came into the living room. 'It's Busby, dear. He says it's important.'

Dennis took his cigar out of his mouth and set it in the ashtray. 'Never play cards with a newspaper editor,' he said. 'You never get the chance to win your money back. Do you know something, I think he arranges for these guys to call him up on purpose?'

Grant went through to the hallway and picked up the phone. Enid stood close behind him, and for no reason at all found herself looking at his elbows, wrinkled and red. Grant said, 'Hello, Busby, what's the latest?'

Busby sounded fractious and tired. 'I just heard. They found another body, 955 West Grand Avenue. Same ritual-type killing. Woozy's coming around to pick me up, and we're going over there straight away.'

'Have you called Gordon?' asked Grant. 'Good, okay. Well, I'll talk to him myself. I want as much out of you as you can get. When you've finished at the scene, talk to the police commissioner. And get young Jenny out to talk to what's-his-name, that psychologist fellow who wrote that paper on the Heirens case.'

'DuQuesne,' said Busby. He knew everything and everybody connected with the Heirens case.

'That's him,' said Grant. 'And, listen, Busby, this feels to me like it's going to be a big one. A potential circulation-grabber, and an important criminal and social story altogether. If the *Star* can get a break on the killer, it's going to lift our prestige not only with the cops but with the whole community. Get all of your people out there quick. You can use Harry again, if you need him. I'll get on the line to Gordon right now.'

He put down the phone. Enid was watching him. 'What's wrong, dear?' she asked him.

'They found another body. I may have to go in to the office.'

Dennis came to the living room door, a glass of whiskey in his hand. 'Another body? You mean, hacked up, like the other one?'

Grant nodded. He picked up the phone again and dialed the *Star*'s famous telephone number SUperior STAR. Gordon answered almost straight away. He sounded quite calm, inspite of the fact that the early editions were already printing and he was going to have to kill the front page and break open pages two and three. Because of the long-running typographical strike, the paper always had to start printing early, and 150,000 copies had been run with the headline HACKER WILL STRIKE AGAIN! when of course the Hacker had already struck. Still – they hadn't embarrassed themselves as seriously as the *Tribune* had, during the presidential elections last year, when they had carried a front-page headline in their early editions claiming DEWEY DEFEATS TRUMAN, only to have to change it during the night to DEMOCRATS MAKE SWEEP OF STATE OFFICES as Truman steadily captured the country. Colonel McCormick of the *Tribune* had never quite managed to live down that particular gaffe, and Howard had never grown tired of reminding him about it.

Gordon said, 'I've called in six extra girls to handle the varityping, and Hunziger's going to engrave the plates personally. If Woozy's quick, we may be able to run pictures of both murder scenes side by side.'

'Keep in touch,' Grant told him. 'I'm ready to come down to the office if you need me. And, by the way, how about an editorial? See what Frank can come up with. Maybe something along the lines of what turns a man into a ritual killer. The need for attention, the need to get revenge against society, Frank will know what to do.'

Gordon jotted all that down, and then asked, 'By the way – do you have any idea at all where Harry is? I've called him at home but he isn't there. I've called him at his mother's. I'd like to get him along to back up Busby.'

Grant lifted off his eyeshade. 'Where Harry Sharpe gets himself to in his time off is one of those questions I don't like to ponder on too deeply. But you could try O'Leary's.'

'I tried O'Leary's first.'

Grant put down the phone and returned to the living room. Dennis was waiting at the card table for him. 'Do you want to raise me?' Dennis asked him.

Grant shook his head. 'I'm sorry. Let's carry on tomorrow maybe. I can't keep my mind on the game tonight. This Hacker story is really breaking big, believe me. This is going to be one of those stories they quote for years to come. God – it makes you shudder, doesn't it, Dennis, to think that there's a man out there in the city tonight who can kill women and cut them into pieces, and he's probably sitting in a bar or waiting for a bus or riding on the El, and other innocent people are sitting there right beside him.'

Dennis sniffed, and grimaced. 'You know your problem, Grant? You've been working for the prints so long you're beginning to *talk* like them. I think the whole question is, where are the cops? Where are Chicago's finest, now that we need them? Oh, sure, they're always around when you're making an illegal U-turn, or parking in front of a hydrant, but when there's a hacker loose, where are they, that's what I want to know? Whittling assholes for hobbyhorses.'

Grant poured himself another whiskey, and sat back in his chair. 'You know something?' he said. 'When I was a young feature writer in Philadelphia, I always dreamed of editing my own newspaper. The newspaper I really wanted to edit was the *New York Times*. But, you know, what I never realized then was the responsibility that a newspaper editor has toward the city that he covers. It's almost more burdensome than being mayor. At least the mayor has his clear legal duties and he has the executive power to be able to carry them out. But when you're a newspaper editor, do you know, your duties include everything you can think of – from making people laugh to taking a serious interest in their broken drains. You're expected to help the weak, support the strong, be loyal to your city, tell the truth, expose the villainous, compliment the charitable, and at the same time amuse and entertain everybody from crib to burial box without offending or upsetting any section of your readership religious or ethnic. All this without displeasing your publisher, and more importantly, without displeasing your advertisers, from whom all revenue springeth. Sometimes, Dennis, I think it's all too much.'

Dennis sucked a tobacoo leaf off the front of his teeth, and extracted it between finger and thumb. He thought for a moment, and then he called, 'Enid!'

'Yes, Dennis?' said Enid, appearing in the doorway.

'Enid, your husband needs some of your poor-boy sandwiches, and quick. He's beginning to wax philosophical.'

Grant couldn't help laughing. 'You know something, Dennis, you're incorrigible. Enid – forget about the sandwiches, he's not serious. Just because he's in the catbird seat in this one game, he wants to carry on until he's cleaned me out.'

The clock in the hallway chimed midnight. Enid said, 'I'm going to bed now.'

Twenty minutes after Enid had closed her bedroom door, Busby Brill and Woozy drew up outside 955 West Grand Avenue, a narrow four-story brick building next to a garbage-strewn waste lot and a low factory building belonging to the Miller Peerless Mfg Co. To the south east, only a mile away, the glittering towers of the Loop district rose into the night sky. To the east, the wealthy apartment blocks of the Gold Coast shimmered like Camelot. But this district was like a tidal pool, into which at various seasons waves of different races had washed, and then receded again – Swedes, Germans, Italians, Polish and Russian Jews, Puerto Ricans, Negroes and southern whites. Busby sniffed dryly. Whenever he was tired, his sinuses began to irritate him.

There were five squad cars and an ambulance from the coroner's department parked in the street. Car radios blurted and chafed, and red lights flashed. Already a large crowd of silent people had gathered behind the police barriers, most of them black, but a few orthodox Jews as well, in spectacles and black suits.

Busby was not at all surprised to be greeted by Police Commissioner Philip Spectorski, in full parade uniform, beneath which Busby's cynical eye took note of the puffed-out chest and pinched-in waist which was the characteristic result of wearing a Sears moleskin obesity belt. Commissioner Spectorski's face was the color of prosciutto, and he was in a patent condition of blustery panic. He hated to be questioned by the press: he always shouted back at them as if they were making prurient enquiries about his mother. Busby loved questioning him. It was Busby's calling in life to irritate people.

Woozy immediately took a picture of Commissioner Spectorski, and Commissioner Spectorski swatted impatiently at the flash of the camera, and shouted, 'No unofficial pictures! You got me? No unofficial pictures!'

'I'm sorry, Commissioner,' said Busby, in a silky tone. 'I'll make sure you're warned next time, so that you can smile. Mind you, this is no smiling matter we have here today, is it?'

The usual crowd of raggle-taggle reporters had showed up. Vincent Geruso, James Gavin, Bill Keen, with their attendant photographers. James Gavin said, 'Are we seeing the mortal remains this time, Commissioner? If so, can we get it over?'

'Follow me,' said Commissioner Spectorski, with tightly suppressed contempt, and led the way up the three steps to the red-painted front door of 955. Police and reporters trooped loudly through the hall and up the stairs. The plaster on the walls bulged with damp and fungus, the lining paper hung down from the ceilings in sinister drooping swathes, like winding sheets at a cemetery. There was a foxy smell of urine and decay. On the second-floor landing, there was a bicycle frame with no wheels and a cardboard box filled with twenty or thirty whiskey bottles, all empty.

'Looks like the wire-service people got here ahead of us,' joked James Gavin.

Commissioner Spectorski turned around and glowered at him from under the polished peak of his cap. 'Nobody's been here, except witnesses and police and medical examiners. Do you understand me?'

James Gavin saluted. 'Yes, sir. Got you, sir.'

They were ushered into a third-story apartment. It was dark and chilly, like a nest for demons. To the left of the front door, there was a small galley of a kitchen, with an old-fashioned gas cooker, and a sink cluttered with dirty dishes. There were half-empty bottles of sour milk, a tipped-over carton of Grape Nuts, and a collection of cans – tuna, apricots, baked beans, some of them with spoons in, all of them stinking.

'Not exactly the Drake,' said James Gavin.

It was the last humorous remark that any of them made. Without a word, Commissioner Spectorski led them through to the living room, a high-ceilinged room with a blanket hung over the window instead of drapes, and walls smeared with dirt. There were only two pieces of furniture, a side dresser with no doors on it, and a large Grand Rapids armchair. A bare bulb gave the room a ghastly and depressing cast of shadows, but illuminated the woman's dead body in undiscriminating detail. A Negro woman, what was left of her. No artist or film maker would have lit her body so harshly. No stage director would have left her right in the very center of the room. The effect would have been criticized by tomorrow morning's papers as 'overpowering even for the most sensitive stomachs.'

Busby stood with his hands in his coat pockets staring at the woman's remains and wondering almost for the first time in his life what questions he was going to ask. What more could you possibly wish to know about a woman who had died like this? The flashbulbs flickered on either side of him, summer lightning. Even if good taste prevented them from publishing pictures of the body today, somebody would want them in years to come, as soon as they became historical.

'Her name was Catherine Burnham Mead,' intoned Commissioner Spectorski. 'She was a prostitute and a dope addict, twenty-one years old or thereabouts, and she lived here with her eight-year-old son Wilbur. So far we haven't located Wilbur, nor have we located Miss Mead's one-time partner Jeffrey Attwooll. The old lady who lives on the fourth floor says that Miss Mead very rarely took any clients on Sunday, on account of she wanted to go to church in the morning and spend the rest of the day with her son. She was always telling the old lady that one day Jesus would save her.'

Nobody had any smart remarks to make about that. It seemed grotesque to talk about what had been left in the armchair as 'Miss Mead', but Busby supposed that was the only way to talk about it. He supposed Commissioner Spectorski could have called it 'the victim' or 'the bits'.

Catherine Mead's attacker had cut off her head, her arms, and her legs. Then he had propped her torso in the armchair, upside down, and split it open from vagina to breastbone. He had pushed the head into the gaping abdominal cavity, so that Catherine Mead's blood-smeared face was looking out at them from inside her own body. The legs and the arms had been stacked in front of the torso, quite neatly. There was so much blood that it looked as if it had been dropped on to the chair from fifty feet up, out of a bucket.

Busby pointed to the body with the end of his pencil. 'Is there anything ... apart from the way this has been done ... is there anything to connect it with the homicide of Mrs Leonidas?'

Commissioner Spectorski nodded. 'The preliminary findings show matching footprints, same type shoe sole. Mind you, they were British Walkers, very common shoes, so we can't be conclusive until we've got them under a microscope. There are no fingerprints this time, Miss Mead's assailant used gloves. Added to that, nobody heard nothing, nobody saw nothing. Even if they did, they probably wouldn't have looked twice, on account of men were coming up and down here all the time.'

'Any sign of murder weapons?' asked James Gavin.

'Not this time, no. But it would have taken a particularly sharp type knife to cut clean through the abdominal wall, and it looks on preliminary examination as if some instrument like a butcher's cleaver was used to sever the head and the arms.'

'Do you have any idea how she was actually killed in the first place?' asked Vincent Geruso. He kept his eyes on his notebook; he didn't look across at the dismembered body. All of them knew that they were going to have nightmares about the way that Catherine Mead was staring at them glassy-eyed out her own carcass.

Commissioner Spectorski said, 'So far, we don't have any conclusive evidence on that.'

'You going to catch this guy?' asked Busby.

Commissioner Spectorski's nostrils flared out. 'What kind of a question is that, Brill?'

'The kind of question that every defenseless woman in this city is going to be asking herself as soon as she finds out that the Hacker has hacked again.'

'You listen to me, Brill, this is a random killer we're dealing with here. A maniac with no rhyme or reason. One day he chops up a housewife; the next day he chops up a prostitute. Who knows what kind of a man he is? Who knows what goes on inside of his brain? But we're going to find out, and we're going to find out quick, and we're going to make an arrest just as soon as is humanly possible, so don't you start climbing up my back, expecting me to collar this guy even before the body's gone cold.'

'Okay, Commissioner, keep your wig on,' said Busby.

Vincent Geruso walked around the blood-painted chair as if he were examining a piece of modern sculpture. 'What do you think, Commissioner? Some kind of religious maniac?'

'I can't comment on that,' Commissioner Spectorski replied. 'Obviously we've got detectives checking through ethnological records to see if this type killing bears any relation to some known religious ritual.'

They all trooped out of the apartment and returned downstairs. The sidewalk was floodlit now, and movie cameramen from Movietone and the television news were waiting for Commissioner Spectorski to make a public comment. Busby and Woozy didn't wait around any longer, however. They climbed into Woozy's car and sped straight back through the empty bright-lit streets to the *Star* building. Busby drove while Woozy wound the film out of his camera. There was a messenger boy waiting for them on the corner of Wabash Avenue as they passed the front of the *Star*. Woozy tossed the boy his film and he ran inside to have it urgently processed.

'I just hope they catch this guy soon,' said Woozy, lighting a cigarette in the elevator in blatant contravention of a Smoking Prohibited sign. 'I'm not sure how many more of those disassembled ladies I can take.'

Busby lifted an eyebrow but said nothing. His mind was already writing his story; and he was turning the facts of the homicide over and over, like a man examining a newly fallen meteorite, seeking some clue to what it was made of, and where it had come from, and why.

He had never come across killings like these before. Usually, when there was some kind of ritual dismemberment, there was a strong sexual link. There would be evidence of torture or rape or drinking of blood. In this case, however, although the genitalia had been savagely cut open, there was nothing to suggest that the killer had been interested in anything else but murdering Catherine Mead simply for the sake of murdering her, and then arranging her remains in the grisliest and most horrific way possible. There was a disgusting showmanship about it, and that was what disturbed Busby more than anything else.

He went straight to his desk, lifted off his coat, loosened his necktie, lit his leather-covered Longchamps pipe, and shucked a sheet of copy paper into his upright Underwood. They were the practised, uncomplicated gestures of a man who had been returning to the office for twenty years and going through exactly the same performance. He rattled off the first paragraph without hesitation (it had all been composed in his head in the elevator).

hacker 1   bb
Detectives were frantically searching through books on primitive religious rituals today in the hope of understanding the reason

why a brutal killer dismembered two Chicago women over the weekend.

He continued:

> Their bodies – with arms and legs and heads cut off – were both discovered by neighbors in what Police Commissioner Philip L. Spectorski described as 'horrifying sacrificial arrangements.'
>
> And Spectorski warned that the two-time hacker could very well strike someplace else in the city – and soon.

As he reached the conclusion of each paragraph, he tugged the paper out of the typewriter and held it over his right shoulder without even looking to see if a copy-boy was standing there to take it. Of course, there usually was; but there had been one or two occasions when Busby had written an entire story, dropped it over his shoulder on to the floor, and then walked away and left it where it was, for the copy editors to pick up.

Only after the fifth paragraph did he pause for a moment to light his pipe. He sucked away at it for a while, and then continued typing, more steadily now. The lighting of the pipe was also a signal to Gordon McLintock that he could emerge from his office and come up to Busby's pigpen to see how things were getting along. A copy editor was already marking up the first paragraphs of Busby's story, 7D on 8½pt Regal clc × 10½ ems – that meant a type size of seven points with one-and-a-half-point space in between each line, capitals and lower case, across a column width of ten and a half ems. The copy was then taken by hand down to the girls waiting on the varitypers downstairs. Usually, copy was whisked around the *Star* building by pneumatic tube, but this story was too urgent to risk it going astray.

'Well?' asked Gordon, his hands in his pockets, watching Busby's nicotine-stained fingers rattling over the worn-down keys of his Underwood. 'What kind of a story do we have?'

'Straightforward two-time homicide so far,' said Busby, his teeth clenching his pipe stem. 'But there's some interesting ramifications for the afternoon paper, what kind of a man is the Hacker, that kind of stuff, especially if Jenny comes up with some good psychology. And if we're *really* on our toes, I think we might be able to track this joker down – either with the cops or without them.'

'Sounds like four pennies times one million to me,' said Gordon, with cautious satisfaction.

Busby finished another folio, and handed it back to the copy-boy. 'Any sign of Harry yet? I'd like to get him out and about.'

'Nothing so far. Maureen rang him about a half-hour ago, still no reply.'

'Well, that's a pity. Trust Harry to go fishing just when I need him bad. How about young Wollensky? What's he doing?'

'I sent him to North Green to talk to the dead woman's parents.'

'North Green on a dark summer night like this? Rather him than me.'

Busby finished his story and handed the last folio of copy paper to the boy who ran up to him just in time to catch it. Then he swiveled around in his chair, and asked, 'How about Frank's editorial? Do you have it in yet?'

'He phoned it through ten minutes ago. David! Do you have a copy of that Hacker editorial? It's the usual *donner-und-blitzen.*'

David Tribe came over, his shirt sleeves rolled up, a pencil stuck behind each ear, a large thumbprint on the left lens of his spectacles. 'It's being set already,' he told Gordon. 'But here's a black.'

A 'black' was a carbon copy. David handed it over and Busby flicked through it quickly, sniffing and pipe-puffing. 'Amazing, isn't it?' he commented, when he had finished. 'I think Frank can write this stuff in his sleep.'

'This weekend, two women were viciously murdered in the city of Chicago. Today, their killer remains on the loose, a specter of terror, thirsty to kill again.

'As we wait with stopped heartbeats for the painstaking investigations of police and reporters to bring the killer to justice, we ask ourselves some penetrating questions. Questions about the very nature of our city and our society.

'We ask – has a city where titanic wealth and grinding poverty stand shoulder to shoulder in the same street given birth to a new and bizarre kind of killer? Has a society in which the rewards of success are skyscraper-high but in which the consequences of failure are skid-row low produced a personality which murders and dismembers not for lust or for profit but as a ritual act to guard against those two most savage and conclusive of American ju-jus – being poor and being unnoticed?'

The editorial went on and on for thirty paragraphs in a similar vein, heaping cliché on top of cliché, until the reader was left with a dizzying sense of confidence that the *Star* really cared about the Hacker murders – that the Croft Tate newspapers demanded not only the better protection of innocent women, and the immediate arrest of the Hacker, but a radical change in the social structure of Chicago so that no such killer would ever emerge again. The copy editor had headlined the editorial BITTER FRUIT, after the famous line from the *Shadow* radio show, 'The weed of crime bears bitter fruit.'

They went down together to the press room in the basement of the *Star* building. There was an uncanny echoing silence down here, considering it was two o'clock in the morning and the presses should have been running at full blast. The press room was two stories in height, with green-painted walls, and housed 126 black press units, twenty-three color units, and twenty-four folders, all arranged in four long rows, a city block long. Each of the new Goss Headliner presses weighed twenty-five tons, and was mounted on specially designed springs, which themselves were mounted on steel and concrete caissons which had been sunk 110 feet below the floor down to solid bedrock. This kept vibration throughout the *Star* building to a minimum; which was especially important for their radio and television studios.

Herman Short – a stubby crew-cut German who was in charge of the presses at night – came over to Gordon and Busby, wiping grease off his hands with a rag. 'You people finished giving me ulcers?' he wanted to know.

Gordon said, 'Are you ready to run?'

'All but. They're locking in the last plate now.'

'How late are we going to be running?'

'An hour, maybe fifty minutes.' He went over to what he called his 'office', a steel table cluttered with wrenches and rags and mugs of scummy coffee and pieces of printing press. Taped to the wall behind the table was a complicated timetable of press-running schedules, as well as a poster on how to treat electric shock, a postcard of palm trees from his sister in Tampa, Florida, and a pin-up painting of a girl in a sheer black nightdress opening her front door at three o'clock in the morning to let in her small beribboned kitten.

'I've got one line down to overhaul the ink fountains, but if I can get that running by half after, I might be able to cut it down to twenty minutes late.'

'All right, see what you can do,' said Gordon; and even as he spoke the warning siren screamed, and the rheostats started the motors, and gradually the huge presses began to turn over, building up speed like three massive locomotives to nowhere, until they were running at their top pph of 60,000.

Here was power: the power of giant machines, capable of printing ninety-six-page newspapers with full-color pictures at a rate of more than sixteen copies a second, and the power of the press itself, the dissemination of more than a million newspapers to more than two and a half million readers, from Busby Brill's typewriter and Woozy's camera to the newstands all around Chicago, in less than forty-five minutes.

The noise of the presses was thunderous. Press-men wearing square newsprint hats climbed all around the half decks, checking the tension of the web of newsprint as it streamed up and down through the presses, keeping a watchful eye on the conveyors, folders and stackers. At the far end of the press room, a line of fifteen bright scarlet Chrysler trucks was parked, tailgates hanging down, waiting for the first bundles of newspapers to be driven up the ramps and out into the streets. It was twenty-five minutes after two. Gordon McLintock stood with his hands on his hips watching the presses and it was one of those moments when he knew for certain that he never wanted to do anything else.

Herman Short waddled in his baggy white overalls down to the stacker and whipped out two copies of the newspaper without even disturbing the evenly advancing row of folded copies. He brought one back for Gordon and one for Busby.

'What do you think?' he asked, in his thick Teutonic accent. 'Reckon the guys deserve a bonus for this one, ya?'

The front page carried two pictures, side by side – one of the bloodstained hallway in the house where Mrs Leonidas had died, one of the chair in which Catherine Mead's body had been found, but photographed from the back, so that her actual remains could not be seen. Underneath the pictures ran a page-wide headline HACK TWO WOMEN TO DEATH Cops Seek Ancient Ritual Clue In Double Murder.

Busby's story ran underneath the main headline. Harry's earlier story, rewritten to fit the discovery of the second murder, ran beneath it. Pages two and three were taken up with a variety of special reports on the murder, interviews with Mrs Leonidas' friends and relatives, a police drawing of a possible suspect, and the BITTER FRUIT editorial.

'Who knows what evil lurks in the hearts of men?' asked Busby, folding up the paper and tucking it under his arm. 'I'm going over to O'Leary's for a quick one before it closes. You want to join me?'

Gordon shook his head. 'I'll stick around. Call me when you leave O'Leary's, I want to know where you are. The way this guy's going, he'll probably have hacked up three more women and a goat by morning.'

Herman Short interjected, 'That guy ain't allowed to hack *nobody* or *nothing* until we finish this run. Otherwise he's going to have to answer to me, personal.'

Busby left the *Star* building and crossed Wabash Avenue to O'Leary's. Roy Chamberlain saw him coming, and his 'burra-peg' of Canadian whiskey was waiting for him by the time he reached the bar.

'Hard day at the office, dear?' asked Roy.

A Negro maid had laid out a light supper of cold cuts, crackers, cheese, and dry white wine, with a cold bottle of beer for Harry if he wanted it. Harry and Marcella had sat on the floor and started talking to each other, cautiously at first, but then loudly and broadly and happily, laughing a lot, enjoying each other's company, relishing each other's straightforwardness. There was no question about it, either – Harry found Marcella highly stimulating to look at, especially when she reached over to cut herself another piece of cheese and that silky black V-neck slipped aside and revealed for one tantalizing instant the curved white underside of one breast.

'Don't think that I haven't thought about the moral dilemma I'm in, being my father's daughter,' Marcella had told him, munching Longhorn cheddar and Bath Oliver. 'I must have thought about it twice a day every day since I was old enough to understand that my father wasn't the kind of father who goes to work at the Prudential every morning and comes home at night with the evening paper and a bunch of flowers.'

Harry had popped an olive in his mouth at the same time as huffing in amusement at the notion of Enzo Vespucci in a gray flannel suit, working in insurance.

But Marcella had asked him, anxiously, 'What can I do? I've thought about all kinds of ways of reforming him. I've thought about asking Cardinal Langella to visit him, to explain that he's doing wrong. Don't laugh, I'm serious. I've even thought about going to the State's Attorney's office, and ratting on him, so that they'll send him off to Joliet for the rest of his life, where he can't hurt anybody but other criminals, and himself. I've thought about cutting myself off from him – never speaking to him – emigrating to Peking, or at least to Boise. But I can't get away from the fact that he's my natural father, Harry, my *father*! I sprang out of his loins, if you want to be Biblical about it; but I'm his daughter and even if I'm guilty of collusion and conspiracy in all of those dreadful things he does, I can't sell him out, I can't deny him, because I love him, and he loves me.'

Harry had thoughtfully sipped his wine. 'What you're telling me is that you love a man who keeps thousands of human beings in conditions that you and me wouldn't even keep our pet slugs in. Am I right?'

Marcella had dropped her gaze down to the diamond and sapphire rings on her immaculately manicured hands. 'Of

21

'How about some breakfast before you go?' Marcella suggested. 'There isn't a mobster's daughter in Chicago who scrambles better eggs.'

Harry pushed his hand through his hair so that it stuck up like Stan Laurel's. 'What time is it?' He looked at his wristwatch. 'I don't believe it – nearly four.'

'Time flies when you're having fun,' Marcella smiled.

Harry was sitting cross-legged on the rug, with his back against the couch, and he stiffly unwound himself and stood up. 'The first thing I'd better do is get myself some sleep. I have to be back in the office by nine.'

'You can sleep here if you want to. And you can always borrow a clean shirt. My mother has stacks of them. In case of gentlemen callers, you know. Some of those shirts have beem moldering in the closet since before the war. More shirts than callers, you see.'

Harry had arrived at Marcella's apartment promptly at eleven. He had been irrationally inspired to wear his Sunday suit, which was blue chalk-stripe with wide padded shoulders and wide lapels that always hung sadly forward, no matter how many times he tried to flap them back. Marcella had greeted him at the door in a ravishing black silk wrap, with pleated batwing sleeves and a deep V-shaped neckline. She had led him into an opulent living room decorated in peacock blue and silver, with gilded antique furniture and a fluted marble fireplace, and a portrait of her mother hanging in one corner. A dark, hauntingly attractive woman, just like Marcella; the kind of woman who looks more like a queen from a fairy story than a living, breathing, practically minded mother.

course you're right. I'm not denying it. I've seen those slums for myself.'

They had talked for over an hour about the tangled morality of Marcella's family; not evasively or guardedly but with complete directness. Now, at six minutes of four in the morning, Harry felt that he had a glimmering understanding of what it was that drove Enzo Vespucci to behave the way he did, to grasp whatever he could, and God damn the human consequences. It was chilling; it was enough to leave the taste of blood and distrust in anybody's mouth; but it helped Harry to grasp the nature of the man whose life and corrupted works he was determined to destroy.

Marcella led the way through to the marble-tiled kitchen, and opened up the huge domed Frigidaire. 'We have eggs, we have bacon, we have cold spaghetti salad.'

'Some coffee would do me fine,' said Harry. He lifted the window blind a little and looked out over the lights of Lincoln Park. He turned back to Marcella and smiled and said, 'Just coffee.'

'What are you going to do about your fire story?' asked Marcella.

Harry pushed his hands into his pockets. 'There's not much I can do. I'm only a minion. The management have told me to keep my nose out of it. Not just my editor, the big-caliber management. The way I understand it, the legal department have convinced Howard Croft Tate that if we try to tie your old man in with the torching of his own slum properties, he's sure to sue; and not for Boston dollars, either.'

Marcella opened the ceramic coffee jar. 'Have you asked yourself why Howard Croft Tate is so worried?' she asked.

Harry narrowed his eyes and looked at Marcella carefully. 'Do I detect the accents of somebody who knows more than they're telling?'

'You're too sharp, Harry Sharpe. One day you'll cut your own tongue.'

Marcella switched on the kettle. 'I thought your paper was afraid of nobody. Why should your management be so frightened of offending my father? You know what my father is. How do you think his word would stand up in a court of law against the fearless honest words of somebody like you? Against your newspaper?'

Harry smoothed down his hair. He didn't answer.

Marcella brought two breakfast cups down from the shelf. 'You should ask *yourself* questions, you know, as well as other people.'

'Such as?' said Harry.

'Such as, will this lady help me in any way at all? Has she perhaps been looking for a way to punish her father, without having to commit herself personally?'

Harry reached into the breast pocket of his shirt and took out a crumpled pack of Luckies. He offered one to Marcella but Marcella shook her head. 'I guess without realizing it I've been looking for a long time for somebody like you,' she told him. 'Somebody with no phool-ium, hokey-ium, or baloney-ium. Maybe I'm a coward. Maybe I'm going to regret talking to you for the rest of my life. But when you told me you were after my father there was a light in your eyes and I could see then that you believe in what you're fighting for.'

She hesitated. Then she said, 'I love him, but there has to come a time when somebody tells him, enough already.'

Still watching her, still silent, Harry lit his cigarette.

Marcella said, 'I can't finger him personally. I won't. That sounds like a mobster's daughter, doesn't it? "Finger." But, well, I'll tell you what I can do – I can tell you who it was set light to that building on 31st Street. I heard my father talking about it on the telephone when we were out at the track. "Don't forget to pay off Medill," that's what he said.'

'You heard him say that?' Harry asked her. 'How do you know he was talking about the fire?' He was trying to remain very calm and unimpressed, although his heart in actual fact was falling off skyscrapers.

'I just know. You'll have to take my word for it.'

'Do you have any idea who Medill is?'

Marcella said, 'No. But I think he must work for some city department. My father kept talking about the "inside dope on City Hall." I didn't hear very much more.'

Harry looked serious. 'You understand that if I can find out who this guy Medill is, and if I can prove that he torched that building, and if I can also prove that your father contracted him to do it – then your father may be looking at a jail term? Not very long, if his lawyers are any good – but it's a possibility.'

Marcella stood very silent and still. She was a beautiful girl.

Where her father had the looks of a venal priest she had the looks of a dark-haired saint.

'His name is Medill,' she repeated, in a firm whisper. 'That's all I can tell you; that's all I know.'

'Okay,' said Harry. He looked around for someplace to stub his cigarette. 'Let's have that coffee, shall we?'

They sat together in the living room, very close together, Marcella saying almost nothing. Gradually, behind the drapes, the sky began to lighten, and it was Monday morning. Harry drank his coffee, smoked, and wondered what he was going to do next.

'Have I worried you?' asked Marcella. Her face was as pale as milk, and there were dark circles under her eyes.

Harry said, 'No, I don't think so. It takes a lot to get me worried these days. I worry when I lose a sawbuck at Washington Park, who wouldn't? I worry when my mother tells me I'm getting thin. But those are serious matters, you know. And, anyway, I'm not in love with anyone right now. Being in love is one of those things that makes you worried. I think love and worry are two sides of the same coin. Think about *Romeo and Juliet*. What the hell was that all about? Two people, worrying. The only difference between love and worrying is that you can't have babies through worrying, although one time when I was worried about getting a job I can tell you I just about laid an egg.'

At the very moment he said the word 'babies', Harry heard a clogged-up intake of breath from another room in the apartment, following by the first cackling of a baby's cry. The rest of his sentence was simply mouthed, syllables filled with nothing but air. He stared at Marcella, and said, 'That's a *baby*. I said "babies", I said "you can't have babies", and what happens?'

Marcella smiled. 'Let me get him.' She unexpectedly kissed Harry on the cheek, and went through to the bedroom. When she came back she was carrying a frowzled-faced baby boy of ten months old, who blinked and frowned at Harry, and then buried his head in Marcella's shoulder. He wore a pale blue sleep suit with a buttoned back-flap and elephants embroidered on the collar. His hair stuck up like a little black wisp of smoke.

'This is Eduardo,' said Marcella. She nuzzled the little boy's head. 'I think he wants me to change him.'

'He's yours?' asked Harry, in surprise.

'My first and only. My mother said that it was criminal of me to keep him, I should have had him adopted. But look at him. How could I give him up?'

'Here, give him here,' said Harry, and Marcella handed the boy down to him. Harry sat him on his knee and jiggled him up and down. Eduardo stared at him with grave uncertainty.

'What does his grandfather think of him?' asked Harry. 'Come on, chum. Kidjy, kidjy, kidjy.'

'His grandfather spoils him,' said Marcella. 'Poor Eduardo, to have a grandfather like that. Poor me, to have a father like that.'

Eduardo's mouth suddenly turned down at the corners and he burst into tears, and Marcella had to take him back. 'He's not used to me yet,' Harry told her.

Holding Eduardo on her hip, Marcella walked across the room and tugged the drapes. Outside, the early morning sky was that particular color called Amish blue. There was something melancholy but expectant about the streets below, the few people already walking to work, the occasional autos, still with their sidelights winking.

'Do you think that God will forgive me?' asked Marcella, turning back and looking Harry straight in the eye. 'For telling you about Medill, I mean.'

Harry shrugged. 'I don't know. I don't know where "honor thy father and thy mother" begins and I don't know where it ends.'

He came up to Marcella and held out his pinkie, so that little Eduardo could take hold of it. 'Do you still see his father?' he asked.

'Now and then. Not so much recently.'

'Don't tell me his father isn't proud of him.'

Marcella shrugged. 'His father has another life to lead. He pays money to keep him, he sends him gifts. But he hardly ever comes to see him.'

Harry leaned forward and bipped Eduardo gently on the nose. 'Don't you worry, kid. I'll come see you. You want to know how to play baseball? You're looking at the stylishest pitcher that Roseland ever knew. As soon as you can walk, I'll take you over to Soldier's Field for some practice.'

Marcella said, 'Will you call me, if you find Medill? And

please don't let anyone know that I told you. My father is a vengeful man.'

Harry kissed Marcella's cheek. Her skin was very soft and she smelled of some musky perfume he couldn't identify. 'Listen, Marcella, let me tell you this – more than anything else in the world I want to see your father cut down to size – more than anything else in the world I want those slums cleared away – but if there's any risk of anything happening to you . . .'

Marcella shook her head. 'There won't be, so long as you never mention my name. It's time, Harry. If I don't do this now, I never will.'

Harry said, 'I'm still willing to forget you ever said Medill. And, believe me, that goes against my instincts.'

Marcella reached out and laid her hand palm-flat against his chest. There was a look in her eyes which was too complicated for him to be able to interpret exactly. Concern, determination, but affection, too. Harry didn't believe in love at first sight, but he knew that something had happened between them the moment they met.

'I want to see you again,' he told her.

'You will,' she assured him. 'Call me.'

Harry left her apartment block and returned to his yellow Woodie, which he had parked on North Dearborn. The windows were fogged up because of the early morning humidity, and somebody had prized off its last remaining hubcap. He climbed in, and drove through streets that were striped with sunshine to his own apartment building on Ashland Avenue, two blocks north of the offices of the Polish *Daily Zgoda*, the Polish-language newspaper where he had once worked. He had written his first column there, a collection of local news and gossip called 'Chit-Chat'.

His apartment was in the loft of a narrow four-story brick building owned by a Polish widow called Nina Czerwonka, a small fat motherly lady who always dressed in dusty black and who expected her tenants (all male, all single, all lonely in their individual ways) to call her *matka*, mother, and kiss her on the cheek when they left for work in the morning (always the cheek with the hairy wart on it).

Harry went up the stone steps in front of the building and let himself in. It wasn't quite five yet, everybody was still sleeping. The hallway floor was covered with green flecked linoleum, and the walls were papered in brown flowers. From the half landing at the top of the first flight of stairs, green and yellow sunlight filtered into the hall through a stained glass window. There was a strong smell of Fels-Naptha and salami fat.

Harry climbed as silently as he could to the top floor, and opened the brown-painted door of his rooms. There was a largish sitting room, with a huge old-fashioned sofa in the style once known as a 'Roman Davenport'. One side was supposed to let down, to form a bed, but it had been let down so often that now it stayed down. There was a rolltop desk in one corner, with a portable typewriter on it, and it was here that Harry had been trying to write his epic novel about Polish immigrants in Chicago in the 1900s. A thin lifeless carpet was spread on the floor, and on the walls there were lithographs of 'American Farm Scenes', dour-faced men and women going dourly about their daily tasks. Harry went through to the narrow kitchen, opened up his tabletop icebox, and took out a bottle of orange juice. He drank three swigs of it out of the bottle, standing in front of the open icebox, and then he put it back again.

He went through to his bedroom. It was small and square, with just enough room for a single bed covered with a blue candlewick bedspread and a sawed-oak closet where he kept his clothes. He sat on the bed and wearily undressed, rolling his soiled shirt up in a ball. Then he went back to the kitchen naked and washed himself at the sink with tepid water and Ivory soap. He dressed, and then shaved with a razor he should have changed two weeks ago, his face hovering in the mirror on the back of the kitchen cabinet door.

Mrs Czerwonka knocked. 'Harry! Is that you, Harry?'

He opened the door, tying up his necktie one-handed. Mrs Czerwonka immediately took hold of it, and tied it properly, tugging it from side to side to make sure that it was straight. 'Five times the paper called if once they called,' she scolded him. 'And where are you, out all night? How can I take good care of you if you don't live here no more? You pay your rent, live here, the place is yours. Somebody else would charge you three times! You want breakfast?'

'No thanks, *matka*, I'll eat at Irving's. I have to get down to the office right away.'

'Well, that's right! They called five times! Mr McClontick! I'm so worried, he said, where's this boy Harry? How should I know, I said. Himph!'

Harry brushed his hair, shucked on his coat, and left the house. It was ten after five now, and Mr Pincus' newstand at the intersection of Ashland and Milwaukee was opening up, so Harry crossed the street and bought a pack of Luckies and the *Star*.

So that was why Gordon had been calling him so frantically. HACK TWO WOMEN TO DEATH. And all the time he had been sitting in Marcella's apartment, whiling the night away with philosophical conversation and cups of coffee.

'Women aren't safe no more,' said Mrs Dzuba, who always passed here early in her moulting feather hat on her way to clean up at Alliance Printers.

'Women never were,' responded Mr Pincus, gloomily.

Harry drove a zigzag course down to the *Star* building by way of Division Street and Wacker Drive. As he crossed over the river, he was momentarily dazzled by the golden sunshine on the water. He glanced again at the newspaper lying on the seat beside him. So, the Hacker had hacked again, and he had missed out on it. Still – if he could locate the arsonist who had burned down the tenement on 31st Street, he would more than redeem himself, especially in Grant's eyes. He knew how sorely Grant wanted to get his teeth into Enzo Vespucci and the slum problem.

The *Star* offices were almost deserted when Harry arrived. He made himself a mug of coffee and read the paper from front to back. Dundas the copy-boy appeared, looking white-faced and tired. He perched himself on the edge of one of the pigpens and began monotonously to strum an elastic band which he clenched between his teeth, like a Jew's harp. Harry, his feet up on his desk, wreathed in cigarette smoke, said, 'What time is your audition with the Symphony Orchestra?'

At nine, when City Hall opened, Harry started making calls. First of all he talked to Judy Maloney, a secretary in the personnel section, and a one-time date (baseball, pizzas, no sex). Judy demurred at first, but in the end the promise of an Italian dinner persuaded her to check through the staff records for the name Medill. An hour later she called back to say that the city of Chicago had employed nobody of that name for over sixty years.

'Are you sure you have the name right?' she asked him, tartly.

'Medill, M-e-d-i-l-l. I'll pick you up Wednesday at seven. Do you like calamari?'

'I like any kind of cheese.'

'Well, that's nice, but calamari is squid.'

Harry turned to the telephone book. There were nine Medills listed in the Chicago metropolitan area, two Medalls, and one Medil. He called them all. Mr Medil had died early in March, Mr Medall and Mr Medall were father and son, and were both tailors. Six out of the nine Mr Medills answered their telephones, none of them had ever worked for City Hall. That left three Mr Medills still to be checked.

Harry drove to Weed Street on the North Side where Mr R. Medill lived. One of his neighbors leaned out of a second-floor window and shouted that Bob Medill had left his wife and gone to live in Madison, Wisconsin, and who could blame him. Then Harry drove to East Cullerton Street on the South Side and found Mr K. Medill, who owned a carpet store, and who almost persuaded Harry to buy a brown Smyrna rug with a picture of a dog on it. At last Harry went down to South Indiana Avenue, once one of the most fashionable streets in Chicago, but now peeling and tired and crowded with parked cars and pushcarts and garbage.

Because this was the last Mr Medill in the telephone book, Harry had the illogical but firm conviction that this was going to be the man he was after. He double parked his Woodie beside a broken-down Ford pick-up with flat tires, and crossed the sidewalk toward the entrance of a large old red-brick building with a sign outside that said ROOMS. As he did so, the doors opened and a slim young man with a pencil mustache and slicked-back hair came out, burrowing in his pockets for change or a key or something else he had forgotten.

'Does Mr P. Medill live here?' Harry asked him. The young man stopped and stared at him.

'That's me, P. Medill,' he retorted, in a snappy South Side accent. 'Who wants to know?'

'Mr Medill, I'm from the *Star*. I've been looking for three days now for everybody in Chicago called Medill on account of Mr Horace Medill the meat-packing millionaire died last week, and left twenty-five thousand dollars each to all of his distant relations. It's a great story, a wonderful opportunity, you could be rich.'

The young man eyed Harry suspiciously.

'You do *know* Horace Medill?' asked Harry, pointedly.

'Well . . . sure,' the young man replied, in a slow voice. 'I can't say that I ever met him, but I *know* him.'

'That's a good start, then,' Harry grinned at him. 'All I need to know now is what your mother's maiden name was.'

'Frankel,' the young man told him. Harry jotted it down as if it were important.

'And . . . what's your occupation, Mr Medill?'

'I'm a fireman, why?'

'Oh, you're a fireman, that's interesting. Which company are you with?'

'Twenty-nine, is that something you have to know?'

'Oh – we don't have to ask too many details, Mr Medill. If you could just give me your first names? It looks pretty much as if you're one of the relations we've been looking for.'

'Is that so?' said the young man, licking his lips, and stepping closer. 'You mean I might get twenty-five thousand dollars?'

'It's on the cards,' smiled Harry.

'Well, my first names are Peter Axelrod.'

'Ooohhkay,' said Harry. He folded up his notebook and pushed it back into his coat pocket. 'If you can stick around town for a day or two, Mr Medill, we'll be checking up to make sure that you're entitled to your share of the Medill millions, and call you just as soon as everything's signed, stamped, and delivered.'

Peter Medill took hold of Harry's hand and pumped it up and down. 'That's something! That's something! Well now, sheesh. You wait until the guys get to hear about this.'

Harry lifted a finger. 'I'd rather you kept it to yourself, at least until I've sent you the letter of confirmation. You see, we get so many impersonators, people pretending to be Medills when in fact they're really Browns and Gassmans and Hackenbushes. You wouldn't want to jeopardize your own legacy, now would you?'

'No, sir. I'm with you! Don't you worry, I'll keep mum. But don't you take too long getting back to me, will you? If that's my money, that twenty-five thousand, I want it quick!'

'Of course,' smiled Harry.

On the way back to the *Star*, he rehearsed again and again Peter Medill's clipped, abrasive accent. 'Umma fyman. Is dat summon ya hafda noh?' He was sitting at the traffic signals on State Street, saying over and over again, 'Umma fyman, umma fyman,' and a van driver waiting next to him leaned over and said, 'Hey! You forgot your hose!'

Back at the *Star*, there was a message on Harry's desk that Busby Brill wanted to see him, but first of all Harry picked up his phone, switched on his tape recorder and dialed the Fire Department. When they answered, he asked to speak to Chief Bryan.

There was a long wait. Harry could hear Chief Bryan's distinctive laugh in the background. Then at last the receiver was picked up, and Chief Bryan said, 'Bryan here. Who is this?'

Harry's heart tightened like a prodded sea anemone. 'It's Peter Medill here, Chief.'

'Medill? What the hell do you want? You know better than to call me here!'

'Chief, listen, something's come up. It seems like somebody's been talking. I met a guy in a bar last night and he said that he'd heard I was torching buildings for hire. He wanted me to burn down a place on Cottage Grove Avenue.'

Chief Bryan was almost apoplectic with anger. 'You listen to me, Medill, you've been paid your money for lighting that fire on 31st Street, I don't expect you to light any more. You understand me? I don't care how much you get offered, you don't do it.'

'Come on, Chief, he was offering twice what Vespucci paid,' said Harry. 'Maybe we could split it.'

Chief Bryan sounded suspicious. 'How do you know Vespucci paid for this job?'

'Chief, I live in the district, I work in the district. The only buildings around South Normal that Vespucci doesn't own are the newstands. Who else would have paid to torch one of Vespucci's rat-traps except for Vespucci?'

Chief Bryan was silent for a moment. Then he said, 'This is Peter Medill? You sound different somehow.'

'I got a cold. You know what it's like being a fireman. One minute you're hot, the next minute you're freezing.'

'This isn't Peter Medill!' Chief Bryan raged. 'Who the hell is this?'

Harry dropped his fake South Side accent. 'This is Harry Sharpe, Chief, Chicago *Star*. Everything you just said was recorded on a tape recorder, and I intend to use every word of it in the paper. Do you have any comment about that?'

Chief Bryan slammed down his receiver without uttering another word. Harry wound back his tape and then played it from the beginning. Chief Bryan's voice was loud and clear, and unmistakably the voice of Chief Bryan.

Harry dialed Marcella's number. Marcella sounded sleepy when she answered.

'Marcella? This is Harry Sharpe. I found Medill.'

'You were so quick!'

'I looked in the phone book, that's all. He wasn't hard to find. And, what's more, I got all the evidence I need linking him to Chief Bryan at the Fire Department, and Chief Bryan to you-know-who.'

Marcella was silent for a while. Then she whispered, 'God, I'm scared.'

'You don't have to be scared. You're not implicated in this in any way. Once we go to press, your father will probably have two hundred lawyers down here, and two hundred more down at police headquarters, and all that he'll get is a tut-tut from the State's Attorney. But it will give us the ammunition we've been looking for to support Mayor Doyle, and start loosening your father's grip on the slums.'

Marcella said, very quietly, 'I'm pleased.'

'Listen,' Harry told her, 'I have to go now. There's a whole lot to do. But can I see you tonight?'

'Yes,' Marcella told him. 'Seven o'clock. Come around here. You left your hat behind. Eduardo's sucking the brim into a wet pulp.'

'Well, you know what they say,' Harry replied. 'Never give a sucker an evening hat.'

He put down the phone, then picked it up again and called Woozy. He was so bullish he could hardly contain himself. 'Wooze? Get your tail up here. We're out to make a citizen's arrest. Star Reporter Apprehends Mob-Connected Firebug. That's right. And bring that wooden billy-club thing they gave you in Canada. The guy doesn't look too fierce but you never know, even small farts can bowl you over.'

Grant Clifford came weaving his way through the pigpens, well-shaved and dignified in a gray summer suit and a gray silk necktie. 'Well now, Harry, where were you last night? We could have used the extra hand.'

'Sure,' Harry acknowledged. 'I'm sorry, I was called away, kind of. My mother's Labrador had puppies. You know how it is.'

'Your mother's Labrador had puppies?' Grant repeated, with a disbelieving smile.

'This is some story,' said Harry, nodding toward the double murder on the front page. 'You want me to get involved?'

'What are you working on right now?'

Harry reached into his shirt pocket for a cigarette, and shrugged.

'You're following *something* up,' smiled Grant. 'You want to tell me what it is, or is it supposed to come as a shock?'

Grant expected his reporters to roam free; and to be creatively nosy; although he also considered that the full and proper coverage of the daily metropolitan diary was sacred. Grant knew and Harry knew that Harry was supposed to go out to Kedzie Avenue today to interview seven schoolgirls who had won a Statewide tap competition. Harry could have appealed to Grant to be taken off the item, but then he would have had to tell Grant what he wanted to do instead, and he dearly wanted to come back to the office with the Medill story all wrapped up as a surprise package.

'It's just a kind of a vague lead,' said Harry.

'Concerning?'

'Well . . . corruption, I guess.'

'Corruption?' Grant enquired.

Harry gave Grant an appealing, open-eyed look. Please, just this once, can I go out and get it without having to tell you what it is? He knew for a drop-forged fact that Grant would never sanction a citizen's arrest. When it came to the law, Grant did things by the book, and if there were any criminals to be caught, that was the task of the Police Department. Grant regularly had lunch at the Chicago Press Club with Commissioner Spectorski in the interests of better communication between the police and the press; and those monthly meals were prickly enough without having to explain why his junior staff were trying to play cops and robbers.

'All right,' said Grant. He looked at his Chicago and North Shore pocket watch. 'Just make sure you're around here by three o'clock. We're having a general conference on the

Hacker. And just make sure you turn in that tap-dance story.'

'Yes, sir,' said Harry.

'And be careful,' Grant added. 'I don't want you to get yourself into any trouble. You remember the phoney caviar story.'

Harry looked suitably chastened. 'Yes, sir. I remember the phoney caviar story.'

22

Morgana was still in bed at eleven o'clock when Eleanor tapped on the door of her room and let herself in. Her breakfast lay untouched on the white wicker tray beside her; her morning newspaper was unopened. The white rose which Millicent had picked from the garden and set in a small Lalique vase was already beginning to droop. The drapes remained drawn, closing out the morning sunshine.

Eleanor asked, 'May I come in?' Her voice was very gentle.

Morgana gave her a noncommittal glance. She wore a pale peach nightdress especially designed by Omar Kiam, and her dark hair was spread across the linen pillow like Ophelia's hair across the surface of the river. She was pale. She felt pale. She probably hadn't slept for longer than two hours all night.

Eleanor took away the breakfast tray and set it down on the bureau. Then she came over and broke her own rule of etiquette and sat on the side of the bed. She held Morgana's hand.

'How are you feeling?' she asked.

Morgana said, 'All right. I didn't sleep very well.'

Eleanor looked across at the bedside table and saw Morgana's engagement ring lying there, next to the pavé-diamond star. She said, sympathetically but firmly, 'Phoebe came in last night and told me what had happened. She was very upset.'

Morgana nodded. 'I can imagine. It isn't every day that you're caught *in flagrante* with your sister's fiancé of only forty-eight hours' standing.'

'This wasn't the first time,' said Eleanor. 'Phoebe was – well, she was quite frank about it. She told me everything.'

'I should have listened to you, shouldn't I, Momsy?' Morgana replied. 'You told me that John was going to be a romantic disaster. So did Oscar Hammerstein. It seems as if everybody knew what a broken reed he was except me.'

Eleanor said, 'My principal concern, my dear, is that this family doesn't get completely torn to pieces.'

Morgana looked her mother up and down. 'From you, Momsy, I think that's something of an impertinence, don't you?'

Eleanor drew a tight breath. 'What happened between me and Robert Wentworth is quite over.'

'Of course it is. Especially for him.'

'What I mean is that I regret it and that it will never happen again. I have told your father that already.'

'Does he believe you?'

Eleanor lowered her eyes. 'I don't know. He's going to fly to Los Angeles this afternoon. He says he wants to think.'

'Does he know about Phoebe and John?'

'Not yet. I think that he's been hurt quite enough as it is. In fact, one of the things I came to ask you was not to tell him just yet. Not just for Phoebe's sake or my sake, but for his sake. I've wronged him, I know it, but I desperately want us to stay together, and if he gets to hear about this – well, he may consider that living with all these untrustworthy women is just too much for him to take.'

Morgana stared at her mother coldly. She had never felt so cold to her before. 'Correction,' she said, 'not *all* these untrustworthy women. *All* implies three or more. Ask Grant, if you're concerned about the grammar. There are only two untrustworthy women in this house.'

Eleanor said nothing for a moment or two, but then she looked toward the window, and asked, 'May I open the drapes? It's a beautiful day.'

Morgana didn't answer so she stood up and drew back the curtains. The bedroom was filled with strong warm sunshine. Morgana sat herself up in bed, and reached for her hairbrush.

'How long will Popsy be away?' she asked her mother.

'I don't know for sure. About a week.'

'I can't say that I blame him. I feel like going away myself.'

'You could,' said Eleanor. 'The house at Sarasota is open.'

Morgana shook her head. 'I have things I want to do down at the office. I'm supposed to be having lunch with Grant today.'

'But surely –'

'I'm not *going*, Momsy. I'm not being driven out of my own house and out of my own life by a mother who can't stay faithful to my father and a sister who can't keep her hands off my boyfriends. Do you remember George Phelps? And the way she was all over Lennie Ross!'

Eleanor stood in the sunlight. She looked sad but quite beautiful this morning. Her hair was gathered up and she wore a silky dress by Pauline Trigere with a wraparound waist and a diamond brooch in the shape of a spray of honesty. She said, in a voice like rubbed ivory, 'You're quite right to be angry, I suppose. I just hope that nothing like this ever happens to you. It's very easy to be censorious when you have youth and popularity and all the money you're ever likely to need. But for most of us it's quite different. I married your father for his style and his wealth. I was something of a gold digger, I suppose. But it took only three years of marriage for me to realize that men who are powerful and rich are the very weakest of husbands, and the clumsiest of lovers, and that if they meet somebody who can't be bought or bullied, then they're totally confused. Not only confused, but enraged, and sometimes vengeful. I suppose that's why I warned you about John. Not because I don't like him, because I do. Not because I don't think he's handsome and attractive and endlessly courteous, because he is. But you're a different kind of person, Morgana. You have something in you which one day will sweep the rest of us away.'

'So what are you saying?' Morgana demanded, white hot with anger and frustration. 'Are you saying that I should surrender John to Phoebe? Hand over my fiancé to my sister like an unwanted birthday gift?'

Eleanor picked up the ring and the diamond star from the bedside table. 'You already have,' she told her.

Morgana looked at her mother and understood that what she was saying was probably true. After all, Morgana had always been brought up to expect the best, and after sleeping with Phoebe, John was no longer the best. The ironic part about it was that John would be twice punished for his unfaithfulness; because now that Morgana no longer wanted him, Phoebe would no longer want him, either.

'Momsy,' said Morgana, quietly. 'Do you think we will ever get over all of this?'

'You will,' Eleanor replied.

'And you?'

'I'm not sure. It all depends on whether your father can accept a heart that is still his, but which bears the marks of having once briefly belonged to someone else.'

She was silent for a little while. She smiled to herself. Then she came over to Morgana and kissed her forehead with dry lips. 'You know what James Thurber once said – "it's as well to fall flat on your face as to lean over backward too far." I'll see you later. Are you staying home for lunch?'

'I was going to have lunch downtown with Grant.'

'Are you going to talk to Phoebe?'

'Is she still here?'

'She came back just after midnight. I suppose we must have talked until two or three. She's asleep at the moment.'

Morgana said, 'I don't know. I think it's going to take me a little time.'

'Morgana – if he felt that he could make love to your sister while he was engaged to you, then he wasn't worth marrying. Fortunately, it's happened before we've made any public announcement.'

'I thought it was going to be in the paper this morning,' said Morgana. 'That's why I haven't looked at it yet.'

Eleanor shook her head. 'They held it over because of the murder story. Your father insisted he wanted his daughter's engagement announced right slap bang on the front page, and of course he didn't want it next to some terrible story like that.'

Morgana picked up the newspaper and opened it. 'He's killed another woman,' she said, in horror.

Eleanor said, 'Your father said the photographs of the bodies were so shocking they couldn't print any of them. But then men have so many ways of destroying women, don't they?'

Morgana let the paper fall back on to the floor. 'Momsy –' she said.

Eleanor stood by the door. She seemed almost ethereal, more like a memory than a living mother, a pale image from family photograph albums, a wistful smile between pages of cobweb-patterned tissue paper.

'Give it time, Morgana,' she said. 'Somehow, it will all work out.'

Morgana called for Loukia and dressed in a pale gray linen

suit which had been made for her at the beginning of the summer by Mainbocher. Then Millicent came in and dressed her hair for her, sweeping it severely back from her forehead and fastening it with tortoiseshell combs. She kept the focus of her make-up on her eyes, widening them, and emphasizing her cheekbones only softly. She put on the ring that her parents had given her for her twenty-first birthday, no other.

Howard was standing in the huge marble hallway, wearing a brown business suit, and almost ready to leave. The doors were open and the dark blue Chrysler Imperial was waiting outside to take him to the airfield.

'Popsy,' said Morgana, and came across the hallway to hold him close. He kissed her cheek, then held her away from him so that he could look at her.

'You're all right?' he asked, his eyes crinkled with concern.

'Yes, Popsy, I'm all right. Hurting a little, but I think that's all.' She was caught by surprise by a lump in her throat, and a sudden feeling that she might cry, but she managed to smile, and fussily to brush a thread away from her father's lapel.

'I guess these things are sent to try us,' said Howard. He thought Morgana looked tired, a little bruised by what had happened, but somehow more striking than he could ever remember. Perhaps she had grown up, during the night. People do undergo such transformations, when their lives are turned upside down. Perhaps he could see in her now the pain that he was feeling himself, the pain of having been deceived. And worse than the pain of having been decived, the pain that few betrayed lovers care to admit even to themselves – the pain called loss of face.

'You're not staying away too long?' Morgana asked him.

'Four or five days. I have business in Los Angeles. It could have waited a week or two, but I brought it forward. A few days' thinking won't do either of us any harm, me or your mother.'

'You won't leave her, will you?'

Howard smiled, and squeezed Morgana's hand. 'I don't know. That's not really what I'm going to be thinking about. I'm going to be thinking about what it was that tempted your mother to have a relationship with somebody else, a young man like Robert Wentworth. I'm going to be thinking about myself, what kind of a husband I've been. I'm going to consider my duties to my family, you included.'

Winton Snell came cakewalking across the marble floor with a smile on his face like a red rubber glove turned inside out. 'You ought to leave now, sir. Your first meeting in Los Angeles starts at seven thirty.'

Howard kissed Morgana, and said, 'Take care, honey. I'll see you in a few days. I'll call you.'

He walked off across the hall and he was reflected in the polished floor as if he were walking on ice. He climbed into the limousine, and Morgana saw his hand lifted at the window in a goodbye wave. Millicent came up to her, and said, 'There's coffee for you in the conservatory, Miss Morgana.'

Morgana asked for her new car to be brought out, then she went through to the conservatory to drink her coffee and finish reading the *Star*. She wanted to see what her horoscope had in store.

Millicent poured out coffee from a delicate flower-patterned Limoges service. There were fresh-baked madeleines, too, and crumbly choux pastries, all still warm from the Weatherwood kitchens. Morgana read the Hacker story, then Gasoline Alley, then leafed through to her horoscope. Madame Tzizane (Your Stars in the Star) predicted that 'somebody close to you will disappoint, but beware of feeling vengeful.' Somehow, that wasn't what she had wanted to hear.

Just then Winton Snell came into the conservatory holding a white rococo telephone on top of his splayed-out fingers.

'There's a telephone call from Mr Grant Clifford, Miss Morgana. He wishes to speak to your father; but I told him that Mr Croft Tate had already departed for Los Angeles.'

'That's all right, Winton, I'll take it. I wanted to talk to him anyway.' Grant, sounding ruffled, said, 'Hello? Howard? This is a terrible connection.'

'This is Morgana, Grant. What can I do to help you?'

'Oh, good morning, Morgana. Can you hear me? I can hardly hear a damn thing. Listen – I have to speak to Howard very urgently. It's about that fire Friday. Harry Sharpe has found out who set it. He's found the arsonist, and he's made some kind of damfool citizen's arrest. Almost got himself killed doing it. But the arsonist is right down here at the office now.'

'Harry found him! That's wonderful!'

'Well, one step at a time,' said Grant. 'The arsonist is actually a fireman, from the same engine company that put the blaze out. Ironic, isn't it? He's prepared to implicate Chief

Bryan, and better still he's even prepared to implicate Enzo Vespucci. In fact he's so anxious to keep himself out of jail that he's prepared to implicate almost everybody in metropolitan Chicago. He's given us facts and dates and names. He's even given us the brand name of the gasoline he used. The lawyers have already agreed that we have more than enough solid information to run a full-scale story exposing Vespucci's fire-raising activities on the South Side.'

'That's marvelous!' Morgana enthused.

'What did you say? I didn't catch that.'

'I said that's marvelous!'

'It's a start, no doubt about it. And his honor the mayor will be dancing one of his Irish jigs. But I do need Howard's okay. He gave me specific instructions this weekend that the *Star* shouldn't run anything on Enzo Vespucci or the slum problem. He said it was all too downbeat, too depressing. Legally hazardous, too. But this obviously changes things completely. We have the story and we have the facts and we even have the man who did it. But I must get an answer now. We can't keep this arsonist tied to an office chair for very much longer, Commissioner Spectorski will have our variety meats to feed his dogs on. Your father has to give us a yes or a no. It's his paper. I can't run this story without his categorical okay.'

'Grant –'

'Please, will you get him to the phone?' asked Grant.

Morgana frowned. 'Didn't –' and then she suddenly understood that Grant couldn't have heard Winton telling him that her father had already left for Los Angeles. The phone connection had been too crackly.

Grant said, 'What was that?' but Morgana was seized with a perfect idea, and she told Grant, 'It's all right, nothing. Hold on for just a moment. Popsy's just about to leave for California. He's outside. Let me go call him.'

She put the phone on the coffee table and waited, her hands clasped together in her lap. This might be very wrong; but she knew what her father was like, him and his complicated way of looking at things. As far as Morgana was concerned, the issue was blood simple.

She picked up the phone again. She made herself pant a little, as if she had just hurried in from the hallway. 'Grant? He had to leave. He has a meeting in Los Angeles at seven thirty, he couldn't hold up the airplane any longer.'

'Damn it,' Grant replied. 'Did you tell him what it was all about? Did you tell him how urgent it was? As soon as we hand this arsonist over to the police, every other paper in town is going to get their nose into the trough.'

'It's all right,' Morgana reassured him. 'I spoke to Popsy and explained what had happened, and he said it was fine.'

'What do you mean, fine? We can run the story?'

'Front page, seventy-two-point headlines.'

'You're sure about that? You did explain to him exactly what had happened, and what we're planning to do?'

'Absolutely one hundred percent sure,' said Morgana.

Grant let out a long breath of relief. 'Well, that's tremendous. I was sure he was going to tell us to hold off.' Morgana heard him turn around to call out, 'Harry! It's okay! Mr Croft Tate says go ahead!'

There was a general whoop of excitement in the background. The *Star*'s editorial staff had been eager to roast Enzo Vespucci for years. This was the moment, at long last. And they were going to be given the pleasure of lighting a bonfire under Chief Bryan at the same time.

'Are we still having lunch?' Morgana asked Grant.

'Sure thing. Meet me at the office at twelve thirty. I promised you fish, didn't I?'

Morgana put down the phone and finished her coffee. She felt elated and frightened at the same time, almost as if she had drunk too much champagne in a hot overcrowded room and then suddenly stepped outside into the cold. She stood up, and for a moment she saw stars.

Outside in the hallway, she hesitated. White gladioli in a delicate vase trembled in the slight draft. She could have gone upstairs to talk to Phoebe. Perhaps the sooner this whole business about John was settled between them, the better. But, after a moment's pause, Morgana decided against it. She was still too angry, still too upset. And besides she needed the pain of having John taken away from her to follow its full course; in the same way that those who have been bereaved have to suffer the full extent of their grief. Her Sportabout was waiting for her outside the front door. The day was as bright as glass. She collected her pocketbook, sprayed herself lavishly with Chanel, and left the house without saying goodbye to anyone.

23

Lunch with Grant was a warm, close, friendly affair, in a private booth at the Well of the Sea. Grant was in excellent humor because of the breaking of the arson story, spry and amusing, and full of stories about his cub-reporter days in Philadelphia. To her own surprise, Morgana found herself laughing, especially after they had shared a bottle of pre-war champagne and eaten two fresh soles Walewska.

'We've really got something to celebrate here,' said Grant, lifting his champagne glass. 'Here's to a happier Chicago, a Chicago without men like Enzo Vespucci.'

'I'll drink to that,' said Morgana.

After lunch, Grant returned to the *Star* building; while Morgana went to Marshall Field to console herself by buying some new dresses. It was a warm afternoon; the breeze flowed through the crowded dusty streets. Taxis honked, trucks blared, elevated trains rattled noisily around the Loop. This was Chicago at its busiest, a steel town, a mill town, a packing town, a newspaper town, a seaport at the very heart of America, one thousand miles from the sea. It roared with energy; with street traffic and construction work and the extraordinary massed drumming of a million pairs of shoes on the concrete sidewalks.

Outside Marshall Field's elegant frontage stood six tall Moline elms, which appeared to grow directly out of the sidewalk. They had appeared overnight less than a year ago, and so to many passers-by they were still a novelty. They had been planted in six specially prepared concrete pits which Field's had arranged to be constructed when the State Street subway was built.

Morgana turned into East Washington Street and went in

through the separate elevator entrance that led to the 28 Shop on the sixth floor. She bought her clothes here regularly, especially her basic accessories. The shop was reached through an oval foyer, with beige walls of hand-rubbed oak, beyond which was a large central rotunda, with a domed ceiling and a series of alcoves all around it hung with beige and turquoise draperies.

She was greeted at once by the manageress. 'Miss Croft Tate! We haven't seen you for two weeks! My goodness, we read about you in the newspapers. I don't know how you could have been so *brave*!'

'Well, me neither,' smiled Morgana. 'Could I take a look at some hats?'

'Well, of course. We have some *gorgeous* little hats just arrived from Dior. Mrs George Barrett was in here only this morning, you know what she's like. There's this really pretty bicorne, we have this in mauve and green and also in pink.'

Morgana tried on six or seven different hats, and then went through to one of the dressing rooms to try some New Look skirts. There were twenty-eight different dressing rooms at the 28 Shop, decorated in pairs. One pair was black and peach with lace curtains; another pair was pink and green; yet another was apricot and rose with plushly upholstered banquettes. Morgana's favorite was all mirrored. An assistant brought her a cup of Russian tea while she tried on a dozen new skirts and a range of cocktail dresses by Norman Norell. The least expensive of the dresses was $600. Morgana had twice been sketched for Marshall Field's famous 'Women of Chicago' advertisements . . . 'You'll know her anywhere, the Chicago woman and the fashions she's made famous'.

She had already decided to buy one turquoise dress, and was turning slowly around and around trying to make up her mind about a peach-colored dress with a large bow at the back when the dressing room door opened and Phoebe came in. Phoebe stood in the corner watching Morgana, while the 28 Shop assistant tugged and primped the cocktail dress to show Morgana exactly how it would look.

'The color is *you*,' the assistant kept telling her. 'It really is *you*.'

Phoebe looked almost ghostly. Her face was white and for some reason she had chosen a blue eye shadow which gave her the appearance of being very ill. She wore a white summer suit and a white veiled hat which served only to drain the last tinges of color out of her. She was smoking a cigarette in her long white holder.

Morgana felt the floor surge up beneath her feet. She knew she was blushing. She said to the assistant, 'Would you leave us for a moment?'

'Well, certainly,' said the assistant, and went off with her bangs bouncing. Phoebe stepped back to let her pass, then looked toward Morgana sharply through the curling smoke of her cigarette.

'I guessed that you would be here. Where does any girl go when her heart has been broken?'

Phoebe didn't say this cuttingly or sarcastically. She was simply admitting that if the same thing had happened to her – if Morgana had slept with one of *her* best boyfriends – this is where she would come, too. To dress up, to glamorize herself all over again, to change her appearance so completely that when she looked in the mirror she wouldn't even recognize who she was; and to discard her chagrin on the dressing room floor, unfolded, for somebody else to pick up.

'I really didn't feel like talking to you just yet,' said Morgana.

Phoebe shrugged. 'There isn't very much to say, is there? I've been a naughty sister again. If it's any consolation, I'm sorry. In fact I'm *very* sorry. I suppose I was rebounding from Donald. I needed somebody to make me feel wanted.'

Morgana turned her back on Phoebe but kept on watching her face in the dressing room mirrors. 'He was going to be my husband,' she said. 'You didn't just take away my boyfriend, you took away my future.'

Phoebe said, 'I think I've probably done you a favor. John didn't really love you.'

'I suppose he told you that while you were fornicating with him?'

'Not quite, my dear, but almost.'

'Well, I still don't feel any better about it. And I certainly don't feel any better about you.'

Phoebe sat down on a small Regency chair. 'Do you want to hear the truth? I mean – for all I care, we need never speak to each other again. But I love you, Morgana. I know that I'm wicked sometimes, but I don't do it to hurt you.

We're sisters, and you can't change that, whatever happens.'

'No,' said Morgana, with considerable bitterness. 'Unfortunately, I can't.'

Phoebe said, 'He doesn't love you, you know – not in the way that the man who's going to be your husband ought to love you. You should hear how much he praises you! Your looks, your style, your intelligence. You impress him so-o-o much! I think he's especially impressed by the fact that you're going to take over the *Star* one day, and he's going to be the consort of a newspaper publisher. That impresses the aitch-ee-double-ell out of him.'

'So you were doing me a favor, were you, going to bed with him? You were deliberately putting me off him, and rescuing me from a miserable marriage? That's very selfless of you, I must say. If they gave medals for that kind of service to your sister, I'm sure you'd get one. The Congressional Medal of Loyal Fornication, with fig leaves!'

'I've said I'm sorry,' Phoebe retorted. 'I don't know what else to do.'

'Well, I think you've done quite enough,' said Morgana. She was so angry at Phoebe that her eyelashes prickled with tears, and her face felt as hot as a furnace.

Phoebe was silent. She crushed out her cigarette, and put away her holder, and stood watching Morgana with regret and bafflement, unable to think what she could possibly do to make amends.

Morgana said, 'I suppose you're right, in a peculiar way. If he's capable of going to bed with you, he's capable of going to bed with anybody. Better to find that out now, rather than the day after the wedding. But, do you know, he said he loved me so much. He said he admired me and respected me more than any other girl he'd ever met.'

'I think that was the trouble,' Phoebe said hoarsely.

'Well, I don't know,' Morgana replied. 'What am I going to do now? There isn't much point in my looking for anybody else, is there? You'll only find some way of getting into his pants, whoever he is. Or perhaps I should be content to share?'

'It wasn't my fault he made a pass at me!' Phoebe snapped. 'I mean, I'm quite willing to admit that I was weak –'

'It wasn't your fault!' Morgana raged at her. 'How you have the gall to say that when you were hiding in John's apartment last night while John was entertaining me; after which you went straight to bed with him.'

Phoebe took one smart step forward and tried to slap Morgana's face, but Morgana was too quick for her and snatched her wrist. The two of them wrestled for a moment, squealing and panting, and then Phoebe caught at Morgana's hair, tugging it painfully and pulling out one of the barrettes. Morgana shouted, 'Ow! You bitch!' and knocked Phoebe's hat off.

Phoebe screeched and took hold of the front of the cocktail dress Morgana was wearing, and wrenched it downwards. Morgana hadn't yet fastened the dress properly at the back, and it tore all the way down to the waist with a hideous ripping noise. Phoebe wrenched at it again, this time baring Morgana's breasts.

'This – dress – costs – six – hundred – dollars!' shrieked Morgana, and caught hold of Phoebe's skirt and yanked at it wildly. Both sisters grappled and tussled and hit each other, and then they lost their balance and fell on to the plush blue banquette. Morgana managed to struggle her way on top of Phoebe, naked to the waist except for her pearl necklace, and sit astride her, pinning her down by her wrists. Phoebe twisted first one way and then the other, but Morgana refused to get off.

'You think you're so perfect!' she screamed. 'So damned holy!' She thrashed her legs wildly up and down, and one of her white high-heeled shoes flew off. It went sailing toward the dressing room door, to be caught with unnerving aplomb by the shop assistant, who was hurrying back in some alarm to find out what all the screaming and the bumping was.

'Miss Croft Tate!' the shop assistant gasped. 'Oh, Miss Croft Tate! And –' and here she looked down at Phoebe – 'Miss Croft Tate.'

Morgana climbed off Phoebe, pulling up the cocktail dress to cover herself. Phoebe climbed off the banquette.

'I'm sorry,' Morgana gasped. 'I think we were – well, I think we were slightly carried away.' Her hair was hanging down wretchedly on one side of her face, her lipstick was smudged so that it looked as if she were snarling, her shoulders were covered in red finger marks. She was out of breath, and her heart was beating inside her chest like a native drum in a Tarzan movie.

The assistant approached her with deep but immaculately contained horror. At Marshall Field's, the customer was always right, no matter what the circumstances. She circled around Morgana, staring at the ripped cocktail dress and slowly raising her thumb to her mouth, so that she could bite it. 'Do you – do you wish to *take* the dress, Miss Croft Tate?'

There was a long silence, punctuated only by the sisters' desperate breathing. Phoebe stared at Morgana and Morgana stared back at Phoebe, and neither of them knew whether to laugh or to burst into tears or to spit at each other and stalk out. But, in the end, Phoebe said, softly, 'It's all right. It was all my fault. I'll pay for it. You can charge it to me.'

'*Phoebe* –' Morgana began, but Phoebe shook her head.

'Let's talk later,' she said. 'I have to go downstairs and buy some of that night cream for mother.'

Phoebe quickly straightened her hat in the dressing room mirror, then smiled briefly and wanly at Morgana and left. Morgana stepped out of the cocktail gown, and dressed again in her own suit. The assistant watched her, still biting her thumb.

'Can you have the dress repaired?' asked Morgana.

'Yes, Miss Croft Tate; it's only the stitching that's gone.'

'I do apologize for what happened here,' Morgana told her.

The assistant grimaced.

Having repaired her face and hair, Morgana arranged for her purchases to be delivered to Weatherwood and then left the 28 Shop and hailed a taxi to take her to the *Star* building. She sat back in her seat and thought about Phoebe. She was still furiously angry at Phoebe for going to bed with John, and there was nothing she could do to obliterate from her mind's eye the picture she had of Phoebe and John together – a picture of compellingly lewd detail; a picture with sounds and perfumes and ineradicable color. Yet she felt somehow that the incident had brought her closer to Phoebe, rather than taking her further away.

The taxi driver said, 'Didn't I see your picture in the newspaper?'

Morgana called back, 'No, I don't think so. It must have been somebody else.'

'In that case, lady, you suffer the same problem as me. I look a lot like Madman Muntz, don't you think so? You know the used-car millionaire? Almost everybody says, hey, didn't I see your picture on a billboard, are you Madman Muntz? What do they think Madman Muntz is doing, a millionaire, driving a hack?'

Morgana didn't answer. The taxi drew up outside the *Star* building, and she stepped out into the sunshine. She didn't feel perfect; she didn't feel holy; but for some reason she felt very much better.

24

At three o'clock that afternoon, four police officers arrived in the *Star*'s newsroom to take Peter Axelrod Medill into custody. He had already confessed to *Star* reporters that Chief Bryan had summoned him to headquarters after he had been caught stealing money from another fire officer's coat, but that instead of punishing him, Chief Bryan had offered to 'forget the whole thing' if Medill would 'scratch his back'.

The 'backscratching' had involved raising a fire at the tenement block on 31st Street, in such a way that arson would be difficult or impossible to prove, and with the minimum risk to the tenement's occupants. When Medill had asked who the building belonged to, and why they should want to burn it down, Chief Bryan had said, 'You're doing this for one of Chicago's great benefactors, Mr Enzo Vespucci. The money he makes out of burning this building is all going to the sick children's hospital.'

Even Medill hadn't been so gullible as to believe this, but he had decided that it would probably be healthier to do what Chief Bryan wanted, especially if Enzo Vespucci was involved. By all accounts, he had told the *Star* reporters, Enzo Vespucci was 'not a man to blow your horn at.'

Harry had been keen to keep Medill tied up at the *Star* offices until tomorrow's early editions hit the streets, but Grant had been adamant that he be handed over to the police. They had a full and detailed confession, which none of the other papers would be able to get until Medill had been interrogated by detectives, as well as photographs of Medill trying to run down Indiana Avenue with Harry clinging on to his back.

Walter Dempsey had eyed the photographs disparagingly,

and then said, 'Your riding style is atrocious, Sharpe. You're much too far back in the saddle.'

The front page headline ran NAB MOB FIREBUG, with a strapline which announced Killer Arsonist, Caught By Star Staffer, Exposes Fire Chief, Mobster. Underneath ran Harry's melodramatic story of how 'an underworld tip-off' had led him to Peter Medill; and beside it was Medill's full confession, printed verbatim between giant-sized quotation marks. There were photographs of Chief Bryan and Enzo Vespucci. Harry had called both of them to ask for their comments, but Chief Bryan had already brought in his lawyer to fend off the press, and Enzo Vespucci's housekeeper had told him that Mr Vespucci was 'indefinitely on vacation, and in any case never comments about barefaced lies.'

This wasn't all. Inside, on page two, Frank had written a thousand-word editorial on the evils of Chicago's slum landlords, and Enzo Vespucci in particular, drawing on all the stories of arson and intimidation and corruption that his fellow reporters could dig up. Most of the stories had previously been spiked because of vetoes from the *Star*'s lawyers or from Howard himself. Now that the *Star* had a reliable witness, and now that Howard had apparently given his okay to an all-out editorial campaign against the slums, almost all of them were updated and cleared for publication.

'At long last the tyrants of the slums are revealed for what they are. At long last we can point the finger at men like Enzo Vespucci and Francesco Lorenzo and Orville O'Keefe and fearlessly say, Oppressors of the Poor, Exploiters of the Weak, Captains of Misery, Kings of Despair.'

Harry tilted his chair back in satisfaction, his feet on his desk, smoking a cigarette. In the next pigpen, David Tribe was hammering out a piece on the new popularity of deep-freeze food for the home.

'This damn article is making my mouth water,' he complained. 'Turkey pie, jambalaya, beef casserole! All I had for breakfast was a stale bowlful of Ralston's worst.'

Harry checked his watch. 'Come on over to O'Leary's. I think I'm in the mood for one of Betty's All-British All-Singing All-Dancing Steak and Kidney Puddings. Not to mention a celebratory drink.'

David handed in his copy and they went together to the elevators, both tying up their neckties. Harry had borrowed four neckties from members of the staff to keep Peter Medill secured to his chair; probably the first time in criminal history that a suspect had been detained by two hand-painted kippers with palm trees on them, one red and yellow four-in-hand with soup stains, and a thin brown woven affair with a frayed end.

The elevator doors opened and Morgana and Grant stepped out. Harry immediately doffed his hat, and hastily blew the cigarette smoke that he had just inhaled out of the side of his mouth.

'Miss Croft Tate, we meet again! Well met by daylight, fair Titania!'

'How are you, Harry?' asked Morgana. 'I was wonderfully pleased to hear that you caught that arsonist. And he was a fireman, too! How on earth did you manage to track him down?'

'Well, that's kind of a trade secret, known only to two reporters, and one hunchback, and one nun, and each of them knows only a quarter of it.'

Morgana smiled. 'You must be pleased with yourself, though, really.'

Grant said, 'He did a first-class job, Morgana. Pity about the citizen's arrest. A little flashy, but I guess it worked out for the best. We've all been itching to get our teeth into Mr Enzo Vespucci for years and years. Now it looks like we've managed to buck the bull off the bridge. And I'm especially happy that your father has changed his mind about it. It couldn't have been easy for Howard to swallow all of his previous opinions on the matter; but then, well – that's what makes a good publisher a *great* publisher, I suppose.'

Morgana's smile began to look a little waxy. 'I'll pass on the compliment,' she said.

Harry said, 'Listen, I'm going round the South Side tomorrow morning with Mayor Doyle. He's absolutely delighted that the *Star* is attacking Vespucci so openly. What he's going to do is take me on a guided tour of some of the worst of Vespucci's tenements, so that we can do a big photographic feature on it.'

He paused, and then he added, 'I know what you feel about the slums, Miss Croft Tate. I wonder if you'd care to come along.'

Grant asked, 'Do you want to? It won't be any picnic.'

Morgana thought for a moment, and then nodded. 'Yes,' she said. 'I'd love to come. What time are you starting?'

'Early. We're having breakfast at City Hall at seven o'clock, and then we're starting out around eight.'

'I'll be there, thank you.'

Grant took hold of Morgana's arm. 'We have some pulls of tomorrow's front page over here. Come take a look.'

Harry and David went downstairs to the *Star*'s ultra-modern lobby. Harry went across to the reception desk and leaned over toward the redhead, who was talking on the telephone to someone who sounded like an irate reader. 'Anymore calls from Ogden Avenue, Mandy?' he asked. The redhead shushed him with a wave of her hand, and said to the reader, 'Yes, sir. I'm sure you were, sir. But I regret that the quality of the goods advertised is not the responsibility of the *Star*.'

'How about a drink?' Harry asked her.

Again she shushed him, and frowned. 'Well, sir, we do everything we can to ensure that all of our advertisers are bona fide, sir. But sometimes one or two disreputable companies do slip through.'

There was a yapping noise on the other end of the phone like a small dog chasing after its dinner. Harry waited impatiently for a moment, and then took the receiver out of the redhead's hand.

'Sir? This is the quality control manager. Can I help you?'

'You bet you can!' the irate voice ranted at him. 'I answered a classified advertisement in your paper Tuesday last for a failsafe method of getting one hundred percent better gas mileage. That's what it said, those were the very words, failsafe method of getting one hundred percent better gas mileage, send three dollars.'

'Did you send the three dollars?' asked Harry.

'Like a damn fool I did! And do you know what they sent back? A little scrap of paper, saying Leave Your Auto In The Garage.'

Harry said to the redhead, 'What's your name, honey?'

'Nancy,' the redhead smiled.

'What time do you finish?'

Nancy smiled. 'My husband comes to collect me at five.'

'Oh, well, can't say that I blame him, the bum.'

'What did you say?' the reader demanded, on the other end of the phone.

'I said the *Star* will gladly refund your three dollars, sir, just leave your name and address with the ravishing beauty at the desk.'

Harry and David went out through the revolving doors and across Wabash Avenue to O'Leary's. It was noisy and crowded and smoky in there. Walter Dempsey had preceded them by two or three minutes, and was already toasting the downfall of Enzo Vespucci in undiluted brandy. Harry went to the bar and asked Roy for his usual, and a couple of steak and kidney puddings.

Walter was bellowing out, 'Much as I resent the talented labor which I lavished in vain on my article on Mr Vespucci's string of racehorses, now of course spiked, it is beyond doubt that Mr Vespucci is not only satanic in the extreme, a murderer, a villain, and a living embodiment of turpitude *in extremis*, but that he is guilty of the most questionable taste in vests which it has ever been my misfortune to encounter. Purple sateen, to accompany a Harris Tweed hacking jacket! He should have been machine-gunned years ago, by hired killers from the *Tailor & Cutter*.'

'Walter's on form,' remarked David, sipping his cold beer.

'I think he decided to skip his usual hangover, and just go from one drunk to the next without stopping,' Harry replied. 'His usual logic is that if you stay continuously drunk all your life, you're only going to suffer a furry tongue and a severe headache when you're finally laid to rest. He calls that his Monumental Hangover theory.'

Betty brought over their food. 'Two steak and kiddly puds, dear,' she said, and bent over them as she set the food down, giving them an uninterrupted view of hot perfumed cleavage, deep and dark and maternally erotic, the kind of cleavage a man could have climbed into headfirst, never to be seen by his friends or relatives ever again.

They started eating; but as they did so a tall well-built man of about sixty-five or so came into the pub, and stood for a moment in the open doorway with his hat in his hand, surrounded by shafts of smoky sunlight. Harry put down his fork and looked at the man with interest. There was something familiar about him, yet Harry was quite sure that he had never met him before. He nudged David, and said, 'Who's that? I'm sure I know him.'

The man closed the pub door behind him and walked slowly to the bar, his footsteps hesitant with arthritis.

Harry finished his steak and kidney pudding. It was one of those meals for which he developed a regular craving and yet when he had eaten it he invariably wished that he hadn't, because it lay on his stomach (in Walter Dempsey's words) 'like an ugly baby.' As he pushed away his plate, he looked up and saw that the white-haired man was peering at him acutely, and that Roy was obviously pointing him out. Roy gave Harry a nod, and the white-haired man was shuffling over.

'You're probably going to think that this is very rude of me,' he said. He had a plain farmer's accent, and sounded like the kind of man who might have said something like 'well, that really cleaned my plow!' whenever he was surprised by anything. He passed his hat from his right hand to his left, and shook Harry's hand very firmly and warmly. 'I asked Roy to tell me when you came in. I'm afraid you fellows are all new faces to me. I don't drink any more, doctor's orders. I was over at Billy Goat's once or twice in the summer, but I have to keep myself out of temptation, but deliver me from evil.'

'In a funny way, I recognize you,' said Harry.

'Well, you're a *Star* reporter, and that's what I used to be. Everybody still says, "Anymore calls from Ogden Avenue, Mandy," and that's because of me.'

'Well, this is tremendous,' Harry grinned. 'You're Lenny Mutken! Our one and only Pulitzer-prize-winning demon reporter! It's an honor to meet you! I'm Harry Sharpe, this is David Tribe.'

'I know *your* name, Harry,' said Lenny. He took out a pack of Camels, and offered them around. Then he lit up with a Zippo lighter that roared like a wartime flamethrower.

'I'm surprised you have any eyebrows left with that thing,' said Harry.

'I'm too old to care about eyebrows,' Lenny replied, easing himself into a chair. 'I guess I have six years left on this earth, I don't care whether I spend them with eyebrows or without eyebrows. I have never been a stickler for eyebrows.' He coughed, a light fusillade that rapidly deteriorated into a harrowing series of great dredging wheezes. Harry and David glanced at each other and exchanged silent but wide-eyed expressions of alarm. At last, however, Lenny recovered himself, and wiped his mouth with a handkerchief, and sniffed, and sat back. 'The doctor says I have to give up smoking, as well as drinking. Regrettably I find it impossible to give up both at the same time. If I don't drink, I smoke like blazes. If I don't smoke, I drink until I'm flat on my back. It turned out to be a pretty close-run thing, but in the end I decided to smoke instead of drink. Reach for a Lucky instead of a Scotch.'

Harry said, 'Can I get you something? Maybe a club soda or an RC?'

Lenny shook his head. 'I'll stop on my way home and have a coffee.' He sniffed again, and cleared his throat, and Harry was worried that he was going to start coughing once more. But instead, he puffed quickly and lightly at his cigarette, and eventually said to Harry, 'You wrote that *good* piece on the Hacker.' He made it sound as if the *Star* had published a good piece and a bad piece.

Harry nodded. 'That's right, Mrs Leonidas. I saw the body.'

'I could sense how shocking it was by what you wrote,' said Lenny. 'Fine, sensitive writing. A dreadful subject, seriously and vividly handled. There isn't much of that kind of talent left any more. Where are you, James O'Donnell Bennett? Where are you, Will Barber? Gone to dust, all of them, those great reporters. And those who haven't gone to dust have lost their glory now, like me. There used to be a time when Edward J. Kelly would cross the street to shake hands with me. Now what am I? Nothing more than the man who wrote some of those stories that lie moldering in the *Star* building's morgue; stories that nobody will ever want to read, ever again. You don't get remembered by history, you know, even when your job is reporting history. You fade, you turn yellow, you get blown away by the winds of time.'

Harry swallowed beer, and then said, 'You shouldn't get too depressed, Mr Mutken. You won a Pulitzer prize, everybody at the *Star* remembers your name. And, you're right – yes – even Mr Croft Tate goes on saying, "Any more calls from Ogden Avenue, Mandy?"'

Lenny frowned at Harry, and then shook his head. 'I feel

as if I'm dead already. It's a terrible feeling, can you understand that, to think that your life's work is forgotten even before you've expired? And, please ... don't call me Mr Mutken. It's a very long time since anybody knew me well enough to call me Mr Mutken. I'm Lenny. Lenny, the Conscience of Chicago. That used to be the name of my column. "The Conscience of Chicago". You should have read the piece I wrote on daylight time. Powerful? My God, it was more devastating than an A-bomb!'

'Actually,' said Harry, 'I did read it. I had to write a long article about daylight time when we came off fast-time at the end of the war. I read your piece as background information.'

Lenny focused on Harry as if he had uttered the words of a miracle. 'You read it?' he asked. Then, wonderingly, 'You *read* it? Well, now. You read it.'

He looked across at Harry again, and said, 'You know something, when I saw your story on the Hacker – the part of the story that was bylined to you – I sensed at once that here was a kindred soul. Here was a man who could *write*! Wasn't that extraordinary? Because how often do you think that such a thing can happen? Such a feeling of empathy between two people who haven't even met each other? You read my piece on daylight time; I read your story about the Hacker. Well, now.'

Harry said, a little uncomfortably, 'Is there something you're trying to get at, Lenny? I mean, is there some kind of a point you're trying to make?'

Lenny beckoned Harry closer. 'You'll excuse us, won't you?' he said to David Tribe, with an unsympathetic grin. David shrugged and lifted his drink to his lips and said, 'Whatever.'

'What is it?' asked Harry. Close to, Lenny Mutken smelled very strongly of tobacco and two-day-old shirt and something odd and unpleasant like vinegar.

'You have to understand, Harry, that in my own neighborhood I still have something of a reputation. A lot of the old folk especially think that I still work for the paper. They give me little tidbits of gossip, they come around and ask for advice. So – whenever anything important happens, I'm usually the first to know.'

Harry wished very much that Lenny Mutken would hurry up and get on with it. Lenny sucked at his cigarette at the end of every sentence, and so each subsequent word peppered the air with smoke and halitosis.

'Now . . . this Hacker,' said Lenny. 'I was sitting at home on Sunday morning when my telephone rang, and a voice said, "I've chopped up one woman and I'm going to chop up another." Then the phone was put down, straight away. I didn't even have time to ask who it was, or why he should be calling me.'

'Did you tell the cops?' asked Harry.

Lenny briskly shook his head. 'I didn't think anything of it. Why should I? I'm always getting absurd phone calls. One woman phoned me up once and asked me if I was a friend of St Francis of Assissi. When I said I wasn't, she said, "That's funny, I thought St Francis of Assissi was friends with *all* dumb mutts." So – when this man called me up – what was I supposed to think? There was nothing about any murder in the Sunday papers, and my radio's been on the fritz for weeks. So I assumed it was a joke! A pretty distasteful joke, of course, but still a joke.'

'Then what?' said Harry.

'Well, then I got up this morning and bought my copy of the *Star* and saw that my friend had done exactly what he had said he was going to do. I was shocked, of course.'

'But you still didn't call the police?'

Lenny said, 'I had my hand on the phone. I had the Police Department number right in front of me. But before I could dial the phone rang again, and the same voice said, "Lenny Mutken, this is the man the newspapers are calling the Hacker. I've hacked two women and now I'm going to hack another two, both at the same time."'

Harry stared at Lenny close to. 'He's going to hack two more? *Together?*'

'That's what he said.'

'Did you ask him why?'

'I did, and this time he didn't hang up. He said there was a reason, a very important reason. He said that he was going to hack two more women, and then – once he had done that – he's going to explain exactly what this reason is.'

'He really said that?' Harry demanded. 'He's really going to call you up and tell you why he's been committing these murders?' Even David Tribe couldn't help himself from leaning forward in excitement.

Lenny raised a silencing hand. 'He's going to do more than that,' he said, with great solemnity. 'He's going to meet me at a prearranged place at a prearranged time and give me a face-to-face interview.'

Harry sat back. He was highly excited, but he couldn't stand very much more of that vinegar smell. 'What are you going to do, Lenny?' he asked. 'Are you going to talk to the cops? Come on, you're going to have to. Commissioner Spectorski's going to grind your bones to make his bread if you keep back information like this.'

'Well, that's a risk I have to take,' said Lenny. 'The Hacker categorically requested that the police should be left well out of it. If there was any hint of a police ambush, he said, he would go out and kill *four* women all at once, in revenge.'

He crushed out his cigarette. Then he said, 'It's a terrible choice, believe me, but my considered feeling is that the police will stand more chance of catching the Hacker once I've been able to talk to him than they will if they try to go after him on what little information I have already. Let's face it, Harry, so far I don't have anything to go on, except two telephone calls, a muffled voice, and two threats that could have been made by anybody. No – two women may die today or tomorrow – but I don't think that my going to the police is going to save them. The very best chance I have of helping the police to catch this man is to find out as much about him as I possibly can. His height, weight, general build, accent, mannerisms. He'll probably hide his face, but he won't be able to hide his mind.'

Harry thought about this, and then made a *moue*. 'I guess you're probably right. But where do I come into it?'

'You're going to be my herald,' smiled Lenny, revealing darkly tobacco-stained teeth. 'You're going to announce my glorious return to the *Star* – and introduce my articles on the Hacker. I can't do it myself, modesty forbids it. Only you can do it justice. Pulitzer Prize-Winning Police Reporter Emerges From Retirement To Quiz Hacker. And underneath that, in bright red spot color, the words World Exclusive!'

Harry said, 'When's the Hacker going to call you again?'

Lenny shook his head. 'I don't have any idea. But when he does, I'll be ready.'

At that moment, Woozy came into O'Leary's, with his

camera case slung over his shoulder. 'Harry? You ready for that Kedzie Avenue job? The tap-dancing champeens?'

'I don't believe it!' Harry exclaimed. 'We bring in a front-page scoop, and Grant still sends us out to girls' schools to talk to little girls who tap.'

'The daily bread of a daily newspaper is the daily doings of ordinary people,' Woozy quoted, one of Howard Croft Tate's favorite phrases.

'Okay, okay,' Harry complained. 'Here – take my keys, would you, and go down to the parking lot and fetch the Woodie out? Meet me outside in two minutes. I just have to finish talking to Lenny here.'

He tossed his keys to Woozy and Woozy ducked his head and caught them in the brim of his hat. Then he looked smartly downwards and they dropped into his hand.

'Don't you ever do *anything* the ordinary way?' Harry wanted to know.

Woozy looked nonplused. 'Don't *you* catch your keys like that?'

Harry said to Lenny, 'When the Hacker calls you again, what will you do? Will you call me straight away? I'd better give you some numbers where you can reach me. Sometimes I'm actually at home.'

Woozy crossed Wabash Avenue with his hands in his pockets. He was feeling in a good-to-excellent mood today. Monday was his evening off and Moira, who worked in the *Star*'s mailing department, had agreed to come to the movies with him to see *All The King's Men*, with Broderick Crawford. The afternoon was warm and windy, much less oppressive than the weekend. The wind lifted his necktie like a semaphore signal.

Down in the basement parking lot, Tomahawk Billy was leaning on his desk reading a comic book and steadfastly chewing tobacco. His eyes followed Woozy as relentlessly as one of those paintings of Christ. Woozy grinned and waved at him, and walked across to Harry's Woodie. He slung his camera bag in the back seat, and started up the engine.

At that moment, two bulky-bodied men in gray tailored suits and fedora hats came walking on very highly polished shoes down the concrete ramp to the parking lot. Tomahawk Billy eased himself up off his elbows, and watched them with grave suspicion. He had never seen either of them before, but they had a look about them he didn't like. They glanced neither to the right nor to the left, and they walked with the steady determination of men who have a job to do and are quite prepared to trespass in order to do it.

Tomahawk Billy came to the open door of his booth, and called, 'What you want? No unauthorized persons allowed down here.'

One of the men detoured a little towards him, and lifted one hand in warning. 'Stay there, Geronimo, and you won't get hurt.' The other man approached Woozy just as he was about to drive off, and tapped with his knuckle on the Woodie's window.

Tomahawk Billy said, 'You beat it, or I call for the cops!'

The man standing close to him replied, tersely, 'Don't even think about it. You want to go to the Happy Hunting Grounds special delivery? Don't even think about it.'

Sitting in the driver's seat, smiling, unsuspecting, Woozy wound down the station wagon's window and said, 'What's going on here? Can I help you guys?'

The man in the gray suit said something indistinct. Tomahawk Billy later swore that it was, 'Here's a little gift for you, friend.' But whatever the man said, there was no doubt at all about what he did. He lifted a nickel-plated .45 Colt automatic out of his coat, and fired at Woozy without hesitation at point-blank range, right into his left eye. There was a flat-sounding bang, with no echoes, as if somebody had slammed a warehouse door. The Woodie's windows were instantly sprayed with red. Its engine screamed for a moment, then died. The parking lot was silent as the two men walked stolidly back up the ramp, leaving the Woodie where it was, half in and half out of its parking space, the blood on its windows sliding into glutinous festoons, and Tomahawk Billy standing shocked and distraught.

It was ten minutes before Dundas the copy-boy was sent running over to O'Leary's to tell Harry that Woozy had been shot dead. Harry crossed Wabash Avenue, the sunlight blurring his face like an over-exposed photograph. He was tooted at by a Tucker car, one of those eccentric Chicago-built autos with a central headlight in the middle of its nose. He turned around to glare at the driver, a middle-aged man in a wide-brimmed hat, with a cowering wife; but he hardly saw either of them. They could have been Martians, for all he knew. He couldn't believe that Woozy was dead.

The rest of the afternoon was chopped into frames like a comic strip. Squad cars howled into the *Star*'s parking lot, red lights flashing, and then howled out again. An ambulance came and went, droning a premature dirge. Police officers drew chalk outlines everywhere, the Woodie was here, Tomahawk Billy was there, the killers did this, the killers did that. A fat detective in a camel-colored suit smoked a stogie bombastically in every corner of the parking lot, and then clapped Harry on the back in sympathy and brotherly love, and said, 'I know what it's like to lose a partner. My last partner was t'rown in-a lake.'

'Sure,' said Harry, trembling.

The fat detective looked around. 'You know who might-a done this?'

Harry shook his head.

'Come on, I'm not stupid, you're a newspaper reporter. The only reason that anybody ever kills newspaper reporters is because they're getting close to the troot. God help us that should happen so seldom.'

'Woozy was a photographer. What did he know?'

The fat detective grinned. 'Woozy was driving your wagon, don't forget that. Those two killers was contract killers and contract killers wouldn't of known who you were by sight. Agreed? So if photographers don't take nothing more offensive than pictures, why was they targeting him? And the answer comes back, they wasn't targeting him, they was targeting *you*. Your car, let's face it. They was after you.'

Harry looked at the bright-yellow Woodie with its blood-spattered windows, and knew that he would never be able to drive it again.

'I threw him the keys, you know?' he told the detective. 'I threw him the keys, and he caught them, just like this, right in the brim of his hat.'

'The brim of his hat, hunh?' the fat detective repeated. Then, with far less amusement in his voice, 'You should know who did this.'

'What do you mean?' asked Harry.

'Come on, don't try-ta cold-deck me,' the detective told him. 'You know what stories you was working on. You know who might-a tried to take a crack at you.'

Harry said nothing, but turned away. The fat detective watched him with one eye closed against the smoke of his stogie. He looked uncannily like the star of one of this year's most successful movies would one day look, Orson Welles, in *The Third Man*. Harry glanced around at him momentarily, and then started to walk away up the ramp.

'Call me, if it comes to you,' the detective shouted after him.

Harry lifted a hand in acknowledgement but didn't look back.

25

Marcella was dressing to go out when her maid Eunice knocked at the bedroom door to tell her that Mr Vespucci was waiting for her in the living room. It was seven o'clock, early evening. Marcella had already heard on the radio that a mob-connected arsonist called Peter Medill had been charged by police after a citizen's arrest by *Star* reporter Harry Sharpe. She hadn't yet heard however that a *Star* photographer driving Harry Sharpe's station wagon had been shot to death by contract killers less than an hour afterwards. She might have been more cautious if she had. Swift and merciless revenge was an Enzo Vespucci special. He didn't taunt his victims the way that Capone used to. If he was offended, he killed.

Marcella carefully finished lining her eyes, then tied her wrap more tightly around her, and went through to the living room. Enzo was sitting on the sofa holding hands with a young olive-skinned girl in a pink pleated dress. Ambrogio stood behind them, his meaty hands cupped over his genitalia as if he were posing for a football photograph. Enzo was wearing a beautifully cut suit of cream-colored wool, with a pink carnation in his lapel. The girl was probably sixteen, but looked twelve.

'Marcella, my own angel,' said Enzo, standing up, and holding out his hand. 'You must meet Isabella.'

'Well, well, another one, father,' said Marcella. She smiled indulgently at the little girl, and blew her a kiss from her fingertips. 'We must get to know each other. I'm sure we have an awful lot in common.'

Enzo stared at her frigidly. 'You're going out somewhere?'

'The Colburns are having a cocktail party. Mark Colburn

won some yachting race over the weekend, they're celebrating.'

'Ah,' said Enzo. And then, for no logical reason at all, 'Isabella plays the piano. She played me Beethoven last night, the Moonlight Sonata.'

'I didn't think you cared for Beethoven,' Marcella replied, off-handedly. 'Have you come to see mother? Is it check day already? You could pay the money straight into her bank, you know. You wouldn't see how grovelingly grateful we were, but it would save you a journey.'

Enzo's smile was stretched over his teeth like catgut. 'You're an angel, Marcella, haven't I always called you my angel? But, don't try to be amusing. Women are never amusing.'

'Believe me, father, I know. Would you care for a cocktail? I'm something of a killer at mixing up Pisco Punch. Several of my friends have been hospitalized after taking just one sip.'

Enzo said, 'I'm here to talk serious, Marcella.'

'You are? Well – I never assumed for one moment that you were here to talk silly.'

'Marcella, you were talking at the track yesterday with Harry Sharpe, that reporter from the Chicago *Star*.'

'And?' Marcella challenged him, although her heart felt as if it had suddenly slipped sideways.

'And, you must know that Harry Sharpe is one of those journalists who feel that it is their sacred mission in life to discredit me.'

'I thought *every* journalist felt that way, without exception.'

Enzo came over and laid his arm around Marcella's shoulders. 'Come here,' he said, and guided her out of the living room into the hallway. He pressed her against the blue and brown wallpapered wall, and said, very quietly, 'You must not play any kind of game with me, Marcella. I am not the man for games.'

'If I knew what you were trying to tell me –' Marcella began, but Enzo seized her back hair by the roots, and tugged it downwards so violently that she felt her scalp crunch. She screamed out loud.

'You were talking at the track to Harry Sharpe yesterday afternoon. Today, Harry Sharpe found and caught a man called Peter Medill, who happens to have done a little private work for me. His arrest is very embarrassing, not only to me but to many high officials in the city of Chicago. It is all lies and slander, of course, what Harry Sharpe is suggesting that Peter Medill is supposed to have done for me; but what I would be very interested to know is how in the first place Harry Sharpe managed to discover his name.'

Marcella's eyes were glittering with tears. 'Father, I'll kill you,' she whispered. 'By St Theresa and St Antony, I'll kill you.'

Enzo stared at her without speaking for what seemed to Marcella like endless minutes. His eyes were hooded and inquisitorial; there was a vein in his forehead which steadily pulsed underneath his translucent skin.

At last he released her hair. 'So, you would kill your own father. You would break the fountain that gave you life. Well – now at least I know where I stand. Now I know how shallow your gratitude is for everything that I have done for you. Your schools, your fine clothes, your horses. Look at this apartment! Who pays for it? I do! Every month, religiously, I pay for this apartment, and for everything in it, including the food that goes down your throat. Do I hear words of gratitude and thanks? *Anh?* Do I hear words of affection? Oh, no. I hear, "Father, I'm going to kill you!"'

Marcella leaned back against the wall, hurt, and silently weeping. Enzo cocked back the tails of his blazer, and stood with his fists on his hips, glaring at her malevolently. 'Was it you?' he demanded. 'Was it you who told Harry Sharpe that Peter Medill had been working for me? Believe me, I will find out the truth, and when I find out the truth I will cut out the tongue of whoever spoke! Whoever!'

Marcella wiped her eyes with the lapel of her bathrobe, but volunteered nothing, no confession, no apology, not even a burst of anger. Enzo leaned forward and stared ferociously into her face.

'How come you don't speak? Don't you have anything to say? Not even, "I'm sorry, Papa, it was me who ratted on Peter Medill"? *Enh?* What are you, what kind of a daughter are you?'

Marcella said, 'Eduardo's crying.'

'Oh, so Eduardo's crying. With a mother like you, he should certainly cry!'

'Father, it wasn't me. I didn't tell Harry Sharpe anything. In fact, I didn't care for him at all. He was ignorant and arrogant.'

'Hignorant and harrogant,' Enzo repeated, scathingly, in his caricatured English pronunciation. 'Heeegnorant and harrogant. Well. I don't know what to do. What should I do, tell me? You think maybe I too ought to break down and cry?'

Marcella said nothing. Enzo thought for a while, rubbing his lower lip with his fingertips as if he had a very small patch of dry skin which he was having difficulty in locating. 'What do you think?' he asked Marcella at last. 'Do you think Mr Howard Croft Tate would have anybody working for him who is heeegnorant and harrogant?'

'Maybe,' said Marcella, unsteadily. 'He's pretty ignorant and arrogant himself.'

Enzo nodded, and paced up and down the little corridor. On one wall there was a dull reproduction of a red-caped cardinal mournfully contemplating a geographical globe. Underneath, the caption ran, *Aide-toi, le ciel t'aidera*, help yourself, and heaven will help you. All at once, Enzo stopped, and snapped his fingers, and called out, 'Ambrogio, bring me the black girl!'

Ambrogio appeared after a moment or two, nudging Marcella's maid in front of him. The girl was obviously nervous; she could sense the menace in Enzo's demeanor, in spite of the fact that he was smiling. Enzo beckoned her to come closer, and cautiously she did.

'What's this?' Marcella demanded. 'What do you want with Eunice?'

'I want to test your *truthfulness*,' said Enzo. 'To me, the truth is very important. To tell the truth, daughter to father, that's the first test of family loyalty.'

'Leave her alone,' said Marcella, although her voice was much shakier than she had meant it to be. 'She hasn't done anything, all she does is work here. Leave her alone.'

'But, Marcella, I'm not testing *her*, I'm testing *you*! I want you to tell me the truth. I want you to tell me whether you happened to mention to Mr Harry Sharpe the name of Peter Medill; even if you mentioned it accidentally; even if you mentioned it without *thinking*. I want the truth, Marcella, my darling.'

Ambrogio reached into his pocket and produced a large horn-handled switchblade knife. He released the blade, and held it up. Eunice rolled her eyes at the sight of it, and let out a moan. 'What they doing, Miss Marcella? What they doing?'

Enzo grinned. 'Eunice, you hear me? You tell your mistress to speak the plain truth. You know what the plain truth is, young lady? The plain truth is something you can swear to, in front of God. The plain truth is also magic; and do you know why it's magic, young lady?'

'No sir,' whispered Eunice, without once taking her eyes off the switchblade.

'Well, you listen to me good, young lady. The plain truth is magic because it can make all the difference between being beautiful, like you are now – and being ugly.'

Marcella pleaded, 'Father, this is frightening and ridiculous. And, listen, Eduardo's still crying.'

Enzo reached out gently and held the sleeve of Marcella's robe. 'Eduardo can cry for a little while. It's good exercise for his lungs. Maybe one day he's going to grow up into Caruso.'

'Father, I've told you the truth already. I talked to Harry Sharpe but I didn't say a word about this Peter Medill of yours. All we talked about was racehorses.'

'What does he know about racehorses?'

'Not much. That's why he wanted to talk about them.'

Ambrogio brought the knife up close to Eunice's face, until the pointed tip of it was only an inch from her cheek.

'Have you ever seen this done?' asked Enzo, as dryly and as matter-of-factly as if he were lecturing Marcella on salmon-fishing. 'The point of the knife is inserted into the side of the mouth, only the point, and then snatched backwards, just the same flick of the wrist as cracking a whip. *Phut!* Just like that, and it cuts a crescent-shaped slice from the side of the mouth to the bottom of the ear, right through the cheek; and always the tongue flops out, I don't know why.'

'How dare you behave like this?' Marcella shouted at him. 'Look at her, the poor girl is *terrified*!'

'Well,' said Enzo, modestly, 'I was hoping that she would be. Now she can beg you for the sake of her beauty to tell the truth. Such a cut leaves a hideous scar.'

'*Miss Marcella!*' Eunice shrieked. She tried to drop to her knees on the corridor carpet, and to seize hold of Marcella's robe, but Ambrogio caught her around the chest and dragged her forcibly backwards. He grasped her chin in one huge hand, and lifted up the knife in the other, until the point was quivering right at the corner of her open mouth.

'I just want the *truth*,' said Enzo.

Marcella looked first at Eunice, and then at her father. Eunice was too frightened to say anything now, quite apart from the fact that Ambrogio was gripping her jaw so tightly. Enzo slowly chafed his hands together as if he felt a sudden chill; or as if he were looking forward to the sight of blood being spilled.

Marcella said, in a hushed but steady voice, 'The truth is that I said nothing to Harry Sharpe about this man Peter Medill. Why should I? Every evil thing that you do reflects on me. I am ashamed of what you do. Why should I boast about it? And you never hide what you do, do you, from anyone? How can you give away secrets when you are always barefaced enough to commit your sins in public?'

Enzo thought about this for a moment, and then turned to Ambrogio and winked. Ambrogio snicked the switchblade into the side of Eunice's mouth, just enough to cut the sensitive corner of the lip and make her bleed. Eunice squealed, and wrestled herself away, clasping her hand against her mouth. Ambrogio folded his knife away, laughing; while Enzo smiled with perverse satisfaction.

'You're a good girl, Eunice,' he said. He reached into his billfold and took out a twenty-dollar bill, which he held out towards her, and encouragingly flapped. 'Here – never say that Enzo Vespucci isn't generous. Always generous! To family, and to friends! Come on, Eunice, lips heal quick. Just don't eat any salty chitterlings just yet!'

Marcella pushed past him to Eduardo's room. Eduardo was sitting up in his crib, hot and flushed and sobbing mournfully. Marcella lifted him up and held him tight, and stayed like that, in the drape-drawn darkness of his room, while Enzo stood outside the doorway and watched her and smiled.

'My grandson,' he said. 'My grandson the big-shot. You'll see, one day! Blood always tells!'

Marcella told him, without turning around, 'Get out of here, father. I'm not in the mood for your practical jokes!'

Enzo shrugged. 'Well, my love, I am pleased. You have a good Vespucci sense of humor. Believe me, if I had thought for one single moment that you had talked to Harry Sharpe I would have cut that girl's *head* off, and yours, too.'

'Get out of here,' Marcella repeated.

Eduardo smelled of baby formula, steamy urine and talcum

powder. Marcella kissed the top of his sticky little head and shushed him. 'It's all right, my darling, the boogy-man's going now. Mommy will feed you in a little while.'

Enzo laughed. Marcella had never heard such a laugh, even from him. It was like a clown's slapstick cracking, sharp and vicious. He beckoned to Isabella, who was sitting in the living room watching him with vacant eyes. She got up and came over to him. She put her arms around him and rubbed her knee against his trouser leg, over and over, to show him that she was on heat. Enzo didn't even look at her.

'I'm a patient man,' said Enzo. 'But all this Peter Medill business is causing me grief. If you want to be a good daughter to me, keep your ears open. And don't talk to anyone, not one word. This is a time when I need my family to be loyal.'

It was only after the door had closed behind him that Marcella allowed herself to let go. She sobbed so much that she had to sit down on the nursery chair, and her tears dripped on to Eduardo's sleep suit.

Eunice came to the door holding a padded handkerchief against the side of her mouth. She too had been crying. She came over and the two women held hands, while Eduardo snuffled and coughed.

'I have to change him,' said Marcella, after a while. She wiped her nose.

'I'm all right, Miss Marcella, I'll do it. Your father was right about lips, they always heal up quick.'

Marcella handed Eduardo over, and then went across to the door to switch on the light. As she did so, there was a ring at the front door. Marcella and Eunice stared at each other, unsure of what to do, convinced that it must be Enzo again. But then the doorbell rang again, a tricky little swing riff that couldn't possibly have been Enzo, *brrrnngg, brrr-brrr, brrrnngg, brrr*, and Marcella went through to the hallway to answer it.

It was Harry. He looked pale and disheveled, and he was carrying a half-empty bottle of Four Roses.

'Harry!' Marcella exclaimed. 'Come in quick! My father was here only two minutes ago!'

Harry eased himself into the hallway and leaned against the wall, his eyes out of focus. 'I saw him on the way in,' he told Marcella, and coughed. 'He was . . . just coming out of the building. Had that . . . walking snowstorm with him. And some girl. Very persona – very personabubble, I thought. Very personabubble indeed.'

'Harry, what's wrong? You're so *drunk*!' Marcella guided him into the living room, and sat him down on the sofa. He sprawled back, with his head to one side, and closed his eyes. 'You're right,' he muttered. 'I am very drunk. I haven't been as drunk as this since . . . VJ Day. Except last year, on my birthday. I was very drunk then, on my birthday.'

He opened his eyes and frowned at her. 'I hid, that's what I did. When I saw your father coming, I hid. Do you think that was . . . cowardly of me? Do you think I should have faced him man-to-man? Well, perhaps I should have done, but I didn't. I got down on my hands and knees and I hid behind that potted . . . palm . . . thing . . . down in the lobby.' He burped two or three times, quite violently, and then he looked down at the bottle of whiskey.

'It's driving me crazy, this bottle. The more I drink . . . the slower it seems to go down . . . I started off with a quar, with a quawduh of a boddle, and now I've got a half a boddle. Maybe if I drink smore, id'll . . . fill itself up. You know, compleely.'

He stared at Marcella pink-eyed, and began to laugh, high-pitched intermittent bursts of laughter that sounded more like a woman at a cocktail party. Marcella said, 'Listen, you're going to have to sober up. Stay here, take off your shoes. I'll make you some coffee. And, here –' she reached out for his bottle of whiskey '– you're not having any more of this.'

Harry tried to snatch back the bottle, but missed, and fell sideways. 'That cost me – hey that cost me three dollars and sixty cents. America's favorite bouquet . . .'

He lay on his side on the sofa, not laughing any more, while Marcella went through to the kitchen to perk some strong dark-roasted coffee. She looked at her face in the glass of the kitchen cabinet, and slowly rubbed the back of her scalp where her father had pulled her hair. She had never hated her father before; she still wasn't certain that she hated him now.

However, Marcella had learned two things this evening, and one of them was that Enzo certainly would kill her if he ever found out that she had betrayed him. She wished more than anything else in the world that she hadn't. She stared at her indistinct reflection and thought to herself: why? Why did

I do it? even though she knew the answer as clearly as she knew that he was a man not just of brutality and callous greed, but of creative viciousness, a man who delighted in keeping all around him in a constant knife-edge condition of absolute fear. She had been afraid for too long, and for one brief moment in the company of an ordinary and sympathetic man, she had allowed her self-discipline to crack.

She had spoken the name Peter Medill, and it had been like speaking the words of a mythical spell; a name that would bring down empires. A name that would bring down lives, and reputations, and buildings.

Harry was sitting up straight with his hands in his lap when Marcella came back into the living room. He was openly weeping. Marcella set the cup of coffee on the small marble table beside him, and then sat down next to him. 'Harry, what's wrong? What's happened?'

He sorted through his pockets and found a handkerchief to blow his nose. 'Do you know what they always used to say when I was a kid? Blow your horn if you don't sell a fish. Did you ever say that?'

'Harry –'

'Yes,' said Harry. 'Harry. The great and fearless reporter. Wit, raconteur, hot-shot writer and potential Pulitzer prizewinner.' He turned to face her, his eyes reddened with tears and alcohol, and said as distinctly as he could manage, 'You and I have set something in motion, my dear. We have *really* set something in motion. It's the power of the press, that's what it is, and the trouble with the power of the press is that those who are afraid of it, or contem, *contemptuous* of it – those who have no respect for law or for life – well, they always hit back harder than they otherwise might. Because, you see, there's only one way to muzzle the press, and that is to frighten it to death. Not the press barons, not the publishers, they don't care, in their gilded towers, but the ordinary notebook man in the street, who is loud of mouth when it comes to reporting the news, but who is almost always a congenital chicken when it comes to looking down the barrels of .45s.'

'Harry, what are you talking about? Why are you so upset?'

Harry laid his hand on Marcella's knee. 'This afternoon, shortly after Medill was taken into custody by the police, two things happened. One was that Medill was immediately bailed for $50,000, and will no doubt vanish like one of the Great Surpriso's white rabbits. The other was that my photographer was shot dead in the basement of the *Star* building while he was sitting in the driver's seat of my car.'

Marcella stared at him. 'Mother of God,' she whispered.

'You see what we've started?' said Harry. 'That father of yours is extremely angry, isn't he? He looked angry, even from behind the potted palm. Mind you, I can't say that I've ever seen him when he's happy.'

Marcella stood up, and walked around the back of the sofa, turning this way and that, as if she were in a cage. She felt shocked and light-headed, and she could hardly believe that any of this was real.

'Your newspaper story – have you published it yet? Will it appear in your afternoon paper?'

Harry shook his head. 'It's all set up for tomorrow morning. They start printing the early editions at eleven.'

'Do you think they might be persuaded to leave it out?'

'No,' said Harry, shaking his head. He leaned back and looked at her closely.

Marcella covered her face with her hands for a moment. Then she looked at Harry, and said, 'I think I made a mistake. I think I made a terrible mistake.'

'Come on, you didn't make any mistake.'

'But now my father has killed somebody! Your friend!'

'Yes – and that's precisely why we have to go ahead with the story. Do you think we're going to let him die for nothing?'

Marcella came around and sat down beside him again. 'I made a mistake. I feel the death of that man on my own conscience.'

'Well, you're wrong,' said Harry. 'The whole population of Chicago is guilty, particularly its aldermen and its elected officials, particularly its business men and its police officers and its public servants, and everybody else who allows men like your father to stay in business. Your father should have been locked up years ago. You know that as well as I do. That's why you told me Peter Medill's name.'

He paused for a little while, and then he said, 'Maybe this news story will convince a few other people to act the same way. You know – all those people who think it's smart to rub shoulders with mobsters. The people who take tainted money and don't care where it comes from. The people who put a quiet life first.'

'And supposing my father kills again?' Marcella breathed. 'Supposing he goes on killing until your newspaper is quiet and the city settles down again and everybody says okay, that's enough, we won't say any more about it?'

'Not this time,' Harry told her. 'This time we're going to fix him for good.'

Marcella stayed with Harry that evening. She called the Colburns to say that her mother was sick, and that she wouldn't be able to come to the cocktail party. Eunice fed Eduardo at nine and then went home. Marcella paid for a taxi for her because Eunice was irrationally but understandably afraid that she would be followed home by Ambrogio, and attacked. Harry gradually sobered up as the twilight settled into darkness. Grief was more sobering than any number of cups of coffee.

'I don't think anybody can understand what it is to have a father like mine,' Marcella told him, sitting close. 'I have always had such a terrible longing to be like other girls, to be normal. I suppose when I realized that it was impossible to change him, I tried to blind myself to what he really is. But you are quite right, I have been living like that for too long, just as the people of Chicago have been turning a blind eye to him for too long. If you are not afraid, then I am not afraid, either.'

The ormolu clock on the marble mantelpiece struck ten. Harry said, 'I'm beat, I'd better go.' But Marcella took hold of his hand.

'I have to go,' Harry told her. 'I want to be there when the paper comes off the presses.'

'You can stay for a while,' said Marcella. 'Then we'll both go out and buy an early edition, together, before it's light, yes?'

She led him as if he were a small boy through to her bedroom. It was high-ceilinged, decorated in the palest of greens. There was a set of horse-riding prints on the wall, Currier & Ives, framed in green. The silk quilt was the color of daffodil leaves.

Marcella switched on the bedside lights. She whispered, 'Sit,' and Harry sat on the end of the bed, round-shouldered and exhausted, while she stepped out of her watered-silk mules. Then she loosened the tie of her bathrobe, and let it drop. Underneath she was wearing a beige silk teddy. Her breasts swayed under the silk; a ruby and diamond pendant swung in her cleavage. With her curly tangled hair and her feline eyes, she looked in the lamplight like some passionate savage.

She slipped the strap of the teddy off her shoulders. Harry watched her drowzy and hypnotized, although he could feel himself beginning to uncurl. Marcella began to sing, a breathy little snatch of operetta, la-la-la, and dance for him, bare toes with crimson-painted nails stepping and counter-stepping on the off-white rug. Keeping her back to him, she slid the teddy down to her waist. Her back was broad and olive-skinned with a pattern of moles on her right shoulder-blade. A woman fashioned like an Etruscan vase, isn't that what Walter Dempsey had said one night, trying to describe some long-lost love from 1925.

She turned around to face him, her hands cupping her breasts, lifting them up a little because they were so big and full, glossy-skinned, patterned like Italian marble with pale blue veins. She danced up to him, swaying her hips, la-la-la-ing to him, lips shining, eyes shining, perfumed and warm and encouraging, and he smiled one of those really slow smiles like a man waking up from the happiest of dreams.

She took her hands away from her breasts, baring nipples dark pink like tea-rose petals, with wide dark-pink areolas. She entwined her arms around Harry's neck, and kissed his hair, and then his forehead, and then his eyes, and then his cheeks.

In turn, he kissed her nipples, cupping each of her breasts in his hand in turn, tugging at her gently with his teeth until the nipples stiffened and he could drum them against the roof of his mouth with his tongue-tip.

She held herself against his face. He felt that he would leave a life-mask impressed on her skin. For a moment, he could hardly breathe anything but perfume.

'*Ow*,' he protested, as she kissed his chin.

'What's the matter?' she asked him softly. She kissed him again.

'That's where that nag of yours kicked me.'

'But there's scarcely any mark at all! One little red bruise!'

'He must've cracked the bone.'

'Cracked the bone! *Ahh*, you poor fellow? You're quite right, aren't you, about reporters being chicken? I think Eduardo's braver than you!' She laughed, and kissed him some more, so many kisses.

He said, still smiling, but much more sadly now, 'It's no use, Marcella. I am sorry.'

She stared at him, very close. He could feel her breath on his face. 'You're too sad, aren't you? At least, you think you're too sad. You can't stop thinking about your poor friend. You can't stop thinking that it should have been you.'

Harry shrugged, and swallowed, and there was something in his throat that felt like a twisted lump of gristle and grief. 'He was going out on a date tonight. A girl in the mail room. You should have seen the blood.'

Marcella loosened his necktie, and began to unbutton his shirt. 'You know, there's a toast which people sometimes drink, after Italian dinners. They lift their glasses, and say, "To you! May the saddest day of your future be like the happiest day of your past!"'

She eased him out of his shirt. She kissed his shoulders. His chest was stocky and quite muscular, a little out of condition. There was a small crucifix of dark hair in the center of his breastbone.

'Don't you think that I'm just as sad as you are?' asked Marcella. Her hands smoothed over his bare skin. Her nipples brushed against his arms. Her lips grazed his ears, and dabbed again and again at the bruise where Secret Kiss had kicked him.

He lay back on the bright green quilt naked and it was cool and slippery against his back. Marcella's hand strayed down his stomach and between his thighs, grasping him warmly and firmly, and gently tugging and massaging at him until he couldn't help but swell. But after a while, he subsided again, even though she kept on fondling him; and by the time the clock in the living room chimed ten thirty, he knew that it was no use at all. Too much whiskey, too much thinking, too much sadness.

Marcella sat up. 'Perhaps I should make coffee.'

He reached out and ran his fingertips down her back. 'I hope you forgive me.'

'There is nothing to forgive. Apart from that, I am not a priestess. I do not have the power to forgive.'

She bent forward sharply and kissed his penis. He had never been kissed like that before, not by any woman, and he felt a sudden twinge of arousal. But he was too tired to do anything but sit up on his elbow and kiss her back, and gently touch her black curly hair.

When she returned to the bedroom with two cups of hot black coffee, he was asleep, his hands held up in front of him as if he were pretending to be a rabbit or a kangaroo, his mouth open, his hair touzled. She sat on the edge of the bed and watched him, sipping her coffee. She shook his thigh once or twice, but he didn't stir. Anesthetized by three quarters of a bottle of Four Roses, his mind was now plunging deep beneath the events of the past weekend into a place where it was dark and cold and clear, and absolution could be had for no charge at all.

He never knew what she did to him while he slept. She eased off her teddy, and stepped out of it, until she was completely naked. Then she climbed on to the bed next to him, and took hold of his somnolent wrist, and guided his hand all around her breasts and over her body. At last she lay back and opened her thighs wide and brushed his lifeless fingers backwards and forwards over her parted sex. She began to sigh, and to sing again, not operetta this time, but a song from her childhood. She kissed his fingertips one by one, then she carefully opened herself and pushed his fingers inside her, two, then three, then four, as deeply as she could; then closed her thighs together again so that his wrist was clasped between them.

He never knew that it had happened. He never knew what feelings she felt, what urges she indulged. She panted and gasped; her olive skin shone with perspiration; her eyelids flickered. He was a living man, naked and completely unconscious, and she used him in every way that she could. She did things so daring that they made the muscles in her stomach tighten. There was only one time when he murmured something muffled and tried to turn his face away, but she stroked his forehead and soothed him until he was settled again.

It was four o'clock in the morning when he opened his eyes. The room was already growing light. He sat up and frowned all around him. There was a deep dull ache at the back of his neck. He licked his lips and there was a strange sweetish taste on them, and the skin on his face felt tight. He heard soft breathing and there was Marcella lying beside him, fast asleep.

'Holy Maloney,' he said, hoarsely, and swung his legs out of bed.

He was dressed and down at the *Star* building by four forty. Herman Short came waddling up to him with a fresh copy of the bulldog edition and snapped it at him like a paper thunderclap. 'You look like something the dog sicked up.'

'Thanks, Herman.' Harry opened the paper and there it was. A full-page photograph of Woozy's body lying under a sheet on the floor of the *Star* parking lot, and the headline SLAIN.

Harry left the press room and went back to his office, the newspaper tucked under his arm. Somehow, now that Woozy's death had been published in the paper, it didn't seem to hurt so much any more. Maybe nothing hurt so much, once it was printed in black and white. Maybe the newspaper was a kind of confessional, a means of rationalizing the wild disparity of days that could start with kisses and tap-dancers and end with blood. People might die, people might laugh, people might hurt each other. Trains might fall off the Elevated into the street. Airplanes might explode over Lake Michigan. A rich and silly girl might get married. It was all marked up in seven point Royal on an eight and a half point slug, over ten and a half ems; it was all reduced to grayness and uniformity, the same way that people are all eventually reduced to gravestones.

Harry eased himself into his chair, propped his feet up on his desk, and turned to page three, to which his NABS MOB FIREBUG story had now been relegated. He was still sitting there reading when Grant Clifford came over, looking pouchy-eyed and very tired.

'Harry?'

Harry swung his feet down. 'Hallo, Grant.'

Grant perched himself on the side of Harry's pigpen. 'This is a sad day for the *Star*, Harry. We never had anybody killed before, not even when we ran those Bugs Moran stories.'

'Don't worry, Grant. I'm going round to tour all of those slums today. Believe me, you'll get a follow-up you can be proud of.'

Grant nodded. 'I know you won't let me down.'

Harry lit a cigarette. He offered one to Grant but Grant shook his head.

'What did the old man say about Woozy?' Harry asked him.

'Mr Croft Tate? I haven't been able to talk to him yet. He went to his meeting last night with Redman Radio, and then he had dinner with Mrs Watson of the Commerce Bank of California. After that . . . well, nobody's quite sure where he is. I've left two or three messages at the Beverly Hills Hotel.'

Harry lifted an eyebrow, but said nothing. He supposed that every man was entitled to some hanky-panky, now and again; and he was also beginning to wonder with some embarrassment what hanky-panky he might have been up to himself, without even knowing it.

26

Morgana had been to the Colburns' yachting party; mostly out of courtesy to Mr and Mrs Colburn, who had donated $48,000 to the *Star*'s fund to help children in Europe who had been orphaned by the war. Mark Colburn was a spoiled and arrogant twenty-two-year-old who couldn't think of anything better to do with his life than race yachts. His parents had paid over $125,000 for his latest yacht, *Pandora II*, and so it was hardly surprising that he had won every single race in his class.

She had left early; and she had been driven by a well-meaning boy called Carl Pockett. Carl had buck teeth and a quiff, and he had apologized over and over again for the smell of his auto. 'I took my sister's cat to the vet. I'm sorry, it wasn't a very seasoned traveler.' He had pecked Morgana on the cheek before opening the door and letting her out, but he obviously hadn't had the courage to ask if he could see her again.

Millicent hurried to meet her. 'Mr Birmingham's here. He's been waiting for you since seven o'clock.'

'Where is he?'

'In the music room, Miss Morgana. Your mother told me to take him there.'

'Is my mother still in?'

'Yes, Miss Morgana; in her writing room.'

Morgana went upstairs and along the corridor to her mother's doorway. She knocked twice and called, 'Momsy!'

Eleanor opened the door almost immediately. She seemed to be very well composed. She was wearing a cobalt blue velveteen skirt and a white organdy blouse with a ruffled front. 'Morgana, you're back early. Come in.'

Her mother's writing room was small but elegant. There was a pretty walnut desk, with gilded decorations, and a rack for letters and envelopes and pens. An engraving of a sad cherub looked down from the wall. There is sadness, even in Heaven.

'*John's* here,' hissed Morgana.

'Yes,' Eleanor nodded, equably. 'I was in two minds whether I ought to admit him or not. Turning up in person was very bad manners, he ought to have written. But I didn't really see how his manners could possibly be any worse, after Sunday; and after what he's been up to for a very long time. So I thought yes, let him in, let him wait, and let you and him have it all out between you.'

'Momsy, I don't want to have it all out! As far as I'm concerned, we're finished! There's nothing to say!'

Eleanor gave her a maternal smile. 'I've been thinking today that your father and I ought to be all washed up. Beached on the shores of age and indifference, not to mention infidelity! But we still have plenty to talk about; at least I hope we do.'

'Has Popsy heard about what happened?'

'About the shooting? No, not yet. Nobody's been able to get in touch with him. He's supposed to be back at his hotel, though, later – and I've left a message for him there. That's if he doesn't hear it on the news first.'

Morgana sat down at her mother's desk. There was a half-written letter on the blotter which began, 'Dear Cyrus . . .' She didn't read any further. Cyrus was Cy Wentworth, Robert Wentworth's father. Morgana wasn't really interested in what her mother had to say to him; or to any of the Wentworths. It was very difficult for her to imagine her mother in Robert Wentworth's arms: to think of that good-looking brown-haired profligate holding her mother and smiling and talking like a lover.

'Dear Cyrus, I am still so stunned . . .' Morgana had to admit to herself that she had read that much.

'Can't you just tell John to go away?' she asked her mother. 'Tell him I don't want to talk to him at all.'

Eleanor said, 'I think you ought to. I think you ought to settle this matter one way or another, for good and for all.'

Morgana lowered her head. It made her mother feel a little wistful to see how alluring she looked this evening, her own daughter by Howard Croft Tate. She was wearing a dark red cocktail dress by Dior, with an off-the-shoulder neckline and a closely cut skirt. Her hat had been made out of matching dark red silk, with a spray of dyed osprey feathers.

'All right, then,' Morgana agreed, taking off her gloves. 'I suppose it's the courteous thing to do. Will you come down with me?'

Eleanor shook her head. 'This, my dear, you must do for yourself.'

John was sitting at the piano when she walked into the music room, tinkling out a few erratic bars of Chopin. He looked up and his head and shoulders were reflected in the highly polished lid, so that he could have been a knave on a playing card. He pushed back the piano stool and immediately came across to greet her, his hands outstretched, his cuffs brilliant.

Morgana stayed where she was, and clasped her hands around herself, and stared at him with utter coldness.

John hesitated, and then dropped his hands, and lowered his head, and shuffled his feet, and did everything he could to make himself look as hangdog as possible.

'I guess you're not going to believe me if I say I'm sorry,' he told her.

'You guess correctly,' Morgana retorted. Her voice was cutting enough to make the crystal chandelier start ringing.

'I wanted to apologize,' said John. He lifted his head again – a little too soon, Morgana thought, for a man who was supposed to be so contrite. 'I also wanted to explain.'

'Your apology is noted,' replied Morgana. 'As far as any explanation is concerned, I would have thought that it was redundant. What happened was quite self-explanatory.'

'Morgana, listen to me, please,' John begged her. Morgana looked him up and down, and thought to herself, I could have loved him. I still do. He's so suffocatingly handsome. He's so flawlessly smooth. He's all style and smiles and perfectly cut pants, and of course he's going to be successful at the Bar. She could remember the firmness of his arms inside the sleeves of his tuxedo. She could remember the smell of his sweat and his cologne. He came under the heading of Attractive Male, no doubt about it.

Morgana said, 'All right. You want to explain. Explain.'

John walked across the music room, one hand in his pocket, the other uplifted as if he were speaking to a jury. 'First off,' he said, 'I have no defense whatsoever for what happened with Phoebe. It was wrong, it was selfish, it was misguided.'

'*Misguided?*' Morgana exclaimed.

'Please,' John appealed. 'You've given me the chance to explain. Let me do it, and then judge me.'

Morgana said, 'Go on, please,' with intense sarcasm.

'The point is, darling, that as soon as I first made love to you, I knew that I wanted to marry you. I wanted you to be my companion for life. You have qualities that I have never ever come across in any other girl. But – I've always been brought up to believe that a husband treats his wife with deep respect – and that a husband-to-be doesn't compromise the honor of his bride by sleeping with her before the wedding. I mean, what do we want, those nasty asides when you walk down the aisle – "I don't know why she's wearing white" – that kind of thing?'

'That still doesn't explain your eurythmics with Phoebe,' said Morgana.

John spread both his arms wide, the lawyer appealing to the men of the world in the jury box. 'Morgana – I'm a man. Every man has his animal urges. It's part of what a man is. If it hadn't been Phoebe, it would have had to be somebody else. A B-girl, maybe a streetwalker. Don't you think it's healthier, though – don't you think that it's more a compliment to you – that it was your sister?'

Morgana's eardrums sang with disbelief. She stared at John for a very long time without saying anything, and all the time John kept giving her little encouraging looks, little c'mon Morgana, be-a-pal looks. Morgana at last went over to the piano. On top of it stood a tall Baccarat vase, filled with waxy-white lilies. She lifted one of them out and said, 'You know what lilies are supposed to represent, don't you?'

John came over and stood right next to her, smiling. 'Morgana, I love you and I need you; and I promise to wait until we're married. You'll see. I'll be the most celibate man in Illinois, just for you.'

'John – you had sex with my sister!' Morgana's profile was sharp-cut with anger.

'But, lookit, Morgana – only because I couldn't decently have sex with you!'

Morgana said, 'You mean, then, that your mind is completely controlled by your trousers.'

'Morgana – every man of my age feels the same way! You talk to any half-dozen guys in any mid-Western frat house, they'll all tell you the same thing! It's just the way that men are! Don't tell me you haven't read Kinsey! Men have a fire, and every now and then that fire has to be put out!'

Morgana closed her eyes, then opened them again. 'Come here, John,' she said, quite softly. John approached her.

She turned to look at him. There was a challenge in her eyes. 'Kiss me, John,' she demanded. She just wished that her heart would stop lindy-hopping around inside of her ribcage. John cautiously put his arm around her shoulders, drew her closer, and kissed her.

'Don't you close your eyes when you kiss?' she asked him.

Obediently, John closed his eyes. At the same time, Morgana reached sideways for the vase of lilies, and lifted them off the piano. Then she smartly stepped back, yanked open the waistband of John's perfect black evening pants, and emptied the vase into his underpants.

'*That*,' she said, banging the vase back on to the piano, '*that* was to put out your fire.'

Rigid-faced, John looked down at his soaking pants. Slowly, he drew two or three lilies out of his waistband.

'Well,' he said, after a while. 'That just about sums it up, doesn't it? You've always put the damper on things, haven't you?'

'John,' she said, 'I don't need your insults, I don't need your jokes, I don't need your songs, your arrogance, your unfaithfulness, your explanations, your anything! Now get out of this house and don't you ever come near me again!'

John said, 'Okay – okay. If that's the way you feel. There's just one thing, though, and considering we were officially engaged for two days, I do think I'm entitled.'

'What's that, my dear? An illuminated citation? A Purple Heart?'

'Morgana – what the hell are you talking about? I want my ring back. It's a family heirloom!'

Morgana looked at John open-mouthed for a moment, and then laughed. 'My dear John, of course you shall have your ring back! I shall have it sent round. But, in the meantime, I'd really consider it a favor if you'd leave.'

'Very well,' John sighed. He gave her one last pained, handsome look; one of those looks that he had obviously practiced in the mirror. 'This is really the end then, is it?'

'Yes, John,' Morgana insisted, and she was beginning to feel more confident and aggressive, almost like a young lioness who has made her first killing. She knew that she wasn't yet happy, but that she would be, in time, once the hurt had died away.

John walked out of the music room and was given his hat at the door, while the chauffeur brought his car round to the steps. Winton Snell (to whom nothing that happened in the Croft Tate household was a secret) stood beside him to ensure that he didn't try to attempt anything ridiculous, like some of the girls' previous suitors. Winton glanced down at the polished marble floor and noticed that a small pool was collecting around John's left leg. He smiled at John icily and John smiled back at him. Then John suddenly realized what he had been looking at. He lifted up his left leg and shook it.

'Oh, that – that isn't – hey, you mustn't think that –'

Winton Snell inclined his head politely, but said nothing.

John said, 'All that happened was – some flower-water was spilled on my pants –'

Morgana was watching from the head of the stairs. She smiled to herself, and then went up at a dignified pace to prepare herself for bed. She had an early start tomorrow.

27

Howard returned to the Beverly Hills Hotel at six o'clock Tuesday morning in a taxi. The morning was already sunny and bright; all around the medicine-pink hotel buildings the California quail were fluttering, and the yuccas rattled in the breeze like castanets. Howard paid off the taxi and walked into the hotel lobby smoking a first cigar.

He felt satisfied that he had had some sort of final revenge on Eleanor. He had spent last night in Westwood, at the house of a young red-haired movie actress whose acquaintance he had first made two years ago, when he was setting up the Croft Tate television studios in Burbank. The actress's real name was Lois Heufenbacher. She was pretty as fireworks; intelligent as Einstein; and her sexual appetite always left Howard sweating. He was especially excited by her additional tuft of red plumage, and the whiteness of her skin. She liked pink champagne, and necklaces.

The hotel bellman came smoothly across to intercept Howard halfway across the circular lobby. 'Mr Croft Tate? Good morning, sir. There has been a message from the *Star* office in Chicago, urgent. Also, sir, I have been requested to give you this.'

He handed Howard a large manila envelope. Howard clenched his cigar between his teeth and slowly opened it, while the bellman politely waited. Inside the envelope was a copy of this morning's *Star*, flown out airmail. Howard scanned the front page, then turned inside to pages two and three.

'Is there anything I can do, sir?' the bellman asked him.

Howard stared at the bellman as if he had already forgotten who he was. Then, his face gray, he marched quickly through the lobby and out to his cottage in the hotel grounds. He unlocked the door, and his hands were shaking. On the pillow of his bed, untouched, were three gold-wrapped candies and the message, 'The Beverly Hills Hotel wishes you a pleasant night's sleep.' Howard tugged his necktie loose, unbuttoned his shirt, and picked up the telephone.

'Operator? I want a Chicago number. SUperior NEWS. That's right. And as quick as you can.'

Gordon McLintock answered; Grant Clifford was still at home, sleeping. Immediately Howard screamed at Gordon, 'I just got this morning's paper! What in hell is going on? I specifically said no slum stories! I specifically said no personal attacks on Enzo Vespucci! What the hell has gotten into you people! You're fired! The whole damn lot of you!'

Gordon waited for Howard to quieten down a little, and then said, 'We did try to talk to you earlier, sir. The hotel said you were out.'

'What kind of a smart remark is that, Gordon?'

'I'm sorry, sir. I'm not trying to be smart. But you did authorize the arson story, and one thing kind of led to another. Very sadly, it led to Woozy being shot, too.'

'Now, hold up a minute,' Howard raged, 'I didn't authorize any arson story. I didn't authorize any story at all. This is complete news to me, all of this. I gave Grant and you and everybody else in the newsroom clear and unmistakable orders that we were to launch no crusades against Enzo Vespucci.'

'Yes, sir, I'm aware of that, sir, but we called through to the house yesterday just when you were leaving, and asked your daughter to tell you what we were planning to do. She said that you gave the story the go-ahead.'

Howard's hand was tight and sweaty on the telephone receiver. 'Are you talking about Morgana?'

'That's right, sir, Morgana.'

Howard let out a long, unsteady breath. He licked his lips, and they felt rough and dry. The morning wind stirred the net drapes that covered the windows of his room, and the California sunshine rippled across the rug like a shallow river of pure light. Gordon said distantly, 'Mr Croft Tate? Are you still there?'

Howard nodded, and then said, 'Yes, Gordon, I'm still here. I think I understand what's happened. I'm going to talk to Grant if I can get him, then I'm coming straight back to Chicago. Have my car meet me at Midway.'

'Yes, sir. Have a safe flight, sir.'

Howard called Grant. Enid was reluctant to get him out of bed at first; he had only just managed to get to sleep. But when Howard impressed on her that it was a matter of real life and real death, she went to fetch him.

Howard was brisk and abrasive. The first thing he said was, 'I've read this morning's paper and before you say a single word I want you to know that these stories against Enzo Vespucci were run without my knowledge and without my consent, and that what you've done here is going to have very far-reaching implications that may cost you your job.'

But Grant thought about this for a moment, and then replied, 'I've just been woken up, Howard, and that fact may be affecting my judgement. But my immediate reaction is that you have no right to talk to me that way, and that before this discussion goes one sentence further I want an apology.'

Howard roared, 'Christ Almighty, Grant, don't you get pompous with me! I'm your publisher! This damned story is ill-considered, libelous, dangerous, and infinitely damaging! What's more, it's been run on the front page of my flagship newspaper in direct defiance of my personal orders!'

Without any comment whatsoever, Grant put the phone down. Howard stared at the silent receiver in disbelief. Then he furiously jiggled the cradle to get the operator back to reconnect him.

'*Grant?*' he said hoarsely, when Grant picked up the phone again.

'Yes, Howard?'

'Grant, I apologize. It wasn't your fault. The way I understand it, Morgana gave you the impression that she'd discussed the story with me, and that I'd okayed it. As it was, I didn't know anything about it; and so I can only assume that Morgana took it into her head to authorize the story on my behalf. I haven't called her yet, I don't know for sure, but that's the way it looks. I'm sorry. It's just that this story puts me personally into a very embarrassing position.'

Grant said, 'Can I ask what this embarrassing position actually is?'

'I'm sorry, Grant, I can't tell you over the telephone. I'm

flying back pretty well straight away. I'll talk to you just as soon as I get back to the office.'

'What do we do now?' Grant wanted to know.

'What do you mean, what do we do now?' Howard demanded.

'We have a front-page follow-up story in the works, and I've sent Harry out this morning with His Honor to bring back a full-scale in-depth piece on the South Side slums.'

'We can't run anything like that,' said Howard. 'You'll have to spike it.'

'Howard – one of our people was shot and killed yesterday. A kid, who wasn't doing anything more than his everyday job. We can't let Enzo get away with that! And what the hell are our readers going to think of us, if we never mention the matter again? What is the *Tribune* going to start saying about us? "Oh, the *Star* – they won't say boo to a goose." Or should I say Guinea Fowl?'

Howard closed his eyes and pressed the eyelids with finger and thumb. He had been afraid that something like this would happen. He had been afraid of it ever since that party at the Blackstone Hotel, and of course it had gradually grown worse and worse, more and more complicated, less and less explainable to those who might have forgiven him. It was his own fault, he had allowed himself to be drawn into each succeeding complication, and never once sought an honest and sensible way out. He remembered the old adage about those who supped with the devil being cautioned to use a long spoon. He should have remembered that earlier.

Grant said, 'The feeling in the newsroom is that we have to do everything we can to bring Enzo Vespucci to book. I share that feeling, Howard, and I can't imagine any personal difficulty, no matter *how* embarrassing, taking priority. Let me put it country simple, Howard, if you try to stop this crusade against Enzo Vespucci, you're not going to have a newspaper any more. Your people are all going to walk.'

Howard opened his eyes again. The sunlight looked blurry. 'I'm going to talk to Enzo myself,' he said. 'Don't start running anything until you hear from me.'

'It would help a lot if you could tell me what your problem is, Howard. A problem shared, and all that.'

'In this particular case, Grant, I think it would turn out to be a problem shared, a problem doubled.'

'Suit yourself. I'll see you later. But don't leave your conversation with Enzo too long. I might just be tempted to run this follow-up story and to hell with the consequences. There's always a job for me in Philadelphia.'

Howard put down the phone in slow motion. He was almost tempted to leave the Beverly Hills Hotel, walk out along Sunset Boulevard until he reached the Pacific, and then keep on walking, to see if he could reach the horizon. It always looked so distant and golden out there. He was not a complicated man; and sometimes the easiest answer to tangles like this seemed to be to get up and exit, and to leave everybody else to sort them out. He would leave a note saying simply 'ends' – which was what his reporters typed at the bottom of their copy.

He called to arrange for a private DC3 to fly him back to Chicago. Then he asked the operator to put him through to Enzo Vespucci. Carmino said that he would bring Mr Vespucci to the phone *subito*, but it was almost five minutes before Enzo picked up the receiver and said, flatly, 'Howard. You're calling from Los Angeles?'

'Hello, Enzo. I just saw this morning's *Star*.'

'Yes, Howard. I hope you're very proud of it. Packed with mouthwatering lies, as usual. I sometimes wonder why your reporters don't become fiction writers. Western stories, true romances, hanh?'

'Enzo, come on now, we have a very difficult problem here.'

'No, no, my friend. It is not *we* who have a difficult problem, it is *you*. You are the one with the difficult problem.'

Howard said, 'Enzo, shooting that photographer was way beyond the limit. If you think for one moment that I'm going to –'

'I don't think for one moment that you're going to do anything,' Enzo interrupted. 'I think quite simply that your newspaper is going to publish a prominent apology in tomorrow's edition, front-page apology, and that you are never going to mention one word about me or my business activities ever again, period. That's what I think.'

Howard slowly rubbed the back of his neck. 'You did shoot that photographer, then?'

'Are you crazy? What kind of a crazy accusation is that? I didn't shoot nobody! You know what I am, I'm a businessman. I don't even own a gun.'

'But you had him shot.'
'Howard – I thought we were friends.'
'Enzo, you and I can never be friends.'
'Well,' said Enzo, 'I'm very hurt to hear you say that. I'm very hurt indeed. I always thought you were a man of class. But, what you said in your newspaper about me – there's no class in that. Howard, I'm going to have to say to you, that's it, that's enough, you say you're sorry and you never print no more. Front-page apology.'
'And what if I don't?' asked Howard, in a thick, dry voice.
'What you say?'
'I said, what if I *don't*?'
Enzo laughed. That same sharp slapstick laugh, enough to crack windows. 'Howard! How can you ask me such things! You know what's going to happen if you don't. Everybody in the whole *world* is going to find out about you! Everybody! And they're going to be shouting it from the rooftops!'
Howard said, 'All right, Enzo. You've made yourself plain. Take a look at tomorrow morning's paper. Then we'll talk some more.'
'Howard, you're the most reasonable man I ever met in my life,' said Enzo, with a cheerfulness so caustic that it could have cleaned the sulphur off silver eggspoons.
Howard laid down the phone again. He stood up, and walked stiffly into the bathroom. He needed a shower and a shave. His face in the mirror over the washbasin looked like the face of a classification-yard vagrant, a true Chicago bum. It was in Chicago that the German word *bummeln* became absorbed into the American language, and perhaps Howard in his own way was one of them. He had all the tattered nobility of the true bum; all the proud self-destructiveness. He had inherited everything except the ability to survive.
Whatever the consequences, he knew that he was going to have to allow Grant and Gordon and Harry Sharpe to continue their crusade against Enzo. Maybe things would have been different, twenty years ago, in Big Bill Thompson's day. But Howard as much as anybody could sense the changes that were coming in Chicago, the public and private urge to bulldoze the slums and clear out the ghettos and see Chicago rise on the lakeshore lofty and proud and glittering, a city fit for the '50s.
One personal secret could never be sufficient justification for holding back a whole city's destiny.

He called Marcella. The telephone rang for a long time before she answered. When she did, she sounded highly suspicious. 'Who is this?'

'Marcella, darling, it's me, Howard.'

'Howard! I've seen the paper. I've talked to one of your reporters, too, Harry Sharpe. He told me everything that was happening.'

Howard said, 'What about your father? Have you heard from him?'

'He was here yesterday evening. He was very angry. He hurt Eunice, but not too badly. Don't worry – he didn't touch Eduardo.'

'Why was he so angry?'

'Well, he thought that it might have been me who told your newspaper about this man who lit the fire.'

Howard cleared his throat. 'Was it?' he asked her.

'Was it what?'

'Was it you who told the *Star* about this firebug?'

'What do you think, Howard? You think I would do such a thing?' Marcella retorted.

Howard sniffed. 'I don't know, maybe you would. But, anyway, it's too late, it's done. There's nothing we can do about it now. I talked to Enzo myself, only a couple of minutes ago. He said that if the *Star* went ahead with any kind of crusade against him – well, he'd shout everything out from the rooftops. And you know what *that* means.'

Marcella was quiet for a while. Then she said, with great gentleness, 'What are you going to do, Howard?'

'I don't see that I have very much of a choice. Something like this was bound to happen sooner or later. Your father isn't the sort of man who holds a running flush and then keeps it to himself, out of the goodness of his heart.'

'My father isn't the kind of man who does anything out of the goodness of his heart.'

Howard said, 'Marcella, listen to me. I really think it's better if you and Eduardo quit town for a while. You know what I mean, safer. Things are really going to get bad. You can go down to Florida if you like, and use the house at Sarasota.'

'Howard, Howard, I'm not running away. I never deserted you before, why should I desert you now?'

'I'm thinking about Eduardo.'

'Eduardo will be safe. My father would never hurt Eduardo.'

'Well . . . it's up to you,' said Howard. 'But if you run into any kind of trouble at all . . . please, just go. I can have a private plane take you down, at an hour's notice.'

Marcella said, 'I'll be all right, Howard, and so will Eduardo. Please, just take care of yourself.'

Howard said, 'I'm sorry.'

'What for? Perhaps you should have done this a long time ago. Perhaps you don't realize that I've been trying to force you into it.'

'He's your father, Marcella.'

'Yes! But he is also Enzo Vespucci.'

'I'll call you later,' said Howard. Over the past two years, he had talked for hours with Marcella about her father, and what she felt about him. He didn't want to get into that now. He added, quietly, 'I love you, you know that, don't you? And I love Eduardo, too. Sometimes I wish I were a different man.'

'If you were a different man, Howard, I wouldn't love you. And nor would your son. We will always love you.'

'*Ciao*, Marcella.'

'*Ciao*, Howard.'

The Eagle Air-Charter DC3 lifted off from Los Angeles shortly after nine, and turned its silver wings against the sun, heading north-east. Howard sat staring out of the window at the blue-gray Pacific, his briefcase on his knees, while the engines thrummed and vibrated, and the airplane's fuselage bucked and dipped in the air turbulence over the Santa Monica mountains. Then, after a while, he sat back, and closed his eyes and said a silent prayer to himself, the same prayer that his mother had always said to him late at night.

> Abide with me from morn till eve; for without Thee I cannot live.
> Abide with me when night is nigh; for without Thee I dare not die.

28

Kenneth Doyle was in cracking spirits. He gave Morgana and Harry a breakfast of ham and eggs, hash-browns and grits, with pots of hot coffee and tea. They ate in his office at City Hall, with a white linen tablecloth spread over his desk, and a vase of red and white carnations to brighten it up. Kenneth was wearing his loudest Irish suit, a green ensemble with an orange check, and he was so delighted that he could scarcely eat.

'I would have laid money that your father wouldn't have turned against Vespucci! A hundred dollars, I would have bet! He was so set on being impartial, your father, no condemnation without proof, that was his line! But when I opened up my *Star* this morning, glory be to God I could have cried crimanentlies! The wife thought I was sick, I whooped so loud!'

Morgana managed to eat very little, a forkful of grits, a little ham. She had slept last night for less than two hours. At first she had thought about nothing but John, but in the small hours of the morning she had began to worry about the unauthorized approval she had given to the *Star*'s stories on Enzo Vespucci. It had begun to occur to her gradually and naggingly that her father might have had a very good reason for not wanting to upset Enzo Vespucci. She hadn't quite been sure what this reason could be, but never in the past had she known her father to set himself so categorically against the eager campaigning of his editors.

All the same, Kenneth Doyle was jigging in pleasure, and Harry Sharpe seemed to think that this morning's paper was the beginning of a great crusade against crime and corruption, and the mood at City Hall was generally so bullish that she must have done something right.

After breakfast, they climbed into a Plymouth eight-passenger station wagon, and set out for the South Side. They were joined by Sylvia Leno, the deputy press officer, a brusque young lady with an Ava Gardner hairstyle and a beauty spot on her cheek, and a crisp white square-shouldered blouse with the collar turned up; as well as one of the *Star*'s senior photographers, Sidney Kress. Sidney was a model of cynicism. He had photographed the Marines at Guadalcanal and Betio and Morotai Island, and after carrying his Kodak through two and a half years of whining bullets and bursting hand grenades and roaring flame throwers, he thought very little of photographing women's clubs, tea parties and school outings, and as far as he was concerned, the South Side was paradise on earth, after Betio.

'You think these are slums? You shoulda been on Tarawa Atoll. Muck, maggots, mud huts, you name it.'

Sylvia Leno said crisply, 'The difference is, Mr Kress, that the inhabitants of the South Side of Chicago are not at war with Japan.'

Sidney snorted. 'They'd be better off if they were. At least they'd get medals.'

They were driven down to South Cottage Grove Avenue, where they stopped outside 2621, a three-story red-brick building with white brick arches over the upstairs windows. The ground floor was taken up by a storefront window advertising the Bland Roofing Co. and a sheet-metal works behind. Three Negroes were sitting on the sidewalk with their backs against the storefront, their brown suits patched and dusty, sharing a bottle in a brown bag.

Kenneth Doyle walked over to them and hunkered down on the sidewalk and said to the nearest Negro, 'How's things?'

The Negro smeared his nose with the back of his hand, and looked down the street as if he expected somebody or something miraculous to appear from that direction, like Santa Claus on a sleigh. 'Well, you know, man, I'm just like the bear. I ain't nowhere.'

Kenneth glanced up at the building. 'Do you know who owns this place?'

'Never did, man, and probably never will.'

'Well, who collects the rent?'

'The rent. That's every Friday; every Cemetery Day, that's what we call it, on account of you can't find nobody here that ain't dead. An Eye-talian collects it, what's who, calls himself Mr Minestrone, but sure as hell that ain't his real name.'

'Do you know who Mr Minestrone works for?'

'Come on, man, I'm like the bear's daughter, I ain't got a quarter.'

Harry immediately reached into his back pants pocket and produced a roll of bills. He stripped off two dollars and handed them down. The Negro took them, sniffed them, waved them around, and then carefully folded them up and tucked them into his breast pocket. 'Minestrone works for a man calls himself Amboge.'

'Ambrogio?' asked Harry.

'That's the man,' the Negro told him. 'But don't you go saying it was me that tole. Cause all *I'm* going to say is I was beating my gums.'

'Do you live here?' Kenneth asked him.

'Off'n'on,' the Negro nodded.

'Can you show us around? We want to take some pictures for the newspaper.'

'Whaffor you want to do that?'

'We want to show people how bad you have to live, so that we can get something done about it.'

The Negro clapped his hand over his chest. 'What you trying to do here? You trying to embarrass me or something?'

His companions screeched with laughter, and slapped their thighs. 'Go on, Jonas, you show them around. You ain't *never* embarrassed! Sir! Sir! You should see this man! He'd embarrass a elephant!'

Dazed, unsteady, but with irrepressible confidence, Jonas climbed up on to his feet, and led the way toward the side door of 2621.

'In here,' he said, beckoning all the time, as if the world that lay beyond the door were another dimension. 'Follow me.'

Kenneth lifted an eyebrow to his companions, and went in first. After all, he was the elected mayor of this fair city, in which this dilapidated building stood. The rest of them shuffled in behind, Harry and Morgana and Sidney Kress, while Sylvia Leno took up the rear in the hope that it would give her time to think, and to retreat, if necessary. She had never been down to the South Side before, to what were called euphemistically 'the old neighborhoods'. She was already wondering how on earth she could explain rationally such dismal slums to the average well-fed well-housed reader of the Chicago *Star*, or even to herself. Words like 'neglected' and 'undeveloped' just didn't seem to be adequate.

The hallway looked as if it had been recently bombed with a combination of bicycles, baby carriages, and paper sacks of wet trash. Underfoot, there were urine-soaked boxes of Flako Pie Crust and Nunso Dehydrated Sweetcorn, while half-empty cans of Scout Cabin pumpkins grew pale with florid fungi, and month-old jars of Libby's Deep-Brown Beans festered like props from a Karloff movie. The smell was staggering: sweat and piss and sour vegetables and half-rotted chicken.

They cautiously climbed the stairs, Jonas swaying ahead of them, and singing to himself. 'I done live in this ole house too long, I sure done live in this ole house too damn long. Oh wop Lordy kick my ass I sure done live heah in this ole house too damn long.'

Sidney Kress muttered, 'I wish I was just anyplace else but here in this damn house one damn minute longer. General MacArthur, where are you now that I really need you?'

The stair treads creaked and sank beneath their weight. The banister-rail was gappy and broken, and the plaster on the walls looked as if it had contracted bulging leprosy. There was a single window at the top of the stairs, but only one pane remained intact, the rest of it had been covered up with flattened sections of grocery carton.

Morgana said nothing as she climbed the stairs, but several times she reached out for Harry's hand. She had expected filth and squalor. She had known that the slums were bad. But somehow she hadn't expected the intense, sickening smell, the smell that she had no choice but to take into her lungs with every breath, other people's bad sweat, other people's excrement, other people's discarded food, the stomach-churning invasion of her own senses by other people's social and physical collapse. She began to think that one of the greatest privileges of wealth was that it bought distance from one's fellow human beings. At that moment, as she was climbing up those stairs, escape from other people seemed to be the most precious commodity in the whole world.

When she walked through the rooms of the house, however, she gradually realized that splendid and sanitized isolation meant nothing. After the second room, she took the handkerchief away from her face, it was too blatant an insult to the people who had to live here. If she cared about them, even slightly, she had to experience for herself what they had to live through, day by day.

'This is the dining room,' Jonas announced, leading them into a dingy room with tattered sacking nailed up at the windows. With all the detachment of visiting ghosts, four white people stood in the doorway and stared at the eleven black people who were crouching on the bare-boarded floor, and who stared back at them with equal curiosity. There were half a dozen old folks here. Two of them were wrapped up in blankets, shivering, in spite of the suffocating heat and the overwhelming humidity. The others lay back half-naked against the wall, their eyes dull, the skin on their ribcages like the wrinkled skin on hot chocolate.

'The dining room, huh?' asked Harry, as Sidney stepped over arms and legs, taking flash photographs straight into the old folks' faces.

'Thass right,' grinned Jonas, 'and you know why I call it that? Cause every night you hear them crying out loud, hey, we're dining here, help us, help us, we're dining here.' He thought this was so funny that he slapped his thighs, and smacked his hands together.

One of the old men lifted his hand and called out to Kenneth in a croaky voice, 'Scuse me, sir, I've been cold in hand for quite a while now, you wouldn't see your way clear?'

'Cold in hand' meant broke, and Kenneth knew that. He also knew that if he started handing out dollars to this old man, no matter how badly the old man needed money, he would end up with the whole of South Cottage Grove Avenue standing in line for a handout. He stepped his way across and took hold of the old man's hand and said, 'I don't have a dime, old friend, and I'm sorry about that; but in any case that's not what I came here for. I came here to see if I could help you, to see if the city could find you somewhere better to live, somewhere clean, somewhere healthy. And that would be better than a few pennies, wouldn't it now?'

The old man's head sank down on his chest. 'Man, I say to you, the hell it would. I'm going to be climbing into my burial box within the month, and noplace cleaner nor healthier than that.'

They went through the interconnecting cross-and-Bible

door to the next room. Jonas said, 'You don't want to mind the noise in here, on account of this is where all the children get theirselves put.'

This room was even gloomier than the first, and the stink was so strong that Kenneth went completely white. 'Jesus and Mary, you could cut this air and sell it as ripe Gorgonzola.' Seven children's cribs were crowded in here, all of them occupied by sobbing, filthy, bare-bottomed babies. There were at least another eight or nine children playing on the linoleum floor, only one of them dressed, the others naked. Their only toys were tin cans and torn cardboard and wooden spoons. They crawled around the bare floor like stunted creatures out of a nightmare, urinating unconsciously wherever they crawled, so that they were paddling in their own urine. Sidney Kress was into his stride now, he understood without having to ask the nature of the tragedy they were witnessing. These children were just as much casualties of battle as the dead Marines lying on the beach at Betio, and he stepped around the room taking picture after picture, making sure that he caught the glutinous sores and the pustular eyes and the blowflies which clustered around the children's faces. Morgana had to look away for a very long moment, and close her eyes, and try to summon up the moral and physical strength to continue.

Harry laid his hand on her shoulder. 'Are you all right? You could wait in the car if you wanted to.'

Morgana shooked her head. 'I'm fine. If these people can stand it for ten years, I'm sure that I can stand it for ten minutes.'

Harry said, 'Do you understand now why I was so angry the first time I met you?'

Morgana said, 'Let's go on.'

Their half-hour tour of 2621 South Cottage Grove Avenue was like an endless journey through some dark medieval purgatory. Glimpsed in one of the filthy lavatories, a naked thirteen-year-old with corn row hair, nodding unconscious with a needle still dangling out of her arm. Upstairs, in a cramped room that must originally have been used as a closet, a grotesquely fat man, explosively swollen by degenerative kidney disease, dying in wheezy silence on a mattress that was already torn to ribbons by rats. Leaning their thin black elbows on an upstairs windowsill, two emaciated women with haunted eyes, normal in every respect except that their hope and their human dignity had long since died, and with their hope and their human dignity, their sanity. They talked about cakewalks at the Derby Hotel, and the price of fancy shoes. In a corner in the same room, dressed surprisingly cleanly and prettily, a little girl of no more than ten, with a hugely distended stomach.

'What's the matter with you, child? You seen a doctor?' Kenneth asked her, gently.

'I seen a doctor.'

'And what did the doctor say?'

'The doctor says the baby's due September twenty-second.'

'The baby? You mean you're going to have a baby?'

'A baby of my own, that's what the doctor say.'

Harry said, 'Who's the father?'

'Who's my father?'

'No, no, I didn't mean that, who's the father of your baby? Who gave you that baby?'

'It's my father's baby, that's what the doctor say.'

Kenneth left the room and caught hold of Jonas's arm. 'That's enough now, Jonas. You've been a good guide. Will you lead us out now?' Then he turned to Morgana and his face was deeply engraved with emotional pain. 'Did you hear that? Look at the age of her, and she's giving birth to her own brother. God in Heaven.'

They left the house, but remained outside on the sidewalk for a while, recovering from the shock of it. In all, they had counted or been told of seventy-six people living at that same address; seventy-six people crowded into one three-story building over a sheet-metal shop, some newly born, some almost dead, some hopeless, some desperate, some mad, some sick, yet trying to stay alive, trying to stay alive, even though all seventy-six of them had either forgotten why they should, or had never found out.

Kenneth opened his cigarette case and lit up quickly. 'Do you see now what a crisis we have. Admitted, this house is one of the worst. I brought you here first just to shock you. But wouldn't you rather die, than live like that? I know I would.'

'Do we have any evidence that Enzo Vespucci owns this building?' asked Harry.

Kenneth shook his head. 'The registered owners are Lakeshore Realtors, Inc.'

'And who controls Lakeshore Realtors, Inc.?'

'A corporation in Nevada called McLaughlin Enterprises. None of whose corporate officers is Enzo Vespucci.'

Harry glanced up at the flaking brick building. 'He keeps himself clean, doesn't he? More than anybody can say for his houses.'

'Come along,' said Kenneth. 'I want to show you some more.'

They drove all over the South and West Sides that morning, South Wabash, Federal Street, Vincennes Avenue, Hastings, Throop, and Loomis. By eleven o'clock Morgana had become blind and numb to poverty. They visited old-fashioned brick houses that were sagging and dilapidated; shacks and shanties and lean-tos; they found families that were living in huts made of beaten tin cans and cardboard and old car tires. They discovered two families living outside 1400 Hastings in a broken-down bus. After visiting a half-collapsed wooden house on the south-west corner of Clinton and Liberty Streets, next to the Soo Line railroad tracks, Harry tersely noted down the following, 'Ten people, five families, no toilet, no outhouse, no electricity.' His notebook was already half-full: a shorthand catalog of degradation and despair in America's second-largest city. And this wasn't 1890 – this was 1947.

Their last call was to 'Outhouse Alley', the notorious stretch of Honore Street between 35th and 36th Streets. They walked past the wooden porches and the washing lines and the rows of privies in tired silence. There was nothing more to say, except that there was so much squalor that it was impossible for anyone who lived a normal decent life to take it all in.

'What happened to that privy?' asked Morgana. 'It looks as if somebody's been using it for target practice.'

'Well, that's exactly what happened,' said Kenneth, with some joviality. 'In fact that's a new landmark, that rivals the steps of St Patrick's. That was the privy in which they found that gangster on Sunday, isn't it now, Harry?'

'I didn't cover that story,' said Harry.

Sidney Kress sniffed. 'I did. I came down here to take a picture of it. Carlo Aceto, that was his name, some small-time character from out of town. The police think that he probably upset one of the big boys. They sat him on the jakes and blew him away.'

A lanky black boy in a zoot-style coat and a wide-brimmed

hat came sidling up to them. 'You talking about that outhouse?'

'That's right. That was the one that gangster got himself shot in, wasn't it?'

'I was here, man,' the black boy said, his eyes hidden in shadow but his teeth grinning white. He spun the extra-long watch chain that hung from the waist of his pants, so that it whistled. 'I was here and I saw it all.'

Sidney said, 'When I was here with the cops, sonny, everybody for three blocks around said they'd suddenly gotten a fly in their eye.'

'Well, you know that's jive,' the black boy grinned. 'This here shooting was the most well-attended event since the All-Stars baseball.'

'And you saw it?'

The black boy screwed up one eye, and said, 'You the mayor, ain't you?'

'For my sins.'

'You been coming down on these guinea dudes, ain't you? I mean you really been coming down on them?'

Kenneth said nothing. Morgana swatted away a persistent blowfly. It was hot and stinking in these gardens, and she wished very much that this black boy would get to the point so that they could all go back to City Hall. She would have paid a hundred dollars for a glass of iced tea.

The boy looked around him, still twirling his watch chain. 'If I was to give you the word, man, would you guarantee me some kind of protection?'

'You could be held in protective custody.'

'How about the greens?'

Harry said, 'That depends, kid. If somebody goes to the slammer, you get paid, and paid good. Otherwise, all you get is a blip and a kick up the back of the lap.'

'Well, this information is genuine,' the boy told them, quite offended. 'I ain't just breaking out at the mouth.'

'Fifty,' said Kenneth, like a ventriloquist, without even moving his lips.

'Fifty?' said Sidney, in disbelief.

'Fifty'll do it,' the kid said, still whirling his chain, but clearly quite impressed. He had quite obviously underestimated the urgency of Kenneth's desire to have the streets cleaned of slums. So had Harry and Morgana and Sidney.

They all knew that Kenneth would probably have to pay that fifty out of his own pocket. Harry made a note in his book, $50!! and Sidney coughed and looked away.

'You got some wheels?' the kid asked them; and Harry nodded toward the station wagon parked at the end of the alley.

'Okay,' said the kid. 'You drive around the block, I'll be waiting for you on the corner of 36th.'

They spent a few more minutes wandering up and down the alley, talking to some of the residents, an old woman who had no running water, a young man dying of emphysema. Then they returned to the station wagon, and Kenneth instructed his driver to take them round the block. The black boy was waiting for them, as he had promised, outside the boarded-up storefront of G. Scruggs Cleaners. They opened one of the back doors for him and he climbed in, next to Sidney, who shifted well away from him, and watched him the whole time he was sitting there, rolling a toothpick from one side of his mouth to the other, and sniffing.

'All right, my friend,' said his honor, turning around in his seat. 'What's your name?'

'Earl Knapp, Jr, sir, that's "Knapp" with a kay.'

'Okay, Earl Knapp Jr with a kay, tell me what you saw.'

'It was Sunday, sir, I was messing around with some pals of mine back of the buildings. We saw the whole shooting, the whole thing. The guy didn't make no effort to hide what he was doing. We knew who he was, and he knew *we* knew who he was, and that was the whole reason he knew we wasn't ever going to say nothing, on account of he's the muscle who works for the landlord. I mean, you speak out against the landlord, even to the welfare lady, you're liable to get yourself beat so bad you can't never walk no more, and you're sure as certain to lose your apartment.'

'If it's such a risk, why are you telling me?' Kenneth asked him.

'Somebody has to tell, some time.'

'What do you mean by that?'

'I mean that you're never going to put those men away, less'n somebody speaks out, even if it's only the once.'

'You realize they might try to kill you, if they know that you squealed?'

'Sheesh, I could be long gone. I was due to leave for

New Orleans whatever. My brother's got himself a welding business down there, wants me to come.'

'All right, then,' said Kenneth. 'Just so long as you understand the risks. Who did it? Who shot Carlo Aceto?'

'You heard of a man calls himself Ambojo? Big guy, guinea, sometimes he comes for the rent.'

'Ambrogio,' Harry corrected him. 'We know Ambrogio. Ambrogio works for Enzo Vespucci.'

'Well, hold up a minute, I didn't say that,' the black boy protested. 'I didn't say nothing about no Enzo Vespooky. Come on now, this got to be fair. I saw Ambojo do it, I saw Ambojo shoot that man, just like thirty or forty other people saw Ambojo shoot that man. But I didn't see no Enzo Vespooky, and no more did they. Enzo Vespooky, that's a closed vol-yoom, man.'

'Brother,' sighed Kenneth, 'you said a mouthful.'

'Would you be willing to testify to what you saw in a court of law?' Harry asked him.

'Sure,' Earl agreed. 'On two conditions, right? One is that you square your case with the D.A.'s office before you go to court, so that you know for a hundred-percentile fact that Ambojo's going to go to the slammer. The second condition is that you have two train tickets waiting for me, first class, prepaid, heading due south on the Illinois Central.'

'And the fifty dollars, of course,' smiled Kenneth.

'Well of course the fifty dollars, you think I'm sacrificing my own precious existence just for squat?'

'Such a consideration never entered my brain,' said Kenneth, with a smile.

Earl Knapp Jr stared at Kenneth and shook his head in amazement. 'Is that how you get yourself elected mayor? I mean, speaking like some kind of dude from space?'

They let Earl out at the corner of 28th Street, then they drove back toward North LaSalle Street and City Hall. Harry said to Kenneth, 'What do you think? That's a first-class witness you've got yourself there.'

Kenneth smeared his face with his hands. 'It's a break, I'll agree with you. But it's not enough to take it to trial. Maybe he saw what happened, maybe he didn't. If he were white, and middle class, and a war hero, I'd say thanks to be God, we're practically home and dry. But the fact of the matter is that he's black, and he wears a zoot-suit, and no jury is going to convict one of Enzo Vespucci's hirelings on the uncorroborated evidence of a South Side cloud, especially when half the judges rely on Enzo Vespucci mortgages and Enzo Vespucci loans and Enzo Vespucci liquor and Enzo Vespucci everything else.'

'What more do you need, then?' asked Morgana.

Kenneth made a thoughtful leprechaun-like face. 'I need at least one more witness, my dear, and he has to be a white witness of fairly commendable background. After that, well – things may be different. Ambrogio's lawyer may convince Ambrogio that it would be worth squealing on his master for the sake of his own liberty, and this is certainly an offer that *we'd* be making, too. It's Enzo I want, not Ambrogio. The whole world is shoulder to shoulder with mental deficients like Ambrogio. But there are not too many Enzo Vespuccis, they're clever and they're very difficult to catch.'

They drove back to City Hall, where Kenneth gave them lunch, cold cuts and salad, and a bottle of chilled white wine, and then at last they returned to the *Star* building. Morgana said to Harry, as they went up in the elevator, 'I'd like to see what you write, when you've written it.'

'Why don't you write something too?' Harry asked her.

'You mean, the same way I wrote something about the fire?'

'That was different. This time, I think your work is going to be appreciated.'

Morgana lowered her eyes. 'All right,' she said. 'I'll try. To tell you the truth, though, I don't know where to start. It was all so awful.'

'That's where to start,' Harry told her. '"What I saw this morning was all so awful I don't know how to begin to describe it." Once you've written that, you'll find that it isn't true – you *can* begin to describe it.'

'This won't just be words, though,' Morgana asked him, 'shocking today and forgotten tomorrow?'

Harry took out a cigarette, and tucked it into his lips, although he didn't light it. 'I hope not.'

They reached the editorial floor and Harry ushered Morgana out. As they walked along the corridor, he lit his cigarette, and said, with carefully rehearsed off-handedness, 'My mother invited me for supper tonight. It struck me that you might like to come along, too.'

They had reached the newsroom, with its thundering typewriters and its jangling telephones and its stockyard shouting. 'Copy! Copy!' 'David, this is for you! Urgent!' 'Where the hell is my notebook!' 'Speak up! I can't hear you, for Christ's sake!'

Harry said, circuitously, 'It's just that we worked on this feature together, you know, and I thought you might like to discuss it a whole lot further. There might be some follow-ups, and . . .'

He raised his eyes and gazed at her. She looked tired but maddeningly attractive and he almost lost his nerve. 'Of course, if you're busy or something –'

'No, no,' said Morgana, smiling. 'That would be lovely. I'd love to come. What time?'

'Say eight o'clock? Should I come up to Weatherwood to collect you?'

'You don't have a car now, do you?'

'I can borrow Peter Donleavy's.'

'It's all right, I'll meet you at the Blackstone. Let's have a drink there, then I'll drive you.'

Harry said, 'Listen . . . my mother's place . . . well, she's proud of it, and I'm proud of her, but it's just an ordinary place.'

Morgana took hold of his hand, and kissed him on the cheek. All of a sudden Harry realized that the newsroom was silent, all the typewriters had stopped, and everybody was staring at him. Morgana looked around, too, and all the typewriters immediately started up again.

'I'll write something about this morning, and I'll bring it down,' Morgana promised.

'That'd be swell, McBell,' Harry answered, and made his way over to his own pigpen.

Just then, Gordon appeared, with a pencil perched behind his ear and a thick sheaf of galleys under his arm. 'Ah, there you are!' he said to Morgana. 'I hope you've prepared your defense!'

'My defense?' asked Morgana.

Gordon leaned forward conspiratorially. 'Grant and I are right behind you, don't have any worries about that. So is the rest of the newsroom.'

'I don't understand.'

Gordon leaned back again, and blinked. 'Haven't you

heard? Your father just got back. He's upstairs now, with Grant.'

'My father?'

'Yes – and he's not wholly delighted with the go-ahead you gave to our slum story. In fact when he called me from California this morning he was breathing molten lava down the telephone.'

Morgana took a deep breath. 'I see. Well – I think I'll just quietly disappear and do some shopping.'

Gordon smiled, and indicated his head toward the elevators. 'I'm sorry. I have strict instructions to send you directly up to the eagle's nest without delay. On pain of death.'

Howard was standing by the window of his penthouse office, his hands clasped behind his back, staring out at the golden haze of the lake. Grant was sitting uncomfortably in one of the Charles Eames chairs, looking unhappy. Howard's secretary announced, 'Your daughter, Mr Croft Tate,' and left Morgana by the door. Morgana tried out two or three different expressions – woeful, humble, confused – but decided that there was no alternative to open-faced honesty.

'Hello, Morgana,' said Howard. He turned around, and to Morgana's surprise he was ruefully smiling.

'Popsy?'

Howard came over and kissed her, and put his arm around her. 'I've just been having a long and luminous talk with Grant here.'

'Illuminating,' Morgana corrected him.

'That's right,' said Howard. 'It seems that I gave Grant my personal authority to go ahead with a crusading story against Enzo Vespucci.'

'Yes, Popsy, I'm sorry.'

'Well, you don't have any real need to be sorry,' Howard told her. 'I guess this crisis has been long overdue. It's my fault, not yours. In fact, it has very little to do with the slums, and it has very little to do with Enzo Vespucci. It's all to do with me and your mother.'

'What do you mean?' asked Morgana.

Howard squeezed her affectionately. 'I've been explaining it to Grant here. I guess I should have told him a long time ago. There are times when a man can keep silent, but there are times when he ought to trust the friendship of the people around him; and Grant's a friend.'

Grant suggested quietly, 'Why don't you tell Morgana what happened, right from the beginning, the way you told me?'

Howard looked at Morgana, and then nodded. 'I owe you that much, I suppose. And you are twenty-one. Would you care for a drink? A cup of coffee, maybe? Grant, fix me another whiskey, would you. This kind of confession is hard on the nerves.'

When his drink had been refilled, Howard went back to the window. Morgana came and stood beside him, just a little way away, so that she could watch his face as he spoke. He sipped whiskey, and then he said, 'You mustn't misunderstand me. I've always loved your mother, right from the very moment I met her. It was one of those storybook affairs, love at first sight.' He paused, and then he said, 'She had everything I wanted – looks, poise, wit, intelligence. And first of all I was easily able to impress her, in return, because of being wealthy, and powerful, and owning all of these newspapers and radio stations and whatever.'

'Go on,' Morgana urged him.

He let out a breath. 'The trouble was that, over the years, my lack of – what can you call it? – breeding, education, you name it – all began to show. Your mother could talk to writers and artists and ballet dancers and politicians. She could be amusing and entertaining, and everybody loved her. I began to feel like a rube, for all of my money and for all of my newspapers, and believe me that's not a confession that comes easy. I began to feel, rightly or wrongly, that I couldn't keep up with your mother, and that I just wasn't interesting to her any more.'

'Popsy –' said Morgana. She felt as if her father had taken hold of her heart and wrenched it completely out of place.

Howard quickly shook his hand. 'No, no, let me finish, please. I know that I was probably wrong, and that what I felt about being so clumsy and so unattractive was probably mistaken. But, I felt it, and it built up a kind of a wall between us, between your mother and me, and of course it got worse and worse. I have to tell you that we haven't had what you might call a normal marriage since the end of the war. You understand what I'm saying?'

'Yes, Popsy,' Morgana whispered.

Howard cleared his throat, and waited for a while before continuing. Then he said, 'One result of this wall going up between us ... was that your mother, understandably, began to look at other men. One of the men she looked at was Robert Wentworth – and, well, you know all about that. It's been causing enough disturbances at home. I can't say that I wasn't bitterly hurt when I found out, because I was, although I want you to know now that I think I can get over it.

'The other result was that – well, the other result was that I started looking at other women. I guess I needed to have my morale boosted. I wanted somebody who was pretty and charming but not too bright, somebody who wouldn't threaten me. I'm not a psychologist and I don't know anything about psychology, but when I start to analyze what I did, and why, I know that's the reason. I guess it's the reason that most men cheat on their wives.'

Howard swallowed more whiskey, and it made him shiver. 'A couple of years ago, I went to an opening party at the Blackstone, and while I was there I was introduced to a young Italian-born lady called Marcella Mascagni. She was very attractive, very warm, and we hit it off right from the start. I have to tell you that we didn't have an affair for almost four months. I took her to dinner, took her to the theater, that kind of thing. It was her companionship I valued most – the companionship of somebody whose social style didn't make me feel inferior.

'We became friends; and then, for a short time, we became, well, lovers.'

Morgana retreated a little, and drew up one of the Charles Eames chairs. She could see how difficult it was for her father to have to say all this. He had never before said sorry; she had never known him confess to weakness. What he was saying now was destroying not only what she thought of him now, but what she had thought of him ever since she was a small girl. It was as if her mind were a sculpture gallery, in which all of the images she had ever had of her father were displayed in alcoves, and somebody was walking through it alcove by alcove, smashing each image to chalky fragments.

Howard said, 'Marcella met me one day at the Racquet Club and told me she was going to have my baby. I said that I could arrange to get rid of it, Dr Keller would do it without any fuss, but of course Marcella is a Catholic and she wouldn't hear of it. Besides, she said she loved me, and even if she never saw me again, she wanted a child to remember me by.

'Then she came out with something that shocked me even more. She said that she had told her mother she was pregnant, and that her mother out of respect had told her father. Up until then, I had never met her father, only her mother. I had presumed that her father was dead. I asked her who her father was, maybe I should meet him; but she said that I knew him already. In fact I knew him very well.'

Howard turned to Morgana and he saw on her face something that he had only half-dared to think that he might see; sympathy, and caring, and daughterly love, too.

'Marcella's father is Enzo Vespucci,' he said, although he didn't hear himself saying it.

Morgana whispered, 'Oh, Popsy . . . so *that*'s why.'

Howard nodded, tightly. 'I know now that I should have confessed to your mother right from the start. I should have made a clean breast of it. But I was frightened enough of losing her as it was. If she knew about Marcella, and if she knew about the baby . . . I thought that would be the end of it. And when the baby was born, and turned out to be a boy, somehow that made it even worse.'

'Has Enzo Vespucci been blackmailing you?' Morgana asked him.

'Not in so many words, not until now. But the implication has always been there. And you can imagine what would have happened to the *Star*'s reputation if it had got out that I was the father of Enzo Vespucci's grandson, and that I had deliberately given instructions to my editors not to run any critical campaigns against him. Quite apart from my own reputation, of course, my chairmanship of the church committee, my chairmanship of the Chamber of Commerce, my standing in the Democratic Party, my whole public and private life . . . the whole thing would have collapsed all around me, and around you, too. You and Phoebe have a half-brother who is related to the single most evil mobster in the United States of America.'

Morgana said, 'I think I'll have that drink now.'

Grant stood up and laid his hand on Morgana's shoulder. 'I want to say something,' he said. 'I want to say that whatever mistakes Howard has made, he has impressed me today like no man has ever impressed me before, simply by coming back here and admitting everything that happened. What's more, he hasn't made any excuses for himself. He's been quite open about where the blame should be laid. For that alone, I believe he deserves the support of his staff and the support of his family.'

'What are you going to do now?' Morgana asked her father.

Howard finished his drink. 'First, and most important, I'm going to go back home and tell your mother face to face exactly what I've told you. I'm scared as all hell, I admit it, and she may throw me straight out of the house, with considerable justification. But, it has to be done. Then – I'm going to come back here and I'm going to lead this newspaper into the most relentless crusade that it's ever launched. I'm going to break Enzo Vespucci once and for all, and damn the personal consequences.'

Tears suddenly sprang into Howard's eyes, and when he spoke again, his voice was cracking with strain and emotion. 'Vespucci killed one of our people. He set out the terms and conditions. So – if it's a fight to the death that he wants, he's going to get it.'

Grant looked across at Morgana and for once Morgana was unable to read his expression. All she could understand was that from this moment on, her life would never be the same again.

29

'This is Roseland, this is where I grew up,' said Harry. 'Here, pull in here, right behind that green Buick, this'll do fine.'

Morgana turned the corner into 111th and pulled up outside the lighted storefront window of Zyzniewski's Food Mart. Harry jumped out of the car and ran around it to open the door for her. She switched off the Sportabout's engine and climbed out, looking tall and practical and smart in a pale-blue Pauline Trigere dress with a little square-shouldered jacket to match. She hadn't wanted to dress to kill, not for an evening with Harry's mother on 111th Street, but at the same time she hadn't wanted to seem patronizing by dressing too plain.

'I have to bring back some dessert,' said Harry. 'This won't take a minute.'

He led Morgana into the brightly lit interior of the food mart. There were sausages hanging up everywhere, hundreds of them, like pilgrim's crutches at Lourdes, and behind the glass-fronted counter there were pierogis stuffed with cottage cheese and ham and sauerkraut, and cheeses, and sliced salamis, and bowls of cold potato salad and Warsaw salad with sour cream and apples, and fresh rollmop herrings with their skins shining silver and blue.

The store's shelves were lined with jars of pickled cucumbers; pots of preserved cherries; and cans of pork. The aroma was astonishingly sharp – smoked meat and vinegar, with an appetizing cabbagy undertone.

Mr Zyzniewski appeared, as perfectly rotund as a wooden matrioshka doll, his face varnished walnut-yellow with well-being. 'Good evening, young man,' he greeted Harry, pretending to be stern. 'Why haven't you visited your mother for two days?'

Harry shook hands. Then he introduced Morgana. 'Mr Zyzniewski, I'd like you to meet Miss Morgana Croft Tate. She's my boss.'

Mr Zyzniewski bowed his head, and shook hands. 'Good evening, delighted,' he said. Then, to Harry, 'How come your boss is so pretty? Look at my boss!' And he nodded his head toward Mrs Zyzniewski, who was teetering right at the top of a small wooden stepladder restocking some of the upper shelves with cartons of sugar, a mightily bottomed woman whose legs could have supported a triumphal arch.

Harry chose a thick cream-covered Warsaw torte with flakes of almond embedded in it, and Mrs Zyzniewski carefully packed it into a cakebox for him and tied it with ribbon. 'This cake is the very finest,' he declared. 'Mrs Zyzniewski likes them so much, she always eats three for breakfast.'

He and Harry immediately cracked up laughing, although Morgana was mystified. She had not yet been introduced to the surrealistic teasing which forms a large part of Polish vernacular humor. Nor had she yet been introduced to Mrs Zyzniewski, who obviously didn't think her husband's remark was funny either, because she came creaking down from the stepladder, steps and stays creaking equally, and began fiercely and systematically to lay about Mr Zyzniewski with a yellow plastic fly whisk, until he laughed so much that tears streamed down his cheeks.

'When God was giving out manners, you were asleep under the meat counter!' she shouted at him.

'Mercy! Mercy!' begged Mr Zyzniewski, sobbing with laughter.

Harry had to take out his handkerchief and wipe his eyes. Mrs Zyzniewski waved the fly whisk at him, too, and said sternly, 'I remember you coming in here in short pants, Marek Sczaniecka, wanting a penny's worth of halva! So don't you laugh at me, you young pigling!'

'Pigling' finished Harry off completely, and Morgana had to take the torte for him and nudge him out of the store. Once outside, he leaned his back against the window and wiped his eyes again. 'Those two, they always kill me. But, you know, they're like two whales.'

Harry sobered up a little, and nodded. 'Whales choose a

mate for a lifetime. Once they're in love, they're biologically inseparable. The same with the Zyzniewskis.'

'I guess that Mr John Birmingham and I weren't sufficiently whale-like.'

Harry glanced at her. 'Well, yes, I heard about that. I'm sorry.'

'You don't have to be. I have to admit that I'm a little cut up, but it's all for the best. Is this where your mother lives, here?'

'That's right, come in. Here, I'll take the cake.'

Harry led her through a green-painted hallway with a black and white tiled floor. It was bare but immaculately clean. There was the sound of a radio playing in a first-floor apartment, occasional bursts of studio laughter; while upstairs someone was practising Dvorak's 'Silent Woods' on the cello, elegant sobs and vibrant sighs. Harry opened the clattering lattice of the elevator gate, and pressed the button for four.

'I hope you're not regretting you came,' he told her. He looked tired under the naked bulb in the ceiling of the elevator car.

She smiled, and shook her head. 'My stars said that when I reached my twenty-first birthday, my whole life was going to be turned upside down.'

Harry made a face. 'You can say that again.'

Mrs Sczaniecka had heard the elevator and guessed that it was Harry. She was waiting at the open doorway of her apartment, a small round woman with round cheeks and round eyes, and a little ski-jump Polish nose. Her gray hair had been decoratively braided and fastened with diamanté combs. She wore a smart black Sears dress with wide lapels and smart black old-fashioned shoes. She was still wearing her apron, and she smelled of lavender-water and flour and onions.

'Marek! I thought it was you!'

'Hello, *matka*. This is Miss Croft Tate.'

Mrs Sczaniecka curtsied, then suddenly realized she was wearing her apron, and blushed crimson, and made a big fuss about untying it. 'All evening I was trying to be ready, and here I am wearing my kitchen apron!'

'Please just call me Morgana,' Morgana asked her.

'Morgana?' asked Mrs Sczaniecka, with unabashed directness. 'What is that, a German name?'

'Kind of. My father publishes a morning paper, so he thought I ought to be called something to do with morning, too. He could have called me Dawn, I suppose.'

'At least he didn't call you Late Extra,' Harry remarked.

Mrs Sczaniecka led the way into her apartment. It was crowded with heavy, elaborate furniture, hall tables and sideboards and display cabinets and bookshelves, each piece of furniture protected by a lace runner and each lace runner protected by a crochet mat. The polished parquet floor was protected by Bismarck rugs and the Bismarck rugs were protected by offcuts of larger carpets. Some of the best offcuts even had rubber mats on them, to keep them clean. The big brown armchairs had antimacassars draped over the back to keep off hair oil, and lace mats over the arms to keep off palm-sweat.

The walls were noisily papered with roses and trellises, and there were framed prints everywhere of Jesus and Mary, the Last Supper, and the Parable of the Sower, as well as photographs of stern Slavic-looking Sczaniecka uncles and aunts, Mr and Mrs Sczaniecka on their wedding day at St Stanislaus Kostka, Harry as a small boy standing in the snow frowning at the camera as if he could break the lens, the Sczanieckas on Harry's graduation day from High School, and taking pride of place on the sideboard a studio portrait of Harry's father framed in black ribbon.

Mrs Sczaniecka told Morgana to sit down while Harry poured each of them a glass of sweet white Hungarian wine. As a rule, Morgana only drank dry French wines, but she accepted this glass quite happily. She felt as if she had managed through taking an interest in Harry's work to escape from the world of wealth and influence to find herself somewhere quite ordinary and homely and plain, and she was secretly pleased with herself. At the same time, she was intelligent and self-critical enough to understand that a large part of this pleasure derived from the fact that she didn't have to live an ordinary life herself, and that she could leave this cramped Roseland apartment at the end of the evening and return to Weatherwood and never have to come here again. But she also understood that it was time for her to take stock of what she was; and what she wanted to be; and something of what she wanted to be was here.

Mrs Sczaniecka said, 'Your dress is wery beautiful, Morgana. Now, I want you to tell me something, how much does a dress like that cost?'

'*Matka*,' Harry protested.

'No, no, I'm not embarrassed,' said Morgana. 'Please. I bought it in a sale at Field's. It cost one hundred ten dollars.'

'One dress!' Mrs Sczaniecka exclaimed. Then she turned to Harry and muttered at him in Polish like a machine-gun firing into a cushion, 'How - could - you - bring - this - lady - home - wearing - a - dress - that - cost - one - hundred - ten - dollars - and - you - didn't - even - warn - me - I - didn't - even - have - time - to - buy - myself - a - new - dress?'

Morgana could guess what Mrs Sczaniecka had been complaining about. She smiled, and said, 'Mrs Sczaniecka, I am the elder daughter of a very rich family. Ever since I was little, I was able to have anything I wanted. Clothes, toys, anything. But it was no fault of mine that I was born rich, any more than it was any fault of yours that you were not.'

'Well,' said Mrs Sczaniecka, not at all convinced by this argument. 'I was *certainly* not born rich! Everything you see here, we worked for this, me and Janek! It was all hard work!'

'Of course it was,' Morgana agreed. 'But what I'm trying to say to you is that it's *you* I came to see, you and Harry. I like Harry and if you'll give me the chance I'm sure that I'll like you, too. I didn't come to see how much money you had, any more than when you visit me – which I very much hope you will – you will be adding up how much money I have.'

'Well, you don't have to inwite me back. I don't expect it,' said Mrs Sczaniecka, her lower lip protruding a little sulkily.

Morgana said, 'Of course I shall invite you back. And let me tell you something else. When I saw you standing at the door, with your hair so beautifully braided, and that black dress, and those shoes, do you know what I thought to myself?'

'Silly old woman, I expect,' Mrs Sczaniecka replied.

'Not at all,' said Morgana. 'I thought: here is a lady who is queen in her own home. Here is a lady of good taste, and fine manners. And I feel very welcome here, and I am very pleased to have met you.'

Mrs Sczaniecka didn't know what to say to that. She aimed her protruding lip at Harry, as if it were all his fault that she had lost her confidence, then she tried to smile, and said, 'hah!', even though there was the subtlest gleam of a tear in her eye. Then she lifted her glass of wine, and said, 'I wish to make toast.'

Morgana and Harry lifted their glasses too.

Mrs Sczaniecka said, 'Toast to Croft Tate, thank you wery much.'

They drank. Then Morgana said, 'I wish to make a toast too. To all mothers who bring up good sons. And especially to you, Mrs Sczaniecka.'

'*Matka,*' Mrs Sczaniecka corrected her.

'Thank you,' said Morgana. 'And especially to you, *matka.*'

After that, the evening grew in warmth and happiness. They drank two more glasses of sweet white wine, and then they went through to the dining room, where there were candles and shining glasses, and Mrs Sczaniecka served out *czarnina*, a hot soup made of duck's blood and prunes and pork and apples, and accompanied by bread baked with *kielbasa* and cheese. This was followed by ham hocks and sauerkraut.

Mrs Sczaniecka told Morgana all about Harry's father Janek, how serious and bookish he had been, and how alike he and Harry had always been, big Janek and little Marek. Harry in his turn described how much his mother had fussed over him when he was little, and how she had always wanted him to be a little girl. 'She made me wear dresses until I was five.'

'That is traditional costume!' Mrs Sczaniecka cried out. 'Look! I show you photographs!'

'*Matka!*' Harry laughed. 'If you show Morgana those pictures, she's never going to –'

He stopped suddenly in mid-sentence, aware that his mind had been running ahead of him. He glanced across at Morgana, and said, awkwardly, 'Well, what I mean is, they're kind of embarrassing.'

Morgana smiled and said nothing, although she could guess what Harry had almost allowed himself to say. But she was not at all unhappy that he should find her attractive, that he should want their friendship to grow. She accepted the fact that she was going to be especially vulnerable to the attentions of other men, now that her engagement to John had so abruptly broken up. But Harry seemed to have a rare straightforwardness, an inability to conceal anger or amusement, and she had never come across that quality before, not in the sons of Chicago's blue-book dynasties, and not in many of the wealthy and the famous, either, and that made her feel less cautious, at least as far as he was concerned.

Morgana told Mrs Sczaniecka all about her childhood, and what life was like at Weatherwood. Mrs Sczaniecka also wanted to know all about the fire on Morgana's birthday. 'Marek came back and said you were silly fool. But also he said you were very brave.'

They ate slices of the Warsaw torte which Harry had bought at Zyzniewski's. Morgana raised her hand when Mrs Sczaniecka offered her a second piece. 'I don't want to end up like Mrs Zyzniewski.'

Harry immediately mimicked Mrs Zyzniewski's shrieking. 'You pigling! I smack your head good! I remember you coming in here in short pants!'

The Viennese clock in the hallway was just chiming ten when the telephone rang. Mrs Sczaniecka went to answer it, and then came back to say, 'Harry, for you. Somebody name of Mutton.'

Harry said, 'Lenny Mutken. He said he'd call me if he heard from the Hacker.'

'Well, quick,' said Morgana. She followed him into the hallway and stood beside him while he picked up the phone. The Virgin Mary watched them both sweetly and sadly from a store-bought icon hanging on the wall.

'Lenny?' asked Harry. He listened, frowning, for almost half a minute. Then he cradled the telephone receiver and looked at Morgana and his face was strained.

'What's happened,' asked Morgana. 'He hasn't killed somebody else, has he?'

'Two of them, just like he threatened he would. Lenny says he called about ten minutes ago. I have to get over to 33rd and Rhodes.'

'I'll drive you,' said Morgana.

Mrs Sczaniecka came into the hallway, too. 'What's this? You don't have to go to work? Not now!'

'*Matka*, I'm sorry. It's been a wonderful evening. You've been absolutely perfect. It's that murderer again. He's killed two women, and I have to go right away.'

Mrs Sczaniecka pouted at Morgana. 'You're his boss. Does he have to go right away?'

Morgana put her arm around Mrs Sczaniecka and smiled. 'I'm sorry, yes. That's what newspaper reporters have to do.

But it's been the most fun I've had since I can remember, and the very best meal. I'll come again, if you'll have me, and you must come up to Weatherwood.'

She kissed Mrs Sczaniecka, and held her close, and said, 'Thank you, *matka*.'

'You speak Polish?' asked Mrs Sczaniecka, in surprise.

'Harry taught me that, before we came. And I'm glad he did.'

They finished their coffee quickly, and then kissed Mrs Sczaniecka goodbye, and went down to the street. In the lighted window of Zyzniewski's Food Mart, they could see Mr and Mrs Zyzniewski still arguing, while their customers patiently waited to be served with *kielbasa* and herring and *pirogi*. They climbed into Morgana's Sportabout, and drove uptown to 33rd and Rhodes. Harry lit two cigarettes, and passed one over to Morgana.

'I'm glad you had a good time,' he told her.

Morgana smiled. 'With your mother and that food, anybody would have a good time.'

They arrived at 33rd and Rhodes, a rundown block of three-story terraced houses in a slummy Negro neighborhood. The police and the coroner were here already, and so were the crowds. Morgana opened her car door and the humid night was still screaming with sirens, like unearthly mourners at a mass funeral. The house where the double murder had taken place had faded red and white awnings, and looked incongruously festive.

Harry took hold of Morgana's hand. 'Thanks for the ride. And – thanks for coming to dinner.'

'Take care of yourself,' she said, softly, and he recognized the invitation in her voice and kissed her cheek. In return, she kissed his lips.

Harry stared at her for five long seconds; he could count them because the red light from a nearby squad car flashed in her eyes five times. Then he said, 'I'll call you. Is it okay if I call you?'

'Of course it's okay if you call me. If you don't, I'll call you.'

'Goodnight, Morgana.'

'Goodnight, Marek Sczaniecka.'

'Ssh,' he said, putting his finger to his lips. 'That's my secret identity, you know, like Superman. All you're supposed to know is that in real life I'm mild-mannered reporter Harry Sharpe. God – how am I going to get through all these people?'

Morgana called, 'Stick your press card in your hat! Then you'll look like a real reporter!'

Harry laughed, and gave her one last wave, and then shouldered his way through the crowds of spectators toward the police lines. Morgana watched him go, and then went back to her car. Three Negro boys were already jumping on the hood to see if they could get a better view of what was going on. Morgana climbed into the car and started the engine and they all somersaulted off with hoots of alarm and hilarity.

As she backed out of 33rd Street, and turned uptown again, Morgana found herself feeling extraordinarily elated, almost as if she were drunk. That burning, glowing sensation had started up again, that feeling that she could do anything she wanted, that nothing was impossible. She began to sing as she drove, 'Mairzy Doats and Dozey Doats', and even though she hadn't yet admitted it to herself, anybody who knew her at all well would have guessed that she was well and truly infatuated.

30

She had only been home ten minutes when Phoebe knocked frantically at her bedroom door. 'Morgana! Are you there?'

Phoebe came in wearing the prettiest of evening gowns, white silk with bare shoulders and a sweeping calf-length skirt. Her blonde hair was all curled up under a little white crescent-shaped hat, sparkling with sequins. On her feet were white 'naked sandals' with sequinned bows on the toes.

She stood for a moment by the door. 'Do you think I'm forgiven?' she said, in one of her throaty apologetic voices.

Morgana peered at herself in the looking glass as she wiped off her eye make-up. 'I haven't made up my mind yet. It's possible.'

'Well, do you feel like coming to the Tropical? Bradley and I are just leaving now. Come on, it wouldn't take you a sec to change. You could wear that super blue Dior, the one you wore to the Casino. Bradley's going to drive us.'

Morgana continued to clean off her make-up. 'What's the catch?' she wanted to know. 'And who's going to be my *date?*'

Phoebe sat down on the bed with a fussy rustle of silk. 'It's not exactly a catch but the thing is that Bradley asked me to come and then this afternoon Donald rang.'

'Go on,' said Morgana.

'It's just that I've been *aching* to see Donald. Croft Tate Daughter Pines For Boorish Movie Mogul. And, well – I'm afraid I asked him to meet me at the Tropical, at eleven thirty.'

'You've invited Bradley and Donald out on the same date? Phoebe! For goodness' sake! You're absolutely hopeless!'

'I knew you'd understand,' said Phoebe, bobbing up and kissing Morgana on the top of the head.

'I don't understand at all, I think you're completely nuts! And what do you want me to do?'

Phoebe tried to look cajoling. 'Well, I was hoping that when Donald showed up ... you'd kind of, well, take care of Bradley for me.'

'Phoebe, I really don't believe you sometimes. Why for once can't you make yourself hard to get? You've practically been chasing after Donald with running shoes on.'

'Oh, please, Morgana, it's only this once. I didn't know that Donald was going to call. I thought he'd cooled me off for ever. Please, Morgana, he's so exciting. He's so rude! Please, please, a thousand times please.'

Morgana looked at Phoebe's face in the mirror as sternly as she could. Then – partly because she was in such a good mood after her evening *chez* Sczaniecka, and partly because whatever had happened with John, Phoebe *was* her sister, after all, and partly because the whole idea of setting both Bradley and Donald on a collision-course struck her as so typically Phoebe that it was almost funny – she turned around on her dressing stool and said, 'Ten minutes to get ready, okay? And make sure that Bradley uses his breath-spray.'

'Morgana, you're an angel.'

'I'm an idiot, more like.'

Morgana called for Loukia to help her to dress, while Phoebe went downstairs to join Bradley and her mother in a manhattan. Howard had not yet returned from the office, but he had telephoned Eleanor during the afternoon to tell her that he had returned to Chicago and to warn her that he would probably be back at Weatherwood in time for a late supper. He had sounded quiet and conciliatory on the telephone; Eleanor had been left with the feeling that the worst of the crisis between them may have passed. Robert Wentworth would be buried on Friday. After that, perhaps their marriage could gradually be pieced together again. She felt calmer this evening, anyway. The pain was still there, the guilt was still there, but even pain and guilt can dry up, once they've been squeezed for everything they've got.

Morgana had said to her mother, 'I talked to Popsy at the office. You know that he loves you, don't you?'

Eleanor had smiled distantly and held Morgana's wrist almost as if she were taking her pulse. 'Yes,' she had replied.

'I do believe that he does. I hope only that he understands that I love him.'

A quarter of an hour later Morgana came waltzing down the staircase to be greeted by Bradley in a white tuxedo. 'Hi, Morgana, glad you could come along. Makes me feel like some kind of a swell fellow, having one pretty girl on each arm! I wish some of my college buddies could see me now!'

'They'd foam at the mouth and fall backwards on to the rug, Bradley, I'm quite sure,' Phoebe humored him. Morgana grimaced at her over Bradley's shoulder. She just hoped that this evening's threesome-cum-foursome was going to turn out to be amusing. The trouble was, Bradley took his walking-out with Phoebe so dreadfully seriously, there was no knowing what he might do if he and Donald came face to face. Especially since Donald was such a razorback hog in wolf's clothing.

Bradley's Packard tourer was waiting outside the front door. Morgana kissed Eleanor and told her that she wouldn't be back late; then she joined Bradley and Phoebe in the front seat. Phoebe said, 'How was your evening with that hunky-looking reporter? Come on, I want to know all about it!'

'As a matter of fact,' said Morgana, 'it was *very* boring, and he was *excruciatingly* dull, and I don't suppose for a moment that I'll ever see him again.'

'Oh,' replied Phoebe, and lost interest. She didn't seem to notice at all that her sexual enthusiasm for any man to whom Morgana felt attracted was as glaring as a bright green traffic signal. Bradley said, 'Do you happen to know who's playing at the Tropical tonight?'

'I haven't a clue,' said Morgana, although under her breath she added, 'I know who's going to be fighting there, though!'

Bradley steered with one hand and sang fragments of 'Bali H'ai', getting the words all mixed up. Phoebe held his other hand and blew into his ear. 'Hey, that tickles!' he cried, and the Packard swerved sideways.

'You're in a good mood tonight,' Morgana told him.

'I always am when I've done a good satisfying day's work,' he replied.

'Is that what you've been doing today? What's satisfying about watching two million cans of pink pork come jiggling off the production line?'

'Oh, you don't know the half of it,' said Bradley.
'Obviously I don't.'

They drew up outside the glittering entrance of the Tropical Club. This summer, it had become one of Chicago's favorite nightspots for the young and wealthy. It was located in the basement of the Erie Hotel, in what had once been the Good Times Club, a place where the white and well-heeled had been able to listen to black boogie-woogie music in the late 1920s, Jimmy Blythe and Natty Dominique, Kid Ory and Jimmy Bertrand, Johnny and Baby Dodds, without having to venture to the Negro dance halls of the South Side.

Tonight, North Michigan Avenue was double-parked with glistening autos, all the way to the Water Tower, and the sidewalks echoed with the tapping of high-heeled shoes. Bradley managed to back the Packard into a tight space left by the Chicago *Tribune* van, and then he took Morgana on one arm and Phoebe on the other, and escorted them into the club. The foyer was already crowded with laughing young people. Bradley and the girls went down the curving spiral staircase to the Tropical Bar, which was dark and mirrored and decorated with chromium-plated palm trees and a shining chromium bar. The place was jam packed with handsome young men in tuxedos and pretty young women in low-cut evening gowns. Jewelry sparkled, conversation tumbled, laughter rose like flocks of bafflehead ducks. Beneath the talk, Morgana could hear the kind of music that John used to describe as low-down dirty jazz, and through the palm-fringed archway at the end of the bar, she could see the dance floor already crowded with shuffling couples.

Bradley manfully pushed his way to the bar to buy them champagne. Morgana and Phoebe were left together in a corner, shouting at each other to make themselves heard. For a moment, Morgana felt a wave of tiredness. It had been a day as long as a week, and jostling with incongruities; from her breakfast with Kenneth Doyle to the harshness of the South Side slums to dinner with the Sczanieckas to this. Morgana began to wonder which of the many different Chicagos she had seen today was the real Chicago. Carl Sandburg had said, 'Put the city up; pull the city down/Put it up again, let us find a city.' But from the diversity of what Morgana had seen, she could easily have believed that there was no one city to be found, that Chicago was as many different cities as there were lives being lived in it: rich, proud, squalid, honorable, agonized, energetic, glamorous, defeated, but still somehow hopeful, all of them, still living together, even though they were living in such different places.

Phoebe said, 'When you see Donald – if you see Donald first – for God's sake make some kind of face.'

Morgana squinted and stuck her tongue out. 'Like this?'

A good-looking young man frowned at Morgana and said, 'Pardon *me*.'

At last Bradley came over waving the champagne, and they found themselves a small corner table and frothed it out into three tall glasses. Bradley raised his glass, and said, 'Here's to the two young ladies who are going to make me famous.'

'You mean us?' asked Morgana.

'One man, two ladies, that kind of thing always makes good copy for the newspapers, don't you think?'

Morgana said, 'Don't let us go to your head, Bradley.'

They drank champagne and then they danced, Phoebe with Bradley and Morgana with a personable young man with a little clipped mustache who introduced himself as Fred Young IV, and who danced almost as well as Fred Astaire. There was a fifteen-piece jazz orchestra, all white, with gleaming brilliantined hair and little glitter-encrusted music stands with KSO embossed on them – the Kelly Soberman Orchestra. The tenor-sax player obviously thought he was something with women, and played the filthiest breaks he could manage, while rolling his eyes and lifting his eyebrows at all the girls who went dancing by. Fred Young IV remarked rather dryly, 'Kind of hard to be alluring with a saxophone reed stuck in your mouth, wouldn't you say?'

At a quarter of twelve, Morgana suddenly saw Donald in the bar, waving at her wildly. She turned to Phoebe, who was dancing close by with Bradley, and hissed, '*Phoebe! Phoebe!*' but the sax-player was being louder and more execrable than ever, and Phoebe couldn't hear her. So Morgana reached over and tugged at her sleeve and squinted and stuck out her tongue.

'Hey, are you okay?' Fred Young IV asked.

'I'm fine, it runs in the family,' said Morgana.

Phoebe at that moment pulled an agonized face, and clutched at her stomach. 'Ah!' she cried out. 'Ah! Ah! Oh! Ooooh! Ohhhhhhh!'

Bradley was distraught. 'Phoebe! Phoebe! What's wrong? Phoebe, are you okay?'

Phoebe staggered to the left and then staggered to the right. 'Of course I'm not okay! I wouldn't be making noises like this if I was okay, would I? Oh, God, it must've been those clams I had for lunch! I can feel them! I can feel each individual clam! They're churning around, Bradley! My clams are churning!'

'Well, well – come on, Phoebe – here, listen – maybe I ought to take you home,' Bradley stuttered.

'No, no! Oh, Bradley, I can't ask you to do that! What about Morgana? She's having a dilly of a time! Please, no, I'll tell you what I'll do – I'll just go to the powder room – okay, and if I still feel bad – I'll take a taxi home. Please, that's what I want to do. I don't want you to see me being so sick.'

Morgana took hold of Bradley's arm. 'It's all right, Bradley. That's the best way. Come on now, you can stay with me, can't you? I'm dying to have a dance with you!'

'But Phoebe –'

'Phoebe's going to be fine, don't worry. She just needs to be left alone for a while. I've seen it before, after she's eaten clams. *She* likes them, *they* detest her.'

Morgana and Phoebe were so practiced at maneuvering boyfriends that Phoebe had staggered off in the direction of the powder room before Bradley had even had the chance to work out what was happening. Morgana excused herself from Fred Young IV with a contorted and toothy grin, and flowed into Bradley's arms as dramatically as Scarlett O'Hara had flowed into the half-reluctant embrace of Rhett Butler. Morgana danced Bradley around so that he wouldn't see Phoebe changing course twenty degrees at the door of the powder room to make her way immediately over to the bar, where Donald was waiting with an expression that was eighty percent relief, seventeen percent annoyance, and three percent total mystification.

Morgana and Bradley kept on dancing. Bradley said, 'I hope Phoebe's not feeling too bad. You don't think you ought to go into the powder room and check, do you?'

'Oh, no, Phoebe's going to be fine. I've seen her like this before. It strikes, you know, and lays her out for a couple of hours, then it un-strikes, and she's right as rain. Come on, let's enjoy ourselves!'

After dancing with the fleet-footed Fred Young IV, dancing with Bradley was rather like wheeling one of the Pump Room's carving trolleys around the floor, quite apart from the fact that his ears glowed pink and he didn't seem to be able to think of anything to talk about. But after a half-hour, and some more champagne, Morgana decided that she had done her duty, and asked Bradley to take her home.

'I must say you've been swell,' Bradley told her, as he escorted her out of the Tropical Club. He opened the door of the Packard for her, and she climbed in, hanging her white mink evening wrap over the back of the seat. Bradley leaned in at the window, and said, 'Hold on a moment. I'd better go check that Phoebe took her jacket. She's going to kill me if I leave it behind.'

Morgana sat back in the Packard's passenger seat and yawned, without even covering her mouth with her hand. As she did so, her wrap slithered off the top of the seat and disappeared behind her. She twisted around, and reached down in back of the seat to find it. Instead of the wrap, however, her hand located the handles of a carryall bag, and when she tried to move it aside, it clanked.

She reached up and switched on the Packard's map light. Then she knelt on her seat and looked down into the back. Her wrap was there, beside the carryall. But the carryall was open, and inside she could see a white coverall, bundled up, and the coverall was heavily stained with blotches of dark brown.

She glanced back toward the marquee of the Tropical Club, to see if Bradley had reappeared, but so far there was no sign of him. With her heart walloping so loudly that she could hear it, she opened the carryall wider, and lifted out the coverall. There were some objects wrapped up in it that clanked; and when she carefully unwound it, she saw what they were. Three professional butcher's knives, all about ten or eleven inches long, with clean blades but deeply blood-stained cocoa-wood handles. She stared at them for a moment and shivered, and then she hurriedly wrapped them back up again, and stuffed them into the carryall. She retrieved her wrap, and climbed out of the Packard as quickly as she could, slamming the door. There was still no sign of Bradley. She crossed North Michigan Avenue and hurried as fast as she could along West Erie Street, glancing behind her again and again to make sure that Bradley wasn't following her.

She tried to hail a taxi, but it was only eight blocks to the *Star* building, and in the end she gave up, and walked. Everything that Bradley had said this evening poured through her mind like a wire-service bulletin. '*Here's to the two young ladies who are going to make me famous.*' '*One man, two ladies, that kind of thing always makes good copy for the newspapers, don't you think?*' And what else had he said? '*I'm always in a good mood when I've done a satisfying day's work.*'

It seemed incredible. It seemed impossible. But the facts were that Harry had received a phone call at ten that evening from Lenny Mutken, saying that the Hacker had dismembered two more women; less than an hour later Bradley had been boasting about 'two women' and 'a hard day's work'. Not only that – he had been hiding a bloodstained coverall and three butcher's knives in the back of his car.

Bradley may have appeared to be goofy and harmless; but weren't the goofy and harmless-looking people always the ones who committed the worst crimes? Weren't they the ones who had the chips on their shoulders? Look at Bradley. He loved Phoebe. He loved Phoebe so much that last Friday he had threatened to punch Donald in the nose. Maybe he had two personalities: the Goofy and the Vicious. Maybe Phoebe's consistent rejection of him had taken him right to the edge, and his Vicious personality had decided to revenge itself on any innocent women that he could find. The very idea of it sent a cold thrill up Morgana's back, and she had to look behind her just once more to make sure that Bradley wasn't curb crawling after her. But soon she could see the lights of the *Star* building up ahead of her, and she hurried into the lobby and under the protection of the huge star chandelier. The presses were already beating with tomorrow morning's editions. There was brightness and light here, and people hurrying backwards and forwards, and friendly faces.

Morgana went to the elevator and pressed the button for the newsroom. As soon as she stepped out, she ran into Grant, who was walking slowly along the corridor with his half-glasses on the end of his nose, reading a galley proof of an article on Communist influences in the entertainment industry. Tinseltown Tinted Pink?

'Grant?' asked Morgana urgently. 'Have you seen Harry?'

'Well, hello, what are you doing here so late?' Grant asked

her, taking off his glasses. 'Even your father's gone home.'

'Grant, this is absolutely critical,' Morgana flustered. 'I think I've found out who the Hacker is.'

'You've found out who the Hacker is? How did you do that?'

'It was a total accident. But I was having dinner with Harry earlier this evening, and somebody called him to say that two more women had been killed.'

'That's right,' Grant nodded, his face serious. 'Busby Brill's down there now.'

'Well, the point is,' said Morgana, 'I had a date later with a boy called Bradley Clarke, you know the Stokie Clarkes who produce Ham-I-Yam?'

'Sure, I know Bradley,' Grant told her. 'I met him at your twenty-first.'

'I was in his car, waiting for him,' said Morgana, 'and I reached into the back seat, and there was a bag full of bloodstained clothing, and butcher's knives.'

Grant stared at her. 'In Bradley Clarke's car? Bloodstained clothing? And knives?'

'Grant, I swear to you, I saw it for myself. I swear it.'

Grant said, 'You'd better come into my office. I'll see if I can get hold of Busby.'

Morgana followed Grant into his office. Tomorrow's edition was spread out on his desk. The front page showed the children's room at 2621 South Cottage Grove Avenue; black faces, white staring eyes. The headline read THE SHAME OF OUR CITY. A smaller story at the foot of the page showed the smiling face of Margaret Mitchell, with the headline Gone With The Wind – Author Dies Of Cab Accident Injuries. Grant picked up the phone and dialed Chicago Police Headquarters. It took him a long time to get through. While he waited, he fastidiously rearranged paperclips on his desk.

At last, he said, 'Hello? Listen, this is Grant Clifford, I'm the editor of the Chicago *Star*. Oh, you know me? Well – I very much need to speak to my reporter at the scene of the double murder on 33rd Street and Rhodes Avenue. I wouldn't usually ask you this, but this may have a vital bearing on the case, and I know that Commissioner Spectorski would approve it. Can you please contact one of your officers at the scene and have him find Mr Busby Brill – then ask Mr Brill to call his office urgent. Well, thank you. Thank you. The *Star* appreciates your help, believe me.'

Grant put down the phone, and pressed his hands flat together in his familiar praying gesture. 'Would you like some coffee?' he asked Morgana. 'It's pretty stewed, but it might help to perk you up.'

It was ten minutes before Busby Brill called in. 'Busby,' said Grant. 'We might have a lead here to the Hacker's identity. Just as soon as you've wrapped everything up down there, get back to the office pronto. No, don't tell the police anything, not just yet. Yes, I know what I usually do, but this is different. If we know who the Hacker is, we want to make quite sure that we get a beat on it. That's right, Busby, this could be your hour of triumph. Is Harry with you?'

Grant covered the receiver with his hand. 'Busby says Harry was there for a while, but then he left. He said he was following up a lead. Something to do with the Hacker, but he wasn't quite sure what. Anyway, Busby's going to be back here in twenty minutes or so. Then we can decide what we're going to do.'

Morgana glanced at the clock. It was a fraction after one. She picked up the paper and riffled through the slum story, but it was too immediate and too poignant for her to want to read it just yet. She said to Grant, 'I'm really sad about Margaret Mitchell; she was such a nice person.'

While they waited for Busby to get back to the office, Morgana wandered through the half-darkened newsroom. In a side room, the wire service teletypes chattered and hummed. A lone business columnist hacked out the last few paragraphs of a Japanese stock-market story, a cigarette twiddling smoke in the ashtray beside him. Morgana went to Harry's pigpen and sat down on his squeaking revolving chair. It felt more comfortable here than anywhere else in the *Star* building, more familiar, even under the stern eye of Thaddeus Kosciusko. The luminescent twenty-four hour clock shuddered to five after one. Outside the windows, Chicago glittered through the summer night, those many Chicagos, with their many dreams.

The whole building vibrated softly with the thunder of the Goss Headliner presses. Downstairs in the basement, Morgana knew that there would be organized pandemonium, newspapers streaming off the presses at full speed, THE

SHAME OF OUR CITY one million times over, folded, counted, bundled, and tossed into waiting trucks. She opened the top drawer of Harry's desk and there was a half-empty pack of Camels. She took one out and lit it with a book of matches from the Allerton Hotel.

At that moment, the telephone rang. She hesitated for a second, and then picked it up. A dry-sounding voice said, 'Harry? Is this Harry Sharpe?'

'He's not here right now,' Morgana replied. 'Who wants him?'

'This is Lenny Mutken. I called him earlier, he was supposed to meet me at O'Leary's Pub at eleven o'clock. Thing is, he never showed up. I'm at O'Leary's now, but I can't stay too much longer. Do you think he might be back soon?'

'You called him about the Hacker,' said Morgana.

'That's right. The Hacker killed two women tonight. He called me just after he did it. The whole thing is, he promised he would give me a face-to-face interview – why he was killing these women, all that stuff, and it's on, the interview's on, that's what I wanted to tell Harry.'

'Why don't you tell the police?' Morgana asked him.

'Because the Hacker specifically said that if I called the police, he wouldn't show up for any interviews, and he'd go on killing. Two women today, four women tomorrow. God knows.'

'Well, listen –' said Morgana, 'Harry isn't here right now, but may be back a little later. I'm Morgana Croft Tate, Howard Croft Tate's daughter. If you want to talk about this face-to-face interview before you do it – well, maybe you could talk to me.'

There was a long silence on the phone, although Morgana thought she could hear a slight clicking noise, like somebody licking their lips. In the end, however, Lenny said, 'You're Morgana Croft Tate?'

'That's right. Howard Croft Tate's elder daughter.'

'Well, of course, I saw you in the papers over the weekend, the way you saved that little Negro girl.'

'You're over at O'Leary's now?' Morgana asked him.

'Sure,' said Lenny. 'Listen – why don't you come on over? But don't tell anybody what's happening. The Hacker sounds real nervous. You know – he sounds like you'd only have to whisper the word "police", and we'd lose him. And a face-to-face interview . . . that could bring him in. And what a beat that would be.'

Morgana didn't hesitate. She could recognize a ripe red apple when it fell in her lap. Right at this moment, she was the only person who knew that the Hacker could well be Bradley Clarke, and that Lenny Mutken had arranged to meet him for a face-to-face interview. That meant that if she went along with Lenny to meet the Hacker – and recognized Bradley – she would scoop absolutely everybody. Not only the *Tribune* and the *Daily News* and the *Sun-Times*, but Grant Clifford and Busby Brill and even Harry Sharpe.

'Five minutes,' she told Lenny, and hung up. She stood up, and was just about to leave Harry's pigpen when she thought to herself that to leave Harry without any kind of a clue would betray his affection for her, at the very least. So she scribbled a note on a piece of copy paper, 'Gone To O'Leary's To R/v With Mutken,' and tucked it under the bar of his typewriter. Then she walked quickly out of the newsroom, making sure that Grant didn't notice her passing his door, and went down to the lobby in the elevator.

She felt excited. To tell the truth, she felt a little panicky. But this was going to be the first big story of her newspaper career, the story that would make up for everything that had happened after the fire on 31st Street. From today onward, she wouldn't be simply the publisher-designate, but an ace reporter in her own right, the girl who cracked the Hacker story.

She pushed her way out of the revolving doors in front of the *Star* building and crossed a silent Wabash Avenue. It was late now, there was hardly any traffic around. Somewhere on the Near North Side, a siren wailed; another death, another life. The wind that blew off the lake was gentle and steady, but there was a hidden chill in it, the night wind, the wind that made the bums and the junkies wrap their coats tighter around their emaciated bodies, and think of other times, when life was different. The wind that made the Southern Negroes open their eyes in their South Side slums and think of Macon, and Baton Rouge, and Memphis, and the wind through the sassafras trees.

O'Leary's was almost empty, except for Walter Dempsey and one or two of his hard-drinking cronies, still cackling on about baseball, and Walter didn't even notice Morgana when she came in. Morgana went straight to the bar and asked Roy for Lenny Mutken. Roy pointed him out. He was sitting on his own reading a copy of *Mitchell*'s, a Croft Tate magazine. General interest, fiction, true-life drama, recipes, home improvements. Circulation, 1.3 million.

Lenny stood up as Morgana approached him, and crushed out his cigarette.

'Miss Croft Tate? This is what I call an unexpected honor. Believe me, I never thought that I would set eyes on another Croft Tate, after I left the *Star*. But here you are; and very comely, too, if you don't mind an old man's compliment.'

'Not at all,' smiled Morgana. 'Can I buy you something to drink?'

Lenny shook his head, and covered his glass with his hand. 'Oh, no, that's all right. This is going to be a big night. Face-to-face with the Hacker! Well — when I told Harry about it, he was really excited! I can't think why he didn't come on up here himself! It's such a story! But you're the boss's daughter, aren't you? You're a qualified newspaperwoman if ever there was one! You can cover the story just as well as Harry!'

'I'd like to think so,' said Morgana.

Lenny swallowed the last of his whiskey. 'I'll tell you what, then. My car is outside. I'm supposed to be meeting the Hacker just across the street from the Marshall Field Garden Apartments, which is where I live. You can come along, just so long as you stay in the car and just so long as you don't let the Hacker realize you're there. Can you do that? You think you can do that?'

'I think I can do that,' Morgana told him.

They got up together to leave the pub. As Morgana was making for the door, however, Walter Dempsey suddenly recognized her, and pushed out his table, and came swimming across to say hello. 'Miss Croft Tate! Miss Morgana Croft Tate! May all the felicitations known to men or gods be showered upon you! May all the felicitations *unknown* to men or gods be showered upon you!'

'Come along, Miss Croft Tate,' said Lenny. 'We don't have any time to spare.'

Morgana smiled tiredly. 'Are you all right, Walter?'

'All right? All right? I am prime, Miss Croft Tate! I am

vintage! I am splendid, magnificent, marvelous, glorious, dazzling, superb!'

'Well, I have to go now,' Morgana told him. 'Mr Mutken here is taking me back to his apartment to meet somebody.'

Walter took one shuffling, unbalanced step forward, and whispered in Morgana's ear: 'Don't take any nonsense from Lenny.'

'Nonsense?' asked Morgana.

'Lemme – let me – put it this way – Lenny's a nice enough fellow, don't you know – but –' and here Walter lowered his voice to an almost inaudible whisper '– *he's not the man he was.*'

Morgana clasped Walter's hand, and said, 'Don't worry, Walter, I'll take care. And you take care, too, please.'

Roy came over. He had been collecting up dirty glasses. 'Don't worry, Miss Croft Tate. Mr McLintock usually comes in to collect him when the last edition's been run.'

Morgana and Lenny left O'Leary's and walked together round to the parking lot. Lenny guided Morgana over to a big old '42 De Soto, in battered beige, with sagging suspension. He unlocked the passenger door for her and then walked around to the driver's side.

'I'm sorry it's not one of those luxury limousines you're used to,' he said, as he started the engine. The leather of the seats was cracked, and the inside of the auto was redolent of vinegar, or some other sour chemical.

'That's all right,' Morgana told him. 'Just so long as it gets us where we're going.'

Lenny shifted into gear with a noise like bones being ground in a butcher's mincer, and the De Soto lurched out on to Wabash Avenue.

'I hope you're not too scared,' Lenny said to Morgana, with a humorless grin.

Morgana unpinned her hat, and brushed her hand through her hair. 'I was scared when I went up that fire ladder, but that didn't stop me going up.'

'Well, the headline was right,' said Lenny. 'You're a heroine.'

31

Donald had been driving for almost ten minutes when Phoebe looked around and said, '*Don*-ald? Where in the two-toned tonkert are we going?'

Donald glanced in his rear-view mirror, then turned the Lincoln west on Division. 'I have to see some friends of mine first.'

'Some friends of yours? What friends? I thought you were taking me dancing!'

'I know. I know I said I was going to take you dancing. But I just have this one business meeting.'

'In the middle of the night? Donald, I don't want to go to a business meeting! I want to go dancing! And then when I've been dancing –' she leaned across the car and whispered in his ear '– I want to make mad passionate you-know-what.'

Donald smoothed back his brilliantined hair where Phoebe had ruffled it. 'It's okay, it's okay, don't panic. We'll go dancing.' He glanced into his rear-view mirror again. 'This won't take a moment, I promise you.'

Phoebe knelt up on her seat and peered through the Lincoln's rear window. She was slightly myopic, but she could see the headlights of another auto only thirty feet behind them. They turned off Division on to North Clybourn, heading north-west, and the headlights followed them.

'Donald, I think we're being tailed. There's another car right behind us and I'm sure it's tailing us.'

Donald didn't even look in his mirror. 'Maybe I can shake them off,' he said. 'Listen, why don't you sit down and I'll go through some of the back streets, then if they're really following us we'll know for sure.'

'I've got a better idea,' Phoebe told him. 'Let's find a police car, and say that somebody's after us.'

'Relax,' Donald replied. He made a sudden swerving turn into Ogden Avenue, then another into Weed Street, so that they were heading back eastwards. He checked his rear-view mirror again, and said, 'There, they couldn't have been following us, we've lost them. No – I'm wrong – there they are again.'

He took another screeching right into North Mohawk, heading southwards now. Phoebe turned around and she could see the headlights coming after them, steadily and relentlessly.

'Donald, I'm frightened. For goodness' sake let's find a police car!'

Donald turned around, too. 'This is ridiculous,' he said. 'I'm not having some punk following me all round Chicago. What the hell does he think he's trying to pull?'

He slowed the Lincoln down and drew it over to the side of the deserted street. The headlights drew up a few yards behind them. Phoebe said, 'What are you going to do? Donald – what are you going to *do*? It could be dangerous!'

'I'll tell you what I'm going to do,' Donald told her, bringing the car to a stop, and setting the parking brake. 'I'm going to go back and have a word with that guy.'

'But supposing he's armed or something? Donald, I'm the daughter of a very rich man, remember, they may be kidnapers!'

'Oh, come on,' grinned Donald, opening the Lincoln's door. 'Who would want to kidnap you?'

He climbed out, then leaned back into the car and kissed her. 'Give me two minutes,' he said. 'If they start shooting, scream for the Lone Ranger.'

Biting her lips, Phoebe watched Donald walk back toward the headlights, buttoning up his square-cut coat as he went. The streetlights shone on his brilliantined hair. She saw the door of the other car open, and a bulky man ease himself out, although it was difficult to see him clearly because of the glare of his headlights. She shielded her eyes with her hand.

She waited. The Lincoln's engine was still running, and it was impossible for her to hear anything that was going on outside. Suddenly, however, she couldn't see Donald any more, and the bulky man was walking toward the Lincoln with a rolling swagger like Bluto in the Popeye cartoons. He opened the driver's door and climbed in, the seat complaining under his weight. He was grinning, and he smelled strongly of lavender-water. Even in the shadows of the streetlights, Phoebe could see the sparkling dandruff on his wide padded shoulders.

'Who are you?' Phoebe demanded. 'Where's Donald? What's going on?' Her throat was so tight with alarm that she could only squeak.

The bulky man said, 'You don't have to worry.' His accent was strongly Italian. 'Your boyfriend had a little accident. He trip over a matchstick and knock his head on the sidewalk. He's okay. Just a little –' and the man circled his finger around and around to indicate that Donald was dazed.

'Donald!' Phoebe screamed, and then wrestled for the Lincoln's door handle. 'I want to get out! Let me out of here!'

The bulky man grasped her arm tightly. She screamed, but almost casually he slapped her face, and she felt a heavy ring hit her on the side of her lip, and burst the skin. She tried to scream again, but she couldn't. She simply didn't have the courage.

'You behave yourself, and nothing will happen to you,' the bulky man instructed her, quietly. 'You understand me? He's okay. Your friend hit his head, that's all. Nothing will happen to you. You will be fine. Just for a while, you are going to be a guest of Mr Vespucci. You know Mr Vespucci? Mr Vespucci is a gentleman. A friend of your father. He's going to take care of you for a while. Now, you sit quiet and everything's going to be hunky-dory.'

Phoebe said, 'I don't understand. Are you kidnaping me?'

The bulky man released the Lincoln's parking brake, and drew away from the curb. 'Kidnap? That's no way to speak, kidnap! You are a guest. You are invited. You don't have to worry. When your father does what he's told, you will go back home and everything will be hunky-dory.'

'He won't give in to extortion, you know.'

'He won't?' the bulky man asked her, almost as if he were amused.

'No, he won't.'

The bulky man made an exaggeratedly downcast face, like a clown. 'Too bad for you, then, enh?'

At the moment that Phoebe was being driven through the Near North Side, Harry was walking into the newsroom at the *Star*. Busby Brill was already there, sitting on the edge of Grant's desk. So were Gordon McLintock and David Tribe. The air was gray with cigarette smoke, and Grant's desk was clustered with half-empty coffee cups.

'Harry!' called Grant, beckoning. 'Come on in here. We're beating our gums about how to handle this Hacker story.'

'That's just what I came back here for,' said Harry. His necktie was loose and he looked tired and sweaty. 'I have a pretty good idea who the Hacker might be. I know where we can find him, too, but I didn't want to pull another citizen's arrest stunt without your approval and without Busby being in on it.'

Grant nodded. 'I'm pleased you've decided to stop playing Dick Tracy. Especially since we know the Hacker's identity, too. We're just formulating a plan of campaign – who's going to accompany the police, who's going to interview the family, who's going to talk to our tame psychiatrist – and most of all, how we're going to break the story before everybody else. I've already decided to go Extra.'

Harry reached into his shirt pocket and took out his cigarettes. 'You know the Hacker's identity? You mean I've been running around to Michael Reese and Calumet Harbor and God knows where, and all the time you knew?'

Busby reached over and gave Harry a light. 'It was a lucky accident, that's all. That – combined with the journalistic talents of Miss Morgana Croft Tate. She's some girl.'

Harry said, 'Morgana? Where does she come into it?'

'Well, she knows him socially, of course, and tonight he happened by chance to give her a ride. She found the murder weapons in the back seat of his car.'

Harry blew smoke and frowned. 'She knows him socially? Since when? She never told me that.'

'Obviously you don't mix in the right circles, old friend,' Busby teased him. 'But this one has everything. Grisly murder, high social connections, intrigue, suspense, Our Star Heroine To The Rescue, you name it. Do you want to see the headline? Where's that headline, Grant?'

Busby lifted his backside a little, and tugged out from underneath it a page form in which the banner headline HACKER: ARREST BLUE-BOOK HEIR had been firmly scrawled in thick blue crayon.

Harry took the page, and then looked from Grant to Busby

and back again. 'Now, hold on a minute,' he said, 'are we talking about the same story here? I mean, are we talking about the same person?'

Gordon said, 'What do you mean? You think that Bradley Clarke isn't the Hacker?'

'Bradley Clarke!' Harry shouted at him. 'You mean *the* Bradley Clarke? The one with the ears? The Ham-I-Yam Bradley Clarke?'

'That's right,' put in Grant. He eased himself back in his chair. 'Morgana found three butcher knives and a blood-stained coverall in the back of his car only about an hour after the double homicide was reported.'

Harry said to Busby, 'For crying out loud, Busby, you've met Bradley Clarke, and you saw those bodies tonight. That guy couldn't hack a meatloaf.'

Busby shrugged. 'One thing I've learned from fifteen years as a police reporter, Harry, you can't tell a book from its cover, and you can't tell a killer from the way he looks. Remember William Heirens, seventeen years old, a nicer-looking young student you couldn't have found.'

'Except that *you* didn't find him,' Harry retorted. 'And you sure haven't found the Hacker.'

'Come on, Harry, you'd better tell us what goes on here,' said Grant. 'If you believe that somebody else is the Hacker, we need to know about it. But quite apart from the knives and the bloodstained clothing, Bradley Clarke made several pointed references to two women, and how he was going to hit the headlines, and how hard he'd been working yesterday afternoon.'

'You have to admit the Hacker worked hard,' put in Busby, nettled by Harry's remark about the Heirens case. 'Two women, both chopped into pieces, and all the pieces mixed up so you couldn't tell whose leg belonged to whose body. Now, *that's* what I call hard work.'

Harry said, 'Lenny Mutken.'

'Lenny Mutken?' Grant frowned. 'You're talking about the *Star*'s Lenny Mutken?'

Harry hauled out his notebook. 'Lenny Mutken approached me after the first Hacker stories were published over the weekend and said that he had been telephoned by the Hacker before the murders took place.'

'You didn't tell me about this,' said Grant, in a level voice.

'No, I didn't, because Lenny said that the Hacker would be frightened off if there was any police activity, but I knew that as editor you would be duty-bound to pass the information on to Commissioner Spectorski.'

'So you took it upon yourself to withhold information from both your editor and from the police?' asked Grant.

'That was my judgement,' said Harry. 'If it was an incorrect judgement, then I'm prepared to take the blame for it.'

Grant was obviously tempted to say something else, but he let out a well-controlled breath, and said, 'Go on. I think we'd better hear you out.'

Harry said, 'Lenny said that the Hacker was prepared to meet him face to face, and give him an interview. He said the reason the Hacker had approached him personally was because he still had a neighborhood reputation as a police reporter. I went along with Lenny's suggestion – rightly or wrongly – because if it had worked out it would have been a sensational interview, and also because I happened to agree with him that it might help the police to catch the Hacker before he killed too many more women.'

Harry looked down at his notebook. His hand was shaking. 'Tonight I went along to 33rd and Rhodes, where those two women were killed. Well, Busby was there, too. I didn't want to look at the bodies but in the end I did, and the trouble was those bodies were so gruesome they took your mind off everything else. Commissioner Spectorski said that only two unfamiliar people were seen entering and leaving the building, one of them black and the other one white. The white man had worn a brown suit and a brown hat.'

Busby took out his pipe, and sniffed. 'That ties in with the man seen on Irving Avenue when that first woman was killed. Brown suit, brown fedora, remember?'

'Sure I remember. But then I remembered something else. Just before she dropped me off at the scene, Morgana Croft Tate said, "Do you have your press card? Why don't you stick it in your hat like a real reporter." And then I thought of something that Dan Rogers had said at Irving Avenue. The man in the brown suit and the brown fedora had something stuck in his hat, like a baseball raincheck or something like that.'

'A press card,' said Grant, solemnly.

'Well – there was no logical reason to think that, was there?

But it was worth considering, right? And suddenly I began to think back on everything that Lenny Mutken had been telling me in a different light. I suddenly began to think, why would a publicity-seeking mass murderer contact an old has-been like Lenny Mutken? I mean, granted that Lenny won our only Pulitzer prize, but I didn't even realize that he was still alive, before this weekend. Somebody who kills like a showman, somebody who kills like the Hacker – well, he'd want to talk to the editor, at least.'

'Thanks very much,' Grant put in, dryly.

'I did some checking,' said Harry. 'I was supposed to be meeting Lenny over at O'Leary's, so I knew that he wouldn't be home. I went round to his apartment and talked to his next-door neighbor. I hope you don't mind, I gave the poor old guy a double sawbuck. He deserved it, in my opinion, quite apart from the fact that I woke him up out of a deep sleep. He told me that Lenny had recently come back from four months at Michael Reese Hospital, chronic liver condition, as well as some sort of mental problem, probably related to alcoholism. Lenny used to have a woman living with him, some sort of companion, but the woman left him, only two days after he came back from hospital. Apparently there was all kinds of shouting and arguing, and the neighbor heard Lenny yelling at her that she was a bitch and a Jezebel and that he was going to get even.'

Busby lit his pipe, and watched Harry closely. Harry said, 'I drove over to Michael Reese, and talked to Dr Cohen; then I went to a private nursing-home in Calumet, where Lenny had lived during the war years. The long and the short of it is that Lenny was given a golden handshake from the *Star* in 1938 because he was suffering from DTs and hallucinations. For years afterwards he suffered from paranoid psychosis. His wife divorced him in 1941, and that's when he began to develop a pathological hatred of women. He was arrested in 1943 for a minor assault on a WAVE out on Streeter Drive by the Navy Pier; and again in 1944 for attacking a woman on North Seneca Street.'

Grant stood up. 'You've done an excellent job, Harry. Busby – let's kill this blue-book story. Gordon, can you get me Commissioner Spectorski on the phone? Well, yes, get him out of bed if necessary. I still think Bradley Clarke needs checking out, but from what you've told me about Lenny –

well, he surely sounds like our man, all right. God Almighty, a former *Star* reporter! This is going to be three times as embarrassing as Jake Lingle.'

Jake Lingle had been a *Tribune* police reporter, one of the best, in the days of Al Capone. However, after Lingle's shooting in June 1930, by a gangland hoodlum, it had been discovered to the *Tribune*'s deep mortification that their ace reporter had been inextricably involved for years in arranging favors for gangsters at City Hall, and that he had regularly acted as a middleman in the setting up of nefarious enterprises, bootlegging, gambling, and prostitution.

Busby said, 'We'd better tell Miss Croft Tate that her big-eared boyfriend isn't a mass murderer after all. Though he still has to explain those knives.'

'Morgana's here?' asked Harry, as Busby walked through to the newsroom.

'Sure – she came here after she found the knives.' Busby paused, and looked around. 'Well – she *was* here.'

Harry went over to his pigpen, and picked the note out of his typewriter. He read it, and then without a word he showed it to Busby.

'Jesus on a bicycle,' said Busby, his pipe still clenched between his teeth.

Right then, Morgana was sitting in the front passenger seat of Lenny Mutken's De Soto, opposite the square brick blocks of the Marshall Field Apartments on North Sedgwick Street. Lenny had left her there only two or three minutes ago, while he went to make contact with the Hacker. It was almost a quarter of two in the morning, and Sedgwick Avenue was broken down and deserted, an Old Town slum, badly lit, strewn with garbage and lined with battered and rusty autos. The Marshall Field Apartments had been an attempt to build quality housing in a low-quality neighborhood, but already the neighborhood had begun to infect the project with neglect and dereliction, vandalism and decay. One day it would be renamed Old Town Gardens; and then another day it would all be pulled down.

Morgana was exhausted and twitchy. In spite of the prospect of a scoop, she was beginning to wish that she had never agreed to come; or that at least she had told Grant Clifford what she intended to do. She felt very alone and very vulnerable, sitting in this vinegar-smelling auto in the middle of the night, in this slummy street. Yet she didn't dare to get out of the car and try to walk; and she certainly didn't dare to go looking for Lenny Mutken. Supposing she bumped into the Hacker before she bumped into him?

She waited for over fifteen minutes. Then she made up her mind: if Lenny didn't come back in five more minutes, she would risk walking back down to Division Street, to see if she could hail a taxi.

Two black men walked past, their coat collars turned up, their eyes gleaming white under the wide brims of their hats. She sank down into her seat, as far as she could go. They passed the De Soto without seeing her, although they were so close that Morgana could hear them talking. She lifted her head a little so that she could check the rear-view mirror, and make sure that they had gone, but they were nowhere in sight. They must have turned the corner, or crossed into the apartment lot; or maybe they had been nothing more than a figment of her fraught and overworked imagination.

Morgana looked at her watch once more. Five more minutes had passed. She peered one more time in the direction in which Lenny had disappeared, and then opened the car door, and stepped out. The night was unexpectedly chilly now, but at least the air was fresh. She heard the drone of an airplane high overhead, as it circled toward Midway; and the high unearthly crying of police sirens, way downtown.

She was about to start walking south, in the direction of Division Street, when Lenny came hurrying across the road in his brown fedora and his brown suit. He seized hold of her arm, and said excitedly, 'It's the Hacker, he's here! I've been talking to him! He says he wants to give himself up!'

'What?' asked Morgana, quite stunned.

'He's here!' Lenny tugged at her arm. 'Quickly! Quickly! He's here! He says he won't hurt anybody else! He says he wants to give himself up!'

'Lenny – Mr Mutken – don't you think we ought to call for the police?'

'There isn't time! He may change his mind! Come on, come on, you said you wanted a scoop! He's here, in my apartment!'

Morgana hesitated for one terrible moment. Her instinct was to run away as fast as she could. But there was a kind of gruesome fascination about the prospect of meeting the

Hacker face to face, and what a story it would be if he gave himself up to her, to Morgana Croft Tate, in person!

'Come on, my dear, hurry!' Lenny Mutken cried, letting go of her arm and dancing back across the road ahead of her, like the scarecrow in *The Wizard of Oz*. Morgana didn't hesitate any longer. She held on to her hat and ran across the road after him, and followed him into the darkness between the square brick apartment blocks.

Harry pushed open the doors of O'Leary's Pub and stalked straight across to the bar, followed in quick succession by Busby and Gordon. Roy unhooked a tankard from above the bar, and asked, 'Hard day at the office, dear? Your usual?'

'Morgana Croft Tate,' said Harry, tersely.

'That's right,' Roy nodded. 'She was here about a half-hour ago. She was over there, talking to old Mutters.'

'They left together?'

'That's right. Didn't say where they were going, though.'

'God damn it,' said Harry.

At that moment, however, Walter Dempsey came floating across, moving like a man wading through waist-deep water. 'Gordon!' he cried. 'Gordon, old man! Is it that dread hour already? Is it time to withdraw from combat, and leave the serried bottles for another day? I'll fetch my cane.'

Harry took hold of Walter's arm. 'Walter – did you see Morgana Croft Tate in here tonight?'

Walter frowned at Harry's grasping hand. 'Unhand me, you ruffian,' he demanded. 'I'll have you know that this suit cost one hundred and five dollars exact, and that was in 1928 when a dollar was a dollar and Silent Cal was President and the world was very different.'

'Walter, for the love of God, think,' Harry asked him.

'Very well, in exchange for one more valedictory libation, I shall disclose the fact that Miss Morgana Croft Tate left in the company of one Lenny Mutken, former *Star* reporter honorably discharged, and that she intimated that he was taking her back to his dwelling place in order to meet somebody, although –' and here Walter lifted his head, and raised his hand, and everybody waited in suspense for what he was going to say '– I have absolutely no idea who. Or whom.'

'Marshall Field Apartments,' snapped Harry. 'And – Roy! – will you call the police and tell them to meet us there –

Marshall Field Apartments – tell them we've found the Hacker! Tell them it's urgent!'

'Furthermore,' said Walter, waxing even more mellow, 'I recall now what it was I wanted to say to you the other day, Harry. No – wait! It is a matter of grade A gravity! When I was arriving at Mr Vespucci's apartment to talk to him about his racehorses, I happened to see that mountainous thug of his manhandling a fellow into his automobile – and now of course my slow but remorseless brain has made the connection! The fellow who was being manhandled, the manhandlee rather than the manhandler, was that small-time hoodlum Aceto – the one who met his Maker in a bullet-ventilated outhouse.'

Harry stared at Busby and Busby stared at Gordon and they all stared at each other. 'Walter,' said Gordon, as calmly as he could, 'if ever newspaper editors developed ulcers it wasn't out of overwork. It was out of reporters like you.'

Harry said, 'That's two witnesses, one witness who saw Ambrogio shooting Aceto; another witness who saw him being pushed into the car by Ambrogio only twenty minutes beforehand.'

Gordon excitedly gripped Harry's shoulder. 'Listen – you and Busby go find Lenny Mutken. I'll call Commissioner Spectorski and Kenneth Doyle, too, and see if we can't get Ambrogio, too. Yes, and maybe Vespucci with him! Hot damn! Hot damn! What a night! Did you ever know a night like this!'

32

Howard was fast asleep when the telephone rang. It took him a long time to dredge his mind up from the smooth dark sediments in which it had been buried, and even when he picked up the receiver and said, 'Yes? Howard Croft Tate,' he was still technically sleeping.

'My dear friend,' said an oleaginous, disembodied voice.

'Who is this?' Howard asked. 'What the hell time is it?'

'Don't you recognize me? Come on, Howard, this is your old friend Enzo.'

'Enzo! What the hell are you calling me for?' Howard, gradually waking up now, groped for the lightswitch. The bedside lamp snapped on, and he frowned frowzily at his Cartier alarm clock. 'Damn it, Enzo, it's a quarter after two!'

'Howard! I never disturb the sleep of my friends unless it is vitally necessary. Sleep is a blessing, given by God.'

'Enzo, I'm going to bless your ass unless you tell me what this is all about. And, by God, it had better be good.'

'Well, it is not good,' said Enzo, with theatrical sadness. 'I have acquired an early copy of this morning's newspaper, and you are running an article on the South Side slums which does not name me by name, but which could seriously jeopardize my business. You are willfully and viciously attacking me, Howard! We were always supposed to be friends, how could you do such a thing? I am going to have to insist now that you print no more such articles.'

Howard barked phlegm out of his throat, and sat up straighter in bed. 'You listen to me, Enzo, and you listen good. I'm not afraid of you, and more than that, I'm not afraid of anything you might have to tell the world about me. If you want to use your own grandson to bring me toppling down, well you can try, because I'll 'fess up to what happened between me and Marcella, and I'll 'fess up to fathering Eduardo, and God damn it I've decided to take it on the chin. So you do your damned worst, old fellow, the *Star* is going to go after you night and day from this day onward, and we're not going to be satisfied until you're behind bars at Joliet.'

There was a lengthy silence. Then Enzo said, 'You can speak bravely, when you want to, can't you, Howard? Maybe some of Morgana's heroism has rubbed off on you! But, you know, I think you're right. It isn't grandfatherly to use Eduardo against you. Eduardo is such a fine young boy, how could I use his name in vain? So – well – I have had to think of some kind of alternative. Some other way of making you see things my way.'

'What are you blabbering about, Enzo? Either kick the bull in the teeth or hang up. I'm tired.'

'Very well, then, Howard, I'll make it quick. Since neither of us wish to see Eduardo put under any undue stress; and since in any case I have always believed that you would sneakily be proud to admit to having a son – *anh!* you see, what a psychiatrist I am! – well then, I have decided there must be other ways of soliciting your cooperation. Like your daughters, for instance.'

'What about my daughters?' Howard demanded, harshly.

'Anh! Now I have your attention! I am talking about your daughter Phoebe! Yes, that's right! Phoebe has graciously consented to be my guest until such time as you categorically agree to drop your newspaper campaign against me – yes, Howard, not just drop it, but publish a front-page apology, and an article on everything that I personally do to help Chicago! Do you understand me?'

'And what if I don't agree?'

'There are plenty of meat-packing plants in Chicago, Howard. Are you going to start opening every single can of corned beef to find which one is your daughter?'

'Enzo, if you don't send my daughter back to me in one hour flat, I'm going to come around there and tear you to pieces with my own hands!'

Enzo made an amused little mewing noise.

'Enzo, you listen to me –'

'No, Howard, this time you listen to me. Stop this libel in

your newspaper. You don't care about the slums, you in your big mansion. Nobody in the suburbs cares about the slums. The only person who cares about any of this is his honor Kenneth Doyle, and what is he? A weakly, dithering Irishman with no influence and no friends. A loser, Howard – and that's what *you're* going to be if you carry on this preposterous campaign. A man who lost his way, a man who lost his soul, and a man who lost his daughter.'

Howard gradually lowered his head. His bedroom door opened, and Eleanor stood there, in a pale peach peignoir. Howard let the telephone receiver drop on to the quilt. Eleanor watched him with her hands clasped over her breasts in pain and sympathy as the tears started to roll uncontrollably down his cheeks.

She knelt down beside the bed in a rustle of silk. 'Howard, Howard . . .' she whispered, and she brushed the tears away from his eyes.

On the quilt the telephone purred softly.

33

Lenny unlocked the door of his apartment, and then turned to Morgana and pressed his finger to his lips. 'Quiet, all right! You don't want to upset him. He's easily upset.'

'Is he actually in there?' Morgana whispered. Her heart flew from side to side like a shuttlecock.

'You bet,' said Lenny. 'Come on.'

Morgana hesitated, and reached out for Lenny's sleeve, to hold him back for a moment. But Lenny was already too far ahead of her. The hallway was narrow and cramped, and there was a strong smell of damp and vinegar. Lenny patted the wall until he found the lightswitch, and the hallway was lit up by a single low-wattage bulb in a shade that was supposed to be made out of a pirate's treasure-map. There was green striped wallpaper like hospital pajamas, adorned by a sporting calendar for 1946 with a smiling sweater-girl on it, and a heap of clothing that looked like a mixture of soiled raincoats and corduroy pants.

'Close the door,' said Lenny, without turning around.

Morgana said, 'Lenny – wait – I *know* who it is.'

Lenny stopped in the doorway to the sitting room, although he didn't turn around. When he spoke his voice sounded peculiarly hollow. 'You know who it is?'

'The Hacker. I found out this evening. I know his identity. In fact I know him as a friend.'

'You know the Hacker as a *friend*?'

'Lenny, he's – someone who's close to my family. That's why I came. I thought that maybe I could talk to him, you know – persuade him to give himself up.'

Lenny paused. Then he said, in that same hollow voice, 'Why should he want to give himself up?'

'Well, to save his family from any more disgrace. And to save himself. And to save any more women from being killed.'

At last Lenny turned his head and looked at her. She could see a single glistening eye over the hunched shoulder of his raincoat. 'Are you afraid of him?' Lenny asked.

'Of course I'm afraid of him! Aren't you? But I *know* him, I can talk to him. I mean, I don't quite know what kind of a mood he's in, whether he's different whenever he turns into the Hacker.'

Lenny jerked his head toward the darkened sitting room. 'You want to tell me his name, so that I can call him?'

'His name's . . . Bradley. But don't you think I'd better call him, instead of you? He knows me better.'

Lenny thought about this, and then said, 'I guess. Why don't you go ahead?'

Morgana made her way further along the corridor until she was standing only a few inches away from Lenny. She glanced at him for reassurance and then strained her eyes to peer into the overwhelming darkness of the sitting room. The drapes must have been drawn tight, or else there were boards nailed over the window. The room smelled very stale and close, as if it hadn't been opened up for a very long time.

'Go ahead,' said Lenny, expressionlessly. 'He's here. Call him. See if he answers.'

Morgana licked her lips. '*Bradley?*' she whispered, terribly afraid now that the Hacker might not be Bradley at all, that she might have made a ridiculous and frightening mistake. Yet the knives, and the blood. It *must* be Bradley. 'Bradley,' she repeated, a little louder this time.

'Gwan,' Lenny encouraged her.

'Bradley, are you there, Bradley? It's me, Morgana! You mustn't be afraid! We can talk this over, Bradley. Everything's going to be fine.'

Still there was no response. Lenny looked at Morgana and shrugged. 'He's here, I can promise you that.'

'You don't think he might have slipped out when you came across to get me?'

Lenny shook his head. 'He's here all right, the bastard. He's here all right. Maybe I should just creep into that room and roust him out, what do you say to that?'

'Isn't there a light?'

'No, no light, that was one of his stipulations. No light. I guess he didn't want anybody to see who he was, anybody who might recognize him straight away. Somebody like you, for instance; but of course you know who he is already, don't you?'

'Bradley T. Clarke,' said Morgana, hoarsely. 'He's the heir to Ham-I-Yam.'

'The heir to Ham-I-Yam, hey? Well, that's something to be heir to. I've eaten that stuff myself. What do they call it? The ham that built America strong. Well, now, is that who he is?'

Morgana suddenly took fright, and stepped back along the corridor. 'Lenny – Mr Mutken – I'm not sure he's there at all. And if he is – well, if he isn't answering, maybe he's not exactly safe to talk to, do you know what I mean?'

'Ssshh-ssshh-sshh,' Lenny calmed her, tapping her sleeve with his fingertips. 'Don't let yourself get spooked. You're a famous newspaper lady, remember? An intrepid female reporter. You just keep yourself calm and I'll go in and roust this fellow out. Heir to Ham-I-Yam, hey? That's something to be heir to. Pity it's *trayf*, hmh?' Lenny laughed dryly at his own little joke.

Morgana said, 'I think we ought to call the police.'

Lenny said, 'You wait, it's going to be all right,' and without any hesitation he made his way into the darkness of the sitting room. For a moment Morgana could see the gray shape of the back of his raincoat, then she couldn't see anything at all. She waited at the doorway, her tongue anxiously circling her lips, expecting at any moment to hear Lenny cry out in pain.

'Are you all right?' she called, into the darkness. 'Mr Mutken? Are you all right?'

Another long silence. The radiator pipes rumbled, and Morgana took two steps backward in alarm.

'Mr Mutken?'

Silence. Then a soft shuffle of feet. Then just at the very instant she began to realize what was actually happening – what Lenny Mutken had actually been leading her into – two powerful bony hands shot out of the darkness and snatched hold of her wrists like bullwhips. She screamed, more of a gargle than a scream, but she was immediately dragged into the room, and her hands twisted around behind her back. She struggled, turned, ducked, and tried to lash out behind her. But her legs were abruptly kicked out from underneath her, and she dropped heavily on to the bare-boarded floor, directly on to her right hipbone. The next thing she knew her wrists were being pinched in something cold and sharp; and there was a decisive click; and she was handcuffed.

Lenny Mutken switched on a standard lamp with a fringed shade and revealed himself. He was standing panting at the far side of the room with an expression of triumph and amusement on his face, naked except for a drooping pair of undershorts. To one side of him was a cheap 1930s sideboard, spread on top with a flower-patterned tablecloth, on which were arranged over a dozen dully gleaming butcher knives, two bone-splitting saws, and at least a score of cleavers and stickers and steels and skewers and other assorted butchering tools.

Behind Lenny, on the wall, hung his Pulitzer prize certificate, framed in tarnished gold, and a color print of Beaver Dam, Wisconsin, in the spring.

Lenny Mutken bowed. His chest was narrow and ribby and white, with a curl of gray hair in the middle of it. His skin looked as if it hadn't been exposed to the sun for thirty years.

'*Voilà!*' he announced, pleased with himself. He pronounced it 'voyler'. 'Here before your very eyes, the Hacker!'

Morgana tried to struggle on to her feet, but her head emptied of blood and she half-fainted, ending up on her knees.

'Is this a story!' Lenny exclaimed. 'Hacker slays daughter of Howard Croft Tate! Is any woman safe? By God, a front page screamer! "Terror stalked the streets of Chicago once more – and this time it was the rich and privileged who were shaking in their handmade shoes!" And the byline Yes! Can't you see it now? By Lenny Mutken, Pulitzer prize-winning ace reporter!'

He lowered his skinny arms, and looked down at Morgana with a rueful, almost petulant expression. 'I'm not trying to pretend that this was inevitable, mind you. Life is not like the movies. Life is life. Life is bad plumbing and cans of Ham-I-Yam you can't open because the grocery didn't give you a key. Life is marble and mud. Life is ... *this*, look around you. They still say that stupid catchphrase when they walk into the *Star*, that thing about Ogden Avenue, and that wasn't a joke or a catchphrase, that was *me*! That was my finest hour.'

Morgana breathed, 'You're not really going to kill me, are you?'

Lenny stared at her as if he couldn't remember who she was. 'Kill you? Mhmh! That's what all the other women said. But, you know, they didn't scream, and only one of them cried. They knew what I was going to do, but they didn't scream. They accepted it, you know – almost as if they felt they deserved it.'

'How could anybody deserve that?' Morgana demanded, although her voice was badly off-key.

'You mean, how could anybody deserve being hacked to pieces?' Lenny asked her, ingenuously. 'Well, I don't know. I'm not saying they actually *did* deserve it. Maybe they didn't. Maybe they were good people.' He rearranged the knives and saws in front of him as if he were Lionel Hampton preparing to play 'Ring Dem Bells' on the xylophone. 'Some people say that a good newspaper reporter doesn't make any judgements whatsoever. So ten businessmen get killed in a private plane crash on their way to visit a cathouse in Nevada. Were they guilty of conspiring to commit adultery? Did they *deserve* to die? Should a newspaper reporter even begin to *ask* such questions?'

He paused, and then he said, 'Ben Hecht once told me that being a newspaper reporter is like being a geographer. You see the world in the round but you have to present it to your readers on a flat sheet of paper. If you tell it like it is, without any personal judgements, it's going to end up distorted, just like a map of the world would end up distorted if you didn't project it differently from the way it is.'

Morgana was unable to speak and unable to move. She wasn't sure if she were really here or not, in this small seedy sitting room, under this starkly shadowed light, kneeling in front of a chattering mass murderer in his undershorts. She felt like Morgana through the Looking Glass; as if her whole existence had been turned upside down and inside out. Her strongest impression was of coldness; coldness of heart, and coldness of intention, and coldness of human spirit.

Somehow, a long time ago, the light had gone out in Lenny Mutken.

He picked up a twelve-inch knife, and hefted the handle. 'It's possible to lose your way,' he said, his voice reedy and catarrhal. 'It's possible to lose sight of your ambitions – and also your friends – and also yourself. In those days –' nodding toward the Pulitzer prize certificate '– in those days I think I knew who I was. A hell of a dog. Well, a hell of a drunk, too, but a hell of a dog. But – I've seen a way back – and what a righteous way back! Back to the front page! Lenny Mutken, the *Star*'s star reporter! And crusading, too! Against sin, and immorality, and unbridled wealth! And the cleverness, the journalistic genius, that I have created the story from nothing at all – by being both the story and the reporter, all in one!'

'Lenny –' Morgana appealed.

But Lenny placed the blade of the knife across his lips as a warning to her to keep quiet. 'Back on the beat!' he whispered. 'Lenny Mutken, back on the beat!'

He stared at Morgana and for one instant his stare was very wild and uncontrolled. His eyeballs swiveled independently, and Morgana let out a whimper of dread. He walked around the table, holding up the wide-bladed knife in his right hand as if he were the Statue of Liberty, and Morgana was completely sure that she was now going to die. Her whole body was seized with a convulsion of misery, like nothing she had ever experienced before.

He leaned close, so that his gray face was only two inches away from hers. 'Do you know what they call it when you clean the meat away from the bones?'

Morgana stared back at him but couldn't speak.

'Filleting,' he smiled, with satisfaction.

He moved the knife across until the point pricked at her chin. 'This one's going to astonish them all,' he said. 'Miss Morgana Croft Tate, Chicago's most eligible heiress, was today disassembled beyond all hope of repair.' He laughed wheezily.

Morgana said, 'Don't kill me, please.'

Lenny withdrew the knife. 'If I don't kill you ... what sort of a story will that be? That won't be a story at all! Hacker Relents? Hacker Goes Soft?'

Morgana said, 'I beg you not to kill me.'

Lenny thought about that and then slowly shook his head. 'I'm sorry. I hope you realize that I'm truly sorry. You remember what Hawthorne said, "What other dungeon is as dark as one's own heart, what other jailer is as inexorable as one's self!" So even if they never catch me, which they never will, believe me, Miss Croft Tate, I will serve my time for doing this.'

It was then that the whole apartment exploded with the

sound of the front door being sledgehammered off its hinges. Lenny stood up straight, and said, in perplexity, 'What?' But then the hallway was suddenly crowded with shouting armed police, and Morgana found herself lifted up on to her feet and pushed away to the opposite side of the room. A harsh voice shouted, 'Get that knife! O'Rourke! Get that knife!'

A strong Irish brogue called, 'Mr Sharpe! Here, Mr Sharpe! Here she is! Oh yes, safe as you like! Here now, don't you worry! Here now!'

A policeman came over with Lenny's keys and – after a short struggle – managed to unlock Morgana's handcuffs.

Another policeman cried, 'Find him some pants, will you? I said *find him some pants*! I don't care who he is, he doesn't come down to headquarters dressed like Tarzan on his weekend off! Use your head, will you?'

'*Miss Croft Tate!*' Lenny shrieked, above the confusion. '*Miss Croft Tate!*'

Harry had appeared from nowhere at all, and taken hold of Morgana's arm. He pushed her along the hallway, while more policemen jostled their way into the apartment, and news cameras flashed so close to her face that she was almost blinded.

'*Tell them why I did it!*' Lenny screamed out. '*Tell them why, Miss Croft Tate! Tell them why! Tell them the girls never screamed!*'

Harry helped Morgana across the sidewalk and into a car. The door slammed; then she was being driven down North Sedgwick Street with the streetlights passing her one by one as if they were timing her heartbeat. She could hardly understand how she had got here. She lifted her wrists and gingerly rubbed them where the handcuffs had pinched her.

Harry said, 'Morgana? Are you all right? Thank God you left that message.'

Morgana found it difficult to focus on him. His face kept blurring, as if he were looking at her through a steamed-up window. She understood with some detachment that she was probably suffering from shock. 'He was going to kill me,' she said, although her voice sounded flat and peculiar, not like her own voice at all.

'Jesus Christ,' said Harry, angry with Morgana, angry with Lenny, and most of all angry with himself.

'He had a reason,' said Morgana.

'A reason for cutting you up? A reason for cutting all those other women up? Jesus Christ!'

Morgana said nothing. She had understood Lenny's reason when her terror had been at its peak, but she was not at all sure that she understood it now – or, even if she did, whether she could explain it to Harry in a way that would make any kind of sense at all.

Harry said, 'I'm taking you home, okay? You can sleep if you want to.'

Morgana let her head rest on the back seat, but she didn't go to sleep. She watched the streetlights sail past, and the black silhouettes of the buildings, and then she turned her head to one side and stared at her own distorted reflection in the window. You see the world in the round but you have to present it to your readers on a flat sheet of paper. That's what Lenny had said. Otherwise, it ends up distorted.

She thought she heard Harry say, 'I love you, you know,' but it could have been something she had heard inside her head; or the wind blowing in the quarterlight; or a steamer blowing its foghorn, out on the lake.

34

Howard called Marcella. It was a minute after three o'clock in the morning. Eleanor stood beside him, her face waxy with strain. She had woken up Millicent a few minutes ago and asked for coffee. Neither she nor Howard would sleep again tonight, and both of them needed something to keep them alert.

Marcella answered sleepily, 'Who is this?'

'Marcella, it's me, Howard.'

A pause, a shuffle of bedclothes, then, '*Howard?* Why are you calling so late?'

'Well, it's not really late, it's early. I'm sorry to wake you, but something's happened.'

'Tell me, what's the matter? Howard, you sound so strange!'

'It's Phoebe.' Howard glanced guiltily at Eleanor, who hadn't yet taken her eyes off him. He had told Eleanor everything tonight – all about Marcella, all about Eduardo, all about his unholy relationship with Enzo. It had brought him to this – begging for his daughter's life with the daughter of the gangster who had kidnaped her. 'Phoebe's been – taken away. Well, kidnaped.'

Marcella was distraught.

'Oh, Howard! How terrible!'

'*Marcella*,' said Howard, and that was all he could manage to say. His voice just wouldn't work. The hot tears poured out of his eyes.

Marcella said, 'Howard? Howard? Please, Howard, what is it?' but in the end Eleanor had to take the receiver out of Howard's hand.

'Marcella,' she said, and her voice was chilled with dignity.

'This is Eleanor. Howard's wife. No – please don't try to interrupt. Howard has told me all about you, and all about your son Eduardo. But the position is this. Your father, Enzo, has been trying to prevent Howard from publishing stories about the way that he runs his slum properties on the South Side. The result has been that your father has arranged for the slaughter of one of our photographers, and now he has kidnaped our younger daughter.'

'My father?' breathed Marcella.

'He called Howard a very short while ago. He made it quite plain that if Howard refused to stop the *Star*'s campaign against the slums, Phoebe would never be seen again.'

Marcella said nothing for a very long time. Eleanor shook the receiver, and snapped, 'Did you hear me? Marcella?'

'Yes, Mrs Croft Tate, I heard you.'

'Is there anything you can do?'

'I don't know.'

'Well, can you at least *try*?'

'Mrs Croft Tate –'

'Yes?'

'Please give me one hour. Two hours, perhaps. I will talk to my father.'

Eleanor pressed her fingers against her forehead. She could feel the first throbbings of a migraine. 'Two hours, Marcella. Then I shall call the police commissioner. You know my number here, I expect.'

'Yes,' said Marcella, and put down the phone.

Eleanor slowly replaced the receiver. Howard had recovered himself now, and was wrapping his bathrobe cord tightly around his waist. He looked at Eleanor as if he were a German Shepherd that had just been slapped on the muzzle with a doubled-up leash.

'I've given her two hours,' said Eleanor. 'If she doesn't call back by five, then I'm going to get in touch with Commissioner Spectorski.'

Howard said, 'All right,' quite flatly, and heaved himself out of bed. Eleanor watched him as he stumbled toward his dressing room.

'Is that all you're going to say?' she demanded. '*All right?* Aren't you going to *do* anything?'

Howard took off his pajama top, and draped it over the top of his chair. 'Eleanor,' he said, 'I'm going to get dressed, and then I'm going straight down to the office, and then believe me I'm going to do something.'

Eleanor said nothing as Howard dressed himself in a blue double-breasted suit, and combed his hair. But when he approached her to say goodbye, she stood up, and she was fearful, although she didn't know why. She put her arms around him, and held him tight, feeling the girth of his body, feeling the warmth that came out of him, feeling his plain solidity. When she lifted her head and looked up into his face, her eyes were glistening with tears.

'Howard,' she whispered, as if she wished with all the desperation in her heart that 'Howard' could have been a magic word, a secret spell that whisked them back to those days when they had first been courting, days of summer lakes and leaves and jazz bands and laughter, Chicago in 1924, kissing and dancing and rolled-down stockings.

Afterwards, when she thought about it, she realized that she had known when they had embraced exactly what he was going to do. But at the time she was powerless to prevent it. Howard kissed her; a kiss of obligation rather than love; husband to wife; and then he went to the door. Then he went out of the door, and he was gone, and Eleanor was left with nothing more than the memory of what his face had looked like, in that very last fraction of a second. Here/gone, here/gone, just like a conjuring trick.

Howard went downstairs and called for the Chrysler to be brought out of the garage. Winton Snell went to the cloakroom for Howard's summer coat and gloves. Winton said nothing. He had been working for the Croft Tates too long to comment on their comings and goings; and tonight it was quite apparent that Howard was not feeling conversational. The coat and the gloves were brought, and put on, and then the two men waited silently in the hallway for the car to be driven around to the front steps.

A faint draft blew through the hallway, stirring Howard's coat.

When the Chrysler arrived, Howard unexpectedly shook Winton by the hand. 'Sir?' asked Winton, suddenly aware that something momentous was about to happen. But Howard simply smiled, and said, 'Carry on, Winton,' and climbed into the limousine. The car's red taillights were already dwindling down the driveway as Eleanor came down in her floor-length robe, hurrying, worried, and stood on the steps in the early morning darkness.

'Can I help in any way, madam?' asked Winton.

Eleanor turned to him, her face white, and said, 'Help?'

Howard sat silent in the back of the limousine as it bore him southwards along Lake Shore Drive. The sky was already lightening over Lake Michigan, a mystical silvery-blue, with the navigation lights of lake steamers twinkling along the horizon like drops of dew on a fence. The apartment towers of the Gold Coast were still dark and tightly sealed, the ramparts of the rich.

The limousine drew up outside Enzo's apartment block. Howard said to his chauffeur, 'Wait here. I won't be very long.' Then he entered the lobby, acknowledging the salute of the night porter, and crossed over to the elevators.

He couldn't remember when he had last felt so much at peace with himself. He tugged off his gloves finger by finger and then folded them neatly.

Carmino opened the door of Enzo's apartment for him, bowing low as he did so. 'Good morning, Mr Croft Tate. Would you care for some coffee?' Howard handed him his gloves and his hat and brusquely shook his head. 'This way, please, Mr Croft Tate. Mr Vespucci is waiting for you.'

Enzo was sitting in his library drinking coffee and reading this morning's *Star*. He stood up when Howard came in, and smiled, and bowed his head. He was still fully dressed in white tie and tails, presumably from yesterday evening's dinner. On the opposite side of the library, curled up on the leather Chesterfield, slept a young girl with long silky black hair, the curves of her body barely concealed by a softly rainbow-colored negligee.

'Please, don't concern yourself about Ana,' said Enzo. 'I could let off a cannon, and she wouldn't wake up. A heavy sleeper, like her mother.'

Howard remained standing. 'I've come to do business,' he said, tautly.

'Well, Howard, I'm pleased to hear it. And I give you my thanks for being so prompt. You know me, Howard, I am always a reasonable man. But sometimes I have to say enough is enough even to my friends. I hope you understand that this little show of force was purely a matter of business. I bear you no personal animosity whatsoever.'

'Is Phoebe here?' asked Howard. He found that he could barely pronounce her name.

Enzo cracked his knuckles one by one. 'She is safe, Howard, I can promise you that. My aide-de-camp Ambrogio has her in his custody. If anyone should try to harm her – *whssshtt*,' he said, and drew his finger from ear to ear.

Howard said, 'I've decided to kill the slum stories. I've decided to print a front-page apology, too, and maybe an inside feature on all the charitable works you've been doing. It's not just a question of having Phoebe released. It's a question of editorial judgement. We've been too hard on you, Enzo. Some of our staff, well, they sometimes get a bee in their bonnet about something, and then there's no holding them ... You know, we're talking about *taste* here, and quality journalism. I don't want anybody to be able to accuse the *Star* of being a gutter paper, not even you. Especially not you.'

Enzo slapped Howard on the shoulder. 'Howard, you have seen the light! You have no idea how much you have delighted me! Now, what shall we do? Shall you call your office, and tell them your instructions; after which, I shall call Ambrogio, and tell him to release Phoebe?'

Howard said, 'I think we can do better than that. Why don't you come down to the *Star* building with me? My limousine's outside. I can take you into the press room, and you can personally order the presses to stop. Now, don't you think that's the way to do things? A grand gesture. And believe me, Enzo – until you've stood in that press room with all those units pounding at full speed, and given the word, *stop!* and then heard the silence afterwards – well, you don't know the meaning of power.'

Enzo clapped his hands. 'Howard, Howard, Howard! What a man you are! The grand gesture, yes! And just to show that I trust you, and that I appreciate what you are doing, I shall call Ambrogio now!'

He picked up his telephone, and dialed a SUperior number. He waited for a moment while the telephone rang, beaming at Howard like a sophomore about to play a prank. At last his call was answered, and he said, 'Ambrogio? Yes. Everything is very well. Mr Croft Tate has been most accommodating! Yes, you can let Miss Croft Tate go.'

Enzo covered the mouthpiece with his hand, and asked Howard, 'Where would you like her to be taken?'

'The *Star* building,' said Howard. 'Can I talk to her?'
'Of course,' Enzo agreed, and handed over the phone.
'Phoebe?' asked Howard. 'Honey, is that you?'
'Daddy,' sobbed Phoebe. 'Daddy, I love you.'
'Are you all right?' Howard wanted to know. 'They haven't hurt you or touched you or anything?'
'Daddy, I'm fine. I just want to come home.'
'Well, that's been fixed, honey. They're going to take you to the *Star* building; then somebody will take you straight home. Don't worry, my darling, everything's going to be all right.'

Howard handed the telephone back to Enzo. Enzo spoke to Ambrogio in Italian, and then smartly replaced the handset. 'Excellent! This is good business! Now, shall we go?'

They left Enzo's apartment block and already the morning was blue with light. Howard said nothing as they drove down to Wabash Avenue, although Enzo chattered constantly, about friendship and influence and power, and how it was sometimes painfully necessary to remind those people closest to you that you were not to be taken for granted.

'It happens!' Enzo exclaimed. 'Take Marcella – even Marcella takes me for granted sometimes – and what else can I do but reprimand her?'

Marcella at that very moment was talking to Carmino on the telephone. Carmino said, 'I'm sorry, Miss Marcella, but your father has gone. Yes, only a few moments ago, with Mr Croft Tate. They were going to the *Star* offices. No, I don't know why.'

Howard's limousine drew up outside the *Star*, and the doorman hurried over to help Howard and Enzo to climb out. Howard told his chauffeur to wait where he was, and then led Enzo into the brightly lit lobby. He went straight over to the stainless-steel desk and asked the pretty Negro night receptionist, 'Any more calls from Ogden Avenue, Mandy?'

'No, sir, Mr Croft Tate. And good morning.'

'Press room's this way,' said Howard, and took Enzo by the elbow. The presses were still running at full speed with Grant's late extra edition CONFESS HACKER KILLINGS. The building throbbed, as if it were being shaken by an endless earthquake. Enzo smiled at Howard, and said, 'Power, yes?

The power of the press!' Howard ushered him into the elevator, and they went down to the press room.

Up on the editorial floor, Grant and Harry and Morgana and Gordon and seven other reporters and photographers were celebrating the Hacker story with coffee cups of whiskey which Harry had found in Walter Dempsey's copy paper drawer. The front page of the extra edition was pinned up on Grant's notice board, with a huge photograph of Lenny Mutken being led away from the Marshall Field apartments by police. Underneath the banner headline was a strap which read I Cornered Mass Dismemberer In His Den, by Morgana Croft Tate. Morgana was absolutely exhausted, dizzy, and more than a little drunk, but she had been determined to write up her story and to join in the celebrations. One day this was going to be her newspaper, and she wanted to be part of it.

The telephone rang. Grant picked it up, and spoke for a moment, then held the receiver up to Harry. 'Harry? It's for you. Somebody who calls herself Marcella.'

Harry finished his whiskey, and elbowed his way around Grant's desk. 'Marcella? This is a funny time to be calling.'

'Harry? You have to listen to me! You probably don't know it yet, but my father has kidnaped Phoebe Croft Tate! Yes! Yes! But there is no *time*, Harry! Listen! Listen to me, Harry, don't interrupt! Howard went to see my father only a few minutes ago, and they have both gone down to the *Star* offices! Yes! But Harry, I know that Howard is thinking of doing something terrible! Harry, you must find him straight away!'

Harry said quickly, 'Okay, Marcella. Okay. Listen – stay on the line. I'll try to locate him. All right, but don't panic. We'll find him.'

Morgana saw at once that something was wrong. 'Harry?' she asked. 'Harry, what's the matter?'

Harry said, 'I can't explain it all now, but your father is here at the office, and we have to find him. David – can you call up to his penthouse, see if he's there? Morgana, could you please call down to the reception desk, and have the girl put out a call? Grant – where else might he be?'

Grant shook his head. 'I don't know. Sometimes he likes to go down to the press room. But what's the problem? Who was that, on the phone?'

Down in the basement, Howard was walking arm in arm

with Enzo alongside the thundering Goss Headliners. They might have been two old chums from the same country club. Howard shouted at Enzo, 'What a sight, hey? When you stop these presses, it's going to be just like stopping Niagara Falls!'

Enzo glanced at his jade-faced wristwatch. 'Ambrogio should be here at any moment.'

Herman Short came over, wiping his hands on his perennial greasy swarf. 'Mr Croft Tate? Anything I can do for you?'

'Give us a moment, Herman,' Howard shouted. 'Mr Vespucci wants to see the power of the press running at full lick!'

Enzo laughed in glee. 'Howard! I misjudged you! You know something, now that you have seen things my way, I believe we are always going to be friends! Tonight, let's have dinner together! You and me, at the Blackstone! My treat!'

At that moment, the press room doors opened and Ambrogio appeared, leading Phoebe by the arm. Ambrogio looked pale and impassive; Phoebe was white and wide-eyed. Enzo lifted his hand to Howard and said, 'Hey presto! Your daughter, safe and sound!'

Ambrogio brought Phoebe down the steel staircase and across the press room floor. Enzo shouted to him, 'It's okay, it's okay, you can let her go now! Everything is okay!'

Howard held out his arms for Phoebe and hugged her tight. For a long time neither of them said anything, but then Enzo tapped Howard on the shoulder and nodded toward the presses and said, 'Eh? A bargain is a bargain.'

'Sure you're all right?' Howard asked Phoebe. 'They didn't hurt you?'

Phoebe nodded.

Howard said, 'Listen, sweetheart, I have a little business to finish with Mr Vespucci here. I believe that Morgana's in the building someplace, probably up in editorial. Why don't you go find her, and then the both of you go home. But call your mother first, and tell her you're okay.'

Phoebe stood on tiptoe and kissed her father on the cheek. 'You won't be long?' she asked him.

Howard smiled. 'Only a minute. Don't wait.'

Enzo was plainly growing impatient. He stood with his hands clasped in front of him and his lips tightly pursed, but Howard waited while Phoebe had climbed back up the staircase, so that he could give her a wave and blow her a kiss as she went out of the press room door. At last he turned around and beckoned to Herman Short.

'Herman,' he said, leaning forward and speaking in the printer's ear, so that neither Enzo nor Ambrogio could hear him, 'what's going to happen now is going to take you by surprise. But I want you to promise me this. No – don't ask me any questions, just listen. I want you to promise that you won't let that big palooka over there get out of the building. You got me? As soon as things start happening, have four of your toughest people jump right on top of him – and watch out, he's probably carrying a gun. Now, do you understand that? Whatever happens, you don't let that fellow escape.'

'Mr Croft Tate –' Herman frowned. 'What exactly do you mean, what's going to happen now is going to take me by surprise?'

Howard clasped his shoulder. 'You're a good man, Herman. I never did care for printers much, but you're okay.'

Howard walked back over to Enzo and shouted, 'They're all ready. All you have to do is come over here and say the word. Then everything will stop.'

Enzo made a circle of his finger and thumb and smiled.

They walked together along the rows of presses. But then Howard unexpectedly hesitated, and took Enzo by the arm, and led him right in between two of the roaring units. Enzo held back, but Howard tugged his arm harder, and shouted, 'Come on, don't tell me the great Enzo Vespucci is scared! It's only noise, after all! I want to show you the new catches we've fitted to the stereo plates, so that they don't fly off when we're printing. That used to be quite a problem, not long ago.'

At that second, Harry was opening the door of Howard's penthouse office. 'Mr Croft Tate! Mr Croft Tate! Are you there?' He crossed the carpet to the huge window overlooking the lake, and jostled the handle of the door which led out on to the balcony, but it was firmly locked. He turned back, and hurried toward the elevator.

Howard said to Enzo, 'You see there – you see right there – no, that's it – that's where the ink gets spread on to the stereo plate – no, lower –'

Enzo bent forward. As he did so, Howard seized the nape of his neck, and forced his head forward under the whirling press cylinder like a man drowning a dog in a bath full of water. Both men roared. Enzo's head was snapped into the whirling machinery, and Howard's arm was snatched in with it. There was a hideous mangling noise, and a screech of shearing metal. Blood and bone and ripped-up clothing flew everywhere. The press instantly and automatically shut itself down.

The rivers of newsprint came to a standstill. There was silence, just the silence that Howard had promised. Herman Short put down his handful of swarf and began to walk quickly toward the unit that Howard and Enzo had been inspecting. He forgot all about Ambrogio, but Ambrogio was too shocked to do anything but stay where he was.

Up in the newsroom, the lights flickered and dimmed, and even though the presses were so far below them, the reporters could feel the sudden silence.

Grant said, 'Something's happened.' He picked up his phone and pressed the button for the press room.

Morgana said, 'What is it? Grant – what is it?'

35

It was Wednesday evening. The plates were all locked in, the presses were ready to run. There was silence in the press room as Morgana came in, wearing a black veil and a black pleated dress. Harry was close beside her, and Grant was directly behind. Phoebe was there, too, also dressed in black. Nobody else had been invited. This was a family moment, a gesture of sorrow that the *Star* and all the people who worked for the *Star* wanted to keep to themselves.

Herman Short came forward and whispered to Morgana, 'We're all set, Miss Croft Tate.'

Morgana said, 'Very well, then. Run it.'

The klaxons blared, and then the presses started to turn over. Gradually they built up speed, the webs streamed through, and the folded newspapers began to pour out of the trimmers. Grant walked down and teased one copy out of the stack, and brought it back to Morgana with a sad and sympathetic smile. Morgana drew back her veil, and held the newspaper up. The front page was taken up with a portrait of Howard Croft Tate, on a happy day not long ago, Morgana's twenty-first birthday. He looked like a man who had the whole world at his feet.

The headline above him read, THE HERO.

36

The funeral cortege held up traffic on North Michigan Avenue and Lake Shore Drive for almost three hours; nearly two miles of sparkling Cadillac and Chrysler limousines, their headlights ablaze, the hearse itself and nine other cars heaped with thousands and thousands of scarlet American Beauty roses, which had always been Howard's special favorite. Their petals dropped in the heat until it looked as if it were raining blood.

At the head of the cortege marched the Chicago Fire Department Silver Band, playing the 'Valse Triste' from Sibelius' 'Kuolema', their bass drums echoing from the buildings on either side, while passers-by removed their hats as if a dead king were passing by.

The day burned relentlessly hot. Tarpaper roofs began to run at the seams. As the cortege passed along Lake Shore Drive, Morgana could see the water lying silver-dark and sullen as though poured out of molten type metal. On the other side, the *Tribune* building and the *Star* building and the Palmolive Building wavered in the hot air like mirages, as if they would fade away like the pyramids of Egypt as soon as twilight began to gather.

Those who gathered at the pink-marble Croft Tate mausoleum at Shaded Oaks Cemetery could have been selected by a discriminating hostess from the blue books of ten major American cities, as well as the minor nobility of Europe. There were five genuine princes, three genuine princesses, two Nobel prizewinners, as well as counts and countesses beyond counting, senators, representatives, governors, ambassadors, aldermen, movie stars, authors, bankers, and assorted mayors.

Eleanor led the mourning. Her face was veiled so that she

looked like a Victorian photograph of a ghostly manifestation. She wore a long black dress by Nettie Rosenstein, and an extraordinary black winged hat that Morgana would later describe as 'Nosferatu, the Vampire.' Morgana herself wore a square-shouldered charcoal-gray dress by Omar Kiam, with black collar and black sleeve details. Phoebe wore the plainest black dress of all, high-necked, with a calf-length hem, and no decoration at all but black silk piping and a jet brooch.

Grant Clifford stood on the steps of the mausoleum and read a requiem for his dead employer and friend. The mausoleum had been designed in 1929 by McKim, Mead & White, the architects for the State Capitol in Providence, Rhode Island, and the Savoy Plaza Hotel in New York. It was a Beaux-Arts restatement of Imperial Roman grandeur, all pillars and domes and cornices; and ironically Morgana thought that there was a bittersweet flavor of Mark Antony's requiem to Caesar in the words that Grant Clifford spoke on its polished marbled steps. He was bare-headed. The assembled company in their black plumage and their black gloves listened and perspired and some of them wept.

Grant declared, 'I don't think that a man should be judged for what he achieved but for what he tried to achieve; and Howard Croft Tate tried to achieve more than most. He tried to be the greatest publisher and the greatest communicator that America has ever known, and although the history books will have the final say, I believe that he was successful in that endeavor. Maybe the trouble was that he also tried to be a human being – a man of affection and warmth and personal integrity.

'Maybe Howard discovered too late that power is incompatible with love; and that success is the very opposite of compassion. Too late, that is, to stay alive; but not too late to redeem his past mistakes, and to be remembered here today as a man of courage and honesty and unfailing loyalty.'

It was a very provocative requiem, very close to the knuckle. But Grant knew what he was doing. He was not only honoring his dead friend and former publisher, he was making a clear statement to Morgana that he would fight with her and work with her, and that he was a Croft Tate man, thick or thin.

Afterwards he came up and grasped Eleanor's hands. Eleanor said, almost inaudibly, 'Very good, Grant,' but when Grant came up to Morgana, she said nothing; although she acknowledged what he had done with a slight sideways nod of her head.

'We have our chance now,' said Grant.

'We've always had chances,' Morgana replied. 'What really matters is whether we take them or not.' She didn't intentionally mean to sound smart: but somehow the words came out that way.

Grant shaded his eyes with his hand. 'You know that Francesco Lorenzo and Orville O'Keefe are already muscling in on Enzo's territory?'

Morgana looked at him for a long suspended moment without saying anything. Then she told him, quite firmly, 'Editorial meeting, tomorrow at eleven.'

'Well, the sooner the better.'

'Grant, you may be burying a friend, but I'm burying my father.'

Grant lowered his hand. Morgana could see that she had stung him. 'Yes,' he said. 'I'm sorry. I guess that was poor taste.'

Morgana took his hand to show no offense had been taken, that they were still friends.

Gradually, after shuffling up to pay their respects at Howard's tomb, the assembly of mourners returned to their cars, while the family remained behind to read the inscriptions on the wreaths and bouquets. 'With deepest sympathy, Col. Robert McCormick and all at the *Trib*.' 'In sorrow, Chicago Police Department.' 'A friend has left us, Chicago Chamber of Commerce.' 'Last putt, Howie, from Kenneth.' On Eleanor's special instructions, a small posy of forget-me-nots had been given pride of place at the front of the floral tributes, with a card that read simply, '*Ciao*, Howard, from Marcella.'

Eleanor was many things; but she was not mean of spirit.

Afterwards, the funeral party returned to Weatherwood, where six marquees had been erected, their entrances drawn back with black ribbons, their foyers filled with white roses. Inside, on plain tables, there was a buffet of cold Virginia ham, cold fried rabbit, barbecued ribs, scrambled eggs Creole, trout, steak, cold poached salmon, and all the plain foods that Howard had liked the best. There were well over a thousand mourners, and they were served with chilled California wine, more than ninety cases of it.

The mourners milled in and out of the marquees, or stood

under the sun frowning. It was very hard for most of them to believe that Howard Croft Tate was dead, even now, after his funeral, and the general sense of shock and loss had not diminished. Conversation rose and fell like surf on a windy day. Milton Berle looked sad. Groucho Marx looked sad. It was extraordinary to see so many famous faces looking bereft.

As the afternoon wore on, the band played selections from Beethoven and Elgar and Grieg. When they played Elgar's overture 'In The South', Eleanor excused herself and moved away from the people to whom she had been talking, and stood by herself by the parapet which overlooked the lawns, and wept silently beneath her veil.

Morgana came up to her and said, 'Momsy?'

'I'm all right,' Eleanor told her, hastily. 'I once had a dream about this, that's all, and now it's suddenly come true.'

'Have you forgiven him?' asked Morgana.

Eleanor shook her head. 'He never needed my forgiveness when he was alive. He certainly doesn't need it now that he's dead. I betrayed him just as much as he betrayed me.'

Morgana held her mother close, but she detected a stiffness in her posture, an unwillingness to become too intimate. 'Times have changed already,' said Eleanor. 'I always knew they would, when your father went.'

'He was very brave,' Morgana reminded her.

'Brave? Well, I don't know. Perhaps he was and perhaps he wasn't. He may have been doing nothing more than taking the easy way out.'

'I don't understand,' said Morgana.

'Well, let me put it this way,' Eleanor told her, taking hold of her hand, 'your father wasn't exactly the armor-plated champion of freedom and justice that most people believed him to be. Those of us who knew him closely – myself, of course; and Grant; and Gordon McLintock; and Kenneth Doyle – well, I think we recognized him for what he was.'

'And what was he?' Morgana challenged.

'Don't get upset, my dear, I loved him, and I still do, and I have no intention of maligning him, especially today. He was good hearted, and well intentioned. He had such enthusiasm, and such an appetite for hard work, and he inspired other people to work hard. But, you know, everything he ever did was done for the sole purpose of impressing his father – your grandfather. Ever since he was little his father had told him again and again that he was worthless and dull and that even to keep on feeding him was a waste of money.'

Eleanor smiled sadly, and then she said, 'Grant will tell you how Howard used to pace up and down his office, ranting about his father!'

'But grandfather died in 1926,' said Morgana, mystified.

'That was the trouble,' Eleanor explained. She nodded her head briefly to acknowledge a sympathetic wave from Dave Garroway. 'Yes – that was the whole trouble. Howard became a hundred times wealthier than his father, a hundred times more successful, but his father never lived to see it. Howard was deprived of the one and only thing that would have made all of his lifetime's work worthwhile – his father saying "Well done."'

Eleanor lowered her head. Her black-winged hat perched on her head like Edgar Allen Poe's raven, perching on the bust of Pallas, just above the chamber door.

'Howard was powerful, yes; Howard had a voice to which the whole of America was obliged to listen. But because he had worked all his life for the sole purpose of impressing his father, he had no real aims, no real morals, and no real principles. Why do you think so many gangsters came around to see him? Poor Howard was so susceptible to pressure. He gave up his principles one by one, as if he were losing a card game. In the end, what was he, but bluster and fuss and easy options? Poor Howard!'

She was silent for a little while, then she repeated, under her breath, 'Poor Howard.'

Morgana said, 'He wasn't taking bribes, was he?'

'Oh, no, he wasn't influenced by money. Money meant nothing, as far as your father was concerned. What *did* influence him, though, was fear; plain cowardice; and the willful characters of men like Enzo Vespucci – men who didn't mind killing for what they wanted, and were never afraid of being killed in return. It's very hard to stand up against men who are completely unworried by death.'

Morgana touched her mother's shoulder. She didn't know whether she believed what she was saying or not. But she told her mother quietly, 'I'm not going to let him down, you know. In fact, I think that half the reason he wanted me to take over the *Star* was because he knew that I wouldn't lose my nerve.'

Eleanor turned away. 'I wish that he were here again, just

for one minute,' she said, and her voice was choked with tears. 'I wish that I could tell him how sorry I am, and how much I understand.'

'It doesn't happen, Momsy, not outside of ghost stories.'

At that moment Laurence Olivier approached, looking pale beneath his California suntan. He was wearing a gray morning suit and a formal black silk tie with a diamond tietack. He took off his hat and kissed both Eleanor and Morgana. 'You can't have any idea of how grieved I am,' he told Eleanor. 'Howard was one of the very few newspapermen that any of us in the acting profession could honestly call a friend.'

Eleanor asked, 'Is Vivien here?'

Olivier pulled a tight smile. 'I'm sorry, I regret not. She doesn't care for funerals, to tell you the truth.'

Eleanor excused herself and went off to talk to Robert McCormick's niece Bazy Miller. Olivier said, 'Shall we?' and took Morgana's arm and together they walked along beside the rows of elms. The leaves gossiped, the sun faded in and out just as it had at the very beginning of Thomas Wolfe's story *The Lost Boy*.

'I understand that the *Star* is yours now,' said Olivier, raising one eyebrow interrogatively.

Morgana nodded. 'Popsy told me on my birthday that he was going to pass it on to me. I had no idea it was going to be so soon.'

'Do you think he had a premonition?' asked Olivier. 'I mean – do you think that he actually had a feeling that he was going to die?'

'I don't know,' said Morgana. She was suddenly beginning to feel that she had scarcely known her father at all. All those years, taken for granted; all those meals, when she hadn't said anything more friendly than 'Good morning, Popsy, would you pass the toast?' All those days and nights, all those words, all those kisses, what did they count for now. A memory, perhaps, but what was a memory? He was sealed in his casket now, his lips unkissable, his eyes closed, his mind stilled.

'Well, your father was quite a crusader, wasn't he?' Olivier told her. 'Now you have a chance to carry on some of his good work. Not every daughter has the opportunity to do something like that.'

He kissed her cheek, and then he said, 'I wish you the very

best of good fortune, my dear. It is very lonely, up there on the peak of the mountain, believe me, no matter how much people love you and adore you. But always remember that you can wave to those who sit on the peaks of other mountains; and they, at least, will understand.'

All through the heat of the early afternoon, Morgana was stalked at a distance by Kenneth Doyle. She made no move to approach him, nor to encourage him to come closer, and for his part he stayed well away until he was satisfied that she had spoken to all of those family and friends who had come to offer their sympathies. A little after three o'clock, however, when most of the guests began to say their goodbyes and drift back slowly to their limousines, Kenneth appeared beside Morgana in the rose bower, where she was talking to Phoebe and Bradley, and drinking a large old-fashioned which Winton Snell had mixed up for her specially. Kenneth stood for a while looking uncomfortable with his hands clasped behind his back. His black funeral suit was too tight across the shoulders, and the collar of his shirt looked as if it had been through five Chinese steam laundries too many. He grimaced as if he wanted to say something. The bees darted in and out of the roses.

Bradley was saying, '– it was *crazy*, of course, nuts, because they hadn't canceled the police bulletin, and I was arrested as soon as I drove up to our apartment – and when I told them that all I'd been doing that day was cutting up pork bellies – well, you should have seen the way they looked at me – and of course it wasn't until they got me all the way down to police headquarters that they found out what had happened.'

Phoebe said, 'I think it serves you right, Bradley. You should never take a girl on a date carrying the tools of your trade in the back of your auto. Especially when your trade is dismembering *des cochons*!'

'I agree,' said Morgana. 'You should have been sent to Joliet for five years for calculated poor taste.'

'Now listen,' Bradley protested, 'I normally keep my work bag in the trunk, but the whole point was that my trunk was full to bursting with joints of meat.'

'In that case, you were guilty of *gross* bad taste,' Morgana told him.

Bradley shook his head. 'You two girls, you're bananas.'

'But you love us,' Phoebe teased him, kissing the top of his wiry hair.

'That reminds me,' put in Morgana, 'how's Donald?'

Phoebe sat up straight and gave Morgana a look that was neat arsenic. 'I went to see him this morning, if you must know.'

Bradley frowned. 'You didn't tell me that.'

'Well, Bradley, I don't have to file a report every time I leave the house. I went to see Donald this morning and there was no change.'

'So he's still in a coma?' asked Morgana.

Phoebe nodded, tight-lipped.

'And is that all?' asked Morgana, her voice gentler now.

'No. I talked to the doctor, and the doctor said –'

Phoebe's voice tightened, but they all waited for her to finish without interrupting. 'The doctor said that he probably wouldn't wake up.'

'You mean *never*?' Bradley asked her, taking off his spectacles.

Phoebe covered her eyes with her hand. 'They give him a ten percent chance of staying alive, and a five percent chance of waking up.'

'Five percent is better than no percent at all,' put in Bradley, optimistically.

'Oh, you dummy,' retorted Phoebe, and began to cry.

It was then that Kenneth came sidling over to Morgana, and indicated with a complicated array of winks and nods and hiked-up eyebrows that he wouldn't mind a word or two in private, if that wouldn't prove too difficult. Morgana knelt down beside Phoebe, and put her arm around her, and said softly, 'He didn't care about you, Phoebe. He never cared about you.'

'That doesn't mean that I never cared about *him*.'

'He helped those people kidnap you. You could have been killed.'

'He still doesn't deserve to die.'

Morgana kissed her sister on the cheek. 'No, perhaps he doesn't. But he took the risk. Popsy tried to meddle with Enzo Vespucci, and look what happened to him.'

Kenneth said, 'Morgana? A quick word?'

'All right,' said Morgana, and gave Phoebe one last squeeze before following Kenneth across the bright-green grass to the sundial in the middle of the ornamental lawn. Kenneth leaned against the sundial and there was glistening perspiration in the furrows of his forehead. 'A very warm day for a function,' he remarked.

'Yes,' said Morgana, very quietly.

'I suppose you know why I want to talk to you,' said Kenneth.

'It's been one of those days,' Morgana replied. 'Everybody seems to want something.'

Kenneth looked at her narrowly. She was beginning to realize just how much influence she had inherited, and just how much power she now held, and Kenneth could obviously sense it. He said, cautiously, 'We could always meet some other time, if you'd prefer.'

'I don't mind talking now.'

'Well,' said Kenneth, 'it's about the slums.'

'You don't have to worry. I want the *Star* to launch the fiercest campaign against property racketeers that this city has ever seen, bar none; and I also want to hear just how you're going to start redeveloping, how you're going to finance it, how it's going to be built. I want to know what sort of a vision you have of Chicago in ten years' time.'

Kenneth looked at Morgana very directly. 'In ten years' time, I want to see the worst of the slum districts flattened to the ground. In twenty years' time, I want Chicago to be the finest-looking city in America. In thirty years' time, no slums at all.'

'It's a good dream, your honor.'

'I'm glad you share it.'

They talked for five or ten minutes about the South Side, and then Kenneth grasped Morgana's hand and wished her goodbye.

'I miss your father,' he said, swallowing back his emotion. 'He wasn't the most heroic of men, I wouldn't say that, so it was odd indeed that he died like a hero. But, you know, he was very kind, and he loved a joke, and I don't think that anybody needs to go to their Maker with any better credentials than that.'

Much later, when it was dusk, and the gardens were strung with lights, Harry appeared, wearing a crumpled gray suit and a shiny black necktie and a floppy-brimmed hat. He came up to Morgana, his cigarette glowing orange in the darkness, and watched her with the cautious eyes of somebody who doesn't want to intrude.

'Hi, Miss Croft Tate,' he said, at last.

'Hi yourself, Harry.'

'How's tricks?'

Morgana turned to him and smiled. 'Not bad, McLad.'

'How about a drive?' he asked her. 'It's kind of funereal around here.'

'We'll be having dinner for all the relatives in a half-hour.'

'Can't dinner wait on the lady who owns the Chicago *Star*?'

'I guess,' said Morgana. Then, 'All right, but don't let's go too far. I'll find my wrap.'

Harry had borrowed a big old Lincoln convertible from one of the sports writers at work. Its muffler was holed and it blew out clouds of smoke, but it was comfortable and it went along. Harry drove them northward, beside the lake, and Morgana sat back and let the warm wind blow through her hair.

At last they parked on the shoreline, and sat up on the backs of their seats looking out over the dark purple water, sharing a cigarette. Harry said, 'How do you feel?'

'I don't know. Numb, I suppose. I still find it hard to accept that Popsy's not here any more.'

'It's the same at the office,' said Harry. 'I'll tell you one thing, though. Nobody says "Anymore calls from Ogden Avenue, Mandy?" anymore.'

'I'll bet,' said Morgana.

Harry smoked for a while, and then nodded towards the dark outline of a ship travelling slowly toward the mouth of the Chicago River. 'Newsprint,' he remarked. 'That's all of Sunday's paper. As yet unwritten, as yet unprinted. The things that are going to fill that paper haven't even happened yet. But there it is.'

Morgana said, 'Did you want to ask me something?'

Harry shifted on his seat, and looked at her. 'What gave you that idea?'

'I just have the feeling that you invited me out to ask me something.'

'I don't want to ask you anything.'

'Everybody else has been asking me things. They've been asking for favors, asking for support, asking for this, asking for that.'

'Well, if you put it that way,' said Harry, 'I *am* interested to know what's going to happen.'

'What do you mean, "what's going to happen"?'

Harry made a face, 'Well, you know – now that you're going to be taking over the *Star* – I mean, are you really going to be taking it over? You're really going to be running it?'

'Does that bother you?'

'Well, no, of course it doesn't bother me! Why should it? I should be pleased!'

Morgana stared at him hard. 'You should be pleased but you're not.'

Harry sucked the cigarette down to the butt and then flicked it away into the darkness. 'It's going to change things, isn't it? Between you and me.'

Morgana suddenly understood what he was saying, what he was trying to tell her without actually coming out and admitting it in verbal headlines. He liked her. In fact he liked her so much that – until her father had died and left her the entire newspaper – he might even have been entertaining ideas that he and she could have spent some time together. What made his question even more poignant was that she liked him, too – much more than he realized.

'We can still be friends,' she told him.

He shrugged. 'Publishers don't usually hobnob with the grease monkeys in the city room.'

'Publishers aren't usually twenty-one and female.'

Harry shook his head. 'You belong in a different world, Morgana Croft Tate. Nothing can ever change that. You have the education, the money, the style, the friends. You don't want to be seen with anybody like me.'

Morgana reached across the top of the seat and laid her hand on top of his. 'Why don't you chance it?' she asked him. 'Why don't you ask me out to dinner?'

He looked at her cautiously. She looked pale and severe in her funeral dress, but also exquisitely beautiful, as if her face had been carved by some melancholy genius out of rubbed ivory, and her eyes had been stained into place with the juice of Japanese plums.

'If you don't want to, all you have to do is to say no. I'm not saying that I won't be disappointed, but I won't sack you for it.'

Harry leaned across and lifted the veil of her hat and kissed her very lightly on the lips. 'In that case, come out to dinner with me. How's Tuesday?'

'Tuesday's perfect.'

37

Over the weekend, Morgana met with Grant Clifford and Gordon McLintock and the *Star*'s senior feature writers, and devised one of the greatest newspaper crusades since the *Tribune* had waged war on Big Bill Thomson and Al Capone. Morgana's instruction was simply this: that the *Star* should dig down to the roots of all the corruption and all the palm-greasing and all the *laissez-faire* that had allowed the heart of America's second greatest city to collapse into the single largest slum in the world.

The paper was to investigate every department at City Hall concerned with housing regulations; to identify the landlords of all the major South Side slum properties, and publish their names and their photographs, alongside a detailed report on the squalor of the buildings they owned; to follow up all reports of rack-renting, intimidation of tenants, arson, forced prostitution, and drug-trafficking. No private individual and no city department was to be spared – police, firemen, housing inspectors, tenants' committee members – everybody's record was going to be scrutinized and held up for public examination.

Gordon came up with the leitmotif 'Clean Chicago', while Grant suggested that there should be cash rewards for anyone giving the *Star* information which led to a slum landlord being successfully prosecuted for breaking housing regulations. Harry and four other feature writers spent the weekend preparing a dummy for their first Clean Chicago edition, due out Wednesday morning.

Grant said to Morgana, as they left the last editorial bull-session late on Saturday afternoon, 'You realize that we're taking a serious risk. Men like Lorenzo and O'Keefe aren't going to take this kind of attack lying down, any more than

Enzo Vespucci did. You're going to be faced with just as much pressure as they put on your father, maybe more.'

Morgana buttoned her gray cotton glove. 'If I back down now, Grant, then Popsy will have died for nothing at all.'

'Just remember that these men don't kid.'

'Neither do I.'

That evening, Bradley drove Morgana and Phoebe down to the hospital to see Doris Wells. She was sitting up in bed when they walked into the ward, drawing a large picture of black ballet dancers in wax crayon. The same large Negress who had been there before was sitting beside her bed, talking to her. She lifted her eyes and stared when Morgana approached.

'Doris?' asked Morgana, leaning forward and smiling. 'How are you doing, Doris?'

The Negress said, 'Are you Miss Morgana Croft Tate?'

'That's right,' Morgana told her.

'You came here the other day, when Doris was asleep.'

'That's right.'

The Negress nodded, and said, 'That time, I call you a bad name. I want to tell you I 'pologize for that. I take it right back. I saw the newspaper, all about your father. Now I know what it is you people been trying to do. You got my respect. You got the respect of all the colored people hereabouts.'

Morgana said, 'You don't have to apologize. I know what you've been suffering. If I were you, I think I'd feel the same way about white people. In fact I think I'd probably feel worse.'

'There ain't no excusing prejudice, Miss Croft Tate, no matter who does it to who.'

Morgana looked down at Doris' picture. 'She's clever, isn't she?'

'Sure, she's clever. She takes after her father. Her father used to draw. Scenes from the Bible, mainly.'

'What's going to happen to her when she's ready to leave here?'

'Well, we've been talking about that. Probably she's going to live with the Green family, they've got kids already. They live kind of crowded, but their hearts are good.'

Phoebe touched Morgana's arm. 'Morgana?'

'What is it?'

'Well . . . I was wondering. I don't know . . . maybe she'd like to come stay with us, just for a while.'

Morgana drew a tubular steel chair across, and sat down right next to Doris, watching her draw for a while in silence. Then she said, 'Doris? When you feel better, and the doctors let you out of here, would you like to come stay with me? With me and my sister?'

Doris looked at her solemnly. 'Hattie said you was a boojum.'

Bradley couldn't help laughing. 'That's what you get, hunh, when you try to be a saint!'

But Morgana smiled, both at Doris and at Hattie, and said, 'You don't mind staying with boojums, do you? We don't live any different from you. And we have all kinds of fun. You can swim, and play tennis, and you can draw all you want.'

The woman called Hattie said, 'That's a kind offer, Miss Croft Tate. Maybe I can talk it over with the girl's uncle, see what he says. He's the legal guardian now. If he says it's okay, and Doris wants to go with you, then it's okay by me.'

Bradley shook his head, and let out one of his high yelping laughs, and said, 'Boojum, I ask you!'

They drove back to Weatherwood. Kenneth Doyle and his wife were coming over to have dinner, and also to talk about the Clean Chicago campaign. As they turned into Wacker Drive they saw a news placard on the corner reading HACKER FOUND HANGED IN CELL.

In spite of everything that Lenny Mutken had been, Morgana was shocked. Bradley drew into the curb so that they could buy a copy of the paper, and she read it as they drove home. 'It says he hanged himself with his own shirt. He left a note saying that he was the greatest newspaper reporter of all time, and that this was his last great story.'

Morgana spent a quiet weekend at home. She walked through the grounds of Weatherwood with her mother, and Eleanor told her more about her father, everything that she could possibly remember, right from the day they had met. Gradually, Morgana began to understand him more, although there were still many facets of his personality which seemed to be contradictory. She could understand how a man as powerful as Howard Croft Tate could also have been so cowardly; she could understand how much an ill-educated man could, in many ways, have been so cultured. Yet it seemed inexplicable that a man who had apparently grown so indifferent toward his wife should have been so upset when she had confessed to being unfaithful.

They talked all through Sunday afternoon, Morgana and Eleanor, until tea was served on the lawn under the large fringed parasol, and then they sat together in silence and listened to the birds calling 'feebee', 'feebee', and the warm hum of the August bees.

At the same time, Harry was round at Marcella's apartment, sitting cross-legged on the floor playing with Eduardo, while Marcella herself was perched in the window seat, taking advantage of the late sunlight to embroider the collar of Eduardo's romper suit. She wore circular spectacles, which made her look studious and vulnerable, and her needle winked every now and then in the sun.

'Where did you learn to sew like that?' Harry asked her.

'My mother taught me; and her mother taught her.'

'A real old family tradition, hunh?'

Marcella gave a small smile.

Harry stacked wooden bricks for Eduardo to knock down, and then he said, 'You saw the piece we ran on your father's funeral?'

Marcella nodded.

'We did try to be discreet,' Harry told her. 'I mean, we had to say "mobster", we didn't have any choice. But we did write up his charity work, too.'

'You don't have to make any excuses. I'm not sorry he's gone. I miss him. I always will miss him. But he was a cruel man.'

There was a lengthy silence between them, and then Marcella laid down her embroidery on her lap. The sunlight was behind her, and Harry could hardly make out the expression on her face. 'You seem to have something on your mind,' she said.

'I do?'

'Yes – all through lunch you were quiet, you were thinking. Usually you are all jokes.'

'I didn't think that jokes were entirely appropriate, to tell you the truth,' said Harry. 'After all – well, you've just planted your old man, haven't you? There's nothing very funny about that.'

'No – it's not that,' said Marcella. 'You were thinking. You were looking at me again and again and you were thinking.'

'What are you, a mind reader as well as an embroiderer?' Harry joked, although his tone was flat and not very humorous.

Marcella lifted her embroidery again. 'I don't know. Perhaps you were thinking that you ought not to see me any more. Perhaps you were thinking that I am too assertive, that the man ought to make the running, and not the woman.'

Harry cleared his throat. 'No,' he said, without looking up. 'It wasn't that.'

'Then you were thinking about somebody else. Another woman.'

'I was thinking about work, that's all.'

Marcella said, 'Would it frighten you if I told you that I liked you very much?'

'Why should it frighten me?' Harry smiled.

'If you are thinking about another woman, then it might frighten you. You might be wondering how to tell me without hurting my feelings.'

Harry didn't reply to that. Marcella sewed for a little while longer, and then came over and sat down on the rug next to him. She ruffled Eduardo's hair, and kissed him on the forehead.

'Why won't you tell me what it is?' Marcella asked Harry.

'I can't,' said Harry. He reached out and buried his fingers in her soft curly hair, letting it twist through his hand like smoke or memories. How could he possibly explain how much he enjoyed her company, how much he liked her warmth and her sensuality, how much pleasure it gave him simply to be here, sitting on the floor, playing with Eduardo? And how could he then explain the effect that Morgana had on him, and the glimpse that Morgana had given him of wealth and privilege and influence? He was just as cynical about his own desires as he was about the desires of the men and women he wrote about, but that was no protection against the allure of a forceful and beautiful young girl, and the cornucopia of fame and money that would be emptied on any man who won her.

For the very first time in his life, Harry had been intoxicated by genuine avarice; and it was the most disturbing feeling he had ever known.

Marcella kissed his cheek. 'Will you stay for supper?'

'I don't know. I have to get up early tomorrow. We're running that Clean Chicago special Wednesday morning. I still have a piece on Mies van der Rohe to finish.'

'All right. Will I see you before Wednesday? Why not come over Tuesday night, after the paper's been put to bed?'

'I'm sorry, Tuesday's out. I'm going to have to stay at the office for most of the night.'

'I understand,' said Marcella. 'In that case, why don't you call me?'

'I'll call you, I promise.'

Harry left Marcella's apartment unhappy, conscious of having told her a lie. He climbed into his borrowed Lincoln and pressed the starter. The motor whinnied twice, and then died. God's punishment, he thought, a flat battery. He climbed out of the car again and went back into the apartment lobby. He pressed Marcella's buzzer and waited for her to answer, lighting a cigarette as he did so.

'Marcella? It's me. Listen, maybe that piece on van der Rohe isn't so urgent after all.'

'Oh – I'm sorry, Harry. My mother called the minute you left. She's coming back early and she wants us all to have supper together.'

Definitely God's punishment, thought Harry. He went back outside, and gave the Lincoln a hard kick in the fender. Then he started walking in the direction of the office, his hands in his pockets, his cigarette stuck between his lips, keeping his hat slanted against the last glare of the setting sun.

38

The Clean Chicago special was roaring off the presses at full speed when Harry came up to Morgana's penthouse office and announced himself. Twenty or thirty Chicago luminaries were already there, crowded around Morgana's desk, where the first sample copies were spread out. Champagne was being poured out by one of the Croft Tate's house boys, brought down specially from Weatherwood. Harry was wearing his gray suit, which he had sent to the cleaners yesterday, and a white shirt that still sported the crease marks and pin holes from being folded up in its box. He had borrowed a green velvet necktie from Walter, and hoped that it wasn't too florid.

Grant Clifford looked up in some surprise when Harry made his entrance. This particular celebration was for his honor the mayor and a select group of aldermen and senior management only.

'Harry?' he asked. 'Anything up? Good story on Mies van der Rohe, incidentally. I think for the first time in my life I might have gotten a hazy grasp of the ins and outs of modern architecture.'

'I've, uh . . .' said Harry, waving his hat toward Morgana's desk. 'Miss Croft Tate and I have a . . . well, engagement.'

Grant turned toward Morgana with unconcealed dismay. Quite apart from the social suitability of the publisher walking out with a low-level news reporter, there could be long-term political implications which Grant didn't like one little bit. If Morgana and Harry actually happened to get on well together (which God forfend), Grant might suddenly find his own position as editor becoming increasingly insecure.

Grant was an instantaneous thinker when it came to office

politics. It was partly a professional reaction: an editor who wasn't in total command of his staff was no longer in total command of his newspaper. But it was mostly personal. He had seen too many management favorites edging editors out of their seats, and he certainly didn't want it to happen to him.

Morgana, however, was oblivious of Grant's disapproval. 'Harry! Come and have some champagne! This edition is *everything* I hoped for!'

She held it up. The headline read RAZE CHICAGO SLUMS, and underneath there was one of the photographs they had taken on South Cottage Grove Avenue, a black woman sitting despairingly on a broken-down step. A strapline announced, with stern intent, The *Star* goes to war on city's squalor.

Kenneth Doyle shook Harry by the hand. 'This is going to strip the enamel off a few people's teeth.'

Grant came over and laid his hand on Harry's shoulder. 'Don't keep Miss Croft Tate out too late, will you, Harry? She has a television and radio conference tomorrow morning.'

'You bet,' said Harry, and looked around at Grant and then frowned. He had glimpsed something in Grant's eyes that he couldn't work out at all. Jealousy? Disapproval? He tried to smile but then he realized that everybody in the room was looking at him in the same kind of way, as if he were a commis-chef who had suddenly walked into the middle of an exclusive restaurant dressed in his greasy apron.

Morgana went to find her wrap and then she and Harry went down in the elevator together. Harry slouched with his back against the wall as the elevator's indicator needle slowly sank to Lobby.

'Is something wrong?' Morgana asked him.

'I don't know,' he replied. 'What do you think?'

'I don't think there's anything wrong at all. I'm absolutely delighted with tomorrow's edition. Where are you taking me?'

'Well, I was thinking of the Blackstone.'

'The Blackstone? Isn't that terribly expensive?' Morgana asked him. She wished almost as soon as she had said it that she had bitten her tongue.

'I do get paid, you know,' said Harry, sharply.

'I know you do, I'm sorry. I didn't mean that. What I meant

was, I go to places like the Blackstone all the time, and what I was really looking forward to was going someplace that *you* like, just like you took me home to your mother's.'

Harry shrugged. 'I booked a table at the Blackstone.'

Morgana reached out and held his hand. 'I'm being terrible, aren't I? I must sound really patronizing. I'm sorry. But I would like to try someplace different, honestly. Look at me – I'm not even dressed for the Blackstone.'

Harry looked at her plain gray Dior suit with its perfectly tailored shoulders and its pencil skirt. 'You look like you're dressed for anything,' he told her.

They argued for a little longer as they crossed the lobby under the huge suspended star, but in the end Harry stopped himself from sulking and agreed to take her to Mikow's Restaurant on Ashland Avenue, about three blocks away from where he lived. Morgana kissed him as he pulled away from the front of the *Star* building, and sat back with a self-satisfied grin. 'I knew I could persuade you in the end.'

'You like slumming? I thought you were against slums.'

'Don't start being bitter,' Morgana retorted.

'Well, I don't know, did you see their faces tonight, when I came up to your office to collect you?'

'Harry – I really don't care what they think.'

'You *have* to care what they think! You're going to have to spend the rest of your life working with those people. You need to keep their respect.'

Morgana said, much more quietly, 'You don't think that they're going to respect me if I go out with you?'

Harry took a right against a red light. 'You've got it in one.'

After they had driven four or five more blocks, Morgana said, 'Why are you being so obnoxious to me this evening?'

Harry glanced at her, and said, 'You really don't know?'

'No,' she told him. 'Maybe I'm too young and too inexperienced. So tell me.'

'The reason I'm being so obnoxious is because, despite myself, I think I'm falling in love with you.'

'And that makes you obnoxious?'

'Of course it makes me obnoxious! How the hell is a guy like me going successfully to fall in love with a girl like you, and notice I didn't split the infinitive. I don't have any money at all, I live in a walk-up apartment in a dreary part of town, and what's more I actually work for you. Now – explain to me in words of one syllable how any kind of relationship in which the foregoing conditions prevail is ever going to get off its fanny? Let alone on to its feet. And I'll tell you something else, I'm not even sure whether it's *you* that I'm falling in love with, or your money.'

Morgana stared at Harry in wide-eyed amazement. Then she started to laugh out loud, and drum her feet against the brakeboard in hilarity.

'You're crazy! You're a crazy Polack! And I think I'm falling for you, too!'

'Don't *say* things like that!' Harry shouted at her.

'Why not? I'm your boss, I can say what I want.'

'That's exactly why you can't say things like that!'

They argued and shouted all the way to Mikow's. Harry jammed on the Lincoln's brakes as they arrived outside, and the convertible bucked up and down on its suspension like a great harpooned whale. Harry opened the door for Morgana and gave her a sweeping sarcastic bow. 'My lady, the palace of excellent chow.'

'Thank you, serf,' Morgana acknowledged.

Mikow's was a tiny Russian-Polish restaurant with steamed-up windows and red gingham tablecloths. There were paintings of Mother Russia all over the yellow streaky walls, and every table had a bottle of tarragon vinegar on it for shaking over the jellyish headcheese which was Mikow's specialty. Harry and Morgana were greeted by Mikow himself: a huge broad-shouldered Ukrainian who seemed to fill up the whole restaurant by himself, leaving hardly any room for customers. He was shaven-headed, pale-eyed, with a face like a happy rutabaga.

'A beautiful lady tonight?' asked Mikow, and took Morgana's hand, and kissed it. 'I will give you my most romantic table.'

Mikow's most romantic table was wedged awkwardly into the restaurant's window, with a view of Harry's car, six trashcans, and the thrift store opposite. Mikow lit a candle, however, and after he had brought them a bottle of cherry vodka and joined them in three successive toasts to the United States with the exception of Indiana which Mikow didn't care for; to beautiful women everywhere; and to Harry and Morgana, Morgana had to admit to herself that a certain feeling of well-being was beginning to creep over her, and that it was pleasant enough almost to be called romance.

Harry ordered as starters *piroghi* stuffed with cream cheese and Siberian *pel'meni*, which were like ravioli filled with chopped pork and served with a mustard and vinegar dressing. This was followed by prime ribs baked with potatoes and cabbage. They finished up with a slice of Mikow's cherry pie.

'Now, that was a hundred times better than going to the Blackstone,' said Morgana.

'If you say so,' Harry replied. He offered her another vodka, but she held her hand over the top of her glass.

'You don't have to fight me,' Morgana told him. She smiled at him through the dipping flame of the candle. Mikow's was crowded now; the atmosphere was noisy and smoky and a fiddler had started up with Russian folk dances.

'You're right, I don't,' said Harry. 'But I have to fight myself.'

Morgana said, 'Do they allow you to dance here?'

Harry shrugged. 'Why not? They can always throw us out.'

They danced together between the tables, smiling and apologizing whenever they accidentally bumped somebody's shoulder. They danced very close together because they had to: there wasn't room for dancing distantly. Harry held Morgana tight in his arms and she felt very warm and very womanly and he knew that it was never going to last. Her perfume was too expensive, her hair was too beautifully cut, her stockings were silk and her shoes were handmade in London. In contrast, Harry was a walking advertisement for Sear's men's department.

Morgana was more than a little drunk. The vodka had warmed her toes and then her legs and then it had slowly worked its way up to her brain. She felt happy and silly. She hadn't felt so happy for a long time. She knew that Harry was worried about taking her out, and even more worried about dancing with her, but he was good-looking and amusing and he felt so solid and masculine under his suit, and just at that moment she didn't want to care about anything else but enjoying herself.

She didn't have to worry about the future, in the same way that Harry did. Even if she never went to work again, she would be wealthy enough to live in luxurious style until she was a very old lady indeed. That, of course, was her stainless-steel advantage, and there was nothing that Harry could do to take it away from her.

Harry paid the check and the entire meal came to $6.35, vodka included. At the Blackstone he would have been lucky to escape for five times that amount. They left the restaurant and the street was deserted and echoing and dark.

'Did you say you lived near here?' asked Morgana, as Harry opened the car door.

'Three blocks south.'

'Is it asking too much for you to invite me in for a cup of coffee?'

'Is that a request or an order?'

'I think it's a little bit of both.'

'Okay, then, you're invited. But don't expect the George S. Isham Mansion.'

More than slightly drunk, showing off, Harry drove the Lincoln in reverse all the way back down to his apartment building, three blocks. He parked, yanked the car's canvas top into place, and then ushered Morgana inside the hallway. 'You do live alone?' asked Morgana, as she climbed up the stairs ahead of him.

'Don't worry, my wife's usually asleep by now.'

Morgana stopped, and said, 'You'd better be kidding.'

'I'm kidding. Now that's the door, there.'

They went inside. While Morgana looked around, Harry lifted up all the windows to let in some fresh air. It was a warm, breezy night. There was music in the wind, Polish dancing probably. Harry took off his coat and slung it over the back of his armchair. 'Take a seat,' he told Morgana. 'Make yourself at home. I'll put on the coffee.'

'Do you think I could have a cigarette?' Morgana asked him.

'Sure.' He shook out two, and lit one for each of them.

Morgana caught hold of his wrist as he passed her the cigarette.

'I don't think I want any coffee,' she said. The suggestion in her voice was quite blatant.

Harry didn't take his eyes off her. 'Are you using me for something?' he asked.

'You shouldn't have such a low opinion of yourself.'

There was a moment when either of them could have chosen to restart the pretense movie in which they had been acting all evening; a technicolor comedy of manners. But the breeze was blowing in music and the night was warm and both of them simultaneously thought what the hell, and Harry took hold of Morgana in his arms and kissed her lips very softly at first and then more strongly, parting them at last with the tip of his tongue, and tasting her cherry-vodka mouth; and Morgana gripped Harry as tight and as close as she could, because he was hard like a rock, hard like muscle, and the feel of him made her almost delirious.

He undressed her in the dim light of his bedroom. He slipped off her jacket; the Dior label shone white. He unbuttoned the mother-of-pearl buttons of her white silk blouse. Nicotine-stained fingers with nails hammered flat from constant typing. The blouse slipped off her shoulders and she was wearing only an underwired brassiere underneath, which made her full breasts bulge out softly. Harry kissed her lips, kissed her cheek, unfastened her brassiere. Her breasts were bared, and he placed the palm of his hand against her nipple, sensitive skin rising up to touch sensitive skin.

'Do you think this is actually happening?' Morgana asked him. He laid her down on the crumpled bedcover, unhooked her skirt, and drew it off over her legs. She was naked except for her garter-belt, her gray silk stockings, her white French silk step-ins. Harry looked down at her and his heart almost stopped from complete admiration and desire. Full-breasted, narrow-waisted, with long legs shining in silk.

He tugged off his shirt, unbuckled his belt. He undressed so quickly that Morgana laughed. 'You're just like one of those speeded-up movies.'

Harry climbed on to the bed beside her. The room was quite shadowy, but she could make out the curves of his muscles in the dark. 'Who're you calling a speeded-up movie?' he growled at her.

He kissed her, quite gently and abstractedly to begin with, but then their mouths locked together again and for whole worlds on end they were absorbed in teeth and tongues and lips. Harry stroked her hair and called her all kinds of Polish pet names under his breath, my little tiger, my little flower, my little darling. He kissed the arch of her neck, and she laid her head back on the pillow that smelled of him and his hair and his cigarettes, and then he lowered his head and kissed her breasts, holding each one in his hand, kissing first one nipple then the other, taking her nipples between his lips, gently sucking and tugging at them, nipping them with his teeth.

Morgana knew that she was drunk. She knew that she should never be doing this. But she kept her eyes closed and pretended that she was some other girl, some wanton and seductive girl who allowed any man to make love to her, just because he wanted to; a rich whore, a wealthy harlot, a woman who lived for forbidden excitements and perverted passions.

Harry ran his hands up and down her warm silky stockings. Then he drew aside the leg of her step-ins and touched her between her legs. She could feel the wetness herself, as the warm summer breeze eddied silently through the room. Then Harry was climbing on top of her, keeping her step-ins drawn aside, so that before she knew it he was pushing bluntly up inside her, blunt and big, and his face loomed right over her.

She reached down with her hand and stroked him, feeling how intimately they joined. Then she slid her other hand down, and held herself wider open for him, so that he could push himself deeper and deeper with every thrust.

He was not a stylish lover. John had made love like a musician, compared to Harry. But there was something rough and direct and strong about him, and as he pushed and pushed and pushed again, she found herself twisting from side to side on the pillow, increasingly breathless, and the bedroom closing in on her, black walls crowding in closer and closer until she felt that she was going to be crushed. Push, and push, and push, and push, until something came rising up inside her that she knew she couldn't stop.

She cried out. She thought she cried out. She shook uncontrollably. The whole room seemed to tilt over sideways. She heard Harry shouting too. Then she was lying on her back looking at a corner of his sweat-glistening face, and at the sloping ceiling behind him, and at part of a window.

Harry said, 'Are you all right?'

'All right?' she asked him, as if she couldn't understand the question. As a matter of fact, she couldn't.

He stroked her forehead, brushed away the perspiration with his hand. 'I guess there are some things that were always meant to happen,' he said. He was panting.

Morgana said nothing. He touched her breast but she

reached up and held his wrist. 'You were all that I could have wanted,' she whispered. She reached up and kissed his shoulder.

'What are you trying to tell me? That you don't want any more?'

She smiled. 'You mustn't ever think that. But just because something was meant to happen, that doesn't mean that it was meant to happen more than once.'

Harry rolled over, and found his shirt lying on the floor. He picked it up and shook out his pack of cigarettes. He lit one for himself, one for Morgana, and for five or ten minutes they lay back in the shadows smoking and saying nothing at all.

'What do you think, then?' asked Harry. 'Do you think we make some kind of couple, or what?'

'Nah,' said Morgana, in a West Side accent. 'I'm too ritzy and you're too good-looking.'

'You don't want to keep on seeing me, do you?' Harry asked her, very softly this time.

'You're wrong,' Morgana told him. 'But we can't go out together, not any more. I'm going to hurt you so badly you may not be able to put yourself back together again.'

'Come on, Morgana, you're not that kind of a girl.'

'Of course I'm that kind of a girl. I'm wealthy, I'm privileged, you said so yourself. I'd be hurting you every single time you sat down for dinner and remembered that it was my money that had paid for it, and not yours. I'm hurting you now, except you're too drunk or too thick-skinned to understand it.'

Harry finished his cigarette, and leaned heavily across Morgana to crush it out in the bedside ashtray. He kissed her once on the lips, and then said, 'How about that coffee?'

Morgana reached up and traced the outline of his face with her fingertips. 'Please understand how much I care for you,' she told him. 'Please don't ever forget it. Don't forget tonight, not ever.'

'I'll stick it in my scrapbook,' said Harry, and rooted around on the floor for his pants. As he was standing in the kitchen, however, waiting for the coffee to percolate, he had to take several deep breaths to prevent himself from sobbing, and even those deep breaths couldn't stop the tears from sparkling in his eyelashes. Drunk, he thought. Stupid and drunk.

The Polish dance music wafted in through the window. The night was warm. Some things are beyond the grasp of ordinary men, and that evening Harry knew that Morgana Croft Tate was one of them.

39

On Thursday evening, during a sudden summer shower, Bradley called for Phoebe at eight o'clock to take her to Bogie Barrett's for supper. Morgana had been invited, too, but she had sent Bogie her apologies. She was too busy with the Sunday *Star*, and a special three-page supplement on the South Side redevelopment. Apart from that, she had no escort; or, at least, no escort with whom she really wanted to go.

She had made up her mind that she wasn't going to go out with Harry again. Not because of his lowly station at the *Star*; not because of his severe lack of social credentials. But simply because she knew that she would hurt him, if she went on seeing him, and that he would hurt her.

Morgana and Harry were two strong personalities; head-butters. Both obstinate, both individualistic, and both incapable of taking no for an answer. Under normal circumstances, they might have managed to get along together well. But Morgana was the publisher and Harry was the reporter, and both of them knew that one day that relationship would break them up, and not only break them up, but grind them into tiny pieces.

Morgana sat in her father's library with a dummy of Sunday's feature spread in front of her, looking both businesslike and exotic in a dressing gown of crimson silk. She blew Phoebe a kiss as Phoebe went by. Phoebe was wearing a black high-collared evening dress with a spray of diamonds at the neck, a black hat and black gloves. In public, the Croft Tate women would remain in mourning for at least three months.

'You should come,' said Phoebe. 'There's still time. Bradley *loves* to have a woman on each arm.'

'No,' said Morgana. 'There's too much to do.'

Phoebe watched her for a while, and then she said, 'You mustn't let yourself become an old maid, you know. All work and no play.'

Morgana smiled to herself, and shook her head.

'Come on,' said Phoebe. 'It won't take you a minute to dress. I'll call Loukia.'

Morgana sat up straight, and laid down her pencil. 'Phoebe, I'm a newspaper publisher now.'

'What does that mean? No dinner parties for the rest of your life?'

'No,' said Morgana, 'it simply means that I have to take things a little more seriously.'

'You're in love,' said Phoebe, her eyes and her diamonds shining in the lamplight.

Morgana said, 'Nonsense.'

'You're in love with Harry Sharpe.'

'Absolute nonsense.'

Phoebe smiled at Morgana archly, 'If you're not in love with Harry Sharpe, why have you been walking around for the past two days looking as if you're posing for your own death mask?'

Morgana said, quietly, 'I do like him, but it's over. Is that enough? Or do you want to know more?'

Phoebe shrugged, and looked airily around the library. 'If you say it's over, my dear, it's over. Newspaper publishers always tell the truth, don't they? Hands on their hearts.'

A car horn tooted impatiently. Morgana said, 'That'll be Bradley. Go on, I'll see you later.'

'Yes, dear,' said Phoebe, and blew Morgana a kiss.

Bradley was waiting for Phoebe in the driveway outside, under a large multi-colored golf umbrella. He opened the car door for Phoebe, gave a cheerful salute to Winton Snell, and then hurried around to the driver's seat.

'Bradley?' asked Phoebe. 'What's the matter?'

'What do you mean, what's the matter? Does anything have to be the matter?'

'You're so jumpy.'

'Jumpy? Am I jumpy? What makes you think I'm jumpy?'

'Well, I don't know. Maybe you're not jumpy. Maybe you're twitchy.'

Bradley was obviously excited about something. He kept smiling to himself for no reason at all, and drumming his fingers on the steering wheel as he drove. Every now and then, he said, 'Ho boy, oh boy,' or 'whillikers.'

'I wish for goodness' sake you'd tell me what's wrong,' Phoebe asked him.

Halfway along North Michigan Avenue, Bradley pulled the Packard into the curb and jammed on the brakes. 'Okay!' he shouted. 'Okay, okay, okay! If you want to know what it is, I'll tell you what it is! I might as well tell you here as anyplace!'

'All right, then,' said Phoebe. 'What is it?'

'It's this,' said Bradley, and out of his pocket he produced a small black velvet-covered ring box. He opened it up, and inside nestled a ruby and diamond ring, with a central solitaire that must have cost at least $18,000. Phoebe stared at it and then at Bradley. 'It's beautiful,' she whispered.

'Listen,' said Bradley, 'I know that meat packing isn't particularly romantic. I also know that I'm not a movie star, by any stretch of the imaginative processes. But I'm a regular guy, and I think I've got a lot to offer, and I happen to love you very much. Therefore I'd consider it something of a compliment if you'd say that you'd marry me, let's say April?'

Phoebe looked at Bradley for a long time. 'I'm going to have to think it over,' she said. 'I mean, it's a very important step.'

'Well, okay, think it over. But take the ring.'

'No, let me think it over first.'

Bradley lowered his head, and closed the ring box. 'All right, I guess it's only fair to give you time.'

'I don't need much time. I'll let you know tomorrow.'

'Okay,' Bradley agreed, obviously hurt and disappointed. He pressed the Packard's starter button, and pulled away from the curb without another word.

'You're not mad at me?' Phoebe asked him, touching the padded shoulder of his tuxedo. Bradley shook his head.

'You're sure you're not mad at me?'

While Bradley and Phoebe were driving to the Barretts' for dinner, Harry was being escorted along the green-painted corridor that led down to the cells at the 2nd Precinct, closely accompanied by the station sergeant, a solidly built Irishman whose close-shaved neck looked from the back like a rolled rib roast. The Irishman whistled and jangled his keys. Harry nipped out his cigarette between finger and thumb and dropped the butt into his coat pocket.

'Here he is, King Kong,' said the station sergeant, and led Harry up to the bars of Ambrogio's cell. Ambrogio was lying on his bunk, his head propped up in his hands, his mountainous belly spread out. He was listening to a baseball game on the radio, his eyes fixed on the ceiling. The station sergeant unlocked the door of his cell and opened it.

'Hey, King Kong. That reporter you asked for.'

Harry stepped into the cell with a tight smile. It smelled of sweat and stale food in there, as well as some other indescribably gray smell which clung to prisons everywhere, the smell of hopelessness and isolation, the smell of being on the skids.

'How you doing, big guy?' Harry asked Ambrogio.

Ambrogio's eyes remained on the ceiling. 'I wanna talk to you private.'

'That's all right,' said Harry. 'You can talk to me private.'

The station sergeant warned, 'I'm going to have to lock you in.'

Harry kept on smiling. The station sergeant shrugged, and closed the cell door, and turned the key. 'Just give me a shout when you want to get out.'

After his footsteps had receded down the corridor, Harry took out his cigarettes and offered one to Ambrogio. The big Italian declined it with an almost imperceptible closing of his eyes, as if he were bidding at an auction.

'You mind if I smoke?' asked Harry, and lit up anyway. He looked around the cell, and remarked, 'Nice place you got here. Could use a little remodeling.'

Ambrogio's mouth knotted up with anger. 'You listen to me, punk. I'm going to go down for first-degree homicide and kidnap. They can ice me for one, or they can ice me for the other, or they can ice me for both. But it just so happens that you know both of the principal prosecution witnesses, am I right?'

Harry listened to this, leaning laconically against the bars of the cell, the smoke from his cigarette striped by the slanting sun. 'Go on,' he told Ambrogio.

'I want to make a bargain,' said Ambrogio. 'The Croft Tates drop the charge of kidnap; Phoebe Croft Tate tells the cops that she went with me out of her own free will. Also, that drunken sport reporter of yours forgets that he ever saw me with Carlo Aceto. Otherwise I come out in court and say what I know.'

'Ah, so this is the crux of it, is it?' said Harry. 'And what exactly are you going to say? You're going to say that Howard Croft Tate had a thing going on with Enzo the Schmenzo's daughter, and that he and she bore an illegitimate son? That's stale news, Ambrogio, we all know about that. You'll have to come up with something a whole lot better than that.'

'I ain't talking about Marcella.'

'Oh, you ain't, ain't you?'

'Don't you mock me, punk, I'm talking about Robert Wentworth.'

Harry looked at Ambrogio narrowly. 'What about Robert Wentworth?'

'I'll tell you what about Robert Wentworth. Robert Wentworth was supposed to have drowned accidental. But Robert Wentworth didn't drown accidental. Robert Wentworth was taken to the lake and Robert Wentworth was held under.'

'By whom?' asked Harry. 'By you?'

Ambrogio shook his head. 'Not by me, but I can finger the guy that done it. Linus Scapelli, if you really need to know.'

'But Linus Scapelli worked for Enzo, too.'

'Sure Linus Scapelli worked for Enzo. It was Enzo who ordered Linus Scapelli to hold Robert Wentworth under the lake and count to a thousand.'

'I still don't think that I'm following you here. What does Robert Wentworth's drowning by Enzo Vespucci have to do with the Croft Tates, or with you getting off?'

Ambrogio heaved himself up into a sitting position. 'Listen, bozo, are you going to listen to this or not? You want me to call the sergeant?'

Harry blew smoke. 'Keep your hair on, dandruff. I'm listening.'

'Well you listen to this,' said Ambrogio. 'The reason Linus Scapelli drowned Robert Wentworth was because Howard Croft Tate had asked Enzo to get it done, as a favor.'

Harry frowned. 'Let me get this straight. Robert Wentworth was murdered because Howard Croft Tate wanted him murdered?'

'That's what I said, didn't I? It wasn't common knowledge, but Robert Wentworth had been messing around with Mrs Croft Tate for months. I got proof, and witnesses. And unless those Croft Tates say that I wasn't involved in no kidnap, and unless that drunken sport reporter of yours starts remembering different, that's what I'm going to say in court.'

Harry stared at Ambrogio without saying anything. Ambrogio remained where he was, sitting on the bed. The radio went on chatting about baseball; then suddenly broke into a Pepsi-Cola commercial.

> Pepsi-Cola hits the spot,
> Twelve full ounces, that's a lot!

Harry went to the bars of the cell and called out, 'Sergeant!'

Ambrogio looked up at him with piggy eyes, and said, 'What you going to do?'

'I'm going to talk to the Croft Tates, that's what I'm going to do. I'm going to check up on your story. And by God, if you're trying to pull some kind of stroke here...'

Ambrogio rose to his feet. 'How would you like me to break your back?'

Harry didn't flinch. 'How would you like me to bring you some knitting magazines? Come on, Ambrogio, your King Kong days are over. Sergeant! Let me out of here!'

Eventually, eating a sandwich, the sergeant appeared and unlocked the door. He eyed Ambrogio philosophically. 'He didn't kill you, then?'

'That pussycat?' said Harry. 'He's so gentle, he says goodnight to the cockroaches, individually.'

Ambrogio glowered. 'You listen, punk. One day, I break your back.'

'Sure you will. And one day, pigs will use toilet paper.'

As Harry walked back through the echoing precinct building, Phoebe was arriving at the Barrett house on Foster Avenue. A grass-green carpet had been laid across the sidewalk, and the Barretts had provided flunkeys in powdered wigs to guide the guests into the building and to park their automobiles. Bradley handed the keys of his Packard to a young flunkey in knee-britches that looked far too tight and frowned in disapproval as his car was driven away with a slither of wet tires. There were lights everywhere, and music, and laughter. Bogie Barrett never did anything by halves.

Bradley escorted Phoebe into the marble-floored hallway. The Barrett house was celebrated for its Art-Nouveau decor. It was a five-story stone-clad townhouse, built in 1907, and

Solomon Barrett had employed C. F. A. Voysey, the English architect, to design the interior. There were bronze columns all around the hall, and lanterns that might have been carried by Diogenes in his search for an honest man.

Bradley and Phoebe were halfway across the vestibule when a familiar voice called, 'Phoebe! I say, Phoebe!'

Phoebe looked around; and there, striding confidently toward her, was John Birmingham Jr, all teeth and smiles, as handsome as ever.

'Phoebe! So good to see you!' said John, and kissed Phoebe on the cheek. Bradley said, 'Herrrp-*hm*,' and John grinned at him, too, and slapped him on the back. 'Bradley! You son of a gun! How's Ham-I-Yam?'

John linked arms with Phoebe, elbowing Bradley out of the way, and said under his breath, 'You and me, we ought to get together again. We were always suited, you know? Two peas in a pod. Two spoons in a drawer. I ought to write a song about that.'

Phoebe said, 'I wouldn't bother.'

'Ah, come on, Phoebe, weren't we good together? Weren't we?'

Phoebe stopped, and twisted her arm free from John's embrace. 'What if we were?'

John raised his hands, as if he were being stuck up by Hopalong Cassidy. 'All right, all right, forgive me.'

'I forgive you,' said Phoebe. 'But that doesn't change anything.' She turned, and said loudly, 'Bradley and I are going to be married, aren't we, Bradley?'

'Mr and Mrs Ham-I-Yam?' asked John.

'That's right, lover. Bradley – show him the ring.'

Bradley was about to take the ring out of the box, but then he hesitated, and shook his head. 'This ring gets displayed after I put it on Phoebe's finger, and not before.'

Phoebe held out her hand. 'Then put it on my finger.'

Bradley produced the box, opened it, and slid the ring on to Phoebe's left hand. 'There,' he said. 'We get married in April.'

John said, 'Congratulations,' as if he were reading the label of a poison bottle. Then he shouldered his way off through the crowds of dinner guests, all shiny hair and bad temper.

Bradley took hold of Phoebe's hand. 'You didn't say yes just to annoy John, did you?'

Phoebe said, 'No. I can annoy John any time. I can only get married once.'

Bradley smacked his right fist into the palm of his left hand. 'Whillikers, Phoebe, I love you!'

Phoebe turned around so that she was facing him. She carefully took off his spectacles and then primped the front of his hair up into something like a pompadour. Then she kissed him on the lips. 'Do you know something, Bradley?' she said.

'What?' he asked her, trembling.

'You *have* to stop saying "whillikers."'

40

Morgana said, 'We have the choice, Momsy. All you have to do is say the word.'

Eleanor sat in her chair in the dimly lit bedroom in a white silk nightdress that made her look like Ophelia, rescued from the river, trailing shadows instead of weeds. Ever since Howard's funeral she had been bitter and quiet; still socializing, still seeing her friends, but much more caustic than ever, as if she were trying to punish herself by being unpleasant, and losing the affection of everybody around her.

Phoebe was there, too, in pale pink pajamas, smoking a cigarette in her long movie-star holder. She looked tired: she and Bradley had been dancing all night and drinking pink champagne. The full implications of naming a wedding date still hadn't quite struck her yet. In the morning she would open her eyes and think to herself: my God, I'm actually going to marry Bradley. But, in a way, she had always known that she would. Bradley was her insurance policy against becoming an old maid; and while he was off butchering his hogs, what was to stop her entertaining an occasional gentleman friend?

Morgana was still wearing the off-white linen business suit which she had worn down to the office that evening. Her hair was pinned up severely with tortoiseshell combs. Somehow the masculinity of her outfit gave her even more femininity than usual; but she was far from being soft and defenseless. The responsibility of running the *Star* had already given her new courage, and a head for facing the facts.

Eleanor said, 'Just because we agree not to testify against this creature, that's no guarantee that he's going to keep the story secret, is it? Or that he won't use it to blackmail us yet again?' Her voice was thin but steady; she was frowning as if she had a headache.

'Is it true?' Phoebe demanded. 'I mean, for all we know, it may not even be true.'

'Harry was pretty sure that Ambrogio was on the up-and-up,' said Morgana. 'He checked with some of his contacts, and Linus Scapelli left Chicago round about the date that Robert Wentworth was drowned and hasn't been seen since.'

Eleanor adjusted the skirts of her nightdress. 'It's so hard to believe that your father would have done anything like that.'

'He was probably jealous, that's all,' said Phoebe. 'You know what men get like when they're jealous.'

'But why didn't he simply confront me with it? Why didn't he say anything?'

Morgana shrugged. 'He probably didn't want you to know that he knew. Perhaps he didn't want to face it himself, the arguments, the discussions. If Robert Wentworth simply disappeared, everything could carry on as normal. Or at least Popsy *hoped* that everything could carry on as normal.'

'He didn't count on you confessing your guilty secret,' put in Phoebe.

'That's right,' said Morgana. 'And that probably made it even worse for him, do you see? – because he *still* had to go through all of the pain and all of the arguments that he had wanted to avoid, and at the same time he had this terrible secret to hide – that Robert had been drowned because of him.'

There were tears in Eleanor's eyes.

Morgana took hold of her mother's hands. They felt cold and sculptured. 'The real question is, Momsy, what do we do now? We can tell Commissioner Spectorski that we're dropping the kidnap charges; and we can ask Walter Dempsey not to testify that he saw Ambrogio with Carlo Aceto. Then nobody has to know anything.'

'But this man Ambrogio is a killer, isn't he? And he did kidnap Phoebe. And that poor man Donald Crittenden is still lying in hospital because of him.'

'All the same, Momsy, think what it's going to do to you, to your reputation. Everything that happened between you and Robert Wentworth is going to be splashed all over the papers. And everybody's going to know that Popsy asked Enzo to have him killed.'

'Your poor father,' said Eleanor, her voice as pale as ivory.

Phoebe said, 'Mother – you have to think of yourself now. If any of this gets out, your whole social life is going to be ruined. And supposing this Ambrogio does go free? The whole city is full of criminals and gangsters and kidnapers and God knows who else. One more isn't going to make any difference.'

Eleanor turned to Morgana. 'What do you think, my dear?'

She asked because she knew. Phoebe knew too, and turned away, her thighs crossed, her lips pursed impatiently.

Morgana said, 'I don't want to sound self-righteous, but this family owns and runs a chain of newspapers and radio stations. We make a lot of money out of it, and we work very hard to make that money. But we have a duty, too, if we're going to go on publishing newspapers and broadcasting news. We have a duty to tell the truth, as far as we know it, and that means a duty to tell the whole truth. We also have a duty to uphold the law, because we serve this community as well as making money out of it.'

'Well, don't worry, you did manage to sound self-righteous,' snapped Phoebe. 'You also managed to sound a little holy, too.'

'Phoebe, I run the *Star*!'

'And the *Star* is more important than your own mother's happiness, is that it?'

'The truth is more important than all of us!' Morgana retorted.

'Oh, well, I don't think that's what you have in mind at all,' said Phoebe. 'What you have in mind is your circulation. Just imagine the story! Newspaper Tycoon Ordered Drowning Of Wife's Young Lover. Where on earth would mother be able to hold up her head, ever again? You'd be killing her – just as effectively as father killed Robert! Just as effectively as father killed himself!'

Morgana took a deep, sharp breath to shout back, but then she changed her mind. She didn't want to hurt her mother any more than her mother was going to be hurt already.

It was Eleanor who broke the silence. 'It seems that Horace was right, doesn't it?'

'Horace?' Phoebe demanded. 'Horace who? Horace Horsecollar?'

'No,' smiled Eleanor, gently. 'Horace the Latin poet.'

'Oh yes, and what gem did he come out with?'

Morgana said it first. '*Delicta maiorum immeritus lues.* Though you are guiltless, you must expiate your fathers' sins.'

'Oh baloney,' said Phoebe.

'No,' said Eleanor. 'It's not baloney at all. We are a family, we have family loyalties. I have loyalties to your father, even though I was unfaithful to him, even though I no longer loved him. Even though he was unfaithful to me.'

'Even though he's dead?' Phoebe interrupted, bitingly.

'Especially since he's dead,' said Eleanor.

'I'd like to know what's loyal about letting everybody know that he took out a contract on Robert Wentworth.'

Morgana put in, 'This story's going to come out, one way or another, one day. You know that as well as I do. But think what it's going to look like if the *Star* is seen to have suppressed it deliberately, for the sake of its owners' reputation.'

Eleanor said, 'Is Grant still downstairs?'

Morgana nodded. 'Do you want me to ask him up?'

They met Grant in Eleanor's writing room. Eleanor sat at her desk, her nightdress covered by a patterned French boudoir robe with padded shoulders and broderie-anglaise trimming. Grant came into the room with the diffidence of a man coming in for a job interview. He was pale-faced and smart, although his bow tie was slightly crooked.

'We've been talking it over,' said Eleanor. Her voice had changed; it was glass-edged now, and decisive.

'Well, it's not easy,' said Grant.

Eleanor raised her chin a little, and then she said, 'This family has been self-indulgent, and inconsiderate, and careless of other people's feelings. That has to change, and it has to change now. By publishing the news, we have accepted a great responsibility; we must live up to that responsibility. We will not let this beast Ambrogio go free for the sake of our own comfort. He has killed and he has kidnaped, and he must be punished. For our sins, and for Howard's sins, we must be punished too. Morgana will tell you how the *Star* is going to handle it.'

Morgana said, quietly, 'I want Harry to check Ambrogio's story in every detail. Then I want to run a front-page story that describes exactly what happened; and how Ambrogio attempted to blackmail us into withdrawing our testimony.'

Grant looked steadily at Morgana, and then at Eleanor. 'You're sure you want to do this?'

Eleanor said, 'There isn't any other way.'

'What will you do?' Grant asked her.

Eleanor let out a sharp, cracking laugh. 'I shall stay right here, Grant, and brazen it out. I don't know one single society lady in the whole of Chicago who hasn't at one time or another taken some suitor into her bed. My crime is the crime of being found out!'

'And Howard's crime?' asked Grant, lifting an eyebrow.

Eleanor smiled. 'Howard's crime was the crime of being a dog in the manger. He didn't want me; but then he didn't want anybody else to have me, either. Howard wanted to own the whole world. Most newspaper publishers do. If they didn't, they wouldn't be newspaper publishers; they'd be postroom clerks.'

'If you say so, Mrs Croft Tate,' said Grant.

Eleanor retorted, 'You don't have to be obsequious. I thought we knew each other better than that.'

'Perhaps,' said Grant; and then turned to Morgana. 'I'll have Harry write up a piece by mid-morning tomorrow. Are you coming down to the office, or shall I have it sent up?'

'I'm coming down,' said Morgana.

Grant returned home; Eleanor rang down for a glass of hot milk; Phoebe went to bed. Morgana went to her room and stood for a long time staring out of the window at the full moon lying across the lawns. The summer storm had passed now, although it was still windy, and the trees ducked and bowed like dancers at a midnight ball. She could almost imagine that her father was there, sitting behind her, watching her, saying nothing, but hoping upon hope that she would do everything she could to redeem his reputation and his immortal soul.

41

On Saturday morning, Harry arrived outside Ambrogio's cell at eight thirty in the morning, carrying a folded copy of the *Star* under his arm. Ambrogio was listening to the radio. When Harry appeared, he switched it off and heaved himself up off the bunk.

He approached the bars, without a word. His eyes were small and expressionless, and nestled in the flesh of his face like the eyes of a whale. Harry smiled and unfolded the paper, holding it up so that Ambrogio could read the banner headline.

NEWS TYCOON TOOK OUT CONTRACT ON WIFE'S LOVER. Allege Howard Croft Tate Paid For Drowning Of Paramour Robert Wentworth.

There were even pictures to accompany the text. Howard, smiling. Robert Wentworth, young and good-looking with a sloping grin, three weeks before Linus Scapelli held his head under Lake Michigan and counted to a thousand.

Ambrogio read the story slowly. Then he lifted his eyes from the newspaper and stared at Harry with that kind of tired, patient expression that you see on the faces of ex-pugilists, when somebody at their local bar has drunkenly challenged them to a fight.

'You shouldna done that,' said Ambrogio.

'That's where you're wrong, dandruff. That's exactly what we shoulda done. And we did it. Now we have the satisfaction of seeing you go to meet your Maker, which is more than you deserve, but then we're not vengeful people, we're just looking for justice. What should really happen, you should be dragged behind a bus, and then boiled in vinegar. But you can't have everything.'

Ambrogio said, 'I'm going to kill you, punk. I'm going to take you with me, if it's the very last thing I do. And that drunken sport reporter, I'm going to kill him, too.'

'Well, don't think that I don't take your threat extremely seriously,' said Harry. 'It just seems to me that you have a kind of logistical problem.'

Ambrogio repeated, 'I'm going to kill you, punk, *and* that sport reporter, and that's it.'

'Listen,' said Harry, 'do you want to keep the paper? "Gasoline Alley" is good today. Skeezix had an argument with Nina, and Chipper broke his breakfast bowl.'

Ambrogio snatched the folded newspaper through the bars of his cell, and ripped it in half. 'You see what I done to this newspaper? That's what I'm going to do to you.'

Harry saluted the station sergeant as he left the precinct building. 'Thanks for everything. I'll talk to the circulation manager, make sure you get a free subscription to any Croft Tate magazine that takes your fancy. You just call him, ask for Ned Wynant, tell him who you are.'

'Okay, pal,' said the station sergeant.

Harry drove back to the *Star* building, and parked his borrowed Lincoln in the basement. Tomahawk Billy eyed him suspiciously as he walked past his booth. Harry said, 'What's running this afternoon, Billy? Any certainties?'

Tomahawk Billy scowled at him. 'You took my people's land. Now you want racing tips.'

'I'll pay you ten percent.'

'That's what President Grant promised, and it was lies.'

Up on the editorial floor, the typewriters were hammering away like a riveting shop at full blast. Telephones jangled, reporters yelled 'copy!', teleprinters nattered and chattered. Harry weaved his way between the pigpens with his coat slung over his shoulder. When he arrived at his desk, Walter Dempsey was there, looking untypically dapper, talking to David Tribe about the glorious days of baseball between the wars. Walter clapped Harry on the back, and cried, 'My dear boy! What stirring news!'

'You mean the Croft Tate business? It's making my toenails curl up. God knows what it's going to do to our circulation.'

'Hike it up, I trust!' said Walter. 'Nothing improves circulation like scandal; and this scandal has absolutely everything! Power, lust, jealousy, organized crime, high society, you name it! Not to mention the spectacle of one of Chicago's most elite families, throwing itself on the mercy of the public! One million copies, and ever upwards, I'll bet you!'

Harry took his notebook out of his pocket and flopped it down next to his typewriter. 'I went to see Ambrogio this morning.'

'Well, now, did you? Did you show him the paper?'

'I surely did.'

'And what was his response? A few simian grunts, I expect, followed by a shower of grape seeds?'

Harry shook his head. 'He wasn't exactly delighted. In fact he swore to murder the both of us.'

Walter slapped his thigh and let out a wild whoop of delight. 'This gets better and better! And do you know what, I shall be having an excellent lunch at the Drake today with Arnie Kunz, followed by a first-class afternoon's racing. What a day! And every other sport reporter will be elbow-nudging and whispering behind his race card and saying "See him, he works for *that* newspaper, and what's more, he's a key witness in the Phoebe Croft Tate kidnap-homicide scandal!" And now a death threat! I love it!'

Harry couldn't help grinning. 'Walter, you should know better.' He checked his watch. 'How about a drink over at O'Leary's, just to get the heart started?'

Walter turned round to David Tribe in indignation. 'How dare this man offer me a drink, when he knows full well that I was going to have one anyway?'

Gordon McLintock came out of his office as Harry and Walter passed by, arm in arm.

'Harry?' he said. 'I want an update on the Croft Tate kidnap story. Five hundred words.'

'Give me a half-hour,' Harry asked him. 'Walter and I have business to discuss.'

'In other words, you're going over the road to read a Four Roses label?'

Harry slapped him on the shoulder. 'Did anybody ever tell you that you might have a career in journalism?'

It was Saturday lunchtime at O'Leary's Pub, cheerful and noisy. Walter settled himself into his usual booth, and Harry sat next to him. Bob Kelly from the *Tribune* was there, looking pink-eyed and slightly unbalanced. 'I don't know what to say about you bastards,' he declaimed. 'You'd never catch Colonel

McCormick taking out a contract on anybody, not even for love! In fact, particularly not for love!'

Walter raised his hand in a papal gesture, and said slowly, 'To those who lead the most dissolute lives shall come the greatest rewards. Amen. And why are these beverages taking so long?'

They had been bantering each other for only ten minutes before David Tribe appeared in the doorway. He looked serious and strained.

'David!' said Harry, tugging his sleeve. 'Sit down and pour yourself a beer! Here, Bob, pass the jug, would you? This man looks thirsty.'

David said, 'I've got to talk.'

'What?'

'I've got to talk. Come over here, I've got to talk.'

Harry gave Walter a puzzled look, and then followed David across the pub to the phone booth. There were shining beads of sweat on David's upper lip. It was hot, and he must have been running.

'What's the problem?' Harry asked him.

'Ambrogio, that's the problem.'

'What do you mean, Ambrogio? Talk sense for Christ's sake.'

'Ambrogio, he's gotten out.'

'Out? Out of what?'

'Out of prison, you stupid bozo! He pretended he was sick, and so they sent him down to the clinic. The next thing they knew, he was threatening the doctor with a scalpel, and forcing one of his police escorts to give him his gun. He's gone, and he's armed, and he's looking for you!'

Harry focused on David carefully. 'Shit,' he said.

'The police officer who was escorting him said that he shouted out, "Now I'm going to blow the heads off those asswipes who work for the *Star*." Do you think that's sufficient evidence, or do you want a polygraph?'

'No,' said Harry, sober now. 'That'll do.'

David said, 'Gordon thinks you ought to come back to the office. You'll be safer there. You and Walter, both. He's called police headquarters, and Commissioner Spectorski has promised to send out a couple of officers to give you personal protection.'

Harry thought for a while, and then said, 'Shit. How the

hell could anybody have let that gristle-brain get away? Hold on, David, I'll see what I can do with Walter. He's already firing on nine cylinders.'

He turned to Walter and beckoned him. Walter waved back. For some reason that he couldn't quite understand, Harry felt a sudden sense of urgency and apprehension. Maybe he'd started drinking too early in the day. Maybe his Shakespearean sense of human drama told him that all acts of sacrifice carry their own penalty; and that Howard's sacrifice was returning to visit them all.

'Walter!' he called. 'Come on, Walter, we have to get back to the office!'

'What the aberration are you talking about?' Walter hooted at him. 'I've just this minute ordered another round of drinks!'

David said edgily, 'You have to get him back, Harry. Ambrogio's armed and dangerous. The police officers have been told to shoot on sight.'

Harry ran his hand through his spiky hair. 'All right, David,' he said, 'I'll do my best.'

At that instant, Marcella was opening the door of her apartment on Lincoln Park and there was Ambrogio standing in the hallway, holding a gun. A whole series of synchronized actions: Harry pushing his hand through his hair, Marcella turning the door handle, Ambrogio stepping forward stiff-legged in shirtsleeves and baggy pants, white-faced, sweaty, wearing no shoes, panting, the police revolver raised high in his hand as if he were just about to start a boat race.

Ambrogio pushed the door open with his left hand, and hobbled his way inside. His eyes were expressionless. They darted up and down, left and right. 'Anybody here? Anybody here?'

'Nobody,' Marcella told him, finding it difficult to catch her breath. Her whole mind was overwhelmed with thoughts of Eduardo, sleeping in his crib.

'Your mother? She here?'

'Nobody,' Marcella insisted. She stepped back, but Ambrogio waved her nearer with his gun.

'Okay,' he said thickly, 'where's your car?'

'My car?'

'I said where's your goddamned car! I'm desperate, right! You know what desperate means?'

'Downstairs, in the garage.'

'All right, then, let's go get it.'

Marcella said, 'I'll give you the keys. You can take it.'

'Oh no, precious, you're coming with me. You think I'm stupid? You'll give me the keys and the cops will be round here before I reach the goddamned garage. Now, let's go, hunh?'

Marcella shook her head.

Ambrogio cocked the revolver's hammer, and slowly lowered the muzzle until it was pointing toward Marcella's head. 'Is that what you want?'

Marcella said nothing, but opened the hall-table drawer and took out her car keys. Ambrogio smiled and held out his hand for them. 'You seen some sense, hunh?'

Marcella followed him out into the hallway and across to the elevators. She turned once to look back toward her apartment door, and she prayed to the Virgin Mary that Eduardo would be all right, and that she would be able to come back safely before he woke up. If she came back at all. Please, Blessed Lady, look after him.

Old Mrs Lennox from the next apartment saw them going into the elevator, and called, 'Wait a moment, Marcella, dear, I won't be a moment!' But Ambrogio immediately jabbed the button for the garage, and the elevator doors closed just as Mrs Lennox was hobbling toward them.

'Well, thank you!' they heard her call, shrilly.

Ambrogio and Marcella drove up the garage ramp and into the sunlit street. The golden Buick's convertible hood was down. Marcella was driving and Ambrogio was sitting beside her with the police revolver covered by a green plaid rug. As they reached the top of the ramp, Ambrogio said, 'You go to the *Star* building, okay?'

'The *Star* building?'

'Sure. There's a couple of punks there I want to talk to.'

'If I take you downtown you're bound to be spotted by the cops.'

'Miss Marcella, that's my business. I got payments to make, you know what I mean?'

Marcella hesitated, but then turned the Buick southwards. It was a warm windy day; the trees glittered like showers of fresh-minted nickels. Ambrogio sniffed, and wiped his nose with his fingers. 'Come on,' he urged Marcella from time to time. 'Come on, step on it.'

Just as Marcella turned into Wabash Avenue, Harry was guiding Walter back across the street from O'Leary's Pub. Walter had not yet reached his peak form, but he was beginning to feel very cheerful indeed, and his neatly knotted necktie had somehow managed to become as intoxicated as he was, and now emerged from his collar somewhere below his right ear. He was trying to demonstrate to Harry the Black Bottom, which he had danced very well as a young man, and he considered that the middle of Wabash Avenue on a busy Saturday morning was an ideal place for lessons.

'No, my dear fellow, that's not it at all. You have to oscillate your nates precisely so! Have you got it! Dear me, dear me, you're so rigid! No wonder today's young people never have any fun!'

They crossed the plaza in front of the *Star* building and reached the revolving glass door. 'A last attempt,' Walter insisted. But Harry tugged his arm, and said, 'Walter, we can dance all the way round the office if you want to. But right now, let's get ourselves inside.'

A young pink-faced cop who was standing on duty outside the *Star* building came across to give Harry a hand. 'What's the matter with your friend?' he grinned.

'Early breakfast,' said Harry.

'Come on, sir, let's get inside, shall we?' the young cop said, and took hold of Walter's arm.

Walter went stiff in protest. 'Unhand me! I am a respectabubble member of the grand order of scribes!'

At that moment, Marcella's golden Buick slid up to the curb with a squelch of whitewall tires. Ambrogio pressed his revolver up against Marcella's hip, and said, 'Don't say nothing. Don't shout to nobody. There they are.'

Only a few seconds afterward, Morgana drew up to the curb right in front of Marcella's car in her bright red Sportabout, and the young cop moved away from Harry and Walter to open her door for her. Morgana thanked him and stepped out, wearing a pale peach-colored summer dress with a V-neck and wide shoulders. As she stepped out, she turned, and saw Ambrogio halfway across the plaza, holding Marcella tightly in front of him. She turned again, and saw Harry and Walter giggling in the doorway. Walter was waving his arms and shouting out something about 'Fun! Fun! Where's your sense of fun?'

Morgana suddenly realized what was going to happen and said, '*Oh God*,' under her breath. The young cop said, 'Yes, ma'am?'

Ambrogio gripped Marcella in the crook of his left arm, lifted his stolen revolver and fired four times, point-blank, into the revolving doorway. The gunfire crackled and echoed; the glass shattered. The doorway twisted around and Walter and Harry collapsed bloodily on to the flagstones. Morgana screamed.

Ambrogio turned toward the young cop, but Marcella twisted away from him, and wrenched herself free of his arm. Ambrogio hesitated, turned around again, and then the young cop lifted his own revolver in both hands and fired twice at Ambrogio's chest. The shots were so loud that Morgana's ears started to sing. Ambrogio twisted on his left leg, toppled and fell.

Marcella ran across the plaza to the broken revolving door. Walter was lying face-down. There was a bullet-hole in the left side of his forehead, peculiarly neat and bloodless, as if he had stuck it on as a joke, but he was plainly dead. Harry was crumpled on top of him, his coat stained darkly all down on one side.

'Harry! Harry, it's Marcella!'

Marcella heaved him up, but his head lolled back and banged against the frame of the door.

'Harry, it's me. Harry, listen!'

Morgana stood a little way away, white-faced and shivering with shock. The young policeman had opened up one of the side doors and shouted, 'An ambulance, fast! And call some back-up, too!'

Harry's eyelids flickered. His cheeks looked swollen and his lips were grayish-purple. Marcella held on to his hand and said, 'Harry! Harry, it's me!'

Ambrogio lay where he had fallen. Blood soaked into the concrete flagstones. Across Wabash Avenue, the doors of O'Leary's had opened, and four or five reporters had come out to see what was going on, although the traffic passed by without stopping.

Harry opened his eyes. His pupils were wide and unfocused. 'Morgana?' he slurred.

Marcella looked up at Morgana. Morgana stayed where she was, her hands clasped across her breasts.

'Morgana?' Harry repeated. 'Is that you?'

Morgana came forward, and knelt down on the flagstones. 'Harry? It's all right, I'm here.'

Harry closed his eyes. Marcella said to Morgana, 'It's all right. I can still feel his heart beating.'

Morgana said, 'Let me take him,' and Marcella nodded, and helped Morgana to cradle Harry's head in her arms.

'I had to leave my little boy,' she said. 'Is there somebody here who could drive me home?'

The young policeman said, 'We'll do that, ma'am. Just wait for the back-up. They'll want to take a statement, too.'

Sirens wailed through the Saturday-morning streets. Morgana held Harry's head on her lap, and stroked his forehead. He bled on to her skirt. He felt cold, but every now and then he murmured and shuddered, as if there was something inside him that refused to let go.

'Harry,' Morgana whispered, stroking and stroking his forehead. 'Come on, Harry, you're going to be fine.'

42

If you want to find out what happened afterward, the place to go is to the newspaper morgue; because every life, no matter how modest, has its headlines.

You could look up the Chicago *Star* for Sunday, April 22, 1950, and read a report on Croft Tate Sisters' Double Wedding – how *Star* publisher Morgana Croft Tate married city desk reporter Harry Sharpe, while Phoebe Croft Tate, her younger sister, married Bradley Clarke, the meat-packing heir, at a lavish ceremony held at Weatherwood, and afterwards at St Stanislaus Kostka. Tears, confetti, *kielbasa*.

You could read, too, how Marcella eventually married Herbert T. Leno, the Kentucky race-horse breeder, and went to live on his stud farm in Streetersville, taking Eduardo with her. You could leaf through a few volumes more, and find out that Mr and Mrs Bradley T. Clarke, after six years of childless marriage, adopted Doris Wells, and brought her up at the family home in Skokie. Three volumes later, you would discover that Doris had become a junior tennis champion, and you could follow her career through year after year of sport reports, all the way to Wimbledon.

You could read how Eleanor Croft Tate left Chicago in September 1949, and lived for ten years in Cannes, in the South of France, where she died in 1959 of cancer.

You could read how the South Side slums were demolished, street after street, and how downtown Chicago was rebuilt to become one of the most dazzling city centers in the world.

You could also read that, even today, some slums still linger, and that babies are still dying on Grand Avenue, undernourished, premature, and poisoned by drugs.

You could read how Morgana Croft Tate Sharpe –

But your daily newspaper can tell it better. Go to the corner, pick up today's Chicago *Star*. It's all there, in black and white, the true story, underneath the headlines.